Praise for the A Breed Apart series. . .

TRINITY

"Dodge bullets, cling by your fingertips to an icy cliff—then fall heart first for a wounded hero and his incredible military war dog. You won't sleep, but please remember to breathe. Ronie Kendig's rapid-fire fiction: Oorah!"
—Candace Calvert, author of the Mercy Hospital series
and *Trauma Plan*

"Dangerous mysteries drive this moving and compelling military dog story. So vivid and contemporary that it could be happening here and now!"
—Kathy Tyers, author of the Firebird series

"If 'care about the protagonists' is the essential element of good fiction, *Trinity* is masterful. A war dog, an intrepid, multiethnic girl, and a healing former Green Beret mix it up with the enemy on the mountain cliffs of Afghanistan. Ronie Kendig has penned a page-turner of the first order."
—Eric Wiggin, author of *Skinny Dipping at Megunticook Lake*
and *Emily's Garden*

TALON

"Action, intrigue, and romance the way only Ronie Kendig can write it—this is an author who knows her stuff. With characters you can't help but love—and a canine you can't help but fall for—*Talon* is an intense ride punched with high-octane drama that will have you bolting through the pages in a single, sleepless night. *Talon* is Kendig at the top of her game. Whatever you do, do not miss this one."
—Tosca Lee, *New York Times* bestselling author of
the Books of Mortals series

"Now I know why they label Ronie's novels 'Rapid-Fire Fiction'! With inimitable style, this book hooks you from page one and machine-guns you to a satisfying finish. Bravo, Ronie!"
—Creston Mapes, bestselling author of *Fear Has a Name*

"*Talon* was a non-stop, heart-pounding adventure full of twists, turns, and romance. Every time I picked it up, I was transported to Talon and Aspen's world and felt every emotion that they experienced. It has a little bit of everything to capture the hearts of all readers!"
—Lisa Phillips, Founder/CEO of Retired Military
Working Dog Assistance Organization

BEOWULF

"Realistic characters, great dialogue, popping action—Ronie Kendig lives up to the Rapid-Fire Fiction label with *Beowulf*. I enjoyed the journey."
—Janice Cantore, author of The Pacific Coast Justice series

"High velocity danger, courage that won't quit, romantic tension, and a massive dog that will win your heart. Yet another 'I couldn't put this down' read from the fabulous Ronie Kendig."
—Stephanie Grace Whitson, award-winning author of
inspirational fiction

A BREED APART TRILOGY

RONIE KENDIG

SHILOH RUN PRESS

An Imprint of Barbour Publishing, Inc.

Trinity © 2012 by Ronie Kendig
Talon © 2013 by Ronie Kendig
Beowulf © 2014 by Ronie Kendig

Print ISBN 978-1-63058-502-0

eBook Editions:
Adobe Digital Edition (.epub) 978-1-63409-152-7
Kindle and MobiPocket Edition (.prc) 978-1-63409-153-4

Scripture taken from the HOLY BIBLE, NEW INTERNATIONAL VERSION®. NIV®. Copyright © 1973, 1978, 1984, 2011 by Biblica, Inc.™ Used by permission. All rights reserved worldwide.

Scripture quotations are taken from the *Holy Bible*. New Living Translation copyright© 1996, 2004, 2007 by Tyndale House Foundation. Used by permission of Tyndale House Publishers, Inc. Carol Stream, Illinois 60188. All rights reserved.

Scripture quotations are taken from the King James Version of the Bible.

For more information about Ronie Kendig, please access the author's website at the following Internet address: www.roniekendig.com

Cover photo: Stocktrek Images/GettyImages

Published by Shiloh Run Press, an imprint of Barbour Publishing, Inc., P.O. Box 719, Uhrichsville, Ohio 44683, www.shilohrunpress.com

Our mission is to publish and distribute inspirational products offering exceptional value and biblical encouragement to the masses.

Member of the
Evangelical Christian
Publishers Association

Printed in the United States of America.

TRINITY

MILITARY WAR DOG

DEDICATION

To a special breed of heroes—military working dogs
and their two-legged handlers.
Thank you for your grueling work and heroism,
which often goes unnoticed or unthanked!

ACKNOWLEDGMENTS

Brian, you will forever be my hero! Ciara, Keighley, Ryan, and Reagan—thank you for enduring fast food, on-your-own nights, and even forgotten meals as I vanished into foreign countries and other people's lives. Thanks to my amazing in-laws, whose support is unending! I love you, Mom and Dad!

To Al Speegle—Thank you for sending me that e-mail that launched the idea for this series. You are a gentleman with razor-sharp wit. It is an honor to count you as a friend!

Various MWD handlers and military "experts" who have replied via e-mail or in person to my plethora of questions, including John Burnam, Richard Deggans, Elgin Shaw.

My agent, Steve Laube, who believed in this series from the first bone I threw his way. Without your encouragement, things would've been—are you ready for it?—*ruff*!

Jaime Wright Sundsmo—Thanks for your help and expertise regarding climbing. Hopefully I didn't inadvertently kill a character with a climbing mistake (which would be my fault, not yours, LOL).

Julee Schwarzburg, editor extraordinaire. I am so humbled by you, sweet lady. THANK YOU for your sacrifice of time/wisdom, your calming and encouraging guidance, and your genius!

My dear writing friends, without whom I could not survive this journey: Dineen Miller, Robin Miller, Shannon McNear, Rel Mollet, Jim Rubart, Kellie Gilbert, Lynn Dean, MaryLu Tyndall, Kimberley Woodhouse, Becky Yauger.

The amazing Burnett Sisters—I hope General Burnett does you proud. I hear he has amazing daughters. Thank you for such incredible encouragement!

Thanks to my Audience of One, who has gifted me with this writing dream, enabling me to follow in His Son's steps by telling stories to impact His kingdom. What a joy and treasure!

LITERARY LICENSE

In writing about unique settings, specific locations, and invariably the people residing there, a certain level of risk is involved, including the possibility of dishonoring the very people an author intends to honor. With that in mind, I have taken some literary license in *Trinity: Military War Dog*, including renaming some bases within the U.S. military establishment and creating a new order of warriors within the Chinese Army. I have done this so the book and/or my writing will not negatively reflect on any soldier or officer. With the quickly changing landscape of a combat theater, this seemed imperative and prudent.

Glossary of Terms/Acronyms

ACUs—Army Combat Uniforms
AFB—Air Force Base
AHOD—All Hands On Deck
BAMC—Brooke Army Medical Center, San Antonio
CJSOTF-A—Combined Joint Special Operations Task
    Force-Afghanistan
DD214—Official Discharge from Active Duty
DEFCON—Defense readiness Condition
DIA—Defense Intelligence Agency
FOB—Forward Operating Base
Glock—a semiautomatic handgun
HK 9mm, HK USP—Heckler & Koch semiautomatic handgun
HPT—High-Priority Target
HUMINT—Human Intelligence
IED—Improvised Explosive Device
klicks—military jargon for kilometers
lat-long—latitude and longitude
M4, M4A1, M16—military assault rifles
MRAP—Mine Resistant Ambush Protected vehicle
MWD—Military War Dog
ODA—Operational Detachment Alpha (Special Forces
    A-Team)
PLA—People's Liberation Army of the People's Republic of China
PTSD—Post-Traumatic Stress Disorder
RPG—Rocket-Propelled Grenade
RTB—Return To Base
SIS—United Kingdom's Secret Intelligence Service, otherwise
    known s MI6
SOCOM—Special Operations Command
SureFire—a tactical flashlight
tango—military slang for target or enemy
TBI—Traumatic Brain Injury
UAV—Unmanned Aerial Vehicle

Glossary of Terms/Acronyms

ACU—Army Combat Uniform
AFB—Air Force Base
AHOD—All Hands On Deck
BAMC—Brooke Army Medical Center, San Antonio
CJSOTF-A—Combined Joint Special Operations Task
    Force-Afghanistan

DBE—Official Blackout from Active Duty
DEFCON—Defense readiness Condition
DIA—Defense Intelligence Agency
FOB—Forward Operating Base
GLOCK—a semiautomatic handgun
HK 9mm, HK USP—Heckler & Koch semiautomatic handgun
HPT—High Priority Target
HUMINT—Human Intelligence
IED—Improvised Explosive Device
klicks—military jargon for kilometers
lat-bags—latrine and lavatory
M4, M4A1, M16—military's small arms
MRAP—Mine Resistant Ambush Protected vehicle
MWD—Military War Dog
ODA—Operational Detachment Alpha (Special Forces
    A-Team)

PLA—People's Liberation Army of the People's Republic of China
PTSD—Post Traumatic Stress Disorder
RPG—Rocket Propelled Grenade
RTB—Return to Base
SIS—United Kingdom's Secret Intelligence Service otherwise
    known as MI6
SOCOM—Special Operations Command
shut-eye—a term for sleep
ranger—military slang for forcefront entry
TBI—Traumatic Brain Injury
UAV—Unmanned Aerial Vehicle

Prologue

Body rigid, ears trained on the sound coming from the dilapidated structure, she waited. Breaths came in staccato pants, the heat of a brutal Afghan summer beating down on her. While the Kevlar vest provided protection, it also created a thermal blanket that amplified the heat. She panted again and strained with resolute focus on the building. This wasn't her first tour of duty. It wasn't even her second. She'd completed three tours and outranked the Green Berets huddled behind her on the dusty road. Trinity lowered herself to the ground, waiting.

When she took her next breath, drool plopped onto the gritty sand.

"Easy, girl." Staff Sergeant Heath "Ghost" Daniels knelt beside his Special Forces-trained military war dog, his M4 aimed at the building where three men had disappeared. This so-called security mission for the sweep team in prep for an HPT convoy had taken a turn toward interesting. So much for intel that said the area was clean.

"Ghost, what's she got?"

At the sound of team leader Dean "Watterboy" Watters's voice, Heath assessed his sixty-pound Belgian Malinois again. "Nothing," he called to the side, noting Trinity's stance and keen focus.

With the sun at high noon, they would blister out here if they didn't get this road cleared before the general's pack came through at thirteen hundred.

Trinity came up off her hindquarters, muscles rippling beneath her dark, silky coat.

Heath's pulse kicked up a notch as his gaze darted over the nearly monochrome terrain. What had she detected? Sometimes he wished he had the sharp hearing inherent in dogs.

Having taken cover behind a half-blown wall, Heath peered around the peeling plaster and stared down the sights of his weapon. He let the crosshairs of the reticle trace the structure in which the rebels had taken refuge, but he didn't see anything. No trace of the men who'd scurried away from the sweep team. Men who'd raised the hackles of every member of the team, including Trin.

Snapping and barking, Trinity lunged. For a split second, her paws rose off the ground as she bolted forward. A plume of dust concealed her movement.

In a bound-and-cover movement, Heath and Watterboy hurried after her, making sure they didn't expose themselves to gunfire or RPGs. As they came up on the house, Heath flattened himself against the sun-heated wall.

A scream hurtled through the now-dusty day.

At the telltale sign of Trinity's hit, Heath hoofed it around the corner.

Screaming, an Afghan male bent toward the snarling dog who held his arm tight and jerked it back and forth. Five hundred pounds of pressure per square inch guaranteed submission. Trained not to rip the guy to shreds from head to toe, she maintained her lock on the target.

Heath came up on the guy's right, noting Watterboy on the left. "Down!" he shouted in Pashto. "On your knees."

More screams, this time mingled with tears as the guy warred with his instinct to fight and the order to kneel. Blood streaming down his arm, he dropped to the ground.

"Out!" Heath gave the release command to his canine partner.

Obediently, Trinity disengaged and trotted to his side as Heath maintained control. "My dog is trained to kill," he said in the man's native tongue. "Do not make any sudden moves or she will attack. Do you understand?"

Master Sergeant Tiller nodded his intention to enter the building, and with Sergeant First Class James "Candyman" VanAllen, they led the rest of the team into the structure.

Cradling his arm, the man frantically bobbed his head and whimpered.

Watterboy moved in to search the man while Heath kept watch. Once they cleared the man of dangerous weapons or materials, Heath led Trinity to the shade where he squirted water into her mouth from the CamelBak bite straw. She lapped it up, then turned in a circle.

"Good girl." He smoothed his hands over her body, assuring himself she hadn't been injured during the encounter.

As he straightened, the others streamed back out of the house, faces smeared with dirt and sweat—and frustration. No way. "Empty?"

"One hundred percent."

Their medic hurried, bandaging the rebel's wound.

Watterboy faced the rebel. "Where'd they go?"

The tearstained face of the rebel rose to the Special Forces unit. He gave a slow nod behind him.

As Heath glanced over his shoulder, his gut knotted.

A new enemy rose, proud and majestic. With his M4 against his chest, Heath gazed up at the forbidding terrain of the Hindu Kush. He'd flown over them dozens of times, each time grateful they didn't have to comb through the rugged mountain terrain. The sun bathed the rocky slopes in an orange glow.

He removed his sunglasses and swiped his sleeve across his damp face. He wanted to curse, knowing they'd probably lost the Taliban fighters.

"Ghost, what's Trinity hit on?"

At the sound of Watterboy's voice, Heath snapped his gaze to his furry partner. Nose to the ground, she sniffed and maneuvered around a pile of rubble. She immediately sat down, ears perked and trained on the wood and cement.

Like a volcanic eruption, wood and cement shot upward and outward. Two men darted across the road.

Trinity streaked after them, her black-and-amber fur rippling beneath her muscular body. He pitied the idiots. Her snapping echoed through the narrow valley that ensconced them.

"Go!" Watterboy shouted.

Heath sprinted after his partner. In fact, she was his superior by one rank. If anything happened to her, it was his head on the platter. But that's not what had him sprinting in seventy-pound gear across the singed terrain. It was Trinity. His girl. His only girl.

Heath homed in on the sound of her barking that helped them

navigate the brutal terrain. Rocks and twigs shifted beneath their thick boots. Trees and shrubs reached over the footpath, as if trying to distract the team with the lure of shade and a slight breeze.

Undeterred, Heath hauled butt up the side of the mountain. As he moved, he glanced up—

There!

Trinity sailed over a crevice and disappeared. A klick up, the path widened. Heath pushed onward, determined to find Trinity. She'd been more loyal and faithful than any friend or girlfriend. She had put her life on the line more times than he could count. He owed it to her to get there and interdict before things went bad.

"Whoa. Hold up," Watterboy mumbled.

Heath hesitated, one boot higher than the other as he glanced at his friend.

Watterboy's face glistened beneath the stifling heat. "I don't like it."

"I second the motion." Candyman took a knee, surveying.

For a split second, Heath took in the terrain he'd vaulted up. Like a sharp V, two sides dropped toward the team. An avalanche would bury them alive. The outcroppings were perfect for snipers.

"SOCOM suspects this area is crawling with Taliban," Tiller announced as he joined them. "Eyes out."

Which meant the real possibility of an ambush. Or an IED. Or both. But Heath knew one thing—due to their extreme effectiveness, military war dogs were high-priority targets with obscene bounties. He wasn't letting anyone get a bounty on Trinity.

Barking reverberated through the canyon. A shot rang out, followed by a yelp. Then. . .silence.

Heath burst into a run. His foot slipped on the rocky incline. The thin air pressed on him. Heavy. He felt heavy. But he wasn't stopping. Not till he found Trinity.

As he came up over a rise, a pebble-strewn path stretched out and around a crest in the rugged mountains. And two dozen yards away—Trinity. Pacing, her right back leg dragging. She'd broken behavior.

Something was wrong.

Thinking past the drumming of his pulse, he eased closer, his nerves prickling with anticipation of an attack. He darted a glance around without moving his head and advanced. "Trinity, down."

She turned, her gold eyes boring into him. Started to sit but rose and paced again, this time slower.

"Trin—" That's when he saw the dark streaks on her hindquarters. *She's shot!*

Instinct shoved him into a crouch, gauging the steep slopes towering over them, knowing the enemy had shot her from some hiding spot. He keyed his mic. "They've hit her—wounded her. She's broken behavior, not responding."

He inched along the crevice, fixing his gaze on Trinity. Her leg. Hopefully they hadn't done permanent damage. If he could get an IV in her, she'd have a chance.

A quick check to his six showed him the team, weapons trained as they slunk through the rocky edifice. Fluid, stealthy, the best—pride infused him. Confidence that they'd cover his six enabled him to turn back to his partner. He crouch-ran the last few feet to Trinity. Dropped to his knees.

That's when he noticed her vest. It lay a dozen feet away. How on earth did that happen? He pushed to his feet and started for it.

Trinity moved in front of him, snarling.

He'd seen the damage those teeth could deliver. "Easy, girl. It's okay." After rubbing her tall ears, he moved around her.

She lunged. Snapped. And again, snarled.

Heart in his throat, Heath stilled and drew back. Swallowed against his desert-dry mouth. He noticed the foam at the corners of her mouth. From his CamelBak he loosened the bite grip and squirted some liquid refreshment down to her.

Stance rigid, she stood off with him.

Concerned, he stroked her head. "It's okay, girl. We've got it." Again, he tried to retrieve her vest.

She lunged. Trapped his hand between her jaws. Five hundred pounds of pressure per square inch clamped through his flesh. Shock insulated the pain—at first. *What're you doing. . .?*

Blood slid down across his thumb. This should hurt. Bad. *Real* bad. Thoughts became reality. White-hot fire tore through his muscles and veins, shoving him to his knees. His pulse pounded in his temples. He growled the command, "Out!"

With a whimper, she released him.

Agony pulsed as he cradled his hand. "Down," he growled.

"What's happening?" Tiller shouted as he came up on Heath's nine.

15

"Her vest is off," Heath hissed.

"Think that wound they gave her is messing with her mind?" Watterboy asked as he caught up.

With his uninjured hand on her, Heath held up his other to stem the flow of blood. "Nah. . ." That wasn't like her. It took a lot to wig her out.

"Let's get her vest and clear out. This place is ambush central." Tiller jogged around them.

A growl rumbled through Trinity's belly. Her upper lip curled into a snarl—

"No!"

BooOOOom!

Wicked and thick, a concoction of haziness and pain pinned him down. His eyes wouldn't obey his command to open. He felt heavier than the time he leapt from that bridge and blacked out as a kid. He'd come to as a friend hauled him, unconscious, to the surface. That same feeling, heavy but weightless. . .

A voice. . .sweet and soft.

Heath stilled his mind and followed the voice from the void. What. . . she—it was a woman, right? He hadn't lost that much touch with reality, had he?—what was she saying?

As if his ears broke the water's lip, her voice became clear.

". . .all anxiety or pain you might be feeling. Finally, I pray you'd be uplifted by His grace and feel yourself enfolded in the peace of His embrace."

Peace. . .drifting. . .away. . .so quiet.

Wait. No. Trinity! Where was she? His arms resisted the plea to lift. Fire lit down the side of his neck. He moaned.

At least, he thought he moaned. Maybe his voice wasn't working—

A gasp nearby.

Still, Heath couldn't move or respond.

"What are you doing here?" Male, older, gruffer. Who. . . ?

"Shh," she said. "You'll wake him."

"This"—warbling in Heath's head garbled the words—"bring him back."

"This isn't about *him*," she hissed. "And he won't remember I'm here."

"What if he does? That's a problem—"

"He won't!"

Heath's hearing closed up, his mind drowned in the words that struggled to find purchase against the pain and emptiness devouring him. He struggled. Tried to focus on her voice. That sweet, soft, angelic voice.

Please. . . God, don't let me forget.

Quiet descended and pushed him back into the depths.

Wakhan Corridor
Hindu Kush, Afghanistan
One Year Later

"Opportunities multiply as they are seized." The words of the ancient warrior Sun Tzu held fast in the mind of Wu Jianyu as he hauled himself up over a steep incline, hands digging into the sharp edifice. Weakness meant failure.

He could afford neither weakness nor failure. Not again.

Squatting, he let his gaze take in the breathtaking view. Hazy under the taunt of dawn's first light, the rugged terrain was terrifyingly beautiful. Already, he and his men had hiked for two weeks, having left the province of Xinjiang, which lay more than a hundred kilometers behind.

When he'd spied the worn path traders, including Marco Polo and the Jesuit priest Benedict Goëz, had used for centuries, he ordered his men away from it and away from prying eyes. To the north rose the formidable land of Tajikistan. Behind him, to the south, stretched the borders of Pakistan. West lay Xinjiang, and east. . .Afghanistan.

His path to honor.

Then there was his path: A central branch that ran through the southern portion of Little Pamir to the Murghab River.

That assumed, of course, one was trying to get into China.

He was not.

Twisting in his crouched position, he drew in a long breath of crisp, cold air. Invigorated, he rose, allowing the mountains and valleys, the rivers that snaked and sparkled beneath the touch of vanishing moonlight, to speak to him. Remind him that he alone had been chosen for this mission. And it was his alone to fail. Or succeed.

17

Two more days would deliver them to the province where he could do what was asked of him. And regain what was rightfully his. What had been stolen, ripped from his line of ancestors.

I will not dishonor you again, Father. In fact, to distance his father from the disgrace that had become Jianyu's alone, he'd taken his mother's surname. Thus Wu Jianyu was born. And Zheng Jianyu died. For now.

With one fist closed and one resting atop it, he bowed his head. Closed his eyes. After many minutes of silence and meditation, he once again reached for that which had always been his—emptiness. The chant of the Heart Sutra drifted through his mind and on the wind. It would work. The monk had told him. "*. . .indifferent to any kind of attainment whatsoever but dwelling in Prajna wisdom, is freed of any thought covering, get rid of the fear bred by it, has overcome what can upset and in the end reaches utmost Nirvana.*"

He needed the hope. To fill the empty places.

No, no. That's not what the monk said. Jianyu ground his teeth.

"*There is only one place you will find peace, Jianyu.*" The voice, soft and silky like a lotus petal, seeped past his barriers. His anger. His brokenness. And melted over him like honey.

"No!" He lowered himself to the ground, bent his legs, and rested his hands, palms upward on his knees. Focused on the Heart Sutra. Repeated the words he'd memorized in the years since she vanished and left him with nothing but dishonor.

One

Chinese Tea House, Maryland

Darci pushed through the heavy red door with the brass dragon handle. On the soft carpet she paused and removed her coat. The hostess looked up from her podium. Her face, with a practiced smile and faked cheeriness, exploded into a genuine welcome. "Darci, so good to see you!"

"And you, Lily."

The hostess motioned toward the back. "He's waiting."

Of course he was. Darci had seen his car in the parking lot. Not that she needed that to know he'd arrived before her. In fact, she was sure he came at least a half hour ahead of schedule every time. He was as cast in his ways as was the porcelain shrine of Buddha sitting behind the central fountain.

Even now, through the opaque rice paper sliding door, she could see her father's shadowed form. Though she relished their lunches, this would be one she would regret. As she always did when her job took her out of town, away from her father.

Hand on the small handle, Darci took a steadying breath. *Be strong. He loves you. He just doesn't know how to show it.*

With a quick smile to Lily, who watched with a furrowed brow, Darci slid back the paper door. As she closed it behind her, she slipped off her shoes. The bamboo mat beneath her feet sent a chill up her spine. Afraid to meet his disapproving scowl, she eased onto the empty pillow at the table across from her father.

Darci inclined her head, gaze down as expected. "Sorry I am late,

Ba." She wasn't late, but apologizing seemed to smooth out his frustrations that had taken such strong root in the last few years. Even more so on days like today.

She poured some tea and sipped it, using the little black handleless cup like a shield as she peeked over it to see his face. Hard lines. Burdened lines. The whiskers that framed his mouth were streaked with the paleness of wisdom. Too much for a man his age. There were secrets, family secrets, that he would not share with her. She'd tried to talk of her mother and brother, but they were forbidden subjects.

"You should trim that beard. It makes you look like a grumpy, old Chinese man."

"That"—his sad eyes met hers for the first time as he lifted his shoulders—"is because I *am* a grumpy, old Chinese man."

"Li Yung-fa is a kind, gentle soul." She smiled. "I know. I'm his daughter." With her spoon, she lifted some rice from the bowl in the middle of the table, her stomach clenching as she watched her father.

The mirth around his eyes faded, the rich brown of his irises seemingly lost in another time. She ached for what he'd lost twenty years ago. What she'd lost. She refused to let their lunch once again take a turn for the depressing. She pushed onward with safer topics.

"How was work this morning?" After setting the pile on her plate, she spooned sauce over it, then chose some beef and broccoli.

"As usual." His graying goatee flicked as he talked. "Same paperwork. Same mindless games. They waste my abilities. If they would just use me. . ."

So much for safer topics. Darci gave a slow nod. His mood was not encouraging, and when agitated, his already-heavy accent would thicken. No doubt, he would soon spin into full Mandarin, especially with the news she had to deliver. Squeezing some meat and rice between the chopsticks, she lifted the bowl closer.

"Where?"

Darci aimed the first mouthwatering bite toward her lips. "Excuse me?"

The slant in his eyelids pulled taut. "In your eyes rests the weight of the message I see you withhold."

All these years in America and still he held to the old ways of speaking, as if he were Yoda. She'd teased him without mercy as a teenager, hoping he would be more American. . .less Chinese. Anything to ply a smile out of the rigid face. There had been few smiles then, and as of late, even fewer.

Darci set down the bowl and sticks, cupping her hands in her lap, eyes downcast. "I leave tomorrow." She sighed. "I am sorry, Baba. I know this upsets you that I am gone so much."

Shoulders squared, he looked every bit the general he had once been. "Where?"

There was no use lying to him or trying to deceive him. The man worked with some of the highest-ranking officials in the government. If he doubted the veracity of her information, he'd hunt down the truth. Direct, strong, relentless. . . She'd gained a lot of her mother's American features with the fair skin, the European nose, but her father's strong Chinese heritage rang through her long black hair, slightly slanted eyes, and fire-like tenacity.

Which often left her wondering why he had not searched harder for her brother.

An eyebrow bobbed, as if demanding her answer.

"Afghanistan."

A tic jounced in his cheek as it often did when he tried to rein in his emotions. "That is very far."

"More like 'too close to China,' is that it?"

Like a provoked dragon, fire spat from his eyes. His fisted hand pounded the table. "Too far—from here." He thumped his chest. "From me."

Darci lowered her head. "He won't find me, Ba. I will be caref—"

"Like last time?" Fury erupted. "He nearly killed you!"

She would not let this happen again. "*He* is in China. I will be in the mountains. . .nowhere near him or any Chinese." Darci wanted one thing from her father. "Trust me. Believe in me. Yes?"

His whiskers shimmered—twitched. Was his chin bouncing? "I do not want to lose you, Jia!"

Her breath snatched from her lungs. So afraid someone would find them, he had not used her birth name in twenty years. Her superiors had chosen the name for this mission, one she feared would be her last.

Darci placed a hand over his as she crawled around the small square table to his side. She touched his back. "You will not lose me. Not before my time."

His chest rose and fell unevenly. Hands resting on either side of his bowl, he drew back his hands and uncoiled them. After a few seconds, he pulled in a long, quiet breath. Then gave an almost imperceptible nod.

"I should only be gone a few weeks."

Another nod. "What you are doing is good. You serve your country." His lip trembled.

An invisible fist reached into her chest and squeezed the organ pumping hard and frantic as she took in all that had just transpired. He'd never been open about his feelings, about his fears. Was it a bad omen?

 **TWO**

Texas Hill Country

*Y*ou'll be tempted to ignore this opportunity, but those marks on your hand have shown you trust that beautiful animal who saved your life. Bring her out. Let her decide if this is right for your team."

Nerves on end, Heath climbed from his truck. Trinity bounded from the bench seat onto the grass that collided with a ten-foot chain-link fence. He pushed the door closed and took in the property that rolled out on each side, as well as the white luxury SUV he'd parked beside.

Trees, some barren of their leaves and others thickly outfitted, and brambles lined the east. A half mile west, a rocky edifice rose a good thirty feet straight up. Twenty feet from his position, within the fenced area, sat training equipment. A complete agility and tactical course set up. Cedar trees hogged the perimeter of the fence. But not a person in sight. He'd half expected someone to emerge from the ranch house perched at the top of the slight incline, but that hadn't happened either.

What on earth?

Rubbing his knuckles along his lips, he hesitated at the unlocked gate. He glanced back down the almost mile-long dirt road that led to the black wrought-iron gate. Sun streamed through the lettering in the arch: A BREED APART. Who was behind this elaborate setup?

"Hello? Anyone here?"

A bitter January wind answered, creaking the branches.

The training facility held too much draw. He let Trinity take in the settings, her attention also focused on the training field. She sniffed along the fence line. "What do you think, Trin?"

She returned to him. Trinity swiveled her head back to the front, her black-and-amber coat sparkling in the sun. He smoothed a hand along her dense fur. Her ears perked and her body went rigid.

Heath slanted a look in the direction in which she'd made a hit. A mass of white-blond curls dipped into a beam of sunlight streaming through the cedars as a woman emerged from one of the house-shaped training structures. She glanced back inside and stalled. After much coaxing, a yellow Labrador lumbered from the building.

Anticipation rippled through Trinity's coat, her muscles taut, all but begging for permission to meet the new dog.

"I know you?" Heath asked. This woman with her gun-shy dog didn't seem the type to know much about training, let alone his past.

She straightened and came toward the gate. "No, do I know you?" She glanced down at her yellow Lab, who sat off to the side facing away from them, his expressive eyes conveying his skittishness. He hung his head, then flattened himself to the ground.

"You're the one who invited me here?"

"No, actually," she said with a smile. "I'm not. My friend Khat lives here with her brother. They invited me." At the gate, she slipped through and waited for her dog, who had given up about halfway across the yard and lain down. She let out a sigh and turned to Heath with an extended hand. "Aspen Courtland."

"Heath Daniels. You say you know who owns this place?"

Clap!

Heath jerked toward the wraparound porch and stilled at the figure that emerged from the shadows. "Khouri? No way."

The low, slow chuckle of a man he knew in the Army rolled through the air as the man strode off the porch. With two legs. How. . .how was that possible? Heath had been there when a Coke-can-turned-IED shattered the guy's leg and career beyond repair. Just a few months before Heath lost his career, too.

"Hello, Aspen. Khaterah got called out. She's sorry she couldn't be here to greet you."

"No problem," Courtland said.

Wearing a red knit cap over long brown hair and sporting a thick beard as if he'd never left the field, Jibril Khouri grinned as he met Heath's gaze again. "I wasn't sure you'd come."

Pulling the guy into a half hug, half back-patting embrace, Heath scrambled to get his bearings. "You always knew how to get my attention."

"Yes, but you always got the girls. We had to distract you so the rest of us would have a chance."

Heath shirked the tease and ran a hand over the back of his head, across the scar that changed everything. "Yeah, well, things change."

"So they do." Sobered, Jibril stepped back with another pat on Heath's shoulder, then bent and offered a hand to Trinity. "Hello, girl. Remember me?"

Trinity sniffed his hand, then turned in a circle, her focus locked on the yellow Lab.

"Ah, Trinity has the right idea," Jibril said with a laugh. "Let's go into the training area while we wait for our last recruit."

Uncertainty rooted Heath to the ground. Too many unexplained variables. Too many unknowns. "Khouri, what is this?"

"Now is not the time to be skittish, my friend." Jibril smiled. "Trust me, just as I trusted you the day Trinity saved my life. Yes?"

Stuffing his frustration and uneasiness, Heath gave a curt nod and followed Jibril, Aspen, and Trinity into the fenced-off area.

"Ah, this is Talon." Jibril squatted beside the Lab, who lifted his head and cast furtive glances at Jibril. "All the dogs and handlers invited to the ranch today are former military war or working dogs. Talon here has seen more combat than I have. You'll meet Beowulf and Timbrel Hogan soon—they're former Navy."

With a huff, Talon slid down to the ground, propped his lower jaw on his front paws, and let his gaze bounce over the yard. Those eyebrows did more work than his whole body, tracking Trinity around the training grounds. He looked like he was as through with the military as it was with him.

You and me both, buddy.

Tension bunched at the base of Heath's neck. He stretched it. "So." He shifted his attention to Aspen. "You've seen combat?" That was hard to believe.

"I was Air Force, but no, I haven't seen combat." She must've seen his confusion. "My brother was his handler. He went MIA and Talon was declared 'excess.'"

MIA often meant dead. Not enough body parts to ship home. Heath now understood the Lab's reaction. Trinity had pretty much done

25

the same thing when they'd been separated, well, except she became borderline aggressive and noncompliant. Talon was. . .gone. As if he'd checked out.

"So you adopted him?" Heath and every handler before and since sent up shouts of praise at a new resolution signed into law by President Clinton a few years back, which allowed dogs to live out the remainder of their years rather than being euthanized after the military decided they were done with the dogs. "I know your brother would be glad if he were alive."

"Austin's not dead." Blue eyes flamed. "He's *missing*."

Heath took about five mental steps away from her and that volley of anger.

Trinity nosed Talon's ears, walked circles around him, sniffed, investigated, sized up the new guy. He showed neither aggression—via a low growl to tell Trin to stand down—nor did he move away.

Arms folded, Aspen studied him. "What happened to you?"

"IED in the mountains." Heath held up the right hand Trinity had permanently marked. "Trinity saved my life, but the concussion from the blast and the shrapnel that sliced my thick skull put me out."

Squinting against the sun, Aspen nodded to Trinity. "And her?"

That was a story he didn't deserve, the undying loyalty and devotion of a creature with a pure heart. "When they sent me stateside, she refused to work with other handlers. So they retired her—gave me first dibs."

Aspen wrinkled her nose and looked at Jibril. "I'll be honest. I'm not sure about this."

"It will take time, but I think it will help him, and you."

"I'm not sure Talon—" Aspen froze as the yellow Lab ducked at the mention of his name. "Oh, I'm sorry, boy." She rushed to his side and knelt. "It's okay," she crooned as she stroked his head.

"Don't baby him."

Aspen looked up at Heath. "What?"

"He's going to read your soft voice as a reward for cowering. He's a trained soldier, a warrior, a killer. Even though some people don't like the sound of that, it's true. He's trained to take down terrorists, men with bad intentions, and rout explosives from hot spots. He's not a pampered pet. Don't treat him like one. Give him some respect."

"But he's scared."

"I guarantee while your brother loved that animal, he didn't baby him. They were partners in combat, not out for a playdate."

She let out a small grunt with a smile. "Point taken."

A dog bounded out of a Jeep and through the gate. *Crap, that isn't a dog. It's the Hound of Hell.*

"Ah, Timbrel. Welcome! I am Jibril Khouri."

Dressed in jeans, a long-sleeved black shirt, and hiking boots, the woman exuded attitude as she tugged down the brim of her baseball cap. The wind teased the brown ponytail dangling out the back. "I never miss a party."

Something in Heath's stomach churned. Young. Immature. What was she doing with a beast of a dog like that? Hadn't Jibril said all dogs were former MWDs? This one, too?

"Beowulf is as handsome as ever," Aspen said.

"I wouldn't have any other man." Miss Jeep sauntered through and latched the gate.

Heath shoved his attention back to the drool-bombing dog. No wonder the woman named him Beowulf. Or maybe it was because of the dog's good looks. Trinity, ears flattened, had her hackles up as the beast let out a bark that seemed to send ripples through the fabric of time and space. Lip curled, canines exposed, Trinity held her ground as she watched the beast out of the corner of her eye.

"Hey," Heath called to the owner. "Get your dog under control."

"Relax, Prince Charming. He's just having fun." Timbrel laughed. "I sure hope your girl is fixed."

Heath's heart pounded. "Don't blame me if your dog goes home with a chunk of his throat missing."

Timbrel seemed to feed off his warning. "May the best dog win, eh?"

"Timmy," Aspen said, her voice soft but reproachful.

"Okay, fine." With one snap of her fingers, Timbrel brought her mountain of a brown-brindled mutt to her side. She bounced her shoulders with a smirk. "If only I could control men with such ease."

Heath wanted to laugh, but something about this chick grated on him. "If you approach relationships the way you do him, I bet you're single."

"Men have two things on their minds: money, which they're not getting from me, and sex, which they're also not getting from me." She crouched and kissed the mutt, whose jowls were coated in slobber. With a slurping noise that made Heath cringe from six feet away, Beowulf returned the love. "Beo wants nothing but to be with me. He protects me and won't leave me, unless"—she stood and gave a flick of her wrist at thigh level—"I tell him to."

Despite his broad, stocky build, indicating strength not speed, Beowulf sprinted down the field and skidded to a stop, waiting. "Now, see? If getting rid of guys could be as easy. . ."

Heath shook his head. "No wonder they put you out of the Navy."

Her eyes flamed but she didn't miss a beat. "Want to see what he does to men I don't like?"

Heath chuckled. "No thanks. My girl would take your dog down, and I'd hate to see you lose the only 'guy' willing to kiss you."

Her eyebrow arched, challenge scratched into her expression. "Oh, Prince Charming." Her caustic, hollow laugh bounced off the obstacle course equipment. "I think you're going to eat those words and beg for mercy."

Heath flared his nostrils. "I never beg."

"Game on, Hot Snot."

Jibril laughed. "That's quite the introduction. But, let me tell you why we're here." He motioned everyone closer. "I've invited the three of you here for a business proposition."

Aspen leaned against one of the ramps. "And what is that?"

"Train your dogs."

"Look," Miss Jeep snipped. "I came out here because Aspen knows your sister and said I could trust her, but. . .this just reeks."

"Like your attitude," Heath muttered. He'd dealt with worse. Heath pointed to the man he'd served in combat with. "Jibril is one of the best men I know. He doesn't talk often, but when he does, it's worth listening to."

"Miss Hogan," Jibril said. "I bought this property so handlers like yourself, Miss Courtland, and Ghost could continue training your dogs, and possibly others."

"To what end?"

"Once you are comfortable with your dog's training and progress, I would ask that you allow me to place each dog-handler team on the grid."

"Grid?" Heath couldn't stop the frown. *Grid* sounded too much like combat. Being messed up the way he was with traumatic brain injury, he wasn't looking to press his luck.

"Yes, make your services available to others who might need your help." Jibril's smile this time hung an inch from genuine. "My sister, Khaterah, is a veterinarian. She's agreed to treat your dogs."

"Then...why do you seem like you aren't happy?" Heath had known Jibril long enough to see through that.

His friend's face fell for a fraction, but when his gaze hit Heath's, he shrugged. "We have a difference of opinion on a few things."

Aspen offered a smile. "Khat is one of the most beautiful women I know—inside and out. She loves animals and hates violence."

"Who likes it?"

"You." Jibril's green eyes held Heath's. "Me—according to her. Since we were in the military, since you train your dogs to protect, she believes it breeds violence."

Heath raised his hands. "Okay. Got it. So, who would be hiring us?"

"It would all be contract work. I've seen interest from companies who have contractors on the ground in Iraq and Afghanistan. I've even seen interest from our own military. They've seen the great benefit of war dogs and will pay nice fees to have a for-hire availability."

Heath pursed his lips, considering the info. "HPT and VIP escorts, etcetera?"

"Roger." Jibril grinned.

"I like the idea," Hogan said. "But what's this to you? Why are you doing it?"

Though tempted to roll his eyes again, Heath remained neutral as Jibril moved toward a central position among the four of them—*is he limping?*—and bent down.

"Two years ago, I was a Green Beret." He tugged up his right pant leg...up...up. Until shiny black and silver metal glinted in the sun. A prosthesis. "Were it not for Trinity and Ghost, I would not have just lost my leg that day. I would have lost my life."

★ ★ Three ★ ★

Hindu Kush, Afghanistan
One Week Later

A cool breeze slid across Darci's shoulders, swirled around her bare neck, and trailed down her spine. She drew her legs closer as she sat on a small outcropping and laid aside her field notebook and pencil. Though she'd climbed higher mountains than the one that cradled her now, there was something forbidding, ominous about the Hindu Kush. Rugged, brutal beauty towered over her, as if daring her to carry out the mission. Her most dangerous to date. But she was up for it. She had to be.

Glancing at her field book, she groaned. A week of field mapping and field checking the Russian geologic maps for validity amounted to seven days of backbreaking hammering, measuring, sketching. . .

"In other words, mind-numbingly boring." She freed her jet-black hair from the elastic and rubbed her scalp, letting the wind whip it free and loose.

Though she'd gone out each night searching, she'd found nothing. No sign of her targets. If she didn't find something soon, she'd have to go back a failure.

She'd never failed a mission or her commanding officer. Her dedication and commitment to her country and its foundations forbade her from allowing defeat.

A yawn tugged at her, and she rubbed a hand over her face, trying to shake off the sleepiness. As she did, a striation in the rock below caught her attention. Darci tilted her head, then brought herself forward onto all fours. Gingerly, she peeked over the lip of the outcropping. Straight down—more than seventy feet. She grinned at the challenge.

But no—her focus. The lighter striation. With care, she dug her fingers into the rocks and wedged her toes into the lateral clefts running along the cliff face. Air rushed up at her. Gravity pulled at her limbs. She smiled as her pulse ramped.

"*What* are you doing?"

The gruff voice struck Darci. Her foot slipped. Rocks dribbled down.

She bit down on a curse as she caught herself, palms sweating against the adrenaline jolt. Peeking up and over to her left, she spied Peter Toque glaring at her. "Tempting fate."

"You've got to be the stupidest, most pigheaded. . ."

Darci blew out a breath and inched away from the ledge. She'd have to check out the striation later—it looked like a hidden path, popular among terrorists to scurry from one location to another. And if that was true, it could lead her to the targets. It fit, didn't it? Well hidden. High in the mountains.

Definitely.

But she'd given bad intel once before, and it had cost. . .too much. She wouldn't make that mistake again if she could help it. She'd verify her suspicions later. Courage rose on the bitter wind, steeling her against fear that had threatened to overtake her earlier.

"Aren't you supposed to be on the other side of this rock?" She glared back as she lifted her field notebook and pencil.

"We finished an hour ago."

"Wow, and you already turned in your field slips and sketches to Dr. Colsen?" Darci would not let this wad of muscle and testosterone get to her. He'd shadowed her every move since they'd landed at Bagram Airfield last week.

"I was on my way back."

"Right." She aimed herself in the direction where her field partner, Alice Ward, worked.

"Hey."

A jerk on her arm spun her around—straight into Toque. If she didn't find him so irritating, she might be willing to admit he had the looks most girls wanted. Angular jawline. Height. Muscle. Blue eyes. But then there was his arrogance.

"What you were doing is dangerous."

She flared her nostrils. "So is touching me."

He released her arm. "Look, I'm just—"

31

"Save it."

"You're not the only one here. And this isn't exactly Central Park."

"If you'd put as much effort into your job in the field as you do in trailing me like a lovesick puppy, maybe we'd be done and back at Bagram, analyzing the maps and able to figure out our next steps."

"Lovesi—" Toque clamped down on the words and shook his head.

She rounded a bend in the path and almost collided with Alice. Despite the jet-black hair—dyed, not natural like Darci's Asian-black—nose ring, and kohl-lined eyes, the girl was as sweet as they came. And she had a Texas-sized crush on the cad behind Darci.

"Jia." The girl's voice and gaze dropped when she saw Toque. "Are you done?"

Darci nodded to the red streaks in the sky. "Night's coming. We should head back."

When they stepped into the cluster of tents set up on the plain central to the area they were testing for lithium deposits, Darci stomped toward her tent. Five tents formed a circular perimeter with a fire pit in the middle. One half of the larger tents served as the communications hub, replete with computers and equipment Darci could barely spit out the names for, while the other half sported a long table with two benches used for conferences and meals.

"Hey, Jaekus. You missed all the fun." Toque grabbed a tin cup and poured himself a hot drink from the large steel drum. "Jia there was scaling the cliff when I found her—should've been there with her."

Something about Peter Toque unsettled her and left her guessing. Darci couldn't put her finger on it, but she would. Soon enough.

Perched atop one of the field chests, Jaekus raised an eyebrow at Darci. "Rock climbing again, eh?"

Darci shrugged. "I saw some unusual striations in the rock. Wanted to check it out."

"You have killer instincts, Darci. Trust them." The general's admonishment years ago had come at a high cost—her first and only training failure.

"Well, no more of that." Dr. Colsen ducked as he stepped out of his tent. His muddy brown eyes glared as he dropped into a chair around the hub of chairs and makeshift tables. "I won't be responsible—or have this expedition canceled—because someone took unnecessary risks and got herself hurt or killed."

"It was *necessary*, and remember? I'm a certified rock climber." She might not have the alphabet soup behind her name that he did, but the crash course the general had secured for her enabled her to perform on a level regarding geology with those around her—at least enough to buy time. Dr. Richard Colsen objected to her overseeing the lead on the team, but the man objected to just about everything that wasn't his idea.

"I don't care what you are—except a member of this survey team. If you—"

"All right, all right, old man." Toque pushed off the chest. "Give it a rest."

"You listen here," Colsen said, his face reddening. "This is my project and my name. If I say—"

"Dr. Colsen," Darci said as she joined the team, resting an arm around him. "What results have you found about the samples we brought back already? Are they showing significance?"

The ruddiness bled from his face until the normal, pale color returned. "No." He looked like a grumpy, old man right now. The professor's failing health relegated him to rock analysis instead of the rigorous workout required to carry out the research. Just shy of seventy, how long would he last up here with the thinner air, the rigorous hiking? Maybe it was a good thing he'd elected to remain at the camp while they hiked to check out the terrain today.

It also allowed her time to recon.

"However," he said, snapping her attention to him. "One of the samples Jia brought back from the northeastern grid does show promising signs." His gaze rose to hers, and she saw the approval and thanks for rescuing yet another souring conversation among the team. "We'll look into it further back at the base. When we return in a week, hopefully we can map it out and get the full scope of what's out there."

That worked in Darci's favor. She needed to report in, gather her thoughts, and figure out a contingency plan. That odd striation in the rock plucked at her conscience again. If she could get to the path—*it has to be a path!*—she was certain she'd find a gold mine. She needed to collect samples while she collected information. But Toque was on her back 24/7.

Which meant when they returned, she'd have to ditch the shadow.

RONIE KENDIG

Swaying as if urging Heath onward, the branches shook their limbs at him, void of leaves and weight in the cold February morning. Heath hit the trail that snaked through the trees. The path coiled up and around A Breed Apart's beautiful, expansive setting. Jogging cleared his mind and strengthened his body—and Trinity's. She kept pace without a hint of complaint.

A month. They'd been at this a month, running and training, pushing as he pressed toward the goal of shedding his weakness, headaches, blackouts. The Army had severed his career with the Green Berets because headaches and subsequent blackouts, which occurred when the exercise became too strenuous, left him unreliable. A danger. To himself. To his buddies.

But thirty-two days of fresh outdoor exercise and stress-free workouts in the hills had brought about a significant difference in his stamina and nudged his body toward health. His mind toward all he had to be thankful for these days.

With each foot he planted, Heath felt closer to victory, to "normal."

As he ran the trail, going higher and longer each time, he couldn't escape the irony. First, he and Trinity had been paired up, put through the dog-handler program at Lackland Air Force Base. Nearly five months of training spent there in San Antonio with brutal, suffocating heat, then further training for Special Operations Command. All so they were there that day to save Jibril, who came home—alive. Started A Breed Apart, which gave Heath hope that he hadn't reached the end of his usefulness.

Who was saving whom?

Because of his PTSD and TBI diagnoses, he wouldn't be cleared to return to his Special Forces unit, but maybe he and Trinity could provide some benefit if the chaplaincy fell through. That was his first goal—make chaplain so they'd send him back to the action. To the adrenaline. Serve with the guys. Be one of them again.

At the summit, Heath stood on a ledge that protruded from the cliff, noting the throb at the base of his skull. In recent days, the effects were much reduced.

Lowering himself to the rocky lip brought Trinity to his side. He wrapped his arm around her, the sun glistening across her tan hues, making the amber color richer. Around her broad chest, shoulders, and hindquarters, it looked as if an artist had shaded her coat with charcoal. But what made him fall in love with the Belgian Malinois was her almost completely black mask. At times, when the sun set just right on her coat, it almost seemed as if her black mask were the burned sections, indicative of the fire brimming beneath. And man, was there ever fire in this dog's belly that streamed out through her amber eyes.

"Hey, beautiful," he mumbled as her keen gaze locked on the wilderness. Legs dangling over the ledge, Heath tugged the bite valve from the CamelBak and took three long drags from it. As the cool water swirled around his mouth, he aimed the valve at Trinity and squirted her.

Her head snapped around, and she lap-licked at the water. Sated, she shook out her fur.

"Hey." He shielded himself as water sprayed him. "Payback, huh?"

She nudged the paper sticking out of his waistband.

"Can't ignore the inevitable, huh?" Heath plucked the white envelope and stared at it. The U.S. Army logo stamped in the left-hand corner. Inside, words that formed his future. They had to let him in. It made sense, having been a Green Beret, to get assigned to SOCOM as a chaplain. It was his dream. His yearning.

What if they rejected him? He should've had his new stats sent to them. That would have given him his clear shot. They didn't know, though, how much better he was doing. How improved he was.

Trinity sniffed the envelope.

"Yeah, yeah," he grumbled as he shoved his finger between the flap and the envelope, ripping it open. The wind tapped against the paper, crinkling it in his hand. Heart in his throat, Heath scanned the words, his courage slipping, pebble by pebble like the dirt on the ledge.

"We regret to inform you. . ." Lips moving with no sound, Heath shook his head. "Augh!" He balled up the letter. What? Even God was rejecting him? Telling him he wasn't even good enough for the chaplaincy program?

How could that be? He grew up Baptist. Knew scripture—he'd won every Bible drill in youth group! Faithful and Christian. How could he get denied?

Just like everything else. Shut off. Cut off. Closed off.

He punched to his feet, paced. What type of person got rejected from the chaplaincy? With a growl, he kicked the dirt off the ledge. Trinity stared at him, ears perked. He ran a hand over his face and the back of his neck. "Unbelievable!"

A few minutes later he returned to Trinity's side and they sat in quiet solitude. It brought back so many memories of doing the same—in combat. Sitting for hours on end, watching a settlement. Waiting for a target. Climbing into heavy air as they tracked down Taliban rebels in the brutal hills and mountains, where the fighters had the advantage over the team but not over Trinity, who'd seized many a bad guy.

Expelling a long breath, Heath stared out over the land. Those days were long gone but maybe not as much as he'd feared. The chaplaincy. . .

But isn't it hard to preach what you don't believe?

Heath shook off the thought. "Why are You doing this to me, God? You keep closing doors. . . ."

A sparkle snagged Trinity's attention. She craned her neck forward, watching the sun glint off a windshield. Digging his fingers into her coat, Heath watched Jibril's SUV lumber up the drive to the house. He'd worked with the guy for less than a year, but even then, Heath figured out Jibril was made of steel inside. Now, with this ranch, Heath knew he'd been right. Now that he didn't have the chaplaincy, this ranch, these gigs, were his only chance to feel like he had a purpose.

Heath patted Trinity's side. "C'mon, girl. Let's see how he's doing." The jog down was no less treacherous, but it was less arduous. They cleared the trees and made their way to the fenced-off arena.

Jibril stood at the gate waiting. "Morning!"

Panting and mouth dry, Heath nodded as he let Trinity inside. "You're here early."

Trinity trotted to a small trough, where he lifted a hose and provided the water. She lapped as he sipped from his bite valve.

"You must like the ranch," Jibril said. "You've been here every day for the last four weeks."

Heath eyed his friend.

Jibril shrugged. "The security logs show you accessed the gate every morning at the same time—except on Sundays, when you come earlier."

Retrieving Trinity's ball, Heath tried not to read into Jibril's happiness—or nosiness. What was the guy doing tracking his movements? His buddy was a dichotomy at best. On the phone or through e-mail, you'd never guess he'd grown up in a home with an Iranian father. Or that his first language was Farsi. And you'd never pick him out of a lineup as a terrorist with those green eyes and light brown hair, unlike his sister who had most of their father's features with black hair, brown eyes, and an exotic look. Heath had to admit she was a beauty.

The anger over the rejection needled him. He was stuck here. With them. As a nobody. He whipped the ball down the arena.

"Are you well?"

Trinity bolted, her body streamlined as she tore up the ground getting to it.

Heath jerked a glance toward Jibril. "No. Not really. They refused me for the chaplaincy. Said my last eval rated too low." Tail wagging, pleasure squinting her amber eyes, Trinity trotted back to him. "Trinity, out."

After a few more chomps on the ball, her teeth squeaking over the rubberized toy, she deposited it at his feet.

"Good girl," he said, rubbing her ear. He shifted in front of her and held out a hand to her. "Trinity, stay." He backed up several paces, then shifted and flung the ball down the grassy stretch. "Trinity, seek."

Again, she launched after it, her gait firm and purposeful.

Heath let her get about halfway, then called, "Trinity, down."

She went down, her nails clicking on the pebbles as she flattened against the ground. It seemed her body trembled with the broken anticipation of retrieving her toy. But her attention never wavered from her target that lay so close yet out of reach.

"Good girl." He waited and let a few seconds fall off the clock. "Trinity, seek."

She lunged into the air and closed the distance, seizing her toy.

"Trinity, heel!"

At his side within seconds, she kept the ball.

"She's magnificent," Jibril said.

Heath ate up the praise. He loved his dog and knew she was an impressive animal. She made him proud.

"Will you take her through the course?"

"Yep. You wanna put the bite suit on?"

Jibril's eyes widened. He swallowed. "Uh, sure." A fake smile. "She won't hurt me, will she?"

"You just said she's magnificent."

Arm held out, Jibril rotated it. "So is my arm! I'd like to keep this limb."

Heath's intestines cinched. *Smooth move, ex-lax.* "Aw, man. I'm sorry." The guy already lost his leg and Heath wanted to put him in a bite suit so Trinity could attack him? "I didn't—"

"No," Jibril said with a stern expression, gaze darkening. "We're friends. Don't do this. I'm very grateful for my life." The light returned to his eyes. "I just make it with one skin-and-bone leg and one microprocessor-and-noble-anthracite leg."

"Microprocessor?" Okay, it sounded space-age just saying it. Something like the movie *I, Robot.*

"It senses my full body movement and compensates."

"No kidding?"

"Nope." Jibril crossed the yard and retrieved the padded bite suit that made him look like a trimmed-down Michelin Man. "Just remember—"

"Ya know, this may not be a good idea, you getting in that suit. You'll have to run, and she'll chase you."

Jibril laughed. "I know how to run." He stepped into the thick suit.

Something seemed inherently wrong with this. Heath had been trained to protect guys like Jibril, who might think they knew what they were doing but really had no idea what they were getting into. "Okay, listen, just hold your arm out—she's trained to go for the part that's sticking out the farthest. We won't have her chase you."

"Are we doing this or not?"

"Trinity, heel." Heath waited as she sat beside him. Eyebrows bobbing as she peeked at Heath, then back to Jibril, she seemed to ask, "Now? Can I? He's getting too far away. . .you'd better hurry or he'll get away."

Anticipation rippled through her coat as she awaited the command. Jibril held out his arm and nodded to Heath.

"Trinity, seek!"

With a bark, she burst into action, straight for the would-be attacker. Sailed through the air with a grace and elegance that belied her purpose.

Her jaws clamped on the suited arm.

Jibril grunted but pulled away, making sure she had a good bite. He turned a circle, Trinity tugging and growling. Whipping her head side to side.

Heath jogged over to them. "Trinity, out!"

After another test bite, she released and unhooked her teeth from the material and returned to her handler.

"Good girl, Trinity. Good girl. Heel." On the other side, he rewarded her by tossing her ball. She sprinted after it, tackling the thing, then chomped it before returning.

Jibril laughed as he shed the extra heat. "She's amazing. You both are. I've always admired how well you work together."

Heath grinned, an arm hooked over a training window. "She's my girl."

After Jibril returned the suit to a hook, he joined Heath, all seriousness and business. "I was contacted about you and Trinity."

Stilled by the news, Heath waited. More bad news? Did someone else say he wasn't good enough?

"The PAO would like you to go over and speak to the troops. Show them what Trinity can do. Tell them your story."

Public Affairs Office. Great. They wanted his story—a sob story. "I don't know. . ." He'd hated the people who came over acting like they knew all about military life, knew what it was like to be soldiers in combat. In some of them, he saw the judgment. The thinly veiled belief that he was a killer. In most, he saw fear mixed with awe.

"They know you, Heath. You've been there, done that. You got hurt but came back stronger."

"Stronger?" Heath snorted, hands planted on his belt, gaze on the field, on the emptiness before him. "I don't think so."

"It's true. They need to see that if something happens, if they lose something—a piece of their heart, mind, or"—Jibril tapped his prosthesis—"body, it's not over."

Yeah, you'd have to believe that to dish it out.

"Will you go?"

It'd all be a sick reminder that he could never be the man he wanted to be. But he couldn't say that to Jibril. *Especially* not Jibril. Mr. MicroKnee.

"Yeah, I'll go."

Four

Soldier & Airmen's Home
Washington, DC

I'm going back," Heath whispered into the semidarkened room. Bent forward, elbows on his knees, he threaded his fingers and stared at the form lying on the bed.

Crisp white sheets tucked in around the once-strong body peeked out from a gray wool blanket. Hall light stretched across the darkened room and snaked over the safety bars and myriad tubes and cables surrounding the hospital-style bed. The silent feed of oxygen pumped the vital air into the lungs of the sixty-two-year-old man.

General Robert Daniels.

His uncle. More like a father. The man who'd raised him, loved him, nurtured him after his parents' deaths in a car accident when he was two. Uncle Bobby was Heath's hero. He'd served more than thirty-five years in the Army, a short stint in 'Nam, Panama, the Gulf War, and the War on Terror—the war that ended his career and trimmed a year or two off his life.

Well, if you could call breathing through a machine and being fed by someone else a life. It wasn't much by normal standards, but it enabled Heath to hang on to his uncle a little longer. Clinging to the hope that Uncle Bob might come out of this. They told him it wasn't possible. It'd take a miracle.

And Heath was too aware of how rare those were.

"Not to war—well, yeah, to the combat zone, but not as a soldier." He snorted. "They wouldn't even let me be a chaplain." The wound over those words was still raw. He rubbed his knuckles, aching for the man who'd guided him through many a bad decision to speak up, tell him if this was the stupidest thing he'd ever done. "Trin's goin', too—I know how much you like her, got a kick out of her."

A cool, wet nose nudged his arm.

Heath slid his hand around Trinity's shoulder and patted her chest, massaging his fingers into her dense fur. The staff at the home allowed her as long as he let her "perform" for the veterans and wounded. It was a small highlight in their day, and seeing those faces light up after, no doubt, hours of boredom, made his day, too.

He sighed and rubbed his hands over his face as he slumped back in the chair. Head against the wall, he looked at his uncle. Two years like this. Moments of amazing clarity suffocated by long stretches of comatose-like absence. More gone than not in recent days.

If Heath went back in this condition, would he end up like Uncle Bobby? What if he *wasn't* better, improved? Just because Heath wasn't with the military in an official capacity didn't stop attacks. Americans were Americans—prime targets. War dogs and specialized search dogs were high-value targets. Terrorists paid big for dead military working dogs. Couldn't exactly explain to an RPG that you had peaceful intentions.

Then again, hadn't he wanted to be like Uncle Bobby all his life? Wasn't that why he joined up in the first place?

"Heath, live your own life. You don't have to follow in my boots, son."

That willingness to let Heath pursue any career, that care and advice, was the reason Heath joined at seventeen, with Uncle Bobby's approval and signature for an early sign-up. Heath walked the stage at his high school graduation with honors, skipped the parties, and flew to Fort Benning Monday morning.

Leaving his uncle now, after vowing to take care of him for the rest of his life—he felt a deep conflict. He owed his uncle. Owed him the respect of seeing him live out his remaining days with dignity after all the hours he'd invested in Heath, in the nation. What if something went wrong—if the Old Dawg finally gave it up after all this time? What if the doctors needed Heath to sign off on something?

Dude, chill.

He was overreacting. It wasn't like his missions with Special Forces where he didn't have contact with his family for months at a time. This was a PAO gig. Two weeks over, then back home.

41

No big. No worries.

A shadow broke the stream of light and Heath's concentration. Straightening, he glanced to the side and smiled at the brunette leaning against the door.

"I thought I could smell wet dog. Oh, and you brought Trinity."

Her tease pulled a smile from Heath. "Hey, Claire. How's it going?"

Nails clacking against the vinyl, Trinity sauntered over to Claire Benedict and nosed her hand.

Heath pushed out of the chair.

The fiftysomething woman smiled. "Good." She tossed her chin toward the bed. "Has he been awake at all?"

Surprise lit through him. "Awake?"

"Yep, the Old Dawg woke up this morning when I was here." Her voice, always filled with honey, held a fondness that made Heath ache. If his uncle had been. . .well, not been laid up, would he have remarried after Auntie Margaret died ten years ago? Maybe married Claire? She'd entered his life right before the general headed over for his final tour.

Heath grinned. "He always was partial to you."

"That's only because I didn't let him treat me like one of his recruits, nor did I let his bark scare me off."

He laughed. "There is that."

Eyebrow arched, she gave him a look. "You okay?"

"Yeah, sure."

"You'll have to do better than that if you want to convince me." Always ready with cheese cubes, Claire tossed one to Trinity. "So, what's eating you, Heath?"

He leaned back against the wall. "I have a gig for me and Trinity. It's a morale-boosting thing."

"For you or them?" Wariness crowded her mature but attractive features. "Where?"

"Northern Afghanistan for a week, then heading south."

She sighed and tossed another cube to Trinity. Standing, Claire folded her arms. "He'd tell you to go, that you have a warrior's heart." Her gaze drifted to his uncle's bed, and her lips twisted and tightened. "War didn't scare him. Being weak did." Her eyebrow arched again. "That's what you're thinking, isn't it? That because you're not over there, you're somehow weak, or less?"

Heath stared at his boots. "Wasn't thinking anything of the sort." Though it might seem odd, him talking to a woman not related to him, they'd both spent many hours watching over his uncle. She had leverage in his life not many did. "Besides, I wasn't looking for it. This gig came to me."

"How?"

Still. . .talking to this woman always made him want to close up. Claire had an uncanny ability to read him, to cut open his heart and expose things he hadn't seen or didn't want to see. But he told her about A Breed Apart, about Jibril, about his new training regimen that had helped him overcome most of the TBI effects.

"I feel good, focused, for the first time in eighteen months."

Quiet draped the room, punctuated by the bleeping and hissing machines. When seconds turned into minutes and he felt the bore of her gaze drilling him, he finally closed his eyes. "Go on. Get it out. I know you want to say something."

"You're not weak, Heath."

His attention snapped to hers.

"Going back, doing this—it may be a good thing—but it's not going to give you back what you think you lost. You're a strong, amazing young man. Bobby always said that. He was very proud of you."

But Uncle Bobby didn't know today from ten years ago. He didn't know that Heath had lost all he'd worked for, all the general had lauded and clapped him on the back for.

"Yeah, he *was*." Heat and pressure built in his chest. He rolled it up and stuffed it away with his humiliation and shattered pride. "I'd better get going." He called Trinity and started down the quiet hall.

"Heath." Her voice chased him.

He hesitated at the juncture that led to the elevators as he met her soft gaze.

"The man Robert loved is the man whose character got him where he was. Not the career he chose or the uniform he wore—or doesn't wear." That tone again, the one that slipped past his barriers—like a slick coating on a sour pill that made it go down easier—forced him to listen. "No matter what you do or where you go, your character is what will always make your uncle proud."

"Claire, he's not even conscious. When he's awake, the doctors aren't sure if he's lucid. He believes I'm a soldier, an elite soldier. That's what he remembers." His throat thickened. "I'm not that man anymore."

Lackland AFB
San Antonio, Texas

"It's not personal."

"Bull!" Heath's temples throbbed as he faced off with Jibril.

When a uniformed presence made itself known shifting into his periphery, Heath lowered his voice so the MP would leave off. "You and I both know this is very personal. Two days ago, this was *my* gig. The PAO asked for me. I agreed. Now, everyone's going?"

"Heath, please—it's not—"

"Don't lie to me, Jibril." Heath cocked his head. "We're too good of friends to go there."

Jibril held his gaze but didn't look away. Silence hung rank and rancid between them as they stood on the tarmac, the C-130 engines ramping up with a whinnying screech. The jumbo plane would ferry them halfway across the world so Heath could begin the speaking engagements.

Heath glanced down at the crate that held Trinity. Just like his partner, he felt caged by the TBI. Would he ever be free? What was this, some enormous lesson on trust? *Is that what this is, God? Because I think I already wrote the book on this with the surgery.*

Jibril broke the silence after a jet roared into the sky from another runway. "It makes sense, Ghost. This is the first mission for the organization. I was coming anyway, and it's logical to bring Timbrel and Aspen. We all need to feel this out. Their dogs aren't coming though."

Pulse whooshing through his ears, Heath reared up. "This. Isn't. About. The. Dogs." If only it were. It wouldn't feel like such a colossal ambush. He took long, deep breaths, trying to calm himself, head off the thumping that warned of a migraine. "It's about me." He poked a finger against his own chest. "You don't think I can handle this. I'm not a cripple."

Calm and ever serene, Jibril said, "No."

Swallowing hard, Heath felt like a heel. The man before him was missing a limb. Before his prosthesis, he'd been a "cripple."

"But you are diagnosed with TBI. And I have a responsibility—

especially with regard to insurance and protecting the organization—to make sure you arrive alive and return in the same condition."

"This is bunk." Heath wanted to spit. "Would you be sending all of us if it was Hogan?"

Hesitation provided the answer.

"I don't believe this." He spun around.

"Please, Ghost—"

"Whatever. Forget it." Heath raked a hand through his short crop. Despite the affront, despite the intense feeling of failure, of not having his friend believe in him, Heath held his anger in check. Anger would only ignite the TBI. It'd inflame an already tense situation. And what if he got so upset he blacked out? Yeah, that would help.

A car rolled to a stop near the private jet waiting.

"Heath, please. Understand my situation—"

"I do." Man, he hated to admit that. Because admitting it tanked the frustration. Tanked the anger. And right now he wanted to be angry. As much as he didn't want to face it, as much as it angered him to almost be called a liability. . .Heath understood the position this put his friend in.

Time to suck it up. To look at the flip side of this coin. "Thanks."

Mouth agape, Jibril blinked. "For what?"

"For believing in me. I know you wouldn't let me go, you wouldn't put ABA at risk if you didn't believe in me." Swallowing his pride, Heath sighed. "Thank you."

Two thuds stamped through the air.

Heath glanced at the car where Hogan and Courtland waited. Aspen wore guilt like a neon *chador*. Hogan on the other hand held her ground. She must've had the world handed to her and didn't care who she ran over getting to the top. Spoiled brat.

"I'll meet you on board," he said to Jibril, then headed up the ramp into the plane. He made his way past the cargo hold stacked with equipment. Techs anchored the pallets with straps.

Getting out of the Army, he thought he'd escaped the looks of pity and actions that bespoke hesitation and concern about his ability to perform his duties. So much for that idea. The truth was spelled out on the three faces of the other ABA members: They didn't trust him to do his job. They expected him to fail.

Heath entered the small cabin area and stuffed himself into one of the seats. After fastening his belt, he pressed the back of his skull into the headrest with his eyes closed. God just wouldn't give him a break. Strip the beret from him. Strip the chaplaincy from his hands. Strip the respect for him from his own team. Anything was better than facing the team he had already failed. Failed with a capital *F*.

Because that's what it boiled down to, wasn't it? If they already felt they had to protect him, then they'd hover over him on the trip. Nobody would be productive. Everyone would be stressed. Especially him.

Why had he agreed to this again?

Oh yeah. Because he thought he could bury the past. Be of help to others.

Hard to do when failure is your middle name.

"Commit your actions to the Lord, and your plans will succeed."

Heath groaned. "I tried that. It didn't work!" He'd made plans. God shut them down. Where was the verse for that?

"We can make our plans, but the Lord determines our steps."

Frustration tangled his retort. Heath pinched the bridge of his nose, letting the agitation and—yes, he had to admit—hurt leech out. He groaned again. *Enough with the verse tug-of-war, God.*

Cool air swirled around him as a light floral perfume intermingled with the treated air. "It was concern that pushed us to talk to Jibril."

Heath shifted but said nothing to Aspen. At least she sounded contrite.

"Heath, look at me."

Jaw clenched, he rolled his head to the right and met clear blue eyes. Dull lights from the cabin ceiling bathed Aspen's porcelain features in a somber glow, adding to the look already in her gaze. "I lost a brother over there." White-blond curls tumbled around her face as a gust of wind carried into the small seating area. "Please understand that I didn't want to lose anyone else. That's the only reason I went along with Timbrel."

Heath leaned forward, anger roiling through his body like an undammed river. "You don't control who is lost and who isn't."

Unfazed, she remained stoic. "Perhaps, but there's safety in numbers."

"Bigger numbers also mean easier targets. Easier to find."

Aspen sighed. "We care. Is that a crime?"

"No, it's not." He adjusted in the seat so he faced her. "But I need you guys to trust me. I wouldn't go over there if I thought I'd put anyone in danger." The words tugged at his conscience. He hadn't even considered anyone else when Jibril mentioned the speaking gig. He'd been so anxious to have a purpose for existing, to bail on boredom and leap headfirst into the action. "Don't say your going is about concern for me. Tell me you wouldn't like to take a look around and maybe find out what happened to your brother."

Her face flushed.

"So, don't put this off on me, okay? I'm healing."

Then why was his vision graying? What was the hollow roar in his ears? Heath dropped against the seat as the world went black.

★ ★   Five   ★ ★

Bagram AFB, Afghanistan

*L*ook *him in the face. Tell him the truth. It would hurt for the first few seconds.*

Darci nodded to the MP guarding the door, and he turned the knob to General Lance Burnett's office. The door swung open to reveal the stuffy interior. Salt-and-pepper hair highlighted by the overhead lamp, the general looked up from his desk. She snapped a salute.

He acknowledged with one of his own. "Kintz! Why do you look like someone killed your cat?"

"I hate cats, sir."

He let out a booming laugh and motioned to the steel chair in front of his metal desk as she heard a click from behind and knew they were alone. "What do you have?"

Seated, Darci let out a long breath. "Nothing, sir." The words were bitter and sour at the same time. She hated bringing back nothing. Hated the very taste of failure.

The wheels on his chair squeaked as he leaned back. "Not what I'd hoped to hear."

She wasn't sure what was more painful—her father who would never let her into his heart because she was a reminder of the wife he'd lost, or the general she would never be able to please after a near failure on one of the biggest missions of her career.

Darci put on her confident facade. "I know, sir. I'll have more for you after our next run. We've only been out there a few days, and that netted me about six hours to reconnoiter alone."

General Burnett stared at her for several long minutes, then narrowed his blue eyes as he dropped forward in his chair. He moved to the small portable fridge that sat beneath a table and pulled out a Dr Pepper. Imported straight from the factory in Waco by his wife, Marilyn. The tiny carbonation combustion hissed through the room. He took a slurp as he turned—his eyes hitting hers. "I'd share, but these are pure gold."

"Of course, sir."

Can cradled in his hands, he sat on the chair beside her. Took another sip, then set the burgundy can on his desk. Clasping his hands together, he took a breath and let it out. "Darci, I need to ask a question."

Oh boy. Here it comes.

"And I want the truth." His blue eyes probed hers. He'd always seen to the truth of things. Which worried her. Especially now. "Is this mission, this location, too. . .close?"

Her nerves fidgeted under his scrutiny. "Sir?"

"Darci," he said, his warning clear: Don't play dumb.

Darci swallowed and darted a glance to his soda. She sure had a lot in common with that sweating can. "No, sir. It's fine."

He roughed a hand over his jaw. Youth clung to his chiseled features—angled jaw, slightly hooked nose that was masculine and strong. Gray streaks in his hair hinted at his midfifties age.

With a growl, he plucked his soda from the desk and returned to his chair. "Look, fine. I won't bring up the past—"

"Thank you, sir."

He hesitated, then plowed on. "But if you don't get me something, I've got to yank you and send you home. Bring in someone who can find what we're looking for."

She wet her lips. "I—"

"Lieutenant."

Pulled up straight by his use of her rank and his "general" voice, Darci stilled.

"This area has seen unprecedented violence in the last few months, and yet we can't figure out where they're coming from. The Chinese are here setting up that mine, and while I'm ticked so much I can't see straight that US research efforts regarding the ores in those mountains on behalf of the Afghans are lost and sold to the Chinese, I need this wave of violence over. Stabilization is the key. We can't do that if we can't find these terrorists." His battle-worn face hardened. "Am I clear?"

Defeat clung to her like the sand out here that seeped into every pore. But she'd brought this on herself. Now she had to fix it. "Sir, yes, sir." She wouldn't look down. She'd withstood much worse interrogations. She'd been beaten within an inch of her life by a man she thought she'd fallen in love with.

But General Burnett. . .he'd plucked her from the mind-numbing boredom of analyzing reports back at DIA. Chosen her for her ability to see what others missed, for her ability to speak Mandarin as fluently as she spoke English. He'd believed in her and recruited her into the covert field she now worked. He'd mentored her, invested his best in her training.

And she'd let him down.

Again.

"I'll find something, sir." If it took her last, dying breath.

Smile lines crinkled at the corners of his eyes. "I know you will, Darci. You're just like your father. That's why I put you on this." He studied her for a minute, then nodded. "That's all."

Weighted by the disappointment in his expression, Darci rose. "Thank you, sir." Why on earth were her eyes stinging? She blinked and rolled her eyes, trying to ward off the tears.

"Darci."

Door open, she stopped. Bolstered her courage. Glanced back. "Yes, sir?"

"You look tired. Take a couple of days off. Check out the entertainment tonight? Might do you some good."

"Thank you, sir, but the geology team heads out in the morning."

He scribbled something on a notepad, called in his MP, handed him the slip of paper, then grinned at Darci as the young specialist slipped past her. "Not anymore. Departure delayed due to activity in the area."

Entertainment was the last thing she wanted. "Yes, sir."

"Lieutenant." He scowled. "That's an order."

Irritation skidded through her. "Understood, sir." Was he trying to butter her up? Soften his blow? Or was he trying to tell her something by ordering her to the entertainment show tonight?

"You okay, ma'am?"

Darci jerked her head to the side, surprised to find another specialist in place. "Fine."

Just fine. He'd grounded her. Again.

She strode from the building, muscles tense, mind buzzing. Why did it feel like her entire career was on the line? She had to ramp things up. Quit playing it safe. She'd avoided a couple of opportunities while in the mountains with the geology team, afraid of being discovered. Well, she'd connived her way out of many a situation. She'd been gifted with a quick mind and tongue. But she hadn't completed her mission—yet.

Her boots crunched on the dirt road between Command and the mess hall. She'd grab a bite for dinner, then head over to the field for the entertainment. She'd be there in body but not in mind—she'd be tracking routes and exploring possibilities.

Movement collided with the clap of a bark, pulling Darci up short as a large dog bolted into her path. It jumped and pegged Darci with its front paws—almost knocking the breath and life from her—then dropped back and barked twice. Alarm died down as Darci stared at the dog. Tail wagging, the canine seemed to have something on its mind.

"Hey"—Darci craned her neck to the side and peered at the dog's underside—"girl. What's up?" She bent toward her, noticing the tattoo on the left ear. Darci jerked back up. MWD. Which meant no petting. "So, you're not just a stray."

The dog sat on its haunches, pink tongue dangling out the side of her mouth. Gorgeous coloring, rippling with power and yet restraint. On all fours again, she backed up, prancing and tossing her head as she barked. Wagged her tail. As if she recognized—

Darci sucked in a hard breath. This couldn't be happening. . . She leaned closer to make out the dog's identification numbers.

It was him—her.

Darci took a step back, feeling the heat and nausea of fear spiral through her veins.

The dog tensed.

I am dead meat.

A beast of a Mine Resistant Ambush Protected vehicle towed a Humvee, severing Heath's visual cue seconds after seeing Trinity's spine go rigid. He slapped the MRAP and scurried down its line. "Move!" Between the two, Heath saw a lithe woman bend toward Trinity. "No! Don't touch her." The brakes of the larger vehicle ground, suffocating his words.

Heath tightened his lips. If Trinity saw her as a threat—

He hit the back of the MRAP again and rushed through the two steel hulks, his gaze locked on the woman and his partner. "Trinity, out!" He doubted she could hear him with the noise of the compound, but he had to try. He threw himself over the hitch and beelined toward her.

The woman took a step back.

"No, don't move!" Heath slid to a stop, his boots stirring dust plumes. "Trinity, out!"

His girl stood down and trotted to his side. He eyed the woman as he clipped Trinity back under his control. "Sorry." He straightened, holding the lead taut so there was no give for her to take off again. "She broke behavior. That's unusual for her. Sorry."

Pretty almond-shaped eyes stared back. What was that? Fear? No, not fear. Sluggish movements. Dazed eyes. Open mouth, as if words hung frozen. Shock? What. . . ?

Heath scanned her body to make sure Trinity hadn't bitten her. The woman wore black tactical pants like his, and that gray-on-black North Face jacket wasn't military issue. Long, black, silky hair pulled away from her face. Pink lips. Attractive—*very*. But no wounds as far as he could tell. And no words.

Heath signaled for Trinity to heel. "Did she hurt you?"

As if he'd thrown a bucket of water over her, she hauled in a breath. "What?"

A protective instinct rose within him. He touched her elbow. "Hey, you okay?" Man, if Trinity shook her up this bad—what was she doing out here in a combat zone? Who was she? Civilian?

She shook her head again and pulled away. "Fine." Her gaze flicked to Trinity. "She. . .she seemed to want to play."

"Yeah, sorry about that." He looked back the way he'd come. "Can't believe she did that. She never breaks behavior like that." She was trained not to. This could spell out a disaster, especially on a base where there was constant action and threats. "We need to work on proofing. I guess she's out of practice."

"Aren't we all?"

Her words caught him by surprise, considering her toned physique and confidence that surged to the front all of a sudden. At her transformation, he didn't believe for a second she was out of practice. But he was. He stopped his hand midair—subconsciously reaching for the scars that had shaken the confidence he'd once had in approaching women. "Maybe so."

Though her eyes slanted a bit, she looked half Asian. But she was all beautiful. Her skin—one word came to mind: alabaster.

Okay, now he was losing it. Who even used words like that anymore? He extended his hand. "Heath Daniels."

"Jia."

Her fingers were cold and small in his, yet strong. "Nice handshake." He liked that. A lot. "My uncle says you can tell a lot about a person by the strength of the handshake."

A subtle tinge of pink hit her cheeks. Was she blushing? Man, when was the last time he'd done that to a woman? Maybe he hadn't lost his touch.

"Yeah?" She folded her arms over her chest. "And what does mine say?"

"Confident." Heath nodded, as if agreeing with his own assessment. Yeah, now that she shook off the shock of meeting Trinity close up and personal, this woman had confidence oozing out of her pores. "You aren't afraid to try something new."

"Interesting." That wasn't quite an affirmation, but the way her lips quirked told him she wanted to smile. But wouldn't.

Why? Could she see his scar? He adjusted the black A Breed Apart ball cap, smoothing his hand down his shorn hair. She hadn't seen the back of his skull, so she couldn't have seen the scar. Right?

Shift gears. Don't obsess or stress.

Laughter billowed on the cool wind as the sun set. Heath glanced toward the building guarded by sandbags at least six feet high and deep. Hogan, Aspen, and Jibril disappeared around the door. Chow time.

"We're heading to the mess hall. Want to join us?" It seemed logical, and maybe it'd give him a chance to unwrap the mystery before him. She'd given almost all one-word answers. Was she always this stiff? Or had Trinity rattled her?

Nah. She wasn't the type easily rattled.

Which meant something else was behind her standoffish behavior. The training in him made him want to find out what she was hiding. Or maybe it was the soft brown eyes against that fair skin that tricked him into inviting her to dinner.

Heath took a step toward the building and away from those thoughts.

"I . . ." She wet her lips.

53

"It's a nice quiet dinner with...about five hundred grunts and bad food." He chuckled, trying to ease her nerves. Heath coiled his hand around Trin's lead, noting his partner full at ease so he didn't have anything to be worried about. "I promise, Trinity won't drool on your food tray"—he paused for a smile—"much."

"Sorry, I've got to get to work."

Yeah, should've known a pretty woman wouldn't want to hang out with a washed-up wannabe when there were men around who had all their well-muscled pieces in the right places.

"No worries." He tugged open the door and stepped into the mess hall. Why he even created that personal invitation to rejection he didn't know. He rubbed the back of his neck and entered the cafeteria. Something about her...he couldn't put his finger on it. But she seemed... familiar.

Six

The whumping of rotors had nothing on her pulse.

Darci stalked back into the command building and down the hall. Did the general know? If he knew and hadn't told her... How could this happen? Breathing hard, she hurried around the corner. And skidded to a stop.

No guard.

Meant no general.

Darci spun. What was she going to do? She darted her gaze around the narrow hall, as if the gray cement and walls would provide the solution.

The general would tell her if he'd known Daniels would be here, right? Had the Green Beret returned to duty? He had his dog. He looked fit. Into her mind flitted the image of his black performance shirt stretching over his chest and biceps—*definitely fit.*

Had he been cleared to return to duty?

Okay, this wasn't a big deal. He was here. She was here. But they were on different missions. It wasn't like she'd be working with him or anything.

Then again, little missteps could blow her entire cover.

"Why don't you check out the entertainment tonight? I think it might do you some good."

The general's order pushed her back outside and to the activities building. Inside, she headed to the bulletin board where schedules were posted. A wave of heat rushed through Darci as she stared at an eleven-by-thirteen poster with a handler and his dog. The headline seemed lit in

55

neon lights: FORMER GREEN BERET TO SHARE HIS STORY. There, along with the time and date was an image of Daniels and his Belgian Malinois.

No no no. Darci stepped back, mouth dry. This couldn't be happening.

Okay, calm down. He doesn't remember. According to the doctors and experts, he should have no recollection of her or the first few days after that incident. So, there wasn't a problem. Right? She wet her lips and trudged back into the darkening evening.

But what if he *did* remember?

"One way to find out," Darci mumbled as she pivoted and entered the mess. Then stopped. If he was in there, he was with friends. She wouldn't be able to direct the conversation.

Okay, so. . .then what?

Maybe if she showed up at the activities arena ahead of the scheduled time, she'd catch him before he went onstage. Waiting around wouldn't work because they were flying out first thing in the morning to dig in for the next week for more work. And her only chance to get back to the site and figure out what those striations meant. If her instincts were right. . .

Two hours. She'd have to kill two hours. And she knew just how to do it. In the activities building, she snatched the poster and went to her cot. There she retrieved her laptop, powered up, and while she waited, let her gaze sweep the poster again. He was good-looking, but that wasn't why she had to know about his background.

She typed in the organization *A Breed Apart.* The first page of results provided a link to the website. After scanning the mission statement, she clicked on TEAMS and found a close-up of Heath and Trinity at the very top with a link to his bio. Energy surged through her. This was what she wanted.

A highly decorated Green Beret, Heath Daniels and his military war dog, Trinity, served several tours in Afghanistan, Iraq, and Somalia. Two weeks before returning home for some R&R, Heath and Trinity were involved in a mission that received bad intel. Trinity hit on explosives and stopped Heath, leaving him with permanent scarring on his right hand, but the soldier who tripped the bomb died in the blast.

Never one to give up, Heath fought his way out of the hospital. Diagnosed with traumatic brain injury, he battled excruciating headaches and occasional blackouts. As a result, Heath was medically discharged.

Darci stared at the words, choked up. He'd been discharged. She'd heard the men on his team saying he'd rather be dead than not serve. Is that why he'd joined the private contracting dog team?

She scanned down a little more and read about their journey toward a civilian partnership. Impressive that the dog had become too attached to be reassigned to another handler.

He was a hero. One of the real ones. And even though she had more information on him now, she still didn't know what he remembered of the incident or the days after.

A distant noise—no, barking! Darci punched to her feet. Outside, she spotted Heath and his dog crossing the compound. Heath flung a ball down the road, and Trinity bolted after it.

Back at her cot, Darci powered down and stowed her laptop. She snatched a clean shirt and stuffed it on, then brushed out her hair. As she checked her teeth, she stopped. *What're you doing? It's not a date.*

True, but maybe if she was a little refreshed, she'd be more on her toes.

Yeah, go with it.

Within minutes, she entered the outdoor "theater," if one could call it that. It amounted to a field where chairs had been set up and a black stage that stretched the width of the front. The two times she'd been here before had been for celebrities. Once with country crooner Craig Morgan, and the next time she had the privilege of witnessing the genius that was the Lt. Dan Band with cofounder Gary Sinise.

Darci edged around the fenced-in area, careful to cling to the shadows at first.

Onstage, Heath walked back and forth with Trinity on a lead. They made it to stage right, and he released her lead. Though he said something to the dog, Darci couldn't make it out. Then he walked to the middle and lay down.

Trinity watched him, 100 percent focused on her handler. In the spotlights of the stage, the amber shading of her coat seemed more vibrant than usual. Her black nose all but vanished against the black curtain.

Trinity launched forward and raced to Heath's side in what looked like two large bounds and heeled at his side. Incredible. What signal had he given? Darci hadn't noticed one.

Heath sat up and rubbed her ears. She licked his face.

"Daniels!"

Darci flinched as someone came up on her six, glanced at her, then continued toward the stage.

Heath squinted at them, apparently blinded by the glare of the lights.

"They're moving your show up," the man announced. "You've got thirty. You good with that?"

"Sounds like the choice was made for me."

The man laughed. "You got it." He spun and stalked away.

Darci eased out of sight.

"Jia?" With one hand on the ledge, Heath hopped down from the stage and Trinity with him. The guy's muscles rippled and stretched his shirt taut.

Those were things she should notice as a part of her job. Because it told her he had the muscle power to take her down. Of course, it shouldn't elicit a traitorous, involuntary reaction from her body. But it did. How crazy was that?

She stepped into the open. "Hi."

His cockeyed grin made her heart skip a beat. *Grow up, Darci!*

"You checkin' up on me?"

"Actually, yes."

He raised an eyebrow. "Yeah?" Why did he seem so pleased? It was meant to put him on the defensive, not make him happy.

"Saw the poster in the activities building, so I looked up A Breed Apart." She walked with him to the side of the outdoor theater. "And your bio."

"Ah." Heath's smile faded as he looked down.

"I'm glad Trinity came home to you."

He shot a sidelong glance to her, then to Trinity. "Yeah, I was lost without her. When they called and said she was declared 'excess,' I flew into action. Paid to bring her back and picked her up after the vet cleared her."

"You're a good team." Thank goodness, her mistake in the field hadn't created a permanent separation.

From his pocket, he produced a ball. Trinity pranced, turned, scurried a few feet, then glanced back. Heath flung it down the aisle of the seats. Trinity tore off after it.

He leaned against the platform that formed the soundstage. Hands resting on the wood on either side of him, he looked at her. "So, you know my story—"

"Not all of it."

He cracked another smile, then tossed his chin at her. "What's your story?" He slumped back and folded his arms over his chest. "What're you doing out here on a military base? I mean, I have yet to see you in ACUs or battle dress, and you don't salute the officers."

Wow, he hadn't missed much. Although she did salute General Burnett. But him alone.

"Geology. I'm with a geological survey team." Why did that lie feel like a mouthful of the rocks they'd been studying? "We've been here a few weeks already, and we head out first thing in the morning."

Soldiers trickled into the arena as Trinity trotted back with her ball. Heath retrieved it and tucked it in his pocket. Trinity paced, then sat back on her haunches at Heath's side.

"What are you surveying?"

"Rocks."

"Wow, I never would've guessed."

Darci laughed and relented with the information. "There are reports of lithium up in the mountains, so we're trying to determine if mining will be lucrative or a waste of time and resources."

He shrugged. "Yeah, but the Chinese are stealing all our gigs. Why do the work for them again?"

Darci eyed him. He'd paid attention to what was happening here. She couldn't say the same for many of the soldiers or most people she knew. "Thankfully, my job is just to determine if the deposits are large enough to warrant mining. I'll let the politicians argue out their differences."

He nodded, watching the men and women filter in.

"But I would hope that no matter who mines the lithium, Afghanistan can become a stable, formidable country."

"Amen."

"Religion?" She kept the curiosity from her tone.

His smile twisted to the side. "Sort of bred into me. Grew up in church, my uncle dragging my angry teen butt in every Sunday." He glanced at his watch. "Hey, I need to head backstage." He took a step away, his gaze on hers. "Are you staying for the show?"

Darci saw it all over his face. Expectation. Hope. What was even stranger was she felt it. A hunger within her to be wanted, to have someone who cared, gnawed at her defenses. "I wouldn't miss Trinity in action for the world."

Amusement twinkled in his pale gray eyes. "Good. Would you. . . ?" He checked the crowds again, then hauled his attention back to her. "Up for a walk afterward?"

Her chest squeezed. "I. . ." She had to get some sleep. They were heading out early. "Sure."

"Great." He looked down at the lead in his hand, then peeked at her again. "I know this will sound crazy since we just met, but I like hearing you talk. Your voice sounds familiar."

"The men and women beside you are your friends, your partners. You're on the same team," Heath said at the close of his presentation as he stepped off the stage, walking the center aisle, pleased that he hadn't fainted, blacked out, or choked up. "You hang out, you grab rec and rack time together—well, no coed, or you'll have officers breathing down your neck."

Laughter rippled through the packed-out area.

"But you're there for each other. You've got each other's backs."

Beside him, Jibril—dressed in full practice gear—stood and lunged at him.

He heard the collective gasp and knew the plan had worked. Turning, he saw Trinity sail off the stage, over the heads of a half dozen soldiers and right into Jibril's back. Which shoved Heath—and his head—straight into a chair.

Whack. His teeth vibrated against his skull. Pain speared his head and neck.

But he regrouped. Shoved aside the pain. Focused on Jibril, who'd gone down beneath the weight of Trinity, who'd chomped on the heavily padded arm.

Heath hauled himself upright. "Trinity, out!"

Disengaging, she shook her head to release her teeth from the fabric, then trotted to his side.

The crowd erupted in applause as he helped Jibril to his feet and out of the suit. Concern clouded Jibril's eyes as he whispered, "You okay? Your head hit—"

Heath winked, about all he could do with the searing fire in his neck and back. Afterward, he'd down a few ibuprofen and be fine.

He returned to the stage as the applause died down. "As you can see, Trinity is trained to protect me with or without commands, with or without a lead. She's got my back. The funny thing is—that fateful day, she warned me." Man, he hated to admit that. "Told me there was something bad, and I didn't listen—that day, *I* broke behavior. Another guy on my team hadn't noticed Trinity's warning. He lost his life, and I almost did, too."

Heath looked down, remembering Tiller. "Sometimes, we do that to God." The words served as a gong against his conscience. "He prods us, gives us warnings, and we just ignore it. Do life our way." The truth clogged in his throat.

Heath swallowed and went on. "Then when things go bad, we blame Him. Get angry." *Oh yeah. Definitely.* "In fact, I'd bet someone in this crowd is ticked at me right now for even bringing this up." He held up his hand with the scars from Trinity. "Don't put God in a position where He has to scar your sorry carcass. I did that. Then I was ticked. Beyond ticked!" *Still am!* "I hated God, hated life. Laid up with TBI and discharged from the one thing I wanted in life—being a Green Beret—I blamed God for everything."

Shame gripped him, thinking of Jia listening to him. What would she think? He had this overwhelming need to see her reaction, yet as he scanned the crowd, he couldn't see her. Or worse, what if she learned he still felt that way? Not as much. . .but the aftereffects lingered.

He shared how he'd begged God for a miracle—to heal him. When it was obvious that wouldn't happen, he sunk even lower. In his darkest hour, he'd begged God for one good thing to happen. When nothing happened, he vowed his days of begging were over. Never again. But then a ray of sunlight struck his storm-riddled world—he got the call that the Army had decided to retire Trinity.

"God has your back." Toes dangling off the edge of the stage, Heath stared out at the faces of those who put their lives on the line. "You aren't alone. He's there. Always. And I pray you find the strength to reach out to Him." He drew in a long breath and smiled. "Just because things don't go the way *you* planned, doesn't mean God left you. He may have just put you on a new course. Follow the adventure!" He held up a hand. "Thanks for listening to me tonight. I'll be around to talk if you have questions."

Jibril took the stage to explain A Breed Apart a little more, then turned over the stage and night to one of the soldiers, who dismissed everyone.

A steady stream of admirers walked by Trinity, but—thank goodness—they remembered he'd warned them not to mistake her for a domestic dog they could pet. Trinity was working. Always.

He shook hands, signed some miniature scrapbooks, and took pictures with others. All the while, he searched the crowds for Jia. Where had she gone? Heath hoped he hadn't said something from the stage that scared her off. Being brutal-honest with the audience opened himself up to ridicule. But. . .the thought of her thinking worse of him rankled.

Weird. Why would he care what some chick thought? He never had before.

Yeah, and you've never tried to soften up a woman since your life wrecked.

Man, his head felt like someone drove a tent stake through it. What happened? Maybe it was just all the excitement of the night. Or that collision with the chair. He pinched the bridge of his nose.

"Great job," Jibril said as the crowd petered out. "You're a natural." His smile rivaled the lights on the stage. "I knew I picked the right man."

"Thanks. Hey, have you seen—?"

"Your Chinese friend?"

Heath jerked, stunned.

"I saw you two talking before the show." Smoothing his beard, Jibril studied him. "Is she stationed here?"

Heath clipped Trinity's lead on. "She's not military. Civilian with military contract to scout for minerals. She's leaving in the morning."

"I am sorry," Jibril said, his expression somber. "I saw her leave about halfway through your presentation."

"Oh." What did that mean? "Maybe she got a call."

"It is possible." Jibril patted his shoulder. "Are you okay? Your head is hurting?"

"Just too much excitement, I guess."

Jibril looked unconvinced. "This has been a long but good day. Now, I must rest. We head south tomorrow, so be sure to rest up. I'll see you in the morning."

"Right. Okay." But Heath's brain cells were engaged on wondering why Jia had left.

He tugged Trinity's lead toward the tents where contractors bunked. Maybe Jia wasn't feeling well. As he stared down what looked like an endless row of tents, he realized the futility of his personal mission.

Gutting up the disappointment, he headed for his own tent. He rounded a corner and almost stopped, but his old training kicked in and kept him moving. Jia stood with a general, hovering in deep conversation. Jia, a contractor with a *geology* team. With a general. He'd like to hear the explanation for that.

The general's face darkened beneath the large, powerful lamps that shattered darkness in the compound. He stabbed a finger at her, his voice loud but unintelligible.

What's up with that?

Trinity pulled taut, watching the showdown, too. Heath didn't like it, and apparently Trinity didn't either. She stopped short, as if she'd gotten a hit—on Jia. Good thing he'd tethered her, or Trinity would've taken off.

"Trinity, come."

Jia glanced over her shoulder and saw him. She said something to the general, then walked toward Heath. She let out a long sigh as she approached. "Sorry I missed the last part of your presentation."

Heath shrugged. "No worries." He nodded to the general who disappeared into the command building. "What's with that? He looked ticked."

"They're giving us grief over our paperwork again. And I think Dr. Colsen, who's the lead geologist, is being less than gracious—again." She smiled, but it didn't reach her eyes. "So, still up for that walk?"

"Absolutely." Heath headed toward the canine practice field, knowing they'd have the area to themselves. But her story didn't sit straight with him. Why would the military hassle them over paperwork if the team already had been here for three weeks? And why did she seem buttery-sweet all of a sudden?

What was she trying to divert his attention from?

Seven

Copper Mine, Jalrez Valley
Wardak Province, Afghanistan

*H*ear no evil, speak no evil, do no evil.

Carved out of stone, the statue before him epitomized the old proverb, since its head and hands had crumbled and disappeared with time beneath the harsh elements in which its temple sat. And yet, some might think the armless and headless condition of the statue indicated the broken power of the gods.

To the left, another broken stone figure stood on the other side of an entrance. Through that opening lay the mine China had begun to excavate copper from. Frustrating China, the mine bore the great tragedy of being situated at a 2,600-year-old Buddhist temple. What should have been a quick insertion of Chinese progress through mining ore morphed into a nightmare in preserving the reputation of the People's Republic of China by protecting the Afghans' history through archaeology.

Colonel Zheng Haur glanced once more at the crumbling relics. Was it a bad omen?

"So much for the power of their god." Captain Bai smirked.

"No god has power. Only man." How many times had General Zheng said that?

"Colonel." A Chinese lieutenant rushed into the open. The sun struck him as if illuminating his presence. Was that a sign as well—was a god shining on this man who saluted him? "I did not know you were coming. What can I—?"

"I am here to speak with Colonel Wu." Haur kept his focus like steel.

The man's gaze darted around the area as he frowned. "I. . .so sorry, sir. But the colonel left a week ago."

Cold spread across Haur's shoulders. "What do you mean he left?" The orders given to Jianyu had been to remain here till the general sent for him. "His orders were to oversee this mine."

The man nodded and half bowed. "Yes, sir, but he said he was recalled to China."

Haur raised his gaze once more to the stone god. What secrets lay beneath his lap besides archaeological finds? Did Jianyu send this errand boy up here to deceive Haur?

He glanced to his left, where Captain Bai stood ready. The look in the eyes of the man he'd trained and worked with bespoke the suspicion Haur felt. "Search it."

In Chinese, the captain shouted, "Search it!"

A dozen men climbed out of the deuce-and-a-half and trotted through the narrow opening with their weapons in hand.

"You will not find him, Colonel. He is not here." The man shifted nervously. "Please—this site is very old. Your soldiers will disturb the relics and archaeologists."

"We respect your work here, but we have our orders." Haur considered the implications if Jianyu actually had left.

As Haur's men returned to the truck, tension rose.

"When did Colonel Wu leave?"

"I told you, one week—"

Impatience snapped through Haur. "Date? Time? What direction?"

The lieutenant cowered. "I. . .I don't—"

Captain Bai lunged. "Do not—"

"No!" Haur held up a hand to his captain, then redirected his focus on the lieutenant. "A week ago. Was it Thursday? Or Friday—right before the holiday?" Chinese New Year had always been important to Jianyu.

The man's eyes widened. "Yes, yes. He said he was going home just in time to celebrate with his father."

Haur studied the man. There was more to this story, but whether the old man knew it or not was another thing. "Morning or evening?"

"As soon as the sky lightened."

"Let us both hope you are telling the truth." Haur would prefer that this man was not telling the truth, because the implications were too great otherwise. If Wu Jianyu was not here, where was he? What was he doing? And with a group of China's elite, the Yanjingshe warriors?

Haur returned to the Lexus SUV and closed the door. He pulled out his phone and dialed. When it connected he said, "General Zheng, he is not here."

The long pause stretched painfully. "Explain."

"Jianyu left a week ago. He told the miners you called him back."

Silence choked the connection, but as the car pulled over the dirt road, Haur thought he heard hard breathing. No doubt his brother had yet again disappointed the general. He ached for the pain that stretched through the silence. "Should I return—?"

"Find him!"

Haur's chest tightened at the rage in the general's voice.

"Find him and bring him back to me."

"Of course." Haur ended the call and slid the phone back into his pocket. Hand fisted, he pressed it to his mouth and propped his elbow on the window ledge. Staring out over the rugged landscape, he probed the possibilities of where Jianyu had gone. What intention did he have in this game he had begun?

Watching Jianyu collapse beneath the weight of the general's scorn after the spy had been discovered—

Haur diverted his gaze. Even though the incident was in the past, the general refused to discuss the breach and the records had been sealed. Beyond their building at Taipei City, nobody knew of the American spy who had penetrated their so-called secure and advanced systems.

And Jianyu's heart. Something Haur never thought possible. He had wished to have met this spy, the one who broke his brother.

Since the day she had fled back from wherever she had come, Jianyu had become a stranger. His father refused to speak to him. Refused to acknowledge he had a biological son. In the last thirty-six months, *son* became a term applied not to Jianyu but to Haur.

And Jianyu despised him for it.

"This is bad. Here, so close to American and British soldiers. . ."

Plucked from the past, Haur nodded at Captain Bai.

"The general will kill him."

The words hung ominous and true. There was no wrath like that of the enraged General Zheng. Ruthlessly powerful. Yet. . .so gentle and kind—to Haur.

"What do you think he is doing?"

There could only be one reason for Jianyu's disappearance: He wanted to restore his name and honor to his family. To do that, he would of course need some great plan to win his father back. "Whatever he is planning, it is not good."

"Where should we start?"

A glint in the sky lured his attention back out the window. Two small, dark shapes glided along the horizon. Black Hawks. Americans.

Inspiration floated down from those helicopters. Haur straightened. "There. Stop." He pointed to a clearing and snatched the GPS from the dash. As the plan congealed in his mind, so did a horrible certainty.

To see it through, he would not live.

Bagram AFB, Afghanistan

Conversation with Heath had been easy and comfortable. More than it had ever been with any other man besides her father. Hands stuffed in the pockets of her North Face jacket, Darci eyed the man. About six-two, well-built, sandy blond hair cropped short. The guy had a subtle charm that drew its strength not from a cocky attitude, as she'd seen in other men like Jianyu, but a quiet presence that ensnared her curiosity worse than heat-seeking missiles to infrared radiation.

Now he jogged the course with Trinity, leading her up, over, and through the various obstacles. The Belgian Malinois moved with grace and speed, at ease as if she did it every day.

It wasn't Darci's smartest move, seeking him out. Researching him. The whole thing just made her ache. As an operative, she couldn't have the kind of life she dreamed about. A husband, two-point-five kids, and a house in a suburban location.

Even if she could, she didn't deserve it. Not after what she'd done. Not after what her father had done. Darci wrapped her fingers around the cold wire of the chain link, as if holding on to that would somehow enable her to hold on to her dream. Hadn't she spent the last eight years working to regain some honor for her family, for her father? He couldn't have stopped her mother's death. Darci wasn't angry at him. She just wished things could've been. . .different.

A thunderous clap snapped her attention back to Heath.

He and Trinity trotted back into the triangle of light from the lone field lamp. Heath slowed, his feet dragging on the hard-packed ground as he rubbed his temple. But then, as if he hadn't just looked like he was in pain, he lifted the ball and in a fluid move spun around and threw it back into the darkness. Arm swinging around, Heath's gaze locked onto Darci.

Trinity burst after the ball.

As he came toward her, Heath gave a smile that warmed her all the way to her toes. It was more than a friendly hello smile. It was one that showed pleasure in her presence, pleasure that she'd come to him.

"Bored?"

"Tired," she said as she joined him, leaning against the fence. "It's been a long day."

"I'm sure the general's tirade took its toll."

Darci preferred to keep that conversation tucked away. "So, you said you head out for another base?"

"Yep. We'll head out around sixteen hundred tomorrow." He clapped at Trinity, who trotted back into the light in a lazy run and pranced around them, as if to taunt them with "Ha! I caught the ball." She dropped it at Darci's feet.

Wow, wasn't that like breaking some dog-handler code? Darci checked with Heath. "May I?"

Another approving smile shaded his jaw in the uneven lighting. "Sure, I'll deal with the traitor later."

She lifted the slobbery ball from the ground, took a practice step, then sent it sailing through the air.

"Whoa! Nice arm. Where'd you learn that?"

Reveling in his praise, Darci turned as Heath moved away from the fence, stunned. "I played softball in high school and college. Shortstop."

His gaze skated over her with an appreciative nod. "Remind me to never get in your line of fire."

Darci laughed. When was the last time someone made her feel this special? Probably too long, but there wasn't anything to lose here. They would go in opposite directions soon, so no loss, no gain. Well, maybe a small gain. When she was out in the mountains, she could remember Heath's smile. Or the way the sinews in his arms rippled as he threw the ball for Trinity. Or his approving smile. Fantasize that he was the man filling the role that could never happen—husband.

Okay, way too weird.

She needed to be careful. There were certain pieces of classified info that would tank any chance at a relationship—not that there was one. . .

The slower pace of the last twenty-four hours and being with Heath kneaded out some of the kinks in her neck and shoulders. Trinity returned, made her way to the trough, and dropped her ball in the water, then lapped up some refreshment.

"So, you going to tell me?"

They both started toward the gate as if communicating on some hidden signal. The camp had quieted but still bustled with activity as was the MO during wartime operations.

Darci wrinkled her brow as he linked up with Trinity. "Tell you what?"

At five-ten, she appreciated the height on Heath. And his soulful gray eyes. The almost bashful way he behaved.

Hands in his pockets, the lead looped around his wrist, he looked down at her as they walked across the camp. "Whatever it is you're not telling me."

Ouch. Never think a Green Beret is bashful. They were trained to ferret out inconsistencies and get to the heart of the matter. But this was a matter and a heart he couldn't intrude upon. Not this time. As much as she'd wished otherwise.

As her tent came into view, she slowed, then turned to him. "You were a Green Beret long enough to know if I'm not telling you, then I can't." Why did she go and say that?

"Thought so." His gaze raked the blackened sky, disappointment lurking in his eyes.

Time to cut this rendezvous short before she gave in. "Look, it's been nice hanging out with you. Talking. But. . ." She hated this part. But it was necessary. Wasn't it? "You're going on tour, and I'm going into the mountains." She shrugged and shook her head. "Let's not ruin a great friendship with complications."

Despite the creaking of axles and rumbling engines and shouts, the only sound she heard around them was the rhythmic panting of his dog. Though she looked up to read his emotions, she stopped at the one that affected her the most: hurt. It was hard to remember that hardened grunts like him could have soft hearts.

"Complications." He pursed his lips, his chin dimpling. "Right. Yeah." With a quiet, disgusted snort, Heath caught the lead and drew Trinity up. "Well, good night—and good-bye—Jia." He did not wear disappointment well. In fact, it weighted his shoulders. "Hope things go well for you."

She'd taken the abrasive, aggressive road of telling him they'd never see each other again, and he wished her *well*. He the hero, she the villain.

As his form hulked through the darkness, Darci told herself to stay put. Or better yet—go into the tent.

Instead, her feet carried her after the war-dog team. It took a stretch, but she caught his arm. "Hey, wait."

In a lightning fast move, Heath spun around, his eyes bright beneath the floodlight as he flipped their grips so his hand wrapped around her wrist.

Frozen in time and shock, she stared up at him as his fingers slid along her forearm, then back to her wrist until he entwined his fingers with hers. He grinned down at her. "Thought so."

Stunned, Darci mentally pushed him back. . .a dozen feet. But she clung to the husky words. Two simple words that outted her. Strangest thing was, she didn't mind.

Standing toe-to-toe with him did crazy things to her stomach. Though she couldn't resist, she should stop staring at their intertwined hands. She'd *never* reacted like this with a guy. And in those time-warped seconds with their gazes locked, it dawned on her that he'd known she wasn't immune to his charm.

"Just give me a chance, Jia."

Oh, but she didn't like that name on his lips. Darci. She wanted him to call her Darci. "To what?"

His gaze darted around her face, as if studying a political map. "To prove I'm not like whoever hurt you so bad."

Beneath the teasing caress of his husky works, her brain caught up with her stupidity. She freed her hand and swallowed—hard. "It won't work." She wanted to punch him. How had he gotten through her defensive perimeter?

He smirked. "You haven't tried yet."

"Look, it's not that I don't want to. . ."

"Hey. I'm interested. You're interested, but. . ." Heath shrugged, his high-powered smile gleaming as he held up his hands as if in surrender. "I won't beg."

Darci took a step back, her stomach clenched. "I'll e-mail you."

"Cheater."

"Excuse me?"

"It's your get-out-of-jail-free card. You walk away under that ruse, I'll never hear from you again."

It was her turn to smile. A sad, heavy smile. "RockGirl@rkmail.com." With that lie, she pivoted and hurried into her tent. At least he knew the truth.

Eight

Last night had been the best night of his life. . .but it'd also been the worst.

Had Jia blown him off because of the scar? Or because he just wasn't good enough? Like everything in his life he didn't measure up for?

"What happened?"

Heath shot a look at Aspen as they strode into the workout room. "What do you mean?"

Hair pulled back with sprigs of curls framing her face, she rolled her eyes. "You've got more bite than Trinity this morning. What happened?"

Oh. That. "Nothing."

"Did she turn you down?"

Heath ripped open the zipper of his gym bag and grabbed the hand wraps. He straightened and looked toward the corner. "Speed bag."

Aspen's wry grin needled his mood. "Hey, Ghost."

Wrapping his hands, Heath tried to ignore the woman. The yellow roll slipped out of his hand. He grunted.

Aspen stepped in, rolled it back up, then used care in wrapping his hand. Tight. She knew how to do this. "Heath, she's a smart girl. When she realizes what she's missing out on, she'll be back."

He tugged free. "She gave me the kiss-off. Besides, she headed out this morning."

Aspen made quick work of prepping his other hand, too. Heath grabbed his boxing glove and tugged it on using his teeth. She smirked. "I guess that explains why she just came in."

71

Aspen was looking over his shoulder, and he followed her gaze.

Oh, man. Jia. Black workout pants. A red tank. Hair pulled back. Donning gloves.

Unexpected impact against his gloves jerked his attention back to Aspen. "Free the oppressed, right, Hot Shot?" Aspen nodded. "She looks oppressed."

He wasn't a Green Beret anymore, but the ingrained motto guided him regardless. Still, Heath's courage slipped through the slick gloves. If Jia didn't want something to work between them, then "freeing" her wouldn't make a difference.

But what if she *did* want it to work? Heath considered that possibility as he made his way to the universal punching bag. Warming up, he threw some light punches, bouncing back and forth for a good cardio workout but also good boxing posture.

A few right hooks, an uppercut, and he shifted to his left, jabbing.

Since his career change, Heath had steered clear of female involvement. A few thought it was cool that he'd taken a hit during an ambush. But the cool factor waned at the headaches and depression. More and more, he felt himself turning into Uncle Bobby.

That scared him. Right out of dating.

Not that he thought less of his uncle, but the man had lost his will to live when the chopper he'd been in went down and left him paralyzed in both legs. Strong military hero reduced to a wheelchair. How many times had his uncle groused about that?

Left-right-left. Heath moved around the bag, blocking. Punching. Blocking.

He took a step back and shook out his arms and stretched his neck.

She was beautiful. Light brown eyes. Sweet smile.

"It won't work."

Heath led with his right foot and nailed a hook. The impact rippled through his arm and up into his shoulder. Felt good. Strong. The days of grueling physical therapy reminded him that anything worth having— getting back on his feet—was worth fighting for.

Jia.

A left uppercut. A right cross. *Whoosh. Thud. Whoosh-whoosh. Thud.* He repeated it.

As he bounced on his toes and hung his head back, staring at the ceiling, he sensed someone at the bag beside him. He took a step to the side. Jia had a wicked throwing arm. Nice figure. A laugh that embedded itself into his memory and made him want to hear that sound a lot more. He had a feeling she didn't laugh nearly enough.

Argh! Why wouldn't she get out of his head? Heath ducked, blocked with his left, and threw a hard right. A left hook. A right.

Whoosh. Thud. Whoosh.

The echo of his movement registered. He started to look to the side, but he had enough distractions. This workout would be his last for a while. After this, he'd retrieve Trinity from the kennel and take a run.

Left up, he jabbed several times with his right. He'd hit a nerve when he took that leap, mentioning someone had hurt her. In fact. . . that was when her defenses went to the highest state of alert. He toed his way around to the other side, out of the line of fire from the other boxer. So, who had hurt her?

He slammed a left hook into the bag.

The person boxing beside him came around the back. Heath angled, using the challenge to slip between their bags without getting hit.

Thud! At the impact against the back of his head, Heath blinked away stars. Resisted the urge to tell the guy to bring it down a notch. But he wasn't in charge here. Not anymore.

Right. Left. Left uppercut. Right hook.

The movements were echoed again. To his left.

Heath cocked his head slightly. What was with this person?

A foot flew toward his face.

Heath jerked away, arching backward. "Hey!" He straightened and found himself staring at those perfect brown eyes.

"Sorry." Without another word, Jia threw jabs and hooks into the leather-padded column.

Uncertainty slowed him as he returned to his workout. He moved through his routine, one he'd established while doing PT. But as he worked, he noticed his movements mimicked. What, was she challenging him? He did the regimen faster.

So did she.

Heath stretched his neck and moved to the side farthest away from her. What was she doing here anyway? She said they were bugging out. Did she lie? Or did the plans change?

His bag lurched toward his face.

He angled right, narrowly avoiding a face-plant with leather. *That* wasn't an accident. Jia tracked him to the back. He threw a right. So did she.

Right. Left upper. Right hook. Right jab.

Heath moved around, gaining the front and Jia trailing—banging into his back.

"Sorry."

"Sloppy work, RockGirl."

If he'd figured out her little game, then after another left hook—

Her foot swung out.

Heath ducked and stifled his smile. "Let's hope your work in the field is better." He took himself through the routine again. Waited for her foot. Heath dropped and swung his leg around, catching her foot and sweeping her off her feet.

Jia flipped back. Her body thudded against the mat, yanking a grunt from her chest.

Heath bent, his arms resting on his knees. "If you need boxing lessons, I'm available. Anytime."

She shook her head, chest heaving from the workout as she fought a smile. But it fought back. Won. And pried a laugh out of her.

Heath liked what he saw. The healthy flush on her cheeks. A girl not afraid to take him on. Able to laugh at herself. And at him.

"Train me?" She angled a look at him. "It took you ten minutes to figure out I was next to you."

"Five." He extended a hand as an olive branch. As she stood, Heath steadied her. "And I was distracted."

Jia's smile was warm. Like the rest of her in his arms. "Yeah? What could distract a former Green Beret?"

"A beautiful woman who said it wouldn't work."

Her smile slipped. She took a step back. Lifted a gloved hand to her forehead where she swiped loose hair from her face.

Man, she was more skittish than Aspen's Lab. What had her on the run? The real question, did he have the stamina to pursue?

"Want to shower up and grab some chow?"

She laughed. He could get used to that sound. "You don't let up, do you?"

"Not on you."

Jia stared at him. Then looked around, which was when he noticed a few spectators. She yanked off her glove. "Okay." Jia eased back, her eyes darting everywhere but his face.

"Out front, fifteen."

Sweat sliding down her temples, she gave a curt nod, then strode out of the main workout room toward the showers.

Heath's heart pounded as he used his teeth to pry off the Velcro band of his gloves. What was he doing? The scar. . .the TBI. . .

Jia.

He spun, grabbed his bag, and wrangled out of the wraps as he headed to the showers.

"One joy scatters a hundred griefs."

Darci stared at herself in the mirror of the showers. One joy. Heath definitely qualified. It'd been stupid, really, to goad him. She felt foolish, as if she'd returned to junior high.

But his expression. . .

A giggle slipped past her tough facade. Covering her mouth with her hand, she used the other to brace herself against the porcelain sink. *What are you doing?*

"Crows everywhere are equally black."

What was this? War of the ancient Chinese proverbs? Darci tucked her chin. The point was—just as crows were black in China and in America, men were. . .

No. There was a world of difference between Jianyu and Heath. She saw it. *Felt* it. Heath's character had a moral base. He didn't even know her, and already she felt challenged. How did he know? She searched the mirror for signs of distress on her face. How did he know someone had hurt her?

Heath wanted the chance to prove he wasn't like Jianyu.

But that meant being vulnerable.

She squeezed her eyes tight. She wanted it. Wanted a family. Wanted to *not* be alone anymore. What he said, what he did. . .it was what she wanted. *Yearned* for.

But you don't deserve that. You sold your soul in Taipei City.

Heath would never understand. Darci straightened, then blew out a breath. Enough pining over the hunky dog handler. Time to return to reality.

Her gaze struck the Exit sign. She pivoted, tugged her pack off the

75

bench, and strode out the door. Grief and regret nipped at her heels, but she stomped onward. She made the right decision, no matter how much it yanked out her heart.

Icy wind slapped her face, hard and unwelcoming.

"Ready?"

Darci stopped cold as Heath came off the back wall of the building, sporting a field jacket. "What are you—?"

"Come on. I've got two hours to change your mind."

Mortar rounds in the distance echoed those in her chest. "About?" He knew she would try to skip out on him. The guilt felt a thousand times worse than if he hadn't. She was an absolute heel.

He winked and eased her pack from her hands. He slung it over his arm and guided her down Route Disney, the main thoroughfare through Bagram.

"Where, exactly, are we headed?"

"There's a Thai restaurant down by the shops." He stuffed his hands in his jeans.

"How'd you know I like Thai?"

"I didn't." He grinned. "It's my favorite. Sorry—being selfish here. Last good meal for a while."

Why did she not believe that? Because Heath seemed to anticipate every move. Every thought. It hit her like the bitter wind roiling through the base: if he'd known, she probably would've gotten more nervous. Would've backed out.

Which is what she needed to do.

Darci stopped and turned. "Heath."

With his lightning-fast reflexes, he slid an arm around her waist and pulled her close, his jacket gaping and forcing her to press against his T-shirt. Warmth tingled against her fingertips. Awareness flared through her. That hunger. . . *No no no.* It roared for prominence, for satiation.

"Jia." Every morsel of lightheartedness vanished as he looked down at her. "It's one date—lunch, if that makes you more comfortable."

Her throat constricted. She lifted her hands from his chest, from feeling the rhythm of his heart beneath her right palm, then let them rest again. "Why. . .? Why can't you just let it alone?"

"Because." He craned his neck to the side to look into her eyes.

At that moment, she was lost. Lost to her own mechanisms that kept her safe. That suffocated her lone dream.

A slow smile slid across Heath's face as he smoothed his knuckles along her cheek. "Because of what's happening right here..." He lowered his head toward hers, eyes on her lips.

Swirls of warmth and cold, exhilaration and dread, spiked simultaneously. *I can't.*

But she couldn't move.

Heath's breath caressed her cheek.

She lifted her head, pulse thudding against her own inner warnings. If she did this, if she let this happen...

A face ignited from the past.

Darci shoved Heath back. Blinked. Shook her head. "No." She spun on her heels and started away.

Heath hooked her arm. "Jia."

She stopped. "Please..." It hurt. To hope. To feel what she felt with him. It scared her. Beyond any imagining.

"I'm sorry." He ran a hand over the back of his neck. "You're right. That was too fast. I just..."

"What?" She didn't want to ask that, but she needed to regain her fortitude against his stealth romance.

"I want this to work."

Her heart misfired. "Why?" Vulnerability skated along that single syllable, but if he was going to pull out the stops and be blunt, so was she. "Why do you want this to work?"

"Because I've never felt anything like this. I can't stop thinking about you. I want to kill the guy who hurt you, and my dog likes you."

A chuckle leaped up her throat. "Your dog?"

"Hey, Trinity's a very discerning animal."

She couldn't help the laugh. Because she knew he was right. She'd seen those dogs in action. Knew their loyalty rested with their handlers and no one else.

The muscle along his strong, angular jaw bounced. "If you want to take it slow, we will. But don't shut me out. I see it in your face, hear it in your words, Jia."

Darci.

"You want 'us,' too. So let's figure it out, RockGirl."

Her lips tweaked in a smile all their own. "I'll never live that down, will I?"

"And lose one of the ways I can make you smile?"

She swung her gaze to him. He wanted to make her smile? Willing to take things at a different pace just for her? "Are you for real?"

"Let me kiss you, and then you tell me."

"Ha." Darci laughed harder, too pleased with the attention and determination of Heath Daniels, and started walking. "Are we going to eat or what?"

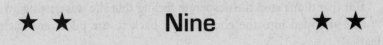

★ ★   Nine   ★ ★

Dawn cracked the day with a splinter of blue. That lone sliver of light through the dark sky allowed Heath to take in the bustling base. Teams gearing up to head out for patrol. Others in formation for drill. Beyond the barricade that held in the patriots and kept out the terrorists—in theory—loomed the mountains. In the distance to the north, he saw the same shape that had stolen his career.

No, a bad intel decision and an ambush stole it. Not some innocuous scrap of land. God shut the door on his career and his hopes.

Heath slowed to a lazy jog as he and Trinity skirted the airfield on their third circuit. A stream of people crossed the sand to a waiting Black Hawk. Among them—Jia.

Impulse stopped Heath. Trinity sat, but her panting and a small whimper indicated she had spotted her, too. Stretching his arms over his head, he watched the team board. Yesterday had defined things for him. He wasn't so sure about her. More accurately, she wasn't sure what she felt. Probably too tangled up in the past, tangled up in whoever had hurt her that she was terrified to risk a relationship again.

A guy about the same size as Heath spoke to Jia. She glanced over her shoulder to him, the backwash from the rotors whipping her hair into her face. Across those eyes. A smile, shy and still uncertain, flickered across the distance.

Why did he care? She wouldn't commit to save her life. And he'd pulled out all the stops. When was the last time—*never*. He'd never been that bold or direct. He was messed up.

79

And yet. . .he stood here, like a lost puppy, wishing she'd been willing to try.

The desire was there, buried deep in her past. It was okay. He wasn't going to rush it. Wasn't going to stress. Something in him said this wasn't the last time he'd see her.

But that didn't stop the desperate feeling that she was getting away.

She strapped into the chopper, her back to the pilots and facing Heath.

Trinity barked.

A smile slid into Jia's face. Her hand lifted an inch.

So. That's it: good-bye.

Why was he acting like a chump? He had her figured out, really. That inch of a raised hand was a mile for her, which meant she *was* trying. He could live with that. For now.

He ruffled the top of Trinity's head. "C'mon." He made his final circuit, passing several other choppers. Lucky ducks would get a fast trip to wherever they were going. Of course, they were twenty-million-dollar targets for RPGs. Then again, the MRAP and Humvees that would ferry him and the A Breed Apart team to their next gig, though not as expensive, were just as vulnerable.

Vulnerable. . .yeah, he'd exposed his backside to Jia for a nuke of a rejection.

But then he'd pushed it back into her court, cornered her as best as he could. Convincing her not to repel what she felt for him was like trying to get a cat to take a bath.

At his tent, Heath placed Trinity in her crate with some fresh water and headed to the showers, ready to wash the dirt, grime, and frustration from his body. It was okay. He wasn't in a place where he could nurture a relationship—or more important, where he wanted to. They had time. And his life was screwed up enough with his uncle in the soldier's home and his own failings, thanks to the TBI. He hadn't even told Jibril about blacking out on the way over. Thankfully, it was a short one.

Most people who weren't familiar with the blackouts would never realize what happened because they came and went in seconds. It'd seem as if he was just disoriented or lost in his thoughts. Still, it was a problem. But if he stressed about it, the symptoms would grow worse.

Back at the tent he shared with the other ABA members, he noted all of Jibril's belongings packed and gone. Heath double-checked his watch. Not late. But he should get his ruck and head to the rec building to meet up with the team.

He let Trinity out, and she jumped up on his cot and stretched out. "Spoiled." Pink tongue hanging out, she squinted beneath the rising sun as if to say, "Yeah, so?"

Ten minutes later, he and Trinity ambled across the base to the main gate where two MRAPS idled. Four soldiers stood around talking. The others were already assembled. "Did I miss an earlier rollout time?"

"No," Jibril said.

"What's the matter? Lose track of time after your hot lunch date?" Hogan smirked. "She seemed to be into you."

If Hogan didn't have such a stinking attitude, he might find her attractive. She was as annoying as a kid sister.

A swirl of rushed movement from the side severed his biting retort. A dozen men rushed toward a chopper, armed to the teeth, determination carved into their faces. Heath took a step in their direction. Saw their patches. Heat zapped through his shoulders, the familiar *tsing* of adrenaline. It was—

Couldn't be.

He took a few quick steps.

One of the SOCOM guys, eyes shielded by Oakleys, looked his way—and slowed.

Watters!

Heath's body lurched into action two steps before he told himself to stay put. The pounding of the helo's rotors thudded against his chest. The wind whipped and tore at his face. He offered a two-fingered salute to the man.

The skids lifted, and Heath stepped back as the chopper rose. Its nose dipped down, then leveled and rushed forward to save the troops.

That used to be me.

And what was he now? Comedic relief. Entertainment. The thought burned and scraped as he swallowed the painful dose of truth. He gulped adrenaline and disappointment by the liters, very aware of the emptiness in his chest. First, Jia. . .now. . .

If only they hadn't gotten bad intel on his last mission. He'd love to wrap his fingers around the neck of the person who had cost him his career.

"Hey, Prince Charming, you coming, or do I inherit your beautiful dog now?"

Heath dropped his gaze, regrouped, and dumped the depression that had swooped in once again. He turned to Hogan. "I'd like to see you try." Because Heath knew that even if he died, Trinity would never leave him. Her training was now as inbred as her instincts.

Jibril and Hogan headed into the second MRAP, while Heath and Aspen climbed the three steps into the first one. As they settled, the driver became immersed in radio chatter.

"Yes, sir. We'll wait, sir." Over his shoulder, he hollered to Heath and Aspen, "We've been ordered to hold."

Heath slumped into a seat, Trinity on the seat next to him, and looked at Aspen, who shrugged.

Ten minutes later, the driver cursed and muttered something to the soldier in the seat next to him. Heath rose and peered out the front heavily fortified window. Two generals and at least a dozen special-ops guys jogged toward them.

Noise drew Heath's attention to the rear, where the door sat open so he could see another MRAP pulling up behind. Heath leaned in and patted the driver. "What's happening?"

"Hanged if I know. They told me to wait, so I wait."

Heath glanced at the guy. He looked young. Too young. "How long you been here?"

"Yesterday."

Something strange twisted in Heath's gut. "You ever been off this base?"

"No, sir, but I'm ready."

Heath choked back his groan as he bent in half, swung around, and threaded his way around Aspen and Trinity to the rear door. "I'll be right back."

"Heath—"

A man appeared in the doorway. "Make a hole!"

Heath eased back into his seat. With only four seats in the vehicle, he wasn't sure where this guy was going, but the authority with which he spoke pushed Heath back down. In his seat, he gripped Trinity's collar and lured her to a spot between his legs.

The soldier dropped into the seat next to Aspen. Another flipped down the spare jump seat. As he did, Heath noted the trident on the guy's arm. A SEAL. Interesting. That swung Heath's attention back to the guy next to Aspen.

His gaze hit the rank on the man's vest, then ricocheted to the man's face—eyes burning holes into his own. It was the same general who chewed out Jia last night.

He took in the lettering on his chest. BURNETT.

The general paused as he stared down Heath. "Of all the. . ." He muttered something about being cursed, then banged on the hull. "Get it moving, Specialist!"

The back door clanged shut and they lurched into motion.

Though the four-star might want to play the silent game, Heath didn't. "Is this a personal escort to our next site?"

Blue eyes met Heath's. "If you want it to be."

Placating him. Heath would have to dig a little harder without ticking him off. "You and I both know those stars on your chest are more of a homing beacon for trouble than a shield."

Gaping, Aspen sucked in a breath but said nothing. Her own military training probably dumbed her into submission.

But like Trinity, his training was as much instinct now as ever. He didn't play dumb. He got info and made a plan. His experience told him something big was happening if two generals were added last-minute to an entertainment convoy.

Heath nudged Aspen's boots. "This should make an interesting addition to my talk with the troops tonight, don't you think, Aspen?"

"Don't drag me down this hole." Her pale cheeks went pink.

"Oh, c'mon. You know the troops would get a kick out of hearing how two four-stars hitched a ride with us."

General Burnett leaned in.

In a heartbeat, Trinity read the aggressive move and leapt to all fours. Had her side not pressed against his leg, Heath might've missed the low growl of warning that rumbled through her chest.

Burnett was undeterred as the SEAL aimed his weapon at Trinity.

"Hey!" Heath shouted, throwing his hand into the line of fire. "Trinity, out!"

"Unless you want a personal escort to a detainment cell, Mr. Daniels," the general said with his own snarl, "I'd suggest you keep this little endeavor to yourself."

Heath's head pounded as he coaxed Trinity down, just as he did his own pulse. Seeing that SEAL take a bead on his partner. . . He looked to the general. "Understood. Sir." As he eased back, Trinity once again relaxing on the steel floor, Heath closed his eyes. Focused on calming down. *What was that, Daniels? Getting info is one thing, but getting stupid's another.*

In the back of his mind, he wondered if his aggression toward the general wasn't some reaction to the way the man had treated Jia.

The generals were making a secret trip. Where? Why? Was Air Force One in the area? Dignitaries meant to bring peace and unity often brought death and destruction—to their own troops with the invisible target painted on their heads.

Heath settled in, wishing for all he was worth for an M4A1 to level the playing field. The general had a sidearm. And the SEAL an M4, an M16, and a modified handgun.

Prepared. Armed to the teeth. *What's going on?*

Whatever drew them out, it was big. And Heath hoped they lived through it.

Dead stop.

In the second he heard the driver mumbling about something in the road, Heath went for the weapon he didn't have. His gaze struck the general, who was in motion, too.

"Why did we stop?" Burnett demanded.

"Back up!" Heath shouted at the same time the general spoke. He locked gazes with the steely-eyed general.

"Not sure, sir. Something about a roadblock."

"Back up, back up!" The general's face reddened. "Get us out—"

The vehicle lurched. Shoved Heath out of his seat. Into Aspen. Her blue eyes went wild as the MRAP dropped down and bounced. He stood and pushed himself back, mind racing.

"Go, go, go!" Heath shouted to the driver.

BoooOOOOOooomm!

Whipped into the air, Heath tensed. His hearing hollowed. His vision went black.

Coughing, Heath snapped awake. A sweet, metallic taste filled his mouth. He couldn't breathe. He dropped his head back and coughed again. Again.

A warbling sound came from his right.

There, the general knelt, his mouth moving in hollow shouts.

Heath blinked. Shook his head—and the whole world spun. Man, why couldn't he breathe? It felt like something was on his chest. He craned his neck—and let out a soft grunt. Stretched across him in a defensive posture, hackles raised, teeth bared, Trinity snapped. Growled—he felt it rumble across his ribs. He rested a hand on her flank and dropped his head back. With another cough, his head cleared. Trinity snapped at the general, who attempted to get closer.

Aspen's fair skin was smudged with black. "She won't let us help."

"Trinity, out," Heath said with another cough.

She ceased aggression and licked his face.

"Good girl." He scooted to the others, throat burning. "What's happening?" Wiping the grit out of his eyes, Heath tried to get his bearings. By the way things were playing out, he hadn't been out more than a few minutes. Was it the TBI? Or had he hit his head?

Aspen swiped a hand across her forehead, smearing black over her pale complexion but looked otherwise unscathed.

A streak of blood ran down the general's temple, but it seemed his helmet absorbed most of the impact. "RPGs. Got our driver. Backup's en route. But we still have a shooter out there. Idiot about took my head off."

The MRAP sat on its side, having been divested of passengers. The SEAL knelt at the front, staring out in the direction from which they'd been hit. Heath sidled up next to Aspen.

"You okay?" His throat burned as if he'd swallowed a blowtorch.

She nodded, the helmet cockeyed on her head.

Heath rubbed Trinity's ear, letting her know she'd done a good job protecting him, as he scanned the area. In front of him a cement wall lined the road they'd been ambushed on. Following it to the far side, he recalled the zigzag at the corner. Two shops sat at the end, then the row of apartments, in which the shooter had taken refuge.

As he scoped it, a man rushed from the side of the building, glanced in their direction, then tossed something aside.

"Target! Give me a gun!" Heath shouted.

"Are you crazy?"

"Completely."

The general grinned and tapped the SEAL, who passed him the

small fully automatic. "You're not authorized to engage the enemy, Mr. Daniels."

Heath jerked toward him. "Trinity and I can find him. Take him down. Or do you want this punk to kill more of your men?"

"Lieutenant Wilson, go with Daniels." Fierce eyes probed Heath. "Temporarily activated."

Heath rose and Trinity with him. Using the dilapidated wall as cover, he sprinted down the street with Trinity a full length ahead of him. "Trinity, seek!"

The command fueled her desire. She surged ahead and barked. Across the intersection, which was ominously empty, and into the building.

Heath raced after her, knowing that while she was trained only to attack those in an aggressive posture, she hadn't done this in a while. The doubts were new. She had her vest—one thing he'd insisted on, knowing how much terrorists wanted MWDs dead.

Snapping and barking ahead pushed him faster. "She hit on something," he shouted to the SEAL behind him.

"Let's hope it's a *someone*," Wilson retorted.

They hustled up to a corner, and their actions were seamless. The SEAL eased around and cleared it. Heath rushed into the room and pied out. Nothing. *Where is she?*

Paint curled off the walls, reaching for them, as if looking for escape from the neglect. Plaster pocked with holes seemed as dejected as it looked. This place bore the marks of abandonment. *Years* of abandonment. But the carpet, table, pillows, and, in particular, the steaming cup of tea told him someone had been in here recently. Very recently.

"Tea." His single word alerted Wilson to trouble.

Another bark.

"She's close." Heath sidestepped and eased into the hall. The tip of Trinity's tail was low and flicking. Back legs spread, she snarled.

Heath rushed forward. Took point, then let the SEAL again clear it.

The guy stepped into view.

Tat-tat-tat.

Wilson jerked back, stumbled. Went down.

Trinity vanished.

A feral scream stabbed the tension and replaced the gunfire.

Heath rushed the room, weapon aimed, knowing Trinity had taken the tango down. The assailant lay on the floor, screaming, his arm between Trinity's powerful jaws. Heath hurried to her side, Wilson rushing the combatant. "Trinity, out!"

With a stretch of her jaw, she released her quarry and came to his side.

Cowering and simpering, the man held his arm.

In Pashto, Heath said, "Down on your knees. Do not make any sudden moves. My dog is trained to attack on or off lead. Do you understand?"

A frantic nod.

"Hands behind your head." Wilson grunted and held his side. "Slow."

As he complied, the man darted looks to Trinity and tears streamed down his cheeks.

Weapon trained on the terrorist, Heath backed up. A half-dozen shapes swooned to his left. This was it. He'd die. Never see Jia, make her face what she felt for him. If that was possible. They were all going down. Heath swung his weapon to them.

"Friendly, friendly," one shouted.

Standing down, Heath indicated to the room. "We need a medic."

"We've got it from here," a SEAL said as his team went to work securing the prisoner and aiding their comrade, whose vest had intercepted the bullets that would've put him six feet under in Arlington.

As Heath waited in the forward room, he took a knee and smoothed a hand along Trinity's coat. Panting, she smiled up at him, her amber eyes sparkling. If she had a voice, she would be thanking him for letting her get back in action. He wasn't as glad.

"Good girl." He smoothed a hand over her head and rubbed her ears. "You're a top-notch soldier, Trinity."

"Wow," Hogan said as they regrouped. "If you had talked to that Asian chick as nice, I bet she wouldn't have left. Or maybe that was the problem—you were too nice."

A retort was on the tip of his tongue, but as Heath came to his feet, he spotted General Burnett. The man seethed.

The SEALs came through, Wilson with a hand over his side, his face knotted in pain. No doubt the bullets had left a bruise. The last two warriors brought out the attacker.

"Did he do it?" General Burnett asked.

"Yes, sir," a SEAL said.

The general's brow furrowed as he considered the man. "Did he know *who* he was hitting?"

The SEAL shook his head. "Only that he was hitting Americans."

A disgusted look washed over the general's face, replacing the worry that had been there seconds earlier. "We'll have to hunker down till nightfall. Choppers are on a rescue op south of here and can't get to us till then."

Aspen handed Heath a water bottle. He took a swig, then held the bottle out for Trinity, who lapped it so fast, half of it missed her mouth. She shook out her fur as if to shake off the attack itself. Heath crouched in front of his partner and stroked her fur.

"See you got our man."

Heath looked up at the general. "Let's hope so, sir." Some Afghans hated Americans and would make any claim that made them look like a hero when the real villains could still be lurking on the rooftop.

"They cleared the roof. Found the tube." Gruff and to the point as always. Without a "thank you" or "job well done," the general pivoted.

Jibril frowned as he moved into Heath's path. "Are you okay?"

"Yeah, sure." He gave the answer everyone wanted. But there was something in him, something deep and forbidding, digging into his brain. A thought he never imagined he'd have. Maybe he was just out of practice. Maybe it was the general's attitude. But Heath couldn't evade the warning that something was very wrong here. And that if he stayed in this country that had tried to snatch his life once, he would die.

Ten

Parwan Province, Afghanistan

Night descended with a wolfish devour. Cold and biting, all the winds of Asia seemed to roll over her, ripping at her jacket. Burrowing against the bitterness, Darci pressed her body into an elongated, cuplike formation. Rock and twigs poked into her belly as she settled. She tugged the wool hat down over her ears and lowered her chin so she could recirculate the air she breathed in the hopes of keeping herself warm.

From her small pack, she retrieved the night-vision goggles. Cold against her face, the goggles morphed the darkness into a monochromatic mural of greens and whites. Rocks. Trees. Slopes and rises. All spilling down toward the valley guarded by the mountain range.

The howling wind snapped at her cheeks, but she focused on the distance.

She'd seen them.

Zooming with the NVGs brought the image into sharper focus. Good. She scanned left and counted eight. . .no, nine—ten! A cluster of ten tents straddling the valley floor near a mud-brick home. Here the two-story structure with a perimeter wall would be considered a mansion. The wealthiest of—

Her lens hit something. Darci hesitated. Retraced the wall. Portions were missing. In a normal village, the wall would've been repaired, their "noble" taken care of by the people. Farther down, she could see diagonally from one side of the house through to the other side. . .and out. Crumbling and spitting mud and plaster from a hole, the wall mocked the white tents flapping outside.

Interesting that there was no rubble pile from the missing section. Which meant it had either been cleaned up—unlikely if they were willing to let the hole go unrepaired—or it had blown. Like from an RPG. Or high-powered rifle.

The thought traced an icy finger down her spine. To make that shot, the attacker would've been. . . *Right where I am.*

If that was true, then the Afghans would've had sentries monitoring this spot.

Darci froze and listened. The roar of the wind and the defiant rustle of her coat made it impossible to hear anything. If someone wanted to sneak up on her, she'd be dead and never know. Then she'd never have to feel the guilt again of giving Heath the fake e-mail address.

Swallowing, she pushed her thoughts to the dilapidated "fortress." No light twinkled through a curtain or blanketed opening.

Abandoned?

She flicked her gaze to the tents. When a glare of white burst through the lens, she resisted the urge to tense. More than a hundred yards from the camp, there was no way they would know she was here. But it still left her feeling naked, more so with the unusually cold night.

The men wore *qmis*, loose-fitting shirts that reached their knees, and *shalwar*, full trousers tied at the waist with a string. Heavy jackets concealed whether or not the men wore vests, but she was sure their *chaplay*, the thick leather shoes, provided little protection against the cold night. At least not the same protection her Columbias provided.

What made her hesitate was the *pagray*. The turbans were not worn high off the forehead as normal—necessitated for touching of the forehead during prayers—but instead they were low and pressed against their brows.

Odd.

Move on. It was cold, and she'd been gone too long already. Someone—Toque—was bound to notice.

She dragged the NVGs over the camp, counted heads and tents, memorized the layout. Another odd thing. It wasn't set up like a village, with clusters of tents close together for families. They were all huddled together. Not family-like. More. . .like the military.

Well, they were Taliban. And she had their numbers and location. Which was what her CO wanted to know. But did a small cluster like this justify the great increase?

Tugging the jacket hood up over her head, she dug down into her coat and retrieved the phone. Capitalizing on the protection of cover from her hood to shield the blue glow from the night and sentries, she turned it on. Punched in her lat-long, her data, and the date and time. Sent it spiraling to the satellite somewhere overhead. Then powered it down, tucked it back in her pocket, and nudged the hood out of the way.

Once again, she used her NVGs to study the valley. The people. The layout. Learn everything she could. Trailing the neon-green along the upper portions of the valley, she traced the hills. The plateaus. Searching for caves and other possible groupings of fighters.

Small for a Taliban camp, this settlement broke too many molds and unsettled her. But analysis wasn't her job. Recon and reporting were.

"Just tell me what you see." Burnett had been adamant that she not put herself in danger. Darci cringed every time he warned her to be careful. She and danger had a love-hate relationship: She loved to avoid it. It hated to miss her. Invariably, it not only found her, but hunted her down. Sort of like Heath.

No, no. Can't go there. Not now. Not ever.

"If you don't go into the cave of the tiger, how are you going to get its cub?"

Darci ordered the voice to shut up, to leave her alone. Going into that camp—or going there with Heath—would not bring trouble to her doorstep. She'd walk into its den!

But if she didn't, the little inconsistencies about what was happening out here wouldn't be answered. What if something was going on down there? They were less than two hours from Bagram. From thousands of American troops and their allies.

Darci pushed onto her knees. "Don't do this." She tucked the NVGs into her coat and zipped it as she started down the side of the mountain. "This is really stupid," she muttered.

True. But Burnett had kept her in this job because of the very instincts that had her hustling down into the veritable den of tigers. The night before she left the base, he'd all but vowed to send her packing if she didn't find something.

Her boot slipped—rocks, pebbles, and dirt dribbled down. She froze, swallowing hard as she waited to see if the wind had carried the noise to the Taliban. Satisfied it hadn't, she hurried along. Kept herself tucked into the shadow of a cleft that gave protection against the angry wind and the probing eyes of the men down in the settlement.

She scurried along the shelf to where the mountain tiered down to the valley floor with what looked like hand-carved terraces. Once used for farming, no doubt. For her, they served as stairs and a quick path— but also an exposed one.

Squatting at the base amid a tangle of brambles and boulders, she peered over a large boulder toward the far right where a fire roared. Men laughed and talked. If she was caught, they'd kill her. After a brutal gang rape, no doubt.

She squelched the thoughts. No use going there except to remind herself to be quick and careful. No mistakes. In and out. Back to the campsite—

Stupid, stupid, stupid. If someone figured out she was missing. . .

Half-bent, Darci sprinted the fifty feet across the open and scrambled up behind the building. Back pressed against the wall, she felt it shift.

Rocks and dirt rained down on her. Dust plumed around her face.

She blinked and choked back a cough. Cautious, she peered around the corner. Laughing continued. So did she. On her feet, she crouch-ran along the wall to the far side where she'd seen through to the other side. Enough would be missing to allow her to gain entry without being noticed. True to her expectations, she found the hole. Glanced over the twelve-inch ledge—and bingo! The debris spread over the ground. Inside.

So, what was going on? Why were the men outside when they could patch this place up and take shelter for the winter and from the coming blizzard?

Darci slunk through the darkness, blinking against a gust of wind that nearly knocked the breath from her chest. Inside the home, she confirmed her suspicions. Empty. Abandoned. She moved to the wall and peered around the cloth that still hung in the window.

A dozen men now gathered around the fire.

Where are the women?

The realization hit her in the gut. No women. This wasn't a Taliban *settlement.* Her gaze pinged over the men. Laughter barreled up from one side. Two men roughed around, tangling with each other. A pagray tumbled free. The man who'd knocked it loose threw his head back and cackled, his laughter howling with the wind.

The man who'd lost his turban retrieved the length of material from the ground and straightened. Like a dance of demons, firelight flickered over his face, revealing his origins.

Darci sucked in a hard breath. *Him!*

Eleven

What were the Chinese doing hundreds of miles from their border and dressed like Taliban fighters? Darci jerked away from the window and pressed her spine against the cement-block wall. She slid down, her mind thundering with what she'd just seen. Panic swirled and whirled through her body, overloading it with adrenaline and heat. In particular, what was Tao doing here? And if he was here, then so was. . .

Oh man. Out now. *"He nearly killed you."* Ba's warning haunted her. She had to get out of here before they discovered her.

This was bad. No, no. This went beyond bad. This was Threat Level Red. DEFCON 1. Threat Level Critical. And any other "extreme" world system panic code.

Heart jammed into her throat, she pushed back against the cold cement and stared up through the hole-laden ceiling to the blanket of black. *Don't do anything stupid.*

Steadying her pulse was the first objective. If she couldn't get herself under control, she wouldn't be able to think. To devise a strategy and get out of here alive.

If they found her—

No. She *would* get out of here. Get back up that mountain without being seen. Get the team back to Bagram where there were lots of guns and battalions of men trained to fight.

No go. Chopper wouldn't extract till morning.

Yet. . .she felt her pulse slowing, calming. If she could sneak back into the rugged terrain without these men seeing her, then she could

93

hoof it back to camp, night would pass, and the chopper would come. No one would be the wiser, but Burnett would have his information. The team would be safe. She would be safe.

The last time she believed that, she'd almost died.

So did he.

This can't be happening!

Chinese in Afghanistan—hiding and far away from the mines they were authorized to work. It didn't make sense. What were they doing here?

Darci slowly rose to her feet, lifted the NVGs to her face to construct more data, knowing full well she'd have to give a complete report. Were all the men Chinese? Or just some?

She slid aside the panic and adrenaline and replaced it with the uncanny ability that had gotten her recruited into military intelligence: her ability to divide her fear from her reason and carry out the mission all the same. Some might call her coldhearted, or a colorful metaphor. To her, it was just intuition. Instinct. A gift for survival.

Yes, Chinese. All fifteen. They had weapons. But they also had crates in their tents—nicely fitted tents with rugs and pallets, cooking stoves. But nothing else. Like vehicles. How had they gotten here? Which route delivered them to this Afghan province? How had they not been seen and reported?

The clothes. They dressed like Taliban.

Move it or lose it, Darci. Using every ounce of training, she shifted toward the hole she'd climbed through minutes ago. Sound took on a deafening level, as if each step shouted her presence. Halfway across, she lifted her booted foot over a crate and set it down. Then her other foot. Relaxed. Focused. Stealthy.

Rolled rugs cluttered the dirt floor. She used one to step around the others. A strange noise hissed from the carpet. She leapt aside, staring at the dark bundle. A sickening feeling tightened her stomach.

No, no time to sort it out. Just get back to the hills.

Toeing her way to the entrance, gaze locked on the sliver of space that afforded her a view of the Chinese encampment, she kept moving. Wind ripped the thin material covering the window and jerked it back.

Darci froze, afraid the men might see her dark form shift in the night.

But with the wind came a scurrying sound. She stilled and let her eyes rove the interior. Something. . .something wasn't right.

The rug she'd just stepped on, the hissing one—okay, that made her sound like a loon—it had shifted. That's not how it had been a second ago.

Another sound. This time it almost seemed like a whimper. An old stove huddled against the far wall. A shelf dangled on the wall, a pile of pottery shards on the floor. Rugs. A low-slung bed frame without a mattress. A blanket draped over it. Whites of eyes peeking back at her.

Darci shoved herself back. Gasped.

The whimper rose.

Her gaze shot to the window. The laughter and insanity continued—stupid men thought they were impervious and invincible—so no one was the wiser to her presence. It was just her and whoever lay beneath the bed, which. . .too small a space to conceal an adult. That pushed her toward the frame.

Slowly. . .she stalked closer, her hand going to the small of her back. Darci went to a knee. Craned her neck to the side and peered under.

Tears slid from wide dark eyes, dusted by bangs and jet black hair. A small child peered back. Hand in her mouth, the girl seemed to be stifling her cries. Face screwed tight, she drew back.

"Hello," Darci whispered in perfect Pashto. "Where is your daddy?"

With slobber-coated fingers, the girl pointed to the middle of the dwelling. Darci didn't have to look to know the girl was pointing to the pile of rolled-up carpets. The very ones Darci had stepped on.

"Your mother, is she. . .here?"

The girl shook her head, freeing more tears. Dead, too, it seemed. How on earth had this little girl managed to hide? And from the Chinese men who'd slaughtered her people, who just happened to be in the wrong place—their own home!

Double snap. This complicated things. She couldn't leave the child. But taking her into the mountains could get them both killed. Something about this little girl reminded her of the mission Darci almost didn't survive. She'd expected to be abandoned, she'd been so near death. But she fought to stay alive. Fought to find a way out. And she did.

Just like this little angel. She'd stayed alive against impossible odds. No way would Darci abandon her now. *Time's short.* "We must leave. Before the men see us."

Another frantic shake of her head.

"They are bad, yes?" she continued in the tongue of the little girl, who readily agreed. "I have friends in the mountains who can help us. We will go to the Americans."

A sniffle.

Darci held out her hand. "Please? Before they see us."

The little one reached up and pushed back the blanket. She stood. Even in the darkness, Darci could see the blood that coated the girl's clothes, making her ache. Had she witnessed her parents' murders, hidden here? The girl couldn't be more than three or four. Darci lifted the girl, who kicked free of the blanket that tangled around her feet. Her foot hit the frame.

Thud!

"Augh!"

She clamped a hand over the girl's mouth. "Shh."

"Check it out," came the terse command, followed by thumping of booted feet.

Darci pinched her lips and hurried to the opening she'd come through. Adrenaline jolted through her veins, heating her. The child was heavy, which made Darci's steps louder. But if the girl walked on her own, she'd slow them down. Darci scrambled to the safety of the low-lying wall. They were doomed.

God. . .

Why she'd even gone there, she didn't know. God hadn't helped her mom. Why would He help her? She believed in Him. She did. She just wasn't sure—

Just move!

Holding the girl tight against her chest, she peered over the wall to the men clambering into the building. Rowdy and sloppy, they pushed and taunted each other, clearly not taking the noise as a serious threat.

Good. Eyes on the mountain, Darci plotted her path. Once she got far enough away, she'd unzip her jacket and tuck the slight frame of the child into its warmth. Wind tugged at her as she darted to what looked like an abandoned well. Crouched, she checked the men.

Still oblivious.

"Just a little farther," she said to the girl, then scurried out into the open, aiming for a cluster of shrubs and brambles that lined a dry creek bed. Halfway there and still safe. Her panic began to subside. At least, the edge of that panic. She knew better than to let her guard down until she was at base.

Squatting, she set down the child and unzipped her jacket. She motioned the girl back into her arms, then instructed her to wrap her legs around Darci's waist. Once in position, she tugged the jacket, tugging hard to make it zip.

"Okay," she whispered. "Hold very tight. Do not let go."

The moon reflected off the obsidian orbs peeking from below dark bangs. The tiny arms tightened around her. "Tighter." The girl complied, but it still wasn't nearly as much as Darci preferred.

When an explosion of laughter ripped through the valley, Darci seized the chance. She shoved up and launched toward the mountain. She plunged onward, feeling as if she had a fifty-pound rucksack strapped to her front. The ground before her rose enough to make the run harder. Her breath came in snatches.

With one arm she braced the girl's bottom and pumped for speed with the other arm.

A shout rang out.

Crack!

Dirt burst up at her, peppering her face. Rifle fire!

★ ★   Twelve   ★ ★

Camp Eggers, Kabul, Afghanistan

Amazing. It hadn't changed in the two years since he'd left. Barren, flat, tan—it's the reason the country was named Afghani*stan*. But then again, when he glanced down the heavily fortified and fenced road to the gorgeous Hindu Kush—formidable, daunting, stunning—nothing was barren about this place.

A gust of wind stirred up a sand demon that prowled the monochromatic scene dotted with splotches of green from occasional shrubs. Small trees reached toward the heavens with bent, gnarly hands, as if begging for water. Fear and awe wove a wicked tapestry through him as the quiet terrain erupted with ghoulish memories. Bombs. IEDs. The *tat-a-tat-tat* of M4s.

Heath jogged down the steps to the temporary bunk, Trinity's lead in one hand and his duffel in the other. His performance last night came in a distant second, considering the attack. Between the adrenaline, the performance, and predawn rise this morning, exhaustion weighted his limbs. He was out of shape. Plain and simple.

A furry head nudged beneath his hand. Without taking his eyes off the phantom plain beneath the sun's unrelenting oppression, Heath rubbed Trinity's ears. Could she sense it, too? The ominous feeling he'd felt thick and rancid after that attack? Was she remembering that horrific day that left her with a small scar and him with one bigger?

A Humvee squawked to a stop just feet in front of Heath, pulling Trinity into work mode. "Easy, girl."

Two men piled out of the vehicle. One strode toward him.

Heath held up a hand. "Approach slowly. She might not be government issue now, but she's still got razor-sharp instincts and teeth."

The specialist smiled beneath his helmet and sweat, compliments of the mountain of clothing, vests, and gear. "Daniels?"

Sack slung over his shoulder, Heath extended his hand.

"Specialist Randy Farley. I'm your tour guide back to Bagram."

Specialist. The specialist who'd driven the MRAP was dead. Would this one end up that way, too? What about Jia? Where was she? Was she safe, out of reach of the Taliban or other extremists? Man, that near-kiss... was something. . .like near-stupidity.

Shake it off.

"First stop—the training field."

"No rest for the weary." Heath glanced back at Hogan who trudged down the steps of the portable building they'd crashed in last night. She wore a frown the size of "who authorized you to disturb my beauty sleep?"

Stuffing a hat over her standard ponytail, she grunted. "Couldn't we do this tour after lunch, or even better—never?"

"If you want to sleep, you should've stayed home." That she'd manhandled her way into coming still bugged him. That she thought he needed babysitting downright angered him.

He had, after all, handled himself fine with that terrorist who had the rocket launcher.

Farley shot Hogan a nervous look. His face turned red.

Figures. Hogan had attitude that rivaled Cruella de Vil but the looks that went with any homecoming queen. Soldiers would fall all over themselves to talk to her. And Aspen, though reserved, with her white-blond hair and blue eyes, might be mistaken for a new Marilyn Monroe, minus the sex-symbol status. He just couldn't see Courtland prancing around in a gown, blowing kisses to the camera. Boxing a camera? Definitely.

Heath cleared his throat. That was way more imagery than he needed about Courtland. Or any female. *Except maybe Jia.*

Augh. He needed someone to smack him upside the head to dislodge the thoughts of the mysterious woman.

"Ready?" Farley climbed into the Humvee, and Heath claimed the seat behind him. "There's a few teams training nearby." He looked at Hogan. "Thought y'all might like to check them out."

"Who's training?" Zipping his jacket against the cold winds, Jibril asked from the front seat.

"We've got a regular menagerie training." Randy glanced back. "There are a half-dozen dogs out there." He grinned at Trinity, who sat on the seat beside Heath. "Oh, and SOCOM sent some guys in here late last night, so I think you might see them. But they don't talk to us grunts. They keep to their own."

I used to be part of that "own."

Jibril turned to Heath, his green eyes boring into him. Heath didn't want to talk about it. He shoved his attention out the window and stroked Trinity's fur. SOCOM. Special Operations Command. The source of his discharge. Trinity's classification as "excess."

They headed off base, and the ride was pretty typical as they passed embassies and schools, homes, shops, and just about everything else, making their way out of the city. Soon the Humvee lumbered over a rise, then the front end dipped and provided a perfect view of the valley below. More of the same, flat terrain for another half hour before they reached Forward Operating Base Robertson, where they'd separated from General Burnett two nights ago.

Heath sighed as they were unloaded at a gate where MPs waited. Two dogs made their circuit around the vehicle, then the MPs waved the vehicle past the checkpoint. Inside, they drove a short distance and exited the established perimeter of the FOB into a cordoned-off area with a dual-rutted path before coming to a stop at a small camo canopy.

Heath climbed out with Trinity and surveyed the land. Familiar, yet not. The same, yet different. Natural and unnatural. Watching the men in training maneuvers, the experience not a part of his life for the last eighteen months. All the same, he could remember it, taste it like the dust in the air.

On her lead, Trinity tugged against the restraint. She wanted to play. Catch the bad guys. So did he. They had a little of the action yesterday, and she seemed still a part of that game. To have purpose and meaning. To matter. At least Trinity did.

What hurt more, bothered him worse, was that he recognized the men leading the training exercise. Watters. He'd seen the fierce warrior heading out at Bagram. What were the chances he'd end up here, too? Watterboy shouted orders to the soldiers. The Green Beret had loved his moniker, despite it sounding trite and demeaning.

"Nah," Watterboy had said. "It's a role of support, encouragement, refreshment. Can't have a better mantra."

The guy always did have a unique way of seeing things. Like the way he saw the man jogging at his side—James VanAllen, aka Candyman. A guy with a long line of military ancestors, including some elusive connection to a Revolutionary War general named "Mad" Anthony Wayne. Candyman insisted Mad Anthony was misunderstood—he wasn't crazy in the head. He was crazy in the heart—for his country.

"Just like me," Candyman had said, grinning within his wiry brown beard and olive skin.

That's the reason he donated all the candy and goodies from his care packages to hand out to the Afghan children while on patrol. One candy bar went a mile in public relations. To Candyman, he was buying the hearts of the children one chocolate at a time. Behind those Oakleys rested piercing eyes that had melted far too many feminine hearts.

A greedy, icy wind swirled around them, winter clinging on for one last hurrah. Hands slick, Heath stood at the edge of the training field marked with rocks and sand-filled barrels. Anything to demarcate the perimeter. Other handlers worked with their furry partners, clearing buildings, detecting explosive materials, and taking down one heavily padded "bad guy."

Man. It'd been. . .forever since he'd hung out with these guys. It'd also been all too near since they stood over him at the hospital after the ambush. Beside him, he could feel the questioning, waiting gazes of Jibril, Aspen, and Hogan. Let them wait. He wasn't going out there till the acid in his stomach turned from a puddle of anxiety to a solid mass of courage.

Then again, at this rate, that'd be the day after never.

Trinity nosed his hand.

"Yeah, yeah. I know." He rubbed her ears. "Don't get pushy." But his girl always knew best. The scars on his hand reminded him to listen to her.

Bolstered by her anxiousness to get to work, he stalked onto the field. Steps crunched behind him, assuring him that the other A Breed Apart team members had his back. He was grateful they hadn't pressed him, urged him onward. Especially Hogan. Her emotional magazine was loaded with aggression and very little patience to temper that fight-now instinct.

As the four of them crossed the field with Trinity trotting ahead, sniffing, and tail wagging, Heath noted Watterboy hesitate as he spotted them.

With a laugh that carried the fifty feet, Watterboy clapped his hands. "Knew they couldn't keep you away for long, Ghost." When they met, Watters gave him a one-armed hug, back-pat greeting. "Sorry I couldn't stop and talk at Bagram."

Heath shook his head. "Man's got work to do."

A half-dozen feet away, attention focused on the grunts, Candyman spun. "Ghost?" He locked gazes with him. "Speak of the devil. . ." Two long strides carried him close enough for a strong-armed hug.

Heath's chest squeezed at the welcome. "How's it going?"

The two men lowered their hands for Trinity's assessment. Her nose twitched, then she turned and scoped out the action on the field.

Both men eyed the others with Heath. "Who's your posse?" Candyman asked.

"Oh, sorry." He'd so expected a scowl-faced greeting, their acceptance rattled his cage. Heath turned to A Breed Apart's owner. "This is Jibril Khouri—"

"Yeah, sure." Watterboy shook Jibril's hand. "I remember working an op with you three years back. Helmand Province?"

"Kandahar." Jibril smiled. "I'm surprised you remember."

"Never forget a face." Watters held out his hand to Aspen. "Dean Watters."

"Aspen Courtland, and this is Timbrel Hogan." She freed her hand and motioned to Hogan. Was the heat getting to Courtland, or was she blushing?

"A pleasure, ma'am." Watterboy smiled down at her.

"What's the holdup?" Someone shouted as they drew closer.

Trinity lunged into a protective position, snarling.

"Trinity, out." Heath eyed the black-haired guy who wore the same patch Watterboy and Candyman sported.

Watterboy gripped the man's shoulder. "Rocket, meet one of our own—Heath Daniels."

"One of our own?" The guy appraised him, distrust stiffening his posture.

Candyman elbowed him. "Dude—it's Heath Daniels. You know, *Ghost.*"

Rocket's eyes widened. "Seriously?"

Grinning, Candyman nodded. "We talk about you and that mission all the time."

"Mission?"

"The one that 'bout took us all out."

Rocket offered a hand. "Nice to meet you, sir."

Warmth not related to the sun soaked Heath. Hearing their approval, knowing they'd talked about him to newbs and that they still called him one of their own. . .

Man it was good to be back.

"So, what brings you to this godforsaken desert?" Candyman asked.

Truth or dare. He knew this time was coming, so on the plane over, he'd practiced the most casual answer he could muster. "Brass thought you grunts could use a motivational speech."

Rocket shouldered between Heath and Candyman, who held out a hand to Hogan. "Thanks for coming all this way to inspire us, Miss. . ."

Hogan's expression remained impassive. She gave no response.

Rocket slapped Candyman. "Knucklehead. Ghost's the speaker."

"I know."

A frown tugged at Hogan's lips. "Then why'd you thank me?"

"A face like yours would inspire any man to get home alive."

Watterboy groaned. "Down boy. Back to the fight." He shoved Candyman toward the training field and chuckled. "You'll have to pardon him. He's wiry—"

Hogan crossed her arms. "More like needs his mouth wired shut."

Another shout from the field drew Candyman round. He jogged a few steps then spun, walking backward. "How long you here for?"

"A week."

Candyman nodded. "I'll try to catch you later."

"Sounds good." Heath watched, envious, and remembered the day when he'd been in charge of training, in the thick of combat-training maneuvers. He missed it. Missed being part of something bigger than himself. Missed being strong. A hero. The highs.

What he didn't miss were the lows. Hard to miss something you experienced every day. And the emptiness that gripped his throat right now at *not* being a part of that team. Of not being one of the guys running down there and barking orders.

"Want to look around?"

Heath grinned. "It'd be nice, but I won't beg."

"Never would," Watters said with a laugh. "C'mon. I'll take you around."

Parwan Province, Afghanistan

Fire lit through Darci's shoulder.

A guttural sound escaped her lips as she stumbled forward. Her fingers scraped the ground, but she pushed on. The little one clinging to her cried out.

"Shh, shh." Darci ignored the wet warmth sliding down her arm and raced into the anonymity of the mountain. Over one crest—

Rock blasted her face.

She ducked and hurried around a boulder, zigzagged upward. Slipping into a narrow crevice, she used it as a shield to protect them from more shots. But it also forced her to walk sideways, shuffling— slower. If it would just give them a barrier to get high enough that they could lose anyone following. . .

Maybe the Chinese would think she was a settlement survivor, that she wasn't worth pursuing.

Yeah, keep telling yourself that.

In the darkness, she scrambled onward. Slipped. Her foot dropped. Her weight shoved it into a gouged area—stuck! She grunted and jerked her leg, trying to free it.

Shouts below grew louder. Nearer.

"Hurry," the little one said with a sniffle.

Rock cut into her palms as Darci jerked and yanked to free her foot. Still no good. She pulled hard—flopped backward.

Out into the open.

Thwat! Thunk!

Shattered rock pelted her cheek, stinging. Darci rolled, arching her back as she went over the little one strapped inside her jacket, and pushed to her feet. She found a trail and used it to gain distance and speed. Couldn't stay on it much longer or she'd lead them to the camp. Her legs grew leaden. She stumbled but did not stop. Stopping would get them killed.

And to think—she'd thought getting out of the valley would be the hard part. Finding a safe passage with a three- or four-year-old child up through the mountain. . .

Remind me to never do this again. Heath would probably take care of that for her. The thought pried a smile out of her weary soul. Not at him calling her on it, but just. . .him.

Clattering through the darkness, she pressed on. Ten minutes later, she moved off the hard-packed path and climbed upward, over rocky ledges, and around bushes. Anything to conceal their movement and direction.

After heading north for several minutes, she eyed a ledge about four feet straight up. She'd never be able to get up there with the child. But maybe. . . With their options down to zero, Darci had to try. Kneeling to the side, she unzipped the jacket—and froze. Where was the phone?

Frantic, she scanned the area. No sight of it. Shouts and the bobbing light beam told her she didn't have time to search for it. But without the phone, how would she get out of here, warn Burnett? Save the team?

The girl's whimper pulled her sanity back together. The girl tensed, her muscles constricting around Darci.

"What is your name?" Darci asked in Pashto and a soft whisper as she helped her climb out of the warmth and onto the ground.

"Badria." Moonlight reflected off the girl's large, dark eyes. She shifted back and glanced down at her clothes. Dark spots splattered her tunic.

Darci peeled back the shoulder of her jacket and inspected her wound. "See? Not bad. Just a small scratch." Though to this little one, it probably looked like more. But now was not the time to distress her. "Badria, you've been so brave. We must climb up there. I'll help you. Ready?"

The girl shook her head.

"I know you're scared, but it's okay. I am, too." Only as the words left her lips did she realize how very true they were. A deep, heavy fear had settled over her since. . .well, since when? Since starting this mission? No. It was more recent.

She huffed a smile. Since leaving Heath.

Get over it. He's not here. There's little chance you'll see him again. It'd been why she was willing to have lunch with him. Play the game. Though, with the way he seemed to anticipate her, she half expected to see him around the next corner. Okay, not literally, but. . .

Darci lifted the girl, cringing as fire raced down her shoulder. That might be a graze but it hurt like crazy. Tightening against the slice of pain that accompanied the movement, she hoisted the girl onto the ledge. "Climb up and lie flat."

Surprise snaked through Darci when the girl did as requested. This wasn't the first time she had to hide, and that rankled Darci. No child should have to live like that.

Grateful for her love of rock climbing and the numerous adventure trips that gave her experience, Darci bent and rubbed her hands in the dirt. Not as good as chalk, but it would help. Then she wedged her toe into a gouged area and pulled up.

Pain sluiced through her again. *Gut it up and get moving.* She pushed herself up, caught hold, and dragged her legs over the ledge before rolling onto her back. With a breath of relief, she gazed at the stars. Wind tugged at her, whistling over them. They had to make it back. She had to tell Burnett about these men. Something was going on down there, and it couldn't be good if they were masquerading as Taliban.

Her gaze traced the edifice that rose another twenty feet. Only as she lay there did the tree dangling over the ledge register. It was less than fifteen minutes from the camp. But getting up there. . .climbing that height with the child and an injury. . .

Shouts came from her right. She peeked out and down toward the voices. Shadows flickered in and out of the moonlight. Beams of light danced up and over, some bobbing in a strange dance against the face of the mountain as the men hurried. Snap. Had the entire camp come after her?

Okay, choices just vanished.

They *had* to go up. If she tried to take the route she'd come, the Chinese would be on her in minutes. She had to buy time by scaling the cliff. It'd be okay. As long as Badria could hold on tight. And Darci's injury wasn't deep and poisoning her or bleeding her out.

A strobe of light struck overhead.

Darci flashed a hand to Badria. "Don't move." She turned her head toward the cliff face as the light dropped on them. Her breath kicked into the back of her throat as the beam slid over her body. At least she'd had enough sense to wear a black jacket and jeans—it'd help her blend into the shadows.

Keep moving, keep moving, she mentally urged the men.

The beam traced the rock, slipped down the path, and vanished into a tangle of trees and shrubs.

Once sure the men weren't searching this location anymore, Darci pushed onto her knees. She removed her jacket and guided Badria onto her back. She slid the jacket back on and zipped it. "Okay, I need you to be brave and strong." She patted the girl's hands knotted around her neck. "Hold on tight—and don't look."

Darci tucked dirt into her pockets, then reached for the first hold. Keeping her movements slow and meticulous, she began their ascent. With each rise, Badria's arms tightened around Darci's shoulders and squeezed. Sweat broke out over Darci's brow. The rubbing against the wound made it raw, burn. She blinked past the pain, determination hardening her resolve to make it.

In a secure toehold, she freed one hand and dug in her pocket for dirt. They were within three feet of the upper ledge when the voices once again returned. Not right under them, but she and Badria would soon be discovered if Darci didn't hurry. As she tried to secure another foothold, she wished for the professional climbing shoes. Not the heavy boots she'd donned to withstand the bitter Afghan mountain nights.

Her foot slipped. Scraped along the rock. The slip jarred her shoulder. Badria cried out and wrenched her legs.

At the stab of pain, Darci bit down to stop from crying out, too. Arms placed to the side as if she were a giant spider, she hung her head and let her brow rest against the rock as she regained her composure, shoved aside the burning.

Shouts below.

Her eyes snapped open. Straight down, she saw men.

They'd been discovered.

Tempted to hurry, she knew they couldn't. One wrong toe placement…

Then again, if the Chinese started shooting again, toes wouldn't matter.

Darci rammed her foot into a hold. Used all her remaining strength and threw herself toward the upper ledge. She caught. . .then slipped.

Rocks dribbled down.

"No," she ground out as she scrambled. Her fingers clawed dirt.

Rocks.

Sliding debris.

Gravity snatched them.

★ ★ Thirteen ★ ★

2 Klicks outside FOB Robertson

Cold poured into their Humvee without mercy. Dull and aggravating, a throb annoyed Heath as they trounced over the hard-packed roads through the training area. He should've eaten a good meal before heading out. If the headache continued to increase, he—

No. He wouldn't go there or let that happen. He freed his CamelBak straw, clamped down on the bite valve, and inhaled. The water felt good, but the throb didn't ease. Probably because the pounding wasn't from water deprivation. But from stress. From the TBI. He had to make it. Couldn't go south now with his health.

A wet nose nudged his cheek. Then a wet tongue.

"You want some, girl?" Heath aimed the valve at Trinity and squeezed. Water squirted her nose. She jerked back but then lapped the liquid, half of it splashing on him at first. He chuckled as she settled next to him and seemed ready for a nap.

Heath swiped his arm over his face and mouth as he squinted out the windshield at the maneuvers. He'd seen a sniper take out a target without being spotted. He'd seen a Ranger battalion on the range, and he'd seen tanks and MRAPs practicing.

"Where are the dogs?"

"Come again?" Watters steered around an incline, then ramped up another.

"Specialist Farley said there were some working dogs out here."

"Oh. Yeah, yeah." Watterboy adjusted his weapon strap. "Command ordered them down to Helmand. Got some HPTs coming in, so

108

they sent the dogs."

Heath nodded, remembering the mission that had been his last. "My last gig was for HPTs, remember? They're expensive."

Watters nodded. "No kidding. Cost a lot in equipment, training—and if things go bad, body count."

Heath held up his hand. "It goes bad."

"It was a close call. At least you'll never forget—and neither will I."

As he lowered his arm, Trinity nudged his hand up and licked it, pulling a laugh from him. Heath didn't need to see behind the Oakley sunglasses to know Watters's hazel eyes studied him. He nodded to Trinity. "Think she remembers that mission?"

"I guarantee it, but she doesn't spook easily." *Wish I could say the same for me.*

The thought of a spooked dog pushed his gaze back to Aspen. Just as he turned, her curls bounced as she turned her head away. Maybe now would be a good time for a topic change. "So, you guys seeing a lot of Taliban up here?"

"You know how it was a hot spot here for a while, so we were ordered into the mountains. Then things quieted down and we were sent south." Watters shrugged as he pulled up along another Humvee. "Now the bad guys are back." A broad white smile stood in stark contrast to Watterboy's very tanned face and dark beard. "So are we."

Stepping out into the cold seemed to invite the Afghan desert to drum on his skull. Heath winced as he strapped his helmet back on. The thing felt like a ton of bricks. A little more water and he'd be okay. All he had to do was stay in the shade as much as possible. Hydrate. Avoid stress.

Right.

They rounded a bend, stepping down a narrow gorge that emptied into an open valley guarded on all sides by limestone. The shape of the terrain reminded him of an upright tunnel.

Squinting, he peered up at the unrelenting sun layering its way into the gorge. Shade. "Right." After one more sip of water and a squirt for Trin, he kneaded the back of his neck.

"You okay, Prince Charming?"

He eyed Hogan and knew she was waiting for him to fail. To prove her right. To be weak. "Peachy."

She gave a cockeyed grin and stepped past him. "Be glad Beowulf's not here. He can smell a liar."

Heath hesitated.

Hogan laughed.

And the sound plucked on the frayed ends of his nerves, pushing a scowl into his face. The knotted muscles added to the thunder rumbling through his thick skull.

Jibril touched his shoulder. "Easy. She just likes getting you worked up."

"She's good at it."

"My sister has the same talent with me." Jibril smiled, his beard fitting in with the dozen Spec Ops soldiers they trailed into a makeshift shelter.

Three MRAPs sat in the northern quadrant with a tarp stretched over them, providing the only source of shade. The immediate relief to his throbbing head almost made him wilt in gratitude. Huddled around their leader, the men talked as if lives depended on their chatter.

Heath could sense a shift in the force. Scowls. Tensed shoulders. Hands fisted. Lips set in determined lines.

"Hold up," Watters said. "Looks like something's happening. Stay here."

Suspicions confirmed, Heath lowered himself onto the bumper of one of the MRAPs and rubbed Trinity's head. She whimpered, scooting forward every few seconds. She could sense it, too. Huh. Maybe his subconscious had picked up on her antsy behavior, and that's what alerted him, since dogs had heightened senses. No doubt by the scent of fear. Maybe even aggression.

It was in the air, too. As if the spirits that roamed this country were. . . Were what? Alive? Of course they were. The Bible spoke about the spirit of a place. So why did it surprise him? "Because it's almost tangible."

"What?" Aspen looked at him.

"Nothing." He tightened his hold on Trinity's lead.

"What do you see?" Jibril lowered himself to the bumper.

"They're planning. Something on the spot, need to move fast. Probably got wind of suspicious activity nearby." Otherwise, they'd be packing up and rumbling back to base camp. "Not too urgent, or they'd be yelling back and forth with SOCOM."

Watterboy and Candyman approached.

Heath stood and Trinity with him. "What's up?"

"Command got word of a potential drug lord's location about ten klicks east. We're going to check it out." Watters squinted as he looked at them, then to the ladies. "You're cleared to go along, but you stick like glue to us."

"Let's move," Hogan said.

Heath glanced at the girl, who didn't seem to understand what a threat was, that they could go into this village. . .and never come out alive. Wait a minute, wasn't this what he'd wanted three weeks ago? To get back in the action, prove he still had what it took?

Parwan Province, Afghanistan

He'd never taken kindly to traitors. Staring down the face of the cliff where Jia struggled to maintain her grip, he toyed with letting her drop.

But Peter Toque needed her. Needed to know what her mission was here. Because one thing was certain—she was a part of the geological survey team, in name only.

A yelp yanked his better judgment to the front. He hooked an arm around a tree that shot up out of the rocky terrain and swung down, catching her arm.

The sudden shift in her weight jerked them down. Wide, almond-shaped eyes came to his, the moonlight glowing off the whites. The tree cracked. Popped. Gravel dug into his belly as he strained against her weight.

She slapped her hand up and coiled her fingers around Peter's forearm. "Don't let go."

Don't tempt me. He gritted his teeth, dug his heels in, pulling himself into a hunch, then hauled her up. Shouts and clamoring voices drew closer.

She twisted and flopped onto her back, rolling away from the ledge, and thudded against a rock. A grunt hissed out.

He half expected her to lie there, but in a lightning-fast move, she hopped to her feet and sprinted away.

Peter cursed his hesitation and darted after her. He'd—once again—underestimated the Asian woman. Since they'd met in the warehouse and she'd shown more awareness of the geopolitical nature of the area than the geological makeup, he'd watched her. Back at Bagram, she'd been pulled into a meeting with a general after saying she'd filled out paperwork wrong. She returned an hour later, and all paperwork questions vanished. Good thing he didn't believe her geology student status.

Rock and dirt exploded, peppering his cheek. A piece flicked against his brow. He cursed and ducked, wanting to stay intact, and propelled himself around the next corner. Pumping his arms faster, he vowed to get the truth out of Jia—if they survived tonight.

He broke through a small cluster of trees—and rammed straight into Jia, shoving her forward. She yelped. Why wasn't she moving faster? "Move! Go! They're right behind us." Peter pushed her.

She stumbled, recovered, then ran again. But her legs seemed tangled in vines. After a few missteps, she regained her footing, and they hurried farther and farther from the gunshots.

They tumbled into the camp almost on top of each other.

Jaekus leapt from his canvas chair by a fire. "Whoa!"

Jia dropped to her knees with heaving breaths.

"We've got trouble. Get everyone up." Peter spun to Jia. "What have you done? Where did you go?"

Eyes hooded in pain, she barely acknowledged him as she fumbled with her zipper.

Only then did he notice another set of eyes peeking at him. A child—in her jacket! "Who is that?"

The little girl wiggled out of Jia's coat, dark spots sprinkled against her clothes.

"She's bleeding!"

"No," Jia said with a gulp. "She's okay." After another labored breath, Jia looked to the right and slumped back onto her legs.

Alice came from the tent. "What's happening?"

Jia nudged the little girl toward the only other female in the camp. "Alice, get her clean clothes and some food. She's been alone for a while."

The nymphlike girl rushed into action, ferrying the child into a tent just as the professor emerged from his quarters, firelight accenting the bags under his eyes and the askew salt-and-pepper hair.

Even as the others fretted over the little one, Peter knew something was wrong with Jia. She'd been a pillar of strength and defiance since their first meeting at the university. When she tried to stand just now and tripped, his suspicions were confirmed.

"It's you. That was your blood on her."

Not responding or even acknowledging him, Jia pressed a hand to her shoulder, pushed onto her feet. "Everyone pack up. We've got a truckload of trouble about to hit us." She trudged toward the tent she shared with Alice, her boots dragging heavily on the dirt. As she reached the opening, Jia paused and looked back.

Jaekus and the prof stood around, dazed.

"Move, people! They're coming to kill us, not have tea." Despite the vehemence in her words, the strain couldn't be missed. "Move! Now!" She wavered.

Peter stepped into her path as she eased into the darkened interior. "Get off me. Pack up."

"Screw the stuff. You're hurt. Let me see it." He pointed to her cot. She shoved him back. "Get out! Don't you get it—?"

"Yeah, I get it. You're Lara Croft's sister and don't like her showing you up. But if that"—he pointed to her shoulder—"kills you, nobody will have to worry who's stronger."

"Nobody should be worrying—period!" She reached under the bed and grabbed her pack. When she swung it onto the cot, she jerked and held her arm. She recovered, then dug in the pack. Sweat beaded on her pale face.

Her stupidity would get everyone killed.

Not if I can help it.

Peter snatched the Glock holstered at his back.

★ ★   **Fourteen**   ★ ★

Gun in hand, Darci spun. Staring down the barrel of a Glock, she hauled in a breath. Her gaze jumped to the owner. "Toque." His name came out like a breath. A disbelieving breath. "What are you doing with a firearm?"

He knocked his against hers. "I could ask the same." A smirk. "Thought I had you pegged right." He cocked his head and nodded toward her HK 9mm, then his weapon. "Same time?"

Yield? Was he crazy? "I'm eating your barrel and you want me to stand down?"

"Together."

"Who are you?"

"Weapon first." He motioned toward her cot with his free hand. "On the bed."

Clenching her jaw, Darci considered the showdown. She should've been alerted to him. In a way she had, with the way he stood out, annoyed her, trailed her. But she hadn't clued in, and that was a deadly mistake. When had she last made such a grievous error?

Who was he? He couldn't have known her mission, so what put him on her team in the middle of Afghanistan? This couldn't be a coincidence.

"You said we had to hurry," he said in a calm, smooth voice.

Darci flicked her wrist so the firearm pointed toward the ceiling of the tent. Eyes locked on Toque, she backstepped away from him and bent as he did the same. She set the weapon down and backed up.

Mentally combing her belongings. Where had she put the Gerber?

Toque set his Glock down and straightened. Hands on his belt, he flashed that cocky smile. "So, what part of the alphabet soup are you?"

"If you had any brains, you wouldn't ask."

"Let's just say I'm short on those at the moment."

His arrogance kneaded her frustration. Cold wind flapped against the tent opening and swirled around her hands and face. "We can play Scrabble with our letters, or we can get everyone packed up and out of here—alive."

"Who's coming? You never said."

"Does it matter? The brand doesn't matter when it's a bullet through the skull." Truth or Dare. If she told him it was the Chinese, he'd never believe it. She sure wouldn't have if she hadn't seen their distinctive faces with her own eyes.

"Matters a lot to me."

"Then you can die alone." Darci dug into her pack. She'd learned long ago how to get by on little. And survive on less. She glanced at him as she tugged out the blast-proof box. Spinning it to the right combo, she tried her best to ignore the man standing over her.

"You're spooked. So I'm going to guess it wasn't Taliban. What? Has someone with a vendetta found you at last?"

She popped the lid, removed the canister of oxygen, then pressed down twice in rapid succession. *Click!* Darci dug her fingernails into the hair-thin space between the platform and the interior hull and pried up. The false bottom gave way. She pulled out the tiny satellite phone.

"Last resort, Kintz. A call from that phone should precede your death by seconds." The general's warning boomed through her mind as she powered it up.

Toque cursed.

Darci recognized the move that followed his curse and dove for her weapon.

Dead weight dropped against her arm. Pain snapped a yelp from her.

"Who?" Toque growled, his face against hers.

"Idiot!"

"Who followed you?"

"I am not authorized to divulge that information."

"American?"

Darci met his hard expression, their noses an inch apart. She knew what he was asking—since she had slanted eyes and high cheekbones—was she loyal to the Asians or Americans? And she hated the operative before her for even questioning her loyalty.

"You're the spook," she ground out. "You tell me."

He didn't budge.

"What—what's going on?"

At the startled voice of Alice Ward, Toque stood. In the second it took him to stand, Darci flipped the blanket over their weapons, folded it up, and tucked the bundle in her pack. "Nothing. We're packing up. Toque was getting fresh."

Toque spun, his gaze skimming the bed, then nailing the backpack as she slung it over her shoulders and secured the straps around her waist. "Hey!"

"Out of time." She looked past him to Alice. "How's the girl?"

"Clean." She swallowed, still disconcerted and not buying the cover Darci had thrown over their standoff. "She's asking for you."

"What about the others?" Darci stepped around the cot.

"Jaekus is packed and waiting. The professor is muttering and not doing much of anything else."

"Alice, make him! Or he'll be dead within the hour." Darci rushed toward her. "Now!"

Mouth open, eyes wide, Alice took a step back. Nodded. Then another step backward. "Right." She spun and hurried into the morning that washed with the blue specter of dawn. Odd. She'd never thought of dawn in that way, but knowing daylight could reveal them if they had to hide...

Fire ripped through the back of her head. Her world tilted upward.

Toque had her hair in a fist. He hauled her against him. Something pinched her throat.

A knife!

Planting one hand on the handle and one on the blade, she forced herself not to fight him. To set him off balance and seize the chance. "You won't get anything out of me like this."

"It seems there's no way to get anything out of you. But I have a feeling you'll talk if I go after that girl."

"N—" She clamped down on the panic.

He chuckled. "Thought you might reconsider. Now cough it up."

The girl wasn't just a child she'd gone soft for. Badria could possibly identify who'd murdered her family. Yielding now insured Darci could get the girl back to Bagram, back to the general and the experts.

"Who's coming, Jia?"

"Release me."

"We tried it your way."

"You're going to get us killed."

"No, you wasting time is getting us killed."

Anger tightened her chest. "Fine." As soon as she said it, the pressure on her throat eased. She pushed the knife away and straightened, moving toward the tent-pole support. If she needed to, she'd use it somehow.

"I want my Glock and the information."

Thunder rumbled through the predawn hour.

Wait! That wasn't thunder.

"Chopper," Toque said. Three large strides carried him to the entrance.

Darci was at his side. She whipped open the flap.

"Good," the professor announced. "They're just on time."

"Who? Who's coming?" Darci hurried forward, fury coloring her vision red.

"I called the Army, told them we needed to—"

"Fool!" Toque shouted.

Darci gulped the adrenaline as she lifted Badria into her arms. "You've led them straight to us."

"Of course I did," the professor said with a chortle. "Wasn't that the idea?"

"Not them, the *enemy!*"

White hair rimmed wide eyes. "What enemy?"

Toque leaned toward Darci and placed a hand on Badria's black hair, severing the dance of firelight on her face. "Who is it, Jia?"

It wouldn't matter in a few minutes. "Chinese."

His eyes rounded. He spun toward the chopper.

As if in response, a stream of hellfire dotted the dark sky as if lighting the way for the missile streaking toward the helicopter that now hovered above their camp. But Darci knew—the dots were the missiles.

"Run!" The backwash of the rotors drowned her words.

Darci crushed the girl to herself and dove away from the chopper. Two routes presented themselves: through the main tents, down the path that led to the gorge where they'd collected water and showered. Or to the right, up the rigorous terrain and deeper into the unforgiving Hindu Kush.

High ground has the advantage.

She dove to the right. Sprinted between the base-camp tent and her own. A hand on her shoulder told her she wasn't alone. No time to look back. To consider who was with her. Who was against her. Pain niggled at her, reminding her of the graze. She reached for another crag.

Night turned to day. Brilliant white. For an instant.

Darci tensed.

Booom!

An invisible hand shoved her face-first into the rock. White-hot pain flashed through her skull. Then blacker than black, night devoured her whole.

★ ★   Fifteen   ★ ★

10 Klicks outside FOB Robertson

The village felt haunted. Emptied, yet he knew it wasn't. Couldn't be if Command had sent them here. Heath peered through the slats of the MRAP as it lumbered around a row of buildings. Arabic script ran down the walls on either side of doors. Some sported both English lettering and Arabic. Closed doors. Closed windows. Closed hearts. Heath had seen it time and again in Taliban strongholds. The only thing some wanted from Americans was death—of said Americans. Every now and then that distinct feeling wafted on the wind and brought with it a warning.

This was one of those times. His words from the night before about God having their backs echoed in his mind. He sure hoped he hadn't lied.

"Looks like they knew we were coming," Candyman called to Watters.

"Yep." Watters shifted and glanced down.

Heath traced his line of sight. Pride swelled as he realized Watters was assessing Trinity for signs of concern or agitation. But his partner sat at his feet, snout resting on his knee. Until he put her into action on the ground, she wasn't interested. He ruffled her head and shrugged at Watters.

Watters banged the hull. "Let's get up close and personal."

The MRAP slowed to a stop.

Two sergeants at the back climbed out, one taking point on a knee, the other flanking him. "Clear."

119

Heath and Aspen waited as the rest of the detachment filed out. Waiting and acting like a spectator. As he bent and stepped from the steel coffin, he realigned his mind. Civilian or military, he was in a hostile situation. Not being ready mentally could get his head blown off.

Trinity tugged on her lead, straining. She looked at him, wagged her tail as if to say, "Ready to play?" then sat down and stared at her objective.

Heath glanced at Watters, who was giving his team orders. "She's got a hit."

"You aren't—aw heck, never mind." Watters motioned to Candyman to take a team and scout north. Watters would sweep south, and they'd meet up in the middle again. With four guys behind him, he nodded to Heath. "Lead on."

Heart pumping fast, Heath released Trinity. "Trinity, seek!"

With a small lunge, she barreled onward, nosing the ground. Her head turning right, then left as she continued. Exhilarated, Heath looked to his friends, only to see Hogan's narrowed gaze behind Aspen. Something needled his conscience. But what? Trinity loved this. Heath might have a pounding headache, but Trinity was pounding the ground.

Jogging behind his canine partner, he felt the telltale thud in his skull. *Too much.* He'd done too much in too short a time. He knew it. But slowing down equaled defeat. And he wasn't going there.

Trinity stopped, sniffed, then sat back on her haunches and looked at him. Then at the closed door.

Heath signaled to the team leader.

Watters and his team edged in, weapons up. "U.S. Special Forces," he shouted to those inside. "Come out with your hands in the air." He shouted the message again, this time in Pashto. Then Arabic.

Heath clipped the lead back on Trinity and took a firm grip.

The door eased open.

Trinity lunged. Barked.

Sucking in a breath, Heath grabbed a tighter hold on the lead and pulled her back. Which was about like trying to harness a tornado. "Trinity, out!"

An Afghan man screamed, then bent away, covering his head. Cowering.

The rest of Watters's team rushed into the home. Shouts came from several directions. Down the dusty, hard-packed street, Heath saw the other team members clearing a store. Heath walked Trinity in a circle around the small crowd of Special Forces troops and the family of six or eight who stepped into the cool morning. A good hit, but that was enough. The weakness in his legs and arms told him so. The erratic heart rate told him so.

Then why couldn't he just let it go?

With a fair distance between them and the others, Heath let Watters do what he did best and took a knee next to Trinity. He wrapped an arm around her thick chest, proud that even after thirteen months off the grid, she still had what it took. "Good girl."

Trained on the others, Trinity was distracted just long enough to turn her head to him, swipe her tongue up his cheek, then refocus on the action unfolding. She missed it, the action, being useful, being part of a team.

He patted her side. "Me too, girl." He sighed. Or did he?

In his periphery he saw Jibril, Aspen, and Hogan monitoring the progress of the SF team. It hit Heath then—*I have a team, a new team.*

Trinity's ears flickered. Swiveling like satellites, they twisted to the rear. She looked over his shoulder. In a split second, she launched over Heath's shoulder.

The lead ripped out of his fingers.

Heath spun—so did his head. He shook it off as he shoved to his feet, searching for Trinity. Scanning the structures, he tried to make sense of the almost monochromatic setting. Brown roads. Brown buildings. Wait—there. To the right. Third building. Trinity once again took up an aggressive stance, snarling and snapping.

"Trinity, heel!" He glanced to Watters. Should he shout for help? When he turned back to Trinity, his heart stuttered. She was gone!

"Trinity!" He took a step forward. Crap. He wasn't cleared to engage hostiles. Then again, he wasn't leaving Trinity to end up dead. She hadn't left him—he wouldn't leave her. Again, he double-checked his six.

The villager was arguing with Watters, his team helping with small children from the home.

Too busy.

Heath rushed after Trinity. *This is real smart. You have no weapon. No backup.* He didn't care. He wasn't losing Trinity. Not now. Not here. At least he had a vest and helmet. With each plant of his boots, Heath steeled himself. His head felt like it was taking assault fire. *Boom. Boom. Boom.*

His vision blurred.

No!

He pushed it aside. It resisted. He shoved forward. Farther. "Tri. . ."

Everything went black.

Panic snapped his eyes open. Heath glanced around. How long had he—? *On the ground. I'm on the ground.* On a knee. Heart and head still pounding. That was good then, right? Meant he'd only been out a few seconds. Right? *Please, let it be right.*

"You okay?" Hogan shouted as she ran past him. "I got her."

"Yeah. . ." The answer proved weaker than his legs. Walking through pudding would've been easier. He trudged onward.

An Afghan male stepped out of the hut.

Armed. Aiming at Hogan.

A strangled yelp whipped out of her. She skidded, trying to stop, and landed on her rear.

Heath hauled in a breath as the guy shouted, *"Allahu Akbar."*

Heath's breath backed into his throat. A million thoughts pinged off his addled brain: Where was Trinity? Was the guy alone? Had he killed Trinity? *I don't have a weapon. I'm going to die. Hogan's going to die.*

As the telltale crack of an M4A1 split his thoughts, Heath watched the guy fall to his knees. A dark spot spread over the tan tunic he wore. He flopped into the dust.

"Yes, indeed." Candyman laughed as he trotted toward Hogan. "God *is* great. But maybe not his god." He grinned at Heath and knelt to check his pulse. " 'Cuz I'm thinking my god—whoever he is—just won."

Behind them, a team snaked into the house. Trinity tore out a few seconds later. Heath gathered her into his arms, his biorhythms off the chart. Face buried in her fur, he clung to the wriggling mass of energy. "I thought you were a goner, girl." Once he'd regained his head, he ran his hands along her amber coat for injuries. Clean. Weird.

Boots crunched as a sergeant approached. "He shut her in a room."

"Why didn't he shoot her?" At the thought, Heath ran his hands over her body again, wondering if he'd missed something.

The sergeant shrugged. "Hey, I'm not a psychologist. And he's dead, so I can't ask."

Heath nodded. The question was dumb. One they wouldn't be able to answer. But he could thank the Lord for watching out for both of them. As he got to his feet again, he had one thought: *I don't belong here. . . .*

It wasn't the first time he'd thought that since setting down at Bagram, but this time a deadly danger hung over the words. He'd nearly gotten himself, Trinity, and Hogan killed.

Hogan came up next to him, arms folded. "You enjoyed that."

But he couldn't let on to his fears, not in front of the others. "What? Seeing you fall on your butt?" Heath grinned as he fed Trinity a treat. Had to play it cool. "One hundred percent."

"Ha. Ha." She nudged his shoulder. "I meant being back in action. You got so happy-slappy, you nearly did a face-plant."

"Nearly. But not quite." The five-second blackout. . .what if it'd happened after he made it to the building? If the terrorist pointed the gun at *his* head instead of Hogan's? A shudder rippled down his spine. The others would've had brain soup for chow.

Yeah, he needed to distance himself. Squinting, he brought his gaze back to Hogan and saw in her wheat-colored eyes, something. . . *She knows.*

Would she call it? Tell him—or worse, tell Jibril—that he was unfit for duty?

It'd happened once before with a colonel who felt Heath had become more a liability than an asset. He'd yanked Heath, tanked him, and sent him packing.

I'm not going back. Metaphorically or literally. But he had a responsibility. To Trinity. To the men and women around him.

Thunder streaked through the heavens.

Something went still in Heath. A knowing. A deep knowing. "That wasn't thunder," he muttered as he turned a circle—and stopped cold.

In the mountains, a cloud plumed, thick, black, and angry.

Parwan Province, Afghanistan

Can't breathe!

Someone had a hand on her throat. Darci jerked up—but saw nothing. She coughed. Again. No, not a hand. Smoke! The blanket of darkness smothered her. Her eyes watered. On all fours, Darci scrambled along the ground.

"Alice? Ba—" Another cough choked off the little girl's name. Where was the girl? Darci had her in her arms when the explosion knocked her out.

Explosion. The geological survey team.

She squinted, trying to see past the pillar of smoke. No-go.

Okay. She had to find Badria and get to lower ground, out of the small fire eating through one of the dense green sections of the mountains. Darci ripped off a stretch of her shirt and tied it around her face. "Badria! Where are you?" she asked in the girl's language.

Scooting along the route she'd taken, she searched for the small form, praying the little one hadn't survived the slaughter of her family to end up dead.

Her fingers traipsed over the rocky edifice. Forcing herself to recall what she remembered of the shape, Darci crawled, afraid she'd plunge down a drop-off she hadn't noticed before. Though determination held her fast, her priority had to be getting out of sight. If a gust of wind cleared the air, she'd be visible. Whoever had taken down the chopper would no doubt be looking for anyone escaping.

Darci dropped down a two-foot ledge—her ankle wobbled on the uneven surface. She shifted, then realized—a leg!

She traced the body. Too big for Badria. "Alice?"

A small groan. The legs moved. Arms. "Wha. . .?"

"Are you hurt? Is anything broken?"

Coughing, Alice shifted onto her side. "No. . .I don't think so." In the haze, Alice's face appeared close. Her thick black hair tumbled free of the binding she'd had it in before the blast.

"Where's Badria?"

With more coughing, Alice shook her head. "I don't know. She was with you."

An urgency gripped Darci she couldn't shake. "We can't leave her." She wouldn't leave the girl behind. "Help me find her—but stay low."

Wide brown eyes watered and turned red. Not from crying but from the smoke and ash eating the sky and oxygen.

Rocks and sharp shards digging into their knees and palms, they searched the surrounding area. But to no avail. Darci's heart pounded. She couldn't leave the girl. Not the way—

She stilled. *Not the way, what?* Her psyche warred with her past. *Not the way Ba left my brother.*

Slumping back against the mountain that rose several feet over them, Darci tried to catch her breath. This wasn't about her family. This was about a national—no, *international* crisis. If China was up to no-good here in Afghanistan, it could unseat everything.

Then, as if an invisible hand reached down, the cloud of smoke shifted to the east.

And before her, thirty or forty feet down, a hunk of twisted metal lay scattered over the remains of what used to be their camp. Small fires pocked the flat space. Gathered in a northwestern corner, about twenty shapes.

Darci pulled back. Too many fires still burned, stirring up ash and smoke, making it impossible to see who was down there. Who among their team had survived. She'd need to get closer if she had any chance—

"What's going on?" Alice whispered from behind.

"They've rounded up survivors." Darci scooched forward, her boots too loud for stealth. She slowed and made deliberate efforts to lift and place her foot with each step.

As she rounded a corner and hid behind a boulder, something in the southern corner, near a large piece of wreckage, caught her eye. A flash. Where was that coming from? She scoured the black, charred remains—

There. Again. Another flash.

She narrowed her eyes and leaned in. A shadow? No! A burst of relief shot through her. Not a shadow. It was Toque. Covered head to toe in ash and soot, he crouched next to the belly of the downed chopper. Had he rolled in the ash?

Another flash. A thought niggled at her brain. Was he sending her messages?

Pay attention, Darci.

Patting herself down, she searched for something to let him know she was listening. Wait. No. If she did that, the attackers would see her. She looked down. Against her North Face jacket, her hand would stand out. She gave the move-out signal.

The glare of whatever he was using scorched her eyes. But she forced herself to read the message. It came through:

.‑ .. ..‑‑ .‑‑ .‑‑. .‑.‑.‑ ‑.. .‑‑ ‑. .‑‑‑‑. ‑ .‑.‑ ‑‑‑ ‑‑‑ ‑.‑ ‑.... ‑.‑. ‑.‑ .‑.‑

E-T H-E-L-P-D-O-N-T-L-O-O-K-B-A-C-K.

. . .et help. "Get!" *Get help. Don't look back.*

125

She relayed her understanding, but. . .she didn't understand. What did he mean, don't look back?

As if in response to her question, Toque rose and stepped around the hulk.

No! You're exposed!

Hands raised, he shouted at the enemy.

Gunfire erupted.

"No!" Darci lunged forward but just as fast threw herself back down. Rocks exploded around her.

She'd drawn their attention. Her pulse thundered through her chest, reverberating off what she'd just seen. No. He couldn't be dead. He might've been a spook, but if anyone had a chance to help the team, it would've been Toque.

Something tickled her back. Something small, spider—

Darci whirled.

A pair of beautiful brown eyes stared out from a small hole. Badria! The little girl pushed aside some rock and rubble. On her belly, she wiggled backward, waving Darci to follow. As the girl cleared the opening, Darci saw it—

A tunnel!

Sixteen

Camp Eggers, Kabul, Afghanistan

All the demons of war must have him on their hit list. He'd made an impact here, saved thousands of lives from burning in hell. And the immortal beasts wanted him gone. His grandfather, Woundedknee Burnett, would've told him it was the spirits. But his grandmother, who'd drawn the grouchy ol' Cherokee from his reservation with her blue eyes and firm Christian faith, would've said he was right. The demons wanted to stop the Kingdom from advancing.

Right now, Lance didn't care who he was fighting as long as he won. With a four-man crew, he stalked down the long corridor that bisected the large building. Ahead stood General Early and his entourage.

Lance offered a salute. "General."

Early did the same. "Sorry about your adventure in that village."

"Comes with the territory. Had things to take care of, someone got a lucky hit in." He shrugged as he motioned to the steel door marked with a number 5. "So, we're both here now. What've you got?"

General Early nodded to one of his lieutenants, who swiped a badge down a reader. The light swam from red to green with a quiet beep before he tugged open the door and stepped aside.

"I tell you, this is the darndest thing. About zero-two-hundred, I wake up to the guard dogs going berserk, MPs shouting, and soon after Lieutenant Zeferelli here"—Early stabbed a finger at the lieutenant who'd accessed the room—"is banging down my door."

Lance smiled at the L-T who ducked, nerves jangled. "Don't you know privates have been sent to Leavenworth for less?"

The man's stiff composure softened beneath the joke. "Yes, sir. I've heard that, General, sir."

Lance laughed. "Get hold of those nerves, Zeferelli, or you'll wet yourself." He couldn't help but grin at the red spreading through the young man's face. "Go on."

Zeferelli looked to Early like a good dog. "Well." He licked his lips. "MPs rang my room, said they had a Chinese national. Three, in fact."

"And why would this news alarm you so much that you'd interrupt the precious sleep of your base commander?"

"Because, sir, the men asked for General Early by name."

"And every Afghan and Taliban terrorist roaming this godforsaken area knows that name."

"Yes, sir. But they don't know yours."

Lance stilled, listening to the whir of the minimal heating unit battling the exterior elements to afford a minuscule degree of warmth. "Come again?" His presence here wasn't common knowledge. He'd made sure with his delicate work of protecting operations and operatives.

"He asked for you. By name, sir. Said he would not talk to anyone but you."

"I thought he asked for Early."

The L-T nodded again. "Actually, his words to the MPs were, 'Tell General Early that if he wants to stop an international incident to get General Burnett here.'"

What was he saying about those demons earlier? "You gotta be kidding me," Lance said to General Early.

Shorter, grayer, and more wrinkled, the man fooled a lot of grunts with his size and age. "You been dancing with the wrong man's daughter again?"

Lance would've laughed at the memory, but this wasn't the time. He eyed his friend as they stepped into a monitoring room. Through the one-way glass, he found their guest.

And for one second, one painful, past-hurtling-to-the-present second, his heart stopped. Then his Catholic faith rushed up his throat in a hoarse prayer, "Sweet Mother of God. . ."

"My son! My son is still there."

"We'll get him out."

"No!" The man buried his head in his hands, sobbing. Finally, he hung his head, shaking it. "You cannot—they will be watching him. Watching his

every move. If they suspect, they will kill him."

"I can get him. I'll do it myself."

"No, no, you cannot." *The man lowered his head, and he slumped in the hard plastic chair. He wept.* "He told me—" *A shudder severed his words.* "He say, 'They watching me. If we all go, we die.'"

"What was that?"

General Burnett dropped into the rickety, creaking chair at the table stretched before the rectangular window. He picked up the shattered pieces of the past and cleared his throat. Put on his game face. A handful of people were privy to that mission. But nobody in this room. "What do you know about him?"

Zeferelli lifted a hand in defeat. "Name, rank—only by his uniform."

Lance nodded, his gaze skimming the PLA uniform. The rank on the shoulder. The gold aiguillette. But the one thing he couldn't tear his gaze away from was the familiar eyes.

"We've spent the last few hours digging up information while we waited for your arrival. His name is Colonel Zheng Haur," Lieutenant Zeferelli said, his dark hair rimming a young face. "According to our brief research, he is the personal aide to General Zheng, the minister of defense."

Why on earth would Zheng put Haur into enemy hands? Lance had tried to send in operatives to retrieve this young man, convince him to switch sides, but nothing—*nothing*—could draw him out. Because General Zheng had so thoroughly brainwashed and leashed him.

So what changed? Were they seeking revenge?

His breath backed into his throat—did they know Darci's location? No. No way they could know she was in country.

Or had Zheng sent Haur to prove his allegiance once again? Unfortunately, Lance couldn't share what he knew with anyone in this room, or the next. Forbidden territory, all of it.

But. . .could he snatch this kid? Have him vanish from this very building and disappear into thin air—thin air called anonymity? Would Haur go? Or would he fight him?

Lance didn't know enough. He'd have to ply information out of Haur. Figure out where he stood. What he wanted. Man, Lance could use a Dr Pepper about now.

"Let's find out what he knows." Lance pushed out of his seat, surreptitiously wiped his palms on his slacks, then strode to the door.

"Z," he said to the L-T as he swiped his card to gain access to the galley between the two rooms. "Did he say anything else?"

"No, sir." Zeferelli glanced at the general with his card poised over the reader.

Lance gave him the go-ahead. The light zipped green and a soft click echoed in the steel-reinforced chamber.

The L-T posted himself at the door as Lance moved to the table. The face before him so familiar, yet way too old for the few years that had passed.

Haur stood. "General, thank you for coming."

For cryin' out loud. The kid even sounded like his old man. Lance felt like Atlas, with the weight of the world on his shoulders. With the fate of one family he'd ripped apart twenty years ago dangling before him. But he had to play this right. Be the deputy director.

"First things first, Colonel." Lance stuffed his hands in his pockets, not wanting to put the man on the defensive. "We need your name, rank—you know the drill."

With a curt bow of his head, he assented. "Maj—Colonel Zheng Haur with the Ministry of Defense. I am here to speak with you on an urgent matter."

"If it's so urgent, why wait for me to show up? And what's wrong, can't you remember your own rank?" He tapped the table with a finger. "You know what I think? I think you're wasting my time. You didn't want to talk to me. You're buying time while your cohorts are out there plotting to destroy the base."

The man stiffened. "Of course not."

"Then what's the story? Why not talk to General Early—it's his base, for cryin' out loud. He can do anything I can."

Haur's face twitched. "No, sir. Not this time."

Little alarms buzzed at the back of Lance's head. But he told himself to play along. Play nice. No strong-arm tactics. Unless it became necessary. "And why is that?"

"You are familiar with the minister's son, yes?"

The conversation just took a giant leap toward Darci. "A hotheaded fool."

The tense brow smoothed, bringing a slight smile. "We agree."

Not the answer he expected. What he wouldn't do to plug this kid into a machine and figure out if he was playing them or what. Then again, Lance's own operatives were trained to defeat lie detectors, so he could expect no less from the Chinese officer standing before him at attention. "I'm sorry, Colonel, but I'm not here to deal with paternal issues. If the minister—"

"Colonel Wu has gone rogue."

That may be the worst news the man could've delivered to Lance. Colonel Wu, born Zheng Jianyu, had more patience, which wasn't a good thing in this case. It was a lethal thing. Jianyu knew how to play his enemy, taunt him, bring him into submission until he crushed his spirit so he'd never be the same again.

Lance had seen the man's handiwork with his own eyes.

"What in Sam Hill do you mean? Rogue?"

"His assignment was to oversee the integration and implementation of the teams working the mine in Jalrez Valley in Wardak Province. When I arrived to escort him back to China—"

"Why are you escorting him back to China?"

Haur's jaw muscle flexed, strength and anger bouncing on the nerve. "When I arrived, the mine director informed me that Colonel Wu had left the site."

Another yard closer to Darci.

"Good, he went back home." Lance said it to remind Colonel Zheng of the only acceptable answer. The way things should be.

"No." Frustration oozed out of the colonel, just as Lance intended. "He lied to the director of the mine, told them the general had recalled him. That is not true. He left with few supplies save his elite warriors."

Yanjingshe. The fiercest fighters and trackers Lance had ever witnessed. If they were out there. . .

One more baby step.

Mother, may I, please kill him?

Keep it cool. He had to keep it cool till he had cold, hard proof that Wu Jianyu knew the location of one of the Army's most prized assets. "Again, I'm not here for father-son fights. I have a region to stabil—"

"Then let me speak plainly, General." Haur let out a long sigh, fingertips pressed against the table. "You and I both know you are not here to stabilize anything."

Lance itched for a Dr Pepper with its hefty dose of sugar and caffeine.

"You are deputy director of Defense Counterintelligence and

HUMINT Center. You are responsible for dispatching teams of linguists, field analysts, case officers, interrogation experts, technical specialists, and special forces. You've had personnel in countries that could systematically destroy your reputation with the UN and even your closest allies."

Haur leaned forward his chained and cuffed hands jangling against the metal table. While there was no malice in his face, a fierceness edged into his until then calm demeanor. "Would you like me to lay out, in front of all these witnesses, what covert missions you are operating in this region?"

Seventeen

10 Klicks outside FOB Robertson

Smoke snaked into the sky, the snowcapped mountain marred by the black pillar stretching high over the spine. Dark and angry, it told Heath this wasn't a wood or forest fire. Black and billowing meant fuel and oil. And lots.

"Not exactly a small campfire, huh?" Aspen asked quietly. "What do you think happened?"

Green Berets huddled around the MRAP drew his attention. "Let's see if we can find out." Heath trotted that way.

Tense, quiet conversation carried between Watterboy and Candyman, hunched over a relief map. Of the mountains, if Heath guessed right. Candyman stabbed a finger at the one-dimensional topography, his expression intense. Watters held up a placating hand.

Slapping both hands against the hull of the MRAP, Candyman growled, "This is bull."

With a step back, Watters leaned in as if to say something to Candyman, then noticed Heath lurking. Man, he felt like some criminal eavesdropper.

Heath cleared his throat and gave a nod to them. "What's going on?"

Candyman turned to him and rolled his eyes. "Classic bureaucratic bull." He stomped off.

Asking again would agitate the man he'd worked with, so Heath waited.

Watterboy jerked toward him, a squall of anger hovering over the storm in his eyes—but it dropped flat as he sighed. "Look, I'd like nothing more than to tell you, but I can't. It's—"

"No worries." Hand held up, Heath cocked his head. "I get it."

Into a secure phone, Watters said, "Yes, sir. Holding."

Holding? Heath chewed that nugget as he returned to his team. Was that "holding" as in holding position and not returning to base, or holding on the line? By Candyman's frustration and anger, Heath bet it meant staying here. In hostile territory. No RTB orders and no going in to help with whatever had happened in the mountains.

"What did he say?" Jibril's brow knotted in concern and consternation.

"Nothing. He won't tell me what's going on because I'm not authorized personnel. But I heard him say they were holding."

"Holding?" Aspen folded her arms. "Holding what?"

"Position, most likely." Jibril's gaze rose to the lingering smoke. "The fire is still burning."

"That wasn't a house fire," Hogan said as she adjusted the helmet that bobbled on her head. "Something bad happened up there."

"You got that right." Candyman's voice erupted behind them.

Heath glanced past Hogan to his old buddy. Hogan arched her eyebrow at Heath, and somehow he knew what she was going to do.

"So, it's bad?" She sounded like a doe-eyed woman.

Candyman hesitated as he looked down on her, their nearly twelve-inch difference exaggerated with them side by side. "Baby, don't work me up if you're going to work me over."

Hogan laughed. "I like you."

"Mutual." Candyman smiled, then looked at Heath. "Running this morning, I saw one of my former buddies hustling to a chopper. They were sent out for an emergency extraction of some stupid survey team up in the Kush."

"Survey?"

"Yeah, checking out the rocks or something. Hanged if I know, but why on this insane planet anyone would be up there in the first place if they aren't wearing an Interceptor and carrying"—Candyman hoisted his M4—"at least one of these. . ."

An image erupted in Heath's mind. Warm almond eyes. "Wait." He gripped Candyman's vest. "Survey team. You mean the geological survey team?"

Candyman shrugged. "Yeah, maybe. Don't know."

Aspen shouldered in, her blue eyes locked like radar onto Heath.

"You think she was with them?"

"Who?" Candyman glanced between the two of them.

Jia. Heath wanted to look at the smoke-streaked sky, but it'd give away his concern. *Play it cool.* She wasn't anything. . . . Except the only person who'd made him consider the future. The woman who made it easy to talk and be around someone of the opposite sex. The woman who—

Was so scared of what she felt for him, she wasn't willing to feel it. That fake e-mail address—RockGirl—told him he wasn't worth the effort to get to know. Which he could've informed her from the beginning. But no, he'd let himself off-lead when it came to her. And been downright brazen about their mutual attraction.

She was up there. . . . His pulse hiccuped at the thought of her being near—or in—that explosion.

A wet nose nudged his hand.

Yeah, Trinity knew. She always knew when he was off-kilter. Knew when he needed space to breathe. He lifted her lead and mumbled to the others, "Excuse me, I think Trinity needs to do her duty."

"Heath." Hogan's voice trailed him, but he kept walking.

Watterboy intercepted him. "Hey, stay close." When his gaze rammed into Heath's, he must've seen the panic. "We've got unfriendlies here still. And with whatever just happened"—he motioned to the mountains—"who knows where we'll end up by nightfall."

Heath caught on. "It'd be smart to move a little closer. Get us out of here where we've got headhunters breathing down our necks. Then we'd be closer and in position. If needed, I mean."

Eyes crinkling, Watters slapped him on the back of his shoulder. "Good thoughts, Ghost." He stalked away.

Heath walked Trinity to an area where the dead grass matched the hard-packed roads. After taking care of business, Trinity trotted over to a building and flopped down in the sliver of shade provided. Pink tongue dangling, she panted, eyes squinting sheer pleasure. She thrived on this scene. Loved working.

Heath started toward her, smiling. Somehow, that seventy-pound fur ball made everything seem okay. When everything wasn't.

Just above her right ear cement erupted.

As if punched in the chest, Heath sucked in a breath. "Trinity, down!" He dropped to a knee, knowing the shooter was somewhere behind him. "Taking fire, taking fire!"

His beloved canine flattened herself against the earth.

Heath used his torso as a shield to break the line of sight between the shooter and the only girl who'd ever protected him. She fastened those amber eyes on him. He signaled with his hand. "Come," he said, quiet and hoarse.

Trinity low-crawled toward him, a stealthy thing that made his heart balloon with pride. She was incredible, her trust implicit, her loyalty thorough. Her snout puffed dust around her. When she reached him, Heath covered her. Trinity was a prized asset, but more than that, she was his best friend. Soldiers and civilians alike knew whoever killed a war dog lived well for the next decade.

They'll have to go through me first.

"Ghost!"

With Trinity huddled beneath him, dust and grit billowing into his mouth as a cold wind pulled at his clothes, Heath shot a glance to the side. Amid another plume of dust, Watters and Candyman knelt by the MRAP for cover. "Where?"

"Shooter," he gritted out, inching his way toward them. "My nine o'clock."

As soon as the words escaped his lips, the team pelted the building. Heath scooped up Trinity and sprinted. A half-dozen feet from safety, something plowed into his back. Like the mighty hand of God shoving him face-first into the dirt. He released Trinity, who skidded out in front. On the ground, he felt himself dragged to safety by two or three men.

Hauled out of the line of fire, he scrambled to see Trinity. She sat beside him on her haunches, tail thumping, as if this had been a day in the park. "Only you, girl." Chuckling, he ruffled her fur—pain snapped through the tendons and ligaments in his arm and back.

A slap on that same spot about made him come out of his skin. *Augh!*

"How's that shoulder?" Candyman asked.

That thing would leave a nice, shiny bruise. Pushing to his feet, Heath grunted. His back felt as if someone had driven a stake through it. "Much better now that you hit it." Rotating his arm to test the range of motion, Heath took up Trinity's lead with his other hand. When he turned, he met malice-hardened eyes.

Four men wrangled an Afghan to his knees a few feet away.

"Here's your dog killer."

"Or attempted killer," another sergeant said.

Gaze locked on the shooter, Heath lunged.

So did Watters. "Hey!" Caught him by the arm. Swung him around. Candyman was there in a heartbeat, too, both strong-arming Heath back a safe distance.

"He tried to kill Trinity—took shots at her. I'm not—"

"Ghost." Watters shoved him back with his shoulder, then braced him with two palms against his chest. "We've got him." His calm, in-control gaze stilled the fury in Heath's chest. "He's not going anywhere, no more weapons."

Only as he saw the concern in his former buddy's face did Heath grab hold of his sanity. *What is wrong with me?* Nerves buzzing, he stood down. Blew out a breath as he turned a circle.

Rather than longing to be in the middle of combat, taking a bead on the enemy, suddenly Heath wanted nothing more than to jog the trail at the ABA ranch. Escape. Again, it hit him: *I don't belong here.*

Parwan Province, Afghanistan

"Push in, push in," Darci said, scooting along, palms flat against the wall of the cave, her mind hooked on Toque's sacrifice. Why? Why had he done that? The shot she'd heard as she dove into the cave and tripped. . . had that been the signal that he was dead?

Think positively.

Darci squinted to see the thin thread of light that filtered in from the opening thirty feet back. But slinking farther into this cave to hide was as bad as trying to hide in a coffin. Dark, no air. . .death.

Think. Positively!

Her shoulder ached, a sticky mess after all the exertion and trauma. Darci gritted her teeth against the pain. She had to get Badria and Alice to safety. Back to Bagram.

"Why are we in here? Won't they find us and. . . ?" Alice's voice trailed off.

"This area is home to thousands of tunnels," Darci said, crouch-walking inch by inch. "It should lead us to a safe location."

"And if it doesn't?"

Darci sighed. "Let's keep our options open, okay?" If they didn't, they'd give up before they started. But she was determined to find a way home. She wouldn't abandon her father, no matter what he had done in the past.

"Right." For a young, naive girl from the country, Alice had a strength about her that surprised Darci.

"Trust me, we'll be fine."

"What about the others?"

Frustration coiled around Darci's mind. "Let's not talk for a while. We have no idea if they've followed us, and we don't need to be a homing beacon." Besides, she needed mental space to think and work out a plan.

"Right."

As darkness gathered them into its arms, Darci knew she had to push her mind somewhere pleasant or she'd suffocate herself. Okay, so. . .where? Home? With her father?

No. . .

On the training field. A dog barking. Warm gray eyes that led to a very deep, rich—but tortured—soul. He'd been so crushed when she tried to lower the boom that they didn't have a chance that she'd wanted to take back the words, feed him empty promises. And yet. . .yet, he'd pressed in. Yanked the truth out from behind her barriers like some thief. Some guy who thought he owned the world.

And yet. . .he didn't. What a strange dichotomy in him. Broken, but strong. Confident, yet uncertain.

She'd left their lunch date without handing out promises. That had been intentional, and his hurt lingered in her mouth like a bitter herb. But she wouldn't. She worked targets and objectives. She wouldn't work a guy she. . .liked.

Look how things ended for all of James Bond's girls—dead or gone to the dark side. No thanks. She wouldn't bear the blame for things like that.

If only the double life she led could compare to the glitz and glamour of James Bond. And yet Bond had a string of heartbroken women in the wake of his speedboat-style life. That's the reason Darci never went there.

Okay, so the mission in China had taken longer than usual. Jianyu had gotten under her skin, under her defenses. The biggest mistake of her life. She hadn't seen the real him. And when she had. . .

A shudder ripped through Darci. She blamed it on the clamminess soaking her shirt. But she knew better.

"Why'd you stop?" Alice's whispered words skidded into the darkness. "What's wrong?"

"Sorry." Darci hadn't even realized she'd stopped. "Leg cramp."

A small hand touched her knee. Darci wrapped hers around the tiny, icy fingers. This far up in the mountains, coiling their way through the innards, lowered their core body temperatures. They couldn't stay hidden from the sun much longer. Holding Badria's hand, Darci used the wall to push to her feet. Hot and cold swirled through her, the pain mind-numbing. "Just a little farther."

"You've been saying that for an hour." Exhaustion tugged at Alice's slow words that bounced off the walls.

I have? Had they really been hidden that long? What if they never made it out of here?

Don't think that!

Why hadn't Darci listened to the promptings that told her this mission would be her last? What made her think she could do this job indefinitely? She didn't want to. Weariness tugged at her the last few missions.

She'd loved this job once. With a brutal passion. It helped her feel like she gave hope to people who didn't have any. Her psych assessment before she took the job revealed she wanted this role because of what happened to her mom. The evaluation didn't make sense to her, but if she somehow honored her mom, helped others who were in danger and didn't know it, then that was a good thing.

But. . .to what extent? What did she have left? What hope did she have?

"Because of what's happening right here." Even at the memory of his husky words, Darci felt the warmth she'd experienced several nights ago in his arms.

If only it could happen. If she could walk away. . .

"How much farther?" Alice said through a yawn.

Too bad Heath wasn't here. With that gorgeous dog of his. Trinity would find her, find an escape. "It can't go on forever." She hoped.

"My thoughts exactly." Alice pulled in a breath. "But what if it does?"

"Alice."

"Right."

Around a corner, the shadows lightened. Air swirled as if... Trekking her fingers along the ribs of the cave, she slowly rose to—

Her head thudded against the ceiling. She grimaced but was glad she could stretch her legs. "Let's stop." As her eyes adjusted to the open area, Darci noticed light streaming through two different locations. Straight ahead and at her two o'clock.

"But that...that's light. It means there's an out, right?"

Yes, but where precisely would they exit? What if they'd managed to come full circle back to the camp? What if they dumped out into a Taliban stronghold? Despite her best efforts at keeping her sense of direction, Darci had only an educated—if you could call it that after so many twists and loopbacks—guess about their direction.

"Is something wrong?" Alice's voice skated along Darci's cheek.

The girl was close. Then again, in a narrow cave tunnel with darkness, everything felt close. "Just resting."

Darci knelt and tugged her pack from her back. She fished through it for her sat phone. Normally she wouldn't take this risk, but they were out of options. Odds said the team had been killed. Toque—

Darci squeezed off the thought as she pulled out the phone. Her thumb slipped into a depression. A hole? Since when did her sat phone have a hole? She angled it toward the lone halo of light and stilled. A bullet blinked back at her, the light glinting off the surface. They'd hit her—the phone—and she'd never known. Heat speared her stomach at how close she'd come to dying. She couldn't even recall feeling the impact. Adrenaline had shoved her through the opening. Besides, after the pain from the first bullet, with another Death would come knocking.

"Ah, Death, the spectre which sate at all feasts!"

As if hearing her Poe quote, the light beam straight ahead fractured. Darci pushed back, drawing Badria into her arms. "Quiet," she hissed to Alice, whom she expected to start peppering her with nervous questions.

Shouts slithered into the cave. They bounced off the walls as if searching for them.

Positive thoughts gone. *We are dead.*

Eighteen

En Route to FOB Murphy, Afghanistan

Despite the chill, body odor and tension radiated through the steel hull of the MRAP as they lumbered out of the village and gained speed. At the village, the Green Berets requested and received clearance to move to FOB Murphy. Eighty minutes had passed since the explosion. Though no official orders had come down, the new location would put them closer to the base and the mountains.

Watters was no dummy positioning his team in a prime location. Heath could tell by the way he was moving his team and staying on top of updates. That's the way of it in the military. If you suspect your fellow American troops are getting hammered, military branch divisions and rivalries vanish. You help. You help fast.

Then later, after saving the rivals, remind them constantly who saved whom.

Chin resting across Heath's and Hogan's legs, Trinity yawned and moaned as he ran a hand along her back. Hogan smoothed her coat, too, eyes closed. No doubt she took comfort in Trinity's rhythmic breathing. He had. Did now. Even during furnace summers out here, it never felt hot or suffocating to have his furry partner stretched across him as he waited in the field. Laid prone on lookout, her side pressed to his.

At the FOB, soldiers went one way while A Breed Apart entered a three-story structure that housed a small eating area and multiple rooms with bunk beds. Grabbing rack time when possible kept soldiers alive and alert. Heath opened an MRE and dropped onto the bunk beneath Jibril. Meals-Ready-to-Eat had other infamous, derogatory names, but they supplied enough calories to keep him from caring. Across from him Aspen and Hogan occupied the other bunks.

Heath fed half his meal to Trinity and provided her a bowl of water from a cooking pot he'd reallocated to himself from the kitchen. When they geared out, it'd be returned, with the addition of some slobber. Served them right for cutting him and the team out of the mission briefing.

Munching a chocolate candy-bar stick-looking thing, Heath rose and went to the window, clouded by years of grime and dust. Blending with the landscape made a ragtag huddle of buildings that served as a checkpoint almost indiscernible. For years, locals paid what little they had to clear the checkpoint, contributing to the bloated recreational funds of corrupt officials and their perv underlings. Liberal media outlets might call this war useless, but try telling that to the average Muslim trying to make his or her way across a land polluted with corruption and greed. Now they could traverse it without selling their souls.

Jia.

As the name lodged into his still-pounding skull, he looked to the mountains, but his mind looked to that heart-shaped face. The kiss he'd almost stolen, wanted bad. Though his TBI had been an excuse to pull back from the world, Jia made him want to reenter it. Be there with her, for her, beside her. . . .

Was she up there? The explosion—did she die?

He kneaded the ache in his temple, thinking through how he'd find out if she'd been on the casualty list—if there was one. That was the thing of it. Nobody knew what happened.

Correction: They knew. He didn't.

In fact, he had little doubt they were getting briefed on it as he stood here.

"You weren't ready."

Heath felt the words as much as heard them. Coarse, tight, controlled, but vitriolic all the same. He looked over his shoulder.

Hogan hovered less than a foot behind and to the side. She glanced back, and that's when he noticed the others had cleared out. "Where'd they go?"

"Don't ignore what I said."

The challenge pulled him around. "I'm not." He stared her down. Though she couldn't be more than five five, the woman made up for it in attitude. "But what I do and when I do it—that's not your concern."

"It is when you black out in the middle of a gig." On her toes, she leaned in. "When you put my life, and Trinity's, on the line."

Heath cocked his head. She'd just accused him of putting his dog's life in jeopardy. "Step off."

"No."

Heath drew himself straight. "Hogan—"

"Look, I get it."

"I don't think you—"

"You wanted this." Intensity flamed through her irises. "But that scar you got wrecked everything. So you get this chance to be back here and you grab it." Her expression softened. "But you weren't ready. . .yet."

Amazing that a three-letter word could stand him down when a 120-pound woman couldn't.

Her brown eyes searched his. "Heath, I saw you black out."

Could she hear the shelling of his heart? She had said nothing to the others. When he didn't respond, she plowed on as Hogan always did. "I have a feeling it wasn't the first time since the plane touched down. And you've had a headache the whole time, haven't you?"

Heath swallowed. The last time he felt dressed down by a woman, Auntie Margaret had chewed him out for skipping football practice his senior year. That was two summers before she died. He'd joined the Army a month later.

"And then that Asian chick. You freaked out, thinking she was in that explosion, right?"

"I—"

She thrust a finger in his face. "Don't bury feelings. She may be the only piece of heaven on earth to keep you sane. I'm not saying you have to get all gooey over her—God knows I don't need to see that—but feel what you feel." Sincerity pinched her eyebrows as she bobbed her head at him. "Don't bury it. You're stressed out of your mind, and that's what's making the headaches worse."

He blinked. She was right. He knew she was. But owning up to it. . .

"Despite my objections about you coming, I think there's a reason you're here."

Heath stared at the fiery wonder. For an annoying, mouthy woman, she was all right. *Little sister* came to mind. "You covered me." It was hard to read her expression thanks to the bangs that fell into her eyes.

"Out there, in the village when I went down."

She gave a curt nod.

As voices floated down the hall, Heath glanced toward the closed door, then to her. "Why?"

"You get whacked out and A Breed Apart is shot." She backed away and climbed onto the top bunk. "You think you're the hot snot now, but wait till I get Beo under the spotlights."

"His drool alone would wipe out the audience."

Grinning, she flung a wad of MRE trash at him.

He caught it, his mind weighted by the profound conversation. One he'd never expected from Hogan. He'd underestimated her. And on every count, she was right.

Talk about cutting a man down to size. Big chunk of humble pie, hand-fed by a woman he'd detested a week ago.

Heath glanced at her. Looked down, ashamed. "Thanks."

"Don't thank me." Arms stretched behind her head, she closed her eyes. "I'm trying to convince you to get out. I want your job."

Parwan Province, Afghanistan

"Back." Darci caught the edge of Badria's shirt and tugged her backward. "Farther." She bumped against Alice, who scrambled back into the gaping maw of darkness.

Darci's world spun, a feeling of lightness and swimming all at once. She shook her head, strained to see. If her head felt so light, why did her legs feel like lead weights?

Stumbling, she gripped Badria tighter, tumbled into the cave wall. Fire lit down her arm again. Darci steeled herself against the wave of nausea and light-headedness that wrapped her in a tight cocoon. When was the last time she ate? Or had anything to drink? At this rate, she'd never get Alice and Badria to safety. Propped against the wall, her arms still around the precious girl, Darci swallowed and let out exhausted breaths.

"What—?"

"Quiet!" That whisper had razor-sharp precision, severing Alice's question. Though guilt bit at Darci, desperation and pain chomped into that guilt. She rolled her head to the side, to the other route of darkness, knowing that a dozen feet that way were two more tunnels. Two avenues of escape. They couldn't see the light beams, so they didn't know if they were being searched. And in the cave, noise echoed and popped off every surface with maddening clarity, making it impossible to know from which direction the noise originated. To the right, the way back to camp. More than an hour's journey. They couldn't do that. She couldn't do it.

Banging her head against the wall did nothing to shake off the haze. Panic fisted itself around her heart—if she was blacking out, she wouldn't know till. . .

Well, she may never know if they killed her.

Okay, genius. Do something.

To her left lay the dual tunnels. There people were searching. No doubt the Chinese. Nobody else would be looking for them, at least not on foot. Not this fast.

So, if she led them out the wrong tunnel. . .

Searing, an image of Badria soaked in blood popped before her.

Darci squeezed her eyes tight. Okay, no good. Why did it feel like a brick sat on her chest?

Shake it off, Darci. Get them out of here—alive.

"Okay," Darci said in a whisper to her right, to where she imagined Alice hunkered. "We have to split up and—"

"No!"

"Listen!" Darci took a breath. "I'll distract them, then backtrack."

Only heavy breathing met her words.

Arms trembling, she guided Badria over her legs and toward Alice. Cold fingers latched on to Darci's, the tiny fingers digging into her flesh as the little one yelped.

"Shh, shhhh." In Pashto, she explained to Badria that she needed to go with Alice to save the others, that they'd meet up at the foot of the mountain. "It'll be okay," Darci said with little confidence. "Alice, take her. Get down the mountain. Get to Bagram, ask for General Burnett. Don't stop for anyone and don't talk to anyone else. Burnett. Nobody else. Got it?"

"What about you?"

"What was his name? Tell me who you're going to talk to."

"Only General Burkett."

"Burnett. *Nett,* Alice."

"Right. Burnett." She huffed. "What about you?"

"I'll be right behind you. Even if you can't see me, just keep going. I'll find you at the base." There was a greater chance of not being able to evade the Chinese, of getting drilled full of holes. "Okay?"

"I. . .yeah."

Mouth drier than the land around them, Darci gulped. She didn't have much time. And she had to *buy* them time. "Then let's do this."

"Darci, wait." Alice's fingers swiped over Darci's side, then caught her arm. "Are you. . .what are. . .?" A weighted breath. "Please don't do anything. . .heroic."

"Who?" She winced at the knife that sliced through her courage again. "Me?" Slinking back into the somber glow, Darci looked for movement.

"I hear something!" a voice shouted.

Darci pointed to the other tunnel. "Go!" She nudged Alice to prevent her from arguing.

Wobbling into a crouch, Darci fell back against the tunnel wall. A gasp behind her told her Alice was hesitating. "Go," she ground out and pushed herself off the rocks and toward the opening.

Her feet felt like writhing snakes, tangling and thick. She had a mission. She had to get this done. Had to protect the others. The river of light drew closer, spilling over the rocks and glinting in her eyes. No, not just glinting. Glaring.

Hand just inside the lip of the cave, Darci paused. She closed her eyes, shutting out visual cues that would deceive her and trained her mind on the sounds outside. Wind. Cold, bitter wind. The temperature had dropped since they'd entered. Would Alice and Badria be okay? Would the storm hit before they made it to the base?

A bird squawked in the distance, but she could sift no other sound from the surroundings. They must've—

Rocks dribbled against each other.

A grunt.

Darci smiled. *Ready or not, here I come. . .*

She drew in a breath for courage and blew it out. *God, help me do this. Help me to not get killed, so I can go home and have tea once more with Ba.*

A rumble of noise and shouts froze her. But only for a second—they'd spotted Alice!

Darci stumbled into the open. A three-foot ledge provided minimal protection against a fifty-foot drop. Her stomach squirmed as adrenaline exploded through her veins.

She straightened and turned toward the noise. "No!"

Her panicked shout stopped several men.

She widened her eyes in a pretense of fear.

Though she pretended to scramble away, Darci glanced back. To her pursuers, she'd look like a terrified woman. But for her, it was her reassurance that Alice and Badria would get away.

"There! It's her—Meixiang! Grab her!"

Yes, come and get me.

She went down. Glanced back and threw her arms up to protect herself against their blows.

Two men still followed the girls.

"Please," Darci said loudly. "Don't take me to Colonel Zheng!"

In her periphery, the other two hesitated.

"Please," she said in a begging tone. "Jianyu will kill me." Okay, there was too much truth to that for her to fake. They saw it, too.

With one last glance to Alice and the little one, Darci surrendered to her fate. The major towering over her leered, then raised the butt of his weapon and slammed it into her temple.

Nineteen

FOB Murphy, Afghanistan

Stretched out on his back, Heath stared at the slats of the bunk above where Jibril slept, a snore filtering the awkward quiet. *Scritch. Scritch. Scritch-scritch.* Heath lolled his head to the side where Trinity lay pressed against him, her legs racing to an unseen dream destination. Maybe she was making the same route he was—straight to Jia.

Three feet away, Timbrel lay on her side curled into the fetal position. Vulnerability cloaked her in a somber embrace. But he knew better than to think that girl was vulnerable. Then again. . .maybe she was. That tough-mama persona, the GI Jane attitude, probably concealed wounds beneath that stone mask. He'd never tried to find out.

Good thing he hadn't made it into the chaplaincy program—he hadn't been able to look past big attitudes and loud mouths to see a person's wounds.

Because, in truth, explosive anger and powerful defensive mechanisms served one purpose: to conceal and protect what lay beneath the surface of that superficial display of strength.

So, what's eating at you, Hogan?

A swish of material drew his attention to the top bunk where Aspen dropped back against the gray mattress. She stared up. Her chest rose and fell unevenly. She lifted a hand to her face. Wiped something. . .

Concern pulled Heath up, his elbow under him for support.

Aspen glanced over—then jerked her gaze away.

In that split second, her watery eyes cried out to him. No way he could let that go. God had put him here. Didn't Hogan say something to that effect—that he had a purpose for being here? Heath climbed off the mattress. As he slipped over to the bunk, he heard Trinity sit up and start panting. He touched Aspen's arm.

A tear rolled down her face, and as she brought her gaze to his, the tear splatted on the mattress.

Soundless, he mouthed, "C'mon." Heath lifted Trinity's lead from the table and motioned for the door. Behind him came the sounds of Trinity's nails clicking on the cement and the gentle groan from Aspen's body scooting across the mattress. Then the soft thump of her landing on the floor coupled with a sniffle.

"Hey," said a drowsy Hogan. "Where you. . .going?"

"Nowhere. Rest," Aspen whispered as she eased out and pulled the door closed.

Sunlight streamed into the building through a narrow slice between the door and the foundation. Strange to think it was midday since they'd put a blackout blanket over the window so they could sleep.

Heath walked to a bin with water bottles and withdrew two. He handed one to Aspen. "Drink it slow."

Red rimmed her eyes, but they weren't puffy and swollen. Either she hadn't cried long, or it wasn't a hard cry. "Thanks." Blond curls akimbo, she brushed them back and took a mouthful, swished it, then swallowed. "I need to let off some frustration. I need a speed bag."

Arching a brow, Heath considered her. "Speed bag?"

Amused blue eyes sparkled in the sunlight. "I did ten months in Iraq when I was enlisted, but I got stuck in a building doing paperwork all the time." A breeze swept along the alley formed by the buildings and tousled her hair. "Drove. Me. Nuts." She flashed him a smile, and it was a good thing he didn't feel attracted to her because her beauty had killer written all over it. "Austin taught me to box to work off the mind-numbing boredom, but he also wanted me to be able to defend myself against predators."

"And Austin is. . ."

"My brother." She looked down the road, but he guessed what she saw wasn't down that empty road to the mountains but the road to the past.

Heath started walking, Trinity trotting ahead a half-dozen feet, nose to the ground, tail wagging. "He the one you're crying over?"

"Yeah." She took a sip of the water. "He vanished on a mission."

Heath was tracking. "Talon's handler, right?"

Another nod. "He and his team were ambushed. They didn't tell me much, only that in an explosion, Talon was thrown away from Austin and found twenty feet away. Broken leg, but that was it as far as visible wounds."

As they rounded a corner, an armored personnel carrier rumbled out the gates and into the open terrain. Boots crunched. Trinity zigzagged the way she was trained.

"Yeah, it's those *invisible* wounds that get tricky." Heath considered Trinity, who sauntered through combat like a walk through the hills of A Breed Apart. "So that's why he has doggie PTSD."

Aspen sniffed a laugh but nodded. "Yeah, and that's the only reason they let me have him. He had too much baggage for them." She shifted toward him, thoughtful.

"What?"

"Ever heard of someone declared MIA, presumed dead, that came home?"

This was delicate ground. "No, but since we're taught to never leave a man behind. . ." He tread carefully. "You think he's still alive?"

Shoulders drawn up, she stuffed a hand into her jacket pocket. "Don't know." She shoved her fingers into her ringlets, holding them from her face. "Look." She pivoted toward him. "I appreciate what you're doing here, getting me to talk things out." Aspen wrinkled her nose and shook her head. "But I'm not interested in dialogue."

"Only a speed bag." Bottle in hand, he motioned to a tented area. "Will that work?"

Relief swelled, pulling her straight, then it whooshed out. "Perfect." Aspen smiled. "Thanks for understanding."

"No worries." He backed up and waved. "Trinity and I are going to take the grand tour."

"Okay, catch you later."

Jogging wouldn't alleviate his headache but he'd feel better. Heath whistled to Trinity nosing through a couple of crates outside a building. She loped into a run and caught up with him. This team thing with the people of A Breed Apart might just work after all. And to think he'd joined to find purpose again, to feel useful. To get back out here, in the action. Okay, so he never expected to actually fulfill that dream, but it'd happened.

Heath slowed, hands on his sides as he walked the fence to snuff out the burn in his chest and muscles. He'd gotten his dreams back—well, somewhat. But if he could book some more gigs through ABA, then who knew what opportunities would arise.

A niggling wormed into his thick, pounding skull.

Hand a few inches from the fence, Heath hesitated, listened for the familiar hum of electricity. Convinced it wasn't hot, he gripped it and arched his back, stretching muscles wound tighter than a primed trigger.

He dropped back against the links and held his knees. What was bothering him? Why couldn't he ferret out the truth the way he'd ferreted out terrorists in the desert?

Heath mentally reached for the tenuous threads of that niggling. What was it? What was hanging there like a phantom? Present but intangible. He felt it—not with his hands. It was stronger than that. Bigger.

God, I'm missing something here. That probably wasn't anything new to Him. *Just. . .help a guy out, okay?* God had shut down his career. Removed the chaplaincy option. Now. . .what? What was he doing here, in a place where it couldn't be clearer that he didn't belong anymore?

What do You want with me?

Trinity lunged, rattling the chain links as she pounced against the fence. She barked.

Heath flattened himself against the ground and rolled, expecting to see someone there with a weapon. Wouldn't be the first time. But only as his gaze streaked the horizon did it register.

Her bark. Not aggressive. It was. . .

Trinity whimpered, stalked back and forth. Attacked the chain link. Pawed at it. Another whimper.

Heath pulled himself off the ground, squinting as he searched the road and field of brown, tan, and pocks of green. Heat plumes wavered—

Wait. It wasn't hot enough for heat plumes.

That was someone. . .coming, wavering, staggering like a drunk.

Or one seriously dehydrated. Or wounded.

Heath spun around and sprinted to the tower guard. "Nocs, where are your binoculars?"

Wide-eyed, weapon resting against his chest, the specialist handed him a pair. "What's wrong, man? D'you see something?"

"Get your boss out here. Now!" Heath darted back in the direction he'd come, vaulted up on an MRAP to see better.

"Hey!" someone below objected.

Trinity raced around the vehicle, then sprinted back to the fence, barking.

"Good, girl." Heath knelt awkwardly on the steel trap and aimed the binoculars toward the figure.

Commotion ensued around him. Several asking what was up, others jogging to the fence to figure out what he saw.

Seconds after a door banged against a wall came Candyman's shout, "Whaddya got, Ghost?" His voice and pounding boots drew closer.

"A woman—she's. . ." He strained to focus the lenses. "American!"

Curses and orders flew through the cool wind. A vehicle revved to life.

Heath craned his neck, as if the few inches would make that much difference. Whatever she held in her arms made her steps uneven. Clumsy. Something near her shoulder moved. His heart catapulted over what tunneled through the lenses to his brain.

"She's got a kid with her." Just as the words left his lips, the woman collapsed.

"Move, move, move!"

Camp Eggers, Kabul, Afghanistan

"I don't like it."

The words grated on Lance's conscience, and he glared at Zeferelli. "That's a lame line from a bad book."

"Yeah, but he's right," Early grumbled.

"I don't care if he's right." Lance pushed to his feet and paced in front of the one-way glass. "Nobody likes this. Besides, every time someone says that, something bad happens. And I don't know about you, but I think we've got enough bad without adding to it."

Zeferelli and Early exchanged a look.

Fingers pressed to the cold table, Lance leaned over the surface. "What?" The growl in his voice seemed to prowl the walls.

Zeferelli touched his nose, then spoke. "There's a blizzard whipping up, pretty mean, over the Kush. It'll hit here in a day, two at most."

He needed an exorcist to get rid of those demons. What else could go wrong? Head tilted back, Lance held then let out a long breath. They didn't know about Darci, so he needed to tread the fine line. They also didn't know about her mission because of its extreme sensitivity. And if Early figured out Lance had placed an operative in his territory, he'd go off like a scud.

He traversed a very slippery rope. With Darci out there, Wu Jianyu skulking through the country, and Zheng in here. . .

Maybe two exorcists. "How bad's the storm?"

"Bad. We're prepping supplies for the troops and SOCOM guys in remote locations. Command suggested pulling our guys back from FOBs till this blows over."

"Oh, and Burnett," Early said. "I think you best haul those geology freaks back before that storm hits. Lord knows I don't want the deaths of civilians on my head, too. The media would scream holy terror." Early leaned back in his chair, stretching.

Lance couldn't yank Darci now. She'd been convinced something was there. He'd seen the light in her eyes, and before they had another string of attacks against the men, they needed to know what sort of numbers they were dealing with.

He wanted to curse. "You know what kind of money we put into that team? If we don't let them get this done, that grant money is down the tubes. That's going to look real bad when I go up against the Hill trying to justify our funding and programs."

"Imagine how bad it'd be trying to justify leaving them there and dragging home frozen corpses."

"It just can't get any worse."

"Unless someone comes through that door with bad news." Early chuckled.

Lance glared at Early. Yet at the same time, a squall of warmth washed down his spine and pushed him into a chair. "If someone does come through that door, I'm pinning it on your head, Early."

Laughing, Early and Zeferelli shot nervous looks to the steel barrier that kept them safe from the surrounding chaos.

Mischief-laden eyes locked on Lance as the general thumbed toward the door. "Frank, take a load off the general's mind, please, and lock that."

With a rumble of laughter, Frank came out of his chair. "Yes, sir."

Lance again shot another glare at Early for taunting him. "Sit down, Lieu—"

Bang! The distant, hollow thud of a door hitting a wall reverberated through the building. Shouts climbed the cement hull and snaked along the floors, stretching closer. . .closer. "General. General!"

The weight of the next few seconds anchoring him to the chair, Lance cursed. God forgive him, he didn't mean to, but he did. He waited with the foreboding that had been inescapable since he rolled out of the rack this morning.

"Where's General Burnett?"

At the sound of Major Otte's shout, Lance shoved to his feet. He pivoted and strode for the very door they'd almost locked. He yanked it open and stepped into the coffin of a hall. "Otte."

The lanky officer turned, eyes bulging. "General." The rush of relief flooded his words. He pulled himself back in line. "Sir." He saluted. "Sir, I have news." His gaze drifted over Lance's shoulder to where he could sense Zeferelli and Early hovering.

Another flurry of noise filled the narrow space behind, and Lance knew the void where the ominous news lingered would soon be filled with anger, revelation, missions. . . "If you'll excuse us, gentlemen." He took his aide by the shoulder and guided him into the room. As he closed the door, he essentially closed out the other two.

He flipped the lock. Sucked from the dregs of his courage and faced the man.

"Sir. We've lost communication with the geology team."

Lance felt prepared for just about anything at this point. "Sat imaging?"

A nod. A breath. "Not good, sir." Panting. "It's a mess. From what we can tell, they were attacked. Fire. Everything's destroyed."

"Who's responsible?"

"Uncertain, sir. Nobody's claiming it yet. And if SOCOM hadn't gotten a call this morning from Dr. Colsen, we probably wouldn't know about any of this."

"The professor?" A scowl crowded Lance's face. "Was he calling to report the attack?"

Sweat slicked the tips of Otte's dark hair as he shook his head. "I don't believe so, sir. He told Command they had to get out of there, that Jia awakened the camp, saying someone was coming after them."

His pulse stumbled at the mention of Darci's alias. "What time did his call come?"

"Zero three hundred, sir."

"That's almost five hours ago."

"Yes, sir, it's taken me that long to authenticate the reports."

The words faded as one name grew loud in Lance's mind: Jianyu.

". . .explosion. It's all we know, sir."

"Explosion?"

Otte nodded.

"From what?"

"The Black Hawk, sir. SOCOM went to rescue the team." Otte said it as if he'd already mentioned it. Maybe he had.

But Lance's mind couldn't surrender the thought of Darci up there in the middle of an attack. What was the probability that Jianyu had found her? "What happened?"

"They were shot down."

He'd need to get an assessment team up there to find out who. . . "The geology team." He looked at Otte. "Are they alive?"

"Unknown." His aide paled.

Lance knew what was on the line, *who* was on the line with that team. His heart tangled over the news and twisted into a hard knot. Otte wouldn't be here as if he'd lost his first pet if the team was alive and in communication with the base.

Otte continued. "At this time, we are officially listing them as MIA."

In other words, presumed dead.

Parwan Province, Afghanistan

Free-falling snapped Darci awake. Her arms shot out and she yelped. Rocks scored her palms as she slid along the ledge. Her face smeared the ground. Head spinning, wet, warm stickiness sliding down her neck and chest, she groped for her bearings. Something fluttered down around her. White. . .light. . . Snow?

"She came at us from out of a tunnel like the snake that she is."

Inwardly, Darci cringed. She knew that voice. Knew that meant she was in a very bad position.

"Did you think you could escape with our secrets and not face the consequences?"

"Jia," a hushed whisper sailed amid the Chinese flowing like the fat white flakes around them. Cold bit into her fingers still planted on the ground, thanks to the boot pressing against her back. She blinked and rolled her gaze around, trying to find the source of English.

She spotted Toque, pinned between two guards.

"Get her up."

The world swirled in a mural of white and olive green as the uniform gave way to the hauntingly familiar face of Wu Jianyu. Hair grown out and pulled into a ponytail, he leered at her. "Why are you in these mountains?"

"Enjoying the view," she spit out in Mandarin.

His jaw muscle popped as he walked to the side, pulling her gaze with him. He stood next to Toque. Walked behind him.

No. No, don't do it.

He was testing her reaction. If she showed one, he'd kill Toque. But she would not give him one. Instead, Darci locked her attention on him as he paced behind the survey team. The professor and Toque had been roughed up a bit, scratches clawed into their lips and cheeks. No doubt they'd provided a little resistance.

In Chinese, he said, "You cost me everything."

"The only thing I cost you," she replied back in Mandarin, "was pride. Everything else was your own doing, Jianyu."

Fury exploded through his expression. He shoved between Jaekus and the professor. "No! *You!* You cost me everything."

"If you had been half the soldier you claimed to be, I never would have gotten as far as I did." The words were cruel, and she should've reined them in.

As if a stone mask slid over his face, the anger fell away. "Let me show you the cost of your actions."

He turned, exposing his firearm. Jianyu raised it and aimed at the professor.

"No!" Darci lunged, but two of his elite Yanjingshe fighters secured her, yanking her backward—hard.

The report of the weapon ricocheted through the canyon and through her heart as Professor Colsen slumped to his knees, shock frozen on his face.

With a kick, Jianyu shoved him over the cliff.

Twenty

FOB Murphy, Afghanistan

Trinity at his side, Heath waited with a medic as the retrieval team barreled through the secured gate. Amid a plume of dust, the MRAP skidded to a stop, spitting dirt and rocks at Heath. He didn't care. The woman—he was sure he'd seen her with the geology team.

The back door flew open, and Watterboy stepped out with a girl in his arms. Their gazes collided for a second. "Dehydrated and scared out of her little mind. Get us a stretcher."

The medic took the child and vanished into a building

"What about the woman? What's wrong with her? Why does she need a stretcher?"

"Ankle's messed up pretty bad, but no other visible injuries. And she keeps asking for Burnett."

Heath peered into the vehicle where Candyman crouched next to a woman. An IV snaked into her arm and disappeared beneath her skin. "Who's Burnett?"

"The boss's boss."

As Candyman stretched to the side to adjust her fluid bag, Heath saw the young woman's face up close. "She was with the geology team."

Watters glanced at Heath with an undecipherable expression.

"Did she say anything about"—Heath swallowed the words that would've exposed his true interest—"the others? Why is she wandering around the desert? Why isn't she with her team?"

"If she'd talk, I imagine she might answer them. Said she'd only talk to Burnett."

Two more medics emerged with a stretcher. "Coming through."

Heath and Watters shifted aside, but no way would Heath let that woman out of his sight. She knew about Jia. Knew what happened to the team. Knew if that explosion they'd seen was connected to the geology team.

Mind buzzing, Heath ignored the hammering against his temples. He grabbed the bite straw of his CamelBak and squirted some water into his mouth along with three ibuprofen. As the medics disappeared with the woman, it took everything in Heath not to follow. Instead, he locked his gaze on the mountains. On the spot where he'd seen the smoke billowing hours earlier.

There was one reason that young woman would be wandering the desert just before a storm, alone, and with an Afghan girl. Something had gone wrong. Terribly wrong.

"Should get a team up there."

Watters clapped him on the shoulder. "You can take the soldier out of the war, but never the war out of the soldier."

Heat infused Heath's face. He lowered his head. "Sorry."

"No way, man. You know the drill, you know what needs to be done." But that expression flickered through Watters's face again.

"What is that?"

His friend shifted. "What's what?"

"That look on your face." Ibuprofen hadn't kicked in yet. And the telltale pressure in his chest told him the anger rising through him wouldn't help. Besides, why was he letting things get to him?

Because he was assuming the worst, that Watters didn't think he should be here. That he didn't have a right to be here.

But Watters had never been anything but supportive and encouraging.

In Heath's periphery, a shape slid into view. Timbrel. Then a cold, wet nose nudged his hand. All signs and warnings that said, *Get a grip, man.*

Mentally, Heath took a step back. He wouldn't face off with one of his only allies here. "Forget it."

"Ghost. . ."

He didn't need to be placated by a warrior brother. "I get it, man." It was a bitter pill to swallow, like pieces of charcoal going down. "Just. . .keep me posted about the geology team. 'Kay?"

Watters looked down, then nodded. "Sure." He spun and entered the building where they'd taken the woman.

Heath pivoted on his heel, and the world spun. He stiffened and waited for the feeling to pass. As his vision and focus realigned, he found the team staring at him.

Aspen stepped forward, chin and shoulders up. "I'm sure she's fine, Heath."

"No." He didn't want to live on false hopes. "Nobody knows that." Curse himself! He'd just indicated his interest in Jia with his roiling emotions. "It doesn't make sense that she'd be out there, wandering the desert alone with that little girl. Something happened."

"Do you think they're still alive?" Leave it to Hogan to be straightforward.

Like a bad action movie, the explosion played over and over in his mind. What he couldn't get around was that it'd take something large and mechanical to create an explosion like that. A chopper. And if she'd been on that chopper, she wouldn't have a prayer.

"Hey." The quiet, firm voice of Hogan snapped—once again—through the self-beatings of his attitude. "Got a sec?"

"No." Heath extracted himself from the familiar and took a jog with Trinity. Alone with the one girl who'd never expected anything from him, except to be there. The only thing God asked of Heath was obedience.

And what had he thrown back at Him? Rebellion in the form of control and anger, borne out of hurt and/or fear. Why had God allowed him to get so messed up? Why had God stolen his career from his fingers?

He wasn't angry, but it rankled.

Well, maybe that wasn't the complete truth. Because if he wasn't angry, things like this wouldn't bug him. He'd deal with them, release them to God's all-powerful hands, and take the next leap of faith.

The thought of something happening that would require him to leap with faith. . .

God. . .please. . .don't. Give a guy a break, okay?

Heath groaned. Already, he could feel it coming. It would hit him head-on. And he'd crumble because he no longer had faith or strength. He'd come out here, insisting this was what he wanted, to be back in the action. He'd never been more wrong in his life.

Camp Eggers, Kabul, Afghanistan

"Think this is connected to the Chinese?"

"Think? Yes." Lance paced the small room, itching for an IV line to a Dr Pepper keg. "Prove? Not at all."

"You going to make Colonel Zheng talk?" Otte asked.

"How? Beat it out of him? And what does that do but tip our hand?" They were trapped right now. Just enough poison to smell and know someone would die. Not enough to know who was contaminated and would fall victim. Besides, Lance would be hanged if he'd let that man out of his sight without figuring out what he knew.

He gulped the last of the syrupy sweetness and tossed the can in the trash. "Get a chopper lined up to take us back to CJSOTF-A. And find out what teams are there."

"Sir." Otte left the room.

Slumped in a chair, Lance steepled his fingers. What Zheng told them and what Zheng knew were two very different things. Lance could feel it. In the deep marrow of his bones. But if he pushed, Zheng would know something had happened. Would know that there was a high probability that Jianyu had struck.

If it was Wu Jianyu who hit the survey team, how in the name of all that was holy did he know Darci—or Meixiang as Jianyu knew her—was here? Her insertion into that team was a veritable locked vault. He could count on one hand the number of people who knew she was DIA.

Coincidence?

That'd be a mighty amazing coincidence.

But stranger things had happened. Like the young colonel sitting in this compound with him.

Lance had to play it slow and careful. But if things were going as expected, he also didn't have time to lose. If Jianyu had Darci—Lance would have to send all the dogs of war after him.

Dogs. . .

That punk former Green Beret who'd been smitten with Darci. . .an MWD handler. . . An idea slowly coalesced—

Boots squeaked and crunched behind him.

"Lance, ODA452 at FOB Murphy just radioed in." Early stood in the doorway. "They've picked up a little Afghan girl and a young woman."

Great. More poor citizens looking for food and shelter. With this storm, he understood the concern. At the base of the mountain, that area would get hit hard by the blizzard.

"She says she was with the geology team you set up."

Lance hesitated as he glanced at Early. "We didn't have Afghans on that team."

"No, the woman was American."

Was it too much to hope? One hundred percent of his attention landed on his old friend. "What's her name?"

"Didn't say. Won't talk to anyone but you."

Thunder rumbled through his chest. It had to be Kintz. FOB Murphy was about five klicks south of the Kush.

General Early bore a grave expression. "Want me to have them bring her in?"

"No." Considering the totality of the situation and the way it seemed to be complicating matters exponentially, this was a good time to get back to where he had more assets and control. "Send a chopper. Get them to Bagram. I want them there when I touch down."

"Anything else?"

"Yeah." He knew Early meant it sarcastically, but his mind raced. "Wasn't that dog handler speaking to the troops with that team?"

"Yes, sir," Zeferelli said from behind Early. "The team was there. Caught in a confrontation earlier. A Taliban terrorist tried to make soup out of that war dog."

He couldn't lose that dog. That dog was key. "Get everyone up there. Now." He stalked to the door. "I need that dog."

"General Burnett."

The loud, firm call of his name stopped Lance before he hit the hall.

"I've known you a long time, and we've worked a lot of years together." Shorter by a head and whiter haired, Early held fast. "Long enough for me to know something is off."

"Then you also know when not to ask."

"What am I not asking?"

"Questions." Period. Early knew better. Particularly in an unsecure

161

location like this. "As soon as I can, you'll know, but. . ."

Early waited.

"You may not like me when all is said and done."

"Who says I like you now?"

FOB Murphy, Afghanistan

Stretched out against some sandbags, Trinity curled up beside him, Heath smoothed a hand over her fur. Neither Watterboy nor Candyman had given him an update in the last eighty minutes. That meant one of two things: either they didn't have anything to update, or the update was bad news/confidential.

And because Heath Daniels no longer held rank with the military, his nose was kept out of the mess.

Except, he felt waist deep in this one.

Jia had been one of the most real people he'd met. Crazy to think that, having spent only a few hours with her. She'd been undaunted by his scars and his status as a noncom.

But she'd also been lightning fast to sever the ties.

It'd rankled him at first, but maybe that was just her way of coping. Maybe. . .

Maybe you just need to let this go.

Even if she was alive, even if the U.S. launched a mission to find her—the thought dragged his gaze to the rugged Hindu Kush with its winter storm clouds that stood over them like an angry god—Heath the noncom would be sent home. Forbidden from helping.

She was right. They'd never see each other again.

Heath sat up, nudging Trinity off his chest. She huffed her objection, then stretched, which drew out a groan. "You and me both, girl." He rubbed her ears. Why did it bother him, the thought of not seeing Jia? It wasn't like he was top candidate material for dating. Imagine passing out on a date when he got stressed over things not going right. But things had gotten significantly worse since arriving here. It was almost like he was allergic to the place.

A wet tongue slurped his face.

Instinct wrapped his arm around Trinity's broad chest, and he tightened her in his hold. "It's okay, girl."

"Ghost."

Heath shot to his feet at the sound of Watterboy's voice. "Hey." He dusted off his backside. "What's the word?"

"Oh." Watters glanced back to the doors. "Nothing. She's not talking. But we got RTB orders."

"Bagram?"

Watterboy nodded. "Grab your gear. Chopper's en route." For a moment, he stood there, as if wanting to say something.

"Everything all right?"

With a sigh, Watters waved. "Yeah. Fine. Tired, I guess." He started to cross to the bunk building, then gave another wave. "Catch you later."

"Right."

A strange ache wove into Heath's chest. He'd been good friends with that man once. They'd shared command and secrets. Laughs about newbs and girlfriends. Now the guy was stiffer than the hull of an MRAP.

"Hey, Hot Snot."

Irritation skidded into his mood as Hogan stepped out of the main building. "I don't need—"

"Ghost, chill." Her brown eyes held not condemnation or even a lecture but a twinkle of something. She bobbed her head to the side. "C'mere." She stalked away and went through a side door.

Trinity looked up at him, beautiful amber eyes sparkling with a "why not" expression. He sighed. "All right. But if this goes bad, I'm blaming you."

Trinity barked, then trotted after Hogan.

Inside, Heath paused to gain his bearings. This looked like—

"Hey." She leaned backward, her torso peeking out from a door to his right.

Heath entered the room. An examination table hogged the room. "What's this about?"

A man moved in the corner. Dark eyes. Dark skin.

Timbrel bounced over to the guy in an Afghan national uniform. The insignia on his chest identified him as an officer. "This is Mahmoud. He's a doctor." Whoa, the smile she shot that guy could blind the unsuspecting.

Ah. He knew what was happening here. Heath held up a hand.

"Look, I've got an arsenal of docs back at BAMC—"

Hogan laughed. "He's a chiropractor." She patted the table. "Face down."

"That's handy"—how many chiropractors were there in this area?—"but no way."

Steel slammed into her expression. She stalked around him, around Trinity, and closed the door. "Listen, you do this or I'm going to Jibril."

"Nothing like taking hostages."

She sidled up next to him, her gaze imploring. "Heath, I talked to Mahmoud here, and we both think that maybe. . .just maybe. . . something might be out of line."

"Yeah." He huffed. "You."

Hogan rolled her eyes. "Just. . .give it a try, will you?"

Heath sized up Mahmoud. The Afghan pumped antibacterial cleanser into his palms, then rubbed them and the tops of his hands with enough friction to create a fire. "You have headache now?"

Heath gave a curt nod.

"Please. Remove your shirt."

"Look, I appreciate—"

"What can hurt?"

Heath sighed. Unbuttoned his shirt. Glared at her. "If this doesn't work. . ."

"Then I still win. You'll have headaches, and I can report you to Jibril."

Somehow in that expression he saw a stunning truth. Hogan had his back. Despite her threats, she was looking out for him.

After a brief exam with Mahmoud tracing his spine, kneading his shoulders—which about made a grown man cry—Heath face-planted himself on the table.

Cold hands, a cold table, a cold chill in the marrow of his bones made for a chilling experience. After Mahmoud had him roll onto his back, he took Heath's hands and held them perpendicular to his body, straight up.

"See? Your fingers not even."

Heath did see—that his right hand rested about a half-inch shorter.

He guided Heath's left arm down and placed it along the side of the table, then took his right, lifted it straight up, then braced the shoulder

164

and rotated the arm across Heath's chest and—

Pop!

Pain shot through his back. And with it an immediate... What was it? He couldn't quite discern. And while he was thinking, the doctor held his neck with both hands.

Okay, not liking this.

Holding a man's neck like this... *So easy to snap my neck. Kill me. He's Afghan. But what reason would he have to kill me?*

I'm a dog handler.

Heath tensed.

The man applied pressure to the lower portion of his neck where it curved, then whipped Heath's head to the left.

Crack! Pop! Snap!

White-hot fire speared Heath.

"Augh!" His arms came up, defensive and ready to fight.

Trinity snarled and lunged.

In the split second that he realized Trinity was defending him, Heath also realized that a cool wash of freedom swam through his neck and shoulders. His heart rapid-fired, thinking of Trinity, his ever-faithful girl, attacking this doctor.

"Trinity, out." Heath swung around to find Hogan held the lead, restraining his seventy-pound dog. Trinity whimpered as her gaze hit his, then she wagged her tail.

"You okay?" Hogan's question held both expectation and concern.

"I sounded like a cereal commercial." He rubbed the back of his neck, amazed. And searching for the pain that had hounded him over the last week.

"How's your headache?"

He rolled his shoulder. "Gone." Wait. That couldn't be right.

Hogan propped her hip against the table grinning like a petulant brat sister. "It was my theory that when you took that hard hit in training, it might have knocked some things out of whack, besides your good sense."

Ya know, for a kid-sister-type, she wasn't bad. "That was some theory."

"But you feel better, right?"

"If you discount the second where I felt like someone drove metal through my skull again..."

"You feel. Better. Right?"

Heath grinned at her terse words. It was so easy to annoy her. "Yeah."

5 Miles from Geology Camp,
Parwan Province, Afghanistan

His body fell from the ledge.

Inside Darci lay a box. One in which she kept all her precious thoughts and feelings. One where she hid what could be used against her by someone like Jianyu. It was there she tucked away the brutal reality that she had caused the death of yet another friend. Jaekus. The poor, gentle soul. A kind and generous person.

Hands cuffed behind her, she stood a few feet from where he had fallen. The bitter wind whipped and tore at her thin jacket and pants, biting into her—but it was nothing compared to the immense sense of failure that chomped into her heart at not protecting an innocent. Would God hold her accountable for that? She certainly did.

Her hair, once wet with snow, now hung stiffly and needled her face.

"See, Meixiang, what you cost those around you?"

Wooden and cold-chapped, her legs at least held her upright. Jianyu had pushed them up the pass and higher into the mountain, higher into the gaping maw of a pending blizzard. "Your idiocy is again showing," she said in Mandarin. "Taking us into the blizzard—we should be moving away. Nobody is dressed for this, not you, not your men. You're a fool!"

"Jia," Toque hissed from the side.

Jianyu's gaze flicked to the last remaining member of her team.

One pawn left.

And if he didn't shut up. . .

Darci whirled and shoved her booted heel into Toque's face. The impact sent him flying backward. The momentum tilted her world. Her legs tangled over each other. She stumbled. Landed on her knees. To the side though, she saw Toque. He'd landed strangely quiet in a bed of freshly fallen snow with a soft thump. Unconscious.

Maybe they'd leave him there. Then Toque would rouse—hopefully before his body had frozen through—and get to safety.

Two Yanjingshe fighters hauled her upright. She shuffled to a stable footing.

"Pick him up." Jianyu stalked to her. His eyes, which she once thought held power and beauty, darted over her face.

She had never feared him. Not for her own safety. But today. . .

He shoved a hand forward—right into her side.

"Augh!" Darci swooned and flopped into the elite guard. Tears squeezed past the agony and escaped her resolution not to be weak. Head hanging, cold, wet hair in her face, she gathered the shattered pieces of her courage. He'd always taken pride in his skills as a fighter. He'd never used them on her though. Times had changed.

"Shoot him."

She jerked her head up before she realized the mistake.

"Wait."

Darci closed her eyes.

"He means something to her. Bring him. He may be useful."

She snorted. "The only thing he's useful for is annoying me."

Jianyu's breath plumed in her face. "Then it appears we have something in common." He inched forward, then grabbed the back of her neck and jerked her closer. "But I told you once I do not share what is mine."

★ ★ Twenty-One ★ ★

Sir, she is injured and slowing us down. We should leave her."

Jianyu turned and raised his weapon, aiming at Lieutenant Colonel Tao. "You would question my authority?"

The man's chin drew up as he swallowed his objections. "Of course not, Colonel."

Lowering the weapon, Jianyu looked at Meixiang. So beautiful. Her skin like the pale blossom of a lotus flower. Her lips not the rouge color he'd tasted more than once, but blue. And trembling. She would die unless they could find shelter.

She had destroyed his plans by showing up.

Yet created the perfect storm by showing up. He'd need to make a marginal change to his plans, but through her, he could show his father what true power looked like. Not just to his father, but many more. Thousands. Hundreds of thousands. Millions.

"She will die, Colonel. It's hypothermia."

Jianyu jerked to the side. "Huang."

The captain snapped to the front and stood stiff as a reed with a salute. "We need shelter. And a doctor."

After a curt bow, the man trotted down the path that wound up the mountain.

"We cannot go farther up. The meeting—"

"Will wait."

The lieutenant colonel's disapproval shone through. If he could not master his feelings, Tao would prove not to be as useful as Jianyu hoped.

"The storm is our delay," Jianyu muttered, so his men would cease their grumblings and accusations, the very ones they thought he could not hear, the ones they whispered when they thought the wind would swallow them.

But they would see. . .they would all see soon enough.

Bagram AFB, Afghanistan

"We leave first thing in the morning."

Heath rose from the chair. "What—how?" Did Jibril really expect him to leave at a time like this? When Jia was out there, maybe bleeding out, dying?

Calm and confident, Jibril lifted a shoulder. "It is time."

"We had one more week here."

"And now we do not. With the storm and the conditions here," Jibril said as if talking about cookies someone had eaten. "Ghost, it is time for us to go home."

"No!" Everything in Heath writhed. Coiled. Poised, ready to strike. He turned a circle, looking. . .for what, he didn't know. Something to hit? Someone to yell at? Something to change this outcome!

When he looked up, Jibril had closed the distance. "There is a great torment in you, my friend." Somber green eyes held his. "I am concerned."

Heath swallowed. "I know." Shook his head and rolled his eyes. "I know. Since I came back here, I've been. . .rigged." Ready to blow. He dropped into the chair hard. "I was so sure that coming back would solve everything. I mean, I was scared, sure, but a part of me was convinced I'd find what I'd lost here, or that they'd somehow realize how wrong they were in putting me out."

Jibril eased into the seat beside him. "And now?"

Heath straightened, elbows on the arms of the chair as he stared at his feet, at Trinity's snout that stretched over his boot. "Just more questions. More confusion. More doubt. More—" He bit off the word, but it hovered and careened against his yearning for wholeness: failure.

"So, you would say that this trip has been a waste, a failure?"

"No." *I'm the failure.* "I've enjoyed this, enjoyed the times I got to share my story, encourage those who are still here fighting, feeling forgotten, alone." Heath shoved a hand through his hair as the extra time spent with Jia sped through his mind like a F-16. "I've met some great people."

"The girl. . ."

Heath looked into a knowing gaze. He smirked, never able to keep a secret from him. "Jia."

Jibril nodded, his longer-than-normal hair dipping into his eyes. "Chinese."

"Yeah." He reclined and stretched out a leg. "But. . ."

"But?"

With a shrug, Heath sighed. "She was into me, I could tell, but she wasn't willing to go the mile." He sat up. "We had lunch, hung out, but there was still a huge emotional mile stretching between us. And now she's up there in the moun. . .tains." Was she even alive?

She needs me.

Which was the stupidest thought he'd ever had, because he couldn't even hold it together during one intense situation. "I guess. . .I just need to know she's okay." He stood and paced to the other wall five feet away. They'd been detained per orders of the base commander as soon as they'd stepped onto the base. "It's stupid."

Jibril smirked. "Why?"

Heath shoved his hands in his pockets and shrugged. "I don't even know her." Scratching the scar on the back of his head, he tried to make sense of it. "I mean, we spent like two days together. That's it." He grunted and returned to his seat. He probably looked like a loon, pacing. "Besides, she told me it wouldn't work. Gave me a fake e-mail address."

"I think," Jibril said as he folded his arms over his chest, "she did not want you pining over her when there was no realistic reason you would ever see each other again."

Heath laughed. Hard and short. "Thanks. With friends like you. . ."

"But you are a warrior, Heath."

Slouched down till his head rested against the back of the chair, he eyeballed his friend.

"You have been trained, and it has been ingrained in you to fight for what you believe is right." Jibril smiled. "Every soldier is taught to hold his ground."

What was he saying? The trap was set, Heath could feel it. And he wasn't about to step into it.

Trinity sat up and glanced at Heath, her eyebrows bobbing. As if saying, "Ask him what he means. I want to know. This sounds good."

"Traitor." Her ears were soft and soothing between his fingers. "Well, go on." He looked to Jibril. "Spit it out before you bust a gut laughing at me."

Laughter spilled through the room. "When was the last time you took interest—like this—in a woman?"

"Jibril, didn't you hear? She cut the tether."

"I think, like you, she is afraid of what could be."

Morose—no, morbid thoughts trapped Heath's mind. "We aren't even sure. . .she might be dead."

"Then why is your heart still fighting?"

A door squeaked open, and a guard thrust Hogan into the room.

"Hey!" She scowled and drew her arms back.

Trinity and Heath lunged—Heath to Hogan, to catch her before she did something stupid. And Trinity to protect him.

"Got it," Heath said to the specialist who'd manhandled her.

The guy's face flushed. "Sorry, sir. We asked her. . .she wouldn't—"

"Understood." Heath nodded. "We'll keep her safe here." When the door closed, Heath turned. "You said a bio break! What was *that* about?"

"Fact finding."

"You mean snooping."

"You spell it your way, I'll spell it my way." Unrepentant and rebellious, she sauntered to a soda machine. Kicked it. She spun toward them. "I was this"—she pinched her fingers till they were millimeters apart—"close to finding out what was going on."

All pretense of civility drained from Jibril. "Timbrel, you must stop this." He went to her. "This organization cannot gain a bad name because you won't cooperate."

She held up her hands and looked the most repentant Heath had ever seen her. "I know. I know. I'm sorry. It's just. . ." She hunched her shoulders. "Something is going on out there. There's more brass here than on the knuckles in LA—and trust me, I know. I've lived there."

Heath couldn't help but grin. "I bet Christmas presents under the tree killed you."

She blew her bangs out of her face. "Why? I already knew what they were."

Heath groaned. "You're hopeless."

"Shut up." The snarl in her words yanked the humor from the conversation.

"Never mind," Jibril said. "We want to be welcome to come back, so we must all"—he even looked at Heath—"be our best."

"Yeah, Ghost." Hogan's eyes flamed.

He'd said something that shifted their worlds. Whatever it was, he regretted it. Heath closed the instance. "Hey," he said in a low voice so the others couldn't hear. "What just happened?"

"Nothing."

He placed a light touch to her shoulder. "You put my nose to the fire earlier over my headaches. I'm putting yours to the fire now."

"Just..." Her narrowed eyes snapped to his. "Don't call me hopeless." She shrugged away and circled the room. "Where's Aspen?"

"We don't know. Two MPs came and asked her to go with them."

"This is stupid!" Hogan sat cross-legged on the floor, petting Trinity. "It's like lining up to see the principal. What'd we do?"

"Nothing, as far as we know. Unless your little bathroom diversion created trouble."

"It gave me information."

"Like what?"

"Like all the brass I saw—"

"Hey, genius. This is a military base. What'd you expect?"

"Two four-star generals, a few three-stars, and you're going to tell me that's normal at a place like this where supposedly all's well?" Her expression seethed. "Then what about the Chinese man in handcuffs, ferried into a building the brass just entered?"

"Chinese?" Heath asked.

"I overhead an MP say the Chinese guy is the personal aide to China's minister of defense."

"You've got to be kidding."

"And the little girl that the Alice chick had with her? She went into absolute hysterics when she saw the Chinese dude." Vehemence tightened her lips. "So, Hot Snot—am I useless and hopeless?"

"I didn't call you useless."

She waved and turned. "Whatever."

Along with Hogan's attitude, they had a wad of trouble on the base. Though he hadn't seen anything that set it off, Heath had sensed an electric hum in the air for a while. Something really big was about to blow wide open.

★ ★   Twenty-Two   ★ ★

Sitting in a comfortable chair with a Dr Pepper in hand, Alice Ward looked like any high school sweetheart one of the thousands of specialists at Bagram had left at home. But this girl knew something.

"Miss Ward?"

Licking her lips, she straightened. "I need to speak to General Burnett."

With a soft snort, he lowered himself to the edge of the table in front of her. He tugged on his name patch. "Right here, Miss Ward."

She deflated. "Finally." Tears welled in her eyes. "I. . ." She tucked her chin and sniffled. "I. . .was so scared. . .but she. . ." Alice shook her head. "I can't. . ."

"It's okay. Just take your time." He slurped his Dr Pepper, determined not to be undone by tears. Give him a tough nut like Darci any day of the week.

Scooting up, she seemed to draw on the last of her courage. "I don't know how she knew, but she knew. And she was so good and fast." Her eyes widened as her gaze met his. "Holy cow, that girl was so fast—like she had *skills*."

He wanted to laugh. "Who?"

"Jia. Jia Kintz." Animated, Alice related the story of Jia rushing into the camp. "She had this little girl with her, and I was stunned. We all were, in fact. Okay, maybe not the professor. He seemed annoyed, but then again, he was always annoyed. Anyway, she was bleeding—"

"Who was bleeding?"

173

"Jia. But she wouldn't slow down to let anyone look at it." Alice brushed the hair from her face. "She told us all to get packed up. She gave me the girl, and I got her cleaned up and put a warm jacket on her—that's when I saw all the blood. I realized it was from Jia, so I went to our tent—and there they were. Locked in a gun battle."

Alarms shrieked through his mind. "Who?"

"Jia and Toque. They both had guns—I have no idea where they got guns. It made no sense."

"Did he shoot her?" Lance tried to remember what the dossier said about Peter Toque, but it was like trying to find a pea in the dark.

"No. I. . .I don't think so." She covered her mouth. "Wow, I hope not. I mean, he could've, I guess. He was up with her. They'd come back to camp together."

"Where had they been?"

Alice shrugged. "Don't know. Jia was always going off on her own. She said it helped her clear her mind."

More like clear an area. She'd been working. As always.

"That's when the chopper showed up. Everything went crazy from there. Jia sprinted between two tents, and I was so scared I followed her. We went into the tunnels." She explained how they'd stayed there overnight, trekking and stopping for rests only when necessary, and how Jia had this shoulder wound. . .

"How did you escape and get down that mountain to the base?"

Once again, tears pooled in her eyes. "Jia." One loosened itself and streaked down her face. "She said she would distract them, then join us, but. . ." Hands to her face, she collapsed into tears.

Lance pushed to his feet. He didn't need the young woman to tell him what happened. Experience, integrity spoke for itself.

Darci sacrificed herself.

He almost couldn't bring himself to ask the final question. "Do you know if she was alive?"

Face still buried, she shook her head. "I don't know." She lifted her tear-streaked face. "I don't know. . . I heard shouts and gunshots and screams. . .and I ran. Ran as fast as I could with the girl." She shuddered. "I should've stayed. Should've made sure she was safe, right? I mean, what kind of person does that? Leaves another—"

Lance nodded to Otte who sat beside the woman, a hand on her twittering hands, and reassured her that she'd done the right thing. That it was a smart move.

Stepping into the hall, Lance left behind the somber, smooth voice of Otte trying to coax the woman out of her sodden grief.

One thing was clear: Jia had found something up there. And someone didn't want her to tell the tale. If she'd had time to alert the team to pack up and get to safety—wait.

The child.

Lance stalked to the preview room where he thrust into it. "Zeferelli."

The man snapped to attention and saluted.

"Where's the girl?"

"In interview room—"

"No, the little girl. The Afghan. Get her for me."

Fifteen minutes later, the lieutenant lumbered back in with the girl and an older Afghan woman. A few minutes of discussion with the older woman and child armed Lance with a nugget of gold. Together, the four of them walked down the hall, the girl clinging to Lance's hand. Reminded him of his granddaughter back home, a few years younger, and Carrie had blond hair.

They stepped into interview room six.

Badria was a half step behind him. When she swung around to the front, she saw the man hunched at the table and threw herself back. Terror's greedy claws stabbed her innocent face. She screamed.

Lance nodded to the lieutenant.

Zeferelli lifted the shrieking, crying child and carried her out of the room.

"Explain that to me." Lance sat back in a folding chair, metal digging into his back. He lifted his ankle and placed it on his knee. Casual and looking comfortable.

Colonel Zheng's face remained impassive. Implacable.

"Imagine that." Lance straightened and folded his hands on the table. "A little girl, found in an Afghan village, goes into terror fits when she sees you." He slid a piece of sugar-free gum into his mouth. "Wonder what that means."

"That she is a little girl who should not be used as a pawn in games of war."

"A pawn?" Lance pursed his lips. "I'm not the one who made her a pawn. Someone who murdered everyone in her village made her a pawn."

Quick as a bolt of lightning, an expression zapped through Haur's face.

"Now, I wonder—"

Two knocks on the metal door.

The signal. Lance went to the door and opened it.

"Sir," Otte said. "She's awake."

"Ah. Good." He looked to Zheng, hoping to make the man sweat. "I'll be right back."

Door secured, he strode down the hall.

"When you mentioned that village, Zheng's thermals went through the roof."

He didn't need thermals to tell him that story worried Zheng. They both had full knowledge that Wu Jianyu was the devil himself.

And knowing that man was in this area. . .

Knowing he had a bloodthirsty vengeance against a young woman named Meixiang. . .

Who was Darci Kintz. . .

The connections and secrets were as vast as the mountains containing the greatest drama of his life.

It was time for some cooperative effort.

On his knees, eyes closed, Haur trained his mind to quiet.

Two decades.

Thousands of compromises.

Millions of words.

Quiet.

There on the precipice before him, he sensed the winds shift. Change. The course would be altered. This journey, this determination to be relentless, would bring him something far greater than he could imagine.

Would he be free? Finally?

It was a vain and selfish hope. He chided himself for the thought. There were things far greater. . .

Palms up, on his knees, he surrendered those dreams.

"What's he doing?"

Zeferelli snorted. "Meditating."

"Well, let's wake him up." Early looked to Lance. "You ready?"

Lance nodded. Together, they entered the room, and as if he rose from the air itself, Haur sprang to his feet.

Zeferelli jumped, reaching for his weapon.

Lance chuckled. "At ease, Lieutenant." He motioned to the table. "Colonel."

With a nod, Haur placed himself in a chair. Unnerving as all get-out was the absolute calm on the man's face.

Ironically, Early's storm overshadowed what was right in front of him. "You've played your cards," Early said, hands folded on the table. "Now I'll play mine."

Eyebrows pinched, Haur leaned in as if confused. "Do you not understand—?"

"No." Early's commanding tone severed the Asian's argument.

"We do not have time—"

"Then shut it and listen." Early had a mean streak the size of the Mississippi, but it only came out when necessary. Absolutely necessary. "This is my base—American base. You don't come in here giving orders."

Plowing his hands through his short dark hair, chains dangling, Zheng pinched his lips into a tight line. He shoved back. Raised his hands in surrender. "Play your diplomatic and political games. But I will not be responsible for what happens by your waste of time."

"And what is that?"

"The general's son," Haur said, his breathing haggard, bloated with frustration. "Wu Jianyu is loose in this country. He is without the approval of our government. There is no telling what he will do."

Lance wasn't flustered. "You have an idea of what that is though, don't you?"

Tension bled through the Asian's body. "Revenge."

Early laughed and slapped the table. "Chinese getting revenge on Americans. Ya'd think he'd be more original."

"Revenge against his father." Haur craned his neck toward Early. "He will do whatever it takes to make General Zheng bleed humiliation for the entire world to see."

"Now why would he do that?" Lance asked but he already knew the story. Too well.

"Jianyu dishonored his father's name, so General Zheng disowned him. It is why Jianyu took a new surname, his mother's. He feels the punishment is not his to bear, that he was betrayed by his own people, so he wants to make his father bleed publicly, just as his father made him." Haur cocked his head to Lance. "He will kill till the blood awakens the sleeping giant. By the thousands, if he is allowed to move unchecked for much longer. He would like nothing more than to pit the Chinese against the Americans."

"That's a tall order for one Chinese soldier."

"Tell me," Haur asked. "What would your government do if they learned the son of the minister of defense antagonized and was personally responsible for the death of thousands of American soldiers?"

Foreboding truth hung like a noose in the room. "They'd dismantle that ministry brick by brick."

"Yes." Haur heaved a breath. "Do you not see? The one man in China who most wants to keep peace is the very man being set up."

"By that you mean, General Zheng."

Haur gave a slow nod.

"Easy words coming from the adopted son of said man."

"The adoption was never formalized. It is—"

"A matter of honor."

Haur inclined his head. "The very honor Jianyu seeks to destroy."

"Says you," Early said with a growl. "See, here's what I'm not understanding, Colonel. If this minister of defense is so committed to seeing this through, why doesn't he stop his own son? Why doesn't he come here himself?"

"To be here would jeopardize a great many things. And—"

Time to throw a pound of steak to the lion. Lance eased forward. "We have located your brother."

The man went stone still.

"Team of civilian geologists up in the mountains were attacked, some taken hostage—"

"Civilians?" Confusion smeared over the Asian's face. "That makes no sense. Jianyu would not do such a thing unless there was great gain."

He was beginning to know these demons by name.

Lance was on his feet. "If you gentlemen will excuse me." He'd seen enough. Had enough.

Haur shot up. "General Burnett, it was you General Zheng told me to seek out. He said you would understand. . ."

The words trailed Lance down the hall. Into the icy night. He stopped under a streetlight and drew in a hard breath. All the forces of darkness, all of his sins, were coming to bear. Oh, he understood all right. Twenty years ago, he should've gone back. Tied up some loose ends. Paid better attention and not allowed Li's wife to be snatched—though even he had to admit the Chinese went to great lengths to stage that event, taking her while Li was out of the country, the kids at school.

And now. . .Wu Jianyu, to restore his honor, may have extracted a blood price from one of the best operatives the U.S. had ever trained.

He had no more time to waste. He wouldn't wait this time. He'd waited, yielded his doubt to the benefit. . .

But now, the answers had come. The brutal, scalding truth that Jianyu knew *who* was up in those mountains, knew who he'd captured.

Lance prayed for the great blessing of being able to kill the man responsible for all this. At the very least, make him pay in a very painful, excruciating way. Snuff out some of these demons. It wasn't a Christian thought. But that's why they say, war is hell.

Twenty-Three

Camp Loren, CJSOTF-A, Sub-Base
Bagram AFB, Afghanistan

Here, have a seat."

Heath lowered himself to the floor, where he stretched out, crossed his legs, and tucked an arm behind his head for a pillow. Since they wouldn't allow the team to leave the room—Hogan had to be right, something was going on—he'd make the most of it and grab a few z's. Eyes closed, he tried to settle his mind, bar it from thinking of a pretty Asian.

The soft click of nails on the floor made him smile. Soon, a soft, furry body pressed against his. With an exaggerated sigh, Trinity slumped onto his chest. Had she sensed his distraction over Jia and gotten jealous?

A cold, wet nose nudged his chin.

I'll take that as a yes. He roughed her fur, then settled into a smooth stroke along her ribs.

As he lay with his girl in his arms, Heath focused on his slowing heart rate. It amazed him that after all these years, Trin still had the ability to bring him to a point of near-stasis. She was more than a military war dog, more than the dog he handled, more than his partner. There weren't many people he'd try to explain that to, because they'd get weirded out. Few understood the incredible bond.

Trinity's head snapped up.

Heath opened his eyes, hand going to the weapon he didn't have, mere seconds before the door opened.

A tall, lanky major stood in the doorway, and Heath noted the name patch: OTTE. His gaze swept the room till it landed on Heath. "Daniels, General Burnett wants you."

Heath pulled himself upright. Glanced at the others. Had he done something wrong? Maybe the whole stint with the villager taking a bead on Trin. He climbed to his feet and reached for her lead.

"Just you. Not the dog."

Heath paused. "Not happening." Too many factors went into his resolve that he wouldn't be separated from her again on this trip, and right at the front of the line was the villager who'd tried to shoot her. Though he knew Hogan and Aspen were dedicated to their canines, nobody would put their rump on the line for Trinity like he would.

"We can make you—"

Heath moved a foot back and lifted his arms, ready to take him on. "Bring it."

The major grinned. "He thought you'd say that." He tossed a nod toward the door. "C'mon. Time's short."

Heath hesitated. Who thought. . . ? What. . . ? What was happening here? He coiled the lead around his hand, shot a look to the others who shrugged. Out the door, down the hall, across Route Disney, and into HQ.

Otte pointed to a chair. "Wait here." He stepped into the room—and in the brief second before the door swung shut, Heath peeked. Packed with all the brass Hogan had mentioned, a table consumed the room. Around it stood a dozen or so men—Watters and his team.

The visual connection severed with the wood barrier. Okay, that looked a heckuva lot like a mission briefing. Or had the airings of one. He wasn't included but instead dragged to the wings. Were they trying to taunt him? Point out that he wasn't good enough?

Head in his hands, Heath closed his eyes. *Lord, what's happening? I—*

"Daniels."

Heath jerked to his feet.

The major stood at the door and motioned him inside.

Sweaty and smelly, the room bore the stench of the twenty-plus bodies crowding it. And that was the word—crowd. Only three paces into the den and there was nowhere for Heath to stand, let alone sit.

"Make a hole," a deep voice boomed.

Like the Red Sea parting, bodies drifted aside, enabling him to reach the table.

General Burnett, who'd chewed Jia out that night, sat at the head to his left.

"Heath Daniels. You asked for me, sir. . .s?" He glanced around the ranks on the ACUs, and Hogan had been right. More brass—

"Daniels, you saved my life and every man on the team escorting me to Eggers." Burnett paused. "Is that right?"

"No, sir."

Burnett eyed him. "Do tell."

"I saw a hostile and engaged with my working dog, sir. If there hadn't been boots on ground, we would've been slaughtered."

Chuckling, Burnett looked around. "What'd I tell you? Team player." He rifled through some papers. "Daniels, you met a young woman while at Bagram. Made friends with her, right?"

Electricity hummed through his veins. Was this a write-up? "I met a lot of people at Bagram, sir."

Burnett leaned forward, his fingers threaded on the table. "But there was only one young woman you spent several hours with on the training field well past training hours after your speaking gig. Only one lady you had lunch with at the Thai restaurant. Is that right, son?"

Despite the heat churning through his gut and face, the snickers behind him, Heath placed his hands behind his back, at ease. "Yes, sir."

"In fact, this young woman mentioned you."

Heath's gaze betrayed him and skidded to the general, who chuckled.

"And I chewed her out, told her to get her head back in the game."

Is that what was happening that night, a chewing out? Something happened up in the mountains where she'd been. . .and he hadn't seen her since. She wasn't here. Had she died? Was Heath being blamed for Jia's death?

"With all due respect, sir," Heath said, his heart pounding, "I think you might've underestimated her. A woman who can tell a guy to take a long walk off a short pier has her head in one place—the game."

"Is that so?" Burnett sat back with a look of disgust. "Then maybe you can explain how she didn't see the attack that was coming."

"Sir, again, with all due respect, she wasn't a soldier. She couldn't have known—"

"That's where you are wrong." Burnett motioned to a man to his left.

"Daniels, have a seat." As the words left General Early's lips, a three-star rose and vacated his spot.

"This is a mission briefing with two purposes: discovery and recovery." Early slid reading glasses on the tip of his broad nose. "Daniels, you will be riding with ODA452. They're going up there to discover what happened. Who attacked, are there bodies, if so, how many. If all members of the geological survey team minus the girl who escaped are not accounted for, we need to know who's missing. If anyone is missing, the team will report back here and then launch the second phase: recovery—recover bodies, then search and locate any missing."

Standard fare. With one exception: Heath. Why was he going? The Special Forces team didn't need a broken soldier and his dog.

But the thought of helping find Jia. . .

It still didn't make sense.

Heath turned to Burnett. "Permission to speak, sir?"

"Not now, Daniels," Burnett said.

"We have sat imaging and the report of one Alice Ward, who was on scene when the attack took place." Early nodded to the lanky major who cut the lights. A projector threw images up on the wall, forcing Watters and his team to shift to view the pictures.

An aerial short of the mountain stretched over the wall. "This was taken about an hour ago. No heat signatures anymore, thanks to the storm rolling in."

Watters's team shook their heads. This was going to be fun in reverse, but they were soldiers. And soldiers didn't complain when things got a little tough. Or in this case, a little cold.

"Now, we have this thermal image from last night."

Candyman pointed to several spots. "Fires." His finger wavered beneath the imprint of the image. "This. . ." He tapped a green spot and glanced at Watters. The grim expression spoke for both of them. Bodies. . .dying.

"You should know there are reports of Chinese military in the area."

Watters pivoted, his brow knotted. "Sir?"

"You heard me." Early tugged off the reading glasses. "Chinese. We don't know why they're there or what they're after, but if you encounter them, your orders are STK."

Shoot to kill? What was that about?

Burnett motioned to the major, who hustled to his side and bent low. The general spoke into his ear, then Otte hurried out of the room.

"Daniels, you'll stay with ODA452, use that dog of yours to see if you can find anything useful."

Again, this was all exciting and thrilling—in fact, it was what he'd wanted—but these men could do the work in half the time, grab a dog team from another unit, and they were good to go. To be honest, he didn't want to put Watterboy or Candyman in harm's way, and that's exactly what he felt would happen.

Heath pushed his attention to the grumpy general. Bulldog. Throw the dog a bone.

"Not now, Daniels," Burnett growled.

Heath let out a huff.

"Sir." Watters's tone was gruff. "Permission to speak freely?"

Early glowered. "Go on."

"Sirs, with all due respect to you and to Ghost—Daniels," Watters said, his face grim and red, "I must lodge a protest against his inclusion on this mission. Sir."

A stake through the heart would not have hurt as much. Heath lowered his head. He never expected that, for a man he trained to turn against him. Even though it made sense. If their roles were reversed, he'd do the same thing, but still. . .

"Explain yourself," Burnett said.

"Sir, I have the utmost respect for Daniels. I worked under him, then with him. He's a good man."

"So, what's the problem?"

"I've seen him in action since his return. He's still there, engaged—until his body shuts down." Material shuffled, as if Watters shifted his feet. "I witnessed him in a four-second blackout. He went down, lost sight of his dog and his team. When he came to, he was disoriented." Watters had gotten quieter with each word. "Sir, out there, in the field, that's the difference between life and death. In all good conscience, I can't put my men at risk like that."

"Understood." Burnett's gaze bored into Heath, who lowered his head once again. "ODA452, grab your gear. Head to the choppers. Dismissed."

Ghost looked haunted. Lance had seen it before. In fact, he'd been there once, back in Somalia. All his dad's shaman talk and his mom's

Christianese didn't do much against those demons that plagued the mind. A counselor and years took the edge off that.

The look on Ghost told him there was more truth to Watterboy's words than Daniels would ever admit.

As if a boulder of guilt sat on his shoulders, Ghost rose.

"Daniels," Lance barked. "Sit."

Surprise clawed into the young man's face as he dropped back against the chair. The dog beside him raised her head. "Sir?"

Lance blew a hard breath against his fisted hand as he considered the young man. Darci hadn't ever been willing to stand up to him when it came to a dating interest. But she had with this former Green Beret. And Darci had been the cream of the crop in assessing people. Even though she said she'd lost that gift with Jianyu, Lance tried to get her to see that Jianyu was a different type of man. One of the most dangerous with his uncanny ability to wait out his enemy.

Back to Daniels. So this man had some good mettle, or the young woman he thought of as a daughter wouldn't go to bat for him.

The room had cleared minutes ago. They were alone. With Ghost's ghouls and Lance's demons. "Is it true? Does that scar on the back of your head go deeper than your thick skull?"

Jaw muscles flexing, Daniels nodded. "I blacked out—yes, sir."

"Do you think you put others in jeopardy?"

His mouth opened but said nothing, an automatic rejection seemingly lodged at the back of his throat. Misery smothered his hope. "Yes, sir. I guess it does. . ."

"I'm hoping you got a mighty big 'but' coming."

The man studied him, and Lance saw the burden, the passion, the warrior hiding behind the mask of failures and wounds.

Daniels shook his head. "No, sir."

Somehow, Lance wanted to reach in and haul that warrior back to the present. "No, let's hear it. Put it all on the table."

He straightened, and the highly decorated Green Beret surfaced again. "I got banged up in a training incident when we arrived. Nothing serious, but it pinched a nerve in my neck. An Afghan doctor at FOB Murphy gave me an adjustment." Heath met his gaze. "I haven't had a headache since."

"So you think it cured you?"

"No, sir." Swift and sure, the answer was the right one. But did the

185

young man realize it? "I wish it were that easy, for me and countless others, but unless a miracle occurs and the scar tissue in my brain vanishes, I'll have problems with headaches and seconds-long blackouts. But before arriving here, I hadn't blacked out for months." He stared at his hands, then his dog. "I want to do this. I want to be there. . .for Jia."

Lance didn't know whether to punch him or thank him. "Well, I hope you're right because I need you out there."

Heath frowned. "Why? You have handlers without my issues. Just assign one—"

"You're the only one who spent time with her."

Daniels quieted.

"Son, what I'm about to tell you is to go no further than where you're sitting." Lance stared at him hard as he pushed out of his seat, came around the table, and hiked up a leg and leaned against the surface. "Am I making myself clear? Because if you so much as sneeze in the wrong direction, I will make sure you can't dig yourself out of the hole I bury you in. You tracking?"

"Sir. Yes, sir." Steady. Solid. The guy had a stellar combat record. Numerous medals. But it was the confidence without cockiness that resonated with Lance. Probably the same reason Darci had been drawn to him.

"That young woman you met is a military intelligence officer."

Gray eyes met his with little emotion.

"You aren't surprised?"

"It explains a few things."

"Like?"

"Like why she would show interest in me, then sever any chance of talking in the future."

"That was my fault. She mentioned you one too many times, and I bit her head off for it." And Darci had never been the kind to get distracted by big muscles or big talk, so there was something to the kid before him. He'd have to trust her instinct. In fact, he *was* trusting Darci by sending this former Green Beret out after her. "I think you saw that confrontation."

Daniels gave a slow nod.

"She's one of our most important assets." He reached back, picked up a folder, rifled through it, and plucked a photo from it. "This man is Wu Jianyu. A week ago, we thought he was the loyal son of General Zheng Xin."

"Minister of defense."

"Exactly." Lance stood and stuffed his hands in his pockets, noting Daniels wasn't surprised yet again. "For years we have seen Wu Jianyu climbing the ranks, to take his father's seat when Zheng retired, we assumed."

"And now?"

"Now, he's a rogue son, bent on sabotaging his father's name, bent on igniting some long-repressed fears of a war between China and the U.S."

Daniels's gaze darted over the image. "He's the one in the mountains?"

"That's our belief. We also have reason to believe he is after Jia."

"Is that her real name?"

"It's the only name you need to know." Lance smiled, weighing what he would say next. "I need you and that dog up there. Jia might be dead, but I doubt it. She's a resourceful operative." He returned to the head of the table. "Get up there, find her, bring her back. Am I clear, Daniels?"

"Crystal, sir, but. . ."

"That sounds like a mighty big 'but,' son."

"Yes, sir." The kid gave a miserable sigh and shook his head, muttering. "This is crazy. I wanted this. . .with every breath, every beat of my Green Beret heart. . ."

"Wanted what?"

"To be back here, fighting, doing what I was trained to do."

"Good. You're back. Bring Jia home."

"No, sir."

The response knocked Lance back a mental step. "Excuse me?" Had this punk kid just told him no? "Want to try that again?"

"I mean. . ." Daniels huffed. "With all due respect, sir. . ." He glanced down at Trinity, and Lance could see the emotions rolling off the kid like heat plumes. Failure. Fear. Inadequacy. "I think Watters is right, sir. I don't belong out there anymore. My head. . .my body—they're too weak."

Lance could take this rejection and let the guy walk. But that would mean Darci might not come back. That wasn't acceptable. In Basic, the newbs were pushed until they redefined the "can't" to "yes, sir." As a former soldier, Daniels knew better than to sling whines and excuses.

Which meant Lance had one recourse. Though he hated pushing this kid, he had no choice. He kicked a chair. "Well, too bad."

Daniels blinked. "Sir?"

"I said too bloody bad." He stabbed a finger at him. "You're going. I need you in there. I need that dog—"

"But—"

"No buts. You were military issue once, and I can dang well make it legit again. And I know you don't want that since you know what it'd mean to your dog." He let the threat hang rank and ominous in the chilled room. "So just get your sorry butt out there and do it, Daniels."

The man's chest heaved. "I can't. I pass out, I—"

"Well. . .don't. You know her. That dog knows her scent. That's what I need. Not some whiny, complaining grunt." Lance stomped to his feet. "You liked her, didn't you, Daniels—Jia?"

Daniels swallowed, and Lance wanted to yank his Adam's apple till the kid squawked into submission. Why couldn't the punk see he had the one thing Darci needed—someone going after her who cared. Someone who *wanted* her safe.

"Her life is in your hands."

Mouth open, Heath stared back at him.

"One more thing." He indicated to Otte, who stood by the door in complete silence during this tête-à-tête, then slipped out without a word. "I'm partnering you with Zheng Haur and his first officer."

This might be a mistake, but there were two lines of thinking here. One: Haur could be an asset. He had a vested interest in stopping Jianyu from sabotaging forward international progress between China and other countries, something for which General Zheng had been a vocal advocate.

Or two: He could be blowing a lot of smoke up their proverbial skirts. In which case, Lance wanted someone out there to protect Darci. Someone with a vested interest in Darci. Unfortunately, she cared about Daniels, too. What he hoped was that the two didn't combine those feelings and come out wanting something more. Lance couldn't lose an asset like Darci.

Heath glanced back, and when he didn't show any surprise at the arrival of Colonel Zheng, the decision was cemented. He'd picked the right man for this mission.

"Daniels, meet your new partner, Zheng Haur, the informally adopted son of General Zheng."

Daniels pulled to his feet.

"We have no reason not to trust him," Lance said. "Except that he's Chinese."

The remark had its desired effect. Outrage rippled through Zheng's expression but then faded to resignation.

Lance clapped a hand on Daniels's shoulder. "Keep a close eye on him, son." He squeezed the muscle. "If you can do this, I might be able to find a way to give you your career back."

Heath went stiff. "Sir. I—"

"Just bring her home, Daniels."

★ ★ Twenty-Four ★ ★

So close. So very close. Yet years and miles away. Being in Afghanistan, without the eyes of General Zheng peering over his shoulder, Haur's fantasy swirled through his mind and took root.

No. It would be too risky. He could not.

They had separated him from his men save Captain Bai. Tactically, it was smart. But it also left a curtain in Haur's hidden vault vulnerable. Behind it. . . He wasn't even sure the door behind that curtain existed anymore.

It'd been so long. So very long.

"Promise me!"

The hissed, frantic words seared his memory.

With a thud and a gust of wind, a large pack dropped on the concrete in front of him. "Your gear. Courtesy of the U.S. Special Forces."

Haur rose slowly, not wanting to appear confrontational. "Thank you."

The man thrust a hand forward, the other resting on the stock of his M4A1. "You can call me Watterboy." He twisted his upper body and pointed to the others. "That's Candyman." A man with a brown beard and sunglasses perched on his head touched two fingers to his forehead in a salute but kept working. "The others you'll get to know. The guy with the dog, your partner, we call Ghost."

"My captain, Bai, and I am Haur."

"Did he say whore?"

"Hey!" The man in front of him scowled. "Keep it clean." He

smirked. "Think maybe we'll just call you 'Colonel,' but don't think for a second we're under your authority."

"We want the same thing, *Watterboy.*" They did not trust him with their names. He understood. Breaking down the barriers, discovering if these men could be of help to him. . .

Smiling, Watterboy backstepped. "Not so sure about that."

"I want Jianyu returned to China." Haur glanced around. "I know him best and can assure you that is, without a doubt, what you want."

Watterboy spun, and as he did, he slowed as he passed the dog handler. The two exchanged a glance that spoke of bad blood. Perhaps it would be useful should Haur need to create division among this team.

A blue glow drew his gaze to the side.

Candyman pecked on a military-grade laptop with its virtually indestructible case. A curiosity itched at the tips of Haur's fingers. If he could just use that for two minutes. . .maybe four. It was all he needed. He could universally shift the course—

"Storm's coming," someone said as he dropped more gear. "A mean, nasty one with a butt load of snow and freezing temperatures."

A rumble of groans reverberated through the room.

His brother might just die before Haur gave General Zheng the pleasure of unleashing his vengeance on his son. To Bai, he said in Chinese, "He will not have prepared for that."

"Perhaps, but little stops his iron will," Bai spoke softly in their native tongue, his face not masking the disgust as he assessed the team. "They are weak. Jianyu will outsmart them."

Haur glanced toward the taller leader and the dog handler. "I would not underestimate them, Bai."

"Ghost."

Haur looked as Watterboy handed off a pack. "Got these from the kennel. Thought you could use it for Trinity."

Ghost hesitated, then took the packages. He unwrapped the smaller. "Doggles, sweet." He smiled, then opened the larger item. "Whoa. No way!" He held up what appeared to be a vest. "Tell me. . .this isn't. . .an *Intruder?*"

Watterboy grinned. "Yeah, don't mention it."

"I can't believe they let you have a Storm Intruder vest. This thing has everything—camera, special harness, life vest, four-channel receiver—dude!"

Watterboy and another man laughed. "Seriously. *Don't* mention it. Not to anyone. Just go with it." The meaning was not to be missed. They'd absconded with one for the man and his team, which made Haur wonder why it was not just issued to the soldier.

Ghost's smile slipped, but he nodded.

"I'm counting on you and Trinity to keep us alive."

Grating and grinding, the large steel door rolled up into the ceiling. General Burnett stood, flanked by a half-dozen men, most in suits. Which meant, not military. "Okay, ladies. Gather up."

Haur started forward, but Burnett held up a hand. "Sorry, Colonel. I'll need you to stay out of this one."

Haur stood mute, frozen. Overwhelmed, once again, by the certainty that he would not come off that mountain alive.

Heath tested the vest once more for a snug, solid fit. He tugged on the front around her shoulders to make sure it wasn't going anywhere. His mind zigzagged over the cost, over the question of whether he'd have to return it—of course he would, it was a forty-grand loan—and how much he wished he could keep it.

Hooking his hand through the lead, he smiled as Trinity looked up at him. She had that "I'm gorgeous and you know it" look going on.

"Daniels! Front and center."

Heath tugged Trinity forward as the team huddled with the general and suits in a corner. "Sir."

"Okay, listen up. This is Agent Bright with the SIS."

"Spooks." Candyman spat.

"That's right," the general said in a tone that explained how happy he was with this whole predicament. "So just shut it and listen up."

Agent Bright stepped forward. "Thank you, General." Chiseled jaw with a scar over his left temple, the British agent slipped into his role with ease. "What I'm about to tell you is confidential."

"And if you tell anyone, you'll have to kill us, right?" Candyman shot off.

Bright seemed to chew down the stub on his frustration. "About five hours ago, one of our operatives activated his emergency code."

"That sounds real 007ish." Man, Candyman was in his element antagonizing the spook.

"Then you'll know that Bond always gets his guy." Bright rolled with it. "And so will we. The transponder emits a signal once every hour."

"What good is that?"

"It keeps my man alive."

Candyman nodded. "Understood."

Spreading a map over his knee, Bright pointed to some marks. "His signal first emitted here."

"Geologist's base camp."

Bright nodded. "Then here, here, and here."

"That's only four," Watters said. "Thought you said he went missing five hours ago?"

"Next activation is in roughly fifteen minutes."

"And this means what to us?"

"My agent was on that survey team."

"Why?"

Bright smirked. "Even Bond never told all his secrets."

Candyman eyed the guy. "Which means you'd have to kill me—or at least die trying—if you told me."

"You're almost smart enough to be a spook, Candyman."

"How d'you know my name?" The man's face fell as he looked around, the others laughing. "How'd he know my name?"

"Listen up, ladies," General Burnett said in his booming, grouchy voice. "You know what we're after. Head up to the camp. Send me the feeds. But then, I want you with the spook at the last-known location."

Watterboy hesitated, scratching his dark beard. "*With* the spook?"

"My guy is missing, too, so I'm going," Bright said.

Several around them cursed, but the extra body could work in their favor. Heath understood the territorial nature and the belief that the more "new" you added to the mix, the more volatile that mixture became for the team. But the spook clearly had access to stuff the military didn't. And for Heath, that increased his chance of surviving this, and if the spook was still alive and sending a signal, then it was possible Jia was, too.

The building rattled as the wake of rotors rumbled in, around, and above the building.

"Your ride's here. Make it quick and clean. In and out. Let's hope for the best, plan for the worst."

"Hooah!"

193

RONIE KENDIG

Deep in the Hindu Kush
20 Klicks from Chinese Border

Hands plunged into the snow, Darci grunted. The icy accumulation bit into her hands, into her strength. She slumped back on her legs and tilted her head up. The gray sky mocked her. Not even a drop of sun to warm her face, beg off the stinging pain of freezing through.

"*Qǐlái*. Get up!"

Jianyu stood over her, leering. The muffled sounds of boots to her left warned her. "*Qǐlái!*" the elite fighter shouted as she locked gazes once more with Jianyu. In her periphery, she saw the man thrust his weapon at her.

Fire and pain exploded through her side, the momentum of his strike shoving her sideways into the snow. She slumped and breathed hard, wishing the iciness could numb the pain. It hurt to breathe. If he hadn't broken her ribs, he'd at least cracked one or two.

"*Líkāi wǒ bèihòu,*" Darci muttered, knowing very well they would not leave her behind. She saw the gleam in Jianyu's eye. Saw the delirious hunger in him to drag her back to his father, throw her at his feet, and regain his honor.

Hands gripped her shoulders.

World spinning, she looked into the eyes of Peter Toque. "Get up, Jia. No time like the present to live." He dragged her onto her feet. His mouth brushed her ear, and out came a rush of warm words. "I have a tracking device."

A crack thundered through the sky.

No—not the sky.

She felt herself falling again.

Peter slumped over her.

"What, have you gained a new lover now that you have left my bed?" Jianyu sneered as he shoved Peter sideways with a boot. "How many have you had, Meixiang? Or should I call you Jia? Perhaps I should kill him the way you killed me in the eyes of my father."

"*Yǒu méiyǒu qítā rén.* Would he believe that there had been no others? She hoped so, because she would never sacrifice another's life to save her own. Cradling her side, she braced herself against the mountain as she tried to pull herself up, but the pain shoved her down.

Jianyu squatted, his left eye twitching as he stared into her eyes, their noses all but touching. There had been a time she'd found him intoxicating. His strong features, his charismatic manners. It'd been her job to break him.

Instead, he'd broken her.

And even now, she did not trust herself. Yes, a primal attraction existed between them. But so did his mean, calloused heart, his thirst for power and wealth. It hurt to love a man like him.

He caught her face in his hand and forced her to look at him, nostrils flaring and war raging in his eyes. "What of our child?"

Twenty-Five

Rage colored the white landscape in a blanket of red.

"There was no child." Meixiang squeezed her eyes closed, cutting off his only avenue to probe her soul. See for himself if her words were true.

It was a trap. She wanted him to believe the baby did not exist. He dug his fingers into her cheeks. "Lying whore!" He rammed her head back against the rocks. A solid crack snapped a yelp from her lungs. She reached for her head, but he saw that steel strength he'd been drawn to when he first saw her in Taipei City.

"Sir—we need her alive."

Jianyu shuffled back, sliced his hand through the air, and nailed his officer in the throat. The man dropped, gasping for air. Quick as lightning, Jianyu pushed his foot against Meixiang's throat.

"I am not lying. There was no baby." She gritted her teeth, her face reddening as she lay stretched against the path and the spine of the mountain.

How did it feel, he wanted to ask, to have the very breath cut from you by one you trusted, loved? And now, she wanted to do it again? "You think I am a fool?" He shifted and grabbed her face again. "I saw the sonogram. I was there, do you forget?"

Face pale as the snow behind her, Meixiang shook her head. Fingers reddened by the bitter bite of winter, she fought for her life. Tears slid free as she kept her teeth clamped tight, her tears a mixture of determination and fear.

Yes, fear. He would have that fear multiplied so she trembled. So she realized the error in leaving him, in betraying him. But he would not—*would not!*—believe her lies ever again.

Grabbing her by the neck, he hauled her to her feet. "What did you do with my son?"

"It was fake!" Her legs wobbled, and she threatened to collapse again, but he pushed her against the rocks. Pawing at his hands with her own cuffed hands, she sagged and straightened. Sagged again. "The technician was paid off to go along with it."

It wasn't true. He'd seen his son with his own eyes. "I saw it! I saw him move!" A path to redemption, to regaining his father's favor was a son.

Her brow knitted into an inverted V. "It was a video." The tears left streaks on her dirty, frozen cheeks and mingled with the heavy-falling snow. "It wasn't real."

Jianyu pushed his body against hers, pinning Meixiang between the mountain and his rage. "You lie!"

"It was the only way to keep you on my side, to stop you from betraying me."

Squeezing her face hard again, he crushed her beneath himself. "You mean, it was the only way to betray *me*." With the fury roiling through his body, he shoved his hand, flattened, into her side, fingers first. The blow would devastate the injury Tao had inflicted earlier.

Eyes popped open, mouth agape, Meixiang sucked in a breath. Her eyes rolled into the back of her head. Limp as a noodle, she slid from his grip. And he let her.

He did not believe her. Would not believe that the totality of that situation had been something she'd conjured up. There were too many facts that said otherwise. Including the photograph of his newborn son.

And now. . .now that he had her back, he would throw her at his father's feet and demand justice. Demand his honor back. Demand his right as a son to rule.

And if his father did not relent, Jianyu would take it from his cold, frozen heart.

Of course, after he killed the old man.

Parwan Province, Afghanistan

Spotted like a dalmatian. Charred spots against the snow gave it the mottled appearance. It's all Heath could think as the Black Hawk circled the campsite-turned-crash site. Uneven, a blanket of snow had spread itself over the scene, concealing whatever lay beneath. He'd worked recovery on a building in Kandahar, and it wasn't pretty. The smell, the shock that hammers into your skull the first time you spot a limb. The revulsion that hits home when you realize the limb isn't attached to anything.

With a shudder, Heath prayed that's not what they'd find here. Hogan had said she thought he was here for a reason, and now he saw the earmarks of Providence written all over this like the charred rubble in the snow.

Or was that just him grasping for meaning and hope? Nah, he'd had too strong a connection to Jia to chalk it up to nothing.

Between his feet, Trinity shifted and leaned toward the opening. The wind battered its fingers through her thick fur. She pulled her tongue in and stretched her neck even farther. The Doggles made it easy for her to look out the chopper.

With the swirling snow compliments of the rotor backwash, the storm looked fiercer than it was. Yet. He'd seen the Doppler for the next several days. If they had to hike through this rugged terrain for long, it wouldn't be pretty. He'd have to monitor Trinity, don the special insulated paw protectors.

The helo swung around, its nose pulling up and to the right, shoving Trinity in the direction she'd leaned. She jerked and backpedaled. Heath couldn't help but smile. The bird leveled, and he felt the lift as it lowered to the lip of the plain.

Trinity leapt from the helo and onto the soft blanket of snow. Heath hopped out behind her and led her to the side, taking a knee until everyone had disembarked. As he did, he petted her, reassuring her—and himself—that everything would be fine. Under the control of the rotor wash, a torn piece of tent flapped as if telling them to hurry into its protection.

As the bird pulled away, the tent flap seemed to grow frantic in its welcome.

You're losing it, man.

Forcing himself to take a look around, Heath braced himself for the worst. Charred bodies to account for each member of the team. Including Jia. The general might believe she was resourceful, and Heath wanted to find her alive, but he'd seen elite warriors go down in flames enough times to struggle with the sovereignty of God yet yield to it.

Heath couldn't explain the connection to Jia and the subsequent ache to see her alive. There wasn't even something special she did, like taunt or flirt with him. *That's because* she *is special—period.*

Yeah, okay, that sounded logical.

The truly logical thought would be that if she'd somehow survived, it meant she was in a heap of trouble. And trouble was a lot easier to work with than death. Heath didn't want to haul her body out of the rubble.

Watch over her, God.

Watters gave the advance signal as he swept the area with his weapon. He pointed to the two Chinese officers and told them to stay, then ordered a sergeant to keep their guests company.

Heath led in a wide perimeter. Flaps of white had been chewed up by the flames and left black and looked moth-eaten. The hulk that had landed almost in the middle of the camp and had been the source of the explosion he'd seen from the FOB was indeed a Black Hawk.

Weapons up, the team snaked in, out, and around the scene. Heath held fast to Trinity's new lead on the Intruder and walked her through the site. Nose down, she trekked through the debris. Her head popped up, she wagged her tail, then sat quietly.

"She's got a hit," Heath said.

Two of the twelve-man team jogged over and started digging. One stood back and cursed. "One of ours."

As they cleared the dirt and chunks of metal, Heath could barely discern the flak vest with most of the material burned off.

Heath tightened his lips and kept moving. *Don't think about it. Don't think about it.*

Trinity barked again, tying Heath's stomach in a knot. Another helo loomed over them, whipping the ash and dust into a frenzy. It deposited a cleanup crew, alleviating Heath's fears that he'd have to locate more bodies. At the back, Watters and Candyman worked to prop up the tent that had tumbled forward, the post snapped as if a man with only one leg.

Jibril. Heath had seen the worry in the man's gaze as he left the hangar and boarded the helicopter.

"Hey."

Heath looked up from where Trinity nudged aside some clothes waffling in the wind.

"It wasn't personal." Watters shifted, his gaze darting around the campsite. "I had to speak up."

"I get it." And he did. But it didn't make the matter any less painful. "You did what you had to. I don't belong here." As the words slipped past his lips, Heath realized those words had taken on a different meaning. He just didn't know what. "But I'm here. And I'm going to do everything I can."

"Hey, look." Candyman knelt beside a locker near a crushed cot. He spread a handful of gadgets over the rubble-strewn ground. An electric razor, a small radio, shaving cream, and a brick phone.

"She was working with the general." Heath tried to keep his explanation vague.

M4 propped over his chest and resting against his knee, Candyman stared at him, then frowned. "That's great, but this wasn't her locker." He pointed to another one that lay split in two, contents—clothes, a handheld radio, and a pair of boots—spilled out. "That's hers."

Watterboy lifted the radio from the pile Candyman studied. "Why would an equipment supplier need a military-grade satellite radio?"

"Or more to the point," came a heavy Asian accent. "Why would he need an electric razor *and* shaving cream?"

Watterboy looked toward the opening where Zheng stood with his officer and a Green Beret. He tossed down the radio and picked up the shaving cream, assessed it, then cranked on the bottom. *Pop! Hisssss.* Watters upended the can into his hand. "HFIDs."

Why did the equipment guy have high-frequency identification discs?

Watterboy cursed into the strong wind. "They're used as short-range tracking devices."

The spook joined them. "The equipment supplier was my man." He retrieved the HFIDs. "Thank you."

Climbing to his feet, Candyman squinted out over the blanket of white against the gray sky. "Who the heck were you tracking?"

"Anyone he felt necessary."

"Is it possible your man placed one on the others?" Zheng Haur asked.

"Sure."

Watterboy nodded to Candyman. "Can you have your people run them and see if there are any hits?"

"Even if there are," the spook said, "the weather and distance will interfere. And they don't last long."

"We can try. Better have Burnett do some deep digging while we're hunting down the missing."

Heath's heart skipped a beat. "So, there *are* missing?"

"Far as I can tell, with the woman back at camp—"

"Alice." Rocket nodded.

Watters hesitated and frowned at his friend.

"What?" Rocket shrugged. "We talked. She's cute."

"She's off-limits."

Rocket snorted. "Sorry, Charlie. She's civilian and of age."

"She's the only witness we have into the deaths of six SEALs." Watterboy tapped his friend's vest. "Until Command clears her, step off."

Heath wanted to choke them both. "So! How many are missing?"

"Three."

"Found a body!"

"Make that two." Candyman slapped Watters on the shoulder and started out of the misshapen tent. "I'll check it." He jogged to where three men stood looking over a ledge.

Heath watched the team moving around the camp with methodical, meticulous precision. He tucked aside the feeling of isolation within a crowd. What happened here was pretty extreme and thorough. Who had come into this territory and wiped out a team surveying rocks? And the bigger question—why?

Watterboy started for the opening. "Let's figure out who's missing first, and we can extrapolate later, hopefully get us out of this winter mess before it sneezes rain and ice all over us." He stepped out from beneath the tarp and joined the rest of his team, counting bodies and IDing them.

Protected from the heavy snowfall by the tarp, Heath loosened his straw and stuffed the valve into his mouth and took a long drag on the water. Trinity looked up at him expectantly. "You too, huh?" He tugged the straw looser and aimed it at her.

She lifted her head, and he squirted water at her. As the water splashed over the contents of Jia's box, he cocked his head to look at a picture. A smile pushed through the depressive mood that had steeled over him. It was an image of him with Trinity. When had that been taken? He didn't recognize it. He bent and retrieved it. When he did, something slid out and landed with a soft thud on the dirt. Heath retrieved it but hesitated as the red and gold ribbon registered. Prying them apart, Heath angled the picture of himself and stilled. Scanned the information. This was. . .pre-DD214. When he was an Army handler. Still in the Green Berets. How did she get it?

"Why would someone have your picture?"

Heath met the steady gaze of his new "partner." A kindness wreathed Haur's face, in contrast to the infuriated, arrogant gleam in Bai's. "I have no idea." Though he hoped he did—he hoped she had the same healthy curiosity about him that he had for her.

Something stuck to the back of the printout.

He slid his fingers between the two.

Hurried footsteps drew his gaze to the lopsided opening. Watters leaned in. "We got a lead on the two missing."

"Yeah?"

"It's the girl Burnett wants and"—he angled a dossier page toward him—"this guy. Peter Toque. Equipment supplier out of Ohio."

"My man," the spook reminded them.

Relief sped through Heath's veins so swift and thick, he wanted to laugh. She was alive.

Watters tugged a phone from his pack and dialed.

While the sergeant radioed in, Heath glanced down to the papers in hand. What he saw made him stop. "What. . .?" Weird. What was Jia doing with a picture of him at Landstuhl?

Twenty-Six

Deep in the Hindu Kush
20 Klicks from Chinese Border

Between the overzealous colonel and the dropping temperatures, they had one hope to stay alive: he must become allies with Zheng. But that would take some convincing, and the only way to do that was to provide real information. Scattered around the circumference of the small site, Zheng's men were alert and jovial. How they could be with the ragged claws of the icy winds and snow billowing around them, he could not fathom.

"I can help," Peter braved, breaking his silence as Jianyu continued staring at the still-unconscious Jia. "I have information about her that would prove useful."

"How can any information you have be useful to me?" The sneer seeped past Jianyu's lips and infected his words.

"I know her real name."

Snickers swirled through the snow.

"You know nothing!" Jianyu punched to his feet. "Do not attempt to become my ally. I have little use for you, American."

"I'm not American," Peter said, allowing the accent he'd hidden these long months.

Appraising eyes narrowed. "British. Spying on your own allies?" He seemed amused.

"Her involvement in the survey team had a smell to it."

Wind whipping at them, snow drifting around their heads like angry halos, neither moved. Or spoke.

203

Then, without a word, the colonel turned toward Jia, squatted, and traced a finger down her face, tucking her thick, black hair away from her face. "What do you know of her?"

The man had a strange sort of obsession with the woman lying at his feet. Was it possible this madman—and yes, Peter knew exactly who this rogue before him was—loved her? What was their history? That was the lone hole in his knowledge.

"Her name is Darci Kintz."

Jianyu stilled. Stood, his gaze still locked on her.

Feeding off the man's apparent interest in the information, Peter pushed on. He *must* get this man in his pocket or he would be as good as dead. "She lives in New York."

Someone coughed. A nervous one, that drew Peter's gaze to the side, but he could not tell who had made the sound or why. When he looked back—

A boot sailed into his face.

The afternoon darkened and swirled to black.

Deep in the Hindu Kush
18 Klicks from Chinese Border

Fire and ice. Pain and peace. Tumbling and turning, writhing through her mind amid screams and haunting silence. Running toward people only to see them slip away. Out of sight. Out of existence.

Dr. Colsen. Looking at her, talking and taunting. Then his head exploding.

Jaekus dropping from a ledge with a ravenous scream.

Darci jolted.

White-hot pain speared her side. She drew up a leg, covered her side, and froze. Her yelp strangled by her tears.

"Easy, easy."

Blinking, she found no difference between eyes open and eyes closed. Was she blind? Or was it dark? Wait—no, there. She could see a differentiation in the shades. She wasn't blind. So, where was she? Pulling herself up, fire lit through her abdomen again.

"Stop moving."

Even as he spoke, the memories stumbled through her mind, one on top of another. The campsite. The professor, Jaekus, then getting knocked out—she sucked in a breath. "Toque?"

"Tell me you didn't forget me."

She couldn't laugh. It hurt too much.

"But if one more Chinese person plants his boot in my face. . ."

She snorted, and a sensation like a live cat trying to claw its way out of her stomach shredded her smile. "Where. . .?"

"An abandoned shack. Not sure how far, but I'm guessing twenty or thirty miles from the Chinese border. He seems to be heading in a very particular direction. I heard him insisting they stick to the schedule."

So, Jianyu was meeting someone.

"Look, Darci, I should tell you, I think he's got some wicked bad allies. I'd wager he's trying to attack the bases, but that's a wild guess."

Pressing her arm to her side, she pried herself up. She ground her teeth, ignoring the throb. Sweat dripped down her face and back. She let out a heavy breath as she pushed herself upright.

"And I think he has plans for you."

"Why would you. . .think that?" Bile rose in her throat at the pain.

"He knows you. Knows everything about you. More than you could possibly imagine."

"Of course he does. His father is Chinese intelligence."

"No, Darci. It's worse. He knows *everything*!"

As if her mind backfired, a crack in their conversation revealed itself. How did he know her name? "Who are you?"

"Are you that far gone? Peter Toque—"

"Equipment supplier. Who isn't an equipment supplier." She steeled herself against the fire in her ribs and for the truth. "Now. Who are you, really?"

Quiet swirled around the small hut. "British intelligence."

He'd told her. Shoot! Opening their secret IDs and placing them on the table meant the situation was much worse than she could have imagined. "I knew something about you wasn't right."

"What," he said from across the hut, where she guessed he'd been tied up. "Didn't I do the Ohio country boy well?"

She eased back against the wall, feeling the bamboo poles digging into her back. "What were you doing"—she breathed hard and swallowed—"with the team? Why were you there?"

"When your name showed up on that manifest, I knew something was up. So did my bosses. They wanted to know what you Americans were after, so being the good spy analysts we are, I embedded to steal all your secrets."

Darci groaned. Ninety percent of intelligence came from assets embedded in innocuous positions, just to monitor goings-on.

The throaty rumble of a vehicle drowned her words as slivers of light streaked through the not-so-weather-proofed walls. Darci squinted against the brightness.

Diesel and loud.

"Sounds big."

"Really big for this mountain pass."

Considering she wasn't up-to-date on their location, she couldn't gauge that. But his notice helped. "Did Jianyu give any indication of what he's doing?"

"If he had, I would've told you."

"And I'm just supposed to trust you?"

"We're captives to the Chinese military. What choice do we have?"

"To keep my trap shut and stay alive."

He snorted. "We have to get out of here."

"You're brilliant, Sherlock."

"Thanks."

Crunching pushed her eyes open, and her pulse thrummed to find his shadowy form standing over her. Wait. . .something. . .something wasn't sitting right. Now he wanted them to work together? "I thought you were tied up."

"No, I just couldn't see you till the trucks rolled in."

Right. He really must think she was the dimmest bulb in the pack. Though her weakened state pushed her to trust him, to *not* have to work so hard, her instincts objected. Pain poked her, and she used it for an excuse not to reply.

"He had one of his men check your ribs."

She snorted again. "That explains the ungodly pain—they're butchers."

"They saw a scar. . ."

Darci stared out of the corner of her eye. Night blindness made it impossible to read his expression, but that sounded like a very leading comment. The rickety cot creaked, and the air whirled as he eased beside her on the bed.

Alarms blazing, Darci felt the first tendril of panic as she realized she would be in no shape to incapacitate him again or fight him off if he wanted to incapacitate her.

"Is it true?"

At least he had the brains to soften his voice. She was right! Indignation wormed through her all the same. He was digging for information. Most likely working for Jianyu. If that was true, then what was Jianyu holding over Toque's head to make him do his dirty work?

She'd play along. Let him dig a wide circle around the truth. He'd never know the truth if it hit him in the face, so she had time on her side. "Is what true?"

"I heard him—on the pass. He asked about a baby."

"Then you also heard my answer."

"But the scar. . ."

It made sense now, putting him in here with her. To bleed her courage. Typically, prisoners were kept apart so there was less chance for collaboration, less chance of encouraging each other, more opportunity to break them.

"Appendix," she said.

A door flung open. Light and soldiers flooded the room, and for the first time, Darci saw that they had not been alone. Jianyu stood in a corner, his eyes narrowed. His expression reeking of fury. Hands behind his back, he stalked toward them.

Toque, who sat beside her, started to rise.

Jianyu shoved him down and did not remove his grasp. "What does he mean to you, *Darci*."

A new heat swirled through her, sparking adrenaline. She looked to Toque, who hung his head. Traitor. She bet he'd tried to barter his way into Jianyu's life with a slip of information. But he had no idea the damage he'd done.

Ba.

Jianyu grabbed Toque by the neck and shoved him onto his knees in front of her, then jammed a weapon to his temple. "What does he mean to you?"

She glared at Jianyu. "What, are you going to kill everyone? What will you do after he's dead? Kill me?" She tried to stand but flopped back down. Pain drove through her side and back like an iron bar. "This is stu—"

Crack!

Warmth splattered her face.

207

Twenty-Seven

Parwan Province, Afghanistan

*T*rust *is not easily gained.*" Though Haur understood this, had been beaten with this over the last twenty years, he struggled in his present situation to accept that the men around him, seasoned in warfare just as he was, viewed him as an enemy and not an ally. It worked against his purpose, against his mission.

That must change.

And he knew just how to do it. Haur placed himself near the dog handler.

Strongly built with intelligent eyes, the man said nothing.

Haur bent to pet the dog.

"Don't." Heath Daniels stepped into his path. "She's not a pet. She's working."

Haur inclined his head. "Sorry. I did not know." It did not escape his notice that Daniels tucked the photos into his leg pocket. They'd provided him virtually no information on the survey team, which was why he'd gone digging for some. He tugged the heavy, oversized jacket they'd given him closer and started out over the swirl of snow dancing over the scene. "It will be a hard storm."

"Always is," Daniels muttered as he gripped his dog's lead and moved toward the others.

He, too, was an outsider. Though he had more intel and knowledge on this mission than Haur, they had kept him out of the loop. He eased next to the man again.

Daniels shifted a step to the side.

"They are not the most trusting."

"Trust is earned."

Haur looked at the sandy-haired guy. "Have you not earned their trust?"

Daniels kept his gaze on the men. The longing, the ache to be included ran through that flexing jaw muscle. "Not this time."

"As it is with me, both here and at home."

This time, the man met his gaze. "What does that mean?"

"I see that no one here trusts me." Haur sighed. "Sent on a mission to retrieve Jianyu, I discover his betrayal and attempt to capture him with American help, yet no one here trusts me past the end of my nose. And because of my father's treason against China, most of my own people do not trust me."

"Do you mean your biological father or the minister of defense?"

Haur gave a slow nod. So Daniels knew more about him than he'd thought. "You go to a park to skate on the frozen lake. You see the ice, you know it's ice, but you do not know how thick it is, how deep its hard facets go."

Daniels watched him.

Haur said no more.

"Daniels, Zheng."

They both looked to the leader, Watterboy, who held up a finger and circled it in the air.

Without a second glance, Daniels moved into the group with his dog, who hadn't given Haur a second glance. That was a good sign, right? The dog didn't see him as a threat.

He moved into position.

"SOCOM is running a UAV over the area to see if we can pin down the location of the missing and their captors. There's been too much snowfall to know which direction they're headed." Watterboy folded a piece of paper and slid it into his slanted chest pocket. "Daniels, once we get that lead, we'll want you to take point. You cool with that?"

The man's eyes glinted with appreciation. "Yes, sir."

Smart guy, giving recognition to the authority. Haur had this lingering feeling that Daniels had at one time been an equal if not superior to the men here.

"Zheng, we'll need you to talk to us, let us know if you expect something, if a situation would make sense." Watterboy's eyes stabbed with accusation. "You came to us, so if you want to find your man, you gotta talk to us. Clear?"

"I am not your enemy."

A shorter man with a vest strapped over a very wide chest snorted. "Yeah, that's what my last dead enemy combatant said."

Heat churned through Haur's stomach, but he squelched the fury. He expected this. Still, he must not be a doormat yet not be a rabid dog at the gate.

"Do you understand?" Watterboy asked, his lips tight. His eyes hidden behind the dark sunglasses. "I don't need trouble from you, and I don't have to drag you on this mission."

"Your message is clear."

Whatever Zheng was up to, Heath wasn't going to be a part. Or a pawn. The guy wanted an ally. Heath could understand. But it wasn't going to be him. He would not be used to hurt his country or those he had vowed to protect fifteen years ago when sworn into the Army. It angered him to think this dude might try to play him.

"Coming online." Candyman angled a handheld device to avoid glare from the low-slung sunlight and the blanket of white.

The mention of the UAV's activation drew Heath's gaze skyward. Though he saw nothing against the swirling snow and sun, Heath knew the UAV had or soon would make its first pass.

"Getting a dual feed," Candyman said.

The Green Berets hovered over the handheld device, blocking his view. No, not just his view—him. They didn't believe in him. Not like they used to when they'd follow him into the blackest of nights.

Maybe they're right. Though the chiropractor adjusted his spine, it wasn't a miracle cure for the brain damage that occurred two years ago.

"Too bad, I need you on that team."

Wind howled and tore at his clothes, the sky darkening. While they were waiting for the UAV information, he could get a leg up on this mission. Heath jogged back to the tent where the survey team had slept. He pointed to the blanket and bedding. "Trinity."

She lowered her head and sniffed the material.

On a knee, Heath rifled through the broken box. Lifted a sweatshirt and held it up to Trinity. Again, she pressed her snout to the fabric, nudged her nose further in, then sat and looked up at him as if to say, "What now?"

She wasn't a combat tracking dog—and what he wouldn't do for that specialty like Aspen's dog, Talon, had training in—but Trinity was a Spec Forces dog. She'd been trained and handled in the higher altitudes, the rocky, uneven terrain, the brutal weather. She could catch a scent and read body language. And take down the worst of the worst.

Though he was asking a lot of Trinity, he couldn't help but question what this would take out of him. If he could even fulfill this mission. Though a migraine hadn't exploded through his head, the ever-present thump was there. But Heath knew he was asking a lot of Trin this time—to find a woman she'd only met for a few hours, on a ground now covered with snow, which would eventually freeze her sensitive snout.

Purpose and meaning spiraled through his veins. He might have sucked down there at the base, working the speaking gig, but up here, his determination renewed that he'd been brought here for a purpose. As he looked up to the sky, the view crisscrossed with mountain peaks and spines, Heath knew meeting her at the base was no coincidence.

You brought me here for Jia, didn't You, God? Maybe that was why he couldn't stop thinking about her, couldn't shake that beguiling smile and no-nonsense charm from his memory banks.

Heath stood, scanned Trin's new outfit, and couldn't help the smile. Sleek and sophisticated, the new vest made her appear top of the line. "You look sexy, girl." Smoothing a hand over her head, he whispered, "Do me proud like always." He released her lead and once again showed his girl the sweatshirt. "Trinity, seek."

She spun around, tail wagging, and headed out of the tent. Now, here was a classic example of trust. Trinity had never let him down. Even when he'd been flat on his back, unconscious.

He stayed within a half-dozen feet, monitoring her, the surroundings, and waiting. . .anticipating that second when she'd get a—

Her bark lanced his anticipation. She sat and stared again.

Good girl. "She's got a hit." Heath jogged toward her.

Trinity's powerful front legs hauled her over an incline, her back legs scrambling for purchase. Rocks and debris dribbled down, dusting Heath's face as he hurried to maintain a visual.

"Daniels, hold up!"

"No, go, go," Candyman shouted. "UAV shows movement in that area."

211

Exhilaration of the hunt propelled Heath onward. He searched for headache pangs, dizziness. . . Nothing.

Zigzagging, Trinity darted along a snow-covered path, her silky amber-and-black coat a stark contrast to the bed of white lying deeper with each hour. Grateful for the boots protecting his feet, Heath would need to monitor her condition. Trinity would keep working till her last breath if it meant completing the task he'd given her.

It amazed him, really. For him, it was a mission to honor his country, to do his best. For her, it was also a mission to do her best, but she lived for one goal: to please him. Loyal, brave. . .

No different than the men hauling butt behind him. To his left, he noticed a man consistently at his side. Zheng Haur.

Around a bend, Trinity slowed. Sniffed. Circled back.

"What's wrong?" Watters asked.

Heath shook his head. She'd find the trail soon. "Just give her room to work." As they waited, wind and heavy breathing from the team swirled together. Heath tugged up his collar and tucked his chin, seeking warmth against the dropping temperatures.

"Snow's probably covering up the trail." Watters hunched his shoulders as his breath came out in steamy puffs.

Heath nodded. True, but if the trail was there, Trinity would find it.

She trotted back to him, circled, then returned to a cleft. Heath walked behind her but noted the others slumping against rocks and crouching. Taking five. Anxiety crept around his shoulders and tightened. *Come on, girl. You can do it.*

A lone bark strapped through the afternoon.

Heath hurried to where she sat. "What is it, girl?"

She scooted forward on her haunches. Nose to the rocks.

"What's she got, Daniels?"

"Not sure." Kneeling, he studied where snow had piled up against the rocks. He brushed aside the loose powder.

Trinity nudged in beside him, her snout acting as an arrow.

And he saw. The snow he'd brushed aside was stained red. "Blood." He cleared away a larger area and the circle grew.

"Human? Animal?"

Heath shook his head as Watters crouched beside him. "No way to know. But with the location, and since Trinity hit on it and had Jia's scent. . ."

"We know Jia was injured—the girl said she was shot. Might be her blood."

Nodding, Heath stood. "Maybe they took a break here."

"Or she fell."

"Possible. Maybe both." Heath turned and surveyed the path. "So, if they came this way. . ." The path wasn't wide and didn't branch off, so there would only be one course of action. "Why can't Trin catch her scent?"

"Perhaps she was unconscious." The thickly accented voice came from behind.

Heath and Watters turned toward Zheng Haur.

Zheng shrugged. "They would have to carry her, which would mean her scent would not be as strong. Yes?"

"No. There are different types of tracking—air-scent dogs and tracking dogs. Trinity is trained mostly for air scent, but she does have tracking, or trailing, training." Heath looked around the scene. "Which makes her losing the scent a mystery." Vertical collided with horizontal. The path disappeared around a bend. What options were there that might preclude Trinity from maintaining course? Hidden trails? The escapees getting choppered out? Nah, the peaks were too jagged and close together to allow that. So. . .

Hand along the cliff face, Heath wondered. . .

Watters leaned in. "What are you thinking?"

"The woman who brought the Afghan child to the FOB said they hid in a cave-like tunnel."

Watterboy spun toward the rest of the team. "Search for a tunnel."

Heath stepped back and peered up at the overhang that partially covered this section of the path. He visually traced it as he moved until a jagged crescent blinked at him. "See that?"

"A ledge broke off—small avalanche."

Heath jabbed his hand into the mound and hauled back a section of snow. The others moved in without a word to help clear it away.

"Got it!" Candyman announced. "There's a tunnel."

Manpower tripled on the site to clear the debris away. Once a hole was made, Watters waved everyone back. "Give Ghost and Trinity room to work."

Nodding his appreciation to Watterboy, Heath motioned Trinity into the opening that yawned in the face of the mountain. The rubble inside shifted as Heath maneuvered into the darkness. Weapon up, SureFire button pressed, he sidestepped into the black hole. Trinity's claws clicked as she moved beneath the beam of light. She barked and kept moving.

"She's got it." Heath twisted and turned back.

When he did, a loud *whoosh* breathed through the tunnel.

Darkness collapsed on him.

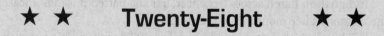

★ ★   Twenty-Eight   ★ ★

Deep in the Hindu Kush
18 Klicks from Chinese Border

Move!"

A weight plowed into her back. Darci pitched forward. Her palms poofed the new fallen snow. Though they'd stuffed her in a heavy jacket, it was several sizes too big and made movement awkward at best.

Gentle hands helped her up.

Though inclined to accept the help, she shoved away. Surprise rippled through her—she'd thought Jianyu had shot him. Thought it was over.

"Hey," Toque said. "I'm just trying to help."

"Help by staying out of my way and mind."

"What in blazes does that mean?"

Shouts collided with their argument. Two of Jianyu's men pried Toque away from Darci. As they supported her, she eyed Toque. Though not an enemy, the Brits had been notoriously antagonistic and arrogant in their presumptions about Americans. She had no reason to trust him. Considering he'd hidden his identity from her, infiltrated her mission, she had all the facts to hold him in contempt and as an enemy.

Spies didn't trust other spies. When one lives a life of constant vigilance, it does not lend itself well to relationships. But oh, she'd like to change that. This mission—she didn't think she'd make it back alive. Not this time. Escaping Jianyu last time had been a miracle. She spent a lot of time in church, thanking God. But she wanted to make it back this time. She had something she wanted to explore. Heath. A relationship.

Jianyu sauntered toward her. Though he had the looks, behind his

215

eyes lay malice. Why hadn't she seen it before. . .before it was too late? How had she ever seen anything desirable in him? Stark and startling, the differences between Heath and Jianyu were like winter and spring. One icy cold and brutal. The other warm and inviting.

"Can you walk, or must I shoot you like an injured cow?"

Indignation flared across her chest, but she batted it aside. "Please." She tightened her mouth. "Do me the favor."

With a flourish, he whipped out a Type 92 heavy machine gun and aimed it at her.

Darci quaked inside but could not show that he held any power over her. "If you shoot me, you can't drag me back to throw at your father's feet."

A small twitch flickered through his lips.

"That is what you're doing, isn't it? Right after you make this rendezvous?"

Raising his chin, he stuffed the weapon in its holster. "Do not try to bleed me for information, Meixiang. I have none after what you did to me in Taipei City."

"You would do no less in the name of China."

"I would not have condemned the one I loved to humiliation and dishonor!"

"Don't be a fool. Of course you would have—you do it *now*!"

His hand flew, the slap stinging against her cheek.

Darci stumbled back into a steady hold. A face appeared over her shoulder. Toque. Again. She shrugged out of his grip. "Don't touch me."

"See?" Jianyu gloated. "She treats even allies as enemies." He swung his arm toward the front. "March."

"We don't have the supplies to make it over the pass." She needled his confidence, at least she hoped she did. Darci thrust her chin toward the slope of the mountain. "That's where we're going, right? Over the pass into China?"

"Move, or I will drag you."

Darci plodded onward, using the steep incline on her right for support. The cold pouring out of the rock seeped into her fingers. Traveled up her wrist and all the way into her heart. As the sun lay to rest in the embrace of the Hindu Kush, she lost all feeling in her hands. Her toes. Her heart.

"You're being idiotic," Toque muttered as they slowed.

"I don't care what you think."

"I'm your ally, Darci. Let me help?"

"An ally in what? Death?" She pushed away from him, shoved her hands in the deep pockets of the coat, and burrowed into herself. Focused on staying alive. Getting better wasn't an option right now. They'd wrapped a stiff bandage around her waist, but she could feel something deeper sinking into her. Maybe it wasn't the broken ribs that bothered her, but the wound in her soul.

Darci planted one foot in front of the other. That was her only goal. But with each step, her legs grew heavier. Her mind slower. Her heart emptier. Somehow, without her permission, her thoughts drifted to a handsome handler and his energetic war dog. He had strength in a way few men did, but something had buried it beneath layers of self-doubt. Still, she could tell he'd once been a no-holds-barred warrior. The way he'd called her out, been unafraid to challenge her halfhearted attempt to shove him out of her life.

Oh, she'd wanted anything but that. In a whirlwind life of betrayals, deception, distance, and loneliness, a warm inviting wind blew during her time with Heath Daniels. He'd noted her throwing arm, a skill she'd honed and few cared about. It was silly, but he seemed to approve.

"Thought so." Those gray eyes of his had caressed her face as he stared down at her after she'd. . .chased after him. Chased? Since when did Darci Kintz, military intelligence officer, *chase* after anyone except a mark?

Darci, you've lost it.

No, no she hadn't. There'd just been something about him walking away, thinking she wasn't interested.

Not that she could pursue a relationship.

Why not? Being human gave her that right. And she was free.

You're an operative. United States Government Issue. Property. Owned. Did that mean she couldn't have a life?

Hesitation caught her by surprise. Until now, she would've said yes because her moral obligation was to her country.

Darci shook her head. Insanity. Here she sat, thinking about the possibility of a romantic relationship with a man who probably just wanted a casual date. Who said he was looking for more?

Besides, none of that mattered right now, considering Jianyu held the reins on her life and intended to drive her straight into Taipei City.

What if Heath came after her? Came to rescue her?

What? Now you're a damsel in distress?

"Might want to drag your head out of those clouds and pay attention."

Darci scowled at Toque.

"Something's happening."

Elbowing past him, she regained her bearings. Unfortunately, he had a point. They'd slowed, and Jianyu now stood with another man at the crest of a hill, radio held near his ear.

Radio? Up here?

Dread swiped through her.

A radio meant two things: He had contact with someone in the area.

And that meant his allies were within range.

A chorus of cheers shot up from the others.

"What is it?" Toque asked.

Darci urged herself forward, and when she reached the edge, a wide valley swept out below them. Several small, dark plumes snaked up across the bed of white. A village. Small but inhabited.

What haunted her was not the half dozen huts huddled against the storm. Nor the smoke rising from offset roofs, but the disturbed snow leading into the village. Tire tracks. Large, wide tire tracks that rushed right up to a gathering of trucks.

Russian military.

Twenty-Nine

Deep in the Hindu Kush
25 Klicks from Chinese Border

Heath froze as he stared at the blackened rubble that two seconds ago had been an opening. Indecision gripped him tight. Should he dig his way through or. . .?

He looked to his left and killed his torch. Was that. . .? He squinted and waited for his eyes to adjust. Was he seeing things? Pulling himself off the wall, he heard shouts muffled by the avalanche of rock and debris from behind. Ahead the darkness seemed to surrender its power to a light source.

Heath bathed the tunnel in light. Two eyes glowed back at him. "Trinity, seek." The eyes vanished, and he knew she'd looked down the far length of the tunnel. Her claws scritched over the rocks. Heath moved fast and with as much stealth as he could muster, deeper into the belly of the mountain. He'd heard about these tunnels, as vast as the blades of grass and rock that peppered the terrain. Taliban had hidden themselves, hidden high-value targets effectively. Too effectively.

Ahead, darkness lost its power. Heath turned off the lamp as he rounded another corner. Light stretched into the tunnel and embraced him. His pulse thrummed at the sight of the opening. Silhouetted by the light, Trinity stood at the mouth.

"Trinity, heel," Heath whispered.

With a flick of her ears, she turned and trotted back to him.

Inching closer, he drew up his weapon. Pressed himself against one side, unwilling to become a block of swiss cheese, compliments of the Taliban. Or any other well-armed, terrorist-minded Afghan.

Heath peered out, breathing a little easier when only a strong wind and a stomped path met him. Easing out, he scanned left, then right down the scope. Footprints matched his theory that this path had been traveled recently. Dark spots pulled him to a knee. Blood.

"Daniels," came an echo-laden call.

Heath shifted and glanced back to the tunnel. "Here. Just around the corner. It's clear." Once more, he scanned the area. No more than four feet wide, the path disappeared in a northeasterly direction, and if he missed that path, the valley floor would be a jagged, painful hundred-foot drop to another swirl of paths ringing a lower, rocky peak.

With the pressure building in his head and his chest, Heath knew they were pushing into higher altitudes. This is where the Kush divided the men from the boys.

"We thought we'd lost you." Watterboy emerged from the tunnel with a shudder. "Man, I hate those things."

"Claustrophobic?" Bai sneered as he and Haur joined them.

"No." Gaze dark, Watters scowled. "I saw a team get ambushed in a tunnel."

"The path is trampled, and you can see blood spots." Heath pointed them out.

"Seems our guys knew where they were going." Watters made way for Candyman and formed a huddle.

Trinity nudged her way past Heath's legs and sat in the middle, panting as she smiled up at him. He rubbed her ears, rewarding her discipline and good trekking.

"Can't say it's a convenient accidental detour." Candyman winked. "Taking one of those tunnels, you could end up in South Africa. It'd be a mighty lucky guess."

"Or perhaps the weather drove them into the tunnel, and they merely happened upon a shortcut." Haur scooted aside so more of the Green Beret team could fill the path.

"Right." Watterboy nodded to Heath. "Let's get moving. We're losing daylight fast, and I don't want to take a wrong turn and fly to my death."

"Agreed." Heath reached for Trinity, and she moved into position beside him.

Dirt and rock spat at him. In the seconds it took to register, Heath heard shouts from behind.

"Taking fire, taking fire!"

Heath pressed himself to the ground, doing his best to shield Trinity. "Where are they?"

"Anyone got eyes on the shooters?"

Heath urged Trinity closer to the rocks, and his girl low-crawled, ears flat and belly against the rocks, to the solid wall. Twisting on his side, Heath brought up his weapon and scanned the outlying area.

Seconds lengthened to minutes as they searched for the shooters.

"Think they left?" Candyman asked.

"Put your head up and find out," Watters said, his face void of the sarcasm his words implied.

A soft pop and dribbling rocks sounded to Heath's left. Then a hard breath.

"Who was stupid enough to lift his head?" Watterboy asked.

"What are they waiting for? They could wipe us off the map."

"Exactly," Heath muttered. "They have us trapped. They live to kill Americans, and they've been waiting for this. No way they'd give it up."

"Agreed." Watterboy's gruff voice rattled the air.

"Then why aren't they shooting?"

Haur's question was a good one. Heath had been wondering about that same thing.

Tsing!

A whiff of gunpowder stung his nose a second before more debris peppered the back of his head. "Down." Heath swept his reticle along the ridge. "They're below us." Which explained why they hadn't been shooting—they couldn't see the team flattened on the path.

With care, Heath scanned the striations on the opposing ridge.

A glint flashed at him. As bad as flashing their backside. He wanted to laugh. The sun had been in the favor of his team, glinting off the reticle of a weapon. Heath used the mental snapshot of where that glint appeared and homed in on the spot. Though he saw nothing that would mark a sniper, he fired.

"What're you shooting at?"

A shape shifted in the reticle.

"Gotcha." Heath waited and saw more forms lined up. His heart pounded. "Lower left ridge, two mil right."

As soon as the words left his mouth, a barrage of weapons fire assaulted the position.

"Ghost, move!"

Heath grabbed Trinity's lead and hauled it up the path and around the bend. Out of sight, he hoped, of the shooters. Using the bend for cover, he aimed in the direction of the ledge and provided suppressive fire as Watters and the rest hustled into the safety and protection of the bend. Once clear, Heath eased out of sight and slunk back to the team, who'd huddled.

"Keep moving, people. Don't give them an excuse to find us." Watters's direction was met with groans but also compliance. They all knew he was right. They had to keep moving, not just to avoid getting shredded by bullets but because of Jia. She was out there, somewhere. Injured, if their guess was right.

Heath drifted closer to Haur—and noticed Bai clutching his arm. "You got hit."

Bai shrugged. "A graze."

"Hold up," Heath called to the front where Watterboy and Candyman led the pack. He tugged Bai's hand away and nodded. Seared by the bullet trail, the flesh hovered red and angry around a hole. "You bit one."

Bai pried away Heath's arm. "I will survive."

"No, you need to have that looked at."

"It is nothing."

"Yeah." Watterboy motioned a sergeant toward him. "Well, my guy will make sure."

Heath tugged Haur aside, away from the captain. "Hey, Jianyu— would he be the type to seek help for his man if he got shot?"

Haur looked at Bai. "Most likely, he would shoot him and finish him off."

Yeah. Exactly. "That's what I thought."

"Why?" Watterboy's voice was close and drew Heath around.

"Jianyu's behavior indicates he has one goal in mind. We don't know what that is, but I don't think he's going to let anything get in his way, especially not a wounded soldier. It'd slow him down, cost him time and resources."

Watterboy tilted his head to the side. "So if the wounded was a soldier, he'd kill to get him out of the way."

Heath nodded. "That was my thinking."

"Or it is Jianyu," Haur said.

Heath considered Haur, the reason behind the suggestion. Was he trying to wear down their defenses, or was he legitimately trying to help them process this situation? "True, but they're moving too fast for their leader to be down."

"Agreed." Watterboy smiled at Heath.

"What?"

Head down, barely concealing a smile, Watterboy shook his head. "Nothing."

Only it wasn't nothing. It was a grin of approval. Finally! He'd done something that merited the proverbial thumbs-up from the men he once considered to be like brothers.

"Incoming from Command," Candyman shouted.

Watterboy clapped Heath on the back and stalked away. "Fire it up."

Still soaking in the pleasure of gaining Watterboy's approval, Heath stared down at Trinity. Yeah, it'd given him pleasure, but not as much as he thought it would've. Tides were shifting.

"My brother will stop at nothing once his mind is made up."

To his left and behind a bit, Haur's voice drifted around Heath in the swirling elements. Heath waited, surprised the man had opened up. But he also seemed to be telling him something, or trying to imply something. "And what is his mind made up about?"

Snow crunched as Haur came forward and his gaze slid to Heath's.

Speaking of tides, Heath felt the tidal shift of two countries. An ominous element shrouded this night.

"Ghost!"

He pried his gaze from Haur's to Watterboy.

"UAV has movement ten klicks north. Team of twelve, holing up in a village." Watters ordered the men to eat and rest up before they headed out to engage or capture their targets.

"General Zheng drove Jianyu from his arms, but my brother bore a wound more grievous. One that drove him mad, changed him."

This wasn't just information for information's sake. The man had thrown down the die. "I'll play your game," Heath said as he tugged his bite straw loose. "What was that wound?"

"A spy, one who infiltrated the highest levels of our government, dug beneath the impenetrable barriers of one of the nation's most ardent loyalists—my brother." Haur lowered his head. "General Zheng discovered the spy's activities before my brother, but he did not tell him.

223

They fed the operative false information, trapping the spy. And my brother. I think it angered the general that his own son could not see what was happening, even though all had been deceived." Haur toyed with the tattered edges of his gloves. "They disgraced Jianyu for failing to detect and stop her."

"Her?" Heath choked on a draught of water. "The spy was a woman?"

Haur gave a slow nod. "Known as Meixiang, she destroyed my brother's life."

Heath's heart chugged through the swampy story the man had just churned.

"It is ironic, is it not, that one of the two Americans missing is a woman." He dragged his attention to Heath. "And the only vengeance my brother has ever sought was to throw an American woman at the mercy of the Chinese government."

"Are you telling me you think the woman we're searching for. . ."

"I do not know who we are searching for, only that it is one American woman and one male." Haur's smile did not reach his eyes. "But the irony does not escape me."

"No kidding." Was it. . .could it be. . . ? What if Jia was this spy? Oh man, that made so much sense. Didn't it? Or did it? In a blink, everything seemed tenuous. Innocuous. Veiled.

"If my brother found this woman"—serene, thoughtful eyes drifted to the darkening horizon—"I would fear for her life."

Camp Loren, CJSOTF-A, Sub-Base
Bagram AFB, Afghanistan

"Enter."

The door creaked and musty air snuck into his office as he glanced once more at the UAV images.

"General Burnett, you have a, uh, visitor." Otte slunk into the office.

"You know I don't have time for this. Tell him to come back." Was this really a Russian tanker sitting in the middle of the Hindu Kush? What were the Chinese and Russians planning? Could he head them off in time?

"Uh, sir—"

"Are you still here?" Lance threw down a pen and groaned. "Didn't

I tell you I was too busy?"

"Yes, sir." The man shifted, nervous. "But. . .but I think you'll want to see this. . .visitor."

"And why would you think that?" Lance snatched some printed images from the shelf behind him. Compared the two. Flipped to the enhanced images. Confirmed twelve men and a woman.

"Because, sir, it's General Zheng."

His mind staggered over that name as he continued studying the images, thinking, plotting. As he did, the title of *Colonel* fell away from his expectation and skipped to what had just been said. "Wait. Did you just say *General* Zheng? As in Zheng Xin?"

Otte shifted on his long, lanky legs. "Yes, sir."

"Why on God's green earth didn't you say so in the first place?" He punched to his feet. "Where is he?"

"General Early won't let him—"

"Good for him," Lance said with a laugh. Anything to annoy the crud out of that arrogant Asian. "Keep the Chinese on their toes." He shoved around the side of his desk.

Lance stormed down the hall to the secure conference room, which—to his dismay—was right next door to the command center overseeing the mission to track down the man's son and Darci.

Voices, raised but controlled, sifted out of the room and drew Lance inside. Early sat at the head of the table, leaning forward and pointing a finger at Zheng. "I don't care what your reason is. This will not fly."

"And what would that be?" Lance asked.

Early pushed back, eyes ablaze. "You were right."

"Yeah?"

Nostrils flared, Early flung daggers at Lance. "I don't like you much right now."

"Ah." So he'd found out about Darci. Ignoring the revelation, Lance shook hands with Zheng. "General, a surprise to find you here. You Chinese are getting mighty slippery, getting past our security forces."

"General Burnett," Early said with a huff. "I think you'll find his story amusing."

Lance stayed on his feet, opting to maintain a sense of control, of which he clearly had none if two high-ranking Chinese officers could slip into this sub-base without his awareness. "That so?"

Face red, Early leaned forward. "Go ahead, Zheng. *Regale* him. Tell him the tale you told me."

Placid and unaffected by the hatred roiling off Early, Zheng took a long, measured breath. Then delivered the death knell. "My son is here on an unauthorized mission."

With a hearty laugh, Lance leaned back and shook his head. "Hate to disappoint you, General, but we already know about Colonel Wu's activities."

The face remained unmoved save a twitch of the man's right eyebrow. "I do not speak of Jianyu."

Lance frowned, his heart powering down.

"I come to you to find and stop the boy I attempted to raise as my own, the boy I tried to influence and provide with a solid, exemplary upbringing." He looked stricken. Ashamed. "It is true, as they say, 'distance tests the endurance of a horse; time reveals a man's character.'" Chest drawn up, he let out a weighted breath. "The one who must be stopped at all costs is Haur."

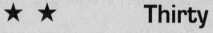

Thirty

Deep in the Hindu Kush
15 Klicks from Chinese Border

Taking risks had a certain amount of stupidity to it. Most times, a person risked that vulnerable part in the belief that things would work to the benefit. And for the most part, Peter Toque had gambled and won, came out on top, ahead of the game, ahead of the target.

Maybe his luck had run out. After all, a man could get so far on raw luck and experience, right?

He fisted his hands as the Yanjingshe, handpicked by Jianyu, huddled around the fire pit in the middle of the hut. Snow twinkled down into the fire, melting before even being kissed by a spark. Blazing, the fire roared, spreading its heat throughout the twenty-by-twenty space. An Afghan village gathering hut overtaken by Chinese warriors.

Once they'd entered the village, the men swept through, ruthlessly overpowering the villagers, who were even now holed up in their homes. Two had been shot and killed in their attempt to defend their village. A village that had put them in a daunting proximity to the Afghan-Chinese border.

In fact, Peter grew more convinced with each passing minute that his gamble on fronting Darci Kintz—a maneuver designed to ingratiate himself with Wu Jianyu and ultimately control the man—had failed. It wasn't because of bad intel that he'd misjudged this man. He'd studied the Zheng dynasty, knew of the bad blood between the young colonel and his father, knew of the former's expulsion from grace and power. A shift had occurred in Wu Jianyu, one that made predicting his actions next to impossible.

Which explained how he'd ended up here without anyone in the "spyverse" knowing. No word had filtered through the back channels about the man's location, so to find him slinking around the mountains of Afghanistan, where he just so happened to find Darci. . .

What were the odds? Had someone tipped Jianyu off that she was in the area? Or was it just dumb luck on the part of the fierce, revenge-driven soldier?

Peter's superiors had monitored Darci's movements since her narrow escape from the clutches of the Chinese. When she'd started the gig for the geology team, they knew something was going down. Forty-eight hours later, he had a new identity—Peter Toque—and an entire new history to corroborate even the most thorough of checks.

Why? Because while Darci Kintz didn't hold the record as the best operative—that title usually went to the more flamboyant, kick-butt operatives—his brief encounter with her a decade ago told him she was someone to watch. His instincts proved correct. She'd gotten into the heart of Chinese intelligence, slept with the enemy as it were, and gotten out alive—she was ahead of the game and a master at her job. He'd been told to try to pull her into working with them, doubling of sorts. But he'd told his people that the loyalty pumping through her veins was too thick to allow her to break that morality code. Peter liked her. Admired her. Held her in the highest esteem.

And you just fed the lamb to the wolf.

And the lamb's father was in danger now, too. Dumb, dumb move. He'd need to send a relay as soon as they got out of here, to alert his people to monitor Kintz's father. Even though he'd given Jianyu the wrong state, the man would no doubt feed Li Yung-fa to the beast of China—his father.

Two for one.

Peter cursed himself.

The door burst in and with it Darci Kintz. Yanked in, she tumbled and landed with a thud against the wood floor. A deathly silence dropped on the room, backlit only by the fire and its thundering cracks and pops. At least they seemed to thunder over the hollow quiet.

Nostrils flared, Jianyu sneered around the room as Lieutenant Colonel Tao eased in behind him and closed the door. If there was ever a doubt about the fear this man instilled in his men, it flickered away like a wisp of smoke.

"Secure her." Jianyu waved a hand toward Darci and smoothed back his hair with the other.

The men were swift as they hauled Darci up and held out her arms. Firelight glistened over her hip. Peter frowned. A fresh circle of blood spread out on the new shirt they'd stuffed her in. A sheen covered her face, which seemed paler than normal.

Lip curling, Jianyu turned to Peter. "You." His head bobbed. "You say you are on my side." He held out a Tokarev. Why use a Russian handgun? So he could blame his new bedmates? "Prove it. Shoot her. Get rid of this woman."

Peter might've been wrong in handing Darci to them, but he knew what road to take now. "I am not on your side. And if you'd wanted her dead, you would've done it yourself hours ago rather than have your surgeon tend her. And I see now you have injured her further."

Uncertainty trickled through the man's face, and he looked at Darci, then glowered at Peter. "You admit you are not aligned with me and expect to live?"

"I admit that I do not take sides. What has passed between you and this American woman has nothing to do with me, save that we're all breathing the same air." *Easy, now.* Jianyu had his heart planted in the middle of this fiasco. And his attachment to Darci was palpable. If he felt Peter was willing to get rid of her. . .wait. . .it was a test. "Personally, I like her. She's smart. Attractive—"

As soon as the man shifted and dropped his shoulder, Peter knew what was coming. Since he wasn't about to eat another boot, he ducked. The strike sailed just millimeters past his head. He stepped back—

Thud!

The hit from behind stung. Peter stumbled forward, pain spiraling through his neck and shoulders. Another blow sent him to his knees. Fingertips on the dirty floor, he coughed, trying to recapture the breath they'd knocked out of him.

Laughter filtered through the room. Peter didn't care—he saw Jianyu's boots moving away. And that meant for now, he was alive.

Easing back to his feet, Peter froze midmove.

Jianyu's men had anchored Darci's arms out, tethering them to the wall. She had a sweet, innocent face, one that—were her features a bit more Chinese and less European thanks to her mother—belonged on a geisha. Fair skin blotched from a blow or two but appealing against

229

her jet-black hair. Even in a dirty brown tunic, tactical pants, and hiking boots, she seemed delicate.

But he knew better. He still had an imprint, at least mentally, of her boot on his face.

Wariness crowded the soft features of her face as she wobbled but braced herself. She swallowed and looked at Peter.

No regret. No anger.

Pure determination—to survive.

"I want to know," Jianyu stood behind Darci, "who worked with you in Taipei City."

"Nobody worked with me," Darci gritted out.

Standard answer. Peter expected no less. But even that single question ramped up his pulse. Darci was in no shape to endure hours of torture. She'd hold on for a while, but if she wasn't rescued soon. . . He gave a slow, almost imperceptible nod, encouraging her to hang in there. Help was coming. At least he hoped it was.

"That is not the truth." Hands behind his back, Jianyu circled her until he severed Peter's visual connection with her. "We have surveillance of you in the Crypt. You're hidden in the shadows, but there is a man with you."

"There was no man," Darci said.

Jianyu's shoulders drew up.

"Except your Colonel Tao."

Rage flung through the colonel's face. He shifted toward her, jabbed a flat-handed thrust into her side.

"No!" Peter's shout mingled with Jianyu's.

A strangled, blood-curdling scream shot from Darci.

She dropped to her knees, limp.

Deep in the Hindu Kush
17 Klicks from Chinese Border

Hunched against the brutal, driving elements, Heath knelt and shielded Trinity from the bitter wind as the team paused to strategize. He tugged his zipper up, wishing he had a thermal suit. Anything to ward off the cold that snuck past the gaps, that whipped into his nostrils each time he breathed.

"Storm's getting bad," Watterboy shouted to the team huddled close together. "Last report said we were going to get buried. We're two klicks from the village."

"Get in there," Candyman hollered. "Get it done. Get out. Get home."

Sergeant Putman looked up from the coms box. "Lost communication."

Watterboy scowled.

"Storm's pulling major interference," Putman said.

"We're losing warmth faster than daylight." Watterboy looked at Trinity. "Ghost, how's she holding up?"

Ears perked and swiveling like equilateral radar dishes, Trinity seemed at home with the elements and the situation. "She's good." Heath coiled an arm around her and rubbed her chest, trying to infuse some warmth and reassurance—for him, not her. She wasn't easily rattled. He was another story. Especially with all that was happening. Wind, snow, stress. Thinking of Jia, wondering why Haur had picked him to buddy up to, fear of failing. . .

With his track record, he should pass out any minute now.

Please, God. Help me.

"God is our refuge and strength, an ever-present help in trouble." The first verse of Psalm 46. He knew it, quoted it. But did he believe it?

Of course, it wasn't God who'd tanked on keeping His end of the bargain. Heath had given talks about God having their backs, about not walking away from faith and belief, and hadn't Heath done that very thing?

What Heath believed in and what he did—they'd become two very different things. Saying those words, spouting scriptures was easy. Almost second nature.

A habit.

His heart dropped against that revelation and landed cockeyed in his chest.

It is not good to have zeal without knowledge, nor to be hasty and miss the way.

Heath stilled at the admonishment. Wished he'd worn his spiritual steel-toed boots for that verse. Was he being—?

Yes. No need to even finish that thought. Hasty was the precise word he'd use to describe his personal mission—or was it a vendetta?—to prove he still had what it took. With all vigor to get back in the game. To feel useful, needed, and important again.

"Hey!"

Jarred from his internal diatribe, Heath blinked through the snow and wind to Watterboy.

"Use Trin's NVG camera to lead the way."

Heath flicked up the camera, which stood perpendicular to the spine of the vest, and retrieved the monitor from his pack. He turned it on, the screen smearing an ominous green glow across the darkness. "It's up and working."

"Good, let's move. I want to get home and thaw out before this storm goes blizzard on us."

"Ain't this a little late for a winter storm?" Candyman said with a growl. "Winter is over in three weeks."

"Wasn't too long ago," Heath put in, "Afghanistan had their worst storm in fifty years. Maybe they're trying to top it again."

"Well, they can stop."

"Okay, move out, people!" Watterboy said.

Trudging forward, his gloved hand gripping the readout, Heath realigned his thoughts with the mission. But there in the chaos of his swirling thoughts and the snow, he wondered what propelled him. What drove him to risk another blackout, to risk his life—and considering these elements, Trinity—to save a woman named Jia? A military operative who had hoodwinked one of the most powerful men in China.

Okay, that was a big leap, but considering what Haur mentioned, Heath couldn't help but entertain the thought. What if she was that operative? Burnett hadn't mentioned her occupation, just that she was military intelligence and needed to be found. But military intelligence could be anything. It didn't mean she was the spy, right?

Even he knew he was reaching with that one.

"That's the only name you need to know."

The general's words whispered on the wind of doubt. It implied she had other names. Who had other names besides operatives? Fugitives. Entertainers seeking to protect their privacy. Since she wasn't in the latter group, and he couldn't think of another category, Heath was left with the option of buying into the fact that Jia was a spy.

Clandestine, then, was her middle name.

Small Village in the Hindu Kush
15 Klicks from Chinese Border

Jolts of fire thrust Darci from the greedy claws of sleep. A scream echoed in her thoughts as she came fully awake. She blinked in the semidarkness, searching for the source of the cry. But as the resonance settled, she came to the gaping conclusion that the scream had been her own.

A shape shifted nearby, drawing her focus to that spot. The blurs morphed into the form of a man. With the light behind him, he stood as a perfect silhouette. Jianyu? He seemed to have the same build, but the angle made it impossible to know for certain. What she did know for certain was the glint and clang of metal told her what was on the menu. Her brain.

So, torture.

Fear wiggled through her gut. Weakened from the broken ribs, beatings, and no food, she wasn't sure how long she'd last. Darci slumped back, fingers trailing what she lay on. A table? It wasn't metal. Wood... thick enough to hold her but not too solid she couldn't break it. If she could just move her feet—no go. Restraints pulled against her ankles.

God...I'm not even sure what to ask.... Just let me know You're here.

"Names, Meixiang," came Jianyu's voice from behind.

Eyes shuttering closed, Darci braced herself.

"I want the names of those who helped you gain access to the highest levels of security."

"I worked alone."

"No! That is impossible!" His warm breath crawled along her ear and down her neck. "What you accessed required security protocols only someone in the highest levels could provide."

"Maybe you provided it," she said, feeling out of breath. Fire again wormed through her side, the spot where the soldier had cracked more ribs. "Maybe you talk in your sleep."

A snicker made Darci still. Who else was here?

"You would like me to think that, but I do not sleep that hard."

"That's true," Darci said. "You're so haunted by your failings and insecurities you can't sleep at night."

Something touched her arm.

White-hot fury bolted through her body, thrashing her secured limbs. Darci clenched her eyes as the smell of burning flesh—her flesh—filled the frigid air. "You coward! Using electrical torture!" She arched her back as the electricity zipped through her body, using the water to conduct its fiery path.

Silence gaped as the current died, and Darci slumped back against the table. Panting and grunting against the agony, she willed herself to hold on.

Hold on for what?

A rescue? In all her years as a military intelligence officer, she hadn't been rescued. No supernatural intervention. But she'd had a lot of situations that worked in her favor that convinced her God was watching out for her. She clung to the faith her mother had died for.

But that was just it: Her mother *had* died. Believing God.

Was that Darci's lot in life, too? To die?

God, I don't want to die. She didn't feel like her life was over. That her usefulness had dried up. Maybe her desire to continue this occupation had dried up, but her will to live, her curiosity over a certain guy. . .

Trinity.

Was it a foolish hope that his dog would help him find Darci?

Right. Twenty-four thousand feet above sea level, in a snowstorm?

Might as well expect angels to float down and cut her restraints right now.

Darci held her next breath, her mind trained on the bindings on her wrists and ankles. Waiting for them to be loosed.

She wriggled her hands. They didn't budge.

Didn't think so.

"Names. I want names, Meixiang."

Humor. She had to keep her humor, keep him operating out of anger so he didn't have time to put thought into what he was doing. "Pinocchio, Cinderella, Aurora—she always was my favorite."

Volts snapped through her body. Her teeth chattered. Bit into her tongue. Sweet warmth squirted through her mouth. It lasted longer, stronger than the previous time. He was escalating. Another indication he wasn't here for the long haul. He had to get answers fast and move on.

That both pleased and worried her. Pleased that she wouldn't have prolonged torture. Worried because he could pull out some big guns of torture. And while she thought she could survive it, Darci would prefer to keep her body parts intact.

Slumped against the wood again, she tried to swallow but found her mouth parched. She stroked the salivary gland beneath her tongue, trying to wet her mouth. As she sucked in heavy breaths, she heard a creaking.

Footsteps.

Quiet.

Lifting her head, she looked around. The light still glared at her. But shadows sulked in the corners. Alone? She dropped back and let out a grunt-whimper. *Get it together, Darci. You can do this. You* have *to do this.*

Soft rustling to her right drew her head around, then a clanging. She stilled.

"Darci."

She let out the breath she'd held. "I thought he shot and killed you."

"Just my leg." He angled it toward her.

Sympathy wound. Still working her. She groaned. "What do you want, Toque?"

"Hold on, Darci. You're doing great."

Twisting her neck to see him didn't help much. She couldn't see all of him. "If I'm doing so great, why don't you switch"—pain stabbed her side, and she jerked with another grunt—"with me?"

"He's still soft on you."

"I'd hate to see your definition of hard."

"He killed the guy who hit your side. Shot him on the spot."

Darci hesitated. He'd killed one of his elite?

"And just now, you couldn't see his face, but I could. I've never seen the guy look so tortured. It was killing him."

Darci laughed at his choice of words. "I think he's killing *me*."

"Listen, I have people on the way. Just hang in there."

"Yeah?" She hissed as her still-tingling extremities ached and her head pounded. "Well, forgive me if I don't buy that."

More clanging, and this time he shifted into view. "I think we can use his sympathy for you. Milk it, get him to stop torturing you. Buy time till my people arrive."

"Your people?" She snorted as the room began to darken. She was fading. "Who? How do. . .know?"

"I have a tracking device. I activated it when the Black Hawk went down. They use it to home in on my location." His voice grew animated. "They'll be here."

"And what if I kill you?" came Jianyu's voice.

Darci snapped her eyes open and looked in the direction of the new voice.

Shadows. All she saw were shadows.

"Jianyu, no."

Bright muzzle flash blinded her.

★ ★ Thirty-One ★ ★

Deep in the Hindu Kush
15 Klicks from Chinese Border

Tucked into a tiny cleft and shielded from the raging elements, Heath tugged Trinity onto his lap to get her paws off the bitter, freezing terrain. From his pack, he tugged out the collapsible bowl, dumped a packet of food in it, and held it while she chowed down.

"We got a feed from Command," Watterboy said as he crouched beside them, munching on a protein bar. "There's a village just around the next rise. We'll reconnoiter." He jutted his jaw toward Trinity. "How's she holding up?"

Heath rubbed her head as she sat back, licking her chops. "Better than me, I think, in this freezer of a mountain."

Watterboy nodded with a smile, then clapped him on the shoulder. "She's gotten us this far. Take care of her so she can get us back."

"Hooah." Heath smiled as he buried his hands in Trinity's dense fur and, unbelievably, found warmth.

Someone landed next to him, shoulder to shoulder, leaving no room. Heath frowned, then saw who it was. Haur.

His captain stood over them, surveyed the shoulder-to-shoulder arrangement, then with a grunt he left.

Had that been done on purpose?

"A friend I knew had a dog like her," Haur said over the howling wind.

Heath grinned. "Not possible." He rubbed her ears. "With her pedigree and her training, other dogs don't compare. Besides, she's my girl." As if in answer, Trinity swiped her tongue along his cheek, then leaned against him, closed her eyes, and lowered her snout to his arm.

Power nap. *Atta, girl. Get some rest. You've earned it.*

"Do you have family?"

Heath paused before answering. Odd piece of dialogue in the middle of a mission. "Don't we all? How else would we have gotten here?" But the bitter pill of truth caught at the back of his throat. His parents had been dead for years. His only father figure lay in a soldier's home dying.

"Then you have your parents?"

"No, actually." Heath chewed over how much to divulge. "Trinity"— her ears flicked toward him despite her closed eyes—"here is my family. I have an uncle I'm close to, but he's. . .well, one war too many."

Haur gave a slow, curt nod.

Family. Why on earth had he brought up family? To point out to Heath that he'd do anything to help his brother? What about his father, the general?

Something niggled at the back of Heath's mind. Had since the guy first started talking. He looked to the Chinese man. "Can I ask you something?"

Keen, expectant eyes held fast to his. "Of course."

"I've noticed you call Wu Jianyu 'brother,' yet you have never referred to General Zheng as your 'father.'" When he didn't respond right away, Heath resisted the urge to backpedal. "Or am I wrong?"

"No." Haur's face filled with an artificial expression, one that spoke of a deep hurt yet. . .something else. Respect? Maybe, but that seemed too. . .good. "General Zheng has treated me well. I owe him great respect. He is a great man in China. To have him provide shelter for me when I was alone, when my family was not there. . .many in China say I owe him my life."

Heath cradled Trinity, but his mind was trained on his talk with Haur. "China says, but not you?"

Haur tucked his chin. "I owe him a great deal. I am very grateful."

"But not thankful?"

"China is my homeland. Of course I am thankful."

"But not to Zheng?"

Haur looked to the right, which drew Heath's attention to Bai, who sat staring into the swirling chaos. *Ah. Got it.* "It's obvious with the loyalty you show that Zheng has no reason to doubt you."

An appreciative smile was his reply.

"When one's father betrays your country, it is hard to be trusted." Emotions twisted and writhed through his words. "I have worked hard to ensure that my name and reputation smother any doubt."

"Gather up, people," Watterboy said as he circled a finger in the air.

Heath nudged Trinity up, then hoisted her onto his shoulders in a fireman's carry so she could have a little more rest.

"Okay, round that bend is a flat plain. It stretches out then drops into a valley. The village there is believed to be the site where the woman is being held."

"And my man is there, too."

"Right." Watterboy shifted to Putman, who shook his head. "We've lost coms, so we're winging this. Probably another two klicks to the supposed site of the village."

"Not supposed. It is the last known location of my agent."

"In other words, no shooting the Brit?" Candyman asked. Then shrugged when the spook glowered. "Just making sure I know my priorities."

"Our priority," Watterboy said, "is getting Jia back."

Heath nodded. About time they mentioned that.

"We want our man as well." Steady, Haur met everyone's gaze. "If at all possible, we want him taken into custody, not killed. He will be removed to China and dealt with there."

"This is getting muffed up," Candyman said. "Too many hands. . ."

Watterboy nodded. "Agreed." He towered over the others by a half foot. "Bai and Haur, we understand your concern, but our orders are STK. If we are being fired upon, we will shoot back."

"If we encounter Chinese soldiers, let me or Bai handle it. They are our people, under our command. We can convince them to listen."

Watters and Candyman shared a look that told Heath they weren't happy, but conventional wisdom said the plan made sense. That is, unless Haur and Bai weren't on the right side of convention, which was something Heath did not believe of Haur. He couldn't say the same of Bai.

Camp Loren, CJSOTF-A, Sub-Base
Bagram AFB, Afghanistan

"What do you mean we've lost communication?" Lance pulled himself from the dregs of sleep and off the mattress. Cold shot up through his stocking feet and pinged off his bones. He stuffed his feet in his boots and yanked the strings taut.

Otte, looking like a bloated sausage in his winter gear, shifted near the door. "The weather, that's what they're saying. The storm is interfering with communication."

Lance fingered his hair, glad in this angry weather that he hadn't gone bald like his father. It paid to have Cherokee blood, even on the days that made it boil. Like today. "What was the last confirmed relay?" He threw on a thick sweater, then reached for his heavy-duty jacket.

"The village location."

Shoving through the door, down the hall, and into the bitter night, Lance searched his memory banks, nodding. But against the fog of sleep deprivation—two hours on a sofa prevented minds from operating on all cylinders—he knew something wasn't right. Village. . .what else—?

He wove around vehicles cluttering the road that separated his home away from home and the command bunker. "Daggummit, where'd all these vehicles come from?"

"They pulled in the teams from FOBs Murphy and Robertson. The storm is going to bury the tactical teams."

"You don't think I know that?" Asking about all the traffic was just his way of venting his frustration. Of off-loading the foreboding that dumped on him as fast as the elements. And playing host to—

"The general." He stopped as an MRAP turned into his path to enter the motor pool, and when the driver saluted, Lance threw him one back, then moved on. "That message about Haur. Did it make it?" Inside the command bunker, he shook off the snow from his jacket and boots.

Papers rustled as Otte consulted his notes. Seconds fell off the clock. Slowly, his semibalding head swung back and forth. "No, sir."

Lance leaned into the major. "Are you going to sit there and tell me those men don't know Haur is a traitor?" His boots squeaked against the vinyl floor as he trudged through the hall so quiet they seemed partnered with death tonight.

"No, sir." Otte blinked. "I mean, yes, sir—they don't know. Or at least, it's not confirmed."

Half the lights were killed, and loneliness clung to the walls. "Where in blazes is everyone?" When he stepped into the command center and the same eerie silence met him, Lance cursed. He slowed, annoyed at the quiet that draped the room that should've been buzzing with keyboards, coms chatter, and general chaos. Instead, only two of the eight monitors were manned.

He turned to a specialist, her hair pulled back tight. "Where is everyone?"

"The storm," the nervous specialist looked up from her station. "Most of the teams have been called back, and there's little to do, so Colonel—"

His pulse pounded. "Little to do?" He thrust a finger back and to the side, in the general direction of the mountains. "We have a team of twelve men, two Chinese soldiers, a spy, and a dog handler stuck in the mountain tracking down what they believe to be a rogue Chinese colonel, and you're going to tell me there's little to do?"

"With all due respect, sir—"

"Shove your respect—"

"Sir," Otte said. "General Early ordered Colonel Hastings to shut things down, give the men downtime."

"I don't give a rip." Lance waved a hand over the room. "Wake them up. Everyone, including Early. Get everyone in here who can operate a machine. We need to find our men and stop them from getting killed."

Wide-eyed, the woman stared at him.

"Specialist, unless you want an automatic six-month extension added to your tour, get moving."

"Yes, sir." After an obligatory salute, she flew out of the chair and out the door.

"Otte." Chest puffing, Lance moved to a computer. "Find my girl." Misery groped for a foothold with him. "Bring her home. I don't want to have to tell her father China won after all."

Deep in the Hindu Kush
15 Klicks from the Afghan-China Border

Trust. A sliver-thin film that stretched over relationships like food wrap. Flimsy enough to be broken. Strong enough to protect. Twenty years he had worked to prove his trustworthiness. Twenty years he'd lived beneath the shadow of his father's actions, his father's betrayal. No one bore the brunt of that betrayal more than Haur. Left alone in a country without a mother and father. Left to face the authorities who'd beaten him unconscious several times in the first few weeks. When they finally decided the fifteen-year-old boy left behind didn't know anything, they turned their efforts toward obtaining convincing proof that his father had committed the ultimate betrayal. Soon after, he was shown pictures of burned bodies. His father and sister. Dead. Their betrayal cost them their lives.

"Where is your loyalty, Li Haur?"

Standing before the minister of defense, stripped of honor and name, he'd screamed at Zheng Xin, raged that they'd stolen his life. Demanded to see his father again. Told them he refused to believe the charges. That he wasn't going to turn on his own family. Or believe their deaths.

Not until the officers showed him a video of his father and *Mei Mei* entering a building but never leaving. . .then another image of a man and little girl in London who bore a striking resemblance. . .not till then.

He'd cried. He fought. Then pulled himself together.

The next day, he was delivered to the minister's palatial home. Shown to a bedroom on the second floor. Told to shower and clean. He was then escorted to the minister's private office. In that room in the heart of Taipei City, his life changed. General Zheng said Haur's fire was borne out of anger at being abandoned, at being left behind by his own father. The same father who had betrayed his friends, including Xin.

Haur vowed his loyalty to homeland China. To the Rising Sun. A brutal fight with Jianyu created not a lifelong enemy, but a lifelong brother. They became allies, battle hardened through life and the daunting weight of being in the public eye on a regular basis as the sons of Zheng Xin.

Even now, that film of trust had stretched taut. . .between him and America, but also—and more important—between him and his own people. It did not escape his attention how Bai monitored him, tracked his moves, never gave him more than a few minutes alone with the American elite warriors.

They know. Both the Americans and Chinese doubted his loyalty. Each for different reasons. His father's choice twenty-plus years ago cost Haur more than he could've ever imagined. *I will never escape this black mark on my life.*

"You seem friendly with the Americans."

Haur slanted a glance to Bai, who watched the men crawling up to the crest of the incline. "Keep your friends close, your enemies closer." With that, he crouch-ran forward, then dropped to his knees in the snow. He crawled up to the dog handler, Daniels.

"Down," Daniels said, then returned his attention to the night-vision binoculars he held.

Haur peered over the lip.

A village smiled up at him, its buildings sunk beneath the heavy snowfall. Roofs peeked out, but the road into the village had been beaten down by large-wheeled vehicles that grouped in the middle of the structures. The mountain resembled a cup with one side, the southernmost, missing. To the left of the team, a rocky incline swooped down toward the base of the village. Probably compliments of a landslide during rainy seasons. The rocky slope would be the best tactical entry point. Able to hide among the boulders and use the color variation to their benefit.

Since the snow had let up, the moon peeked through the clouds, bathing the pristine blanket with a blue hue. That aided him in seeing with the naked eye, but not much.

Haur glanced to Daniels with the binoculars. "May I borrow them when you are done?"

Though the man's distrust screamed, he handed them over.

The dog watched the exchange, panting, her breath puffs of blue in the predawn hours. Head down, she jerked her snout back toward the village. Keen eyes locked on the village, as if she'd seen something. She seemed to be processing the scene as much as her handler. With a small whimper, she scooted back.

"Counting at least twenty, maybe thirty, unfriendlies," came Watterboy's report.

"Roger," Candyman said from his left.

Haur saw only stubby figures, then zoomed in, almost able to see facial features. Half of the men on guard were Russians. He just cared that Jianyu was down there. With Russians. That made Haur tremble. China had long been allies with the Russians, but for them both to be here, it meant trouble. Both for China—they would have to deal with the bad publicity that would come out of attacking American forces—and for the Americans, who would have to face two enemies.

He returned the NVGs to Daniels and hesitated. "Where is your dog?"

Daniels glanced over his shoulder. "Call of nature. Don't eat the yellow snow."

Chuckles rumbled through the area, which confounded Haur. Were they not aware of what trouble they were walking into? The buildings were huddled and around them were sentries. "Impossible."

"What's that?" Daniels asked.

"There are too many. How can you get in and get this girl without being seen?"

"We'll get the girl," Candyman said. "Whether we're seen or not is another matter. Besides, haven't you heard? This is our lucky day."

"You will need more than luck." Haur knew the type of man they were facing, the ruthless determination to do what he felt was right, to bring glory to China.

"We've got that, too." Candyman held up his weapon. "M4, M16. Who can stand against us?"

"China. Jianyu. Any enemy who wants you dead."

"God's got our backs." Daniels stilled, uncertainty in his eyes. He did not believe what he'd said. Were the answers so meaningless? Did he not understand?

"That and my M4." Candyman snorted.

"Quiet!" Watterboy hissed. With quick hand signals, he sent four men scurrying to the west and another four southeast. "Putman, how's our coms?"

"Working on it."

"Get it up. We need Command."

Next to him, Daniels propped himself up on one arm and looked around. "Hey. . ." He pushed himself upright.

Haur knew what he was thinking. "Daniels, where is your dog?"

Daniels tugged a whistle out and blew on it. No sound came out.

Watterboy keyed his mic. "Heads-up. Trinity's missing."

"We've got movement in the village," Candyman said. "And the incline."

Eyes snapped to that spot, Haur itched to look through the NVGs, but Daniels had already moved out to find his dog. "It is a good spot for a sniper, yes?"

"My thoughts exactly."

"Moving kind of fast."

"Yeah. . .and agile. . ."

"Got a bead," someone else said.

"Take the sho—"

"No!" Heath shouted. "It's Trinity!"

Rifle fire cracked the darkness.

★ ★ Thirty-Two ★ ★

Small Village in the Hindu Kush
15 Klicks from Chinese Border

The report of the rifle fire echoed through the valley and bounced back to Heath, thudding against his chest. "No!" He lunged at the Green Beret who'd taken the shot. He tackled him and flipped him over, straddling the guy. "Tell me you didn't hit her! Tell me!"

"I. . .I don't know. I just saw snow dust."

Heath flung himself to the ground, grabbing for his NVGs. *Oh God. Please. . .please don't let him have hit her.* Back and forth, he scoured the pocked slope.

"Anyone got a line of sight on Trinity?"

Heath's pulse roared as the green field blurred. His hands shook with rage and panic. "I can't find her." *Lord, God. . .Lord, God. . .* He zoomed in. Rocks. Shrubs. Snow. Branches. *Lord, I know You didn't bring us out here for her to die on that hill. Please! For her, I'll beg.*

A sickening feeling dropped his heart into his stomach. The thought of her getting sniped. . .of her bleeding out. . . He was going to be sick.

A flicker of movement.

His heart vaulted back into his chest. He whipped back to the left, where the movement occurred. Rocks. Snow. Heath eased the whistle to his lips and blew. Scanned. *C'mon, c'mon.* He blew it again. Scanned.

Eerie green eyes locked on him.

"Got her!" His heart now flipped into his throat, choking him with elation as she stared in his direction, her sensitive ears picking up the high-frequency whistle. He gave her the signal to return.

"You got her?"

"Yeah." Heath mentally prodded Trinity to head back. Her beautiful head trained in his direction, then flitted around, then back to the village. He blew the return signal again.

Instead, she slunk farther down the slope.

"No," he said to her, knowing she couldn't hear that. "Crap!" He pushed to his feet. "She's broken behavior. Something's wrong." He trudged through the snow, each step dropping him knee-deep. "I'm going after her."

"Whoa, no." Watters caught his arm. "No way, Ghost."

"Back off, Watters. I know you didn't want me on this trip, and if I die going after her, you won't have to worry about us anymore." Everything in Heath pulsed with conviction. "You wouldn't leave one of your men behind, and I'm not leaving her. She's *everything* to me."

"I know, Heath." Watters touched his shoulder. "I didn't want you to come because I didn't want you getting hurt. But you're here. Now, you're part of my team. And I won't let you go into a situation that could get you killed. Let's make a plan."

Pulse lowering, Heath nodded. "You make the plan. I'll meet you down there."

"Look, if she's gone rogue—"

"No." Heath drew in a frigid, ragged breath. "Not rogue. She broke behavior. It's different."

"How?"

"Rogue means she's not responding to commands. She responded to my whistle command, but then—I didn't see it at the time, but she was trying to tell me she caught a scent. It's not normal for her to go without me, but she is trained to work off-lead. That's what she's doing—working off-lead." Realization dawned like the sun rising into its zenith. "She's only done that one other time—with Jia at Bagram. I don't know why, but she's taken a liking to this woman." *Just like me.* "I have to believe she must've seen her or can detect her scent."

"That's a stretch, don't you think?"

They'd worked together enough for Heath to know Watters's words held hope, that he wanted to believe what Heath was saying. "Not as big as you might think." Heath grinned. "I'm going down. Cover me, okay? Then bring in the cavalry."

"Candyman, Java, Scrip, Pops—take the spook," Watters said, never taking his gaze off Heath. "Go with Ghost. Keep coms open. Rocket and everyone else, you're with me. We'll flank the south."

"Hooah," Candyman said.

"Remember, orders are STK." Never doubt that Watters was a soldier. "Let's find the girl and bring her back."

"Lock and load." Candyman's grin never faded.

Heath nodded to the team leader. "Thank you."

"You're wasting air," Watterboy said with a grin.

Heath jogged, as much as the deep snow would allow, toward the place he'd seen Trinity scaling the jagged terrain. Alive with the mission of finding and securing his girl, he struggled against the elements that impeded speed. An impression in the snow snagged his attention.

"That her trail?" Candyman voiced Heath's thoughts.

"That's her." Heath used her already-carved path down the slope. Sneak of a dog had plowed through this with such speed he hadn't even seen her doing it. Nobody had. And here, he felt like he was trying to wade through a tub of sour cream. Or quick-drying cement. Frigid wetness chomped into his legs, his pants wet and sticking to him. But he plowed on, determined to find Trinity.

And Jia.

He prayed that what had lured Trinity into breaking behavior and going into the village alone was the woman. The two had taken to each other as if they'd met before. Which was ludicrous. Their first encounter had been at the base. He was good with faces. Rarely did he forget one.

As the snow crowded around the first line of defense the rocks formed, Heath slowed. Searched for Trinity's trail.

"It's like she disappeared," Candyman said.

"Or jumped." Heath's gaze hit on a spot to the right. Paw prints on a rock. Then another trail to the left where the snow wasn't as deep.

"It's like she knew it wasn't as deep."

"She did. She's a dog—she can smell the earth beneath the snow easier." Fueled by finding her trail again, Heath maneuvered his way. Behind him, the rest of the team did the same.

"Down, down!" Candyman hissed into the predawn morning. "Movement, ten o'clock."

Heath's gaze went left. Sure enough, a sentry stalked toward a tree, vanished behind it. What would a sentry be doing way out here? A few seconds later, the man reemerged, then slogged back to camp, whistling.

"Clear," Candyman whispered.

Heath used Trinity's tracks through the foot-deep snow to hide his own steps as much as possible, leading the men in the same path to hide their numbers. Moving on, Heath hopped down a two-foot drop. This was where Trinity hesitated, then ignored his whistle call. He searched for signs of blood. Had the shooter hit her?

"No blood," he muttered as he looked around.

"Then I guess that means you're not going to kill Scrip." Candyman grinned to the man behind him.

"I'm sorry, man. I thought it was a sentry or a wild cat."

"As long as she's not hurt, I'll let you live," Heath teased.

"Then let's make sure that's the case."

"Supreme excellence consists in breaking the enemy's resistance without fighting."

Jianyu took in a long, slow breath of the incense on the table before him. He pushed aside the bitter cold. Folded away the anger. Ignored the doubts. He must find a center, find a way to reach that nirvana and quiet he'd once known.

With Meixiang.

The first time he'd ever thought life had smiled on him.

The first time he'd ever be made a fool of. And the last. He would make sure. A kiss shared equaled a life of honor stolen. Love—

With a growl, he leapt to his feet, shoulder-width apart, hands at the side.

Roiling fury stirred the air around him.

No. He must calm himself. Draw strength from sage wisdom.

Curse the wisdom. She was here! In that hut. Alive, beautiful, and traitorous. She would not divulge which of his men had fed her the information. She could not have accessed their secret military files without that information. Though she'd tried to twist his suspicions back to himself, Jianyu knew better. He only had a part of the codes. No one soldier held them all. The safety protocols were immense. She had to have worked with someone with great power. Or with more than one source.

Jianyu stuffed the incense in the snow, snuffing it out.

He would find out. He would make her spill all of her secrets before he spilled her guts all over that table. It was a waste, of course. A beautiful woman like that.

How had he failed? Should his passions and views not have swayed her?

She had spoken with conviction of her belief in the same values and systems. Were they all lies?

Perhaps he could play on her sympathies. She cared for him—loved him. He saw it in her eyes. He would use that and drag the truth out of her. Then give her one last chance to walk away from the disgraced life of a spy. He would speak to his father, grant a dispensation so she could live.

But would she betray him again? Would his father believe her? Would *he* believe her?

No, he must never give her the chance to make a mockery of him again.

She had stolen honor from him once. Now he would rip it from her, just like the breath from her lungs. He spun and stalked out of the hut.

A guard snapped to attention as Jianyu stepped into the morning and headed to the hut where they'd held Meixiang. Or Darci. That was the name the British spy had given. Once they got out of this valley and could reestablish communication, he'd contact his father. Give him the name and location. Let them ferret out that filthy pig of a man Li Yung-fa.

Dr. Cho looked up from his work as Jianyu entered. He smirked. "Your meditation did not work again?"

"You should worry about your patient and my patience."

The doctor laughed. "She needs a hospital. The ribs are broken. Moving her, torturing her, will risk puncturing her lungs."

Jianyu stood over her, gazed down at her face. So pretty. Fair skin against her black hair. Just like most Chinese women. But there was something. . .serene, peaceful about Meixiang that had always drawn him. "She only needs to live long enough to give back what she stole."

Cho tossed down a bloodied wad of gauze. "That I cannot guarantee, especially if you continue to brutalize her body."

Fire whipped through him. "Do not tell me how to conduct an interrogation."

Cho's eyes crinkled as a placating smile creased his lips. "Would not think of it. You merely said you wanted her to live long enough to tell you what you want to know. I offered my medical opinion."

"Are you done?" Jianyu snapped, his breath heaving.

Cho drew up straight. "There is no sense in my doctoring her if you are going to undo it." He plucked off the bloodied plastic gloves and slammed them in the trash.

"Then there is no need for you here." Jianyu planted his hands on the table, just millimeters from her long, black hair. Between his thumb and pointer fingers, he rubbed the silky strands. Things could have been so different.

Why? Why did she have to—?

It did not matter. He shoved himself upright. He would not mope over this woman, no matter how much of his heart she'd trampled.

Jianyu slapped her face. Hot, clammy. Feverish.

Her eyes fluttered, and she moaned but slipped back out of the present.

Again, he slapped her.

This time, her eyes snapped open. Met his—and he saw the fear roiling off those irises that used to sparkle for him.

"Names, Meixiang. Who did you work with? How did you get so far?"

She groaned and rolled her gaze from his.

Gripping her face, he squeezed hard, forcing her to look at him. "Answer me! Who did you pay off? Who did you buy?"

"I told you," she said between his tight hold. "No...body."

"I do not believe you."

A breathy laugh rose and fell on her lips. "The one time you should..."

He pounded the table and smacked her—hard. "I do not care if you die. You will tell me what you know." He grabbed an instrument from the table.

Her head lobbed side to side as she struggled.

He pressed the scalpel against her throat. "Tell me! Names! Who—was it Ming? Gualing?"

"No," she ground out. A drop of blood slid over the blade, a tear down her cheek. "It was you."

"That is not possible. I never gave you access to that."

"Little by little," Meixiang said. "A piece here, a pie—" She yelped, her eyes wide.

Jianyu realized he'd pushed the knife deeper into her throat.

Blood trailed down her neck faster this time. He could not kill her. Not only because he must bring her to his father.

"I'm sorry," she said, her Adam's apple bobbing as she swallowed. More tears. "I did not mean to hurt you. I. . ."

"Hurt me?" He leaned into her face. "You did not hurt me. You *destroyed* me!"

She shook her head. "No, it wasn't me. They knew. They knew and they used you."

"Lies!" His voice bounced back at him. "You lie."

Pinching up her face, she shook her head, tears and blood mingling in the hollow of her throat. "No. No, I'm not. Your father found out." She drew in a breath, wrought with pain, then slowly exhaled. "He thought you were complicit. It's why I left so fast. If I stayed, they would've blamed you."

Jianyu stumbled back. It wasn't true. Couldn't be. His father said he never doubted his loyalty. "My father trusted me, unlike you."

She met his gaze. "You know better than that. He trusts no one. He's paranoid. He's delusional."

His fist flew before he could stop it.

She lay on the table, nose oozing blood and drainage. Mouth agape.

His breaths came in ragged, difficult gulps.

"Sir."

He spun to the door, stunned to find Tao there. "What?" Jianyu snarled.

"The Russians are here. They're ready to talk about payments."

He turned back to the table, to Meixiang. He smoothed her hair from her face. Lifted gauze from the table and wiped the blood from her face. "Have our men been successful?"

"Yes, sir. They are on the bases."

Had his father doubted Jianyu, even then? "What of the devices?"

"The bombs are ready for your activation codes."

★ ★ Thirty-Three ★ ★

Eyes trained on the nearest hut, Heath waited. Adrenaline wound through his veins, knowing that despite being declared unfit for duty, he was here. In the middle of it.

"Clear." Candyman's word came with a thud against his shoulder.

Heath bolted forward, sprinting across the twenty feet that separated the lip of the bowl-like valley and the hut. Daylight lay in wait, ready to expose them to the soldiers huddled out in the cold and elements.

Pressing himself into the shadows, Heath used his M4 to scope the area. Nothing moved, so he searched for Trinity's tracks. Trailing along the building, they banked right. Out of sight. The swift rustle behind him told Heath the team had moved in.

A soft clap to his shoulder gave him the clear to advance. He hustled forward, weapon up, ears probing for sound, mind pinging with possibilities, expecting every turn to throw trouble into his path. Right shoulder to the wood wall, he tugged the whistle from his pocket and gave the signal again.

He returned it to his pocket and shuffled forward. Candyman slipped in front of him, took a knee as point, and eased into the open to clear the area.

When silence reigned, Heath pied out, stepping into the open. He advanced quickly, sweeping, watching, listening. His head pounded with the rush of adrenaline and the fear that any step could be his last. The fire at the base of his neck warned him of a pending blackout.

Heath shook it off and sidled up to the next building, easing farther

251

into the den of thieves. Candyman was hot on his tail. Shaking off the anticipation spiraling through him, Heath eased forward.

Two claps on his shoulder jerked him back, heart pounding. Spots bled into his vision.

Crap, no. Not now. He couldn't do that now.

"Hold," Candyman whispered.

Over his shoulder, Heath said, "What?"

"Spook is going ape-crazy."

Heath glanced back and sighed as the spook slipped into a hut. "What—he's going to get us killed."

"Keep moving, Alpha team. Spook's not our problem," came Watters's command through the mic.

Pulling in a breath and blowing it through puffed cheeks, Heath braced himself. Squared his mind with the fact that God must want him here. So, if the Almighty wanted him here, then He had his back. Right? All that stuff he'd spouted sounded good in theory. Out here, in the field, with trigger-happy Chinese and Russians breathing down his neck, it was another thing.

No, it's not. It's theory put to practice. Faith in action.

Hooah.

He stepped out.

A shadow coalesced into a man.

Heath froze. In the two seconds it took to register that the enemy stood before him, Heath saw the muzzle slide up in front of a hardened Chinese face.

Oomph!

The man tumbled forward. Slumped into Heath.

Heath caught the man, stupefied.

"Tango down."

With Candyman's help, Heath dragged the body into the shadows. When he shifted, he saw the blood stains in the pristine white. Toeing the snow, he piled it up over the spots. Recovered, they took a second to reassess their position.

As they did, noise from behind drew them around, weapons up. Prepared to fight.

The spook emerged, a body draped over his shoulders. He swung toward Heath and the others, gave a thumbs-up, and headed back toward the rocky incline but stumbled. Clear indication they were in the right place if the spook found his guy. Thumbs-up meant the guy was alive still, right?

Candyman signaled Scrip to aid the guy, then shrugged at Heath and nodded for him to keep moving.

Right.

Trinity.

Jia.

Heath eased through the narrow space between two huts, where the snow wasn't as deep as the shadows. Grateful for the cover, he took a corner, and through a sliver of huts, he saw— No, that couldn't be right. Haur wasn't here. He was with Watterboy on the south side, wasn't he?

Heath cleared the right, Candyman the left, then they both stepped into the open, sweeping the path that led down then vanished around another hut. How many huts were there? This place didn't seem this dense from the mountain.

"Ghost," a voice skated through the coms. "Line of sight on Trinity. North and east of you. Moving pretty quick."

Heath keyed his mic. "Copy." He rushed forward, in between more huts, cringing as his boots crunched on the snow-and-ice-laden path.

"East," the voice instructed.

Heath went right.

"Ahead—wait, she ducked between the last two huts. She's heading into the heart of the village. Eyes out."

Warmth spilled down Heath's neck and shoulders as he plowed onward. Why did she have to be so mission focused? Get the job done. She was a better soldier than many men he knew. Including him. His vision jiggled, slowing him.

Oh no.

Okay. Faith. Focus on faith.

Lord—my faith in action is believing that I won't pass out doing this.

Things were going in their favor—snow had stopped, wind had gone down a notch, they hadn't encountered but one Chinese soldier— so he didn't need to mess it up by passing out. Or put the men in danger. But even the thought of doing that stressed him. Made things worse.

He stumbled over his own feet.

A hand on his shoulder told Heath they had his back.

He drew himself up straight and pushed on.

Barking clapped through the morning.

Followed by gunfire.

"Crap!" sailed through the coms. "Ghost—they got her."

The words threw Heath forward.

"No, back, back!"

Heath pushed on. Wasn't going to leave his girl to die. Wasn't going to abandon her in the midst of chaos.

"Heath, stop. Listen."

"Not leaving her." He hustled, M4 cradled in his arms. Keyed his mic. "Where is she? Tell me!"

"A yard north, beside a truck."

Already in motion, he barreled forward before he heard the rest of the dialogue.

"But there's a mess-load of Russians there." The voice sounded strained. "Heath, she's down. She's not moving. Get out of there. It's not worth it."

"Bull! She's my partner," he growled as he jogged in the right direction. Each footfall sounded as a cannon blast. *Thud! Thud!* Surely, they'd find him. He didn't care as he launched over a pile of wood, his focus locked on Trinity, finding the girl who'd done everything to protect him. Now it was his job to protect her.

As the narrow passage opened up, ahead he could see trucks. Men. Heard laughter. On a knee, he lifted his rifle to his shoulder and peered down the barrel.

C'mon, c'mon. Where is she?

A soft thud to his six alerted him to Candyman's presence. "Anything?" he whispered into the wind.

Heath ignored the question, ignored the thunder in his chest and the whooshing in his vision. He shook his head, trying to dislodge the dizziness. Vision ghosting. . .gray. . . *No!* Not with Trinity down. Gray. . . dark gray. . .

"Help," Heath muttered as the world winked out.

Haze and fuzziness coated his synapses. Weighted, he pulled himself up.

"Ghost, it's okay. We got you." Candyman patted his arm. "And guess what?"

Heath shook his head and straightened.

Candyman handed him a pair of binoculars. "Take a look. At the truck."

Pinching the bridge of his nose, Heath brought the binoculars up. He peered through the lens. . . *Trinity*.

The snow around her a blood bath, Trinity lay on the ground.

"Oh—"Wait! He scanned the body. Wrong size. Wrong color.

"It's not her," Candyman said, his words thick with relief.

"Yeah." The fist-hold on his lungs lessened. "It's a black shepherd." He slumped back and handed off the binoculars, shaking from the adrenaline dump. Then a hefty dose of determination surged through his veins, dispelling the chill the adrenaline left. "Let's find my girl."

Candyman grinned. "Which one?"

Heat swarmed Heath. "Not funny."

"Wasn't meant to be."

A feeling of falling snapped Darci's eyes opened. The room writhed. Ghoulish shapes danced before her. She squinted trying to. . . *Oh, a fire.* That's why the room shimmied and swooned.

She pushed back and tried to lie down again, but her head thumped against something. Only as the haze of sleep faded did Darci realize she was now propped against the center support, hands and ankles tied. Her head drooped as the room spun once more.

Pain seemed to ooze from every pore. Legs, arms, side—broken ribs. Every breath felt like inhaling fire.

"*. . .awaiting your activation codes.*"

The words brought Darci up short. Had she imagined them? She had no idea how long she'd been here or in this—she looked around assessing her surroundings—wherever it was. The village. That's right. They'd brought her to the village. Jianyu tried torturing her. Though he'd ordered the session and oversaw it, he found no pleasure in it. She'd been at the hands of sadistic men, those who enjoyed watching others suffer, and she'd expected to see those feelings roiling through Jianyu after all she'd done to him.

Instead, she saw her own pain mirrored in his expression.

But not enough to move him to stop the electroshock session. Her fingers throbbed, and she strained to see them. Confusion wove through her as she saw the blooded tips. Her stomach churned. Bloodied fingernails. . .wait, no. The nails were gone. They'd pulled out her fingernails? When had *that* happened? She had no recollection. . .

Nausea swirled and spun with the dizziness.

Stay awake. She'd missed too much already. What if they drugged her and pried the truth from her? Truth serums were more James Bond make-believe. They didn't actually make someone spill her guts, but they did make one very prone to suggestion.

Is that why her head was spinning? Why she couldn't see straight to save her life? Is that why the room darkened. . .even now?

Heat bathed her, cocooned her, tempted her to rest in its arms. But. . . something. . .the heat. . .not right.

Crack!

Darci snapped awake.

What. . .what woke her? How long had she been out this time? Was it hours? Minutes? Seconds? Heart chugging, she shivered beneath the tease of a draft that slithered in through the wood slats twined together.

She couldn't stay awake long enough to break out of her bindings— if she even had the strength to free herself. Rescues didn't happen, not in the middle of the mountains, fifteen klicks or so from the Chinese border.

Horror swooped in and clutched the last of her courage, taking it away on a gust of icy wind. What if Jianyu was planning to take her back to Taipei City?

A round of cheers shot through the atmosphere, chilling and haunting. Darci wondered who'd been killed. It sounded like *that* kind of exultant cheer.

She pulled at the restraints. Her shoulders sagged in exhaustion. *Oh, God, I am in trouble.* Worse than ever before. The realization proved heady, suffocating. She struggled for a normal breath, not one strangled with panic. *I won't make it without Your help.*

But God didn't help her mom. She'd died clinging to her convictions. Her faith.

The missionary who delivered the message had said her mom had been unrepentant about her faith to the authorities. She preached to them. *Like Nora Lam.*

A shudder rippled through Darci. At a youth camp, she'd seen the movie of Nora's firing squad testimony. And Darci had bolted out of the building, sobbing, remembering her mother. It'd been way too close to home. She struggled with anger—why hadn't God given her mother that sort of miracle? And if He wouldn't give her mother, who'd died for Him, why would He work a miracle for her?

A whimper squirmed past her hold. "Please. . .God. . . she believed in You. . ."

Defeat shoved her courage back from where it'd come. She couldn't survive on her mother's faith. Isn't that what she'd been doing all these years? Being a good girl, attending church, reading her Bible—when missions afforded her that luxury—but. . .faith. What was it? *The substance of things hoped for, the evidence of things not seen.*

Well, she sure couldn't see her way out of this mess.

But did she believe God would get her out?

Exhaustion tugged at her, encouraging her to fall back into its sleepy embrace. So tired. So much pain. . .so sleeeeppy. . .

No!

No more sleep. She had to stay awake. Stay alert. Darci pushed herself up against the wood. Propped her head back. The fire drew her attention. A story. . .there was a story. . .three men. . .Shad', 'Shach, and 'Nego. They'd told the king that even if God didn't rescue them, they wouldn't bend their knees.

Resolve festooned itself around Darci's wounds, inside and out. That's right. *God, You can. Even if You don't, I believe in You.*

The door flapped open. A cold wind snapped into the hut.

Darci hauled in a breath as a dark shape swam toward her. She moaned a single prayer—*God help me*—knowing she was powerless to stop the darkness drenching her mind and body.

Cold pressed in around her, nudging her from the iron-clad grip of sleep. Oh, everything hurt. Hurt so very bad. Each minute, each breath dragging her closer to death's permanent hold.

Again, cold pressed against her.

Moaning reached her drifting consciousness. *That's me.* Though she tried to sit up, a nagging at the back of her mind lured her to the surface of reality. She groaned.

Cold, wet lapped at her hands.

Darci yelped. What was that?

Beside her, the shadow that had chased her into oblivion the last time shifted side to side. She sucked in a breath and pulled away. Wait— what was. . . ?

Tall, triangular-shaped ears lifted into her view and slowly revealed the glow of two yellow eyes. Holding that breath, Darci felt a swirl of warmth coil around her. What. . .what was it? Uncertainty held her fast.

The shape shifted up onto its haunches.

A tongue swiped over her face.

Trinity.

No. Not Trinity. No way she could be here. Just a stray dog. How did a dog get in here?

Darci blinked as the fire flickered and shadows danced over the fur, which in some places sat in wet clusters. "Trinity?"

A slight whimper as the dog scooted forward. Another kiss on her cheek.

"Trinity." Repeating the dog's name firmed in her addled brain that she was really here. Darci's gaze shot to the wood door. A rescue? Could it be? If Trinity had come, then. . ."Heath."

A louder whimper preceded Trinity in lowering herself and ducking out of sight behind Darci. Wet tongue, cold nose. Against Darci's hands.

She tried to glance over her shoulder to see. Gentle but firm pressure, almost a nuzzling type of motion against the sensitive part of her wrist. The ropes binding her wrists slackened. Hauling in a breath, Darci wriggled her arms. Even as she fought free, she wondered how she'd get out of here. Weakness weighted her like a boulder to the earth. Walking drugged. . .that would be interesting. But she'd do it, because with Trinity here, Heath must be, too. And that meant Darci was getting out of here. Even if it killed her.

A thought stilled her. *She never does that.* Heath had said Trinity never broke from him. And if he wasn't here. . .was he in trouble, too? Had Jianyu or the Russians found him?

Was he alone? Were there other American soldiers here to help?

Trinity leapt up. Her ears rotated like satellite dishes as she threw a glance over her shoulder, to the right. To the door. A broad chest and long legs hinted at the speed and power of this dog.

Darci couldn't help but lean into the godsend. "You found me," she said, her thoughts jumbled and chaotic, tossed around with relief and fear and a thrill. Tears slipped down her cheeks, renewing her hope that she might survive and encouraging her to tug against the ropes. Her wrists burned, but there was enough give that kept her fighting. *You gave up too fast.*

No, you believed just in time.

Trinity's bark shot into the lightening day like the report of a rifle.

"No," she bit out.

Great. Trinity had no doubt alerted every guard and person within a fifty-foot radius. Darci yanked hard—her right arm pulled free. Shoulders aching from the awkward restraint, Darci dragged her arms around to the front. Ugh. She might as well have telephone poles for arms they were so heavy. So sore. Trekking her fingers along the ground, she slumped to the side against Trinity and dug her fingers into the ropes around her feet.

Shouts outside pushed her gaze to the door.

Footsteps rushed toward them.

"Down," Darci ordered Trinity, praying the dog wouldn't be noticed at first, if at all.

The door flung inward.

★ ★ Thirty-Four ★ ★

With a wintry blast, Major Wang lurched into the hut.

Darci yanked her arms behind her back and faked being tied up as he loomed closer. The war dance of flames against his face painted him with a wicked malice that sent alarm spiraling through her veins.

"Stay." Maybe Wang thought she was making an innocuous comment about him.

"Ha!" he said, gloating. "You did not think you would escape?" He produced another needle. "More juice?"

When he knelt at her side and reached for her right arm, Darci rolled, her mind darting over the vibration in the ground—*what is that from?*—and the breathy grunt of Wang coming again.

She flipped over. Out of reach. A scream climbed up her throat. Outmatched.

Air and dirt shifted to her right. In the space of a blink, Trinity flew over her shoulder and nailed Wang in the chest.

He stumbled backward and dropped. Tripped by his own feet.

Trinity caught his arm, growling through clenched teeth.

Darci thrashed against the ropes on her feet, locked on the duel between the beast and the dog. Wang struck Trinity, but she held.

Fumbling, twisting, Darci was unable to loosen the ropes. She searched for a weapon while she dug her fingers in the hemp. Only the logs, half consumed in flames, would work.

She tossed herself in that direction. *Thud.* Her chest slammed into the dirt, spitting the breath from her lungs. She squeezed off the pain that exploded in her abdomen and strained for the log. Dragged it free.

Sparks hissed and popped in protest of being yanked from the fire.

Holding the center tent support, Darci dragged herself upright as Trinity and Wang went at it. The dog proved unyielding, even when Wang rammed the butt of his weapon at her. She yelped but maintained her lock.

Anger tightened Darci's chest. "Hey!" With everything in her, she swung the four-inch-thick log at Wang. It connected with a resounding crack. He staggered, then went down.

Darci thumped him on the back of the head again, hard enough to make sure he was out, but not enough to kill him, even though he'd wanted her dead. He'd helped Jianyu and took pleasure in her torture.

The log began to slide in her hands, the warmed bark raking the pads of her fingers. Darci slumped to the ground on one knee, breath shallow. Trinity nosed her cheek, and she leaned into the dog's warmth. Buried her face in Trinity's neck where dense fur met the stiff nylon vest. Darci's eyes traced the high-tech outfit. She didn't have this on at the base. Where had it come from? She wasn't a certified MWD anymore. And this was a pricey vest. Had someone recruited or borrowed Trinity?

Using the log to hold her up, Darci planted a kiss on Trinity's neck. "Thanks, girl." She rubbed Trinity's ear with the back of her hand. "Couldn't have made it without you."

Her amber gaze flicked to Darci as if to say, "Yeah, I get that a lot." She panted.

"I bet you do," Darci muttered.

"But you should see my handler."

"Oh, I have. He's almost as good-looking as you." Darci smirked at herself. Half dead and having an imaginary conversation with a war dog could get her wrung up for a psych eval.

Time to find out what's going on.

Darci struggled to her feet, the log slipping in her bloodied hands. It was too heavy to carry, and Wang had just donated a fully automatic to her once-empty arsenal. *Ditch the log, try the gun.* It seemed logical. But could she even hold the AK-47?

She bent to release the log.

Movement rustled outside, stilling her.

Adrenaline sped through her veins and tightened her grip on the log. She shot a glance to Trinity, who stood with her ears trained on the door. Ready to attack. Ready to defend. . .*me.* The thought proved a heady tonic to her wounded soul.

Darci took a step back. What would Jianyu do to her if he found her free with his officer out cold? *Nothing good, that's for sure.* Wobbling on her feet, Darci held the log with both hands. Prepped herself. She was not going down. She would not die at the hands of Jianyu or any enemy. Trinity had come for her, and that meant Heath had, too. Staying alive was the best way to thank him for coming after her, putting his life— and partner, Trinity's—at risk.

Again, she looked to Trinity, who spared her a glance, then everything in the beautiful creature realigned on the door.

Darci braced herself.

With another blast of the winter storm, the door swung inward. Light blinded her but not enough to blot out the silhouette of a man with a fully automatic weapon. Sweat dripped into Darci's right eye as she brought the log to bear with a loud grunt.

"Hey!"

Ignoring the spike of pain in her side, Darci raised it over her head.

"Jia, stop!" The silhouette shifted to the left.

Darci's mind tripped on her name as she lost her balance. *Heath?*

Heath braced for impact as the thick weapon in her hand registered. The log wobbled in the air over her head, then toppled from her grasp. Eyes hooded with exhaustion and pain, Jia heaved forward—straight at him.

Heath stepped forward and hooked an arm around her shoulders as she tumbled into his chest. In a dead faint, she was heavy yet. . .light. There wasn't much in terms of weight to this enigmatic woman.

As he lowered Jia to the ground, Trinity trotted to his side and relief swept him. "Hey, girl." He petted her as he keyed his mic. "Primary objective located."

"Retrieve and return," came Watterboy's quick response.

Gaze tracking over the unconscious operative, Heath nodded. Right. Sure. How was he supposed to get her back up the side of the mountain he'd just scaled down when she was unconscious?

"Jia?"

Trinity nudged him, then sniffed his face—then sneezed.

He chuckled. "Good to see you, too." She always hated the smell of tactical paint. He leaned his head toward her, but he scanned Jia for injuries, his heart regaining a normal pattern after thinking Trinity had bit a bullet. "Don't scare me like that again." That fried his brain like nothing else. He couldn't stand the thought of losing her.

Trinity lowered her snout to Jia's cheek.

"Jia, hey. You there?" Man, seeing her like this, pale and unconscious, hurt as much as thinking Trinity had bit one, and that was plain weird. How could he feel that way about a woman he'd met a week ago? Wasn't something he could articulate to himself, let alone anyone else. Whatever it was that had snagged his attention, she had it. And she couldn't die on him. He wouldn't let her.

Heath visually traced the lines of her face. A fat shiner puffed her left eye and blood dribbled down her temple. Dried and cracked, her lips proved her dehydration and the split on the left side matched the one on her temple. Whoever had assaulted her must have been right-handed. He searched for injuries or wounds that would incapacitate her. No head knots or gaping wounds there. He tried to sort out why it was so important to him that she survive. Dark hair spilled toward the dwindling fire, its shadows stroking her black strands.

How could a woman look beautiful even when battered and unconscious?

Because she's a fighter. She doesn't take bull.

"Jia," Heath whispered her name as he smoothed his hands down her shoulders, strong biceps, and forearms, and his mind flipped back to the night at the base MWD training field when she'd thrown Trin's ball with a perfect arc. Athletic, intelligent, but those things seemed so minor. The lunch date when he'd held her close, feeling her unsteady breathing, he wanted to seal their attraction with a kiss.

Stow it, Ghost. He shoved his jagged thoughts aside.

"Ghost, report. What's the holdup?"

"Jia, c'mon." He noted movement behind her eyelids as his hands ran across the stiff binding around her waist. Had she been shot? Cut? What was this?

He hit his mic again. "Target is injured and unconscious." He traced a gloved finger along the red welts on her wrists. Not exactly gentle on her, were they?

"Roger. Candyman—get in there. Grab the package and go," Watterboy ordered.

Crossing her arms over her chest to lift her—

Her fist shot up. No time to deflect it. She nailed his jaw.

Heath tumbled backward. As he did, a swirl of cold air rushed him, snapping his attention to the open door. He sucked in a breath as a form filled it, and he pushed himself upright again.

Candyman stepped inside and pulled the door to, holding the catch with one hand and gripping his weapon with the other. "Inside."

A scream rent the air. Another fist.

Heath hauled himself forward and landed hard on his knees as he gripped her arms. "Jia!" Holding her arms was like wrestling an octopus. She writhed, broke free, but he caught her again. "Jia—it's me, Heath, Ghost!" Like she would remember him, coming up out of it. "American. We're American."

She struggled, then went still. Wild eyes locked on him. A whimper. "Heath?" Her taut limbs went limp, her brow smoothing as the fight drained from her expression.

"Yeah." Dawg, that felt good to hear the way she said his name. "Let's get you out of here." He tried crossing her arms again, then bent to scoop her into his arms. As he pushed to his feet, she hooked an arm around his neck and burrowed into his vest with a shudder.

Something strong and powerful tugged at his heart with that simple gesture. A shudder. . .it wasn't like she'd vowed her undying love. Although he'd take that, too. But the shudder told him she trusted him, she felt safe with him.

"Hey, RockGirl, you okay?" Why did he feel shy all of a sudden? No, he'd never been shy. Confident, arrogant—yeah. But shy? He peered down at her, and though she didn't look up at him, she nodded.

"Yeah. . ." Her grip around his neck tightened as she pulled deeper into his hold. "Now."

Hesitation strangled him and held fast. His lightning-fast mind attached a bevy of meaning to that simple statement. Expectation like he'd never experienced before hung in her words. *Oh, Lord, help. . .*

"You're going to be fine. I've got you." Heath firmed his hold, careful of the delicate package in his arms, mindful of the yanking of his heartstrings. Aware he was willing to move heaven and earth to get Jia home safe and alive!

Against his right hand, he felt the vibration of sound through her back and glanced down at her again. Her lips were moving, slowly.

"up. . .ted. . .grace. . .enfolded. . .peace of His embrace."

Ice and fire competed for dominance in his stomach. No, he couldn't have heard that right. But her whispered words unleashed an angel from his past. An angel everyone said didn't exist, that he'd been dreaming. An angel who voiced a prayer that clung to his soul while he lay in a coma at Landstuhl, hovering on the brink of death.

That angel. . .did she lay in his arms now? He watched her lips moving, stunned. *"Finally, I pray you'd be uplifted by His grace, and feel yourself enfolded in the peace of His embrace."*

"Ghost."

Heath jerked to the entry point.

Candyman shot a look over his shoulder. "Ready?"

Mind singed with the memory, Heath braced her against his uplifted right leg to get a better hold, then nodded. "Go."

"Right, left, left." After the instructions, Candyman peered out the door. Nodded. "Move!"

The door swung open, and Heath rushed into the morning. The steady cadence of his boots crushing the snow beat in rhythm with Candyman's and the soft padding of Trinity at his side. They made the first right without a hitch.

Sidling up against the hut, they came to a juncture. As Candyman took point, his weapon stabbing into the open, Heath again hoisted Jia up farther. In view, Candyman gave a sharp nod.

Heath hustled into the path between the huts and rushed forward, trusting Candyman who moved two paces ahead to guide him to safety. Trinity trotted in between them. This didn't seem right. Hadn't they come—?

"Back!" Candyman snapped and threw himself at Heath.

Feet tangling with Candyman's, Heath tripped. Instinct tightened his grip on Jia, but he went down on a knee. Crushing her to himself, Heath prayed he didn't drop her.

"Augh!" She arched her back and pulled away.

Heath tugged her closer as he caught his balance. "Sorry."

"Quiet," Candyman hissed. "Base, we need an out."

Leaning against the mud-and-thatch hut, Heath ignored the burn in his arms and legs. Didn't know what he was thinking trying to carry her like this. Fireman carry—only way to make this journey. He shifted. "Jia." She groaned and lifted her head. "Gotta change carry."

Her head bobbed in understanding.

Heath set her down, then hesitated, thinking about the injury in her side before he shifted to the other side, hooked an arm under her leg, tucked his head, and let her slump over his shoulder. A steeled grunt pushed warm air along his neck and cheek as he supported her across his shoulders. Heath had a perfect line of sight through the huts. All the way to the main hub. Two men emerged from a hut. One older and vaguely familiar. The other Zheng Jianyu.

Heath pushed up and backed into the shadows, praying like he'd never prayed before that they hadn't been seen.

A minute later, Candyman swung around, patted Heath, then pointed a few huts down. "This way."

As he scurried behind Candyman, Heath realized his coms link had come out. Bracing Jia wouldn't afford him a free hand to replace it, so he'd have to trust—

Fingers tickled his ear. He shrugged off the tickle.

"Keep still," came the quiet command—from Jia.

The coms link tucked back into his ear, he eyed her face, so close to his. . .and sideways. He gave a nod and kept moving. Shouts erupted behind them and served as motivation to move faster. They cleared the line of huts and broke into the open. Heath trained his focus on the rocky incline. Remembered slipping and sliding down it. *This will be interesting.*

"Ghost, Candyman, you've got tails."

Okay, make that very interesting.

Halfway up the hill, rocks and dirt peppered his face.

"Taking fire," Candyman called.

Heath stuffed himself behind a rocky cleft and peered up. Huffing, he knelt and looked at Jia. "Doing okay?"

"Sure."

He panted through a quick laugh. "Good." Eying their route, he felt desperation clogging his veins. At least another fifty, sixty feet up to the ridgeline—but they'd still be prime targets. Then another mile or more to the team.

The verse in Proverbs about God making paths straight teased Heath. He smirked, imagining the great hand of God smoothing a path directly to safety. Then again. . . *You are the God who says all things are possible to him who believes, right?*

Trinity barked to the right.

Heath checked. . .and froze as she darted out of view. Tucked behind a stack of boulders, a path led up the side of the mountain. Smooth. Straight. Protected. "No way." He readjusted, looked to Candyman, who already pushed up from his spot and started toward Trinity.

"Hold on," Heath muttered to Jia.

"Ya think?"

He smiled and broke into a sprint.

Gunfire peppered the ground.

Fire lit through his leg.

Jia sucked in a sudden breath.

The ground rushed up at him.

Thirty-Five

"Cover them!" Watterboy's shout sailed through the air.

Peering through the binoculars but unarmed—at least, they believed he wasn't armed—Haur trailed the trio as they hoofed it back up the mountain, mind stricken with what he'd seen and heard. M4s provided suppressive cover.

He let the extended reach of the lens trace the village. Jianyu's elite were there in force. Russians. . .not so much. Odd. If the purpose of Jianyu's presence here was to align with the Russians in order to attack the Americans, wouldn't there be more?

Maybe they were holed up on the other side of the ridge.

Or maybe there was something different, something more sinister going on here.

Haur double-checked on the threesome and the dog. Making good progress. A tiny explosion of blood on Ghost's leg told of a shot. The man hobbled but made it into the passage.

He'd be fine. So would the dog. And the woman. The spy who'd outsmarted his brother and escaped him twice. Haur would like the chance to talk with her, determine her motives, determine if the love she lavished on his brother was real. Or was in fact a tactic to unseat Jianyu. No one had mastered his brother, the master of all.

Except the woman spy. Meixiang. But that's not what the others had called her. Jia, wasn't it? Thoughts rolled around his mind, laden with curiosity and venom, a hunger to know the power she'd exerted over Jianyu.

He'd tried to exert power, to influence the brother whose thirst for power had darkened his outlook. Oh, how Haur had tried. For more than twenty years. And here he was on an icy mountain, staring at the scene before him, distanced. Cold. Left out.

Again.

Haur studied the village, tried to mesh his thinking with Jianyu's. They'd been close, studied together, planned together, passed exams, and soared through the ranks like twins. But there had always been a particular twist to Jianyu's thinking. The awareness of that element in his "brother" had kept Haur alive.

So, brother, what are you doing here? What madness is behind this mission?

The binoculars hit on movement near the center of the small village. Men ran in all directions. A door spun through the air. Haur trained in on that structure.

A man stepped into the open. His face a mask of indignation and rage.

Giddy warmth slithered through Haur so heated he feared the snow around him would betray his guilty pleasure.

"What do you see?" Bai asked in a low voice. "Do you see Jianyu?"

Haur ignored him, glad he'd kept the smile from his face. "No." The lie was necessary. Especially with suspicions abounding. Especially with loyalties shifting.

"They're clear, but let's keep them safe," Watterboy announced. "Spook, you ready to haul butt out of here?"

"We're ready."

Haur kept his focus on his enraged brother. Who kicked a truck. Punched a private. Knocked a boiling pot from its stand in a fire. Men around it shot up, tumbling backward, away from the spewing maw of the pot and their colonel.

So. Jianyu had discovered the American spy had been recovered. Taken right from his hands. Right out from under his nose. The same operative who'd toppled the Zheng empire.

He should not be so pleased. It was not good to revel in the misfortune of others. His mother had taught him that. But Haur could not help but think even his mother was smiling on this day. Or. . . perhaps not yet. Perhaps soon though.

"Haur," Bai said hoarsely.

269

"They're almost out," he muttered, hoping Bai would beg off and leave him so he could figure out what Jianyu would do now. He wanted to witness this.

"Pack it up, people. Let's move!"

As Haur was about to pull up, a second man emerged from the hut. Heat splashed down the back of his neck, filling him with dread. He knew that shape. Or did he?

No, it couldn't be. . .

Same height but twice the girth. He placed a hand on Jianyu's shoulder, bringing him around. His brother shoved off the hand, arms flailing as he raged at the man. Yet the other man clamped the hand back on his shoulder, brought him back in line.

This. . .this was too familiar. Unease squirmed through Haur's gut.

At this angle, Haur could not see the man's face. But something. . .

Jianyu shifted.

And with him, so did Haur's world.

General Zheng.

"Ghost!"

His foot plunged into soft snow, shin-deep, the second fire ripped through it. Heath struggled to stay upright, to keep from dropping Jia. The weight of the world rested on his shoulders. She was an American operative with information that could put a lot of people in danger and countries at war.

Heath trudged out of the deep snow, staring at the path where Candyman stood with Trinity, each step felt like trying to plunge into a vat of glue.

"Sorry." Jia's apology warmed him.

"For what? This"—he grunted as he pushed up and over a crevice—"walk in the park?" She sucked in a breath that slowed him, worried he was hurting her with the ragged, jerky movements.

"Bomb."

In the split second after she said that word, Heath's gaze hopscotched over the terrain, a blast—literally—from the past still ringing in his ears. "Where?"

"Don't know." Jia moaned. "Jianyu. . .bombs. . .bases."

He braved another step. "But not here?" He couldn't help but assess the ground with more caution now. With the sun about to peek over the tips of the mountain, the pristine snowfall would soon be blinding.

"No. . .bas. . ."

Hands pawed at him. Candyman tugged him into the safety of the passage. "Want me to take her?"

"No." Heath surprised himself at the vehemence of his response. *Easy, chief.* "We're good."

"Tell him," Jia wheezed out, then drooped.

Candyman's gaze darted to him. "Tell me what?"

Thwat!

Heath ducked and went to a knee—which hit hard because of the incline.

"Move!" Candyman shouted as he zigzagged farther into the passage and up the mountain.

Heath pushed himself, ignoring the sweat sliding down his neck and back despite the chilling, bitter wind and the frigid temps. His nerves bounced, wishing he could stop and reassess Jia, but even though they had the protection of the passage, this walled-in passage would provide a perfect ambush point.

He propelled himself up the narrow path and focused on getting back to Watters and the others. It took a minute before they reached the top. Candyman crouched at the opening, Trinity too. She came to Heath and licked Jia's face.

"We'll go up some more, then beeline it for the team. They're waiting and will cover, but going up over the ridge and down a little will provide cover."

"Got it."

Candyman's gaze tracked over Heath and then Jia. "You okay?"

"Sure."

"Let me take her the rest of the way."

"I'm good."

"Bull." Candyman's dogged determination held fast. "Your head's hurting, isn't it?"

"No," Heath said as a thump inside his head argued with his answer. "Okay, a little." Little? The thing felt as if it wielded Thor's hammer. He hadn't noticed.

"Your leg. . ."

Heath glanced down to where blood seeped into the snow. "Just a graze." But standing here, not moving, the muscle contracted and squeezed, sending shards of fire up past his knee and into his thigh.

"You willing to risk her life on that graze and little headache?" Candyman stepped closer, his tone softer. "Ghost, listen—dump the pride. Work with me. We can move faster. You slowed down. You're tripping. Let me take her."

Heath considered the offer. But three things made him hesitate: They had less than a mile to go. The incline had been hard and completely in the open. The other element was Jia's trust in him, her saying she was okay "now," *now* that he was here, now that he held her. And third, jostling her from his shoulders to Candyman's might inflict unnecessary additional trauma.

Then again, if he passed out, went down for five seconds like he had days earlier...

Heath nodded. "Okay." He went down on a knee again, angling his back to his combat buddy. Weight shifted from his shoulders and unbalanced him.

Heath swiftly turned and aided Candyman with adjusting and getting back on his feet. "Got her?"

Straightening, Candyman nodded. "Let's go."

Only as he moved free of her weight did Heath notice the burn in his leg, the pounding in his skull, and the aches in his legs and arms. He couldn't help but make the comparison to the moment of surrender ...with God.

A month ago, he would've been too stubborn and filled with pride to admit that he needed Candyman to share the burden. Just as Heath needed to now admit he needed God's help. He didn't belong here. As much as he'd said he wanted to get back into combat, into the fray...he didn't. His pride had been wounded by that blast. Shoved out the back door by the Army, his self-worth and identity took a hit, center mass.

He'd been so focused on proving he still had what it took, he nearly caused more harm than good. No wonder he hadn't qualified for the chaplaincy.

"Do it," Candyman grunted.

Heath turned to his beautiful partner, invigorated by the life lesson that had just dumped down his nerve network. "Trinity, go!"

She threw her muscular body around and launched along the ridgeline. Heath gauged the incline, making sure they were out of sight.

Keying his mic, he reported in. "Base, Ghost and Candyman en route. One klick."

"Roger. We have you in sight. Covering your six."

And wasn't that just like God, too? Surrender the load, admit you can't do it alone, and He's right there, ready to fight. *"The Lord will fight for you; you need only to be still."* The verse from Exodus sailed across his mind and propelled him toward the team.

Help me be still, God. Not literally, of course, but in heart and mind, in attitude. The fight wasn't his. He needed to surrender the dreams, the hopes, the yearnings. . . God would defend his honor. God would prove the mettle buried deep within Heath Daniels.

A shape rose from the snow.

Heath's breath backed into his throat.

"Ghost!" the form waved an arm.

Heart stuttering, Heath let out the breath. "Watterboy!" He spun around and guided Candyman into the safety of the team's embrace.

Scrip and Doc rushed forward and took Jia. In a two-man carry, they lowered her onto a thermal blanket and litter. Candyman and Watterboy joined the others in lifting it. The spook and his objective were there helping—even though the other man's face looked as beat up as Jia's. A white bandage covered the guy's neck as the team made a quick turnaround and got moving again. They navigated the treacherous terrain for about another klick before pausing near an outcropping.

Scrip and Doc knelt around Jia, probing, assessing. Scrip slid a needle for an IV into her arm.

"How bad is she?" Heath shifted to alleviate the throbbing in his leg.

Doc looked up, then dropped his gaze to Heath's calf. "Let me see that."

Heath tugged the leg back. "I'm good."

"I didn't ask, and I outrank you." Doc wrapped a firm hand around Heath's knee and ripped his tactical pants open around the wound. He grabbed a packet from his field kit, tore it open, and squeezed the clear contents onto the injury. Then he pressed gauze and tape around it. "Just a graze. You're good."

"Except now it stings." Heath couldn't resist the taunt and smirked when Doc glowered at him. "How's the girl?"

"Can't tell—messed up," Scrip said. "Broken ribs for sure."

"Means this hike could make this journey a killer."

273

Scrip shook his head. "Watterboy, we need an extraction. She can't make the hike."

A curse stabbed the tension.

Heath looked at the team leader. "What's wrong?"

"No coms." Watterboy huffed. "Okay, pack her up. Let's get moving. Putman, keep trying coms. First signal, I want to know."

"Roger."

Heath squatted beside Trinity and held her face in his hands, rubbing each ear between his thumb and forefinger. "Good work, girl." Nose cold but dry, she panted and gave him that squinted "You betcha" look. Heath tugged the bite valve of his CamelBak and took a draught of water. Icy cold, but at least it hadn't frozen yet. He sucked hard, then aimed it at Trinity. She lapped the water, but he could tell she didn't have the stamina she'd had twenty-four hours ago.

Heath dug his hand into the fur along her chest, feeling for her pulse. Had she been injured and he hadn't noticed? No noticeable bullet holes. No blood. "You just tired, girl?"

As if in answer, she lowered herself to the snow, pink tongue wagging with each rapid rise and fall of her chest. He slipped on the insulated doggie mitts.

"Let's move. Last established coms was two klicks out."

Heath lifted her onto his shoulders. Though she tensed at first, it wasn't her first rodeo, and she settled into the hold.

The journey proved treacherous and laborious. Heath watched the path in front him, head tucked, gaze down to ensure he didn't step off the path and plummet to his death. When Trinity whimpered, he wondered if she'd be better off walking. At least down among their legs, her back and ears weren't exposed to the frigid air. Gently, he brought her around and lowered her. As he patted her head and took a step—his foot plunged downward. Stomach went with it.

Something tugged him back.

"Easy there, Ghost."

Steadied and moving again, he glanced back. "Thanks, Haur." Shaken that he could've plummeted to his death, Heath mulled over who'd saved him. The Chinese man. The dichotomous one. Whose words always seemed to have double meanings. Or maybe that was just Heath's imagination.

Thanks to the narrow path covered with snow, every cell in his body felt frozen through. Howling winds tore at their clothes and exposed flesh. Heath's head pounded in cadence with each step. He eased two tablets out of a packet tucked into his pocket and dumped them in his mouth. With a dry swallow, he hoped that would cut off the thumping in his skull.

Minutes bled into what felt like hours. In fact, two hours. Still no communication. Shadows overtook the team, drawing Heath's gaze upward. Gray, heavy clouds shielded the earth from the sun. Thick, fat snowflakes swirled and danced on the tendrils of icy air. As Heath's gaze roamed the sky, it hit the foot-deep ledge of snow that stretched over the mountain passage.

A foreboding wormed into his gut and took root.

"All quiet," came the hissed words from the front.

Watterboy, too, had noticed the shelf of snow.

And the danger it posed. They didn't need a missile. Or even a bullet. Just a sound. Just the right frequency, and the enemy could wipe the whole grid off the map and into an icy, suffocating grave.

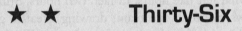

Thirty-Six

They're going to die because of me.

The thought strangled her as the sky twisted into a cauldron of white and gray fury. Darci appreciated the warmth of the thermal blankets and the less-jarring method of carrying her. But that these men were placing their lives on the line. For her. Unacceptable.

In all, she counted four men carrying her, at least four others and Heath closely trailing her. Had he been carrying Trinity? *I thought he carried me.* Two men, shoulders burrowed and heads tucked, trailed Heath. A couple more behind them. A dozen? Why were a dozen men searching for her? Too many! She didn't want to be responsible for that many lives. She'd seen the weight her father bore after her mother's death and being separated from her brother. She didn't want that burden.

She shifted her left arm and felt the familiar pinch of a needle. For what? Darci searched her mind for coherency. She didn't feel addled. That told her they hadn't given her morphine. Saline, most likely. Maybe antibiotics. She was, after all, missing a few fingernails.

Down the length of her body, at the foot of the stretcher that bore her, Darci locked onto Heath. He'd stormed into the hut, all bravado and good looks. Face still streaked with tactical paint, he maintained that grim determination. But beneath it. . .something else spoke. A certainty. A. . .knowing.

What was that? He'd done that at Bagram, too. One thing remained clear to her: When that man decided something, he went after it with war dog-like tenacity. Or was that just a one-day fluke? Would he press her again? Funny enough, it hadn't bugged her the way he'd gotten into her face about hiding her feelings. She liked it. Felt drawn to it. Nothing fake there.

It reminded Darci of her parents. Especially her mother. She'd been so strong, right up to the day she never came home. Friends said she'd been taken from the street on her way home from a Bible study. It still happened today—Christians vanishing into the penal systems of countries like China, Afghanistan, Iran. And the world looked the other way, right into the mind-numbing, moral-erasing conscience of entertainment: television, movies, Internet. Anything to anesthetize their minds to things they didn't want to deal with. Things they felt were out of their control and power. And so. . .they let it continue.

Then there were the men like those around her. They'd sacrificed time with their families, some sacrificed everything—even their lives—to make a difference. Fight wars nobody wanted to fight. Again, more of the same that most of the world didn't want to face.

The sense of justice faded. But not for all. Darci felt the call burning in her from the moment her mother vanished. What put the burning in Heath to be a soldier? To fight battles? To live a brutal life? Who was he, really? What family did he leave behind? Parents? Siblings? A girlfriend?

Darci swallowed. Did he have one? Why wouldn't he? Handsome, funny, inspiring. . . But he hadn't mentioned one at the base when he took her into his arms and all but demanded she admit she liked him. And he hadn't diverted her obvious interest.

"Thought so." At first, he'd come across as cocky. But it wasn't that. He was confident. He knew how to read her. And he called her on her attraction to him. *"I see it in your eyes."* Then he nearly kissed her. But she'd pushed him away. And now, she was afraid she would die before they made it home. Heath would never know how much she wanted to see what would happen between them, how much she regretted pushing away that kiss.

This is crazy.

Voices drowned against the roar of the wind. The team slowed and stopped, her stretcher jarring, sending spikes of pain through her side and back.

One guy shouted to the others, but by the time his words hit the icy din, the sound was lost. Darci tried to read their faces.

Heath's gaze skidded into hers. The left side of his lip slid upward. Then he shot a look to the man who stood shouting. An argument ensued. When he looked back at her, she mouthed the word *bomb*. Had he told them? They were up here in the swirling anger of a winter storm, but down there. . .at the bases. . .was Jianyu finally exacting his vengeance?

The thought of people losing their lives. . .because she'd angered a beast of a man. . .

One of the men supporting the side reached toward her. His large hands bathed in black gloves, he retrieved something near her shoulder. He gave her a firm nod, then slipped an oxygen mask over her mouth and nose. Only as he did that did she realize what he planned. Her gaze cut to Heath's just seconds before a blanket blacked out her visual.

No, no! Blind. I'm blind.

At being covered, head to toe, to protect her from the driving wind and snow, Darci lifted her chin and tried to avoid the suffocating pressure that built in her chest.

No, not your chest. Your mind. It's in your mind. You have oxygen. You're warm.

Being able to talk herself off the ledge was part of the reason Burnett had said she was a prime candidate for an operative. Those who didn't fear were willing to risk too much. Fear kept a healthy balance. Maintained an awareness.

And her awareness now was that this was a smart move, to cover and protect her face and nose from the freezing elements. But she couldn't see what was happening. Couldn't be prepared.

Darci tried to focus on where she knew Heath to be—right at her feet. She trained her ears to listen for his steps. Wind, wind, and more wind pawed at the blanketed environment, rustling out any ability to detect noise.

Faith. Have faith.

A swirl of panic laced through her chest. *I don't have faith! My mother had faith.*

The thought strangled her hope. If she didn't have faith. . .

No, she had to have faith. She'd grown up in a Christian church, her father's attempt at keeping the spirit of her mother and their faith—there was that word again—alive. She'd gone through VBS, memorized the Twenty-Third Psalm, faithfully—ack! would that word not leave her alone?—attended youth group. Dated John Byrd, the most spiritual teen in their group.

When had she needed to stretch herself as she did now? Most likely she had broken ribs, and one wrong move and she'd puncture her lung. Which could be fatal without proper medical treatment. Which was impossible up here in the mountains during a storm.

"With God all things are possible."

Okay, she knew that verse. Matthew 19. . .something.

Darci groped for a tendril of hope, of faith.

What is faith?

Faith is the evidence of things. . .the substance. . .

Augh! Why were all the verses tangling in her mind?

I get it, God. I get it. I've been doing it all in my own power. Living off my mom's faith, not letting You in deep enough to risk vulnerability.

Weightlessness clawed at her, as if she were falling.

Darci started.

The blanket pulled back. Heath hovered over her. "You okay?"

"Where. . .?" She tried to look around but felt pinned to the ground.

"The storm's raging. We had to take shelter." Heath pivoted in his crouched position, looking around. "Not much of a cave, but it'll give us some protection for a while."

Her mind chambered the volatile round. "The bombs. Have you told them?"

Dragging the heavy scarf off his head and neck, he shook his head miserably. "No time. Storm wouldn't let us talk."

"Tell them. It might not be too late."

He nodded. "Okay, tell me what you know."

She eased back, tracing the crooked lines of the granite-looking ceiling a foot above Heath's close-cropped, sandy blond hair. "Just. . . bombs. At the bases." She wet her dry, cracked lips and grimaced. She must be quite the sight. Then again, God had given her the chance to do this, to tell them so they could stop the attacks. *Not in my power, in Yours, Lord.* "They're planning to hit the bases, and they're waiting for Jianyu's activation codes."

"Rest, I'll talk to Watterboy first chance I get."

"First chance?"

Another nod, this one slower, less confident. "They're scouting positions, trying to reestablish contact. He's not here."

"Are we alone?"

"That a problem?"

Her cheeks tingled with unexpected warmth. "I just meant. . ."

"Relax, Jia. We'll be fine. Trust me."

"How do you know?"

He shrugged and pursed his lips. "I. . .just do. Trust me, okay?" Was his face red? "I won't—"

"Beg."

He smirked. At least she thought he did. With the shadows and rogue snowflakes that took shelter with them, she couldn't tell for sure.

He patted her shoulder. "Rest. Hopefully, our time here will be short."

Deep in the Hindu Kush
Village 15 Klicks from Afghan-Chinese Border

The chair sailed through the air, straight toward the rounded wall. *Crack!* Wood splintered and shattered, raining down in a heap at the feet of Major Wang. The man had enough gall not to flinch. Blood and swelling disfigured his face.

"Is this supposed to stay my anger?" Jianyu stormed toward him. "You are already disfigured—no Yanjingshe allows a prisoner to escape. You have failed!" He raised a hand and struck the man. "You have dishonored your family and your name."

"There was nothing I could do! I was knocked out."

Jianyu's temper trembled beneath the cauldron of fury. "Would you bring this excuse to your father, General Wang, and tell him you have allowed the great enemy of China, the one who stole his life work to walk out of this village—alive?"

The man lowered his head.

Hand on his weapon, Jianyu glowered. "I thought not." He lifted the gun from its holster, aimed it at the man's temple, and fired.

Satisfaction thrummed through his veins as he took in three large, deep breaths. Teeth ground, he stared at the lifeblood spilling out just as the man had bled Jianyu of the right to strip Meixiang of the victory she'd stolen from him, his fathers, and his ancestors.

"Feed him to the dogs," Jianyu said as he holstered the weapon and turned back to the table and chairs.

Behind, he heard the scraping of the body as his colonel dragged it into the bitter storm. Jianyu dropped into one of the chairs and stared at the map adorning the wall. He traced the line the Americans would take, the trail he'd sent four of his elite along to track them down and kill those who had stolen from him.

"Be extremely subtle, even to the point of formlessness. Be extremely mysterious, even to the point of soundlessness. Thereby you can be the director of the opponent's fate."

Sun Tzu might have succeeded in that, but Jianyu still had yet to master that tactic. Perhaps he should have withheld his anger, been more forceful with Meixiang's questioning.

"She still holds power over you."

Jianyu kept his gaze locked on the map. On where he imagined her to be. She was badly injured. How did she expect to survive out there, in this, the last of winter's fury unleashed on the mountains? Why would she not listen to him, work with him, let him help her? He'd even summoned a surgeon, who had arrived with the helicopter.

"She will die in the mountains with her American counterparts." But he hoped not.

"Do not underestimate her."

"I have not." Jianyu pushed out of the chair and strode to the map, hands behind his back. "Four Yanjingshe—four of the best—are on their trail."

"A wise decision."

Annoyed with the patronizing tone, Jianyu moved to the soiled earth. He smeared the spot with his boot, then strode to the small serving table and dumped steaming tea into a mug. He stirred honey into the warm brew.

"Honey will not sweeten what is about to happen."

Words meant to reduce him no longer held sway over him. "Retaliation against the ones who dishonored us is sweet enough."

"Do not take pleasure in pain."

"I take pleasure," Jianyu said as he returned to the table, "in delivering justice where it has gone unmet."

"You take too much glory upon yourself, Jianyu."

Seething at the antagonism, he settled in the chair and blew across the top of the ceramic mug. In the hot liquid, he saw his own anger. His own sense of indignation. And like a cool wind, the bitter herb of revenge sailed across it. Sated it. Reminded him to be patient in the journey. To let the leaves settle, the flavor imbued in the hot water, filling every cell of flavor, till the drink was consumed.

The door swung open.

Colonel Tao entered and strode to the table. "It is done. The Russians are dead."

And dead do not talk. Jianyu sipped. Savored. "Enjoy some tea, Colonel."

With a curt bow, he pivoted and served himself.

The man seated at the head of the table pushed to his feet, towering over the colonel, who relinquished the steaming tea to the giant behind him. And bowed.

Jianyu seethed. But he coiled the disgust into a ball and swallowed it with the last gulp of tea. It burned. . .all the way down.

"Any word on Meixiang?" the colonel asked.

Jianyu glowered at him.

"Do not worry about the traitor." The voice still bore the annoying taunt. "She will receive her reward in time."

Their plans were eerily similar yet very different. Jianyu kept his peace, determined not to be undermined in front of his first officer.

"I will deliver that reward—in person."

"No." Jianyu came to his feet. "I put this together. I worked out the details, contacted you—"

"And would you like to answer what you were doing here in the mountains, away from the mine as instructed?" The giant loomed, scowled.

Jianyu swallowed. He would *not* look away. Would not yield his power. "I fed the information necessary—we agreed. Do not take this from me."

Large and powerful, not in size but in the enormity of presence the man wielded, a hand rested on Jianyu's shoulder. "The fight in you is large, but you must master it. Temper it with patience enough to see the mission through. She is out of your reach—for now. But it does not matter. She cannot stop what is already in motion."

"I want her." Jianyu's voice and being shook.

"And you will have her." The man squeezed his shoulder. "In time.

We have an agent with the Americans. In time, he will be revealed." He turned and strode to the table where his emissaries stood in the shadows. "As I have waited twenty-one years, nine months, and fourteen days to have my victory"—he drew up his chin, the resemblance undeniable to even Jianyu—"so will you have yours." Age lines crinkled at the corners of the man's eyes. "But much sooner."

"Are you sure?"

Radio chatter ate up the ominous silence. One of his father's officers stepped into the light. "Sir. They're in place."

A smile creased his father's face. "Completely, my son."

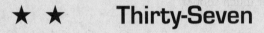

★ ★ Thirty-Seven ★ ★

Deep in the Hindu Kush
Tunnel 5 Miles outside Parwan Province, Afghanistan

It did strange things to Heath's heart to see Trinity cuddled up next to Jia on the stretcher. Jia had even lured Trinity into the warmth of the thermal blanket, and the two were fast asleep. Trinity's amber fur complemented Jia's fair skin.

Okay, that's a weird thing to notice.

Sitting against the wall, legs bent and elbows on his knees, Heath ran the back of his knuckles along his lips. It scared him, what he was feeling and thinking about Jia. She was an operative. Sure, she'd had lunch with him, laughed and talked with him. She'd wanted that missing kiss as much as he had that day. But was he anything more than a player in a mission to her? When this was over, would she skip along her merry way? He'd have Trinity and a lot of heartache.

He tilted his head back, thudding it against the cave wall.

Getting way ahead of the game, Ghost.

First priority: get off the mountain. And there wasn't a single guarantee in attempting that. The storm had unleashed its fury. *Why, God? Why now? When Jia needed a doctor and surgical bay like nobody's business, couldn't You have held off the storm?*

And if God had, would the enemy have found them sooner?

Jia had antibiotics. Color returned to her complexion. And she was sleeping—peacefully.

Peace.

Bomb.

Heath jerked. He hadn't told Watters. Pushing to his feet, he noticed Trinity open her eyes. Her head slid along the blanket to track him but didn't lift. Her "eyebrows" wobbled as she looked up at Heath.

"Not getting up, are you?"

She looked away.

"Traitor." *But I don't blame you.*

Heath bundled into his jacket and inched along the outer edge of the cave toward the others.

Watters stood. "You okay?" he called over the howling wind.

"Yeah, can I talk to you?" Heath bobbed his head to the side.

Watters nodded and followed him, pointing. "Guess she had business to take care of."

Heath caught sight of Trinity squatting in the snow but then focused on Watters. "Hey, listen." He stepped back, away from the others. No need to cause panic with half-baked information. "Jia believes there—"

Boom! CRACK!

Ice dumped down Heath's spine. Watterboy's eyes bulged. Heath whirled toward the cave opening. Saw Trinity tearing up snow toward the cave.

ROAR!

A shadow appeared in the opening. Jia! Propped against the wall, frowning as she aimed those eyes heavenward.

His heart dropped into his stomach. Then vaulted into his throat. He pushed himself, feet skidding on the ice. Gaining traction, he shoved himself toward her. Waving. Hard. "Get back!" Why did it feel like he'd hit slow motion? "Back!"

Ice and snow slowing him, Heath sprinted.

Snow and ice rained down.

The great fury of the winter storm bellowed in his ears. Though he shouted, he heard nothing. Felt only the thunderous vibration of the avalanche.

Snow thumped against his legs. Heath spiraled through the air.

Collided with Jia, whose face said she'd caught up with what was happening. Her arms closed around him as they flew backward. Hard earth scraped and clawed at him as they slid deeper. Heath ducked closer to her.

Darkness. Roaring. Tumbling. Cracking.

Whoosh!

Light shattered. Darkness prevailed.

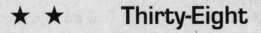

Thirty-Eight

Heath rolled off Jia. "You okay?"

"Yeah," came her weak, soft voice.

He glanced to where daylight and snow raged through the opening. The one that was no longer there. Only darkness existed.

"Trinity?" His voice bounced back at him. "Trin!" He pushed off Jia, careful not to injure her any more than he had. "You okay, Jia?"

"Yeah." Quiet but trembling, her voice skated through the darkness. "Are we alone?"

"You really have a thing about being alone with me."

"No."

At the frantic word, Heath reached through the void for her. He caught her shoulder, surprised when his fingers tangled in hair. It must've come loose when they impacted. "Hey, it's just a joke."

"The darkness—"

"Hang on. Got it." He reached toward his shoulder lamp. "Watch your eyes." He twisted the barrel and light exploded around them. "Trinity?" He turned and checked the corners and crevices. "Crap." Other words filled his mind, imagining his girl trapped, buried in the snow.

The team! Did they get buried. Were they lost?

"So. . .we *are* alo—on our own." Her eyes sparkled, the light of his shoulder lamp glinting off the mahogany irises. Wide. With fear.

"Don't worry. We'll get out."

"How?"

He didn't have the answers, but he wouldn't accept that they would die in this cave. Could they dig their way out? How much snow had heaped on them?

"We'll get out."

"Where are they?"

Ignoring the question, Haur clambered over the mound of snow that had dumped down the mountain, narrowly avoiding him and the others who took shelter beneath the lip of the overhang. Hands plunged through soft, shifting snow. Cold seeped up his sleeves and made his bones ache. Balancing on a boulder that had made the journey with the snow, Haur wobbled. Weak knees, trembling hands. The terror of being buried alive had choked off any bravado or confidence he'd held a few seconds earlier.

That and the conviction that he knew what caused the avalanche. But revealing that would get him killed.

Soldiers skittered back and forth. Dropping to their knees, digging with gloved hands. A couple produced collapsible shovels, then went to work.

"Anyone got them?" Watterboy threw himself over one mound after another, searching. Shouting.

Haur slid a glance to Bai, who stood back, staring. No, not staring. Watching. Enjoying. Haur had had his suspicions about his captain, but the movement out of the corner of his eye in the seconds before he heard the loud crack—which was really a *boom*—could only be one thing.

A grenade. Thrown by Bai up onto the shelf.

Which triggered the avalanche.

And buried Meixiang.

The soldiers rushed around. Frantic. Scared. His stomach churned. Meixiang had more information on Jianyu and the Chinese government than anyone else. He must be certain that information was protected. Kept from the wrong hands.

"Storm's letting up." Watterboy's voice boomed over the unsettled area. "Candyman, we got coms?"

"No coms," Rocket announced from his position.

Just as the storm had let up, the avalanche slowed them.

"Then get it! We need coms—*yesterday*!" Watterboy's face was red, his posture rigid.

"There's no signal," said a shorter, black-haired man who sat on a pile of rocks.

"Then get off your lazy butt and get me one." Watterboy's shout echoed through the narrow valley as he stabbed a finger in a southern direction.

Haur shifted. Glanced up. South? Or was he pointing west? With the sun hiding behind the clouds and storm, there was no telling.

"Hey," Candyman spoke with a hiss. "Lower your voice. Anything could trigger another one."

The dog bounded around the area, sniffing, whimpering. The spook and the man he rescued—a man named Toque—trailed the dog.

A stream of curses mingled with the fluttering snow. "I want them found!"

Candyman knelt beside Trinity. "Where are they, girl? Find Ghost!"

Nose up, she sniffed. Leapt over upturned debris. Sniffing. Bounding.

It was hopeless, was it not? They would not find Ghost or the spy. Not with the way the snow heaped against the opening. Most likely they were buried anyway. That much of the mountain surely filled in the hole.

Watters went to his knees with a shovel and started digging. "They were right here. Let's get them out."

"Think that cave had another way out?"

Haur considered the question spoken with a British accent. "It is possible."

"How would you know?"

Haur understood the animosity, even though he now knelt to aid in digging. "These mountains lead to the Wakhan Corridor and river in China. There are many tunnels and caves there."

"Remember, Jia said she and that little girl found a way through another tunnel."

"That's right."

"But we don't know there was a way out. I went into that cave—there wasn't anything but walls."

"Keep digging," Watterboy ordered.

Candyman shook his head. "What do you think about sending me, Scrip, and Putman on ahead to try to gain radio contact, get us help up here?"

Watterboy hesitated. Pushed back on his knees, sleeves soaked from digging. "Do it."

Haur did not miss that Bai had not taken up the task of trying to find the Americans. He stood to the side. "We should help," he said in their tongue.

"You saw how little regard they had for our people," he replied back in kind. "How can I help save the life of a woman who betrayed and violated all of China?"

"Because you value life, not politics!"

He saw it. For a fraction of a second, Haur saw the sneer bleed into his captain's face. And just as fast, it was gone.

Haur went back to digging, both figuratively and literally. His time was short. To accomplish his mission, to carry out his intentions, he must not let himself be sidetracked by anyone else's leanings. "You will give them the wrong idea," Haur muttered to Bai.

"As you are Colonel Zheng."

He would not be goaded, not by this man, no matter how much he once trusted him. " 'Know thy self, know thy enemy. A thousand battles, a thousand victories.'" Slowly, Haur came to his feet. "It is prudent not to forget the ways of old, the proven tactics of our ancestors." He let his gaze drift to Bai's. "I see your doubts, both the spoken and unspoken. And I see more." He let the words hang in the air. "We have our mission."

"Why did you not go with them into the village to confront Jianyu?"

The moment of truth. Could he convince his captain? "Because the girl has become a higher priority. Do you realize who she is, Bai Ling?"

Question glittered in the man's gaze. "You know?"

"Yes, I know. And do you see my brother here?" Vehemence streaked his words. "I will return her to General Zheng. I will restore honor to the Zheng name."

Bai's head tilted up slightly.

"Do *not* question me again, or I will make that your last."

★ ★ Thirty-Nine ★ ★

F ind anything?" Lonely and hollow, her voice skipped along the curves of the cave.

"No." With that blinding light on his shoulder, Heath returned and crouched. His gray eyes bounced over her face. "You've got a sheen."

She didn't want him worrying about her. They had bigger obstacles to tackle. So, despite the pain and the fire dousing her courage, Darci managed a smile. "If that's your best pickup line, you've got a lot to learn."

"Ha. Ha." He swiveled and went to one knee and tugged off his gloves. Heath pressed the back of his icy hand to her cheek. "You're hot."

Another smirk.

"Don't," he warned.

Darci couldn't help but laugh at him stopping her comeback line. "What? It's okay for you to be direct and forthright, but not me? You shouldn't worry so much."

"Easier said than done." He smoothed out the thermal blanket. "Lie back down. You should rest. Who knows what's ahead. I'll pack ice around your fingertips. They're bleeding again."

"I can do that."

"Don't get all modest on me after making every comment into an innuendo." Heath's smile trickled through his words as he bent over her. "How're your ribs?"

"Some guy just dove into them."

"What a jerk."

"Yeah." Darci turned her face toward the wall, not out of modesty, but so he wouldn't see her face tighten at the pain. She could still breathe, so he hadn't done further damage, but holy cow, it hurt.

Cool air swept up her shirt as he lifted the blanket and took her hand. He hissed.

"That pretty?"

"As beautiful as you are, there's no way something like this can be described as pretty."

Darci's pulse ricocheted off his words and thumped against her chest. Had he really just said she was beautiful? Was he being sarcastic? Only one way to gauge that—the eyes. She glanced back. Thick browridge—a sign of intelligence—hung over eyes laden with concern.

No sarcasm. Did he mean that?

Why was she wishing so hard that he had?

He angled around, then pushed on to his haunches, reaching for something. He turned back and his gaze collided with hers. Softness filled his features. Handsome, rugged, yet. . .soft.

"You just have to complicate things."

White-hot fire shot through her. Then icy cold. She would swear she heard sizzling and realized he was packing snow and ice around her fingers to stop the bleeding. The pain blazed up her digits, through her wrist, and into her arms.

Darci squeezed her eyes and groaned.

A pause was followed by another application.

"Infection's trying to flare up," he said as he pressed a hand to her cheek. Awareness flared through her, but the pain and the severity of the situation doused that tremor of longing.

"I always wonder what my mom's last days were like."

Heath stilled, his somber gaze coming to hers.

She knew what he was thinking—that she shouldn't be talking about last days. But. . .this is how she dealt with things, talking or thinking about her mom. "She was martyred." Why did she want him to know everything about her all of a sudden? "Taken in the middle of the day while my father was out of the country. We never saw her again."

Heath eased down and drew up a leg to his chest. "In China?"

With a nod, she gave away a key piece of information. Weird. Darci didn't mind. She trusted him with this. Besides, if they died. . . "She was a Christian. And my father was very influential and powerful, and of course that couldn't be tolerated. They'd tried to convince him to do away with her, but he loved her too much. He'd been trying to make arrangements to move her back to the States, but. . .."

"Jia—"

"Darci." Oh no. Had she just done that? Okay, well. . .it was okay. "I want you to know my real name."

Something slid through his expression. "Darci. I like it." Though small, his smile was thousand-watt power. "Thank you."

She smiled. *Oh good grief. Can we say "schoolgirl"? Stick with facts. Those I can handle.* "I was born Jia, but when my father and I fled China after they murdered my mom, I took her name for safety's sake."

He nodded.

"Anyway. . .sorry. . .don't know why I'm rambling." Heat again soaked her cheeks.

"I like it."

She rolled her eyes. "Don't get all romantic on me, cowboy."

"How'd you know?"

"What?"

"That I'm a cowboy—well, not really, but I grew up in Texas." He shrugged and looked so adorable and boyish, she couldn't help the smile. "Doesn't that make me an honorary cowboy?"

"Do you mean ornery cowboy?" The laugh made her stiffen, then she relaxed out of the fiery breath. "I'd love to see you in a cowboy hat."

"Nothing doing." He looked sheepish and ran a hand along the nape of his neck. "My head's too big."

Darci threw her head back and laughed. It made her insides hurt, but it also made her insides giddy. Curling an arm around her waist, she pulled herself up.

"Whoa." Heath's smile vanished as he reached for her. "Where are you going?"

"Nowhere. I'm sick of lying down."

"Lying down gets you better."

She cocked her head at him. "It gets me dead."

His lips flattened. "Not on my watch."

A strange twisting and warming melted through her frozen exterior. Was he feeling what she felt when they were together? Did it matter? Burnett would go ballistic if he knew she hadn't severed their connection. She'd lose her job.

"Why do you do it?" he asked as she propped herself against the wall.

"Do what?" Wow, sitting up hurt like crazy. On second thought. . . She slumped a little, alleviating the pressure on her ribs.

"Be a spy."

Darci frowned at him. "Why are you a soldier?"

"I felt called."

"Felt?"

"Exactly." He nodded. "Your story first."

She smiled again. It felt so good. When had she smiled so much? A real smile, not one to get what she needed? "My mom."

Heath watched her, his amazing gray eyes penetrating her barriers. And strangest of strange things—she let him. "Justice. You wanted justice for her."

"Yeah."

"Have you gotten it?"

She let out a soft snort. "Several times."

Arm dangling over his leg, he didn't let up. "And has it worked? Has it given you what you were looking for?"

How had he seen straight to the dark chamber where she kept that secret buried? She hadn't thought it possible anyone would understand that mission after mission left her only with more emptiness. Not a sense of justice. Doing this—spying, intelligence work—had driven her to fill the hole. To somehow give to others what nobody had given her mother—a chance, a way out. She didn't blame her father. . .much. He'd been out of country when the police snatched her off the street.

Heath gave a breathless laugh. "I see. . ."

Why did she feel like clawing that smile off his face? "Shouldn't you be looking for a way out?"

With a stiff shake of his head, he pushed onto his haunches. "Point taken." He angled toward the back, darkness drenching her vision and mood.

Panic swooped in on her. He was gone. Gone! "Heath?"

"Don't worry." Boots scritched over hard earth. "I'm not going far."

Darci laughed at his joke—there wasn't *anywhere* to go. Had he said that because he knew it'd scared her? As stillness and quiet vied for her sanity—pulling at her common sense that there was nothing to be afraid of, that Heath wasn't going to vanish and leave her alone. . .

"Hey."

She sucked in a quick breath at his voice.

"Might'a found something."

"What?" A way out? Would it be that easy, that quick?

"A whole."

"A whole what?"

"No—*hole*. At the very back. Missed it when I looked before. It's not much bigger than me. And. . ."

"And what?"

"It goes straight down."

Heath stretched his arm into the space and wagged his arm. Nothing but icy air, but. . .was that a breeze? Or was that just him stirring up the air? He aimed his SureFire down, hoping to see how far it was.

His stomach flipped when the darkness ate up the light. No bottom? There had to be. Nothing was infinite. Except God.

Lying on his side, he scanned the area around himself for a rock. He dragged a golf-ball-size one within reach and flopped back onto his belly. SureFire aimed over the chasm, he dropped the rock. It whipped out of sight. The darkness ate it, too. Finally, a plunk—distant and almost inaudible.

C'mon. Don't do this to me. They needed to get out of here.

Heath eased away from the chasm, mind chugging. Trapped in here, did they have much of a choice? He roughed a hand over his chin and cringed at the stubble.

"Down how far?"

In a squat, he eased himself out from the compressed space and strode back to Ji—Darci. "It seems bottomless. As far as I can tell, there's nothing but emptiness down there."

"That's not possible."

"I know." He lowered himself to her side, noting she was once again upright. "I told you, you should be lying down."

"Yeah," she said, wrinkling her nose at him. "I never have done too well under orders."

"They weren't orders." Man, she got under his skin fast and deep. "Just strong suggestions."

She grinned, and Heath looked away before his mind could wander. *Could* wander? It already had. What was he. . .? Oh yeah. The hole. Chasm. No way out. Heath ran a hand along his neck and scratched it. They were out of options, but if the gentle stirring of air *was* a breeze, at least they wouldn't run out of air.

Ice could be melted for water.

Three days. They'd be okay for three days.

Food. . .that was another thing. What was in his pack? Heath turned, and the light cut through the darkness to where his pack. . .*had* been. Now lost to the avalanche. Maybe it wasn't buried too deep and he could reach it. On his knees he moved to the barricade of snow, ice, and rocks. Crap. He couldn't even dig—his shovel was in his pack.

Tension wrapped a vise around him. Heath balled up his fists. Couldn't a guy just get a break? He punched the ground. Everything for survival was in that pack. His shovel, his ammo, MREs. . . His fist impacted dirt. Pain spiked through his elbow and shoulder. Jammed into his neck.

"What now?"

"Nothing." He wouldn't fail her. As he bent forward, it felt like his entire brain dumped into his forehead. Heath swung out a hand to steady himself. Pounding returned with a voracious roar.

Hands cradling his head, he clenched his eyes shut. *Father in heaven. . .please.*

Heath. . .Heath. . .

Was that God calling?

Rolling out of the pain, he wriggled his shoulders and neck as his eyes opened—he jerked. Darci knelt in front of him. Her face wrought.

"Heath. . .you there?" She tucked her chin and peered up into his eyes.

Did she have any idea how beautiful she was? How her concern for him felt like a warm salve over his wounded heart and mind?

But it was embarrassing. Humiliating. He edged away. "Yeah. Just. . . a little pain."

"I think you need to go back to kindergarten and learn what *little* means."

"Funny."

"It's killing you, isn't it?"

Cowed beneath the intense pressure, he slumped against the wall.

"Let me try something." She touched his shoulder again. "Okay?"

Heath waved a hand. "Sure." Whatever. It wouldn't work. He'd hoped the chiropractor would help. And it did. But obviously it was limited. Would he ever be pain-free again?

"This won't be fun," Darci said. "But you're a tough guy, so. . ."

Iciness draped his neck. Heath tensed and hissed against it. Waited for it to wear off. Instead, it grew stronger. Colder—was that even possible? He ground his teeth and hissed.

"Grit through it," Darci said, her voice weak.

"You should be—"

"Quit being the boss."

Heath snorted—but quickly lost his humor as the frigid ball of ice bit into his muscles. He fisted a hand. Tight. . .tighter.

"Relax, Heath."

"Why don't you drive a stake through my skull?"

"Would it help?"

Freezer burn had nothing on this. Heath clamped his teeth again. Watched his knuckles whiten. The icy fire streaked through his shoulders.

"How's the head?"

The what? Heath let his shoulders slump. . .searched. . ."It's. . .gone."

"Wimp."

Arching his eyebrow, he faced her full-on. "You just turned my neck into a deep freeze."

"I thought you were a tough Green Beret."

"*Former* Green Beret." The truth hurt. A lot. Former in so many meanings of the word. Mentally, physically, emotionally. Jabbing his fingers through his hair, Heath sat back against the cave wall. But here, with Darci, maybe he knew why he was here. Not just to let go of what he'd lost, but to cling to something he'd found—new faith and. . .Darci.

"Don't think about it too hard or long."

He flicked his gaze to Darci, who curled a protective arm around her side. She was right. Thinking got him stupid, depressed. "Ya know, I think God brought me out here just to show me how wrong I was."

"About what?"

"Everything." Heath breathed a laugh. "Life, myself, what I wanted—"

"What did you want?"

"Action. Adrenaline. The beret. The whole shebang."

"You don't want that now?"

Why did her voice hitch on that question? He rolled his head back and forth. "Not the way I thought I did. It cut me to get sidelined. Injured more than my thick skull—hit my pride."

"You still have a lot left over."

With a smile, Heath nodded. "Ouch."

"You ready?"

Heath frowned as he looked at her. "For what?"

"To go down that hole."

Forty

We are not going down that hole." Heath pried himself off the cave wall. "We don't even know where it leads—if it leads anywhere."

"So. . ." Darci motioned to their surroundings. "We just stay here? And die?" Her head cocked. "I know you're a *former* Green Beret, but even I thought you had more fight in you than that."

"What I have is some common sense." He poked a finger at her. "You're injured—you can barely sit up—and you expect to rappel down a chasm? Our rope won't even reach the bottom."

"It doesn't have to."

He knew where this was going. "You don't know how far it is from the end of the rope to the bottom. You could break your legs—and that's the bright side."

"You're all sunshine and roses, aren't you?"

"Darci." Heath pushed up onto his knees. "Please, I've made a dent using my fingers, but let's give them time."

"What if they don't make it, Heath? What if they were buried?"

"I can't accept that." He swallowed that bitter pill. "Please—let's just wait."

"Only if you beg."

Heath glared at her. "Not funny."

"Why can't you accept that? It's completely within the realm of possibilities."

"Because if they didn't make it, then that means the men are dead. And so is my girl. I'm not going there. Not again." He remembered those men, their funerals he'd missed, the fading in and out, the PT learning to walk, and the scars from Trinity's bite. "I can't lose a team again." This time it was his heart thundering, not his head. All the same in the grand scheme of things though.

Fierceness rosied her cheeks. "That bomb wasn't your fault. You couldn't have known."

Heath stilled. "I should've been more alert."

"It was an ambush. You have to move on and stop letting it color your past."

Heath angled his head, gaze locked on her. "How. . .how do you know about that?"

For a fraction of a second, Darci's eyes widened, then slid shut. And to Heath, it felt like the light in his life blinked out. She hung her head.

He inched closer. "How do you know about that ambush? I never told you. It was above top secret. No reason for you to know."

". . .uplifted by His grace, and feel yourself enfolded in the peace of His embrace."

The fragments came together in that moment as if the bomb that had exploded into shards two years ago flew back together. They were in the mountains. Just like right now. Then the angel who stood over him—

"You. . .it was you at Landstuhl, wasn't it?" They'd told him he was crazy. Whacked on painkillers as he came out of surgery. They vowed over and over that nobody had been with him in the days afterward before he regained consciousness.

"I felt responsible." Darci's words were small as she stared down at her hands. "I didn't know what to do, but I couldn't just walk away. So I stayed there until they convinced me you were going to live."

"You prayed over me." Awe speared him.

"I found it in my mom's Bible—a little gift card with a prayer stamped on it." With a sad smile, she shrugged. "It was all I had to offer, to undo the pain I caused."

Heath tilted his head, confused. "*You* caused?"

Again, her eyes widened. She looked away. Then down.

Realization dawned on him. His gut twisted, and his mind warred with the gravity of what she had just revealed. "You provided the bad intel."

"*Not*"—she jerked her gaze to him, her eyes watering—"on purpose. It was blowback."

Blowback. His ragged pulse lumbered to a slower pace. "Unintentional consequence of spying operations. . ."

"Not just unintended but designed so that when the retaliation comes—the ambush—the public doesn't understand why it happened, can't connect X to Y."

"Amazing." He'd lost his career due to bad intel, provided by her, but then God brought it full circle. Brought them together. Ya know, for the first time, Heath didn't mind the scars so much, if that's what placed Darci in his life. In fact, he'd take a few more for her.

She swallowed. "I am so sorry. Please. You have every right. . .but please. . .don't. . ."

The brokenness in her voice tugged at his heartstrings. "Don't what?"

Big, brown watery eyes. "Don't hate me."

Aw man. She was as bad as Trinity when she tucked her tail and head, then sidled up to him with that pathetic whimper. At least it had the same effect on his heart.

Emotion. Too much emotion.

"Hate you?" Needed some testosterone injection here. "I'm about to go down a rabbit hole for you."

Shhhink. Grind. Whoosh. Thud.

Shhhink. Grind. Whoosh. Thud.

Peter Toque shoveled hard, determined to do his very best to find the girl who'd spearheaded efforts to take down one of the most powerful men in China. And that had drawn the sleeping dragon from his den.

No way was Jia Li going down now. Not this way.

He rammed the shovel into the snow again. Again. Again—*thud!*

Peter cursed.

Another dead end, solid rock.

Shouts from the right drew his attention as he repositioned in a new spot. This was where the opening had been. Would they ever break the two out of the cave?

Watters, Candyman, and the one they called Rocket huddled up, talking. Something was going on. He wasn't sure what, but Peter trained his ears and eyes that way as he started digging again.

"What's going on?"

Peter eyed his handler, Bright. "Not sure." He dug. Thrust, toss.

Thrust, dig, toss. "Maybe they got coms back up."

"That'd be nice." Bright grunted. "Our ride should be here soon."

"I'm not leaving till they have her back."

Bright stilled. "This isn't the time to get romantic."

"You're right. And I'm not." Peter rammed the shovel into the hard-packed snow. "It's about respect. About protecting one of my own."

"She's American."

"She's an *operative*. She covered my back before. I'm covering hers."

"We don't have time for this."

"Then leave." Peter glared. "I know where you live."

Bright shook his head with a laugh and rejoined the effort. "D'you see it?"

Peter tossed another load over his shoulder, sweat sliding down his temple. "What?"

"I'm not sure." Bright's ruddy face twisted beneath the labor. "I thought I saw one of the Asians throw something seconds before the avalanche."

"A grenade." Which is why he wasn't letting the men out of his sight. "Which one?"

"Don't worry about it."

"What are you going to do?"

Peter smirked.

Bright shook his head and held up a hand. "You're right. I don't want to know." He shoved his hands into the snow, no doubt to alleviate the burn from the blisters. Peter had them, too. But what's a bit of blood and blisters when racing to save a life?

Shhhink. Grind. Whoosh. Thud.

"This is senseless, you know." Bright wiped the sweat from his brow. "It's been too long."

"Unless the cave has an air source."

Bright sighed.

Shhhink. Grind. Whoosh. Thud.

"But if it doesn't. . ."

"If you want to stop digging, then stop. Otherwise shut up and let me work."

With another grunt, Bright drove the shovel into the snow. "I'm going to see what they found."

"Please." Peter tossed rocks and snow. "Go."

Foul became his mood. The thought of not getting to her in time. She was a good operative. A kind woman. She didn't deserve this. Nobody did. And he had that mantra, the "do unto others as you would have them do unto you" that he tried to live up to.

Of course, while on a mission, all bets were off. But as a regular citizen, he practically wore a halo.

Another thrust. With it. . .a strange noise.

Peter looked to the side, listening. Nothing. He lifted the shovel.

There—again. Behind him. He twisted his upper body and looked back. Who would be over there? It was nowhere near—

A bark sailed over the still air.

The war dog!

Peter threw down the shovel. "Where's the dog?"

Heads popped up as the others turned their attention to the barking.

Peter jogged around the incline. Oddity of oddities—this stretch was pristine and white, undisturbed, save a trail that snaked down. . .down. . .

A black-and-amber form. "There!"

"It's Trinity. She's found them," Watterboy shouted.

"Not possible," Peter called as he pointed back up over the ridge. "They were up there. In the cave. We didn't make it down this far."

Watterboy hesitated, his gaze bouncing around the area.

"He's right," Scrip said. "It doesn't make sense."

Watterboy raised gloved hands. "That dog is trained to protect her handler at all costs." He looked back down the mountain to the plain where she dug with fervor.

"She's got a hit!" Candyman threw himself down, half sliding, half jogging.

Watters went with him, and so did the Asians. Peter rushed after them, hoping against vain hope that they weren't making a big mistake.

Bright joined him. "This is asinine."

"Did you guys come up this way?"

"Hanged if I know." Bright sighed. "It was dark half the time and the pass so narrow. . .but no, this doesn't. . ." He looked around. "The snowfall changed the face of it. I wouldn't know if I'd lived here."

Toque's face hardened. "Well, let's check it out."

"I have got to be out of my mind." Heath swiped a slick palm down his pants as he adjusted the rope around his hips and waist.

"Maybe for once you're in your right mind." Darci sat at the edge of the hole with him, her voice confident and calm.

"Are you always this annoying under pressure?"

Her smile amplified the beam of his lamp. Then fell as if she'd jumped off a ledge. What replaced it yanked so hard on his heart, he jerked. "Hey." He frowned as he took in her overwrought expression. "What just happened?"

"I. . ." She cringed and held her side. "I just. . ."

"Darci." Heath shifted on the ledge to face her better.

"Do you like me?"

Feeling like a Ping-Pong ball caught between her thoughts, Heath blinked. "Huh?"

"Because if you like me, I can die happy."

Whoa no. No talk of death. "Darci."

"No, seriously. I know it sounds crazy—"

"Yeah, it does."

"I've faced death before—"

"Darci." Heath hooked a hand around the back of her neck. "Stop." He tightened his hold. "Stop talking about death. We're not going to die. You're not going to die and—"

"Will you kiss me?"

Heath blinked. *What?*

"You wanted to kiss me at Bagram, but I pushed you away. So kiss me before you go down there."

What ledge had she just jumped off of? His pulse chugged through his veins. God forgive him, but his gaze bounced to her lips. His yearnings betrayed him, but he finally pushed out a response. "No."

"Why?"

"Because. . ." Heat clawed his face. Two years ago, he wouldn't have hesitated. He liked her. She liked him. But it felt like something bigger, greater was happening here. "Because you're thinking I'm going to die, so you want no regrets." He shook his head, his chest feeling like a mortar range. "And because a kiss would mean something to me."

"It would mean something to me, too. That's why I asked." She shoved the black hair away from her face. "I don't need romance, Heath."

"Maybe." He couldn't believe she was dead serious. "But it's kind of nice. Know what I'm saying?" Taking things slow. Not rushing.

"I just need to know if you're feeling the same thing I am."

Now his brain felt like it was attached to the bungee cord on the ledge she'd just jumped from. His head hurt—and it wasn't the TBI. "How did we just go from death to talk of romance?"

"If I'm going to die—"

"Stop!" He cupped the back of her neck with both hands. "Darci. Slow down." He tugged her in closer, determined she believe him. "Nobody's going to die. I'm going down this hole—doing it for you, remember?"

"You're right." Shoulders sagging, Darci shrunk back. "I don't know what I'm thinking. I'm just. . .tired." She lowered her head. "Sorry. I. . ." Her gaze darted over his face, mouth open about to say something, then she pulled herself inward, crashing down as she pressed her lips into a thin line. "Never mind."

"Hey," he whispered, still holding her neck. "What's going on inside that pretty head?"

Looking up, out from under her eyebrows, she considered him.

"What's wrong?"

"I've never been this scared." A weak smile quivered on her lips as she worried the cuff of her jacket. "Not like this."

Heath nudged her up so he could look into her brown eyes. "Maybe it's because this time you have something to risk."

"Yeah?" Her voice went crazy-soft. "What?"

"Staying alive to make good on that request for a kiss." Heath angled around, bracing himself on the edge before she could see how much that line just embarrassed him. Why did she have to go and get all mushy on him as he was lowering himself into oblivion? It was good incentive, true, but it also made jelly of his iron stomach that someone like her was scared.

Shoulder light fracturing the black void, Heath eased himself down, toes braced against the wall in front. With one hand threading the line, he glanced down. Nothing but pitch black.

Why had he watched all those horror movies? Too many images flashed into his mind, holding him in a vise grip of hypervigilance.

"See anything?"

Her voice already sounded miles away. Heath glanced up at the top. How had he descended that far? "How much line do I have left?"

"Plenty."

Right. Heath considered the depth below. . .waaaay below. He plucked the SureFire from his shoulder and aimed it down. The light danced along a slick wall where snow melted and trickled down.

His beam reflected off something.

Heath angled it again, this time over his shoulder as he strained to see what was down. Unable to see anything, he adjusted his balance so he could turn.

"Why aren't you moving?"

"Thought I saw something."

"No sightseeing."

Heath smirked as he lifted his arm and pointed the beam straight down.

His toe slid free.

His body swung to the right.

He slammed into the wall, his head thudding hard. He flung out a hand to stop the move—in that instant he realized his mistake. "No!"

The *clank-clanky-clatter* of his SureFire tumbling to the bottom—if there was one—reverberated through his mind.

Heath pounded an arm against the wall.

"What's wrong?"

He watched the beam twirling, tumbling—

Splat!

Darkness gulped the beam in a wolfish devour.

"You gotta be kidding me." Heath wanted to punch something. Kick the wall. But he had to keep it together. *Stay upright, calm. . .for Darci.* For her to get frantic, want to cut to the chase when she was all avoidance and distance at the base—panic had its talons dug deep into her courage. And too much distance already separated them.

"Heath." Her voice strained. "What's wrong?"

"Nothing. Everything." He cursed himself for being so careless. He was so far out of his element, off his game. When Darci was depending on him.

And I'm dangling in a shaft with no light.

His studies for chaplaincy rained down verses, one after another, about Jesus being the Light of the World. A staunch reminder that Heath wasn't a shining example of trusting God.

He peered up, no longer able to see Darci's hope and expectation gouged into her face. No longer able to see where he'd come from. And below. . .unable to see where he was going.

Just like my life.

He knew God had a twisted sense of humor, and though he didn't find it funny, the poignancy struck center mass. Hand fisted on the cord below, Heath glanced up and down again. Should he keep going? Or return? The slight tremor in his arms warned him of his weakness.

In more ways than one.

He knew, in his own strength, he could go back up. Get to the top. Be with Darci. But that would get them nowhere. But going down, exploring the unknown. . .hadn't he done the same thing with his life? Familiar with combat and military life, he'd pushed and pushed till he got what he wanted.

And how's that working for you?

Okay, God, enough with the stark parallels. Despite his playful thought, he was wide open to whatever God was doing here. He could sense the life-altering shift. He just wasn't sure how it was connected to this shaft.

Going down was a matter of faith. Exploring the unknown, being vulnerable, was putting action behind his faith. *Faith without works is dead. . .*

Okay. That was beyond stark.

Heath released the belay and lowered himself more.

"Heath?"

Was this stupid? Going farther down, risking getting stuck or never reaching bottom? He continued down.

"Heath?"

Water gurgled below, drawing his gaze downward. A strange glow swirled. . .

The SureFire!

On the surface. About ten feet below.

Heath let out the tension and glided down. . .down. . .to the end of the rope.

Still hadn't hit bottom.

"Heath!"

Her frantic call jerked him out of his focus. "Sorry." If he let go and dropped, he could go straight into the freezing water. With the rabid temperatures, he'd have fifteen minutes—max—before his body temperatures dropped to critical.

So did he feel the way out was there, with the icy water and certainty of death?

"Hang on." His voice bounced off the walls and thudded against his mind.

He stared down at the beam. He couldn't be more than six or seven feet from the bottom. He'd jumped from greater heights in training. The fear that had him clinging to the rope was the question of the water. It'd swallowed the flashlight. Then spit it back up. Deep enough to go down, but not enough for it to vanish.

Noise filtered through his senses. Heath looked left. What was that? To the right? Crazy. There wasn't anything here to make noise.

Again, he felt his toe slipping against the wall and reached out.

Hollow and distant the noise actually sounded closer.

How was that possible?

Thwat. The soft sound registered like a sonic boom. He jerked up, barely able to see the multistrand rope fraying. A strand snapped free.

Playtime over. He had to get down. Now.

Heath quickly lowered himself. The cord snapped taut. *Ploink!* Another snapped.

Do or die, he had to take this literal leap of faith. Heath released himself from the harness. Dropped. Straight down.

★ ★   **Forty-One**   ★ ★

Heeeeaathh!"

Gravity yanked hard.

Straight down. Though it happened in seconds, the fall felt like an eternity.

Icy water clapped its painful talons on his ankles. Calves. Knees. Thighs. Waist. *God, help me!*

He hit bottom of the well. Jarring pain darted up his legs as he impacted. Threw him backward. His head banged against the cave wall. "Augh!" He jerked forward and steadied himself, frigid water cocooning his body.

Seconds. He had just a few minutes to get out of this water before hypothermia set in. But how did you get out of a well that's little more than shoulder-wide with no way out?

The hollow noise he'd heard earlier reverberated again through the water. *Trinity?* No. Now he was imagining things. He shook his head and looked up to where he knew Darci sat. "I'm at the bottom. Chest high in water."

"That's. . ." her voice faded. Quiet. Still. "Not good."

"Ya think?" Heath plucked his SureFire from the water and scanned the walls. The beam stroked the climbing rope. . .too far up to reach.

"What're you going to do?"

Again, the hollow sound—so much like a bark. He had to be going crazy. Hypothermic symptoms included unclear thinking. But he hadn't been submerged long enough for that. . .right?

"Uh. . ."

Water stirred to his right. What on earth would be swimming in ice-cold water?

"What's wrong?"

"I think. . ." He kept his legs and upper body as still as he could, swiveling a bit to look around him.

Darkness rippled through the water.

"Something's in the wa—"

A dark shape stirred a heavy wake.

Augh!

Heath plunged his hand into the water, aiming for his holstered weapon.

Erupting water splashed his face.

He flinched away, but in the seconds where his heart rate hit catastrophic, his mind latched on to the attacker. Who wasn't an attacker. "Trinity!"

Her bark roared through the shaft.

Heath pulled her into his arms. She lathered him with drool, icy water, and elation. His heart chugged as he laughed and hugged her tight. Laughed again. "How did you find me, girl?"

She barked.

"Your dog? How did your dog get in there?" Darci asked, her questions filled with a nervous laugh.

"There must be a hole or something." Heath beamed the light, his body trembling from the cold. "Hang on." Man, to find out where she'd come from, he'd have to submerge—all the way! *Better to lose a few digits than a whole life, I guess.*

He stuffed the SureFire back in place and lowered himself below the surface, ignoring the stinging water. He angled in the direction Trinity had come and sure enough—a hole!

He burst back up. "There's a passage. Let me check it out."

Quiet amplified the cold.

". . .okay."

"Don't worry. I'm not leaving you." Heath willed her to trust him. "R–remember—you owe me a k–kiss."

"Very funny, Daniels."

Her voice sounded lonely but hopeful. He could live with that. For now. He smoothed a hand over Trinity's head. "Ok–k–kay, g–g–girl.

Sh–sh–sh–show m–m–me."

Heath again submerged. Swam for the hole. Hauled himself through the opening. A steep rise made it hard to wiggle up. Panic clenched him in the narrow space. This was their only way out. A blast of cold air stung his face. He slumped to his knees, still partially submerged.

"Hooah!" The shout pervaded the tunnel.

It took a few seconds for Heath to see in the semidarkness. Backlit by pure, beautiful daylight, two silhouetted forms hunkered close by. Watterboy and Candyman.

Hands hauled him up the slope and onto the passage floor.

"We thought we'd lost you."

Teeth chattering, Heath chuckled. "If I d–d–d–don't"—the clatter of teeth on teeth hurt—"g–get warm quick, you w–w–w–will." He hated the way his lip wobbled.

"Where's the girl?"

Heath bobbed his head back. "The t–t–tunnel"—he bit down to stymie the shivering—"leads to a well. . .w–w–water." Violently, he shook. "Twenty- or thirty-foot shaft in the cave we were in. Sh–sh–she's at the t–t–t–top."

Someone cursed. "How are we supposed to get her out?"

"F–fast," Heath said, teeth banging. He bit his tongue and tensed. His arms felt heavy, stiff. Legs, too.

A dark shadow sucked out the light. "Chopper!"

Heath smiled. "This just. . .gets better." Why wasn't he shivering? He slumped against the wall. Felt like an MRAP sat on his chest.

"Hey, get out there." Watterboy shoved Heath's shoulder.

"Get off, man," Heath growled.

Watterboy stilled. "Scrip—get him out of here. He's hypothermic. Do we have extra clothes?"

"Negative." Scrip bent closer.

Heath swatted him off. "Not leaving till. . ." Till what? Where'd that thought go? What was he saying? "Darci." Why couldn't he breathe?

"Scrip, get a litter." Watters angled himself closer to the water, nudging Heath away from the mouth of the shaft, from Darci. "Candyman!" Watters pointed to Heath. "Now!"

He dragged himself past Heath, keying his mic. "Command, this is Candyman. Need warming blankets and prep the medical bay for hypothermia."

"Heath?" Her voice bounced back, empty of promise and void of response. This must be what it was like for the first man on the moon—to look out across the pitch black and know he was utterly alone, save the few on the ship. Heath was...somewhere. Down the shaft. He'd said he wasn't leaving.

Then he did.

Water had stirred, then nothing.

Darci lay back and drew her legs from the ledge. Hand over her forehead and another resting lightly over her side injury, she closed her eyes. A moot point since the pitch black closed in around her, bringing with its totality and desperate isolation suffocating panic.

She swallowed. *Relax. Don't think about it.*

As she had during interrogations, she looked for something recent and pleasant.

Heath and Trinity filled her mind.

Okay, maybe that wasn't the best place to put her thoughts. She had no idea what had happened to him down there. What if he didn't find an out? What if—water. . .he'd mentioned water. In this winter storm? It'd be freezing. What if. . .what if he froze to death first?

The thought punched through her tough exterior, fisted its thorny tendrils around her heart, and squeezed. Hard.

Her eyes burned.

She gritted her teeth. She'd never been a baby. Never been a *cry*baby. She had to get it together, keep it together, until. . .

Until what? If Heath was dead, she had no way out. Already she felt the sharp teeth of frostbite gnawing at the top of her nose, her ears, her fingers, and her toes.

I'm alone. Completely alone. Wounded. Freezing. Dying. . .

Darci felt the odd warmth of her tears against her chapped cheeks. She closed her eyes. *God, I gave my life to You. . .extended my faith. . .my faith, not Mom's. I believe You can get me out of here, but even if You don't. . .*

Just like Shadrach, Meshach, and Abednego.

She recalled her earlier thoughts about the three, but now the story felt personal. They were thrown into the fire. She was thrown into the earth's freezer.

Whatever Your will. . .I want it.

But if she survived this, then. . .where would things go with Heath? Could they work something out, so. . . ?

So, what?

Was she seriously thinking of making a life with him?

A giggle leapt from her chest. *Yeah, I am.*

Idiotic. They didn't even know each other. Although, at the same time, she knew a lot about him, knew the mettle in him, knew the goodness that made him a man of character, knew the tender and funny side. . .

Jianyu had never been funny. She hadn't seen his demons until it was too late. Jianyu's patience had hidden his poison. DIA wanted more information, so she had to buy time by selling her soul. She'd sacrificed everything trying to distract him. Thanks to a CIA operative, she escaped—barely. And spent the next six months in counseling and begging God to forgive her.

And trying to forgive herself.

Splash!

Darci stilled, stifling the tears, ears trained on the shaft below. Heath. . .he'd gone. . .told her he wanted her to live, to make good on that request for a kiss.

Did she really ask him for one? The cold must be getting to her brain. She'd never done something like that. And after they got back, after she recovered, Heath would be on to his next speaking gig with Trinity.

And Burnett. . .sent her. . .away. . .to focus.

Her hands hurt. Her legs. The cold dug into her shoulders, down her spine.

I am focused. For the first. . .home, want. . .home. I want to see my father. I want. . .a life.

Where was her thirst for vengeance? The determination to see justice done?

It's quenched.

Sleep. . .cold. . .it hurt. . .alone. . .so dark. . .

Swooshing dragged her out of the sluggish thoughts.

"Heath?" she barely breathed his name.

No, she was alone. With God. She closed her eyes.

Darci Kintz.

Yeah. Me. Tired. . .pain. . .cold.

"Darci Kintz!"

She opened her eyes. Darkness. Cold. But. . .*my name. . .*

"U.S. Special Forces. Are you alive?"

Yes.

"Can you hear me?"

She realized she didn't put voice behind her answer. "Yes." It came out a mere breath. She coughed—pain! Her ribs. Curled onto her side, she shifted around, dragged herself to the edge of the shaft. Peered down.

Bright light vanquished the darkness.

She grunted and withdrew. "Here." That was louder. But not enough. She pushed herself to shout. "I'm here!"

"Hooah!" Came his response. "Ma'am. Move away from the ledge."

Darci wiggled back, unable to push back.

A strange thwipping sailed through the air. . .louder. . .closer.

Thunk! Clank!

Pebbles rained down, and a snake coiled down from the ceiling. Darci shrunk away—at least, she thought she did. But she squinted. Not a snake. A rope dangling from a grappling hook.

"Thank God," she whispered, her thoughts clinging to her Maker.

In minutes, light and the powerful form of the special-ops soldier loomed over her. Darci relaxed, knowing she was going to make it.

"We're going to get you out of here. Just relax." He shrugged out of a pack and dropped it beside her. He lifted her arm, a small pinch. . .

"Hea. . ."

He said nothing as he wrapped another thermal blanket around her, and then slid her into some type of cocoon. Another soldier appeared beside him. Together they assembled a litter, then lifted her into it.

"We're going to strap you onto me. We'll go down, then into the water, and into the tunnel," the first man said as he drew her toward him. The other secured harnesses around them.

Darci grimaced against the pain roaring through her side. But she'd endure it. To get out of here. To get home.

But the first shift over the ledge jarred. Hard.

Darci tensed and held her breath. Each length he dropped felt as if someone rammed a hammer into her back and side. She dropped her head against his shoulder, unable to withstand the fire eating her up from the inside out.

"Easy," he muttered.

Water trickled and gurgled. Darci felt it encircle the insulated cocoon they'd placed her in. Then her knees. Her waist.

She endured the suffocating feeling as the oxygen mask tightened. "Hold on and hold your breath."

She nodded.

They went under, her back arching. She reminded herself to breathe, not to scream against the knife being driven through her spine. Within seconds, thrashing water and hands pawed at her. Drawn up out of the water, she heard Trinity's bark. . .somewhere.

"Let's move," Watterboy shouted.

They carried her out of the lower cave, and Darci strained to see into the brilliance of the day. Black and dirty against the pristine white, the UH-60 Black Hawk thrummed with life. Rotors whipped the powder-fine dusting of snow. The rescue team huddled around the helo. Two men in flight suits stood at the foot of a gurney, easing into the chopper. Heath. . .

"Make a hole," Candyman called as they hurried toward the bird.

They slipped her through the opening the team made—and her gaze struck Heath. He gave his "Ghost" moniker new meaning with his deathly pale skin and lips. The medics worked to wrangle his hands. He was punching. Thrashing—but in a slow-motion way. Like he was drunk. He almost flopped off the litter.

Darci's heart backed into her throat. Such a strong man. Seeing him combative, confused, clumsy. . .

Others crowded into the chopper around her just seconds before it dipped, then rose into the pale blue sky. She grabbed Watterboy's sleeve. "How long to the base?"

His gaze hit Heath for a fraction of a second, then her. "Twenty."

Twenty *minutes*? Heath didn't have twenty. If he was combative, he'd already entered the severe stage. But at least he was fighting. And not in a coma.

Heath's arm slid down. His other swung wildly, then flopped.

His eyes rolled back into his head.

Forty-Two

Aboard Helo, En Route to Bagram

Intubated, Heath lay on the precipice of death.

Darci lured a whimpering Trinity into her lap and wrapped her arms around the seventy-pound ball of fur, whose only attention lay on her handler. Her partner. Though Darci couldn't hear it for the wind and rotor noise, she felt a whimper rumble through Trinity.

Pale. Heath was so pale. Darci covered her mouth. It pained her to see that thing sticking out of his mouth. The medics hovering, working. Death had never felt so close and violent.

How long had Heath been drenched and icy cold? He'd gone down that shaft for her, to save her. Was it going to cost him his life?

"Pupils dilated," a medic shouted.

"Unconscious."

Wary, Darci shivered uncontrollably, watching Heath slip from this world. *You can't. Please. . .don't leave me when I just met you. Heath. . .*

"Drink." A sergeant stuffed a thermos straw toward her.

She shook her head. "No. . ." Couldn't drink with Heath fighting for his life.

"Drink," he shouted over the roar of the wind and rotors, his expression cross.

She sipped, surprised as sickly sweet warmth slid across her tongue and down her throat. Painful yet. . .better. She took another draught.

"Two minutes," came a shout from the cockpit.

"He doesn't have two minutes!" the medic shouted back.

315

RONIE KENDIG

Warmth tumbled into Darci's stomach, and she wasn't sure it was the drink. Was he breathing? *Heath! Don't do this to me. Not when I found someone worth knowing. Please. . .*

"He's going V-fib!"

Heath looked dead. His chest wasn't moving—or was it?

The next two minutes felt like an eternity. Darci looked away, terrified Heath wouldn't make it. *You owe me a kiss.* Warmth slid down her cheek as she felt the descent of the chopper. She glanced out the door, where three men sat in the opening. Buildings dotted the terrain a few miles out.

Even as they lowered to the ground, Darci saw the medical teams waiting. And a lot of soldiers.

Before the skids touched down, the three men launched out of the way. Settled on the ground, the chopper wound down as the medics hopped out, unlatching Heath's litter.

Behind him rushed a team of six. They transferred Heath to a gurney.

A doc stood on the side of the gurney as the others shoved it away. They shocked Heath. Once. Twice. Three times. CPR. They were doing CPR.

That meant Heath wasn't breathing.

He was dying.

Forty-Three

Craig Joint Theater Hospital
Bagram AFB, Afghanistan

A window peeked out into the night. Snow, falling thick and angry again, drenched the compound. Little movement and even less traffic stirred throughout the American base. Walls creaked and groaned beneath the strong wind, pounding the building with its mighty fists. The last attack of the storm would slow Jianyu's Yanjingshe fighters.

Hands behind his back, Haur stared into the dark night at the mercy of the blizzard. With the fighters delayed, he had more work to do. The bars and lock on the cell, the cuffs on his hands—they were impediments he must figure out how to overcome.

"It sounds bad."

Haur kept his face impassive at the sound of Bai's comment about the weather. On the surface it sounded benign, but when mentioned in light of recent events, he knew they referred to the situation.

"Did you hear, they got the girl out?" Bai's bunk groaned as he shifted onto his side.

Haur said nothing.

"You are planning something," Bai whispered as his dark shape drew closer to the bars on the right that separated them. "Why did you not go into the compound to capture Jianyu?"

Beyond their holding cell, voices rose and fell. The sound of someone approaching pushed him away from Bai. Away from the window. But further into the arms of the storm.

"It is time."

Inside, Darci tried to locate where they'd taken Heath. She heard a flurry of voices and could see shadows and personnel hustling at the far end of the hall, but her team wheeled her into a bay. They laid warming blankets across her chest. Sitting upright a bit, she was ordered to consume more of the all-too-sweet and warm liquid.

"Heath."

"Your core temperature," a doctor attached a probe to her temple, "is just around ninety-three degrees."

"Ninety-four," a nurse announced.

"Good, but we need that higher." He nodded to the thermos in Darci's hand. "Keep drinking."

"I want to see Heath. Where is he? Is he okay?"

"Don't worry about him. If your temperature drops, you'll run some very serious risks. That's what you need to focus on right now."

An orderly rushed in with a machine, which he set up beside her. A steady whirring filled the room, along with warm, moist air.

They were working and moving so fast that Darci took a moment to savor the fact that she didn't have to move at all or jar her ribs. But her mind and heart were with Heath. . .wherever he was. Had she really gone mental on him, asking for a kiss? He'd taken it in stride. During her moment of panic, he helped her haul in the tattered edges of her courage.

The warmth burned a bit, but Darci knew it was just the bitter bite of the frigid temperature wearing off. She closed her eyes and focused on Heath. On seeing him again. Getting warm fast so she could scurry down the hall to where he was warming up, too.

"That's it," the nurse said. "You rest. I'll be right back."

Darci let the quiet descend. . .only, it wasn't quiet. A bevy of noises a few bays down captured her attention. The *tsing* of a curtain jerked her gaze to the side. A nurse rushed down the hall and around a corner. When he did, the curtain slung aside. Just enough. . .

Heath!

Even from here she could see how white he was. Her stomach churned.

Drawn to him, she eased off the gurney but held the blue warm

318

water blanket around her shoulders and trudged closer.

The doctors looked frantic. Nurses, too.

IV bags hung over him. Several tubes snaked into his arms and abdomen. What. . .?

"Get that heart-lung bypass ready."

Hand to her throat, Darci stilled. Bypass? What did that mean?

"Up to eighty-four-point-two."

Degrees?

"That's progress."

"The only progress we've had."

"His heart rate is dropping."

"Losing him!"

Darci dropped back against the wall, hand over her mouth. Tears streaming.

A nurse started out of the bay and stopped. "Oh."

Blinking the tears away, Darci shook her head. Her knees wobbled.

"Help!" The nurse rushed her.

Arms caught Darci as she slid backward. Lifted her—pain stabbed her side—and hurried her back to her bay.

But nothing—*nothing!*—would gouge from her mind the image of Heath dying.

Back on the gurney, the man who'd carried her stood over her.

She looked up into green eyes. The dog handler owner who'd brought Heath over. In his gaze she saw her own pain reflected. Something pinched her arm.

Her vision swooned.

★ ★ Forty-Four ★ ★

A blurry white image loomed over her.

Darci jerked.

"Ah, you're awake."

She straightened, her head feeling like a thousand pounds. "I didn't know I fell asleep."

"Yeah, sorry about that. We had to put you under for your own sake."

Though she should feel ashamed for taking matters into her own hands, Darci didn't. Heath was dying—or dead. "Heath. How is he?"

"I'll let the general know you're back with us."

"Wait."

The nurse left, and in her place came the doctor.

Glowering, he moved to her charts. "You were very foolish to get out of that warming bed."

Darci took the beating. "How is he?"

"Haven't you heard of doctor-patient confidentiality?"

"Can I see him?"

"Not till you're stable and your temperature's much higher." He yanked the curtain around her bed, and outside he ordered the hall cleared, stating it was for medical personnel only.

The nurse returned with a steaming mug and some warm food. "Keep drinking and eating. Get your insides warmed up so you'll stop shivering."

Shivering? Darci glanced at her hand, surprised to see tremors.

"You're doing good. Once you're warmer, we'll take a walk. Exercise is good to get the body heated up."

"A walk?" Darci's yearning to see Heath latched on to those words.

The nurse arched an eyebrow. "Well, not to see anyone. Just to walk around."

Surely she could find a way to convince the nurse. Then a thought struck her—hard. What if Heath hadn't made it? What if he'd died after she fell unconscious?

"Heath—is he alive?"

"Just relax. I can't give out information on other patients. Now, drink."

"Wait." Darci took an obedient sip, more thoughts assailing her exhausted mind. "Have there been attacks?"

The nurse laughed. "You're in Afghanistan."

"No." Darci swallowed. "I mean, bombs—here. On the bases."

Confusion rippled through the older woman's face. "No, not here. Things have been pretty quiet." She tapped Darci's arm. "Ninety-four degrees. Keep that coming up and you'll be out of here in no time."

The nurse disappeared, leaving Darci alone with the chill that seemed to have clung to her bones and the mental fog that made it hard to think straight. No attacks, so. . .Heath had kept his word. He'd told them. But. . .how had they stopped the attacks so fast? Had the rescue team notified Command, and they in turn found the bombs? It seemed too fast.

"Well, 'bout time you came back. Don't you think you've had enough playtime?" General Burnett's voice boomed before he entered the sick bay. His stern features, his gruff voice, felt like the warming jacket she still sported. Then it faded as a smile seeped into his rough exterior. "You should take better care of yourself, or your dad will wring my neck."

Darci couldn't help the smile. "Yes, sir."

He bent over the bed and peered down into her eyes, no personal space between them. "How you doing, kiddo?"

He'd been general first, friend second. But it was a really nice arrangement that provided Darci a base from which to operate in more ways than one. She recognized the concern in his eyes even amid the gruff voice and exterior. "Been better."

"I could've told you that." He straightened and folded his arms across his chest. "That's what you get, trying to take down the entire Chinese army by yourself."

"So, you stopped them—got him?"

Burnett smiled, eyes crinkling. "Thanks mostly to you."

Darci let out a long breath. Exhaustion plucked at every sinew. "Good."

"Get some rest."

"Wait. Heath."

Something indiscriminate flashed through his face. "Don't worry about him. You need to get rested and better."

"I'm fine."

He scowled at her.

"Okay, a little pain—they broke my ribs, but I'm fine otherwise."

"You're an ice cube."

"Water freezes at thirty-two degrees." She pointed to a small box readout. "I'm at ninety-four, so technically. . ." She swung her legs over the side of the bed.

"Whoa." Burnett's large hands steadied her. "Where are you going?"

"I already told you, I want to see him." Even as she moved, the cold temperature made her ankles throb. "Besides, the nurse told me exercise would warm my body."

Burnett squatted in front of her bed, peering up into her eyes. "Darci. Please. Your body isn't ready for you to do this."

"My body isn't, or you aren't?"

"Kiddo, I don't think *you* are ready for this."

Alarm spiked. "What do you mean?"

"It doesn't matter. You can't go in there anyway. Even I couldn't get in there." General Burnett sighed. "Just. . .rest. Okay, Darci? You've been to hell and back. We thought we'd lost you—"

"You did. To the Chinese who captured me."

"Which is why I talked with your dad. He's worried, wants you to go home for a while."

Avoidance. "I want to know how he is, General."

"Your father's—"

"You know who I mean." Though she fisted her hands, her stomach squirmed under his scrutiny. "Heath—how is he? Why can't I see him?"

"Darci—"

Not the tone she wanted to hear. "No. Please don't—"

"Darci, he's not good."

Fire sped through her veins. "What do you mean?"

"He went into full cardiac. Twice."

Darci drew in a hard breath. "How. . .they got him. . .he left. . ." Those gray eyes. . .the strength. . .he'd saved her. . .gone down that shaft. . .*for me.* Tears stung her eyes. "What are you saying?"

"He's in a coma. They don't know why he hasn't woken up. They're arranging to take him to Landstuhl."

"But he'll make it." She looked to the nurse who came back in and stopped cold. "Right? He'll wake up, won't he?"

The nurse shot a glance at General Burnett, then hurried back out. With her went Darci's frantic hope for Heath. "Why won't she answer me?" A tear broke free.

"With the TBI, they just aren't sure what to expect. It doesn't look good."

She threw off the blanket. "I want to see him."

"Darci—"

"Don't." She froze, her heart stamping out his objection. "I know you don't want me involved with him, but. . ." She looked him straight in the eye. "It's too late. I'm invested."

Burnett hung his head as he pushed back to his feet.

"Take me to see him, General—Lance. As my godfather, as my favorite 'uncle.'"

He shook his head. "That's not fair."

"Please."

Escorted by the general, Darci slowly—very slowly—made her way down the hall, each step heavy and awkward. They trudged around a corner, and when they passed through a door, three people came to their feet from the chairs huddled by another door. Heath's dog-handling team.

Trinity. How was Trinity doing? Was she okay? A renewed ache wormed through her chest.

"General." Green eyes bounced to Darci as the team leader greeted her. "Ma'am."

"You're. . .you brought him over here?"

He extended a hand. "Jibril Khouri."

"Darci Kintz. Thank you."

Confusion rippled through his handsome face. He checked with the two women with him. "Thank you? For what?"

"For bringing him. He saved my life."

Sorrow crossed his brow, but he quickly tried to conceal it. "He is a good man, a hero." Jibril put an arm around the blond, whose hair hung in short spirals around her face. "This is Aspen, and also Timbrel." The brunette with a long ponytail.

"How is Trinity?" Darci asked, hands shoved in the pockets of her jacket.

The brown-haired girl jutted her jaw. "Going nuts."

Sweet relief! Darci let out a labored breath. "But she's okay?"

They nodded. Kindness and gentility marked Jibril's face as he inclined his head. "As best as can be expected without Heath."

"Any news?" General Burnett cocked his head in the direction of the door.

"They are. . .tending him now," Jibril said.

It all sounded morbid—and hopeless. She couldn't take it anymore. *Wouldn't* believe that Heath was taking his final plunge. Not when she'd finally set her heart on him. Darci shifted and pushed through the door.

"Hey!"

The loud calls came from behind and in front.

"You can't be in here."

Darci lumbered toward the bed. Lights gaped at him as the doctors and nurses moved around the bed draped with several puffy warming blankets that looked like clear rafts. The same warm moisture that had coated her room filled this one. Heath, tubes running into his mouth and nose, looked peaceful.

Too peaceful.

The thought ricocheted from her chest to her stomach and back. She shuffled closer, surprised when they did not stop her.

"General. . ."

"Let her have a minute."

Relief warred with her panic.

Panic? At what? Heath. . .never opening those warm, caring eyes again.

At his bedside, she leaned against it, using it for support against the tidal pull of emotion. Darci smoothed a hand through his short, sandy blond hair. At least he had some color now. When she'd seen him before. . .death. Not even warmed over. Just icy, cruel death.

"Ghost. . ." she whispered as she drew herself up and sat on the edge of his bed, taking in his large frame beneath the humming warming blanket, which looked more like giant bubble-tube packing, and the warming fan. "You said you'd come back. . .for me." Stubble coated his angular jaw and chiseled features and tickled her fingers as she dragged her finger along it, avoiding the tubing. "Remember?"

Behind her, murmuring. But Darci felt all twisted up and turned inside out over what Heath had done to save her. Again, she touched his face, noting it still was cool. Even with the chill in her own hands, his skin felt icy.

"Remember," she breathed through a clutter of tears and angst, "I owe you something." The general would go through the roof if she mentioned it.

"Let's give her some time," the general's soft words filtered through her awareness.

Soon, the soft thump of the door came.

Darci released the hold she had on her emotions. "Heath," she said, her voice hoarse. "Please. . .come back. Let's figure things out, just like you said. Okay?" She pressed her lips to his temple. "I'll give you a real one if you'll just wake up." A tear slipped over her cheek and landed on his.

Thought so. She could just hear him saying it. Challenging her. And the weird thing was, he just seemed. . .lonely. . .without Trinity.

Darci looked over her shoulder, not surprised to find the dog team watching her through the window. Darci nodded the brunette in.

Timbrel eased into the room. "You need something?"

Waving her over, Darci eased onto her feet. "He looks lonely."

Brown eyes widened. "Don't expect me to help with that."

Smiling, Darci leaned closer to the midtwenties girl. "Can you get Trinity?"

Timbrel's face brightened. "I like the way you think." She spun on her heels and jogged out of the room.

Alone again with the man who had infiltrated her heart, mind, and life, Darci slipped her hand under the warming blanket and coiled it around Heath's. "C'mon, Soldier. Snap out of it." She had no vehemence behind it, but everything in her ached for him to come to attention. "I won't let you die for me, Heath."

Minutes later, Timbrel hurried into the room, accompanied by the soft click of nails. "She went ape when she saw me."

Trinity wagged her tail as she scampered to Darci, then went up on her hind legs, sniffing the bed. Darci drew Heath's hand to the side.

Trinity whimpered, licking his hand as if it were a Nylabone. Digging her claws into the bed, she tried to haul herself up onto the mattress. Darci bent down and gave her a boost.

"Trinity, down," Timbrel said in a firm command that wasn't loud but authoritative, ordering the dog onto her belly.

The dog complied instantly, stretching out next to her handler. She swiped her tongue over his face, then rested her snout on his shoulder and let out a sigh.

Darci ran a hand over Trinity's fur. "Thank you, girl. For everything."

"Hey." Timbrel pointed to the other side of the bed. "There's room for one more."

One more dog? Darci frowned at the girl. Wha—? "Oh, no. I couldn't."

"Oh, for Pete's sake. We're in a hospital. Nobody's going to get the wrong idea." She nudged Darci's shoulder with a fist bump. "Besides, everyone knows body-heat transfer is the best at rewarming others. And we all know you and Heath are into each other."

Heat flushed through her face.

"He needs a reason to come back." Timbrel's expression went soft. "Be that reason."

Forty-Five

I pray you'd be uplifted by His grace, and feel yourself enfolded in the peace of His embrace. . ." Angelic and soft, like a murmur against his soul, the voice drifted out.

Darci's ivory-pale face, almond-shaped eyes, and pink lips dusted his mind. Smiling, laughing. . .leaning forward for a kiss, then pulling away with another laugh.

Stop taunting me.

Then wake up, Ghost.

Wake up? Was he sleeping?

A bark jolted through his hearing. Wet and warm, a tongue slid along his cheek. Heath tried to touch the fur ball but couldn't move his arm. He dragged it out from under Trinity. He wrapped his arm around her as she greeted him with more kisses.

When he tried to lift his other arm, he realized it was pinned, too. But beneath what? Tugging his arm free, he angled to the side, aware of two things in that instant—tubes feeding him oxygen and snaking down his throat, and the blue halo of light against a crown of silky black hair.

Darci? Curled up next to him, in the bed?

No, that had to be a dream.

More like a fantasy!

He wanted to wrap an arm around her, make sure she didn't fall off the bed, but he was afraid to touch her. Afraid to burst this dream

327

bubble. He liked it, a lot. Liked her next to him. Heath coiled an arm around her and closed his eyes. It was so right, so perfect.

"See you finally decided to join us." The voice, though gruff, was quiet.

Heath looked in its direction and grimaced.

Arms folded over his broad chest, General Burnett simmered. "I asked the doc not to remove that tube so you couldn't talk."

Darci still hadn't moved. What was she doing here?

"That woman next to you is very important to me."

"Sh—" *Curse this stupid tube!*

Burnett grinned. "I'll have your neck, back, legs, every piece of you if you hurt her."

Understood, Heath conveyed with a lone nod. In more ways than one. The general was accepting that things were happening between Heath and Darci. He wasn't giving permission, but he wasn't going to interfere either.

"She's been like that next to you for nearly twenty-four hours. The docs ain't happy, but I ordered them to let her and that stinking dog of yours be."

Heath let the glower seep into his eyes. *That "stinking dog" saved your asset!*

"All right, Doc." The general motioned to Heath.

A man moved in and reached toward him. He removed the breathing tube, turned off a machine, then returned. "This will make you gag."

Heath braced himself as the tube—and his lunch—retracted. He coughed. Gagged.

Darci stirred, but Heath firmed his hold on her. She straightened, then jerked upright. Her mouth formed a perfect O when she looked up at him, sleep prying at the edges of her eyes.

"Hey," he managed, and what an effort it took!

"You're awake." She laughed and came out of his hold, but he caught her hand. She stilled for a moment, then kissed the back of his hand.

"Cheater," Heath rasped. She was out of her mind if she thought that kiss would settle her debt.

With a shy laugh, she held his hand next to her face. Tears glimmered in her eyes. His fingers itched to touch her cheek.

"Give me a minute to check his vitals, then I'll be out of your way."

The doctor took Heath's pulse, checked his heart rate, listened to his chest, recorded the information in his chart. . .all while Heath watched Darci. She'd stayed with him? Why was he laid up in bed and she was up and moving around? Genuine concern carved a hard line in her face.

"Wha. . .happ'n?" Talking felt like passing razor blades over his windpipe instead of air.

"You went into cardiac arrest twice," the doctor said. "We've had a tough time getting you to stabilize, then a harder time getting you to come out of it."

"Thickheaded," Darci said, her light brown eyes glittering.

He grinned and felt punch drunk with the way she gazed down at him. Wow, he'd risk his life every day of the year if she was the prize.

"They were prepping you for Landstuhl."

That was the last place he wanted to end up again. "Good thing I woke up." *With you in my arms.* That was amazing. Incredible.

"This young lady and your dog have kept your body temperatures stable. You should be thankful." The doctor perched a straw between Heath's lips. "Sip."

Nasty-sweet and syrupy, the drink squirted down his throat. Though too sweet for him, Heath was glad for the way it soothed the dry, cracked plains of his throat and esophagus.

"Sip this and keep sipping. I'm leaving the saline solution till you down a meal."

Nurses descended on him and over the next fifteen minutes examined, tested, checked—all as Heath kept his fingers entwined with Darci's.

"This doesn't make sense," a nurse mumbled as she recorded information.

Darci looked at her. "What?"

"His electrolytes, blood gases. . .repeat EKG are all perfect." She shared a glance with the doctor. "Like the severe hypothermia never happened. I guess because you were in top shape before, save for the TBI."

Jabbing a finger over his shoulder, the doctor grinned. "That man in the hall has been praying since we brought him in. Maybe it's a miracle."

"Yeah." Heath glanced to the hall where he spotted Jibril. "Definitely—a miracle. That's what it feels like." He downed more liquid. "Amazing. I'm tired but otherwise fine." Weird enough. He even pried himself off the bed. Okay, so his body was a bit sluggish, but they could work with that.

The doctor nodded to the general, then turned to leave. "He's all yours."

Trinity pushed up onto her haunches, panting down at him, those amber eyes sparkling. Heath dug his fingers into her fur and massaged the side of her face. "Thanks, girl."

She swiped another kiss.

Speaking of a kiss. . . Heath turned his attention to Darci, who suddenly seemed gun-shy and wanted to wrest her hand free. He frowned, but before he could say anything, she leaned down. Her lips aimed for his forehead, and his hopes crashed against her modesty.

"Still cheating."

She smiled. "I'll be right back."

"Where are you going?"

"To tell your team you're awake."

Heath couldn't help the smile. Already watching out for him. "You're the bomb—" Heath's eyes widened. "Did you tell him?"

Darci nodded. "Everything's taken care of."

Heath glanced at the general, who seemed peeved, probably over the PDA. "You got the bombs?" Wait. He hadn't had a chance to tell the doc. "How'd you find out about them? Was Haur connected?"

"What do you mean?" Darci asked. "Didn't you tell him?"

"Daniels was DOA. He couldn't tell me nothing." The general went all military on them. "What didn't he tell me?"

Darci hauled in an audible breath. "About the bombs!"

"*What* bombs?"

Forty-Six

Panic and fury erupted in his chest. Lance surged forward, aware of the bleeping that monitored Daniels's blood pressure and other vitals. Aware the increments were shortening. "What bombs, Darci?"

"Wu Jianyu," she breathed, confusion marring her young features. "When I was at the village, his captain said the bombs were ready and waiting for his activation codes." She blanched. "I thought you said you got him. I *asked* you!"

"You asked if I got *him*. And I did—Colonel Zheng is in custody."

"His son?" Her question shrieked as she stabbed her fingers through her black hair.

"Wait," Daniels asked. "That guy you sent with me on the mission?"

Lance nodded.

Darci's voice pitched. "Why is his son in custody?"

"General Zheng came here, told me Haur had gone rogue."

"The minister of defense came here?" Darci's brow knotted. "And that didn't ring fishy to you?"

"Watch yourself, Lieutenant." Lance felt the steel grip of guilt. "Everything was fishy at that point. When a man like that comes into a hostile situation and claims one of his sons is rogue, I listen."

"Wait."

Darci spun toward Heath.

"I think I saw him—the general," Heath said, his voice weak. "At the

331

village. When I was leaving with you, I saw Jianyu with an older man, talking."

"Zheng went back to China." Lance's blood chugged to an achingly slow pace, clogged around his brain, around the brutal information Daniels had just delivered. "He couldn't have been there."

Daniels's gaze lit with challenge. "You verified that?"

What was going on? Nothing made sense. Except that he needed to do as Daniels had suggested. Lance spun and jogged out of the room. Otte pulled to attention. "Get General Early. Call an AHOD of all officers in ten."

"Yes, sir."

"Put SOCOM on high alert. We have a direct threat against military personnel in the region."

Bagram AFB, Afghanistan

"Go!" Heath said to Darci. "Stay with him. I'll get dressed and meet you there." He stumbled out into the hall with Trinity at his side.

Jibril came off the wall. "What—?"

"Help me get to the bunk. I need to dress. Gotta help. . ."

They rushed to the building where his bunk offered him clean clothes, boots, and a jacket. He stuffed himself into the warm garments, savoring the delicious heat coiling around his body. Thank God he lived in Texas, because one thing he never wanted to be again was cold.

"You really gave us a bad scare, Ghost."

On the edge of his cot, Heath stuffed his foot in a boot and shot a grim expression to Aspen. "I'd love a reunion, but there's a very real, very tangible threat right now."

"I'm hearing rumors," Aspen said.

"No rumors." Heath shook his head. "It's real. Chinese have placed bombs on bases."

A voice careened through a loudspeaker, rousing everyone and warning them to grab their gear and get into formation.

Darci appeared with a vest, lead, and harness. "Here."

Man, just the sight of her. . . "Thanks." Heath threaded his arms through the vest—the thing felt like a hundred pounds with the exhaustion from two heart attacks and hypothermia—and secured it before he put on a heavy jacket.

On a knee, he rested his gloves there and donned the harness vest and lead on Trinity. "What're you hearing?"

"Burnett has put the word out." She looked good in clean clothes, even with the bruise and busted lip. She moved stiffly as she handed him an HK USP. "The other dogs are being pulled from their kennels. Ordnance is clearing buildings as we speak."

"EDD. Smart." Heath nodded.

Explosive Detection Dogs were the best at tracking down chemicals and powders. While Trinity could hunt down bad guys like nobody's business, she didn't have the intense training EDDs had. On a base three square miles in size, they had a lot of territory to cover. "This is crazy. No way we'll locate the bombs in time."

"Let's find Burnett." Darci started walking, her movements slow in the thick coat and with broken ribs.

"He's not going to tell us anything."

She eyed him. "I want to talk to Colonel Zhen—"

Crack!

Heath stopped. "That was weapon's fire." He darted toward the building it'd come from. The same building where Zheng Haur was being held. Heath jerked open the door, and Trinity lunged in ahead of him. Weapon at the ready, he moved down the too-quiet halls.

"Don't like it," he whispered to Darci, who bounded and covered with him, her Glock held like a pro.

She shook her head. Sweat beaded on her forehead. The pain from her ribs must be excruciating, but he knew better than to suggest she rest. Or not engage in the hunt.

Bang!

The sound pounded Heath's breath into the back of his throat.

"Door," Heath said, as much to himself as to her. The squeaking and swishing of tactical pants warned them of the incoming flood of soldiers.

Sure enough. Around the corner, a sea of uniforms.

Muzzles swung toward them.

"Whoa!" Heath raised his hands. "Friendly."

The men banked left, so Heath and Darci went right. Down the hall. Clearing one room after another, his heart pumping harder and faster, sensing they were closing in on their quarry. The last room. Heath shoved a foot against the handle. It burst inward. As it flapped back, his heart thudded.

"Hands in the air," he shouted. "Hands in the air!"

Zheng Haur stood over the body of his captain, gun in hand. A guard lay to the side, unconscious. . .but coming to. And still armed.

"Haur, what happened?" Heath shouted, praying the others heard. "Who killed him? Where'd you get the gun?"

Absolute calm shrouded the man. "I want to speak with General Burnett."

"Fat chance." Heath eyed the weapon. "You just killed a man and took out another. Do you really think they'll call Burnett here?"

"Bring Burnett." Haur did not relinquish the gun.

"Not happening," Watterboy's firm voice cut into the room.

"If you want to live, if you want to stop the bombs, bring Burnett here." Way too calm. "I suggest you do it now. Time is short."

Forty-Seven

Camp Loren, CJSOTF-A, Sub-Base
Bagram AFB, Afghanistan

Y ou are Meixiang?"

Daniels stepped in front of the woman, cutting off Haur's line of sight.

Haur gave a halfhearted smile. "I am no threat to you or to her."

Unfazed and undeterred, Daniels held his aim. "I'll be the judge of that."

But Meixiang edged back into view, living up to her reputation as the skilled, bold operative Jianyu had said she was. "I am Meixiang," she said in perfect Mandarin.

With a respectful nod, Haur smiled. "It is a pleasure to meet you at last." She was much paler than he'd expected for his brother's tastes, but her beauty could not be denied. "You created quite a stir in the Zheng dynasty."

Though she said nothing, Meixiang studied him. Intently. She flicked a finger to the body at his feet. "Why have you done this?"

Haur smiled again. "In time, Meixiang."

Shouts and thudding boots reverberated through the building. More military police poured into the room, weapons at the ready, in full tactical gear.

General Burnett stood there, shielded by two MPs. "What is this, Zheng?"

Haur raised both hands, the gun dangling from his thumb. "Thank you, General." Eyes on those before him, Haur dropped the magazine.

Expelled the chambered round. Slid the barrel off. A few more quick flicks, and the weapon lay on the table. "There are times we implicitly trust those who work close with us. We come to believe so fully in their identities, we do not question them." He glanced at Meixiang. "Sometimes that is a mistake."

She eased to the side. Eyes locked with him, she retrieved the barrel from the floor.

"What's your point? Why is Bai dead?"

"Captain Bai is dead because I killed him." He straightened and held his head high. Not that he was proud of his actions, but there was no point in denying the obvious. "I discovered not too long ago that he was not my ally, but my enemy."

Burnett stepped past the guards. "Is that supposed to enlighten me?"

"I was sent to the mine to check on Jianyu. General Zheng ordered me into this country to find Jianyu and bring him home." He tilted his head. "But as the mission progressed, things became less certain." His gaze shifted to Heath. "At the village with your team, I saw something that told me I had been betrayed."

"What was that?"

"I saw my brother *and* General Zheng there. Together." The image burned into his memory. "They hugged. Father and son, happy. Not as the bitter rivals they had pretended to be."

General Burnett planted his hands on his belt. "Why would they do that?"

Haur snorted and shook his head. "I think you, of all people, know why, General."

The older man took another step into the room. "Zheng Xin came to me after you were knee-deep in this mission."

It should not have surprised Haur to hear this. The twists, the betrayals were enough to solidify his determination.

"He said you were the rogue son, Haur."

Words held the power of life and death. And in that moment, a piece of Haur died. The piece of flagging courage that had fallen into the trap of a man he thought he'd made proud. Yet the wound from those words cut deep.

"Now, why would he do something like that?"

"It was time." Three beautiful words that would allow him to keep a promise. "When I was fifteen, my father left China. Defected—with your help, I believe, General Burnett."

The man yielded nothing.

"In the days before my father's escape, I learned of Xin's suspicion of his oldest friend, my father, so I chose to stay behind." Haur tried to steady his palpitating heart, noting the stunned expressions but also the unaffected ones. Meixiang was hardest to read and yet, somehow, he felt he had an ally in her. They'd both been burned by the Zhengs.

"I played the abandoned, grieving son, allowed Zheng to take me in and adopt me so his anger and attention would be deterred. I knew the man would find greater pleasure by drawing me into his camp than by killing me. Making me his son was an act designed with only one purpose—to destroy my father.

"I have endured more than twenty years under the mental and verbal abuse of General Zheng Xin." Haur let out a heavy breath, so relieved to unload that knowledge. "When I realized Bai was not my captain, not my friend, but an asset of General Zheng himself, I knew I had been betrayed."

"How'd you know it was him?" Daniels asked.

"Little things along the way, but the two most revealing—when he threw the grenade that set off the avalanche. He was trying to bury you all alive."

"And the other thing?"

"He had too much information to be a man *under* my authority."

"What does Zheng gain by betraying you to us?" Daniels asked.

"Irony." The word hurt. Stung. "He believed you would kill me. . ." Haur let his gaze linger on the weapons still aimed at him. "My father defected to America, and there would be no greater satisfaction for Zheng than if the Americans killed me—"

"We'd be killing the son of one of the greatest Chinese assets we've ever had."

Peace swarmed Haur as he reveled in the words of the general. "Thank you." He confirmed his secret thoughts, that Burnett was the one who'd helped his father. And the words encouraged him to hope that his father was still alive. "The bombs—I believe it is close to lunch, is it not?"

Burnett hesitated. "I'm warning you, Haur. If those bombs aren't found, I'll feed you to Zheng myself!"

Anticipation hung rancid and thick as they waited with Haur, while the teams searched for the explosives. But something just felt. . .off. Heath glanced at Trinity, but she had curled into a ball in the corner, uninterested. Poor girl had been through enough to sleep for a week. And if she was zoning now, then there was no threat.

Then what was eating at Heath's internal radar? He glanced to the side—

Darci.

Hand to her stomach, she eased to the back of the room.

What was that about?

Burnett advanced. "You expect us to believe you spent twenty years under that man and never tried to escape?"

"There was no need to escape." Haur shifted, as if the words made him uncomfortable. "My father—my *real* father—was safe. Do not mistake my outstanding service record for loyalty to evil men. I did what could be done to keep them from hunting down my father." Serious and tense, Haur held his ground. "I have no regrets."

"Ya know," Heath offered, "I wondered why you never referred to General Zheng as 'father.'" He inched closer, determined to ferret out what was needling him. "You were vague in the mountains when I asked you about your relationship."

Haur nodded as soldiers removed Bai's body and aided the wounded guard to sick bay. "It takes more than a name to make a father. Zheng is a cruel man, who bred a cruel son."

"But you called Jianyu 'brother.' How is that?"

"We grew up together. After my father left and I went to live at the general's home, Jianyu and I were inseparable. I looked up to him—he was fierce, a fighter. Respected. Admired." The man's gaze slid to someone in the back. "He was a ladies' man, which is why I was especially intrigued with Meixiang, the legendary woman who took my brother down."

"Jianyu's weakness took him down," Darci said.

"It is evident, is it not, that while Jianyu and the general accepted me in name, they never accepted me in heart." Haur's smile was genuine. "As I never accepted them. Not fully."

Darci came forward. "Why? Why did you not accept them? You had that beautiful home, wealth, fame..."

Haur glanced down. "Those are poor replacements for family."

"We found them!" Candyman's voice boomed through the room. Burnett glared. "Just like you said."

Heath glanced at the general, who seemed peeved. "Then what's wrong?"

"It's too easy." Burnett pressed his knuckles to the table and leaned toward the thirtysomething colonel. "What's your game, Haur?"

50 Yards outside Bagram AFB

"Go ahead."

"It's done," the voice said. "Ordnance found and disabled the bombs—and Burnett doesn't know, but locals have reported the bodies of the Russians. It's about to blow wide open."

"As expected."

"There's been a small complication though."

Jianyu ground his teeth, feeling the jaw muscle pop. "What?"

"Haur and Bai were arrested upon returning to the compound. Haur killed Bai."

"Understood. Well done."

"I do my job well and count on people like you to make sure I'm never found."

"It will be so." Jianyu ended the call, rubbing his thumb along the spine of the phone as he stared out over the dark night. The final betrayal had come.

"What news?"

Jianyu lifted his gaze from the darkened interior to the wash of moonlight reflected over the blanketed road. "It is done."

"All of it?"

"Bombs have been found, disabled." Still, it unsettled him that Haur had taken extreme measures. "Bai is dead."

A belly-jouncing chuckle filled the interior of the camouflaged vehicle. "Just as we planned." His father pushed open the door. "They're distracted. Let's move."

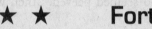

Forty-Eight

Camp Loren, CJSOTF-A, Sub-Base
Bagram AFB, Afghanistan

Y ou're my brother."

His expression—eyebrows tense, lips firm, a slight dimple in the chin—was so like her father's that Darci couldn't pry herself away if she tried.

The boulder of truth hit him. "Meixiang—" Haur's eyes widened. "Oh—how did I not see it? All those days in the mountain. . .even your name. . ."

He pulled her into a hug. It felt right. It felt wrong. She didn't know what to think or do. She'd last seen him as a teenager. But he knew she was alive. Knew their father was alive. And he didn't search for them? She stood stiff in his arms, not sure what to feel.

Growling pervaded the room. Several loud barks.

"Release her," Heath said in a firm voice.

Mind whirling, Darci eased back and looked at Trinity, who was primed on Haur, hackles raised. "It's. . .okay."

Heath eyed her, then Haur. "Trinity, out."

The dog turned a circle, then sidled up next to Heath, panting as she watched Darci.

With a nervous laugh, Haur shook his head. "You were five the last time I saw you."

"And you, so big. . ." Tears stung though she fought them. "I. . .was so mad at Ba for leaving you. I couldn't understand why he'd leave you. He wouldn't talk of you or Mom. But you—why didn't you find us?"

"Didn't he tell you?"

340

She frowned. "Tell me? What?"

"He told no one," Burnett said. "He never betrayed you, which makes me wonder why you betrayed General Zheng. What's the game?"

"No game."

Darci swung around on the general. "You *knew*? You knew that my brother stayed of his own free will, and you never told me?"

He shrugged those broad shoulders. "You never asked. Look, there's a lot to sort out, but not right now. Later." Burnett focused on Haur. "What's going on, Haur? It was too easy to find the bombs—Ordnance isn't even sure they were viable."

Haur frowned. "I do not understand."

"That makes two of us." Burnett growled. "It's like they knew this would happen."

"But. . .that's impossible."

"Unless they were counting on you to finally switch sides," Heath said, his hands tucked under his armpits, probably stealing warmth. "But to what end?"

Haur looked to Darci. "Would he do all this for you?"

She laughed. "Never."

A thoughtful knot formed at the center of his brow as he nodded. "You're right. The general would want to inflict a big wound—"

"Merciful God!" Burnett banged a fist on the table. "He couldn't have known."

"What?" Darci asked, breathless at the fury on the face of the most stoic man she knew.

He looked at Haur. "They were coming after that greatest Chinese asset."

Haur's eyes widened. "He's *here*?"

A curse sailed through the air as Burnett barreled out of the room, MPs and ODA452 on his heels.

It took two seconds for Darci's mind to catch up with the fact that Haur sprinted after the general. They were going to save someone. The greatest Chinese asset.

"Ba!"

Forty-Nine

With Trinity bounding ahead, just feet from Burnett and Haur, Heath ran after them. His heart spiraled into his throat. The infamous Li Yung-fa was here? On this base? Why on earth had Burnett brought the man here?

Beside him, Darci struggled—the ribs, no doubt—but she ran heedless of the pain that had to be punching the breath from her with each step.

As they bolted into the command bunker, Heath slowed at the ominous silence that hung in the building.

"What's wrong?" Darci spun to him.

"It's too quiet."

Burnett hesitated. "He's right."

Candyman and Watterboy were right with them. "Everything okay, General?"

"Lock it down," Burnett shouted as he rounded a corner. "Nobody gets out!"

Heath threw himself after the general as a grinding siren punctured the air. Emergency lights swirled.

Around another bend, Heath barreled over a body. He skidded and glanced back—just in time to see Watterboy and Candyman jogging toward them, armed and serious.

"Got him." Candyman dropped to a knee beside Otte, who groaned.

"Got another one here," Rocket called from the far left. "It's General Early—unconscious." He planted a hand over a wound and dug in his pocket.

At the sound of pounding boots, Heath spun. Darci vanished to the left. "Darci!" He propelled himself after her, praying harder than he'd ever prayed. His body wasn't moving as fast as he'd like, but after being technically dead twice today...

Shouts and thuds reverberated through the hall.

Heath pushed himself. Trinity lunged ahead. A corridor stretched before him. Four doors, two on each side. All closed. No Darci. No voices.

"Trinity," Heath said, looking over his right arm at her. "Seek!"

She zigzagged from side to side, checking doors. At door three, she sat and looked at him. A pat on his shoulder alerted him to the stacked team of ODA452. Heath nodded. He slid up to the jamb and took point.

Watterboy kicked the door in.

Heath stepped in. His split-second recon dumped ice through his veins. And that made him mad. He vowed to never be cold again. To the right, an older man he hadn't seen before sat with a gun to his temple, compliments of the older man he'd seen at the village earlier: Zheng Xin. In that whipped-cream chaos of a moment, Heath couldn't shake the haunting peace that filled the first man's face. Was that Darci's father, Li Yung-fa? Greatest Chinese asset?

A yelp hauled his attention and weapon to the left. Wu Jianyu held Darci in a stranglehold. Eyes ablaze and locked on Heath, he flared his nostrils. By the reddening of Darci's face, Jianyu was squeezing with his arm muscles. Strangling her.

"Let her go." Man, that sounded like a bad line from a B movie. Heath lined up the sights with Jianyu's beady eyes. "*Don't* move."

Trinity's snarling and snapping fueled Heath's anger. Amazing how she'd taken to Darci, ready to defend her.

The hushed rustle of ODA452s swift filing into the room gave Heath little reassurance, especially with Jianyu strangling Darci and his father about to put lead into her father's head.

"Get the dog to stand down," Jianyu said, shielding himself behind Darci.

Coward.

"Nothing doing," Heath said. Crazy. Confusing. So much happening. Burnett and Haur faced off with Zheng, who held Yung-fa captive. Heath kept his focus on Darci.

343

"Unlock the door," Zheng commanded.

"Not happening," Burnett said with a growl.

"I will end this happy reunion if you do not."

"It's already over, Zheng." Burnett held fast. "No matter what happens, you're not walking out of here alive."

Heath knew ODA452 had lines of sight on the tangos. . .or at least they would if he wasn't blocking Jianyu from them. He eased to the side, keeping his weapon on him, determined to place a bullet in the guy if he escalated.

Only as Heath weighed options did he notice Burnett's hand. Signals. He was giving the SOCOM team signals. "You know this isn't going to end the way you want it to, Zheng."

"It will. Twenty years! I have waited twenty years."

"You should have let it go nineteen years ago," the man in the chair said, his voice strong, sure.

"Shut up, Yung-fa! This is my victory. You will not steal it from me." The man's face reddened. "Are you ready to die?"

The question drew Heath's attention.

Jianyu looked around Darci to his father.

Her gaze locked with Heath's. Meaning spiraled through those beautiful eyes. She blinked. Once. Twice. Three times.

"Trinity, go!"

Darci bent forward, hard and fast, driving her elbow into Jianyu's gut.

Trinity lunged, between Burnett and Haur, straight at Jianyu. Grabbed the man's arm and yanked hard. As soon as Darci was out of the way, Heath fired. Winged Jianyu. He was not going to let this guy take anything else from Darci, especially not her life.

Another shot rang out.

Darci dropped, pulse rapid-firing.

ACUs filled her vision. Swarming. Shouting. Taking over.

She had one goal—Ba. She shifted. Backed up. Where was he? Why couldn't she see him?

"Darci!" Heath plowed through the scene and slid to his knees. "Are you okay?"

"My father!" She scrabbled around the others toward her father.

A tangle of bodies made it impossible to figure out what was happening. Shouts. Thuds of fists against bone. One colossal whoosh of action. Then quiet fell over the room.

Boots stepped aside.

Her father looked straight at her and smiled.

"Ba, what are you doing here?" As she scrambled to him, she saw the dark stain on his chest. "No!" She pressed her hand against his wound. "You're shot!"

He held her hand, his goatee trembling. He reached past her. Darci glanced to where he reached and stilled. Haur squatted behind her. She looked back to her father, years falling off his face. "My children," he said with watery eyes and a weary voice. "Together. At last."

"Ba." Haur knelt and bent down, embracing his father. "It has been too long." Tears streamed down his face. "I kept my promise, Ba. I found a way home."

Hand clapped around Haur's neck, their father managed a smile. "Thank you." He sobbed. "Thank you, my son."

Choked at the scene, at the memory of their last time together, Darci let the tears slip free. Her father pulled Haur's forehead to his, murmuring "my son, my son" over and over. Her heart melted at all the horrible things she'd believed of her father, when in fact, she hadn't understood a single thing. His sacrifice—for her. For them. So huge.

A father's love is great.

In that moment, Darci felt an eternal love sprout in her heart. She realized what her mother believed held such depth, such beauty, such truth. Faith. Darci had believed to get out of the tunnel, to see her father once again. . .

And God made it happen.

Medics nudged into the room, taking over. Darci relinquished her first aid to the medics who pressed gauze to her father's shoulder, then lifted him onto a stretcher. "We'll be waiting for you, Ba."

But something warm and sinister swept across her mind. How had Zheng and Jianyu gotten onto the base? Who helped them? A subtle move on the other side of her father's stretcher ensnared her mind. The next few seconds ground to a slow but painfully fast pace. Someone held a gun along his leg. Her gaze traveled up his ACUs to his face—Otte!

He lifted the weapon toward her father.

Darci dropped to a knee and swung her other leg under the stretcher, catching the legs of the man on the other side.

Thud!

Shouts collided with her movement as she whirled around and dropped her elbow hard on the man's face. A resounding crack shattered the noise.

Soldiers dove on top of them.

Flattened on top of Otte and under the special-ops soldiers, she saw the medics scurry her father to safety. Hands pawed at her, drawing her out of the fray and up onto her feet. Swung her around into the arms of Heath Daniels. She clung to him, trembling. "He was going to kill him."

"I know."

"He had a gun."

"Shh."

"But he was General Burnett's personal aide!" She knew him. Trusted him. Talked to him. How. . .?

"You sorry piece of—" Burnett slammed his fist into Otte's nose.

The man crumpled beneath the punch.

"Get him out of my sight," General Burnett shouted, drawing Darci around. She looked over her shoulder as MPs cuffed and dragged Otte out of the room.

"*Mei Mei.*"

Tears blurred her vision at the "little sister" nickname. She tilted her head and looked at her brother. "I have not heard that name in a very long time." She went into his arms.

Haur held her tight.

"I have missed you." Clinging to him, to the piece of family she'd been without, she regained what she lost with her mother's death.

He kissed the top of her head. "You look so much like our mother. How could I not know?"

"And you look like him." She laughed. "You even sound like—"

Crack!

The sound of the shot swung Darci around.

Eyes wide, face taut, Heath stared down the barrel of his gun—aimed in their direction. Slowly, he lowered it, his chest heaving.

"He overpowered me," someone behind her said.

Darci turned around. Propped against a wall, lay Jianyu. Dead.

Shaken, she looked back at Heath. She hauled in a breath that was undeterred when he gave her a halfhearted smile.

Heath winked. "I promised myself he wouldn't take anything from you again."

He saved her. Again. She eased away from her brother—*my brother!*—and went to Heath. "I owe you my life."

A lopsided grin tugged at his face as he stared down at her. Warmth swirled through her belly at the way he looked at her, with those beautiful gray eyes, that crooked smile.

Cupping her face, he stroked her jaw. "You owe me a kiss."

Darci stretched up on her toes, ignoring the fingers of pain scratching at her ribs. They were outmatched by the nervous jellies as Heath's arm encircled her in a firm but gentle hold. She stiffened for a second, darted a look into those steely eyes, then pressed her lips to his.

His kiss was light. . .tender, searching. . .firmer.

Darci melted into his arms as he deepened the kiss.

Applause erupted, along with shouts.

Trinity barked.

"Jealous," Heath murmured against her lips to his partner, then leaned in again.

Epilogue

A Breed Apart Ranch,
Texas Hill Country

It'd been four long, excruciating months. No calls. No letters. No texts. No nothing.

Heath sat on the edge of the cliff overlooking A Breed Apart. He had a lot to be thankful for, the most important one that he could put genuine belief behind those talks he'd give at the bases. And there were more than a dozen gigs lined up since returning from Afghanistan, but he'd asked Jibril to give him a few months off.

He had hoped to spend that time with a certain woman.

But she hadn't reconnected since they'd had to go their separate ways—her, home to D.C. with her recuperating father and her newfound brother. Him, to Texas to reinvent himself, accept God's path, no matter the journey.

No matter the journey.

"Beautiful," came the gruff voice from behind.

Heath nodded, his gaze caressing the cloud-streaked sky. "Better than the view from your room at the Soldier's Home, don't you think?"

"That place was depressing!"

Heath climbed to his feet and moved to his uncle's all-terrain wheelchair. Heath had bought the contraption when he returned to an uncle who'd found his second wind. Crouching beside the old general, Heath sighed.

God had his back. No doubt. That he got some more years with his uncle. . . "Sure am glad you're better so we could share this."

Emotion rippled through Uncle Bob's face followed by a trembling lip, then a jutting jaw. "Bed was uncomfortable."

"Hardened veteran like you? They should've given you a cot."

A smile danced along the weathered lips.

"I'd better get you back down before Claire has my hide."

"I'm fine. She's not my CO."

"No, she's your wife now."

"Same difference."

Heath chuckled, thinking through the whole wife thing. By the time he'd returned, his uncle was up and barking. Claire ordered him to the altar within a month. His uncle complained loud and hard all the way to the chapel, but Heath had never seen the light in the man's face so bright. Claire was good for General Robert Daniels.

Would Darci have been good for Heath? Did it matter? Four months and no sign of the woman. What if Darci didn't want to be part of his life? What if she decided their time together had been too fraught with action and drama? Too risky to risk love?

Because that's where he was. He loved that woman. No question about it.

Trinity trotted to his side, a branch in her mouth.

"Goof," he muttered, tugging it free. "I've got your ball right—"

Trinity went rigid. Radar-ears swiveling as she struck a "seek" pose, aimed in the direction of the house. Heath followed her lead. Sunlight glinted against a white luxury SUV as it wound toward the ranch.

Heath couldn't help the hiccup in his chest. He wanted it to be her. *Please be Darci. . .* But he'd done that for three months with no luck.

The car turned into the drive.

Heath pushed to his feet, watching. "It could be anyone. Another speaking gig request."

"And you called me the fool?"

"Not to your face."

His uncle chuckled.

Trinity wagged her tail.

"Guess we should check it out."

Trinity sprinted down the path.

"Cheater!" Heath released the brake and aimed his uncle back to the jogging path, trailing after Trinity. Ironic how a little hypothermia had somehow corrected—no, that wasn't the right word—warded off? No, not quite right even still—well, whatever. The TBI hadn't manifested since his return, no matter how rigorous his workouts. His physical therapist suggested the good freezing through he'd gotten might have alleviated the nerve pressure that made his brain fry.

Whatever happened, Heath was glad. The symptoms could return, but he was done wrestling God. Clearly, the Lord had a plan for his life. And he would spend the rest of his days figuring it out, one day at a time.

"Slow down before you kill me!"

Heath complied as he broke through the clearing. Two women stood at the foot of the home, talking.

"See?" Pride shone in his uncle's voice as Claire waved and started toward them. "Commanding officer."

"Well, someone has to keep you in line."

His uncle smiled and pointed a shaky finger toward the other woman. "Yeah? Well, she's got your chain."

Heath's blood chugged at the words as he relinquished control of his uncle's wheelchair to Claire, who smiled but said nothing. She didn't have to. Women had *that* look that seemed to say they know everything. Heath slowed at the vision before him. Man, she did crazy things to his pulse.

In a pair of jeans and a white sweater, Darci smiled at him, accepting Trinity's kisses. "I think she remembers me."

"You're hard to forget."

Darci's smile grew. She straightened and strode toward him, her gaze traipsing over the valley. "So, this is the ranch."

After killing the man who'd devastated her, he'd thought of nothing but that kiss at Bagram. And now, he couldn't think of anything else again. "Figured that out all by yourself?"

Quiet wrapped around them as they strolled across the property, driving him crazy, but the comfort of her presence kept his anxiety at bay. She'd come. That meant something. And he hoped it meant something *big*. Heath kept pace, enjoying the simple fact that she was here. With him. No matter how long she stayed.

"I'm sorry it took me so long."

Heath snapped off a branch from a leafless tree. "Did you have doubts?"

"No, I had family." Darci sighed. "I resigned my commission with DIA."

"What...why? I thought you liked it. You were good as all get-out."

A pained expression stole over her beautiful face. "It took too much of me already." She surveyed the surroundings, then slowly brought her gaze back to him. "I think I'm ready for a slower pace."

Rapid-fire had nothing on his heartbeat.

Darci turned. "Haur is taking over my commission. He hasn't accepted it officially, but..." She scrunched her shoulders. "He's staying with my dad in D.C."

What a heady statement. "And you aren't?"

The prettiest color seeped into her cheeks.

He couldn't breathe. *Please, let this mean what I think it means.* "Does that mean you're here to stay?"

"Well." Darci turned and looked back at the house, still blushing. "Jibril offered me a job as assistant manager." Squinting to avoid the sun behind him as she peeked up at him, she shrugged. "His sister invited me to stay with her until..."

Heath grinned. "I like where this is going."

"Where, exactly, is this going? I mean, we don't really even know each other. We spent two weeks together, on and off, in the mountains."

Chuckling, Heath stared down at her, dead certain he wanted to spend the rest of his life with her. "That two weeks took about two years off my life. I died for you, remember?"

Playfully, she punched his gut.

Hooking a hand around the back of her neck, Heath tugged her closer. Kissed her. "I have no doubts I love you, Darci. Some day, when you're as sure as I am, I hope you'll marry me."

Both hands pressed to his chest, she leaned into him. "Are you asking?"

"No." Loving the disconcerted look she gave him, he kissed her again. "I'm begging."

Loyal Protectors

What follows is a true account written by an Air Force handler. I hope you find Elgin and Max's story as inspiring as I did, and that perhaps, we all will realize our military heroes come in many shapes and sizes, especially the four-legged kind.

God bless our troops, veterans, and MWDs, abroad and at home!

Ronie Kendig

"MAX" J216

During my Air Force years, I had the pleasure of being selected and trained as a Military War Dog (MWD) handler. Over the course of my twelve-year Air Force career, I handled and trained many dogs for law enforcement and force protection. Out of all the dogs I ever worked with, MWD Max will forever be my favorite. Max was a 65-68 lbs Australian shepherd–pit bull mix. He was a beige lean-and-mean machine with a heart of gold and truly loved his handlers and all children. The Department of Defense had trained Max as a Patrol Bomb dog.

The month and year was January 1987. Max and I were assigned a graveyard patrol on Fairchild AFB (Spokane). As part of our duties, we were required to do random common-area building checks in search of illegal explosives and weapons. During the completion of one such common-area search, Max and I began to walk across a parking lot to our patrol car. Suddenly and without warning, both of my feet went flying out from under me and down I went, with a crack, onto the frozen asphalt. My head impacted the ground, and I lost consciousness.

I later awoke to the sound of Max standing across my middle torso and growling at my buddies and fellow patrolmen as they were trying to check on me. Max knew his role was not only as my partner, but also as my protector, and Max knew I was hurt. Max was in no way, shape, or form, going to let further harm come to me.

As soon as I had enough faculties to realize what was occurring, I told Max "Out" (the command to cease aggression) and began to talk with him in a normal tone. Max touched his wet, cold nose to my face and then "permitted" a fellow patrolman to lead him back to our patrol car. As I sat up, I looked across the parking lot and saw Max looking directly at me without so much as a flinch. Fortunately, the injury I sustained that night was a bump to the back of my hat holder (head). Nothing very bad.

By Max's actions that night, his undying love for and loyalty to me, I knew no harm would ever come to me as long as he was at my side.

MWD Max J216 lived to be thirteen years old. Postdeath the base flag at Fairchild AFB was flown at half-staff. I later received Max's flag as a gift, and to this day it is proudly displayed in my office in a shadow box inscribed with his name, service number, and dates of service.

God bless you, Max. I miss you, buddy!
Elgin Shaw
U.S. Air Force 1982–94

John Burnam Monument Foundation

John Burnam, a Vietnam-era dog handler, formed the John Burnam Monument Foundation (JBMF) to raise an estimated $950,000 needed to build and maintain this long overdue National Monument to honor the heroic U.S. military dog handlers and their incredible working dogs.

Please consider making a donation in honor of the four-legged heroes who have protected their human counterparts and hundreds of thousands of troops throughout history.

TALON

COMBAT TRACKING TEAM

DEDICATION

ACKNOWLEDGMENTS

Special thanks to military handlers, who prefer to remain anonymous, for their help and direction.

Thanks to Elgin Shaw, a former Air Force handler and reader, who has encouraged me and shared his story of MWD Max in *Trinity: Military War Dog.*

Thanks to my agent, Steve Laube, who remains steadfast and constant in an ever-changing industry. For *not* pushing me off the ledge but holding me back when I wanted to jump.

A million thanks to Julee Schwarzburg—editor extraordinaire!

Thanks to the Barbour team, relentless in their efforts to make our books successful: Rebecca Germany, Mary Burns, Shalyn Sattler, Elizabeth Shrider, Laura Young, Linda Hang, and Ashley Schrock.

Rel Mollet of RelzReviewz—tireless supporter of fiction but also one of the truest and most genuine people I have ever met.

Special thanks to Heather Lammers for helping me connect with MWD handlers.

Special thanks to MWD handlers/trainers 1st LT Brian Sandoval, SSG Jeff Worley, and SGT Andrew Kowtko for sharing a glimpse of the MWD world with readers. You are all heroes!

LITERARY LICENSE

In writing about unique settings, specific locations, and invariably the people residing there, a certain level of risk is involved, including the possibility of dishonoring the very people an author intends to honor. With that in mind, I have taken some literary license in *Talon: Combat Tracking Team*, including renaming some bases within the U.S. military establishment and creating sites/ entitles. I have done this so the book and/or my writing will not negatively reflect on any military personnel or location. With the quickly changing landscape of a combat theater, this seemed imperative and prudent.

Glossary of Terms/Acronyms

ACUs—Army Combat Uniforms

AK-47—Russian made assault rifle

CLU—Containerized Living Units

CTT dog—Combat Tracking Team dog

DIA—Defense Intelligence Agency

FOB—Forward Operating Base

Glock—A semiautomatic handgun

HUMINT—Human Intelligence

IED—Improvised Explosive Device

JAG—Judge Advocate General

Klicks—Military jargon for kilometers

Lat-long—Latitude and longitude

M4, M4A1, M16A4—Military assault rifles

M203—A grenade launcher

MIA—Missing In Action

MP—Military Police

MRAP—Mine Resistant Ambush-Protected vehicle

MWD—Military War Dog

ODA452—Operational Detachment A (Special Forces A-Team)

RPG—Rocket-Propelled Grenade

SCI—"Sensitive Compartmented Information" security level

SOCOM—Special Operations Command

SureFire—A tactical flashlight

TBI—Traumatic Brain Injury

UAV—Unmanned Aerial Vehicle

Kariz-e Sefid, Afghanistan
Two Years Ago

Flames roared into the sky. A concussive boom punched the oxygen from the air. Eating an IED, the lead Cougar MRAP in the convoy flipped up. As if dancing atop the raging inferno. Shrapnel hurtled from the blast.

"Buffalo! Buffalo!" Sergeant Lee Dawson shouted into the mic, hoping to hear from the first vehicle.

"Anything?" Gunnery Sergeant Austin Courtland coiled his hand around the lead of his Combat Tracking Team dog. Talon stood braced, alert. His bark reverberated through the steel hull in warning.

Lee slanted a glance at the "observer" who'd come along. "Report!" Peering through the cloud of black smoke and debris, he searched the chaos to make sure the others were still alive.

A breeze stirred the flames just in time to see an RPG streaking toward the front end of their MRAP.

"Get out, get out, get out!" Courtland and Talon launched toward the back door.

"Oh cr—"

BOOM!

The MRAP bucked against the blast but held. Whiplash had nothing on the ramming sensation pounding into his chest now. Fire burst through the engine.

Fear of being cooked alive or choking to death on smoke shoved Lee from the Cougar MRAP. Coughing and with a hand over his mouth, he choked out, "This way!"

Sand and dirt blasted up, peppering his face. Tiny grains and dust particles swirled under the blazing Afghan sun as he took cover, shouldering his way around the side of the mine-resistant ambush-protected vehicle and out of their attacker's line of fire. Plumes of heat warbled along the hull.

"Find me some terrorists," Court shouted over the roar of the fire, then keyed his mic. "Base, this is Echo One. Ambushed and taking fire!"

Peering down the sights of his M16A4 gave Lee nothing but dirt. . .crumbled building with dirt. . .and more dirt. "I got nothin'."

"Same," came a shout from behind as Truitt "True" Anderson slid up behind him, a nasty cut across his cheekbone. "Where the *heck* did that RPG come from?" The muzzle of his M4 swept Lee's periphery.

Lee kept his sights aligned, adrenaline pumping through his system faster than the blood. "Court," he yelled over the gunfire that crackled in the blistering afternoon, "what d'you have?"

"Nothing!"

Staying behind the disabled vehicle, Lee searched the road. Only two buildings north. Several south. Focused ahead, he studied the structures. He scanned the roofs. Since the RPG's trajectory had been downward, whoever fired it held an elevated position. The roof of one didn't look strong enough to hold someone, and the other had more holes than coverage. He whipped back to the first, waiting. *C'mon! Show your coward head so I can—*

"Quirk, report!" Court shouted to the Buffalo team again.

Only crackling and the shouts of the other teams dragging the lead team to safety met the command. Mind locked on the white plastered structure with the right half of the front wall missing told him that's where the attack had originated.

"Use the drone?" Lee shouted, not lifting his gaze from the scope.

"It's down!"

Lee wanted to curse. Everything had gone wrong. With the drone down, they'd have to do this the old-fashioned, bloody way. *Mano a mano.* Hand to hand.

Dark flashed in his reticle. "Court, two o'clock."

"Let's clear it out."

Sweat raced along the side of Lee's face and spine as he inched around the MRAP. His boot thumped against something. He glanced down—and flinched at the limp body of his buddy. On a knee, weapon still aimed at the building, he gripped the vest of Quirk, the young corporal.

Wide, unseeing eyes etched with the shock of the moment. Pressing his hand against the chest wound, Lee plunged into assessment mode, ignoring the warm wetness that squished through his fingers. The gaping hole— "Sniper!" *Sweet Lord, help us.* They were ambushed. Sniper. RPG. What prayer did they have left?

"Corpsman!" Lee gripped the man's vest straps. "Quirk, hey. Don't do this, man. No quitting."

Another Marine sprinted toward them, allowing Lee to refocus on breaking this ambush site. Breaking the sick cowards who hid and played lethal games of tag with U.S. troops.

He met the steely gaze of his fire-team members—minus one. Another trio of Marines joined them as their cover team. As he lifted the weapon and trained it on the building, he nodded to Court and True, then darted across the fifteen-foot space that separated the partially disabled convoy from the hideouts.

Halfway across, Court dove to the left.

Tat-tat-tat!

The report rang in Lee's ears as he threw himself against the plaster and cement wall.

"Base, this is Echo One, we need that air support—five minutes ago!" Court nodded to Lee before keying his mic again. "Going in."

Stacked—True behind with his M4 trained on the point of entry— Lee waited for the signal.

A tap on his shoulder.

Lee fired a short burst against the door handle. Balanced on his left leg, he slammed his booted heel against the door. *Crack!* It whipped open.

Court stepped around him and tossed a hand grenade into the room. "Frag out!" He jerked back behind Lee, who spined the exterior wall.

Clink...clink...BOOM!

Lee threw himself into motion. Over the threshold, he registered the southernmost wall missing. He swung left. Dust puffed as he rushed the darkened corner. Light streamed in, taunting the smoke and debris rustled by the grenade. Two steps in, one foot from the wall. His weapon grazed the smoke-drenched interior and cleared a path to the left. He heard Court step in and do the same to the opposite corner. Lee hustled toward the left corner, tracking back and forth, adrenaline on high.

To avoid fratricide Lee called, "Next man in," and hurried along the wall, pieing the room to divide up the coverage.

The swish of tactical pants preceded True as he entered. Effectively covering both corners and the door, the three-man team moved forward. To Lee's left a door boasted a spray of bullet holes. Half a window frame drooped against the wide-open maw in the rear.

"Clear," Court called.

A shadow killed the light.

Lee swung hard right. Movement skittered just beyond the hole in the wall. *Scritch-scritch-scritch*—

"Stairs!" He hustled forward, staring down the muzzle of his weapon.

Behind him, he heard the others cluster. To his right, the wall was missing. To the left, cement and darkness—and that's where the mystery guest had gone. They were blind, so they'd have to use extreme caution. He took up a dominant position. Experience told him Court was behind him and True pulled up the rear.

Eyes trained on the corner in case someone rounded it, Lee knelt and focused on the smooth movement of the team. They'd done this dozens of times. Still, one careless mistake and they were dead.

Court's boots crunched against the dirt floor as he pied out to the right as far as possible. Then slowly advanced to increase his angle of fire farther into the dead space.

"Ready," Lee grunted.

"Move!"

They both angled into the open, True tailing. In the blazing afternoon sun, Lee cleared left—stairs! Just as he'd thought. Open, cement steps. No railing. Just a path up to the roof. He climbed two steps, knowing Court would be one step down and to the side. Lee turned to cover overhead, mentally noting his partner oriented to the front, to cover him from getting shot in the back.

Tracing the edge of the upper level with the tip of his muzzle flash hider, Lee backstepped carefully up the stairs, sweeping. Covering. Pieing. Though adrenaline and a need to kill the puke who'd taken out the MRAP and killed Quirk sped through his body, Lee wouldn't take another step without fully clearing the area. As he approached the roof, he bent lower with each level until he crouched, the roof skimming his head.

Lee drew in his fears and harnessed them into taking out some cowards. Glanced to the side—to Court. Then True. Both nodded their readiness. He blew a breath from puffed cheeks. Gave a curt nod.

Court went first.

Lee and True followed, weapons ready. They hurried over the lip of the roof, scanning. . .chairs, blankets, a Styrofoam cooler. . .a small room jutted up from the middle.

Tension high, stomach knotted, Lee hurried toward it. Scissor-stepping, he swallowed hard, expecting an enemy combatant to leap out at any second. He and Court cleared the L-shaped corner with ease. Nobody. He was almost disappointed.

"Where are they?" True growled through gritted teeth.

Lee glanced around. Looked over the front of the building and shouted to the team, "Where'd they go?"

Raised arms and shrugs replied.

He kicked the knee-high wall. Cursed. Swiped the beads of sweat from his face and eyes. Another fire team streamed onto the roof. Confusion squeezed his brain. How could he have gotten away? They'd chased him up here. Lee saw him!

"Looks secure," one corporal said as he stalked across the terrace-like roof.

They needed to clear the other building. "Court," he said, looking around. He frowned. Where'd his partner go? Had he already headed for the other building? Lee started for the stairs.

"Let's see what some terrorists were eating and drinking while they waited to kill some Marines."

An ominous fear washed across Lee's shoulders. "No!" He spun—

Fire exploded. The concussion whipped his feet out from under him. Over his head. Lee felt himself sailing through the air, searing heat licking his backside. Then falling. . .falling. . .black.

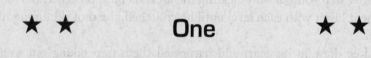

★ ★   **One**   ★ ★

Markoski Residence
Baltimore, Maryland

*T*o live a lie is to remain alive.

Military documents recorded his name as Dane Markoski. That he's the son of an American missionary and Russian father—Vasily and Eliana Markoski. That he joined the military at eighteen, immediately upon high school graduation. That he soared through the ranks and his distinguished career, replete with badges of valor and courage under fire that revealed his natural ability and ambition toward becoming a career Army officer. A man's man. A hero.

None of it true.

Barefoot, wearing only gray sweatpants, Cardinal—his handle, his only form of tangible identity for the last ten years—gripped the rope he'd anchored into to the steel support of his second-story loft bedroom and pulled himself off the ground. Hand over hand, he climbed, legs spider-posed and held out to maximize the workout to his abs and thighs.

When he reached the top, he gripped the ledge-like floor and performed twenty pull-ups. The reps burning, they taught him discipline. Reminded him that he was weak, that opportunity existed with every breath to become better—or weaker. The Gentle Art of Submission—Jiu-Jitsu—helped him harness the poison that threatened his life every day: anger.

Cardinal lowered himself and took the rope. Angling back, he

366

moved hand over hand, backward along the hemp that traced the length of his condo, his body parallel to the floor. Breathing hard, arms and abs on fire, he continued the workout he'd started hours earlier.

A fit body equaled a fit mind, the masters had always said.

So had his father. And it was the one thing the general had said that Cardinal heeded. . .willingly.

Behind him the bank of cantilevering windows sat open, allowing a balmy breeze from the Potomac that did nothing to cool or calm him. The news delivered last night served to be the harbinger of death. The final straw that would break the camel's back—his.

Unless Cardinal found a way to turn this around.

He must. Everything—*everything*—depended on it. Hours training his body and mind to focus and he had nothing. Straightened on the ground, he pressed his palms together and drew in a measuring breath, then slowly blew it out through puffed cheeks.

There, where the sun hit the window, stood a ghost of himself. More apropos than one would expect. What was left of him? Still had the black hair and blue eyes, but what lay beneath those eyes. . .who was it? Was *he* good enough to justify the listing of the commendation medals on his records? At thirty-three, he'd hoped to have more of a legacy than secrecy and anonymity.

Breath evening out, he stared. Willed that person in the glass to find the solution. Solve this disaster. He had a new enemy: time. Beyond the balcony, across the road and stretch of greenery, he spotted a woman jogging with her dog.

A tone flicked through the condo.

Cardinal pulled himself straight and plodded out of the gym, between the sofa and armchairs, to the Spartan kitchen, where he plucked his cell phone from the granite. He registered the number and hesitated. Then pressed the phone to his ear as he watched the woman make her way down the sidewalk. "Yes?"

"Code in."

Cardinal punched a button and the windows slid shut. "Cairo-One-Four-Two-Nine-Nine."

"What do you have?"

They were already breathing down his neck? "It's been six hours."

"I didn't ask what time it was." A long pause strangled the line. "You don't have a single thing, do you?"

"What do you have?"

"This is not good. The longer we sit on our—"

He would not be made into the weakling here. "Do you have something useful to say, or is this just a social call?"

Wait. . .*dog*. His gaze snapped to the sidewalk, now occupied by a young mother pushing a stroller.

"I am *socially* telling you time is running out. If *he* finds out—"

"The only way he would find out is if I am betrayed. And the only people who can betray me are on this phone call. Since we both know the consequences for betrayal, I'll take it he doesn't know." Cardinal folded up his anger and tucked it under a cloak of civility.

"No need to get all James Bond on me, Cardinal."

"Bond is British and highly overrated." What. . .what did that file say? His mind rifled through the documents he'd studied and landed on one phrase: *military working dog*. "I have an idea."

"I knew you had it in you." The man's voice boomed with amusement. "What do you need?"

"I'll be there in twenty. Have a team ready."

Cleaned up and garbed in standard military issue, Cardinal drove down South Washington Boulevard to the geometric five-acre, five-ring structure that was a nightmare to navigate for the uninitiated. He pulled up to the guard hut, showed his ID, and signed in.

"Thank you, Lieutenant Markoski. He's expecting you."

Cardinal drove through and parked. Inside, he made his way to the second floor. A door opened. General Lance Burnett emerged. "General."

"You're ten minutes late," Burnett said, without looking up from the file in hand. He continued down the drab gray hall, and Cardinal fell into step with him. "We got a lead."

Cardinal's heart skipped a beat, but he waited for the general to continue.

"There was activity on his account, but he must've smelled us snooping because the activity ended before we could get a lock."

"What type of activity?"

"Accessing bank accounts, e-mail, etcetera."

"Isn't that obvious? He knows better than that. I trained him."

"Apparently not well enough." Burnett slapped the file closed and smacked it against his leg as he flipped the handle on a door and leaned against it.

"Where?"

"Didn't you just hear we couldn't get a lock?"

"Yes."

The general grinned. "Republic of Djibouti."

Cardinal slowed as they entered a conference room where six men in Naval uniforms waited with another team of six—analysts and experts. "Djibouti. . ." He hadn't seen that coming. "What's he doing there?"

"Hanged if I know."

"It's over 90 percent Islamic." A really bad place to hide when you were obviously white and American. Cardinal nodded to the sailors and took a seat near the head of the table.

The general dropped the file in front of him, roughed a hand over his face, and sighed. "Okay, let's get on with this. Markoski, these men have been briefed on what's happened. Tell us your brilliant idea."

Amadore's Fight Club
Austin, Texas

"Watch your stance!"

Exhilaration swept through Aspen Courtland as she responded to her trainer's shout and realigned her feet, shoulder-width apart. She threw a jab and followed through with a right. Sweat dripped into her eye, stinging. Today. . .the anniversary. . .

Mario, her opponent, threw a hard right then tried a left jab.

Block! The thud against her gloves carried through her upper body. She flipped her mind into the ring again as the impact from his strike rattled down her arm.

Aspen countered and angled to the side. The move could frustrate him by preventing a return hit.

It'd been eight months since the news. But it hurt as if it'd happened today.

Breathing through her nose, jaw relaxed, she engaged a series of redundant punches, all numbing her mind. She couldn't let them get away with this. They had to. . .do something.

An uppercut.

Shielding, Aspen blocked Mario. Hands and shoulder forward. What if. . .what if she went in after him? The thought fueled her boxing. In quick succession she fired off several strikes. Going in there—yeah, real smart. Right into the heart of the Middle East, where Americans were served up with every meal.

A jab. A cross. Angling away.

Mario swung at her.

She blocked. So, she couldn't go alone. She'd need a team.

Again—right. Real smart. How would she get a team into the Middle East to track an invisible trail? She slammed a hard right. Connected with Mario's jaw.

"Nice—face!"

Too late. The counterpunch nailed her cheek. She stumbled backward, stunned.

"Take a break, Mario."

Aspen straightened and turned. "No, I'm good." Batting her gloves together, she drew in a ragged breath, hating the look on Amadore's face as he bent through the ropes and entered the ring. "I'm serious." Another tap of her gloves. "Let's do this."

"No, let's not."

Irritation squirreled through her intestines. "Why? I'm—"

"Fighting with fury." Gentle brown eyes held hers. "Not with focus."

He was right. She knew he was. But she had something to work off, and boxing provided the perfect outlet. "I'm good." Glancing around him, she found Mario still in the ring. "Ready?"

"No." Amadore pointed to Mario. "You do this, you never come in my club again. You hear me?"

Mario grinned and held up both gloves in surrender as he backed away then slipped through the ropes.

As her breathing evened out, she tamped down the anger that spiked. "I'm okay, Amadore."

"No." He cupped the back of her head and tugged her close. "What is wrong with my angel today? You are like a big storm off the coast when you come through that door. What gives?"

Aspen swallowed. Peeked into his eyes. . .and caved. He'd been a part of her life since she was a baby—her mother's father. "It's his birthday." She stuffed her gloves against each other. "He would've been twenty-eight."

The peppering of silver along the sides of his face only made the barrel-chested, former pro boxer look more handsome and distinguished. Even now as the repercussion of her words hit him. "Ah yes. I remember."

Her gaze skirted the boxing ring and fell on the Lab curled up under a bench in the corner, his soulful eyes watching her. "Presumed dead." Her nostrils flared and her eyes stung. "Eight months," she said through ground teeth. "He was only missing eight months and they declared him dead." She fought the trembling in her lower lip. "I thought for sure, he would. . .that we would. . .find him."

"Oh my girl." His other arm came up as if to hug her, but Aspen ducked from his touch.

"No worries." Sucking up the dregs of her crumbling composure, she flashed him a thin-lipped smile. "They might have written him off. But I haven't. I'll deal with it."

"I am not sure your way of dealing with things is the right way."

She folded herself through the ropes. On the floor, she looked back up at him and shrugged. "Whatever works, right?"

"Aspen, wait." He was with her in a second. Nudging her to the side, he urged her toward a bench. "Sit."

With a huff, she plopped onto the wood. Using her teeth, she ripped the band and tugged off the gloves as he sat next to her.

"I worry about you."

She frowned.

"No. I see that look in your eye, and I know—this thing? It will end bad."

"It already ended." At least according to the U.S. Marine Corps. Unwinding the wraps from her hands, she tried to shove back the squall of emotion. "Ya know, what I can't figure out. . ." Her chest rose and fell as the words from the letters and e-mails from the military filled her mind. "Why. . .*why* would they declare him dead when there's no body, no proof he died?"

Sorrow pinched the middle-aged Italian's hard features.

"A little blood." She breathed heavily through her nose. "A dog tag with no evidence of a fight or scratches, and a dog with minor injuries." Her gaze automatically slid to the Lab, who pulled himself out from under the bench and lumbered her way, head down. She smoothed a hand over his head as he sat between her feet. "It doesn't make sense."

"I understand, my angel, but. . ."

"There's no more 'but,' Amadore. Uncle Sam sealed the note." She climbed to her feet, the weight of the letter she'd opened today pushing against her.

He touched her arm. "Be careful."

She scowled.

"This thing you are planning, I see it in your eyes," he said as he rose and stood over her. "Be careful. Your father would kill me if I let something happen to you. Know what I mean?"

Her heart skipped a beat. How did he know? She opened her mouth to deny it, to deny she would go after Austin.

His laugh cut her off. "No, Angel. I know you better than you know yourself. There is a plan in that beautiful head of yours." The smile remained in place. "Which is why I stopped your session with Mario. That head wasn't in the ring. It was at home, still mourning his birthday."

Aspen tucked her chin. "He's all I've got left, *Nonno*." She drew up her shoulders. "I'm not going to let the Marines relegate my brother to the grave without a fight."

Two

Pentagon, Arlington County, Virginia
Two Days Later

Say it again."

Cardinal drew in a breath, tempering his frustration. "This isn't my first rodeo, to borrow your phrase, sir."

"Good. Then this should be better than expected." Undaunted, General Lance Burnett, the deputy director of Defense Counterintelligence and HUMINT Center, popped the top of his umpteenth Dr Pepper of the morning and slurped from the can. With a satisfied sigh, he set it down. "Begin."

Flexing his jaw, Cardinal gave a curt nod. Practice never hurt. Wasted time, but never hurt. "We'll maintain my identity as Markoski. The interview—"

"Sir," Lieutenant Smith announced from the door. "We got Larabie on line 3."

Amusement twinkled in Burnett's eyes. "Let's hope you're as ready as you say."

Cardinal resisted the urge to smirk. "Let the games begin." He strode to the phone, lifted the handset, and pressed 3. "This is Dane Markoski."

"Ah, Mr. Markoski," her voice sailed through the receivers—his and the general's. Cardinal kept his gaze on the old man. "This is Brittain Larabie. You'd e-mailed me about—"

"Please. Can we keep the details"—he added hesitation and concern to his voice to make this work. He'd never had a problem manipulating the media who manipulated the world. Great satisfaction could be gained from maneuvers like this— "Are you able to meet, Miss Larabie?"

"Um. . .yes. Yes I can. I will have a cameraman with me. You understand, for my own safety, I won't meet strangers alone."

"Alone, or not at all. I'm not trying to murder you, Miss Larabie. I want to tell the truth. I want to do what's right." That sounded all patriotic and gallant.

"Of course. What time and where?"

"Are you familiar with Reston ice-skating pavilion?"

"That's in Virginia."

"Correct."

"That's a bit out of my way, Mr. Markusky."

"Markoski." Why couldn't Americans get that right? No doubt they'd butcher his real last name. "And if it's an inconvenience, I can call—"

"No, it's fine. When shall we meet?"

"The sooner the better. Tomorrow night?" Silence plagued the line, and Cardinal tried to ignore the general waving his hand in a circle. "I'm out of time, Miss Larabie."

"That's fine. I had a dinner date, but I can reschedule."

"Eight o'clock." Cardinal hung up and turned to the general. "Everything is in my medical and military history files?"

"You're not the only good operative I have, Cardinal." General Burnett had never asked for Cardinal's true identity. But the old man probably had it locked in that steel vault he called a brain. All the same, Cardinal felt safer with the moniker than with his real name floating around in paperwork and cyberspace.

Burnett motioned to his lieutenant, who slid a file across the table. "Larabie is best friends with Courtland's twin, Aspen."

Why did people name their kids after cities? Cardinal retrieved the file and lifted it. "Odd. What, are they dating?" He glanced down.

"I sincerely doubt that."

Dread poured through Cardinal's stomach, freezing like an iceberg as he met the blue eyes of a curly haired beauty. He darted his gaze to the general. "A woman?" His pulse thunked against the possibility then spun into chaos. "Austin's twin is a woman? How did I *not* know that?"

The lieutenant shifted, shooting a nervous glance to the general.

Burnett grinned. "Maybe you're not as good as you thought."

Cardinal flung the documents back. "Forget it. Deal's off. I'm not doing this." He stormed toward the door. "We'll find another way."

"Cardinal, you are U.S. Government property. You will do as ordered."

"I won't." Rage flung him back around. "I won't work this woman. Or *any* woman. Not ever. That was Cardinal Rule #1 when you came to me." Breaths came in deep gulps. "I'll find another way to get Courtland back." Anger gave way to desperation. He raked a hand through his hair. "Figure something out."

Silence hung rank and thick in the room. Burnett nodded to the others in the room. "If you'll excuse us." He waited for the room to clear then sat on the edge of the conference table. "Cardinal, I respect what you're saying, but it's impractical. Your protégé vanished two months ago in a remote village in northeast Africa—right out from under your nose. You and I both know that is trouble. *If* he is still alive, every second matters. We can't afford to waste another minute, let alone two more months *figuring* something out when you have a working plan right here in front of you."

Cardinal, in a half shake of his head, dragged his gaze downward. "I can't."

Images of innocent brown eyes. . .her laughter. . .seeing her worked over, time and again. *And then the angel flew. . .*

"You knew this." His pulse thumped against his temple as he worked to restrain his temper. "*No. Women.*" Right then, an absolute certainty rushed over him. He stabbed a finger at Burnett. "You." How had he not seen this earlier? Was he too eager to get Courtland back that he hadn't considered all the possibilities? "You knew—you hid from me that Aspen was a woman."

Burnett let out a long sigh. "Son, we've been trying since Austin vanished to find a way to track him and get him back safely. When you came up with this absolutely ingenious plan to use his dog. . .I had no choice."

"We *always* have a choice."

Shoulders slumped, Burnett crumpled his Dr Pepper can. "No, no we don't. And right now, neither do you."

Lips tight, Cardinal glared at him. "I'm not doing this."

"Do this or you're through." He folded his arms over his chest. "Something's haunting you, and I need you to bury that—for now—and do your job."

"You forget," Cardinal spat out, "I came to *you*! I offered *you* my services."

"Yes, but now you're owned. By us." Burnett pushed up and moved to the other end of the table. "I consider myself a nice man who works hard at his job. But that's just it—I have a job. I'm tasked with protecting my country and its citizens. And that means I have to do things I don't like."

Throw that political bull at him, but it wouldn't work. "This isn't my country." Tremors rippled through his arms and legs. What choice did he have? Burnett held more dirt on him, could bury him at the bottom of the sea for ten lifetimes. Or expose his whereabouts to a certain Russian general.

I'm trapped. As always.

Had to get out of there. Disappear. He would not do this. Could not. "I don't owe this country anything. I don't owe *anyone* anything." The words were cruel. And wrong. It was the anger talking. The demons he'd inherited.

"Maybe not, but you *are* a citizen of it. We granted that, remember? And you signed on the line for this job. We own you, Cardinal." Burnett's eyes narrowed. "And that missing boy is your responsibility." He smacked a hand on the table. "Now man up and do what needs to be done!"

Cardinal stormed out of the office, down the hall, the stairs, to the parking garage. In his car, he left the grounds and headed west. Though Reston was only thirty minutes away, traffic dictated the three-hour drive. Familiar with the area, he made his way to a nearby park and planted himself on a bench. He'd promised himself he'd never do this. Never become the epitome of filth and slime that had defined Cardinal's life for twenty years.

Elbows on his knees, he stared at the ground covered in a fresh blanket of wildflowers. Cold seeped into his bones despite the summer heat, but it was nothing like the chill settling over this mission. Over his objective—getting Aspen Courtland to cooperate and think it was her idea.

"I promised," he muttered past his hands, fingers laced and held in front of his lips.

But...Austin.

Cardinal had hand-selected the young man for the field. He'd trained him, guided him, become friends with him. The government intentionally withheld information about Austin's family so Cardinal would not have any impetus or inclination to alter his decision or recruitment.

Nearby a horn honked and snapped him out of his somber thoughts. A quick check of his watch shoved him to his feet. He headed past the hotel, down the sidewalk, and straight toward the pavilion.

The sister—she would want to help, right? This plan he'd concocted depended on the twin's reaction. But he'd thought he was dealing with a guy. Not a woman. A twin was a twin, right? The connection should be there. She should see the imperative nature of using the dog. At least, he hoped she did because he'd take the dog—that'd be so much easier. But they couldn't afford the time or risk to yank the dog and force him to settle in with a new handler.

The dog was the key. And getting to the dog, the key was the sister. Aspen.

He turned into an alley and thrust his fist in the air. "God, why must You torment me? You know what is in me. You know the blood that beats in my heart." Fists over his eyes, he ground his teeth. "Do not...do not let me lose myself."

Was it possible...was it at all possible to complete this mission without becoming his father?

A Breed Apart Ranch
Texas Hill Country

Soulful brown eyes held hers, eagerness and willingness to go the long, hard mile for her pouring out of them. His eyebrows bounced with meaning.

"Hey, handsome."

He scooted closer, his happy impatience melting her heart. She didn't deserve his loyalty. His passionate attention. But he gave it all the same.

Cupping his face, Aspen smiled down at him. "You are amazing."

He smiled.

Or near enough for a Labrador retriever. Talon swiped his tongue along her face, his backside wagging so hard she thought he might wipe out. She rubbed his ears and planted a kiss between his eyes. "Thank you, boy."

"How's it going?"

Aspen straightened and turned toward the voice of Heath Daniels, lead trainer at A Breed Apart. His Belgian Malinois bounded into the training area with zest and zeal Aspen was convinced Talon once possessed. She eyed her blond guy. "We're making progress."

Heath, arms folded over his chest and hands tucked beneath his armpits, smiled at her. "You got him over the hurdles."

Beaming beneath the hidden praise in his words, Aspen grinned back. "Six months ago, I would've thought this was possible." And six months ago, she'd had an uphill battle getting her grandparents to allow Talon to take up residence with her at their sprawling estate. Nana wasn't entirely pleased about having a dog, whose fur sprinkled her marble and gilded décor with yellow hairs. Or Granddad, who had objected to Talon living *in* a house his own father had built at the height of his wealth and power in the roaring twenties. But in time, knowing Talon had been best friends with Austin, they'd relented.

"You're giving him his respect back but also helping him remember he's a dog—the best life." Heath touched her shoulder. "Your brother would be proud if he were here to see this."

Aspen ducked her chin, fighting the stinging in her eyes. "That's just the bear of it, isn't it? If Austin were here, I wouldn't be." The rawness at the back of her throat made it hard to swallow.

"Hey," Heath said, his tone softer. "Don't go there, okay? You can stay true to his memory without feeling guilty about everything. You're doing right by him with the way you're watching out for his partner and best friend." He gave a curt nod. "Understand?"

Surprised at his words, Aspen bobbed her head. "Yeah, I guess so." She clicked Talon's lead on and ruffled his coat, finding as much pleasure in the move as it seemed the six-year-old guy did. "I just don't want Talon to forget Austin."

"Oh, I don't think that will ever happen. Even if it takes years."

"It *has* taken years. Two, to be exact."

"Yeah, but in a dog's mind, I think that equates to two days. They don't forget smells, and he's got Austin's burned into his head. I'd bet my life on it."

A country song sailed through the air. Aspen started and grabbed the phone from her jacket pocket. "I'd better get this. Hope you have a good session with Trinity."

"We will."

Aspen led Talon from the training ground and headed toward her SUV as she pressed the TALK button on her phone. "Hi, Britt. What's up?"

"Girl, we need to talk."

"Okay, go ahead."

"No. I've got something you need to see."

Aspen slowed at the urgent excitement in her best friend's voice. "Okay. . ."

"Can you come over?"

"I had some errands—"

"Girl. Listen." Noise crackled over the line, as if Brittain had put her hand over the phone. "Okay, I can't say too much here, but I think. . . I *think*. . .I interviewed a man last night, a soldier. You have to see this."

"You're not sure you interviewed a soldier?" Aspen loaded Talon in the back of the SUV in his crate then climbed behind the steering wheel.

"Don't mess with my head. Come to my house. It has to be now. You know I wouldn't ask if I didn't think it was important, and this goes to the moon and back on importance."

"Wow, how cryptic." Nerves jangled, Aspen turned over the engine.

"I know. But I have to be. And when I get to the studio, I've got to turn this in to the manager to approve. But trust me, you'll want to see this before it goes live. Aspen, this guy was at Kariz-e Sefid."

Aspen's heart climbed into her throat. "I'm on my way." How she got from the ranch to Brittain's condo, she didn't know because her mind was all awhirl and tumbling from the mention of the Afghan city that stole her brother. Was it possible. . .just maybe. . .that she'd been right? Was he alive somewhere? Maybe held hostage by some radical group?

Talon lumbered toward the door with Aspen. She hesitated, ready to say something positive to the canine who'd been there, who'd seen what happened to Austin but could not speak. "I wish you could—"

The door jerked open.

Brittain's fro spiked out in odd places rather than the perfectly coiffed hairstyle she managed to tame the curls into for her broadcasts. "Girl!" Wide, mahogany eyes held hers. "You are *not* going to believe this."

She reached into the hall and grabbed Aspen's jacket shoulder and pulled. "C'mon. I don't have much time." Halfway across the living room by the time Aspen lured Talon into the apartment, Brittain chattered a hundred miles an hour. "You are not going to believe this man." She threw a look over her shoulder. "But this man? Is *fine*. With a capital *F*."

"What man? How did you meet him?" Aspen shed her coat and trailed her friend to the dining table that cozied up to a bay window in the sunroom.

"That's just it—he e-mailed me. Said he had a story he had to get off his chest. He couldn't live with himself and keep the secret."

Aspen put her hand over her stomach, wishing she hadn't eaten that Angus burger. "What secret?"

Brittain came behind her, set her long, dark fingers on Aspen's shoulders, then guided her to the office and into a plush chair. "See for yourself." She lifted a remote and pressed a button.

Perched on the edge of the chair, Aspen clasped her sweaty palms in her lap. Talon's cold nose nudged her hand. She smiled down at him.

"Could you please state your name for the camera?"

"Are you recording?"

"Yes, is that a problem?"

Pale blue eyes hit the camera head-on. The man shifted. *"No. No, I guess not. My name is Dane Markoski."*

"You contacted me and said you had to clear your conscience."

"Yes, ma'am. I did—do." He sat up straighter. Broad shoulders. Thick chest. The guy was no stranger to fitness.

"Please, go ahead."

"O—okay. I was in the Army. . ." His story went on for several minutes, noting his unit and what they were doing. *"We went to Kariz-e Sefid, and things just felt bad, ya know? We rolled in and things were crazy quiet. Then out of nowhere, we heard the shriek of an RPG rip past our MRAP.*

This was just supposed to be a routine patrol, so. . ." He shrugged. *"Sometimes that happens. And it puts lives on the line, but we don't stop fighting, ya know?"*

"So I've heard," Brittain said. *"Now, you said there was an attack? What happened?"*

"Well, the vehicles were targeted, so we went for cover, tried to find the source of the weapons' fire. A SOCOM team headed to the roof of a building."

"SOCOM?"

"Special Operations Command. A team of Green Berets were there. They said they'd seen something. But. . .that's when things got strange. . ." He looked up to the right and seemed lost in the memory.

"Please, go on."

He blinked as if startled. *"Sorry. I just. . ."* His eyes darted around, as if searching for something. *"The building exploded, and it threw me into the dirt. As we all came up out of that mess, smoke and dust was everywhere. You almost couldn't see."*

"Almost?" Brittain leaned forward. *"But you did see, is that right, Mr. Markusky."*

"Markoski. And. . ." He gave a one-shoulder shrug. *"Yeah, I saw something. Or I think I saw something."* He scratched his head.

"What do you think you saw?"

"Well, that's just it. It's not what I saw then, but. . ."

"But what?"

 **Three**

*W*ell, *the Army seemed really eager to write off one of the men, and then something I saw later. . .one of the men I'd swear was on top of that roof, who should have died. . .I saw him in northeast Africa. I was there helping with a relief team. . . . I thought I saw him there.*"

"Who?"

"I'm not sure we should say that because"—he glanced directly at the camera—"you know."

Leaning back against the black lacquer conference table, Cardinal stared at the wall-mounted screen. Arms crossed, he ran a hand over his jaw as he thought through the answers he'd given. Had he been too obvious? Or perhaps not obvious enough about the implication.

No, if he'd been too direct, Aspen would've detected something. He'd pored over her records since that meeting. She served in the Air Force as an admin for the judge advocate. Meant she had a good brain.

Knuckles against his mouth, he didn't understand. The plan was perfect. Even Burnett had said so. Why hadn't she made contact?

"Hey, you okay?"

Cardinal glanced over his shoulder to the woman who owned that voice. Lieutenant Brie Hastings. "Yeah, sure." He didn't need to be alone with this girl. She'd made her interest in him known all too well.

"That your new mark?"

Cardinal cursed himself for letting his research notes play on the wall. He *X*-ed out of the video on the laptop, noting it vanishing from the wall, then slapped the computer shut. He tucked it under his arm and started for the door.

"You know." Brie turned as he walked around her. "The female population isn't as scary as you think. You ought to give us a try."

Cardinal stalked into the hall and continued toward Burnett's office, praying the general had some news.

"Cardinal!"

The urgent, hissed call pulled him around. Lieutenant Smith jogged toward him, his face wrought until he spotted Hastings, slowed with a stupid grin, shot her a "hey," then refocused on Cardinal as he waved a paper.

Cardinal pointed to the paper in the lieutenant's hand. "Is that—?"

"E-mail just came through."

Snatching the printed communication, Cardinal felt the first surge of relief in a long time.

> *SGT Markoski—I want to thank you, personally, for honoring Austin's memory with honesty and integrity. They've relegated my brother to six feet under without a body to place there. Our country has long worked hard to bring home the fallen, so I don't understand how they can forget about my brother so easily. Thank you for remembering him.*
>
> *It would be nice to talk and trade stories and memories. Austin & I spent a lot of time at Amadore's Fight Club. I'm still there, every Tuesday & Thursday evening, as he and my father taught me to fight to defend myself and to fight for what's right. Semper Fidelis.—A. Courtland.*

Cardinal read the e-mail again.

"Not quite the response you expected, huh?" Smith said.

"No, it's not." Cardinal patted his shoulder. "It's better." He started for Burnett's office.

"Better?"

"Get me on the next flight to Austin." Cardinal folded the paper and rounded the corner.

"Huh? But why? She just said—"

"I'll need a team prepped for Djibouti. We'll need to alert Kuhn we're headed his way." Cardinal carded himself through to the offices of General Burnett and a couple of other four-stars.

From the admin's desk, Cardinal looked through the glass pane and held up a hand to Burnett, who waved him in as he talked on the phone.

He leaned in and held up the paper. "She contacted. We're a go."

Holding up one finger, Burnett spoke quietly into his phone. So quietly Cardinal couldn't hear him. But he could read his lips. *Let me take care of it. I know. . .no, he's not a loose cannon. I can—yes, sir.*

"Problem, sir?"

With a disgusted sigh, the general shook his head. "Always a problem."

Cardinal thumped the e-mail with a finger. "She made contact. I'm on my way up to the Lone Star state."

"Actually, you're not."

Heat spilled down Cardinal's spine as Burnett hung up. He said nothing. Just waited. It always worked better.

"That was General Payne."

A royal *pain* in the backside. Also Chief of Staff of the Army. Burnett's boss's boss. Cardinal knew where this was going. They never approved of the general using him for operations. They questioned his loyalty. Questioned his motives.

Well, one they had no need to question. The other was his business alone.

"Approval for the Djibouti mission has been rejected."

"On what grounds?"

"Nigeria."

Cardinal smothered his reaction. "Unbelievable." He jerked his head down. Looked to the side. Closed his eyes. Then glanced at Burnett. "We have her and that dog. I put eyes on the target. He's down there. We have to go down there and get him out. If we don't—"

Burnett held up a hand. "I know. And so does Payne. They're sending a team—"

"They send anyone who smells like American military down there, the hounds of hell are going to rip out their hearts. Then you'll lose him for good."

Blue eyes held his. "Son, this is not my first rodeo and you're not Cardinal, god of the spy sea."

The terse words pulled Cardinal off balance. The general had never snarled at him like that. Which meant one of two things: Burnett agreed with Payne, or Burnett was ticked off, too.

Either way, his mission just got tanked. Austin's life had been put in dire straits.

There was no battle to fight here. Payne tied Burnett's hands. Which cut off Cardinal's limbs. And possibly severed the heart of a family—the Courtland's.

Not that they'd ever know their son had been abandoned by their country.

Aspen already knows that. She just didn't have the right definition to MIA: Presumed Dead. To her, it meant they couldn't find a body. Cardinal knew the truth—the U.S. buried the body with its complacency and bureaucracy. He respected laws and procedures.

They defined civilizations, prevented collapses.

They also crippled civilizations. Initiated collapses.

He'd seen it too many times. Cardinal gave a nod of surrender. Gritted his teeth, then turned for the door.

"Cardinal."

He opened the door and dragged his attention back to where it did not want to go.

"Don't."

A smile almost made it to his face.

"I mean it." Burnett leaned forward, rested his arms on his desk. "That very propensity to go rogue is why you got benched. Let them handle this."

"Of course."

"I mean it. I'd hate to see you fly off without his stamp of approval," Burnett said. "Then get down there and need help. They'd be all over my hide." A smile twinkled behind the terse words. "I'd have to send my very best after you to drag your sorry hide back here."

Cardinal stared at the general. The man who'd taken him under his wing, guided him, honed his skills, taught him things, learned things from Cardinal. . .and always, always saw things the same way Cardinal did.

"Understood."

Amadore's Fight Club
Austin, Texas

"Good gravy, girl."

Aspen eyed her friend as they headed into Amadore's, assaulted at once with the thick odor of sweat and BO wafting toward them. "What?"

"You only e-mailed him two days ago. What do you expect? He was in DC, for crying out loud. For him to drop everything and come up here?"

Bristling at her best friend's wisdom, Aspen strode back to the women's locker room, which wasn't more than a converted broom closet with a shower well. "He's military. He'll get it. If he was with Austin, then he was a Green Beret."

"Girl, I don't know. I couldn't find record of that."

"You're an investigative reporter, Britt, not the FBI. Records like his would be blacked out or concealed." It was a stretch, but hey, it made her feel better.

Brittain Larabie tossed her bag onto the bench. "What if he doesn't come?"

Aspen turned to her friend. "We went over all of that with the others before I e-mailed him at your condo."

"Yeah," Brittain said, with a roll of her head. "And if I remember, not everyone thought it was a good idea to bring this guy into the plan. In fact, Timbrel said you were digging a grave. And Darci says this man's psych profile showed a lethal dedication to his career. She's not convinced he's right. I was with this guy an hour and he never smiled. I mean—creepy! And—"

"Enough!" Aspen thrust her hands into her hair and tied it back with black elastic as she met Brittain's gaze in the mirror. "We *need* him—he was there with Austin the day of the attack." Yanking the zipper on her bag, she felt the tension tangling her mind and thoughts. "He knows what happened. Maybe I'll have enough to file an appeal or something with the judge advocate. General Gray and his wife still invite me to their Christmas parties. They like me. Maybe he'll listen."

"Yeah, and maybe the Easter Bunny will deliver a gold egg."

Aspen glared at her friend. "I don't need your negativity—"

"It's not neg—"

"I know. It's the facts. *Negative* facts, I'd point out."

Britt let her shoulders sag in an exaggerated way. "What about Austin's fire buddy? He said he doesn't remember this guy."

Aspen rolled her eyes. "Will was a player whose loyalties were with himself." She sighed. "As much as I don't want to put my last hope in this Mar-whatever guy, I will take him over Will any day." When she'd hit SEND on that letter, a thread of hope stitched up her broken, angry heart. She plunged her hand into the bag and drew out her wrist wraps.

Warm hands cupped her shoulders, drawing Aspen's gaze from the yellow wraps she secured around her palm and wrist. Compassion oozed from the milk chocolate eyes.

"No." Aspen stepped back. "Don't do that." She snatched the gloves from the bench and strode into the gym, acutely aware how much her best friend wanted to apply the brakes to this before they got started. But Aspen couldn't—*wouldn't*—let Austin's name end up on some memorial wall. He wasn't dead. She could feel it.

Or. . .could she?

It'd only been in the wee hours of the morning as she wept over his disappearance that she wondered if their twin connection was still alive. Was he still alive?

Batting the gloves into a better fit, she crossed the open floor, passed the free weights, the ellipticals, and treadmills. At the speed bag, she warmed up. When a slow burn radiated through her muscles, she started for the ring.

Mario straightened as she passed, stilling the kickboxing bag he'd just struck. He grinned. "Hey, beautiful. Ready for more?"

Slipping in her mouth guard, she arched an eyebrow at him.

He whooped.

As she reached for the ropes to step in, Amadore, ghostlike man that he was, appeared out of nowhere. "You with us today, Angel?"

With more conviction than she felt, she nodded.

He pointed to Mario. "You hurt her, you answer to me."

Smiling, she nudged his shoulder then bent through the ropes. She strode toward the center and met her opponent. All six feet of the man towered over her five-foot-five frame. Muscles rippled beneath his dark skin as those eyes—Timbrel called them lady-killers—sparkled back at her. In the center, she bumped gloves with Mario, their official start signal.

He threw the first punch, launching them into a rigorous workout. Though they were well matched, he always seemed determined to bring her down. She enjoyed the challenge. Much like this new venture of hers—finding her brother. Bringing him back. Darci insisted Aspen had gone one too many rounds in the ring and incurred TBI, traumatic brain injury, to attempt this. But like Aspen, Darci's mind and heart raced at the thought of doing something everyone else said they couldn't.

Would the guy come? Though she wasn't a former intelligence operative like Darci or a borderline Mensa like Khaterah, Aspen had been gifted with an insatiable thirst for truth and justice. But without this guy, without Dane Whatshisname—who named their kid after a dog, anyway?—she could hang up this plan. He had been there. He knew her brother. Knew the location. The terrain. And he still had connections with the military. Desperately needed connections to get them in and out of Afghanistan. Besides, going in with a team of men alone. . .well, even Aspen wasn't that stupid.

Black slammed into her face with a resounding thud.

Aspen spun away, stumbling.

Mario cursed.

"Hey," Amadore's shout sailed through the cavernous, split-level gym. "What'd you do?"

"Nothin'," Mario said.

Aspen sniffled, smelling and tasting the metallic glint of blood. She wiped the warmth from her upper lip and sneered at Mario. "You'll pay," she mumbled around her guard.

Mario grinned, but even beneath that she saw uncertainty as he darted a gaze to Amadore, who loomed over the front counter, his face aflame. "I warned you, Mario. You hurt her—"

Aspen threw a right cross at the distracted man.

His hand flew up and blocked. He angled to the side and countered.

Her mind had left the ring, and that'd cost her some blood. She wouldn't make the mistake again. And now, she had to pay back this player. Besides, she was tired of Amadore protecting her. The men here needed to know she could hold her own. If she'd proven that in Iraq, she could do it at Amadore's Fight Club, too.

Tracking him around the ring, she deflected several aggressive—and stupid—moves. Mario was running on his victory. He'd die on it, too.

He raised his knee—she shifted, turned slightly, and rammed her elbow down on the meaty part.

Mario flinched and dropped his guard.

Aspen threw a hard right. And connected.

His head snapped back, but he was already in motion. A left jab. Right. Light glinted off the glass-front door—the glare flared across Mario's face. Then Aspen's. Both looked toward the front, ready to holler at whoever had forgotten to pull the curtain to prevent such a distraction.

"Hey," Mario shouted. "The bwind." His mouth guard made him sound like he had rocks in his mouth.

"Sorry, sorry"—Luke, the new hire, rushed and secured the curtain. The streaming sunlight wreathed a tall, muscular figure before the light vanished. Aspen blinked, and when her gaze hit the reception desk in the open-area gym, she froze.

Four

Amadore's Fight Club
Austin, Texas

Can I help you?"

Distrust and disgust stared back from a face that said trouble was best left outside. If Cardinal were the guessing kind, he'd peg this guy as the Amadore whose name stretched across the painted-black window gracing the storefront. Built like a barrel, with hands as big as two ball-peen hammers, the guy had hair that had once been jet black and curly. The proverbial Italian Stallion. And by that no-mess greeting, the stallion had things to protect.

Musty and dim, the fight club had all the glamour and odor one would expect. Light dribbled through the spots where the window paint had flecked off the large panes lining the front of the old warehouse. Dust danced on the light beams, as if locked in their own boxing match.

Cardinal brought his gaze back to the guy who waved off a scrawny kid. "Looking for someone."

"We ain't a date joint," the burly guy said.

Amusing. "Good, I'm looking for a guy."

A shrug of the massive, well-muscled shoulders. "Don't ask, don't tell." The man almost grinned. "We don't judge." He slowly looked Cardinal up and down. "Well, most of the time."

Cardinal cocked his head and met the man's entirely too pleased eyes. "Look, someone asked me to meet him here. A—"

Thwump!

The burly guy jerked his attention to the ring where two fighters, wearing headgear and other protective gear, were heavy into a match.

Thwump!

"Hey!" The burly guy stalked to the other end of the counter. "Mario! What'd I tell you? I'm warning you, punk!"

The guy in the ring held up his gloves in a show of submission.

"Angel, eyes up. Focus!" Scowling, the burly guy backstepped, still watching the match in the ring at the center of the gym.

Cardinal could understand why.

"Up, watch—that's right!"

A woman—had the big guy called her Angel?—bounced around the mat, going toe-to-toe with a bully of a guy. And holding her own. He'd half expected her to be laid-out flat after the way that guy swung.

A hard right. She deflected and threw her own.

"Whoa," the scrawny kid mumbled from the other side of the counter.

"She's good," Cardinal said.

The man's head snapped toward him. "What?" he barked. "What'd you say about my angel?"

"She's a solid fighter. Good form. A little slow on the return, but—"

"Hey, Angel," the man yelled, still glowering at Cardinal. "This punk says you're too slow on the return."

Cardinal laughed. "Hey, it was just—"

She waved her gloved hands. "Bring it!"

He glanced at the ring. Brown, wet ringlets sprung from a pulled-back ponytail, framing the face and doe-like eyes—well, doe in shape. The fury spewing from them made her seem more like the siren who'd coaxed Odysseus from his voyage—mission.

"No, no, I'm here to meet someone."

The burly man laughed, long and loud. "Mister," he said with a menacing gleam, "meet my angel." Finally, he looked away. "Mario, give the guy some gloves."

"No, seriously." Cardinal wanted to punch the scrawny kid who stood laughing at him. "I meant no harm."

"He's just chicken," the kid taunted.

Laughter bounced through the fight club, and only then did Cardinal realize he had an audience. A large one. He wanted to curse.

He rounded on the guy when he started making clucking noises.

The kid's smile vanished, and he backed away. "I'm going. . .to. . ." The guy pivoted and ran.

When Cardinal turned around, something flew at him, thumped against his chest, then dropped to the floor. He glanced down to find gloves and wraps at his feet. Though he retrieved them, he had no intention of fighting, especially not a woman.

He held the equipment out to the man behind the counter. "I'm not here to fight. I'm here to meet someone by the name of Courtland." He looked to the ring, expecting the woman to perk up when he said her name. She didn't. "You know where I can find Aspen Courtland?"

Something dark flickered through the man's eyes. "Yes."

"Where?"

He pointed to the ring.

"Now who looks slow?" came a taunting voice—a female voice. She stood at the side, red gloves hooked over the top ropes. The white tank accentuated her curves—and her toned arms and trim waist. Dark spots—blood?—splattered her shoulder. He'd seen the number she did on that other guy. Though young, short, and athletic, she had a fight the size of Alaska—and as cold—in those cobalt eyes.

The burly guy lifted the gloves. "One round. If you fight fair and remain standing, I'll introduce you to Courtland."

This wasn't the first time he had to buy loyalty from locals. Probably wouldn't be the last. Slowly, he reached for the gloves. "I'll hold you to that." He hesitated, looked at the woman again, then back to the big guy. "Two minutes?"

"As I said, one round. I'm a man of my word."

"So am I."

The man slapped his shoulder. "You can change back there. Luke will get you suited up."

Within minutes, Cardinal had a pair of shorts, shoes, and a tank on. His newfound friend, Luke, led him back into the gym.

"Hey," Cardinal said to the man who'd been in the ring with the girl, "any tips? I don't want to hurt her."

Mario laughed. "Yeah, go easy on her. She's not as strong as she looks."

Why did that sound a lot like "you're stupid enough to believe me"?

Cardinal slowed. "Then what does that make you since she beat the snot"—he motioned to the guy's red nose—"out of you?"

More laughter. Mario bumped his fists against the gloves, a sign of camaraderie. "Don't hold back."

Surprise leapt through Cardinal.

"Angel won't."

Angel. It felt like a sick, cruel joke. The name invoked a haunting memory.

Applause and cheers broke out around the gym, pulling Cardinal back to the present, back to the ring. Surprisingly, most of the others gathered round. Angel waited in the ring, conferring with two other women, who indicated to him as he stepped through the ropes.

The burly guy stood at the center of the ring. He held out his hands. Angel approached, and only as she came closer did he realize she was small. . .and beautiful—er, young. Way young. Was she even out of high school?

"Fight fair. Two-minute bell."

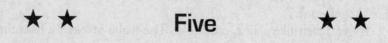

Five

★ ★   ★ ★

Amadore's Fight Club

Generate momentum off the right toe. Keep balance. Take balance away from the other guy. The tall, muscle-bound man rivaled anyone she'd ever matched. In the first thirty seconds of their sparring, she realized he knew boxing. A lot about boxing.

Fair enough. No holds barred.

Aspen backed up, forcing him to come to her. He moved fluidly, which amazed her that a man his size could do it smoothly. Acutely aware of the throng gathered on the bleachers surrounding the ring, she tried to keep her focus. Shake off the words Timbrel had muttered as the guy climbed into the ring: *"A hottie like that—let him win so he'll feel bad and take you out."*

The glove came up, glanced off her chin. She rolled out of it and followed through with a right hook, which he deftly avoided. The jabs and punches came quicker. Apparently, he'd gotten over fighting a girl—the trepidation clear on his face as he lumbered onto the mat was gone. Agitation wound around her stomach. She'd seen that look on every airman who'd been paired with her in the field. They quickly figured out there were bigger sissies back in their bunks. But she hated the assumptions, hated the looks and jeers. This guy had held that presumption for all of ten seconds before unloading.

Hands up, she protected herself against a jab. Though he stood as tall—no, taller—than Mario, the bulk on this guy added some leverage she hadn't expected.

Keep your feet moving. A left, right. She swung hard.

He deflected.

Harder.

A quick strike snapped her head back. Stunned, she backstepped. He eased into the space. She slammed a solid left, which he protected, then she rammed a right. Caught his side. He grunted but swung upward. The momentum carried through, popping her head back. Aspen gasped as her feet left the mat.

Ding!

She landed on her back. *Oof!* Air whooshed from her lungs.

The guy leaned over her. "You okay?"

"Get away from her!" Amadore's shout pervaded the club. "What'd you do, punk?"

Aspen peeled herself off the mat, indignation creeping through her shoulders. She stretched her jaw and neck, amazed. He'd flattened her! Mario hadn't managed that in a long time. Sitting, arms over her knees, she waited to catch her breath.

"Angel, you okay?" Amadore hooked her elbow and helped her to her feet. He twisted around. "You, get out of my club!"

"What a minute."

"Out!"

Dane Whatshisname drew back, glancing between them. "You said you'd—"

Chest puffing, Amadore tightened his lips and biceps. Coiled, ready to strike like the cobra tattooed on his arm. "I said if you survived a round."

Dane glowered. "I did."

"No, you knocked her out. The bell hadn't sounded."

Grit out, she sighed. "He didn't knock me out, Amadore." She patted his side. "I'm okay. Just. . ." She shot Brittain and Timbrel a glance then looked toward the two men hovering near the far corner of the ring. Picking her pride up off the mat took everything she had. At the corner, she offered her glove to the winner. "Good fight."

Confusion and concern crowded his handsome features as he stood on the floor, looking up at her. "You're a good boxer."

Holy cannoli! Was the heat in her face from blushing? No way. "Thanks." She swiped a sweaty curl from her face, hoping she covered the red tint no doubt filling her cheeks. Whipping off the gloves, she smiled. Extended a wrapped hand. "Aspen Courtland."

"Dane Markoski. And for the record, you look nothing like your brother."

"I know. He got my mom's side—full Italian. I got our father's, Irish." She wrinkled her nose. "So, Mr. Mar. . ."

"Markoski. It's not really hard to pronounce."

She shrugged. "I need to shower and change. Meet out front after?"

"Works for me." He turned and walked toward the men's locker room.

Aspen didn't trust herself to talk anymore. Not here, not in front of everyone. And not after ending up flat on her back. She showered and changed, anticipation of talking to Mystery Man pushing her a little faster than usual. Disappointment dogged her steps as she waved bye to Nonno and made her way out the front door, where her friends waited on the wrought-iron bench.

"Something's not right about that guy." Timbrel Hogan, another handler with A Breed Apart, crossed her arms over her chest and stared at the gym doors.

"Is any guy right in your book?" A smile glowed against Brittain's mocha-colored skin.

Timbrel smirked. "A rare few."

Aspen tossed her gym bag in the back of her SUV. "I agree— something feels off. But if he was there with Austin and he knows what happened, then I need to explore this possibility."

"Just don't explore him."

"Timmy," Aspen chided, "I don't care about *him*. Answers about my brother are what I'm after."

Timbrel's eyes narrowed. "But I know you, Aspen—you're soft where it comes to romance. And that guy—he's trouble. He knows how to work people. I can just. . .tell."

Touching her puffy cheekbone, Aspen cringed. "He definitely worked me over." She meant it as a joke to lighten the conversation, but Timbrel seized on it.

"Exactly what I'm talking about. What kind of man would hit a woman?"

Brittain laughed. "Girl, get off your hate wagon about men. Aspen challenged him in a boxing ring. She got what she asked for." Her tall, African American friend brushed Aspen's curl from her face. "All kidding aside, Timmy's right: be careful. We don't know nothin' about this man. And it is strange that he shows up after all this time."

"I know. I know." She touched her fingers to her temple. They were right. It wouldn't be the first time she'd been swayed by blue eyes and smooth talking. Unlike Timbrel who didn't trust at all, Aspen trusted far too easily. She called it optimism. Her friends naivete.

Was it her fault she wanted to believe people were good?

"Why don't I go with you to the ranch?"

Hmm, maybe it wasn't a bad idea. With Timbrel's negative outlook coupled with her own positive outlook, maybe they'd find a safe middle ground.

"Hey, won't Daniels be there?" Brittain nudged her arm. "You said he was good people, that he had a strong ability to read situations."

"She's right. Prince Charming has very good radar."

"Whoa." The wind gust rifled its fingers through Brittain's caramel curls that puffed up in a halo around her face. "Did Timbrel Hogan just pay a man a compliment?"

"It's a fact, not a compliment." Timbrel bristled, but they all knew Daniels had pried a little sister out of Hogan during their mission in Afghanistan last year. The two behaved like siblings and had a mutual respect for each other.

"Here he comes."

Aspen looked over her shoulder.

Showered, changed, and looking quite handsome in a dark blue button down and jeans. . . A breeze tussled his hair and threw it into his face. Cut short along the sides and back of his head, his black hair glittered wet and shiny in the afternoon sun. Longer strands on the top whipped along his forehead and temples as he strode toward them.

"Mmm," Brittain muttered. "Yep, one *fine* man."

"Okay. That's it. I'm going," Timbrel said.

Aspen started to glance at her friend, but Talon let out a low growl. "Out, Talon," she said as she looked over her shoulder.

Dan spoke up. "So, where to?"

"A ranch that's a half-hour drive out of the city."

"Should I ride with you?" he asked.

RONIE KENDIG

"Absolutely not." Timbrel pointed to his car. "Easier for you to leave after she throws your butt out."

Blue eyes, surrounded by olive skin and framed by black hair, held Aspen's. "You do remember you invited me out." He towered over her but not in a threatening way. In the six-inches-taller way. In a way that left her unbalanced and far too aware of a strange current that bounced between them. And the way his jaw was dusted with stubble. "Or did I misconstrue the note you sent via the studio?"

Had he leaned closer?

She took a step back.

"I'm sorry," he said as he looked at the three of them. "I feel like I'm intruding or something." He fixed on Aspen. "You said you wanted to talk to me about your brother. But if I'm making you uncomfortable, or if I crossed some line, then I'll leave."

"No." Aspen cleared her throat, praying that didn't sound as desperate as it felt. "You're right—I asked you to come." She started to touch his arm, a move to reassure him, but she thought better of it. "It's no problem. Timbrel just doesn't like men."

He studied the petite brunette for several long minutes.

Timbrel crossed her arms again, squaring off with him. "What?"

"Nothing." He didn't smile, but his eyes did—weird. "I just. . .if that's your preference, great."

"Preference?" Timbrel's eyebrow arched.

Brittain laughed. "She's not gay. She just. . .hates men, Mr. Markusky."

"Markoski." Confusion whirled through eyes that matched the sky behind him. "Then who do you date?"

"My dog," Timbrel said through clenched teeth as she stomped toward her little import.

His shoulders weren't tensed. Eyes held no barbed-wire accusations, only. . .amusement.

Aspen twisted toward him, her Asics crunching dirt and rock. "You did that on purpose, suggesting that."

"Sorry. I just don't appreciate people questioning my character when they don't know me."

"Don't apologize, Soldier Boy. Anyone who can tie Timbrel's tongue has my vote." Brittain turned, locked gazes with Aspen, and started

398

humming the song "Getting to Know You."

Aspen flashed her friend a warning. Not the most suitable song. There was no king here. And if she recalled, the school teacher ended up falling in love with the king.

So not happening.

Trailing the white luxury SUV left Cardinal with more questions than answers. Things didn't seem to be getting off on the right foot. Or any foot. Aspen was guarded, even more so with her posse of girlfriends. *How do I get under her radar?* What would it take to convince her to trust him?

The truth.

No way. That would risk everything—*everything!* His job and carcass would be on the line. Burnett would fry him. Then stick him in that smoker he raved about.

As they crept out of the Austin city limits and dug farther into the countryside, he evaluated what he'd perceived of Aspen Courtland. The woman had grit, but she also had an…*innocence* about her. Ironic considering she'd been an airman. A pretty tough one from the records he'd seen. And the way she'd gone up against the Brass regarding her brother's status—the very reason Burnett wanted her kept ignorant because this could get ugly fast—and the way she'd taken control of the situation.

At least, she thought she had. He'd anticipated that about her. It'd worked. Exactly as planned. He banged his hand against the wheel.

"You are weak!"

Teeth grinding, he pulled himself straighter in the car. What was that? Dropping out of reality and drowning in the past would get him killed. Create mistakes. The way things were, he couldn't afford a single mistake. He'd keep a line of demarcation between their two worlds. The line in the sand would be reinforced with powerful barriers.

The SUV slowed, snapping Cardinal back to the present. To the country road. He applied the brake as the Lexus turned into a gated drive. The trellised ironwork stretched over his sedan with the words A BREED APART.

The dog!

He eased his car along the tree-lined road. *Head on a swivel. Eyes and ears out.* The old military lingo to watch his surroundings served as a good reminder. Ahead fifty yards, a brown home rose in quiet beauty. Glass and lines marked it with elegance, yet simplicity. Two men stood on a wraparound porch. Waiting.

Aspen's white SUV aimed toward a fenced-in area away from the house. Already her door opened by the time he pulled up alongside. He slid the gear into PARK, eyes on the rearview mirror. Well-muscled, sporting a Glock holstered to his thigh, a former Army grunt, if he ever saw one, approached.

Cardinal stretched his jaw and snagged the bandana from the glove compartment. He climbed out, sizing up the competition who gave Aspen a warm familiar hug.

"How's he doing?" she asked.

"Fine. Trin's got him on his toes."

Aspen laughed.

The man shifted and extended a hand. "Heath Daniels." Though the words were friendly, his posture was not. The man had territory issues.

Take it slow. "Dane Markoski."

Aspen motioned to him. "Dane was on the news—you might have seen him."

Daniels nodded. "Mr. Markoski."

"Oh, and this is Jibril Khouri." Aspen turned, brushing a blond curl from her face. "He owns the ranch."

Cardinal shook the man's hand. "The land is beautiful."

"I couldn't agree more." Khouri's gaze lingered longer than it should have. He was right to be cautious. They all were.

Behind the fenced area came the barking of dogs. Heart rammed into his throat, he looked toward the broad gate marked TRAINING YARD. "Training?"

"Yes," Khouri said as he motioned and started walking. "The ranch is a training facility for working dogs."

"Hey." Cardinal glanced to the side where Aspen walked with them. "Austin's dog—whatever happened to him after. . . ?"

Aspen's expression fell, but she crammed a smile into place.

Cardinal felt like a jerk for asking the question he knew must twist that dagger in her heart, but he shoved aside the feeling.

"He's here." Aspen opened the gate. "I adopted him after Austin went missing."

"I. . .I thought dogs were—" He cut off his words but knew she'd understand where he was going.

"A new law protects the dogs. They're currently classified as equipment, so I had to pay to bring him home once they wrote him off, but it was worth it." Aspen stepped into the training yard and strode toward the center.

A yellow Lab lumbered toward her, ball in mouth.

"Two months ago," Daniels said, "Talon wouldn't lift his head to even look at her."

"Seriously?" Cardinal watched the handler and dog. "What was his problem?"

"PTSD." Daniels's gaze locked on to him. "So, you were with him in Al-Najaf."

Cardinal feigned distraction with the dog. Maybe the woman. She had confidence yet a brokenness that felt familiar. He met Daniels head-on. "Oh. No, Kariz-e Sefid. That's where I worked with Court." Had he noticed Khouri limping? "That patrol, the bombs—it wiped out my career. Put me flat on my back for two months."

"With what?" Relentless, Daniels tucked his arms under his armpits, gauging, monitoring. There was a reason he'd been a Green Beret.

"Broken back. TBI. PTSD."

"You have no noticeable scars."

"It's the invisible ones that get you." Cardinal needed to extract himself from this interrogation. "Excuse me."

Had Daniels figured things out? He'd never been unraveled that fast. And he doubted it'd happened already here, but there was no time like now to put distance between him and the man who'd dig deep enough to find some holes.

Another dog bounded toward them. Lowered her front and tipped up her tail, snarling at him. Cardinal reached out a hand to try to show her he was her friend.

She snapped.

"Trinity, out!" Daniels looked at him and shrugged. "She's protective. So am I."

Something wet nudged his hand. He glanced down to find the Lab sniffing his hand. And prayed hard his plan worked.

To his relief, Talon sat at his feet and stared down the obstacle course.

Wide-eyed, Aspen gawked. "He knows you."

"You sound surprised." Technically, the dog *should* know him if he'd worked with Courtland, so this was a good test marker to also gain Aspen's trust.

A pretty blush seeped into her milky-white complexion.

"You didn't believe me." He tried to sound surprised.

"Sorry." More red. Matched her pink lips. "I've just been fighting to get him back, so it was a little strange that I'd never heard your name till you showed up on the news."

"But you're willing to believe me because of him." He pointed to the dog.

Aspen ruffled the Lab's head. "Talon knows people. Better than I do." She clipped a lead on his collar. "If he accepts you, then I will."

"You didn't before?"

Her lips quirked, and she shrugged. "Your name wasn't in the official report."

Cardinal held her gaze, infusing it with reassurance as he spoke words that could unravel. . .if they weren't the truth. "That's because I don't exist."

WATCHING

St. Petersburg, Russia
Age: 14 Years, 3 Months

The world sped by in a whirl of greens as the train spirited Nikol Tselekova toward Brno. Though he sat with his eyes closed, his mind was alert and rampantly going over every detail. Yes, his bed was made. No wrinkles or ripples. Windows spotless. Footlocker unfettered for inspection. Bedposts aligned with the grain of the wood floors that ran toward the towering window. Yes, all had been in place. He'd made sure. Stood there at the door to his room for ten minutes, inspecting. Obsessing.

He tugged the backpack on his lap closer, tighter. It was worth it. To deliver the gift. To see her face. If only but for a second. It would be enough to hold him over till he could attempt another excursion.

The train slowed as it entered the city. Nikol glanced at his watch, mapping his time and journey. Still well within parameters. Fifteen minutes later, the train pulled to a stop in the heart of the Moravian capital city.

He hoofed it through the streets, avoiding cars and cyclists and pedestrians alike. Invigorated with each step, he headed west, out of the city, up the country road to the missionary's home. As he trudged up the road, he moved out of plain sight. Drifted farther into the trees lining the road. If he was right—

Laughter sailed from a yard. He tucked himself among the trees. Watched. A group of children played among a cluster of small homes. He searched their faces, anticipation thick. On one hand, he wanted to see her—out in the sun, laughing, playing the way she should. She deserved that. And so much more.

403

Reassured she was not there, Nikol moved forward. A young boy threw a ball toward his friend.

"Dobrý den!" Nikol greeted them.

The boy hesitated, then waved. It was not good that the child recognized him. That would be bad. Especially if the colonel discovered the secret. It would be a path straight back to Nikol.

Sitting on the bench, his back to the main road, Nikol smiled at the boy and lowered the pack to his lap. "Petr, jak se mate?"

The boy shrugged. "I'm good."

"Would you do me a favor?" Nikol extracted the white box from his backpack.

Petr sighed. "For Kalyna? Again?"

Nikol nodded. He would have to find another way to deliver the gifts. It was too known. The boy was as comfortable with Nikol as he was with his friends. Perhaps he should just send them via the post.

But then, he would not get to see her open them. And that. . .that was what kept his heart alive.

"If you like her, you should tell her."

The words brought a smile to his face, but Nikol merely nodded. With the eight-year age difference, it was not so simple as liking the girl.

Fisting his hands on his brown corduroy pants, Petr huffed. "What do I get?"

"Smart boy." Nikol produced a bar of chocolate and a green banknote. "First, you must tell me—" He broke off when he noticed the boy's gaze drift to the edge of the field. Following the gaze, Nikol tensed.

A girl stood there.

Watching.

★ ★ Six ★ ★

A Breed Apart Ranch
Texas Hill Country

Wwhat do you mean you don't exist?"

Sunlight peeked through the cedar trees whose branches waved in the unusual summer breeze. Aspen hated the nerves that skittered through her veins. As she waited for his answer, noting that Heath and Jibril now stood a little taller.

The almost-there smile flickered for a second before it vanished, and Dane lowered his gaze. "I was being facetious." He shrugged those broad shoulders. "Have no idea why I wasn't mentioned in the reports. I was there." He motioned to Talon. "He even recognizes me."

Instinctively, Aspen's hand went to the Lab's broad skull. The big lug leaned against her leg panting, oblivious to the tension that had just coated the afternoon.

"Seriously." Dane held up his hands. "If you aren't comfortable with me being here, I can leave."

"No." The word shot out before Aspen could process her response—or the why. The urgency that tightened a fist on her didn't let go. This guy was the first possible good news she'd had in a very long time. "No, I want to hear your story." Something sparked in his blue eyes that unsettled her. "Then, I'll decide for myself if you need to leave."

"Fair enough."

"Why don't we take this up to the house?" Heath said.

"Yes, yes." Jibril started up the hill that led to the house. "I have tea and lemonade."

"You or Khat?" Heath taunted him.

Laughing, Jibril stepped onto the wraparound porch. "It is my house, not my sister's, yes?"

Though Heath and Jibril continued with their banter, Aspen drew into herself. Dane might have the answers. Or he might not. And what good would it do to hear his story for herself? Even if he did see Austin in Africa somewhere, it wasn't proof.

Seated in the cluster of deep-cushioned sofas that overlooked the pool and outdoor area, Aspen motioned Talon to her side. He lumbered to her and flattened himself against the cold tile floor.

Dane folded himself onto a chair next to her. Somehow, the low ceilings and short sofas amplified the guy's height. While he stood several inches taller than her, he wasn't a giant. Though his presence carried powerfully in the room.

"Let me get some refreshments," Jibril said. "Don't wait for me."

Hands folded, elbows resting on her thighs, Aspen steeled herself. "So, Brittain shared the interview with me."

He sat on the edge, forearms on his knees, and nodded.

"So, you were there when the bomb went off."

"I was."

"Tell me what you remember."

"I told Ms. Larabie everything I know."

"I know." Aspen drew in a breath and looked at Heath, whose presence gave her the gumption to push. Not that she was weak. But something about this guy unsettled her. Left her feeling nervous. "But I want to hear it for myself."

"Okay." As he launched into his story, into being down on the ground when the bomb went off, getting knocked unconscious and coming to, it all rang true.

"And in Africa?" Prompting him felt artificial. As if he wasn't willing to tell her what he saw. But he couldn't come this far then drop her off a cliff. Aspen inched closer. "You saw him there?"

He darted a look at her then to Heath before sloughing his hands together.

She touched his arm. "Please. Tell me what you saw."

"That's just it—I can't guarantee what I saw was real." He snorted. "I mean, I saw *someone*, but. . ."

"It could've been anyone." Heath towered over both of them.

Dane's blue gaze rose to Heath's. "Yeah." He skirted her a glance. "I just. . .I don't want to get your hopes up, ya know?"

"I appreciate that." She smiled, noticing for the first time how much depth rested in his face. "But you wouldn't have gone on national television if you didn't think there was a chance it was my brother you saw, not just *anyone*."

Ice clinked against glass as Jibril returned with a tray of drinks. He set them on the coffee table cuddled in the center of the sofas. "Here we go." The ABA owner slowed as he set the tray down. As always, he didn't miss a thing. "Is something wrong?"

"Hot Shot here is getting cold feet."

The challenge soared through the air, and Aspen could tell it hit center mass. Dane rose. Aspen with him. "Hey," she said, catching his forearm as she glared at Heath, "no baiting."

"You know, this was a bad idea."

"Why?" Heath held his ground. "Am I right?"

Dane swallowed. "I don't have cold feet." He started for the door.

"Then what's the problem?"

"I'm not doing this." Dane shook his head and stomped toward the foyer.

"Wait!" Aspen speared Heath with her fiercest glare as she rushed around the U-shaped sofa. "Dane, please."

Sunlight shot through the open door.

She hurried onto the porch. "I want to talk. I need to know everything."

"Why?" He spun toward her. "There's nothing that can be done. The government won't go after him. They won't even listen to me, though they've shoveled threats at me by the ton."

"What threats?"

He snapped back into composure and lowered his chin. "Never mind."

"No. I won't never mind. You have information about my brother and I want it."

"Why?" His brow furrowed, but those blue eyes shone through.

"What are you going to do, Aspen? Go after him?"

Indignation rippled through her and yanked her courage to the front. "If I have to."

"Be realistic. I've been there on a mission. Have you been there? Do you realize the temperature?"

"This is Texas. I'm familiar with hot weather."

He let out a half laugh, half snort as his eyes closed, and he lowered his head again. "I meant the political temperature."

"Oh."

"They aren't friendly to Americans. It's predominantly Muslim. There's an American base there, but that doesn't mean anything except more trouble. If your brother was there, finding him is one thing. Getting him out of there is another."

"Why? What are you saying?"

"I'm saying if he's there, if he went missing—there are myriad possibilities. He could've been snatched. He could've been brainwashed or have amnesia. He could be—" Dane chomped his mouth closed, and his gaze flung to the trees.

Aspen didn't need him to tell her his thoughts. Because hers went there, too. "He could be a traitor." Her next breath felt like it weighed as much as an MRAP. "That's what you were going to say, wasn't it?"

"It doesn't matter. This whole conversation doesn't matter."

"Why? Are you saying my brother doesn't matter?"

"I'm saying we have no way to find him."

She squared her shoulders. "Are you saying you'll go with me?"

He blinked and shook his head. "Aren't you listening to me?"

"I have a team."

"Who?"

"Talon—"

"The dog?" The incredulity in his voice scraped over her spine.

"Yes." She practically hissed the answer. "Talon knows Austin. Better than anyone. He never forgets a scent, even the one of a purported coward."

Dane cocked his head, understanding her accusation. "You said he had PTSD."

"He's getting better."

He ran a hand through his hair. The longer strands swung into his face. "*Getting* better doesn't do us much good in hostile territory."

"Let her worry about that."

They both spun toward the door. Propped against the jamb, Heath had his arms folded again. The proverbial big brother look plastered on his face. No wonder Darci loved that man. Would Aspen ever find a man so protective and gentle, yet every bit the warrior?

"She can worry about anything she wants," Dane said, an edge to his voice. "But taking a damaged dog into who-knows-what—"

"Please." Aspen's heart jammed into her throat as she caressed Talon's head. "Don't call him that."

"I meant no harm."

"I know." Nobody ever did. But it hurt more than anyone could imagine and more than she could possibly explain. "You said you know the last place Austin was seen—"

"*Possibly* seen."

Aspen held up both hands. "Right. But if there's a chance, then that scent is one Talon can pick up. He's our best chance of figuring out if who you saw was Austin." Tentatively, she touched that trembling thread of hope. *Austin. . .* "If we can get a team together—"

"I can put one together."

Point of no return. He'd said the words. Started the opening dialogue of commitment to this mission. With her.

He wanted to curse himself. Cut his eyes out so he couldn't see the hopeful longing in her icy-blue eyes. Eyes so pale they looked cold, yet nothing but warmth flowed from this woman. Angel. The fight club guy had called her that. Now Cardinal understood why. The fire lingering beneath that cool, sultry surface could singe the unsuspecting.

But he wasn't unsuspecting. This was his doing. She'd walked right into his trap. Grinding his teeth, he stood there, waiting as she stared up at him. Expecting. Hoping.

"You can?" A voice soft and pleading like that should be illegal.

Soft, pleading voices had never affected Cardinal. Most often, as now, the woman had no idea how they'd played into his carefully laid plans. But her voice. . .that hope. . .the common thread of knowing Austin.

That's what was different this time. They both knew Austin. That's why it pulled at him. Barreled over his conscience.

"How can you put together a team?" Suspicion oozed out of the former Green Beret. Daniels was bred to mistrust those he didn't know. The Army and multiple tours of combat did that.

"I got a call after my interview with Ms. Larabie." Cardinal avoided the woman's gaze, watching as the Lab and the other dog, Trinity, loped around the porch. "There is a team ready and willing to help." He gave a light, halfhearted shrug. "A high-ranking DIA officer offered it to me."

"DIA?" Daniels perked up.

Act hesitant. Didn't want to give himself away. "Uh, yeah. You know them?"

A wall of granite would've been easier to read than Daniels's face. "Go on."

"Right, okay. Well, he told me they're with me if I decide to do something." Cardinal checked out Talon, now on his belly. "Just not sure about this, especially about the dog."

"Talon should go." Aspen stepped closer to Cardinal.

Pure. Pure trust. Pure beauty. Pure innocence. Pure Aspen. Angel.

And then the angel flew. A cold breeze swept over him. Cardinal hauled his thoughts into line and flogged them. "Are you sure? What if he shuts down or goes nuts on us?"

"He was Austin's partner." Fiery determination sparked in her eyes. "If Talon caught his scent. . .I think there'd be no stopping him."

"But what if there is?"

"We take Trinity." Daniels joined them and leaned back against the railing that stretched the perimeter of the house. "She's Talon's new woman. She keeps him motivated." He smirked. "He'll find his way. If Austin is out there, she'll help Talon find him."

Not good—having the former Green Beret and his MWD on hand would increase the chances of things falling apart, of Cardinal's identity and dealings being compromised. He'd have to find reasons to exclude the man that wouldn't appear artificial. Arrange something. . .

No, he wouldn't put this man in danger. Getting married in two weeks, Daniels should be able to walk down the aisle on his own two feet.

"Give me forty-eight hours." Cardinal had to take control of this before they stepped in. "I'll be in touch."

Aspen nudged into his way. "If something comes up, how can I reach you?"

Cardinal hesitated, ignoring his steel barriers that demanded he spout off some gruff answer like he'd call her. He tugged his wallet out, plucked a card, and passed it to her. "Forty-eight hours."

She scanned the information, tapped it against her hand, then bobbed her head. "I'll be waiting."

The way she said that, why did he find himself reading into those words?

He gave a curt nod to her and the others then climbed into the rental. As he aimed the sedan down the dusty road to the gate, he kept his gaze forward, though in his periphery he could tell Aspen watched. For that reason, he restrained the disgust spiraling through his veins. The urge to punch the dash. The fire that lit across his shoulders.

It worked. Perfectly.

She'd played right into his hands. Easiest deck he ever dealt. It could not have been scripted more precisely. He read her right. Read the men in her life right. Every ploy had been dead on. She responded as if he had puppeted her. He'd known—*known*—what was in her because of the hunger, the deep, burning ache for resolve where her brother was concerned. Resolution.

He could relate. There were answers in his life he wanted, questions eliminated. Loved ones located.

But that man no longer existed. Cardinal. That was his name. His identity. Bestowed on him by Burnett because of their first meeting at the church.

That's exactly what he needed right now. A church. Confession. To purge this evil he had allowed to seep into his soul. Cultivated by manipulating Aspen Courtland.

She trusted him. Those blue eyes. . .so much like—

Cardinal drove his fist into the dash. Pain and fire spiked through his knuckles and darted up his arm, nerves tingling. Teeth clamped, he accelerated. The faceplate of the stereo system cracked. Warmth sped down his arm, dripped onto the gearshift. He snatched his phone and coded in.

"Go ahead, Cardinal."

"I need Burnett."

"He's unavailable."

"Well, you tell him I'm through. I'm not doing this. I'm gone."

Seven

Somewhere in Somalia

Plaster exploded.

Neil Crane threw himself backward with a curse. Pulse hammering, he scrabbled over the dirt, dust, and Sheetrock. Light speared through the hole created by the bullet. As he checked his six, three more beams of light fractured the haven of darkness.

AK-47 cradled in his arms, he sprinted through the darkened hall. "Go, go!" he shouted as he ran. Ahead, he saw her burst from behind another wall. In a dead run, she broke into the searing brightness of another brutally hot day.

He caught up with her. Catching the drag strap of her vest, he prayed for just one more mercy. They'd lived every day of the last three months on nothing but mercy. That fed his conviction that they were doing the right thing. That they had a purpose beyond sucking up oxygen.

"There." He pointed to an alley to the right. "Go!"

As he sprinted with her at his side into the narrow space between two buildings, he heard the shouts of their pursuers behind them. Thudding boots and creaking-groaning vehicles. More shouts. Rock and dirt burst up. From the side, wood splintered.

She tripped. Went down.

He dragged her back into motion.

"There," she gasped, her breath sucked in by the grueling pace.

He searched, uncertain what she referred to. "Wha—?"

With a grunt, she threw herself toward a wall.

A split second of panic snatched the air from his lungs. Was she hit? Then he saw it.

She rolled forward and dropped out of sight.

In a dive, he prayed this worked as he dropped into the darkness. Into the stench.

A Breed Apart Ranch
Texas Hill Country

The trail banked right and down. The cedar leaves provided little protection against the brutal summer heat. Aspen jogged around the bend, sweat dripping down her spine, her neck and temples. The swallow seemed to stick in her throat, the air so dry and dusty. With the lead wrapped around her waist and clipped to Talon, she glanced down at the animal she'd come to think of as a part of herself. Maybe that's the way it'd been with Austin. Living day in and day out with a dog, becoming one, moving as one. She'd never dreamed she'd be able to run with a dog lead coiled around her waist.

His tongue hung out, pink and wagging.

Down the path, she made her way back to the house. At the bottom of the trail, she slowed, walked a few circles with her hands on her hips. She tugged a water bottle from the pouch that hung from the nylon cord. Squirting some in her mouth, she closed her eyes. Swished the liquid that quickly went from cool to warm on her tongue. She swallowed then aimed some at Talon. He lapped it up, tail wagging.

The grief that had been hers for the last five days—well, longer, but amplified over the last several days—tightened around her chest. She smoothed Talon's yellow fur. "Sorry, old boy."

At six, Talon didn't act or look his age, but there was something "ancient" about the war dog. He'd seen more combat than she had as an assistant in the JAG office. The brown eyes, rich and deep, saw a lot.

"I'm sorry he didn't come back, Talon."

The Lab ducked when she said his name. Her heart cinched at the brokenness that engulfed her life. Losing Austin, seeing his once-strong, indomitable dog now cowering.

Remembering what the trainers and Heath had said, she rubbed him behind his ears. The T-touch soothed him almost instantly. She eased up and planted a kiss beside his ear. "I really thought. . ." Emotion in her throat was raw. "He seemed like someone who. . ."

Who would what? Care about Austin as much as you? Champion your cause?

Aspen plopped onto the ground, hugging her bent knees as she wrapped an arm around the bulky build of the Lab. She stared off over the land that sloped down into a valley. "I thought we'd get some answers." Her lower lip trembled, but she let out a shaky laugh. "Even fantasized we'd get Austin back."

Talon twisted around to look at her as if he understood. As if to say he wasn't giving up so she shouldn't either.

Aspen buried her face in his shoulder and gave him a squeeze. "Somehow, we'll get answers."

Oh God, why. . . ? She felt teased, taunted by God. She'd prayed, believed. She'd never stretched her faith as far as she had over the last year, refusing to believe rumors of Austin's death. Just when she'd surrendered and released the idea of finding him, here came this guy who seemed to have the answers.

No, not just answers, but the guts to do something about what he believed—that he'd seen Austin somewhere in Africa. She'd become convinced once again that there was a chance to find out the truth. To resolve this once and for all. For the last two years since the incident, she'd put her life on hold.

Then Markoski vanishes. Just like Austin.

Talon came up off his haunches, his gaze to the north.

Aspen glanced in that direction. A second later, Trinity bounded around the corner, trailed by Heath. Aspen stood and brushed off her backside.

"Hey." Heath came up, his expression tight. "Wanna come up to the house?" The terse way he said that drew her up short.

"Something wrong?"

He hesitated then glanced back. "Just come on up."

Back up at the house, she found Timbrel Hogan there with her infamous Hound of Hell, Beowulf. Beside her at the glass table sat Khaterah, Jibril's beautiful veterinarian sister, who talked with Jibril.

A tray of finger sandwiches sat on the table.

Still catching her breath, Aspen dropped into a chair. "What's going on?"

"Well," Timbrel said, "we got tired of waiting for your troublemaker to show back up."

"*My* troublemaker?"

"Yeah." Timbrel adjusted the ball cap that shaded her brown eyes. "You know, Mister SexyKillerBlueEyes."

Aspen laughed. "So because he has 'killer blue eyes,' he's trouble?"

"One hundred percent." Timbrel reached for a sandwich and tossed it to Beowulf.

"Hey!" Khat objected.

Timbrel ignored her. "That and the way he took you down. I wouldn't trust a guy who'd do that."

Bristling at the way Timbrel was practically telling her what to think about Dane, Aspen shrugged. "I like that he didn't pamper me."

"Pamper is one thing. Pummel is another."

"Hogan." Heath planted his hands on the table as he looked at everyone. "I made some calls today."

Silence dropped like a missile, flattening moods and conversations.

"And?" Jibril sipped his tea.

"I would've turned this over to Darci, but she's out of the country right now. So I put in a call to General Burnett."

Aspen eased forward. "Wait..." Her mind ricocheted over this setup and who he referred to. "You mean the general from Afghanistan—Darci's boss?"

"Former. He's a family friend of hers, so I have his home number."

"Why—I mean, why'd you call him?" Aspen tried to swallow past the lump in her throat. What wasn't he telling her? "What did you find out?"

"Nothing. Burnett, of course, said he couldn't tell me anything if he did find something on the guy, but he said he'd look into it."

Aspen let out a shaky breath. "Oh." She glanced around the table. "I thought you were going to tell me something bad."

"If this guy shows back up, I want to know he's legit. Nobody's going anywhere with him unless he's been fully vetted."

"Wouldn't that be Khat's job?" Timbrel snickered.

Heath stretched his jaw, clearly working to temper his frustration. "Look, something about this isn't sitting right. He went on national television, then came here and talked a good number, then vanishes. I want this guy or his head."

Aspen sat a little straighter. "I really appreciate your protective nature, Heath." Her courage rose to the surface. "But this isn't really your decision. If he turns up again, going with him, searching for my brother is *my* decision."

"Whoa, chickie." Timbrel plucked off her hat, brown hair tumbling free. "It's your decision, but we're a team. A family, ya know? You're not alone, and this decision is a big one."

"She is right," Khat said. "You don't have to do this alone."

"But you aren't going to go, Khaterah, if this happens." Aspen turned to Heath. "Neither are you—wedding in just over a week, remember?"

Timbrel propped her feet on the table and slumped back. "Well, you don't have an excuse to shove me off the cliff of friendship, so don't even try. If this thing happens, I'm stuck like glue to you."

"Why?" The question wasn't meant to be confrontational, but Aspen had never seen Timbrel show that much interest in their affairs. "Why do you care so much?"

"Because." Timbrel narrowed her brown eyes. "I'm not letting him get the best of you."

"Get the best of me?" She tried to keep her words from pitching, but with the heat creeping into her face, it was a lost cause. "I am former Air Force—with the JAG. I am twenty-eight years old and perfectly capable of taking care of myself."

"Oh, don't I know it," Timbrel said. "But two girls who can kick butt are better than one. And if this guy shows me it's necessary, I will take him down. Blue eyes or not."

Austin, Texas

"You grounded me!"

"You went dark. I had no guarantees you weren't dead or under coercion." A laugh erupted. "I still don't."

"I gave you the nonduress code."

"Mm. So you did."

Cardinal bit down on the curse that lingered at the back of his throat. This wasn't about Burnett thinking he'd been captured. This was about the general exerting his *influence*. About the general putting Cardinal's wings to the flame. Or trying to clip them and force him to be his own personal carrier pigeon.

He turned and strode to the window overlooking downtown Austin. Hand on the cold pane of glass, he steadied himself—memories, virulent and agitated, coiled around his mind. Shoved him back. Away from the glass. Away from the drop. Away from the memory.

He fisted a hand, ready to drive it through anything painful. Being forced to do something was one thing. Being trapped was another. He'd been shut down once before. Ten years ago. But it'd been too late by then. Cardinal had already escaped.

"You know I can get around this." He'd become good at going off-grid when he needed to. Burnett knew it, too.

"You're right, I do." Creaking seeped through the line as the general let out a soft groan of relief. "Which makes me wonder why you haven't."

Cardinal looked away. From what, he didn't know. The city held no threat. The phone neither.

"What are you running from?"

The truth. The past. The angel.

"I think you know deep inside, you're supposed to help this girl. I think the fact that you had a hand in her brother's disappearance makes you feel like you owe her something."

My life.

"But. . ." A slurping sound tickled the earpiece. Burnett burped. " 'Scuse me." A breathy grunt emitted as he caught his breath. "There's more to this. You're antsy. Jittery. Do I need to know something?"

Cardinal killed the line. Thudded his forehead against the wall. He turned back to the hotel room and sighed. He slumped on the bed and stared back out over the city. Then the sky. Clear blue sky with a few streaks of clouds. But mostly sun. Lots of sun. Texas heat that had surely fried his brain. Then why did it feel cold and cruel, like winter?

When he'd left Aspen at the ranch, he'd done nothing but drive— that is, after he'd disabled the GPS. No need for unnecessary monitoring by good ol' Uncle Sam. Down to the Gulf. Back up. All day spent trying to unwind his mind and body. His muscles ached.

His heart ached more.

At a moment like this in the movies, the hero would tug out a photograph, stare at it longingly, stuff it back in his pocket, then move on forcefully.

He didn't have a photograph. Refused to allow himself mementos. Anything that could connect him to the past. Anything that could be held against him or used to cripple him. Nobody knew about those things. Nobody would have that much power over him. Ever.

Besides, she'd fallen off the map five years ago.

Bent forward, he laced his fingers and rested his forehead on his knuckles. Going forward with this mission. . .it felt like the complete undoing of everything he'd worked for. But that would mean abandoning the one man he'd mentored. Trained.

Cardinal had failed him. And sitting here not tracking him down wasted time.

But doing this, with Aspen—

"God. . ." The prayer died on his tongue. Cardinal closed his eyes, focused. Yearned for some indication, some sign of what to do.

In the distance, a sound resonated through Austin.

Pulled to his feet at the somber sound of bells, Cardinal grabbed his room key and tucked it into his pocket with the phone. Out on the street, he headed toward the capitol. Light peeked at him between the buildings. Then the shadows lengthened. On Lavaca Street, he hesitated before the prestigious First Methodist Church building. Striking with its columns and pale plaster, it certainly bespoke the austere setting. Pretty. Beautiful even, but. . .no church bells.

Cardinal continued down the street and banked left onto 11th. As he walked the length of the lawn that stretched before the great building of the Lone Star state's seat of power, he admired the structure. The lines, the dome, the architecture. So dominating. Spoke of power. Prestige.

Power corrupts.

He'd seen the fruit of that as a boy. In his father. His father's friends. Even missionaries in country. Everyone wanted power. Those once thought to be nice, kind people had climbed the backs of friends to get to the top.

Cardinal strolled to the corner and looked up and down San Jacinto Boulevard. He crossed the street then glanced right. Block letters adorning a white limestone building drew him down San Jacinto. The darkness in his soul shifted as he crossed onto 10th and strolled along the white stone building to the front steps.

He peered up. Smiled. Bell tower.

As if some force gripped him by the shirt, compelling him into the sanctuary, Cardinal climbed the steps. Inside, he paused. Breath stolen, he waited for the warmth to flood him. He couldn't explain it. Just. . . *knew* things were different inside a church.

The great stained supports that arced over the cathedral reminded him of a ship's bow. The apse bore striking columns that looked like marble, stretching up into the cobalt ceiling, dotted with gold stars. And there in the center hung a stained-glass depiction of Mary. No doubt the one they'd named the cathedral after. And below it, on His cross hung her Son.

Jesus.

Cardinal slipped between two pews. Hand on the row in front, he eased himself onto the gold cushion, his gaze fastened to the altar. The stained-glass windows that gleamed overhead and along the walls bathed him in a warm embrace and a strange glowing wonder.

Here. Here he could focus. Could sort out the insanity that had threatened him.

He sat, thought, silently talked—to whom, he didn't know. . . He lowered his head, shutting out the chaos. The forces vying for his allegiance. His obedience.

As he had every time before, he whispered, "God, if you're there. . . help me." Desperate. Sloppy. But it was all he had. If he said more, he'd berate himself for talking to someone invisible. Intangible. Unprovable. A god for the weak minded.

That's what his father had said of his mother's faith. One of the many *kinder* things he'd said of her and her Christianity.

The comforting rays of sunlight through the stained glass that lined both walls faded and gave way to low-lit sconces. Though his inner self had quieted, he had no answers. For anything. So he stayed. Stared at the likeness of the crucified Christ.

"He was a madman who claimed to be God! Of course they killed him!"

Mary hovering over her son, ethereal and gentle with blue eyes and the Anglo appearance. He'd always smirked at that.

"She was a whore! She got pregnant and lied to cover it up."

Cardinal hung his head with a dangerous thought lodged in his mind. *No, Father. That was what you did to my mother.*

Crack! A scream knifed his soul. He clenched his eyes. Blood. She'd bled so much. . .

A noise. . .repetitive. . .

Cardinal peered up at the altar, attention trained on the *click-click* on the stone floor. What. . .it sounded like. . .dog's nails. Here? In a church?

A shape took form at the end of the pew. A feminine form. He turned his head, coming to his feet. Something swirled in his gut as he looked into pure blue eyes. Hair a halo of white. Just like Saint Mary in the stained glass. Or an angel. The thought pinged through him. Amadore had called her that, and here she stood in this church just like one.

She smiled then looked down the aisle toward the altar. Taking it all in.

His heart beat a little heavier. And faster. He wanted to ask how she'd found him. Here, of all places. He shouldn't ask. It showed weakness. Showed he hadn't been smart enough with his moves. "How did you find me?"

"Heath knows a general who tracked you down. Heath is engaged to a good friend of the general—actually, one of his former employees."

He looked down and shook his head. Burnett. The general had sold him out?

"He said you liked churches." Again, she glanced at the altar. "Cathedrals, in particular."

It wasn't forgivable that the general ratted him out, no matter how vague the tip he'd given. The video camera in his head played out a scene where he stormed out of St. Mary's, shouting into his phone about being sold out. Of him walking away from this.

But that's why Burnett sent her here. Gave her enough information to find him—so she could corner him. So those blue eyes would peel back the years of hardness. To whittle down what little he had left of his identity. To break him.

Force him to face what he didn't want to face: That despite his fears, despite his rigid determination not to, Cardinal knew he had to take this gig. He had to help Aspen find her brother.

Since he already knew the answer, maybe the reason he'd come to church was to toss it back in God's face.

Cardinal focused on the structure of reverence and solace, not on the tumult roiling through him. "It's a lost art, churches like this." His gaze traipsed the bowlike supports, the stained-glass panels standing like sentries around them. . .and collided with those blue eyes.

"It's a good place to be." Her voice was soft, almost a whisper, as if talking might offend the heavenlies.

And yet her words felt like just the beginning. He wanted to know what followed. "When. . . ?"

Aspen shrugged and shook her head. "Always." Perspiration made her face glow. The blush in her cheeks wasn't because of him, so he knew she'd been walking for a while. Searching churches. Searching for *him*. Why did that do strange things to his mind, the thought of her looking for him? Desperation had him culling the possibilities.

Back on track, Cardinal. He pointed to the Lab hunkering at her side. "He probably shouldn't be in here."

"He's a working dog, so technically they can't throw him out. Besides, I wouldn't have found you if it weren't for Talon." She beamed. "About two blocks over he got a hit. Nose to the ground, he was hauling in scents and moving." She giggled. "It was amazing. I haven't seen him do that. . .well, ever!"

Startled, he looked at the dog and tried to school his expression.

"I mean, I know you probably saw him doing it with Austin day in and out, but this was a first for me. Exhilarating." She lifted a red Kong ball from her pocket. "I owe him some playtime now."

"Then maybe he's ready." Oh man, he couldn't believe he was doing this. It was wrong. He'd slip down that slippery slope and there'd be nothing to anchor him. Cardinal started toward the back of the church, the thoughts pushing him out the door.

Aspen's lips parted, her mouth hanging slightly open. Expectancy seemed to hold her captive. "For?"

"A little adventure." He wanted to return the smile that twinkled in her eyes, but he didn't dare. "Eastern Africa." He owed this to his protégé. Owed it to Aspen.

She fell into step with him, Talon trotting alongside. "Then, you'll go?"

Understanding what it meant that she'd come looking for him, that she'd tracked him. . .that if she found out what happened in Djibouti, she'd never speak to him again, Cardinal knew he had to win her now or she'd be lost forever.

And if that happened, Austin Courtland was as good as dead.

UNDISCIPLINED

Brno, Czech Republic
Age: 14 Years, 3 Months

Nikol punched to his feet. Patting Petr's shoulder, Nikol stuffed the money into his hand. "I must go."

The girl took a tentative step forward, her hand raised. *"Okamžik, prosím."*

He didn't have one moment, not even for her. Nikol's feet grew leaden at the soft voice. Move, he had to move or he would be caught. Heat and weight pressed against his chest, but he strode to the trees, toward anonymity.

A man stormed from a home—no, not *a* home. *The* home. The one she lived in.

"Who are you?" She rushed across the small yard. "Why do you bring the gifts?"

Hands stuffed in his pockets, Nikol tucked his head and hurried, his gaze on the trees.

"Please," she pleaded.

She couldn't know. Absolutely forbidden. Leaves crunched beneath his feet.

"Thank you." The shouted gratefulness carried past the crunch of the leaves beneath his feet and the rustle of branches overhead and wrapped around his heart.

A sob punched from his chest, but he choked it back. He stumbled. As the branches slapped his shoulders, he heard voices—adult voices. Closer. Nikol broke into a run. A branch lashed his face, stinging. As he ran, he felt warmth sliding down his cheek. He cursed.

Only as his foot hit the curb of the street where the bus would retrieve him, did Nikol slow. In the devouring chaos of thousands fighting their way through life and crowding the streets, Nikol allowed himself to look back. Clear. No flushed faces or panting men.

At a corner shop he bought water and guzzled it. He had been careless. And for that, he might never be able to make the trip again. Disgusted and discouraged, he made his way to the metro line. Running his hand through his hair, he groaned. Rubbed his face—and cringed. He spun and used the window to eye the cut on his face. Red, swollen around the edges. The colonel would demand to know what had happened.

Nikol needed an excuse. The bus ride back would give him nearly three hours to sort it out, contemplate the fact he might never see Kalyna again. An ache squeezed his chest—the same one that marked her height. His mind flipped back to the yard. To seeing the girl. Cropped just below her chin, white-blond hair wreathed her angelic face like a glowing halo. She had the voice and blue eyes of an angel, too. A voice so soft and sweet. . .

What was it his father had said of his mother? That she had bewitched him with her voice and looks. That loving her had made him weak. Undisciplined.

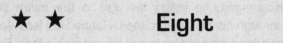

★ ★ Eight ★ ★

In Flight to Djibouti, Africa

Nothing but pale blue atmosphere embraced the plane as it climbed to cruising altitude. Clouds, rare and miniscule in the vast landscape of the horizon, peeked through the portal-shaped windows. Sunlight glinted against the plane's wingtip. Cradled in the seat, Aspen stared out at the sky that held beauty and wonder. It was so incredible. So amazing. The way the universe had been constructed. The way if the planets had been aligned one degree to either side, they would not have the view of the galaxies they had now. Amazing.

And somewhere beneath it all was Austin.

She couldn't let go of the hope that he was still alive. And it fueled her faith that Dane seemed to believe it as well. Otherwise, he wouldn't have agreed to this venture.

Hmm, maybe she shouldn't confuse his willingness to seek out the truth with her optimistic beliefs. She wasn't sure why he'd walked out. If she dwelt on his vanishing act, all sorts of doubts would plague her. The point was he came. And clearly, that decision upset him. He wasn't the same person she'd met at the ranch that day. Something was different about him. Something. . .closed off. But finding him in St. Mary's. . .

The man had a core strength of steel. Even his eyes mirrored it. But the cathedral, peaceful and reverent with the comforting sconce lights and candles, had revealed a vulnerability. It'd been one of the most surreal experiences she'd had, like seeing a reflection of a person in flickering candlelight.

"How did you find me?" His words had been husky. Charmed with the accent of the shadow of stubble and. . .

Something. She wasn't sure what, but it ensnared her mind since that night a week ago. The way he stood there, tension—but also surprise—radiating from his well-muscled shoulders and neck.

Who was he? Dane seemed like so much more than a grunt who'd worked the war zone with Austin. Why would General Burnett know the most likely place to find Dane? Where did he go when he left the ranch? Did he stay in Austin? Or was there a reason—or a someone— that drew him away?

Aspen tilted her head back, stuffed her fingers through the tangled rat's nest of curls, and groaned. *Why do you care?*

Because standing there beside him, wrapped in the serenity of that austere structure, she'd had this insane idea that there was a divine connection teaming them up. Okay, yes—definitely a crazy thought. Probably borne out of her finding him in a church. What was that about? Did he believe in God? Did he hold fast to his faith the way she did? At least, the way she *tried* to hold on to it.

Aspen glanced down at her hands and rubbed them together. Faith. Intangible in a lot of ways, but it felt so soluble, like water, in her hands when she grappled with it in relation to Austin.

A soft whoosh drew her attention to her right.

Timbrel slipped into the seat and groaned. "I hate flying." She adjusted her ball cap, then her jeans, then the boots, wiggled her shoulders as if burrowing into the seat like a dog turning circles in a field to flatten the vegetation. "If I could fly on a Lear with leather seats, champagne, and—" She held up a hand in a *stop* gesture. "Just give me a bottle of sleeping pills." She paused again. "No, just dope me up and knock me out."

Aspen couldn't help but laugh. "You were Navy. Didn't you have to jump out of planes in basic?"

"Jumps are one thing. Crammed in a mostly empty and entirely boring passenger jet, is another." She shifted in the seat to face Aspen. "So, spill."

Aspen raised her eyebrows. "About what?"

"About him, Mr. SexyKillerBlueEyes." A greedy gleam darted through her brown eyes.

Aspen sucked in a quick breath. "Quiet." She peeked between their seats to make sure Dane hadn't heard. Relief swept through her at the way he sat in the seat, head back, eyes closed, and mouth open a little. Sleeping like a baby. "You know as much as I do."

"So not true." Timbrel leaned in. "What dirt did you dig up to force him to come?"

"Dirt?" Aspen shook off the confusion. "I didn't dig up any dirt. We found him at the cathedral like Burnett said and. . ." Why would Timmy think they'd dug up dirt on Dane? "He came."

"And what?"

"And nothing." She shrugged. "He asked how I found him, and I told him. The next thing I know, we're"—she motioned around the cabin—"on our way."

"You're kidding, right?" Timbrel stared at her. Disbelief as distinct as her beauty. Whipping off the hat, Timbrel scowled and pushed herself straighter in the seat. "Please tell me there was more."

Aspen darted another look to Dane then back to Timbrel. "What do you mean? What else am I supposed to know or tell?"

Unease slithered through Aspen's stomach. What had she missed? How many times had Austin told her she was too naive? Though she'd vehemently argued it wasn't naivete but willingness to believe the best of people.

"He walks out, goes silent for ten days, then you find him in a *church*"—Timbrel rolled her eyes—"and suddenly he's back in the game? I don't think so."

Aspen eased back into her seat. "Just because you don't grace the doors of a church with your presence, doesn't mean it's not a legitimate way to seek guidance."

"It's not that." Timbrel wagged the hat as she spoke. "It's the whole thing—who is this guy? Seriously? He was with your brother? Then why wasn't he in the report? Why did he wait two years to give us the goods? To step up to the plate?"

"Timmy, I don't know. But he knows too much *not* to have been there. And now, he's here. He's willing to do something. He got us access to the military base—the same one that all but threatened to take legal action against me for"—she hooked her fingers for air quotes—"harassment. A team is waiting for us." Her anger over the insinuations strangled her excitement. "Nobody has been able or willing to help me get this far. I'm not going to look a gift horse in the mouth."

"I wouldn't look into that man's mouth—or eyes—for anything." Timbrel dropped back against the seat with a grunt. "And I don't like the way he looks at you."

"Don't." Aspen squared off, her heart thumping a little harder than it should. "Don't do this, Timmy."

"Do what? Look out for you when you won't do it for yourself?"

"No, don't rain on my parade. Again." Aspen drew in a steadying breath. "This is my one chance to get answers about my brother. He vanished. Nobody else died that day, nobody else got mangled or ended up with missing limbs. Yet my brother's entire body is blown to pieces—and so many, they can't even verify with DNA?"

Timmy averted her gaze.

Cuing Aspen into the awareness of having lost her temper. She slumped against the seat. Pushed her hair from her face and held it on the crown of her head. She let out a breath. Calmed, she let the tension out of her limbs and released her hair. "Please. Let me have this one chance. I'm not being naive. I'm not being gullible. I'm being reactive to a suspicion. Give me room to be an adult. To cement this once and for all."

"What if this guy isn't on the up-and-up?"

"If he wasn't, I don't think Burnett would've sent us after him." Aspen's pulse settled into a regular rhythm, but the anger hadn't quite settled. "Just give me this chance. I need it. Or I'll never forgive myself or anyone who tries to stop me from following through on this lead."

The petite brunette didn't say anything. She stuffed her booted feet against the back of the seat in front of her. "Look, I gotta protect what's mine, right?"

"Yours?" Aspen nearly choked. "What's yours?" Was she implying Austin—?

"Family." Timbrel's chocolate gaze bounced to hers then away ten times faster. "I've never had family. Not *real* family. My mom—" Red splotched her face, and she dropped her feet. "Well, anyway. I think of you like a sister. And"—she shrugged—"I'm just saying…be…careful." She stood and stalked away.

Aspen peeked up over the seat to see Timmy stalking to the rear of the plane. Family? Timbrel saw her as family? What little Aspen knew of the girl's story—that was as bare as the interior of this 747—wasn't pretty. Not anywhere close. Timbrel rarely spoke of family or her mother. So, to find out she thought of Aspen like a sister. . .

Guilt clutched her by the throat. She shouldn't have chewed Timmy out. Or lost her cool. Not when her friend meant well. And to be honest, Aspen hadn't really had much in the way of family herself since Austin went MIA. Their dad died when she and Austin were young, and her mom succumbed to cancer while Aspen was in boot camp and Austin on his first deployment. Having entered a year after her twin, she trailed him into military service. . .and was still trailing him.

As she eased back into the chair, her gaze collided with steel blue eyes.

Somewhere in Somalia

"*Now* what are we going to do?"

"Walk."

Mouth open, blue eyes wide, she didn't move. "Walk? Are you insane? There's nothing but desert out there."

Neil Crane did his best to stay calm. He didn't have energy to burn on getting angry. Or into a fight. . .again. "And back there are enough countries and ticked-off people to kill us for a thousand years." He stomped down the road, irritation and exhaustion clawing him apart.

"We don't have food or water."

He kept walking. *Thank you for stating the obvious.* He wouldn't give voice to his thoughts because she'd go off the deep end. Again. She'd been borderline hysterical since they'd escaped the last ambush. Fear drove her. That was good, it kept her alive. But it also kept her on his nerves.

Had things been different, he wouldn't have even brought anyone, let alone this woman. But circumstances had tied them at the hip for the last several weeks.

"What if they find us again?"

"I'm counting on it."

"What?" She hustled up a step to catch up with him. "What do you mean?"

"Somehow they constantly know where we are and what we're doing." He didn't get it. How were they being tracked? Going to the mines would be the last place they'd expect him. But he'd gone with some seriously high-tech gadgetry to try to get proof that had pushed him into this underworld. *Come out with the evidence, show it to the world, get my life back.*

That's the way it should've worked.

But the exact opposite happened. They were ambushed, lost their equipment while escaping, and he'd taken a bullet—in the arm. No big deal, he'd already tended it.

What had he done wrong? Mentally, Neil went over his notes, over the plays, over their moves. Just as he'd been taught, and he'd been trained by the best. It just didn't make sense.

As the night deepened, so did the silence and void between them. He'd thought he was in love with her. He'd never forget meeting her at the embassy gala. Man, she looked good in that red silk number. And she knew it. Lina Bissette, admin to a French envoy's assistant. Diplomatic relations swiftly turned to romantic relations between them.

Then things went south.

Neil wouldn't let this trip define their relationship, if they still had one by the time they got back. If she didn't stop blaming him and whining and complaining, he might kill her before then. Nah, he wouldn't kill her. It made sense, her fear and panic making her emotional.

Her hand slipped into his as they trudged down the dusty road. Resignation allowed him to tighten his fingers around hers. It wasn't her fault. Nor his. Getting out of Djibouti had been crucial to staying alive.

"Sorry," she muttered.

Neil pulled her head closer and kissed the top of her dusty, dirty hair. "We'll make it. Just trust me."

Trekking through the barren savanna that was Djibouti fried his brain. But onward he went, hand in hand with the woman who had stuck with him for the last four months. They'd been chased from a mine, hunted across the Sudan, and now walked for four days—well, nights were cooler so that's when they made their way across the land that had no natural resource. Thus the extreme poverty that landed Djibouti on the list as a third-world nation.

431

Get back to the hotel, dig out his secret stash of money and passports, then vanish again. That was his game plan.

"Do you think they'll stop looking for us?"

"Eventually," Neil responded, his mouth dried, his lips cracked. "As long as we don't blow the cover on their operation." The thing was, Neil had no intention of keeping quiet. He intended to rip this thing wide open, once he found the right vein and the right conduit under which to do it. "But I want to stop it."

"Do you have enough to do that?" She hustled a step to catch up with him. "You asked me to go with you—"

"No." Neil stopped and turned to her. "I told you I was leaving. And I said there were a lot of people coming after me—I told you it wasn't safe to stay with me. You could've stayed, made it to your embassy, and worked to prove your identity." She could've, but it would've been a long shot.

"Yeah, but you and I both know someone in that French embassy was involved, too. My passport suddenly invalidated? My name not showing up?" She shuddered then stopped short. Looked at him. "Did you want me to stay behind?"

"Lina, you're the best thing that has happened to me in years." Neil grunted. "Stupidest thing I ever did, leaving. Anyway, come on. We're about fifteen klicks outside Djibouti city."

"Listen." She tugged his hand and stopped him. "I don't think it's so smart to go back to the city. There are too many Americans there, and many who would recognize you."

"Exactly." He felt a smile for the first time. "It's the one place where I fit in, where I don't stand out. We just go in and act like nothing is wrong. Slip into the hotel room, get some food and rest, then. . ." What, he didn't know. He had information that could bring down a lot of people, and most of them didn't want him alive to breathe word of it.

"Then what?"

Squeezing her hand lightly was all the answer he could muster as they plodded down the side of the dirt road that led back to the city that had sent his life into a tailspin. An hour and a lot of blisters later, Neil led her to the bay of the Red Sea.

"Okay, let's dunk."

Lina gaped at him. "Dunk?"

"Trust me." He couldn't help the smile at the way her face almost froze in that expression. He'd seen a lot of that over the last few weeks as they navigated the perils of holding a secret nobody wanted leaked. Neil slid into the water and let the cool liquid rush over him. It felt good, after so many hours of walking dusty, dirty, rubble-laden roads.

He emerged from the water, dripping. Pushing the water out of his face, he grinned. "Ready?"

"For *what*?"

"C'mon." He took her hand and led her up the street to the Djibouti Palace Kempinski.

The bellman's white eyes shone with surprise as he raked them over with a disapproving glare. "May I help you?"

Neil gave a dismissive wave of his hand. "Sorry. We took a bit of a late-night swim. When I left my wallet on shore, someone stole it."

"Very bad luck, sir!" The man opened the door and ushered him to the counter, but his expression warned Neil that he didn't believe them. "Your name, sir?"

"Neil Crane."

The girl behind the counter typed his name into a computer. "Ah yes. Welcome back, Mr. Crane. We were concerned. It has been several days."

"Sorry. We were visiting a missionary in the area and decided to return for some privacy and a bit of luxury." He winked at Lina, who stood beside him playing the coy girlfriend. "Could I get a new room key?"

"Of course, sir." She placed the plastic card on the counter then handed him a piece of paper and circled some names. "Here are the names for the American embassy so you can report your stolen wallet. Your passport—"

"In the room safe, thank God."

"Very good. Thank you, sir. Have a good evening."

"Thank you." At the elevator, with Lina plastered to his side, he smiled at her. Kissed her for the benefit of those watching. Once inside the car, he dropped back against the wall.

"How long do you think we have?"

He eyed her. "Thirty minutes."

433

Nine

Wheels touching down saved him from the void of her acceptance. At least, that's the way it felt—a void that he could vanish in. She accepted him, trusted him. . . . Innocence bathed her fresh confident face. Not naïveté as some might presume. She wasn't naive. He could see it in her mannerisms, in her dealings with others. But she *did* believe people were good.

A fatal mistake. Not that he would intentionally hurt her, but who was he kidding? Manipulating her, playing this game—how could she *not* be hurt? All the same, he had a job to do.

Backpack in hand, Cardinal hustled down the metal stairs and disembarked the plane, leaving behind Aspen Courtland and the baggage of guilt that came with her.

Four men emerged from a building and crossed the tarmac, warbling with heat waves. Compliments, no doubt, of both the heat and the plane's engines. The screaming whine of the jets slowed as the plane shut down.

A tall man with dark hair strode toward him, dressed in his desert camo and a pair of ballistic Oakleys. "Lieutenant Markoski?"

"Yeah."

"Captain Watters of ODA452." He shook Cardinal's hand. "Welcome to Djibouti." He angled a shoulder and pointed to the soldiers. "My team will escort you and the others."

Cardinal gave a curt nod then glanced up the flight of stairs where Aspen appeared with a leashed Talon. Due to anxiety, he'd been crated and sedated during the flight. His strong body hovered at the hatch. Panting in the oppressive heat, he looked down the flight of steps. Then his soulful gaze struck Cardinal and the military unit. Immediately the yellow Lab turned. Tail between his legs, he scurried back inside the cabin.

"Talon." Aspen's gaze darted to Cardinal before she hurried back in after the dog.

"That could be a problem," Watters said as quiet descended on the tarmac.

"Let her worry about that." But the captain had a point. A very sharp one that could poke a hole in Cardinal's plans. He climbed back up the steps. Inside the cabin and bathed in the remnant of cooled air, he found Timbrel slouched against a seat.

"What's going on?"

"Talon doesn't like it." Hogan slid her ball cap back on. "And neither do I."

Cardinal shouldered his way past her. "Well, only one of you is vital to this mission."

At the back of the plane, Aspen squatted at the wire crate that once again housed the Lab. Head down, Talon's brown eyes bounced between Cardinal and Aspen.

"He's shut down on me." Aspen straightened, arms folded. "He hasn't done this in months." She hunched her shoulders. "I don't get it."

"Yeah, but he does." Poor guy. If he already smelled danger and shut down, did they have any hope? "He knows this is trouble." Cardinal crouched at the crate. "Did your brother ever come to Djibouti with Talon?"

"Not that I know of. But then Austin's missions were usually SCI or above."

Cardinal nodded as he reached into the crate and rubbed his fingers along the top of the Lab's head. "Want me to carry him down?"

"No." She sighed. "I've seen him bare his teeth on those who force him into something he doesn't want to do."

Cardinal straightened and glanced at her over his shoulder. "Has he bared his teeth with you?"

She slowly shook her head. "No, but in a normal training session, I would give him a bit of space then reattempt the situation."

"But this isn't a normal training session."

"Exactly." She turned to him. "Look. I want to be honest with you—I'm not sure Talon is up to this. Maybe I got a little ahead of myself." Long fingers traced her brow.

"But we need him." He tucked his chin, feeling the tension tightening the muscles in his shoulders. "You know how to handle him, right?" He waited till she agreed. "And you brought him to find me, which he did."

"Yes," she said, her voice pitching. "But this. . .this base, the noise, the chaos—it's shutting him down. It's out of his comfort zone." Aspen gnawed the inside of her lower lip. "I think if we can get him out there, out of this plane and walk him, let him know there's no danger out there, he'd be okay."

"But there is danger."

She blinked. "Right."

"Can you carry him down?"

"He's seventy-five pounds of muscle and heartache."

"And you carried a sixty-pound rucksack in boot camp."

"That's different."

"Yeah, only in that you strapped the ruck to your back because some burly sergeant shouted at you." He raised his eyebrows and looked around the interior. "Here, it's your choice. You're bailing."

"Excuse me?"

He wanted to grin at the fire that leapt into her blue eyes, and it fed the fire in her gut. And then a fire lit through him realizing he was working her, a maneuver so easy and effective, it almost never failed. "Fear. I see it in your face. You have doubts about this mission. You want to get your brother back, but you're second-guessing yourself. Dump the doubts and the excuses."

"How dare you! That's my brother—"

"Then do something. Find that strength that got you through boot camp, that got you into JAG, and show this dog who's in control." Cardinal's chest heaved. *Easy there. Take it easy.* "Put on that confidence you wear so well and carry him down. Show him you mean business. Show him this isn't therapy. He needs to know you're not afraid. *I* need to know you're in the game to the end. I have a lot to lose if you aren't in the game all the way."

Aspen swallowed and wet her lips. She hesitated before brushing those long, loose curls from her face. Without looking at him, she squeezed past him. Then stopped and looked back. "This is about Austin, about finding out who did this to him. Don't ever. . .*ever* think it's about you."

A war erupted in his chest—pride over her gutting it up battled the disappointment that stung briefly that she wasn't willing to be honest with him. He saw her fear. Read it in her body language. In her hesitancy with Talon.

He stepped back as she squatted and reached into the crate. Talon darted her a nervous look as she hooked her arms around the broad part of his chest and beneath his hindquarters. She hauled him out then pushed to her full height.

Cardinal raised an eyebrow at the sight of her arching her back to balance the large canine overwhelming her upper body.

"What?" She grunted as she angled around him.

"That's a lot of dog—and drool."

Anger still colored her cheeks with a pink tinge. "It's nothing compared to Timbrel's hound."

"He's not a hound," Timbrel called from the front. "He's a bull-mastiff. I weigh his love in gallons of drool."

"That's disgusting," Cardinal said with a chuckle.

"Only to the uninitiated."

"Then, *please*, don't initiate me." He paced Aspen as she navigated down the steps, his heart in his throat at the steep incline and her struggling to see around the dog to place her feet.

At the bottom, she set Talon down. Ears back, head tucked, Talon started lowering himself, but Aspen broke into a jog. "Yes! Let's go." She cast a look in Cardinal's direction as she trotted away. "Where to?"

A woman with stamina, determination, and siren-like blue eyes. . .

He wouldn't come out of this mission unscathed. Neither would she.

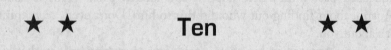

★ ★   **Ten**   ★ ★

If a guy talked to me like that, he'd be next week's leftovers." Timbrel shoved open the door and held it for Aspen, who led Talon into the conference room. With the heat, the confined space smothered her with claustrophobia. The long table and chairs didn't help. Considering the chipped paint, the scuffed cement floor, and the chairs that looked like they were *literally* on their last leg, she got a swift picture of the state of affairs here in Djibouti. She couldn't imagine this room with another dozen or so bodies stuffed inside.

But that was just it—there *should* have been a dozen others. "Guess we're early."

"Or they're late." Timmy hopped up on the table and dangled her legs. "Okay, so seriously—don't let this guy railroad you."

Aspen tugged the red ball from her leg pocket and showed it to Talon. Tail wagging, he panted his excitement. She rolled the ball across the floor since there wasn't room for a good throw. He turned, hesitated as if saying, "Now why did you do that?" then lumbered after it.

"Look, I get it—you're a good girl, you try to be nice." Timbrel hiked a leg up and hugged it. "But that guy? Don't give him an inch or he'll take the whole freakin' world from you."

Aspen reined in her frustration. "Timmy, relax. I'm not letting him take anything." She pointed to the ground, indicating Talon should drop the ball at her side as he returned with the slobber-covered toy.

He deposited it at her feet then settled on the floor. She sat on the ground, her legs stretched out and ankles crossed. Talon reclined against her, his side pressed against her thigh.

"I know you believe that," Timbrel said. "But I've seen you drop your guard before."

"And you don't?" Aspen shouldn't have said it, shouldn't have let her frustration get the best of her.

Tension radiated through the gorgeous brunette's face and shoulders. "Don't change the subject. This guy is trouble if you let him be."

"I'm not letting him *be* anything."

"Then why have you been all morose since we got off that plane?"

Aspen smoothed her hand over Talon's dense fur. Remembering the way Dane had spoken to her renewed her belief that he'd crossed a line. "You're right. He was wrong in the way he spoke to me." She didn't know him. He didn't know her. She took direct talk from her friends, but from a guy she barely knew?

Wariness shadowed Timbrel's features. "But?"

"But...he was right." She cocked her head, looking at the complete surrender of Talon's anxiety as he rested with her.

"How can you say that?" Timbrel planted her hands on her hips. In black tactical pants and black tank, she looked like she'd stepped right out of an action flick. "The dude totally dissed you."

"No, he put it straight. He got to the point. I needed to hear it."

"What are you saying?"

Admitting she was afraid, that she wasn't sure she could find Austin... What an absolutely basic, foundational problem. "What am I doing here?"

"Hey!" Timbrel's gruff, loud word snapped through the sterile room. She hopped off the table and stomped toward them.

Talon lifted his head, and though it was quiet, Aspen felt a rumble in his chest. She placed a hand on his side to reassure him. Timmy read his body language, the way he sat up a bit and eyed her, and slowed.

"Don't." Timbrel crouched on the other side, away from Talon, looking directly at Aspen. "Don't you dare do that."

Tears stung Aspen's eyes. "I'm not a warrior. I'm not a special operations soldier. I haven't even seen combat like you and the others."

"You're Austin's sister, and you have the most to lose if you don't find him." Timbrel's expression flared with fury. "*That* will get you where you need to be. Don't let that jerk get in your head, Aspen."

"He's not a jerk." Why on earth was she defending him?

"You don't get a vote on that right now." She leaned in. "You're the strongest woman I know. We're here to find Austin, and we're not going home without a mountain of proof either way. Don't let Mr. SexyKillerBlueEyes wiggle into that innate soft spot you have. Give him the fight of his life, and make him think twice about playing you again. Got it?"

"Got it." The voice boomed from the door.

Timbrel swiveled around and up as she faced off with him. "No manners either. You could've knocked."

Dane towered over them both by a head and shrugged. "Why? It's a public room."

"Courtesy," Timbrel said as she strode back to the table and crossed her arms. "Doubt you know anything about that."

"Probably not, since I'm a jerk who wiggles into soft spots." The smirk of a smile—did the man *ever* really smile?—squirreled through Aspen's hastily erected barriers, the ones Timbrel said she should have up. Was he taking the jibe she'd dished out in stride, or was he annoyed? Probably both.

"See?" Timbrel turned to Aspen. "The man confesses to it. Maybe *that* is why he was sitting in a church after ditching you—*confession*."

Heat flooded Aspen's face, and she widened her eyes at Timbrel, ordering her to cease and desist. The humiliation was enough knowing Dane had heard their conversation. She didn't need it worse.

But Timbrel had no effect on Dane. "Watters is on his way with the team and the plans."

"Where did this team come from?"

"Burnett."

Aspen hesitated. "Why. . .why would he do that?" How did everything suddenly become so easy and attainable? "I tried for the last year to get them to listen to me, and they told me to move on, get over it." Her pulse raced. Maybe they knew something. Maybe they—

"It's my fault." Dane looked sheepish. "By going public on the news, I made them dig deep and take a serious look."

His charm, his easy mannerisms pushed her back a mental step, forcing her to remember Timmy's warning. "How long has it been since you saw him, again?"

"Two months." A glint registered in his stormy eyes. Recognition. Awareness that she was questioning him, his story.

That awareness folded back on her and wrapped around her own doubts. "Do you think he's still here?"

He lowered his head as he propped himself against the table. "Probably not. If he's alive and hasn't contacted someone he knows, then that means he's either in trouble or causing it."

Aspen jerked. "Causing it?" Even as her words rang in her ears the indignation ripped through her chest. "What on earth does that mean?"

"Exactly what you think it means."

"Listen, Blue Eyes," Timbrel said, coming alive, "you don't get to talk to her like that."

"Yeah?" Dane crossed his arms over his chest as amusement and irritation surfed his rugged face. "So, you think Aspen would prefer I sugarcoat it, feign ignorance and stupidity to make her feel better?"

"Slick snot!" Timbrel let out a disbelieving laugh. "And everyone thinks *I'm* abrupt. This guy is downright mean."

"Not mean. Downright blunt. Being coy, playing roulette with truth isn't going to bring Austin home or get answers." He locked gazes with Aspen, and she felt as if he'd hooked into her soul, drenching her with resolute strength. "I'm not going to play with your emotions by shoveling platitudes down your pretty neck. And I won't give you false hope or play nice." His face hardened. "I *don't* play nice. I play to win. Can you handle that?"

Aspen swallowed, shaken by the ferocity and virility of his words.

"Because if not, then we need to part ways. Now."

Part ways? With the single hope of finding her brother or the truth about his disappearance? "I wouldn't want it any other way. I might be nice or a good girl, as Timbrel says, but I don't quit." She hated when people felt the need to protect her instead of fighting *with* her. "I don't want to be pampered." She gulped the adrenaline then gave him a curt nod. "Thank you for knowing the difference."

Silence dropped as he stared at her for what felt like minutes.

The door swung open, and a flood of uniforms entered.

"Whoa! Thank You, God!" One of the men with a sandy blond beard and Oakleys clapped a hand over his chest. "Be still my beating heart!"

Timbrel groaned. "Not you again."

"Candyman at your service." He grinned and tugged off the shades.

441

"Baby, I was right."

Aspen watched as Timbrel moved a foot back, taking a defensive posture. Yet she didn't move. Didn't punch. Or strike out, not even with words. Hesitation silenced Timbrel as she gave the guy a sidelong glance. "About what?"

"Told you a face like yours would inspire a man to stay alive." He held out his hands. "And hooah! A year later, here we are, and I'm still alive."

Timbrel's eyes narrowed. "I can fix that."

"Down boy," a guy with a dark brown beard intercepted with a grin. "I'm Captain Watters. First op will include medical escort to Peltier Hospital."

Aspen frowned. "Why are we doing that?"

Watters turned to her. "The Djiboutians need our help." He grinned. "And for cover—we can look around, ask questions without attracting attention."

"Without attracting attention?" Dane snorted.

Aspen wasn't following. "What?"

Dane met Watters's gaze. "She has white hair, fair skin, and is pretty. You don't expect her to draw attention?"

Peltier General Hospital
Djibouti, Africa

Loaded into a Cougar MRAP with Talon sitting beside her, staring out the window, Aspen smoothed a hand over his yellow coat. Such a handsome, noble-looking dog. So willing to go the extra mile, to lumber on even though he probably wanted to just go back home and trot around the safe environment of the ranch. She could relate. The mission had already set her on edge, upturned her expectations.

Crammed between Timbrel and Dane, Aspen considered the others. Watterboy, as the others had called him, and Candyman—the man who'd earned the moniker handing out candy bars to Afghan children to win hearts and minds and who'd taunted Timbrel from the moment he encountered her on their first mission—drove the second Cougar creeping toward Peltier General Hospital, where the medical

442

team in the first vehicle would aide with surgeries and the like.

Timbrel groaned beside her as the front right tire hit another crater and jolted them into each other. "If I get bruises. . ." *Thud. Bang.* "You do know the point is *not* to hit the holes, right?"

"Sorry," Candyman shouted back. "Did I miss one?"

Sweat sliding down her temple, Timbrel glowered at the Special Forces soldier driving. "Next one, and I'll throw *your* head into the window."

Aspen elbowed Timmy, feeling the sweat and grime that came with being in an African country during one of their hottest months. Even though they'd just left the base and would spend the day in the city looking around, she already yearned for a cool shower when they got back.

One of Talon's drool bombs landed on Timbrel's tactical pants. She half groaned, half laughed. "If I didn't love dogs so much. . ."

Dane leaned forward, his arm stretched across the back of the seat, affording a little more room. "So, you prefer a drooling beast over a man?"

A caustic look slid into Timbrel's features. "Is there a difference?"

The front end jolted, then the deafening noise and jarring beating the Cougar stopped.

"Blacktop!" Candyman announced as he patted the dash. "Knew you could do it, baby."

"Thank God," Timbrel muttered. "Now, can someone teach him how to drive?"

Candyman shot a wink over his shoulder. "She's crazy about me, can't you tell?"

Aspen resisted the urge to laugh. The two had been dogging each other since they reunited. If she didn't know better, she'd think there was some serious romantic tension beneath all those jibes and cutting remarks. Well, not for Timbrel. But she worried Candyman might be getting some ideas about her.

Though only eighteen miles stretched between Camp Lemonnier and Djibouti proper, the atrocious road conditions slowed them. Now on the paved roads, they might make up a bit of time, but what was two minutes when it felt like the heat would bake flesh off your body?

As they turned onto Avenue Marechal, Aspen eyed the street of white buildings shadowed by trees and littered with women robed in black and their heads covered with vibrant, beautiful scarves. The town looked as if it had been designed in the seventies then never touched afterward. Still. . . "It's pretty."

"This side, yes." Dane sat on the edge of the seat, forearms on his legs. "Go farther north or west, and you'll find a stark difference."

"Why?"

"French embassy." Dane pointed to the building on the corner. "Farther down, a right onto Lyautey, and the American embassy is on the left."

Ah. Of course. Couldn't let some dignitaries or politicians live in poverty.

"Is that your way of saying we need to know where they are?" Timbrel's words held accusation.

"Ignorance is a swift road to death." Dane braced himself as they turned into a drive. The gate's overhead ornamentation reminded her of the outline of a stepped pyramid. The vehicles pulled forward.

Concern rippled through Aspen. "Why are we here?"

Hand on the door, Dane hesitated. "To deliver the doctors."

Her stomach twisted at the buildings around them. This? This was the hospital? She stepped into the unrelenting and balmy heat and stared at the buildings. Perhaps an inner-city clinic might look so dilapidated, but the main hospital for the city?

Talon sat by her feet on the dirt, panting. Aspen looked from one building to another, the familiar arches and the stark white, the smattering of pebbles that almost formed a road through the compound. . . She couldn't fathom seeking medical help in a facility like this. She fed Talon some water then ruffled his fur. Red lettering over the doors—in French, leftover from the French influence and control of the country—identified the buildings. *ORL MAXILLO FACIALE.*

"See?" One of the doctors pointed down the drive a bit. "New facilities. Slowly, they are making progress."

"U.S. has donated a lot."

"Including hands-on help." Aspen nodded as they followed the medical team into the multistoried building.

Over the next half hour, they toured the grounds. No marble tile or slate linoleum that lent a sterile feel to the hospital. Cement served its purpose, and where more sterility was demanded, tile covered 80 percent. Her heart misfired as she saw the building marked *PÉDIATRIE*. Around the entrance of blue-painted wrought iron stood several Muslim women, covered head to toe. Some held the hands of children.

Oh, Father, no. Aspen's stomach tightened. She could endure and tolerate a lot of things, but seeing children in pain or hurting... A touch at the small of her back startled her.

"You okay?"

She peered up into the steadfast gaze of Dane. And felt foolish. "Yeah. Sure." She shot a look at the pediatric unit. A cold, wet nose nudged her hand, pulling her attention toward Talon. As quick as she looked down, he trotted ahead, aiming straight for the children's building. Blue trimmed the windows, curiously drawing her attention to the window AC units that had discolored to a dirty tan. Shrubs poked up from a hard-packed dirt flower bed. Not exactly the lush green lawns found at most American hospitals, but it added a bit of green to the stark landscape.

"This is unbelievable," Timbrel whispered.

"Djibouti struggles," said one of the doctors who led them onward. "Two out of three children will face life-threatening medical problems due to poverty." He grinned and pointed to Talon. "I bet the kids will love to see him."

"He's not a pet," Timbrel warned.

The doctor hesitated. "Will he be okay?"

Aspen smiled. "I'm sure he'll be fine." In fact, she'd taken Talon to parks to help him adjust to sounds, to learn that not every loud noise was a threat. He still had a long way to go, but the handsome guy had come far.

Inside, the doctors quickly made their way to a multibed open area where children lay in hospital gowns, bandages here and there, IV lines snaking in and out. Brightly colored cartoon characters were painted on some walls, their perspectives a bit distorted and odd against the aging wood, peeling trim, and dirty tile. Aspen cringed. This would never fly in America.

As they made their way over to the bed of a little boy, who sat up in the bed, his leg propped on a pillow, Aspen steeled herself. Why was it always so hard to see children suffer? Because they were helpless?

Because it exposed her own vulnerability?

Dr. Gutierrez nodded to Talon. "Hassan would like to pet your dog."

Gathering her courage, Aspen kept the lead loose so Talon wouldn't feed off her tension if she'd kept it tight. "Tell him to hold out his hand, palm up."

Gutierrez relayed the instructions, and the boy extended his hand. Small, brown, marked with scars.

Without any instruction, Talon nosed the boy's hand then swiped his tongue over it, eliciting a peal of laughter from the boy. Pride ballooned through Aspen's chest. It reminded her of what Austin's partner—and superior—had done for her when he'd first joined her family.

Talon sniffed the air. What, had he detected the strong antiseptic odor? He shifted back and glanced to the hall, bathed in shadows.

Trained on the hall, Talon barked. Then quickly sat. Aspen's heart climbed into her throat. She couldn't see anything down there, but Talon was rigid as a board.

The boy jerked visibly. Let out a scream.

Talon bolted.

Eleven

He didn't see that coming. Aspen blurred past him. Cardinal glanced to the rest of the team, already swarming toward them. They broke into a sprint down the hall. She whipped to the right, out of sight. Pushing himself, he fell into the training that was first nature as breathing: memorizing his path, monitoring his surroundings, listening ahead and behind, formulating a plan, then a backup.

Boots and shouts erupted from behind. Another turn. A flight of stairs presented themselves at a cross section. He peered up then right and left. Behind him.

Watterboy pointed to Cardinal's left. "You go right, we'll cover this."

Cardinal lunged down the hall. Empty. He glanced back. The others were already backtracking. Hogan's face bore the fury of fear. "Where is she?"

Thud!

To his right, light burst from another hall.

"Talon," came Aspen's faint call.

She'd gotten farther away than he thought. He hopped back a step and spun around. They were on top of him. He felt the friction of someone else's elbow near his own. That ticked him off. Aspen was his responsibility. His priority to get her back home safely. No way would he be the cause of her death, too.

He burst out into an alley marked with aged buildings, dirt, a few dehydrated shrubs, dirt, a chain-link fence to the right, more dirt, and sun. Lots of sun. It felt like they'd stepped into a sauna. Sweat streaked down his back.

One of the men cursed.

"Aspen!" Timbrel shouted.

"What do we do?"

"I didn't think Talon could move that fast," Timbrel said. "He's been nothing but lumbering and moping since I met him."

"What spooked him?" Watterboy asked.

"No idea." Cardinal stalked south of the pediatric building. There were any of a half-dozen routes they could've taken.

Hands cupped over her mouth, Timbrel shouted, "Aspen!"

Another curse.

"Hey," Candyman said, "watch the language. There's a lady present."

"You wouldn't know one if you saw one." Timbrel called out to her friend again.

Candyman grinned. "She's in love with me."

For that, he was punched by two of his teammates as they fanned out, tense and alert, checking corners, alleys, buildings. Cardinal felt the heat—the 110 degrees and the scalding his conscience gave him for losing his target.

He turned, thinking he'd heard a dog bark. Head cocked to the side, he listened. . .

Hands stabbed at him.

Deflecting the move was instinctual. But he hauled those instincts in as he registered Hogan shouting something. ". . .fault. You better find her." She'd drop him in a heartbeat. That is, if he let her.

"Shouting at me won't help us find her." Cardinal ripped out his phone. Punched in a number. Then a code. "I need eyes." Teeth grinding, he stalked toward the gate, checking in, around, under, and over anything possible.

"Aspen, where are you?" Hogan's shout reverberated through the hospital compound. Curious eyes peeked out of windows. Others stepped outside, watching as if they were some freak street sideshow.

"Here."

The ever-so-faint word threw him around. He sprinted down the dirt road. South. Straight south. That's the direction it'd come from. Aspen. He wasn't one to panic. But this was close.

"Here."

Just as her voice reached him, he saw paw prints in the dusty dirt.

"Over the fence," she called.

Unbelievable. The dog had to have hopped up on that crate and leapt over the fence. It was several feet. But if he never stopped. . .incredible. Cardinal vaulted over it without a second thought. He touched the tarred alley that led back to Avenue Marechal.

Another dozen thumps and he knew the team had made it. He reached the corner, his breathing just above normal. Staying in shape benefited his career. Scratch that. It benefited staying alive.

Across the unenforced intersection, past a cluster of trees, a street led to what looked like a field. He shifted around and looked down the road. . .alley. Nothing.

A flicker to the left snagged his attention.

Aspen around the corner, already on Lyautey, waved before she started running again.

"Got her," he threw over his shoulder. He stepped into the street. The wail of a horn nudged him back. Another car practically kissed the bumper of the first, but Cardinal launched himself over it to get to the other side. He aimed left—then skidded to a stop.

A rippling movement.

There, down that alley that led to an open area.

Talon!

Cardinal plunged down the alley. Pumping as hard as his legs would carry him. Blanketed in the shade of the buildings and the small trees lining the road, he pressed on. Thudding boots trailed him, followed by shouts and streams of communication one of the men had with Command.

He burst into the sunlight again and slowed. Where had she gone? He searched the circular area that looked as if it'd been cleared for building something. He breathed a little heavier, ignored the sweat sliding down his chest. His neck. His back—for cryin' out loud! He was drenched.

Aspen trotted toward them, gulping air. Red splotches glowed against her white-blond curls now a sweat-stained brown. Hands on her hips, she shook her head. "I don't know what's gotten into him."

"He's tracking," Timbrel said.

"Tracking *what*? There wasn't. . .anything in that children's"—she swallowed—"ward," Aspen said with a gasp, still out of breath from the run. "And where did he go?" She threw her hands up and walked out into the middle. "Talon, come." She took a draught from the CamelBak strapped to her spine. She lifted a whistle, placed it between her lips, and blew.

Nothing.

"That thing even work?" Cardinal asked just to open the conversation. He knew it was one of those that emitted a high-frequency signal.

Worry lined her fair features. "He can hear it. Up to two miles."

A string of old buildings lined the property on the northern side. To the south and southwest more recent buildings or those that had been updated. Like the Sheraton and casino cradled at the corner.

"Command ordered us back to base."

Aspen spun toward Watterboy. "I'm not leaving without him. You shouldn't either—he's a soldier, just like you." Her shoulders dropped, and Cardinal could almost read her thoughts, *or he used to be*. She scanned the area. "Just give me five more minutes." Brows knitted, she looked ready to cry.

And in some weird way, that twisted Cardinal's heart. "What can I do?" It was a stupid question. Even as it rang in his ears, he berated himself—*what can I do?* Find the dog! But it wasn't that he asked because he'd had a brain fart.

No, the reason behind that question was far more dangerous. Because with those words, he knew beyond a shadow of any doubt or intention, he would break a Cardinal rule: Never be at the mercy of another.

"Find him." Aspen felt like she'd just placed her heart, her very life, in the hands of a man who had the power to be her undoing. He knew too much. Like the words to say to convince her to do anything. The words to twist her soul into knots until it took hours—as it had last night—of quiet meditation on God's Word to untangle it.

She chided herself, being on this mission to find her brother, but her thoughts constantly straying to this man. Blue eyes. Broad shoulders. Trim waist. Powerful chest and arms. But an even more powerful presence. *Commanding*. He had that effect on most everyone. She was certain of that because of Timbrel's reaction. Like when water hit a hot frying pan. There's that initial explosion then the sizzling till evaporation.

Aspen chuckled to herself. *So, which of those two would evaporate?*

"What's that?" Dane asked, curving his spine a bit to bend toward her.

"Nothing." See? There. He'd done it again. Picked up on a cue she hadn't even realized she'd given off.

"Then you didn't hear me?"

Her heart slipped a gear. "What?"

Dane stretched his long, tanned arm toward the row of crumbling buildings with bent, broken, missing windows. One no longer had a roof. "A couple of those are on brick supports."

"Yeah?"

"He might've crawled under there."

The thought seized her. "That's what he does when he's scared—gets under something."

"Come on."

"What's going on?" Timbrel came up behind them.

"We're going to search the buildings." Aspen nodded toward the structures. "They're on bricks, so—"

"He might be hiding."

Nodding, Aspen fell into step with Dane. A move that felt as natural and comforting as if they'd held hands. *Whoa, chief.* She had to shake these thoughts. Stay focused on finding Austin. "He's been worse since we landed here."

Dane squatted next to a small building then skirted around the foundation curling away from the rest of the house. He tugged it back.

Growling burst out.

Dane grinned. "I think we found him."

"Talon!" Dropping to her knees, she felt a giddy bubble work its way up her throat. She touched Dane's arm. "Thank you." Palms pressed to the dirt, she peered under the building. Were it any other animal, had she not spent the last year coaching Talon through therapy and teaching him how to be a dog again, the hollow gold eyes glowing in the dark would scare the heebies out of her.

She resisted the urge to baby-talk him. Heath had challenged her on that the day dog and handler had met. Keeping her voice calm and controlled would help Talon's mental state. Knowing he could smell her fear, she stowed it. "Talon, come."

A high-pitched whimper.

Aspen dug his ball out of her pant pocket. "Here, boy."

Gravel and dirt shifted in the darkened area.

Repeating the command went against all the training she'd accrued. But she wanted to coax him out. This was different, though, wasn't it? He was in a dangerous place, with the heat and she wasn't sure what else. She did, however, feel like they were exposed and vulnerable.

"Command's ordering us back to the hospital. Temps are skyrocketing."

"Here." Candyman removed his SureFire and crouched beside them. He aimed it beneath the house. Light shattered darkness. "Here, boy." He looked at Aspen. "Want me to go in and get him?"

"No." Aspen lay on her belly. "If you go in, you block his only exit. He'll feel trapped."

Dark blond beard and green eyes considered her. "So, what you're saying is he'll bite my face off."

"That'd be an improvement," Timbrel heckled.

Candyman rolled onto his side and looked up at her, a hand over his heart. "I'm mortally wounded."

"Does that mean I get your weapon and CamelBak when you finally die?"

"Just give me room." Aspen nudged him out of the way. "Talon, come."

He belly-crawled a couple of inches then dropped his head to the ground with another whimper.

Aspen sought Dane's eyes. "This might take awhile." Like. . .forever.

He gave a slight nod then stood. "Why don't y'all get the vehicles and pick us up. Maybe with the tac gear and the heat, he's. . ." Why did that sound whacked?

"What? Having a flashback?"

Timbrel snapped her gaze to one of the men crowding around. "Yes, and if you could smell as well as him, you'd know how much you and your attitude stink."

"Hey," Dane said, cutting in, "just give Aspen some room to work with the dog. If we stress him, this whole gig will be one big fail." He rested a hand on Watterboy's shoulder. "Try explaining that to Burnett without a case of Dr Pepper and protective gear."

Watterboy considered Aspen. "Think you can get him out of there?"

"Yes." Which was another question, but doubts couldn't be part of this equation.

"You've got ten, fifteen max." He pushed back through the group. "Move out."

"I'm not leaving them." Timbrel squared off.

Watterboy stopped, and even with the shades his frustration was obvious.

"I'll stand guard," Candyman said.

"Done." Watterboy and the others headed out.

"I don't need your protection." Timbrel folded her arms.

"Baby, this wasn't about you." He tugged out a packet of jerky and squatted. "Think this will help?"

Appreciation swam through Aspen. "It's worth a try." She took the jerky and ripped it open.

Dane monitored Talon. "He lifted his head."

She tugged off a piece and tossed it to Talon. He wolfed it down. The next piece didn't quite make it to him. He scooted forward to reach it, chewing the dried meat.

"It's working," Dane muttered.

Excitement spiraled as Talon inched toward them.

She pulled the straw of the CamelBak free, took a mouthful, then squirted some water from the bite valve. Talon lapped and lapped. Aspen lazily tossed the last few pieces of meat, forcing him into the open.

"Almost—"

Thwack!

Gunfire!

★ ★ Twelve ★ ★

Fire streaked down Cardinal's arm as he threw himself into Aspen. Adrenaline muted the pain. Drove him. Used his momentum to hold Aspen in his arms and roll. Straight into the building. Heat licked the top of his head. He ground his teeth. "Under, under!"

Aspen folded herself under the building.

As they scurried beneath the crumbling structure into cover, he heard Timbrel and Candyman scrambling. This wasn't the smartest place to hide. But he'd hidden in worse.

"Base, taking fire, taking fire," Candyman shouted.

With about eighteen inches of space, they had no room to maneuver save a belly crawl. Flush against Aspen, he shifted. Or tried. Aspen hadn't moved, and he knew why—Talon's low growl.

"Who's shooting?" Cardinal shouted.

"No line of sight." Candyman sounded ticked. "Why's the dog growling?"

"Seeing your mug is enough to scare even the most-seasoned combat veteran like Talon," Timbrel said, a smile in her voice.

"Ha. Funny."

Though Cardinal couldn't see where Candyman and Hogan were, they were obviously close enough to hear Talon's rejection of this situation.

"He feels trapped," Aspen interjected.

Cardinal drew himself around, shifting and trying to get in a better position. The floorboards of the building scraped his arm. Might as well have poured lemon juice on the slice in his bicep.

As he did, he spied Aspen stretching her hand toward Talon. Cardinal tensed and waited for the dog to snap. Instead, the sound of sniffing blended with the thumps and cracks of bullets hitting the house.

Who on earth was pummeling them? Cardinal pulled himself along the belly of the building, ignoring the warmth slithering down his arm. . .then his underarm. . .and along his oblique muscle. Hand over hand, he used loose boards, exposed pipes, whatever, to drag himself around.

"What are you doing?" Aspen asked.

"Getting out." Cardinal finally had a decent view to the exterior but could not locate Candyman or Hogan. To the left, a thin beam of light fractured then reappeared. The two were holed up at the southeastern corner.

"Backup en route," Candyman shouted.

As if to confirm his words, in the distance screeching tires prevailed against the crack of weapons' fire. As Cardinal dragged himself between earth and wood to reach the north face of the building. Something glinted in the dirt. A rock? Token? The fact that something lay beneath this rubble of a building and was still shiny. . . His fingers curled around it, and he continued on. At the other side, a mere four meters or so, he shoved his feet against the splintering boards. It gave out, light fracturing the darkness.

He glanced over his shoulder.

Light streaked along Aspen—and his heart slowed. Blue eyes locked on him. Aspen had an arm hooked around Talon. "He's trembling."

"Can you get him out this way?"

"I. . .I think so. I have to, don't I?"

It wasn't really a question. And she was already scooting along.

"C'mon, boy." Her voice remained calm and authoritative. "Talon, go. Seek."

And as if another dog took over the Lab's body, scritching told of his movement. The sound of sand and dirt dislodged by his nails and soft pads joined with the affirmation he no doubt needed from Aspen. Something swelled inside Cardinal at the dog and handler. Or maybe it was just the handler. The no-surrender policy she lived out.

Even if it was the handler, what mattered was their movement. They weren't sitting ducks. . .dogs. Whatever.

Cardinal pushed against the skirting. It budged but not enough to release them from the suffocating, narrow void that felt very much like the underworld. Mentally, he ratcheted down the thoughts of the amount of space—or more precisely, the *lack* thereof—and trained his efforts on busting out. He swung his legs around and angled—

Whack!

He jerked back and cringed—he'd hit heads with Aspen.

"Sorry," she said.

He worked on setting himself, flat on his back, at a perpendicular angle to the skirting on the north side. "I probably did more damage with my hard head."

"I'll probably have a shiner," she admitted with a laugh that was anything but convincing.

On his back, Cardinal glanced to the side.

She was. . . Right. There. Wide eyes. Full lips. Prim nose. Innocence. Everything about her radiated a vibrancy that defied the shadowy underground they crawled through.

"What?"

Cardinal flinched. "Nothing." *Cad, you just gave her a black eye.* "Sorry. 'Bout the eye." Gripping the pipes, he shoved his mind back into line and his feet into the skirting.

Light erupted.

A breathy laugh skated along his ear and down his neck, flooding him with a preternatural warmth that had nothing to do with the Djibouti heat. *Get out. Before it's too late.*

"Let's go." He scrambled out into the open and stayed low, eyeing the road that stretched east and west in front of them. Empty. He wagged his fingers toward Aspen. "C'mon."

"Talon, go."

Soon soulful brown eyes twinkled in the sunlight.

"Good boy." Cardinal held out his hand, palm up, so Talon could reassess him.

Dirty blond curls rustled as Aspen broke free. Cardinal helped her up. She drew in a long, greedy breath of air and exhaled it quickly. "I hate tight spaces." She smiled at him—and the red welt on her cheekbone glared back.

Noise from behind yanked him around. He reached for the weapon holstered at his back but stilled the instinct. Candyman and Hogan hustled toward them. "Team's coming."

A blur of tan burst around the corner. Dust plumed out, providing ample cover around the steel-reinforced vehicle. A door flew open. Watterboy jumped to the rear and leaned against the Cougar, watching. "Go, go," he shouted, waving them into the MRAP.

Bullets pinged the hull.

Candyman bolted to the corner and knelt, weapon pressed to his shoulder as he provided suppressive fire.

Cardinal reached back to Aspen, who stood to his five. Pain rippled down his side. He cringed but stuffed it. "Go on," he said with a nod.

She gripped Talon's collar and rushed into the safety of the Cougar, followed close behind by Hogan. Cardinal trailed them into the vehicle, landing hard on a boot, then shifting out of its way as he hauled himself onto a seat. Arm pinned to his side, he tried to quench the fire licking through his shoulder.

Loaded with Candyman and Watterboy, they were in motion.

"What happened?" Watterboy demanded, his face smeared with dirt and anger.

Cardinal glanced at Aspen with Talon sitting between her feet, stroking his ears. She didn't return his gaze, but he could tell she was aware of his attention. "Took fire. Don't know who or why."

Watterboy shook his head. "We're going to get our butts handed to us back at Lemonnier."

"Lemonnier?" Removing his helmet, Candyman snickered. "Captain, I'm worried about Burnett."

Heat spread through Cardinal's back and side.

"How's that shoulder graze?" Candyman asked. "Probably should have one of the docs check that out back at the base."

With a slow bob of his head, Cardinal knew he wouldn't. Medical attention meant medical records. A trail.

Never leave a trail.

Twenty minutes later, they unloaded at the base.

"Hey, that dog going to be a problem?" Watterboy asked, his tone providing the answer he expected. "Do we need to pull this mission?"

"No, I. . .he hasn't done that—"

"He hit on something." Cardinal stepped between them, a hand on

Aspen's shoulder as he guided her out of the conversation. "It means he's back in action." The mere motion of his arm at that angle made his side warm again. Wet trickled down his side.

His eyes closed for a fraction of a second.

Whirring air conditioners and chatter embraced them as they stepped into a building. He didn't know which one till he heard the clanking of utensils and trays: mess hall.

Aspen paused. Her hand came to his side. "Thank—"

Groaning, he arched his back, pulling out of her grip. Hot and cold washed through him. What was this? He'd been riddled before without feeling like this.

Blue eyes widened as she pulled her hand away, stained red. "You're bleeding!"

The weak smile he mustered wouldn't convince her. "A graze."

"Of an artery!"

"No, but thank you for your concern." He inclined his head and stepped away from her.

"Let me help you."

"I'm fine." Cardinal forced his body to comply, to walk out of the building, to head back to the bunks they'd been assigned for the next few weeks. *Let me help you.* She would help him. Straight into the grave. He'd made mistakes out there. Tripped up over a pair of ocean-blue eyes. Swam in them.

The bunkroom sat empty. He dropped on the striped mattress and dragged out his first-aid kit. Stuffed it into his toiletry bag. In the showers, he flipped the shower knob to cold.

Heated water blasted from the head.

Cardinal slumped. Of course. The water purifier only pumped hot water. To kill anything in the water. Maybe it'd kill the bad bacteria forming around his wound. Under the saunalike spray, he washed the wound, dug out the bullet, and sewed it up. Used the searing pain to remind him—not to fail. Not to. . .

She'd been so alarmed seeing his blood on her hand. Not just an apathetic "you're bleeding," but a—

Cursing himself, Cardinal spun the handle and cut the water. He had to gut this up. Get over it. Get the mission done. Get back to Virginia. Maybe. . .maybe he'd even go. . .home.

Djibouti City, Djibouti

"Are you stupid?" She batted her long, black hair from her face. "*Shooting* at them?"

"They're getting too close. They need to go back, leave."

"Leave?" she shrieked. "They aren't going to leave. They're going to come looking for us."

"They won't."

"How can you know that?"

"Because, they're too invested in protecting the dog." It was a theory. One with as many holes as a strainer. "She won't put that dog in the way, not if she thinks he might get shot."

"She was protecting him."

He nodded, remembering how she'd pushed beneath the house to shield the dog with her body. Then the big guy had joined them.

Neil's bullet wound, though stitched, had become red and irritated so he'd gone to Peltier for antibiotics. He couldn't afford to see a doctor and expose himself. But he knew his way around the building. What were the odds the Americans would be there at the same time? And the Lab...

Neil wasn't trying to kill them. Just get them off his back. It'd been too close.

Everything had been too close.

In fact, everything had gone wrong. Two days ago at the Palace Kempinski, he'd taken a two-minute shower, dressed, and was stuffing a pack full of the items he'd hidden in the room when he heard squealing tires. He ordered Lina out of the shower as he checked the window. A dozen cars barreled toward the hotel.

They'd made it out the doors with barely seconds to spare. He hotwired a car, and they vanished down the street, where they abandoned the car ten minutes later. They'd been at the hotel less than fifteen minutes when he heard shouts and gunfire.

"Let's leave, get as far away—"

"No." Neil tightened his jaw. "They stole my life from me. I'm not leaving till I get it back."

RONIE KENDIG

Slumping onto the thin mattress bed, Aspen stroked Talon's fur as he slept on the gray-striped mattress. The words Dane had shot at Watterboy still rang in her ears. Is that what happened with Talon? Had he hit on something? Or was he running scared? What happened had made no sense. They'd been there, he was fine, engaged the little boy, then everything went nutso.

It just didn't make sense.

It's why she came back to the bunkroom, why she'd found that lame excuse about washing off Talon. She wanted to talk to Dane. He had good sense.

Did he really think they'd find Austin? Why did she keep asking that question? Was it her doubt? If she truly believed they'd find him alive, these questions wouldn't haunt her. Right?

She felt the presence more than heard it.

Aspen pushed to her feet, heart catapulted into her throat as she found Dane standing on the other side of the steel bed. Hands at her side, she gulped the adrenaline burst—saw the angry red wound on his side.

"What are you doing here?" He snatched a shirt from his bag and stuffed his hands through the sleeves.

"I. . ." She ran her fingers along the ridges of Talon's lead. "What you said earlier to Watterboy, about Talon getting a hit on something and being back in action. . ."

"Yeah?" Dane ran his hands through his hair, but the strands around his crown dropped back into his face. Beautiful olive skin. A dusting of stubble that made him appear rugged. Those eyes that somehow managed to funnel strength and courage to her heart like an IV.

"I. . ." She sighed. "I'm not sure that's what happened."

"Then what did?"

She looked down at the seventy-five-pound dog, his oh-so-steady brown eyes, and the smile that tugged into his face when he panted. He had panicked. As he'd done before at the ranch. At home. In any new situation. He'd settle for a bit, but once he went into that "vigilance" mode, it was like trying to lasso a mountain.

She'd hoped. . .hoped so dearly that he'd be able to do this. But was it fair to put such high expectations on a dog? A dog with more hurt than courage.

The truth hurt. She braved Dane's gaze again. "I think he got scared and ran off to hide." She shrugged. "I mean, look where we were finally able to corner him."

He held up a hand to her as he retrieved his boots with the other, perched on the edge of the bed next to Talon. "Let's examine your theory." He threaded his socks over his feet—big, flat feet. Nana's old wives' tale about men with flat feet having a bad temper flitted through Aspen's mind. Though she'd seen him determined and perhaps a bit intense, she couldn't imagine him with a bad temper. It just didn't fit.

He let down one foot, booted but not tied, and lifted the other boot from the mattress. "Tell me what you remember—every minute detail."

Rubbing her forehead, Aspen let her gaze skip along the spidery cracks on the floor. "I was talking to the little boy. . ."

"And Talon was cool with that."

"Yeah." She remembered being proud of him. "He sniffed then licked the boy's hand. It was a good connection."

"Tail?"

"Huh?"

"Was Talon's tail up?"

She returned to that memory. "Yeah. . .tail and head. Ears were attentive but not drawn back."

"Right." Boots on, he started tightening the laces. "Go on."

She liked this, the going over details to pick out what happened. She used to do this sort of thing with Austin since their childhood, being latchkey kids—if you could call it that with a maid, a nanny, and a groundsman while Mr. and Mrs. Courtland were busy making millions at the family empire, Courtland Properties. Days gone of an era that she'd once thought gave her happiness. Her childhood hadn't been typical. But she'd come out fairly normal. What kind of upbringing had Dane had? He was so grounded, it had to be a decent one.

Back to the present, Aspen. "Okay, so Talon was fine one minute then barked the next."

"And the kid screamed because it startled him."

"Right, then Talon took off." Scared and looking for a place to hide. Hope deflated in her chest, pulling her courage with it. "So, see?" She was tired. Tired of working her heart out for Talon and believing beyond belief that Austin was alive. Tired of the doubts. Tired of the listing nature of her life. Tired of. . .everything. Even of being tired. She felt the tears burning, the prickling in her sinuses. And hated them.

In a rush, Dane stood over her, hands gently on her shoulders. "Don't go there, Angel." His voice was soft, gentle, like her favorite down comforter. "Don't give up on him."

"He's *not* better, Dane." Her voice cracked. Suddenly aware that her hand was on his side, heat flared through her and she removed it, wiping her fingers along her face to make the removal seem innocuous. "I keep thinking he's getting better, but he's not. How are we going to find out if Austin is here, if he's alive, if Talon can't keep it together?"

"Slow down there," he said, craning his neck to look into her eyes. "Think about it. When Talon barked, what was he looking at?"

"The boy."

Dane started to shake his head then slowed then gave a firmer shake. "Think—"

She drew in a hard breath as the memory spilled over her. Aspen widened her eyes as she drew in a breath. "You're right." A bubble of laughter trickled up her throat. "He was looking down the hall." Her heart beat a little faster. "I think he saw something or someone."

"Which means he had a hit."

"He didn't break behavior." Relief warmed her belly. She laughed. "Thank you!" She tiptoed up, threw her arms around his neck, and hugged him. "You're right."

Awareness lit through her as his arms encircled her waist and tightened. Aspen stilled, the realization sudden that she'd thrown herself into his arms. Then it coupled with the intense exhilaration that blossomed.

But. . .would he take it wrong? Would he. . . ?

Slowly, she eased back to the ground, her hand resting on his shoulder then onto his bicep. He must think her stupid. Or—loose.

She flicked her gaze to his.

And froze.

His fingers swept her cheek. The spot where they'd banged heads earlier. And trickles of electricity shot through her face and neck at his touch. "I was afraid it'd bruise."

Unable to keep her gaze from his for any decent amount of time, Aspen tried to maintain a smile, but everything in her felt ablaze. "I. . . I'm not as soft as I look."

Dane's eyes lowered to her lips.

Oh. . . Her breathing shallowed as his head dipped toward hers.

"No!"

Startled, Aspen drew up short.

Dane swallowed and turned toward the bed, reaching for something.

"No," Timbrel repeated as she stomped toward them. "You stay away from her!"

Indignation squirmed through Aspen. "Timbrel!"

"You don't know this guy, Aspen." Timbrel wore a mask of outrage and protectiveness, but something else was there. "I warned you—told you I didn't like how he was looking at you. Can't you see it? He's working you."

Dane swung around. And what Aspen saw in his face pushed her back a step. The rugged face, the gentility, the quiet powerful presence—gone. In their place, a terrifying fury.

SAFE

Nevsky Prospekt, St. Petersburg, Russia
Age: 14 Years, 3 Months

Back in St. Petersburg, Nikol disembarked the bus. As soon as his foot hit the cement, he stopped. *My backpack.* Breath jammed into his throat, he stared out at the bustling city. How would he explain that to the colonel? Fear swirled through his body, deadening him to the din around him. Was there anything in it that would identify him?

No, of course not. Another thing he had been trained to protect—his identity. Besides his national identity card, he carried nothing with his name or residence on it. The colonel vowed he had sworn enemies who would do anything to get to him.

Believing that was believing in Mikuláš.

A grimy window blurred his reflection—but also reminded him of the cut. *Need to remedy that.* But how? Rounding another corner, he made eye contact with a police officer then veered left and headed down an alley. Skirting a three-story building, he heard the heavy footfalls behind him.

Nikol continued on. Left, then right, he searched. Farther into the darker sections of the city. Should not be too much farther—

"Hey, you lost?"

Perfect.

Nikol turned. "What is it to you?"

The brawny kid came toward him. "This is my territory, that's what."

"As if you could stop me." Showing his back to the guy should be enough.

A gust of wind and a foul smell warned him of the attack. He let it come.

The guy grabbed his jacket, swung him around. In the fraction of a second it took to see the fist coming, Nikol angled his face so the guy would hit his cheek. *Crack.*

Pain shot through his head. His neck whipped back. Stupid kid missed—busted his lip instead.

Nikol drove a hard right at his opponent.

The kid stumbled but came at him again. Nailed him straight on.

Fire streaked through his face and jaw. About time. Nikol threw a flat-handed slice right into the guy's throat. The kid dropped to his knees, clutching his throat.

"Stop!" The police officer raced toward them, aiming a weapon. "Step back."

Hands up, Nikol shuffled away from the thug.

In the minutes it took another police officer to show up, Nikol closed himself off. Mentally compartmentalized. He had accomplished his mission, covered his mistakes.

"You belong to Colonel Tselekova."

Hands behind his head, Nikol merely stared at the officer through a knotted brow.

They laughed as the fatter officer stuffed Nikol's national identity card into his pocket. "He'll get enough punishment at home."

"But you saw—"

"Do *you* want to explain to Tselekova why he had to come down and pick him up?"

"I'll return him to the colonel," the younger officer said.

Silently, Nikol thanked God for the reprieve. Taking him into custody would have made it worse. Having documentation, having to experience the humiliation of retrieving him from a jail, the colonel's fury would be heard throughout the city. It had happened once, and though Nikol had been willing to endure it again this time, he had always done everything in his power to avoid another lesson.

"I ask not for a lighter burden, but for broader shoulders." His mother had said that a thousand times and then would clasp his shoulders and say, *"You will have broad shoulders."*

Nine hundred heartbeats passed before he stood at the door to the apartment, under the control of the officer who announced their presence with two hollow yet booming thuds on the door. Though Nikol tasted the blood from his lip, he cared not.

The door swung open.

Cold dumped into Nikol's stomach as the colonel towered over them both, darkening the doorway. Darkening life. Fury smudged a scowl into the steely features.

"Thank you, Lieutenant Kislik."

Chest puffed, the police officer relinquished control, gave a curt nod, then stomped off.

The colonel moved back without a word. Stood straight and stiff, demanding with his silence that Nikol enter.

Pushing every ounce of contrition into his face and posture, Nikol trudged inside. He paused as the door closed. There would be no dialogue—no excuse was good enough to bring shame on Colonel Tselekova. Or to arouse his anger. The offense didn't matter. A beating would commence. Always had.

Nikol did not care. He had accomplished his mission, and the colonel was none the wiser. Remembering the face of an angel, he turned.

Swift movement tensed him. The butt of a Tokarev collided with his temple.

The blunt force thrust him backward. He hit the wall. Blood sped down his face. As his vision ghosted, he had one thought: *At least Kalyna is safe.*

Thirteen

Camp Lemonnier, Combined Joint Task Force—Horn of Africa
Republic of Djibouti, Africa

Tame the fury.

Gaze locked on Aspen, on the widening of her eyes, the tension radiating through her frame, Cardinal hauled in the hurricane-strength storm that erupted at three words: *"He's working you."*

"I know your type." Red-faced, fists balled, and in a fighter stance, Timbrel stood between Aspen and him. "I know how you work on soft-hearted women—"

"Timbrel—" Aspen moved to the side, closer to Dane.

"No!" Timbrel whirled toward Aspen, who'd moved closer. "No, I'm not going to let this go. I won't let him hurt you. You're too good of a woman."

"And a strong woman capable of making her own decisions," Cardinal said, his heart pounding at her accusations, at the way she portrayed him to Aspen. "Give her some credit."

"Oh, I do, Slick Snot. But not you—and don't think you can put a wedge between me and her with your smooth talk and rugged good looks. Because it's so not happening." Her eyes narrowed. "Step off where she's concerned, or I promise I won't be so nice next time I see you moving in for the kill."

"Hey."

Cardinal wouldn't dare remove his gaze from this little nymph staring him down. But as he looked at her, he saw the truth. "I am sorry you've been hurt—"

"No! You don't get to get in my head. And don't even try to get on my good side." Her lip curled. "I don't have one. And if I did, it'd be booby-trapped to take your head off."

"Hey!" Candyman moved into Cardinal's periphery. "Are you people deaf?"

"Back off." With a shove against Cardinal's chest, Timbrel turned. When Candyman grinned at her, she glowered. "Did you have a reason to be here besides. . . ?"

Interest piqued, Cardinal watched Hogan and the Green Beret. A silent conversation seemed to carry on between the two.

Finally, Timbrel raised her arms. "What?"

Candyman nodded. "Sat chat with the good general." He shot a piercing look Cardinal's way. Then it softened. "Looks like we got a lead." He turned to Hogan. "Can I talk to you?"

"Isn't that what you're doing?" Though there was an edge to her words, it wasn't as caustic as before.

"Outside." The soldier's face betrayed nothing as he stood a step back, eyes linked with hers, and waited for her to move. With one more disapproving glare at Cardinal, he trailed Hogan out of the bunkhouse.

Aspen shifted to face him. "I'm sorry about that." She took Talon's lead. "She means well."

"I know. There's a lot of hurt beneath that explosion she just unloaded on me." He understood more than anyone could believe. But he'd been trained to conceal his anger.

As they started for the door, she hesitated. "Is it true?"

His world slowed into a painful rhythm. Cardinal wouldn't insult her by playing dumb, but he also would *not* lie to her any more than he had to and only where absolutely necessary for the interest of this mission and the safety of his asset.

"Are you playing me?"

"Don't we all do it?" He pointed to the bunk Talon had occupied a second ago. "Isn't that why you happened to be in here with Talon, so we could be alone and talk?"

"That's a pretty jaded perspective."

"It's realistic and logical. Just because we arrange situations to suit our interests does not mean it's bad."

Disappointment lurked in her eyes, but she said nothing. She knew as well as he did that he'd called her hand. But it'd hurt her. And that stabbed his conscience. Hand on the door, he stopped. Shifted toward her, noting that Talon sat.

"Thank you for playing me so we could be alone and talk." The words were meant to tease her, to reassure her—through a roundabout lie that creased his attempts to be honest and direct with her—not open a chasm of hope that lingered in her eyes and tempted him to fall in and never regret. But that's what happened. Especially when she flashed him a coy smile and slipped out into the sunshine, light ringing her white-blond curls in a halo.

Angel.

And you're the Angel of Death, Cardinal. Trust implicit, she had no idea who she was falling for. And falling she was. What made it worse, what made him want to cut out his heart with his own knife was that he wanted her to fall. He wanted the kiss Hogan had stolen. He wanted Aspen to believe in him. He wanted. . .her.

The thought slowed him. Sickened him.

Fists balled, he stowed those feelings. Those misguided hopes. And reminded himself of the venom that ran in his veins.

Pentagon, Arlington County, Virginia

Lance Burnett popped the top of his Dr Pepper, took a slurp. As he let out a slow belch, he spotted Lieutenants Hastings and Smith hustling his way. Hastings held a laptop and papers, while Smith juggled what looked like maps and a phone pressed between his shoulder and ear.

They burst into his office.

"What in Sam Hill is going on?"

Smith turned the blinds and shut the door as Hastings delivered the laptop, her expression hurried. "Cardinal got a lead."

"And why are we hiding?"

"Because, apparently, so did General Payne—on Cardinal." Hastings set down the laptop and pointed to the embedded window. "He's going to call in, but we only have thirty seconds before Payne's team leeches."

Lance gulped his sugary addiction then sat forward. As the Dr

Pepper splashed down his throat, he watched the screen activate with an incoming message. He accepted.

"Sir," Cardinal said, his brevity dictating he knew the call would be traced. "Local feelers report a missionary couple named Justin and Camille Santos sheltered a man matching our asset's description."

Lance grunted. Missionary. Often a cover story for spies.

"Got it," Smith said as he scribbled, his feet already carrying him out to research the names.

"On our last trip into Peltier," Cardinal said, his voice staticky in the connection, "we came under fire."

"An attack?"

Cardinal's gaze was direct and confident. "We're on the right trail." He glanced to the side.

"Agreed. How's the dog and handler doing?"

A flicker on the normally rock-solid face. "They're fine."

Lance frowned. "Good. We need them."

Hesitation lurked through the grainy feed. Then, "Agreed. I'm going dark for a while."

Dark?

"I'll code-in within fourteen days. Cardinal out."

The connection zapped. Lance stared at the screen. What was that about? Cardinal hesitant? Was it because of the girl, the dog, both? Mother of God, if something went wrong and Payne—

"What'd you see?" he asked Hastings, who sub-monitored the video feed and analyzed as the transmission progressed yet recorded nothing.

"A shadowy figure"—she angled the laptop toward him and showed him a reflection in the glass—"is just outside the room. A woman."

"The handler."

"Yes, sir." Hastings straightened, her lips pulled tight.

"Why's he going dark?"

"Most plausible scenarios—"

"No." He hadn't meant to speak that question out loud. Lance didn't need ideas. Cardinal felt it was necessary. Lance would give him the requested two weeks. "What else did you notice?"

"There were others, but they stood too far away for the reflection to be clear." Hastings swallowed. "And Cardinal wasn't himself."

Lance laughed and slumped back in his chair. "Himself?" He

muttered a curse and shook his head. "Hastings, if you know what 'himself' means when it comes to that man, then you're a better soldier than any one of the twenty analysts who examined, interrogated, and psychoanalyzed him."

Her face tightened. "I know a man when he's distracted by a woman."

Laughing even harder, Lance reached for his soda. "If you believe that, you *definitely* have no idea about our Mr. Cardinal." He waved her toward the door. "And don't let your feelings for Cardinal cloud your judgment next time."

She widened her eyes.

"Oh, give me the benefit of the doubt, L-T. You don't think I know what's going on under my own nose? With my own dadgum team?" He shooed her with his hand. "Go on. Do the research on"—he glanced at the transcript that autoprinted from the call—"the Santos couple."

"Sir, I—"

"Dismissed," he growled. At the click of the door, he dropped back against his squeaky chair and pinched the bridge of his nose.

Another rotten nightmare. Embroiled in international chaos.

Hastings was right. Something was off about Cardinal. On his computer Lance coded in, bypassed several security protocols, each one more advanced than the next, till he came to the file he wanted. Time for light reading. About a man he'd met in a cathedral in New York City eleven years ago. A man who'd refused to cooperate. Who refused to become a liar and a stealer of lives.

In espionage terms, in terms of recruitment, he'd been ideal— young, burned by idealism, a burning rage that drove him. Controlled him. Those types of people believed they controlled the anger. It was that illusion of control that men like Burnett turned on their ear to capitalize for the benefit of the United States.

Took a year to lure the guy in. But Cardinal had proven to be a brilliant asset. The kind movies and books were written about. That was exactly why Payne and Morris had vehemently objected to him. If that man went rogue, he could bring down everything. If he wasn't truly turning against his own country to spy for America. . .the damage would be unfathomable.

With the man's fiery conviction and determination to topple one of the most powerful Russians, Lance never worried that Cardinal would betray his trust.

Until now.

But maybe. . .just maybe Lance had a wild card. One that would ensure the loyalty and control of this asset.

Fourteen

Nertz!" Aspen declared as she slapped down the last card.

She and Timbrel high-fived.

Candyman banged a fist on the table. "I liked it better when you two were mad at each other."

Timbrel laughed. "We're best friends. Mad doesn't last for long. Besides, she knows I am just looking out for her."

"But," Aspen inserted, "Timbrel agreed to take it down a notch. Let me handle my own affairs."

Candyman and his teammate Rocket hooted.

Aspen rolled her eyes as she gathered up the cards she and Timbrel had played. "Oh grow up."

"Where is that old man anyway?" Candyman took a swig of his Coke.

"What old man?" Aspen shuffled the deck.

"Markoski."

"He's not old."

Candyman grinned.

"You're incorrigible."

Timbrel took the deck. "Don't *encourage* him."

Aspen laughed but silently wondered where Dane was. He'd vanished since their near-kiss and the fallout. She had counted every minute. At least, it felt like she had. She wanted to see him again. Liked being with him.

Shouts carried down the hall outside the rec room.

"Someone's ticked," Rocket said as he worked the cards like a pro. Sliding them in a snakelike pattern from hand to hand. Then shuffled

473

them in rapid-fire succession.

A loud noise thudded through the building.

"What was that?" Rocket turned, his magic with the cards stopped.

Crack! A crash rumbled across the floor. *Thud!* A primal shout roared through the stale, not-so-air-conditioned air.

Candyman jumped to his feet with Rocket on his tail.

"I'm not going to miss the action," Timbrel said as she hopped to her feet.

Aspen called to Talon and joined the others in the hall.

Papers, chairs, and desks littered the entrance to a small conference room. Blinds hung askew.

"What the heck happened?" Candyman asked to whoever was in the room.

". . .on my life, I will hunt you down. . .no, *no!* This is wrong. I'll kill you. So help me God—you knew this would—*no!*" *Crack!*

Aspen peered around Timbrel and saw Dane standing at the window, his hand freeing itself of the gypsum board wall it'd punched through. He faced away from them, a phone dangling from his left hand. He flung aside the device and planted his hands on his hips. He breathed—hard. She shouldered her way into the upturned conference room and stepped over a trail of papers. "Dane?"

He hung his head.

"What. . . ?" A certificate caught her eyes. Her heart stuttered as she reached for it, recognizing her own name. "What is this?" She couldn't breathe. This wasn't. . .wasn't possible. "Dane? Is this. . .a joke?"

He spun around, face a ball of rage. Stormed past her. Without answering her, he yelled to the others, "Out! Now!"

"I'm not leaving her with you, not like this." Timbrel's objection didn't contain half the ferocity Dane's had.

"If you value your pretty little head, you'll leave now."

Aspen jerked toward them, met Timbrel's bulging eyes. She gave a curt nod, trying to reassure her friend things were fine. But the paper in her hand proved things were anything but. Dane herded the others out of the room. Shut the door. Despite the damage to the blinds, he tried to close them, to no avail. He slapped the glass.

She flinched. Dropped her gaze back to the paper. Numb. That was the only word. "I don't understand. . ."

"Don't try." His voice was hard as he righted the table. From the floor, he retrieved the paper trail. Tossed it on the table. "I need you to understand something."

She snapped the paper at him. "Start with this."

He took it from her. "In a minute." He looked down, closed his eyes, and roughed his hand—with cracked, bleeding knuckles—over his face as he let out a hard sigh. "When they asked me to do this, I..." His chest heaved. Raw power rolled off him. "This isn't how I work," he said with a growl. "I do it alone. I don't need anyone. I don't want or care about anyone else."

"Next time," she said, staving off the stinging reproach, "slap me. It'll hurt less." She tried to stalk past him, her fear, her panic strangling sane thought.

Dane hooked her arm. "Please. . ." His shoulders sagged. "Burnett knows I'm the best chance of finding out if your brother's alive."

She braved his steely gaze. And saw the teeming agony.

"And you're the best chance of tracking him because of Talon."

"What?"

"I refused to work this case. Yesterday, I contacted him, said I was off the case. That I refused to go any further."

"Why?"

"So, he forced me. Forced my hand."

Why wasn't he answering her questions? "If you don't want to help find my brother, then I don't want your help."

"Don't put words in my mouth."

Confusion clotted her patience. "Then *what* are you trying to say? What's the point of this?" She tapped the document in his hand.

"A marriage certificate."

Aspen laughed. There was no way it was real. She hadn't signed anything. Yet even as the thought crossed her mind, she remembered her name. No— "It has my signature."

"And mine." He held it up as if to prove it. "Original seal. Recorded in Virginia."

Panic and ice churned through her chest. "Why?"

"We're going in undercover. You're Austin's sister, seeking closure. I'm your husband, watching out for you."

"That's stupid!"

He shook his head and walked to the window. "You have no idea."

Aspen, fingers trembling, rifled through the other documents. "Birth certificates, passports"—she flipped through the pages, her breathing shallowing out—"Oh my word. They're stamped."

Dane slumped against the far wall. "Apparently, we honeymooned in Greece."

"I've never been to Greece!" The shriek in her voice scraped down her spine. "How can they do this? Get him on the phone. I'm not standing for this."

Dane smirked. Retrieved his phone, dialed, pressed more numbers, then handed her the phone.

Surprised, she took the device.

"I knew you'd call back." A man's voice boomed.

"Yes, this is Aspen Courtland—"

Burnett cursed. "Put that son of a—"

"General, I want you to stop this game."

"I'm sorry. It's done. Get the mission done and you get your life back." The line went dead. She stared at the silver phone. "He hung up on me. Told me to do it and I could have my life back."

Dane's shoulders fell. "I hoped he'd be better than that." He righted a chair and dropped into it. Fingers steepled, he pressed the tips to his forehead and closed his eyes.

Incredulous, she tossed the papers from the table at his feet. "They're fake! Anyone will know."

Grief tugged at his features as he pushed back in the chair and slumped. "They're authentic. One-hundred percent real. Legal. Legitimate."

"I don't care. Make them undo it."

Dane looked down and leaned forward. He threaded his fingers, a heaviness on his brow as he studied the floor.

"You can't possibly be thinking—" She yelped. Spun around. Lunged for the door. "Forget it. I'm leaving."

Hands caught her shoulders. Spun her.

Aspen's fist flew on its own.

Crack! Pain plowed through his skull and neck. Instantly, he felt the gush of warmth. Felt his nostrils closing up. He cursed.

Aspen clapped her hands over her mouth, eyes wide.

He stumbled back to the chair and pinched the bridge of his nose. It felt like someone was driving nails through his eyes. Clenching his hand into a fist, he squeezed his eyes and breathed through his mouth as he waited for the bleeding to stop.

Hell had to be a better existence than this.

He'd shouted obscenities through the phone at Burnett that would've made his mother blush. The general had not yielded.

"Just. . .get the mission done. Use this to cover your trail."

"I don't need this to get my job done. Undo it. Now."

"No can do." Burnett snickered.

"No can do? Or you won't?"

"What would I have to gain by tying your sorry carcass to that sweet girl? This isn't about anything but getting my asset back before someone else gets to him, if they haven't already."

"I'm sorry."

Surprise stabbed through him. Her words were soft. And close.

He opened his eyes—already the swelling was puffing around his eyes.

Aspen stood in front of him, holding what looked like a towel with ice.

He accepted the peace offering. "That's an awesome right hook. I should've remembered." Their first meeting—the fight club.

"My grandfather taught me that when I was five."

Cardinal slowed. "Amadore. . ."

She shrugged. "My grandfather on my mother's side." She squatted. "Please. . .*please* tell me this can be undone."

"Burnett promised as soon as we get Austin—if he's alive— everything will go back to normal."

"You're sure?"

"His words. I can't predict the future." And he certainly didn't trust Burnett as far as he belched.

"I can't believe they can get away with this." She crossed her arms. "Can't we do anything?"

"What?" He pointed to the passports. "If you try to go anywhere with your other passport you'll get arrested. We have two tickets into Djibouti from Virginia—of course, we won't be coming from there, but flight records will probably show that. Most likely, they'll take us to

Egypt or somewhere and put us on the second leg." He sighed. "Look. I know this is asinine, but it will work."

"But why can't we just do it from here, the way things are?"

"Whoever has Austin, if they smell military, we'll get more of the same from Tuesday."

"I thought that was random."

Cardinal gave a snort. "You are smarter than that. They knew who we were. We aren't going to get anywhere with these military grunts breathing down our necks."

She drew a chair over and sat in front of him. "I'm really sorry about your nose."

"Not my first."

"Maybe, but I never wanted to hurt you."

"You know what they say about payback." He'd never forget her horrified expression when she saw the papers. It came pretty close to what he felt as he opened the overnighted box.

"Dane. . ." She worried the edge of her lip. "That certificate is in paper only."

Did she really think he was a cad? He raised a hand. "Give me a little more respect than that. In case you didn't notice"—he waved his hand around the room—"I didn't take the news very well either. I don't want this. I'm not the marrying kind of guy."

Her eyebrows winged up.

He shook his head and it felt like he was under water. "Look, let's just get this done and get out of here."

"But why real certificates? Why not fake it?"

"Technically, they're faked. You didn't sign it. I didn't sign it. But there our signatures are." He'd be mouth breathing for a few days, and the thunder roaring through his head would stop in a few hours. . . maybe. "But they're *not* fake because of who we're dealing with and how convincing we need to be."

"And who is that?"

"We don't know for sure, except that it's pretty high up the ladder."

"How would you know that?"

"Because Burnett sent *me*." He let the full meaning settle in as he applied the ice pack to his nose, cringing at the added weight and pain.

"And who are you, Dane?"

He met her eyes. "Your husband."

Aspen folded her hands and looked down.

He regarded her. Playing her husband was something he feared. And he didn't fear that she'd fail at playing his wife—the word curled around some inner piece of him and made it hard to breathe—or that anyone would doubt they had feelings for each other, because that too was true. He could play the role like an ace. And that near kiss—well, he'd memorized the expectation that hung in her beautiful face as she waited for his lips to touch hers.

No, there'd be no problem pretending. What scared him was how much he'd enjoy it.

I am becoming him.

Aspen reached for the express box and lifted it. Something clunked in it.

Cardinal groaned.

She dumped the item out. A box. Small black box. She flipped it open. Two rings—one a plain, gold band. Another a stunner of a rock poised over a silver band. He cringed—no, not silver. Platinum.

Aspen's eyes widened. "Is this real?"

He smirked. "Are you proposing?"

Pink fanned her cheeks.

"You're beautiful." Only when her eyes flicked to his did he realize he'd said that. *Whoa. Hold up!* "When you're proposing."

She stared at the rings, her eyes tearing.

"Aspen." He reached forward and covered the box with his hand. "I wish we could stop this right now. Call Burnett and—"

"He won't listen." She shook her head. "Just like all the times I called them and told them to find Austin, that he wasn't dead. They ignored me." She shrugged. "You already tried, that's why you were shouting and cursing earlier. And he hung up on me, remember? He won't listen."

"If we both swear out of this, if we walk, they can't do anything."

"But they can." She swallowed—hard. "I can see the fear, the fury in your eyes."

He drew back, startled that she'd seen that. Nobody had seen that.

"I'm right aren't I?"

He felt naked. Exposed. This wasn't good that she could see into him like this. He'd worked too many years protecting himself, erecting barriers.

"What did they threaten you with, Dane?"

He ducked even more.

"I think I deserve to know."

"It doesn't matter." He stood, struggling not to cringe. Again, he stomped around the room. There had to be another way. He couldn't tether himself to a woman. Relationships didn't work. Not for him. Not now. Not ever.

"Look, I'll just get out of here, vanish." That might work. "Tell Burnett it's my fault. He'll let you off."

"Wait." Aspen joined him. "If we don't do this, I don't find Austin. Right?"

"Is it worth going through this?"

She frowned then drew straight. "Yes." She nodded again. "I want the truth about my brother—and now more than ever, it seems like a doozie of a truth."

"Even if it means marrying me?" It was meant to be funny. But it wasn't. He wanted to punch the wall again.

He didn't trust himself to speak. It was the foulest betrayal Burnett had pulled on him yet. And he'd strangle the man if he could get within arm's reach. Burnett knew. . .somehow, he knew what angle to pull with Cardinal. His one weak spot.

Not this fake marriage. Not the putting on of rings.

But his heart.

Get out! Get out, now!

Cardinal gulped back what he felt. The fear. The panic. His anger wasn't about himself—he could walk out of here and never worry about what Burnett or anyone else would do to him. But Aspen. . .this would destroy her. Not finding out about Austin—

Somehow, Burnett had figured out what was happening in Cardinal. Even before Cardinal knew—he was falling for Aspen Courtland. And he'd do anything for her. Including staying.

Aspen lifted the black box, opened it, and plucked the plain band. She lifted his hand, slid the ring on, and looked up at him. "With this ring, I thee wed." Her laugh fell flat. "Boy, that felt weird. But that's all we have to do, right? Put on the rings and off we go."

Into the deepest, darkest pit of hell.

FORBIDDEN

Nevsky Prospekt, St. Petersburg, Russia
Age: Nearly 10 Years

Hunger tore at him as his shoes beat a steady rhythm on the shoveled sidewalks. Icy wind pinched his face and neck, but he swiped a sleeve along his nose and pressed on. Plumes of icy breath danced before him in the March morning as he completed his fifth circuit. Lungs aching, limbs frozen, he savored the warmth of the sun clawing its way over the frozen city and willed it not to hide from him any longer.

"Nikol."

Startled at his name, he looked around.

Mr. Kaczmarek waved from his shop's front stoop on the other side of the street. "Hurry, boy."

Even though he knew the colonel could not see him from here, Nikol looked over his shoulder and slowed. Buildings protected him, but time did not. "I cannot stop, sir."

The Polish baker smiled and stepped farther out, arm extended. Even from here, Nikol could see the warmth rising off the pastry. "You can finish it before you get home, yes?"

Nikol grinned, crossed the street, and accepted the treat. "Thank you, sir."

Yes, he could finish it before he returned to his building. In fact, before he left this street or the possibility existed that the colonel would see him. He took a large chomp out of it. Cinnamon and butter swirled through his palate. Then a cold dread replaced the delicious flavor. Out of sight of Mr. Kaczmarek, he flung the pastry as far over a small home as he could throw it. . .kept jogging, sweating, panting. He bent and scooped up a fistful of snow. Stuffed it in his mouth. Quickly it liquefied.

481

He swished. Then spit it out.

The spittle landed on a fresh blanket of undisturbed snow. And there he saw the telltale brown grains. He repeated the process. On his seventh circuit, nearly five miles, he slowed and paced in front of the building, cooling and slowing his breathing. Back inside he turned on the pot for coffee, quickly showered, then dressed. He stuffed an apple in his satchel, made breakfast. From the cabinet, he took down one white plate and a clear glass. He turned toward the table and stilled.

Two chairs? Why were there two chairs at the table? The colonel never allowed him to eat with him. *"You must learn to depend on nobody, to see nobody's company. To be self-sufficient like me."*

"Why are you standing there like an idiot?"

The booming voice jolted him. Good for him that he did not drop the plate or glass. "Sorry, sir," Nikol said as he set the table as he had done every morning, noon, and night—and without looking at the colonel and proving he was the aforementioned idiot. How had he not noticed the sun that had escaped from the only window on that side of the apartment—the one that was in the colonel's bedroom?

"Set two." With that, the colonel stomped down the hall to the bathroom.

The light beams flickered and danced, drawing his attention to the room. Someone was in there. Nikol dropped his gaze. It wouldn't be the first time the colonel had brought home a woman to have his way with her.

Still, it ignited Nikol's fury. The colonel had tossed his mother out like a prostitute, shouted profanities at her. Beat her. Shamed her. Berated Nikol for crying for her. Then beat him, too. He had not seen her in three years. He dreamed of her but never told the colonel.

"Nikol," came the soft, feminine whisper.

With wide eyes he looked to the bedroom. Wrapping herself in a robe, the beautiful form took shape, wrapped in a halo of light. "Mama!"

She waved him into the room.

He stood there, mute. Terrified. And shook his head. "I'm forbidden," he whispered.

She darted a look down the hall, then hurried across the small dining area to him and drew him into her arms. "Oh, my sweet boy!"

In his mind, he clung to her. Cried against her soft chest. Savored her love that he could sense. She pulled back, cupped his face, and wept. "You have become such a young man."

"I am nearly ten."

More tears.

"Please." He darted a nervous glance toward the hall. "Do not cry. It will make him angry."

She brushed away her tears then nodded. "I am so proud of you, Nikol."

Then the panic started. The thoughts of what the colonel had done to her last time. "Why are you here?" His heart thundered. "You should go. Hurry. Now, before he comes out." Frantic, he tugged on her arm, drawing her toward the door.

"No, Nikol, it is well. He. . .we made a deal." Her smile was small and did not make her eyes sparkle the way he remembered. "It is okay. It is worth it to see you."

"No! You must go."

"Nikol, be calm, my son. He only has the power we give him." She held him again, then knelt in front of him so he stood over her. "Besides, he said if I. . .if I"—her gaze darted to the bedroom and her voice trembled, but she smiled up at him—"if I *came*, I could see you."

"See but not speak to." The venomous voice melded with the words as the colonel appeared, dressed only in a pair of pajama bottoms. "I will not let you poison him, make him weak!"

His hand came down hard on his mother's face. Her head. Curled on the floor, she cried, "You promised! I did what you wanted. You said I could see him."

"Shut up, you whore!" His fist nailed her nose. Blood spurted over her cream-colored robe.

Something in Nikol died that day.

Fifteen

The plane hit cruising altitude, and Aspen settled back, her mind and finger still weighted with the ring she bore. Timbrel had vowed bodily harm against Dane if he made one wrong move. Warned them as soon as they were back in Djibouti they would have eyes on them, and she'd find a sniper to take him out.

Though Aspen warred with the thoughts that she'd somehow violated her belief in the sanctity of marriage, she knew this was a logical path to finding Austin. They wouldn't do anything immoral. Candyman *and* Watterboy threatened intense personal pain if Dane crossed lines. And Rocket alluded to something he'd seen the two do to terrorists who'd kidnapped another special-ops comrade.

It'd taken her the six hours from the time they'd left the others, boarded a military jet, and then made their "connecting" flight back to Djibouti to relax.

Which she couldn't say for Dane.

He hadn't spoken a word.

"I don't remember you two," the Middle Eastern man next to them said as he pointed to Dane's face. "I would have remembered that mess. I'm a plastic surgeon."

Dane smiled, the swelling still obvious. "Like my trophy?" He grinned wider. "Got this when a guy tried to hit on my wife."

The doctor tsked. "Are women worth such a price? How did you get to sit up here? It was full."

Dane thumbed toward the back. "We were in business class. They had an opening—something wrong with someone's papers—and since my wife wasn't feeling well, we upgraded for the last leg."

The passenger leaned forward and peered at her. "Ah, she does look pale. Between your black eyes and her sickness, it's a wonder you are traveling." He grinned. "First class is better, no?"

"Much. It's nice and quiet." With that, Dane closed his eyes.

Aspen wanted to laugh, but she was supposed to be sick. She looked out the window and placed her hand on her stomach, which caused the heavy wedding ring to thump softly against her fingers. *Weird. So very weird.*

"I don't want this. I'm not the marrying kind of guy."

The words had startled her and crushed her at the same time. She had been interested in Dane, was willing to explore things. They seemed to have faith in common. And he was handsome. He seemed to like her, too. But apparently not.

Her mind whirred at what lay before them. Convincing the missionary they were a couple. That would be interesting, considering they'd never even held hands, kissed, or—well, anything.

But she kept coming back to one thought: Dane had tried to leave the mission.

Had she done something wrong?

Or was it because of the near kiss?

She snorted. That's what she got for reading romance novels with arranged marriages. The romantic notions of falling in love with the unlikely man had her going places she'd better not. Dane had wanted to kiss her, then tried to get removed from the mission. And he wasn't the marrying the kind. He'd said so himself.

That made him the last man on earth she'd ever marry.

Hmm, except that you are *married to him.*

Aspen Markoski.

She shuddered. That didn't sound right together at all. Not the way Sam Herringshaw's name had sounded with hers in fifth grade. Oh good grief. She was doing it again.

Timbrel was right—she was a hopeless romantic. Even though this was the most insane thing she'd ever done.

Was it so wrong that she was willing to do anything to get her brother back? Faking a marriage wasn't a sin. Okay, it was lying, so maybe it was. Pushing the damning thoughts from her mind, she focused on finding Austin. Bringing him back home. Reuniting him with Talon. Life would be normal.

Maybe not normal, but a new normal. He'd go into law the way he'd talked about after their parents' deaths. To bring justice. That's what he wanted. She'd been so proud of him. Talon would live out his days happy, and she...

What? What would she do? She'd never really had any goals. And working with A Breed Apart had infused her with a sense of purpose. With Austin taking Talon back, what would she do? Would ABA cut her off?

Life without the saucy Timbrel? Heath—oh heavens, what would he say about this?

Forget Heath. What would her nana say? Oh that would be a sight—and sound!

The plane began its descent and delivered them into the tiny international airport. Even as they disembarked onto the tarmac, she searched for the crate carrying Talon. He was lowered from a pressurized cabin, and she saw him lift his head.

Warmth wrapped around her hand. She stilled and found herself staring up into Dane's blue eyes. He leaned in, pressing a kiss to the sensitive spot beneath her ear. Heat flared through her chest at the intimate gesture. "Your two o'clock. About a klick out."

Shuddering as he straightened from his whispered words, she let her gaze traipse that direction. A vehicle sat idling. ODA452 and Timbrel?

"Let's get our bags."

Tripping mentally to keep up with Dane's natural strides, she chided herself for the visceral reaction to his kiss, which still felt like someone held a torch to her jaw. But he led her into the terminal. She waited with Talon while he grabbed their bags. Whatever was packed in there, she didn't know. She'd only brought a rucksack to Lemonnier.

As they gathered their things, she spotted a man holding a sign that read MARKOSKI. She stilled.

"Ready, babe?" Hearing those words out of Dane's mouth. . .the same mouth that kissed her...

God, help me. I can't do this. I really can't.

Dane was with her in a second. His arm around her waist.

She pressed her hands against his abs. "Don't." Their eyes met as she stiffened. "Let's. . .let's just get to Santos's home."

"Relax." He glanced over her shoulder. "Ah!" He waved. "Here we are." He released her and lifted their luggage.

Drawing on the remnants of her courage, she pushed the dolly with Talon in his crate toward the man.

"You are Mr. Mar—"

"Markoski." Dane lowered a bag and offered his hand. Then he angled back. "This is my wife, Aspen."

The man raised his hands. "Ah, so much like your brother."

Aspen hauled in a breath. "Austin, you saw him?"

Santos's face softened. "Not in a while, dear girl. I am so sorry to say." He waved them toward his beat-up Jeep-looking vehicle. "Let's talk at the house.

At the two-story home, Dane carried the bags up the steps to the upper level, where a beautiful master suite spread out before them. It must have taken up half the second story. Aspen stood by the window, Talon whimpering in his crate.

"Come on downstairs after you have refreshed. We will have lemonade." Santos backed out and closed the doors.

Dane set down the luggage as Talon was freed from his crate and watched Angel. Aspen.

Curse, curse, curse Burnett. That kiss on her neck had been a huge mistake. He'd tried to make things appear natural, but she'd reacted so. . .thoroughly. So had he. It'd taken every microscopic ounce of control he had not to pull her into his arms and kiss her the way he'd wanted to two days ago. Instead, he'd forced his fingers to release her, his feet to move away, and his voice to remain cold and unattached.

The way he should be. Cardinal rules—enforce them or become mastered. Now, he couldn't clear his mind of that or her smell. Light and floral. When he'd noticed her panic at the airport and tried to intercept, she'd gone stone cold.

Talon whimpered and paced then sat down. Whimpered again. Paced.

"Think he can still smell Austin's scent? Santos said he hadn't been here in a while."

He ripped out a piece of paper and scribbled two words on it—*listening devices*—then moved behind her. He stuffed the note in her hand. Then he held up a pen and clicked it once. "We can talk when it's depressed but only for a few seconds."

Her eyes widened as he came closer. She twisted to face him. "You think someone is listening?"

"Never underestimate the enemy. Listen, take Talon and have him check the rooms. I'll keep Santos busy." *Click.* "Fair enough, Angel. But tonight. . ." He laughed and hated himself for the flirting he'd added to the tone for the sake of anyone listening in on them. And hated the fear in her beautiful eyes. Hated that this whole thing would make her wary of his every move. He went to his suitcase and unzipped it. He stared at the clothes. Jeans. Cotton shirts. Underwear. Burnett had been prepared. This wasn't something he'd done on the spur. He'd been planning this.

With a soft thud, her suitcase landed on the bed. She unzipped it and lifted the flap. A soft gasp preceded her gaze ramming into his. Her face brightened to a deep red.

He couldn't help the laugh trickling through his throat. He well imagined what they'd provided for her, especially to make it appear that they were truly newlyweds should anyone rifle through their things while the bags were unattended.

"There's a screen, if you'd like to freshen up." He pointed to the antique hinged panels that stood guard in the corner and raised his eyebrows, indicating that was her out to staying here with Talon.

She hesitated then looked to the screen. "Perfect."

"I'll see you downstairs then in a few." He slipped out and closed the door.

As he stood in the hall, he took in the layout. Two rooms, one to the right, one left. Both sparsely decorated. Bathroom downstairs, most likely. This wasn't the Sheraton, but it would provide shelter and get them answers. . .hopefully.

Cardinal moved down the shadowy stairs and slowed when he heard voices. He angled to look around the corner.

Santos stood talking with another man. Tones were low, hurried.

He strode into the open. "Room's great. Thanks, Mr. Santos."

Santos spun. The door came out of his grip.

Cardinal met the brown eyes of a man who stood about six feet with dark brown hair. "Afternoon." He greeted the man.

"Afternoon."

Could be from anywhere with that British accent.

"Ah," Santos said with a shaky smile, but Cardinal pretended not to notice. "Mr. Markoski, this is Joshua, one of the missionaries who works in another village. He stopped by to warn me of a new flu strain hitting the villages there."

"Sad."

Joshua stared at him. Hard. "Indeed." He gave Santos a smile. "If it weren't for his mad medical skills, we would be hurting a lot worse than we are."

"It is fortunate timing." Santos looked toward the stairs. "Is your wife well?"

"Yes. She wanted to freshen up. A terribly long trip, and a bit daunting, too."

Santos turned to Joshua. "They are looking for her brother."

"Say." Cardinal stepped into the sunlight that crossed the threshold of the open door. "You haven't seen an American, black hair, brown eyes?"

"I've seen a lot of men fitting that description in Djibouti," Joshua said with a laugh.

"Of course." He sighed long and hard. Swiped a hand along his jaw, noting the stubble that had grown to a five o'clock shadow. "My wife has her hopes pinned on this trip." He shook his head. "If Aspen can't find Austin, I just don't know how she'll keep going."

Though there was no change in body language, a look in the guy's face flashed in and out like a bolt of lightning. So fast, so sharp, Cardinal almost didn't see it.

Voices carried up the dark stairwell as Aspen led Talon from the room. She went to the right, to the one with pink walls. The bed cuddled the corner with a pink floral rug at the side and a chest at the foot. A dresser with an oval mirror sat near the small window. Talon walked in and returned to her side.

Nothing.

"Yeah, I'm not crazy about the color either." She turned around and hurried past the stairs, listening to the voices. . .and stopped. She backed up. Laughter, the voices lowered. That was weird.

Talon trotted ahead, sniffing like mad. She followed him and froze.

Cold dread spiraled through Aspen as Talon let out a high-pitched whimper. He paced back and forth in the yellow room, whimpering. Sniffing. Licking. Paws on the edge of the bed, he leaned up and sniffed the pillow. Barked.

The sound felt like a gunshot through her gut. "Talon?" Her heart raced. But Aspen couldn't move. Her eyes traced the setup of the room. The headboard and footboard were at the wrong ends.

Tentatively, she entered the room, feeling the tug on the lead as Talon sniffed and whimpered and yelped over and over. At the wall where the footboard sat, she reached toward a spot in the middle, just a few inches above the board. Slightly darkened spots. *It can't be. . .*

She should get Dane up here. But she couldn't talk just yet. Couldn't bring herself to give credence to what was happening. She turned to the dresser. Glanced at the bed. Then the dresser. Less than an arm's length apart.

It's just a coincidence.

Right. The bed. The wall. The dresser. And—

Talon. The Lab nosed her hip then sat down, peering up at her expectantly. "*I did good, now show me where he is.*"

She took in the room once more. Empty mostly save the dingy curtains, the rug. . .

"*I like to feel the cold floor when I climb out of bed. It wakes me up.*"

Talon paced more. Whimpered. Dropped onto the rug.

Oh man—the rug. Curled up in the corner. Shoved aside.

Certainty rang through her. Austin had been there. So recently the beds hadn't been rearranged. She walked the room, memorizing, imagining—

Why? Why would he be here and not contact her? It didn't make sense.

With a whimper, Talon rose and started wearing a path in the floor as he tread from one wall to the next. Sniffed the rug. Pace. . .pace. . . sniffed the bed. Whimpered.

This wasn't a jail or a prison or a jungle where he'd been taken hostage. Santos had a phone, electricity. If Austin was here, he could come and go as he pleased.

"Talon, come."

He complied. For a minute. Then took up his trek again. Whimper-pace-pace-sniff-whimper.

"Talon, stop."

Why? Why would Austin do this? Leave Talon, leave his friends. . . She shoved her fingers into her curls and fought back the confusion, the tears.

Dust had accumulated on the dresser, save in one rectangular spot. She noted a thin line a few inches from the larger one. A picture frame. What picture had been moved, and recently?

Talon's whimpers grew louder. He dug into the carpet. Settled on it.

What picture had been there? Why was it gone now?

Talon barked, sniffed, then sat back down. Mission accomplished. Whatever he thought he found was here.

She turned 360 degrees, searching, begging for a reasonable explanation. Nothing came to her. Nothing sated the panic swimming mean circles around her mind.

Talon whimpered yet again. "Talon, please. . ." His cries pulled on her heart. He was distressed. And that was distressing her. More of that high-pitched noise.

"Talon!" She ducked and covered her face, hating that she'd snapped at him. The sweet, loyal boy who had a heart bigger than Texas.

Whimpering continued without ceasing.

Her head hurt. Her *heart* hurt.

She wrapped her arms around his chest, hearing Heath tell her not to baby Talon. *Go away, Daniels.* "It's okay, boy." She squeezed him tighter. "Please." Tears stung her eyes, his cries an eerie reflection of what she felt. She buried her face in his fur. "It's okay, boy. We'll find him."

He only grew louder.

I have to get out of here. Get him out of here.

On her feet, Aspen tugged on Talon's lead and hurried toward the glass door she'd seen opposite the top of the stairs.

Do Svidaniya

Nevsky Prospekt, St. Petersburg
Age: 15 Years, 8 Months

Hues of blue, gray, and white smeared the city into a somber landscape. White covered the snow, and the gray clouds hovered deep, forbidding the sun from making its appearance. No sun. Never any sun. Russia was dark and dreary. His life was dark and dreary.

A snowplow lumbered along the street, clearing it again for vehicle passage. Across the way, he spotted a group from his school. Six or eight of them laughing, pushing, messing around. Then she stepped out of the crowd: Svitlana Kitko.

As if his feet had iced themselves to the ground, he watched her wave good-bye to the others and hurry toward the small park that stretched out in front of his building. Their building. She and her family had moved from Moscow. He had heard the colonel speak of Svitlana's father—a Ukrainian scientist. Her mother, full Russian. Pretty light brown curls bounced along the frame of her face, the rest crushed by a cap to ward off the cold. As she stepped onto the sidewalk, their eyes met.

The sun stabbed into the gloominess.

She waved. "*Privet*, Nikol."

His heart stuttered as she said hi. But his mind whirled—*she knows my name*. Of course she knew his name. Everyone did. It was why they walked on that side and he on this one. No, the greater surprise was that she had actually spoken to him. He'd heard the others, especially Matvei Ilyich, tell her to stay away from him, that he was as mean and violent as the colonel. They were right—she should stay away.

But there she was. Boots up to her calves. A thick white coat with a fur-trimmed hood. And that smile. That beautiful smile. He wanted to

492

wave. To smile. Anything to let her know he thought she was the most beautiful girl in all Russia.

He gauged the distance, the angles. They were too close. The colonel could see them if he had come home early. Although he almost never did that, Nikol wouldn't take the risk.

Letting her go inside without acknowledging her presence was rude. He gave her a nod.

She turned from her path at his nod.

He could not let her know the effect she had on him.

"Kak dela?" Hands stuffed in her pockets, she smiled up at him. Her eyes were blue. So pretty. Like the blue of a summer sky. When it was warm.

How was he? Stinking miserable. *"Harosho."* Saying he was fine usually ended the conversation. That was what he needed. They were exposed. He could be seen. It would not go well.

"Fine?" She wrinkled her nose and looked around. "How can anyone on Nevsky Prospekt be fine?" Her laughter could be the flowers in a field on that summer day. He wanted summer. Very much. But it was winter. It was always winter in Russia.

"Then why did you move here?" He should not have asked that. "Never mind. It is not my concern."

"It is okay. My father got this amazing job," she said, sarcasm thick.

"Then you are sad to be here." He started walking. Toward the building. The closer they stood to it, the less likely the colonel could see them.

"I was." She scuffed her boots against the snow. "I had friends in Moscow. I wanted to attend university there."

"You still can."

She smiled up at him again. "Perhaps."

Warmth speared his chest.

"But I am not sad anymore."

"Really?" Everyone was sad, were they not? Really, when they got down to it, what was there to be happy about? He wanted to be happy. But it was just a ruse that got him in trouble.

"Yes."

Snow crunched as they moved toward the building, then along it, leading to the front door.

"Are you not going to ask me why I am happy?" On the first step into their foyer, she turned and faced him. Her cheeks were rosied from the bitter wind. Things awoke in his frozen heart as they stood eye to eye.

Swallowing, Nikol glanced around to make sure they were alone. "Okay." He met her gaze again. "Why are you happy?"

"Because, I met you." She planted her hands on his shoulders, bent forward, and kissed his cheek. With a flutter of a swirl, she turned and hurried into the building. "Do svidaniya!"

Heart pounding, he watched her take the stairs two at a time.

Bitter and strong, an icy wind blew against his sunshine. He flinched, sensing the presence. To his right, a shape loomed closer. His gut clenched as the clouds once again dropped on him and whispered, "Do svidaniya."

Sixteen

Thudding above pulled Cardinal off the wall.

"Sounds like the dog is giving her a good run for her money." Santos smiled.

Calm down, act natural. "Yeah." It did seem like Talon was running. "Sounds like it."

"I think they went on the rooftop. It's good up there. Fresh air. Not much wind, so it is too hot for me."

Having a suspicious nature kept him alive.

It also drove him crazy. And the craziest thought just hit him: *That's my wife up there.* Not in any other sense than on paper. But if he didn't show concern, Santos would question it.

"So, you came all this way to find her brother?"

"Yeah." Cardinal returned to his spot holding up the wall. "Will you tell me what you know?"

"Sure, sure." Santos went to the kitchen, where he pulled bottled waters from the fridge. He offered one to Cardinal. "It's hot."

"I'm good." His gaze swept the home. Two levels—well, three if you counted the rooftop terrace. Plaster painted peach, with tiny flowers scrawling along the upper portion of each wall. "You said it's been two weeks since he was here?"

"I am no good at keeping track of time, but yes, I believe so."

"Why did he stay here?" Cardinal noted the worn furniture, the rickety rocking chair, the pictures that hung crookedly on the wall. The handwoven rug that spread over the entire twenty-by-fifteen living area. Incongruently beautiful in a home with faded, cracking plaster, older furniture. . .

"He was injured."

"But you're not a hospital."

"True, but the beds at Peltier are limited. Camille and I visited there often, to encourage the patients. He. . ." A noise above creaked, and Santos grew quiet. "I hope she is well."

"Yeah, the flight really took it out of her." He peeled off the wall. "I'll go check on her."

On the upper level, he found the rooms empty. He tensed. Then saw a shadow drift across the rooftop terrace steps. He pulled open the glass door and stepped into the late afternoon sun.

Talon lumbered over, nosed his hand, then licked it before returning to Aspen, who stood at a waist-high railing, hands on the plaster, staring out at the Red Sea twinkling in the distance.

"Everything okay?"

A breeze rustled her hair away from her face. Sweat dribbled down her temples—wait. Not sweat. Tears.

"Hey." Cardinal touched her elbow. "What's wrong?"

Her eyes, which he noticed were almost the same blue as the water, met his. "He was here, Dane." Another tear slipped free. "Why would he be *here*? Why didn't he come home?"

Teary depths pulled him in.

She chewed the inside of her lip. Facing the sea again, she went quiet, her chin trembling. "He was here. And recently."

"What'd you see?"

She sniffled through a laugh. "You'll think I'm crazy."

"Hey." He sat on the wall, wedging himself closer between her and the plaster. "I think a lot of things about you, but that is not one of them."

Aspen looked down at him for several heart-thumping minutes then drew in a steadying breath as she once again turned to the sea. "When we were kids, Austin always arranged his room a certain way. I know it sounds insane, but he had this logic to it." She sniffed and shook her head. "I'm his twin and it *never* made sense to me. He always— *always*—put the headboard where the footboard went. And a bookcase near his head." She hunched her shoulders through a laugh. "He was never one for education, but he had this idea that the information would seep into his brain."

"Now, *that* is crazy."

"Yeah." She smiled at him. "But that was Austin. He'd kill me for telling anyone, but that. . .that's how I know he's been here."

"I'm sure he's not the only one who did something like that with the bed."

"True, the real clincher—was Talon. He got a hit."

"Maybe it was a false positive."

She laughed. "It's not a pregnancy test. It's his nose. His partner. His best friend. Talon *knows* Austin. And he *knows* he was in there. He went frantic. The way he whined—" She slapped the wall. "He wouldn't stop whining or sniffing." She turned away, eyes squeezed tight. Her shoulders bounced. "It made me as crazy as whatever he smelled was making Talon crazy. It was like he could smell him but couldn't understand why Austin wasn't there."

She jerked to face him straight on. "Two years, Dane. He's been gone two years."

He slowly stood, knowing he would need to help her find her balance.

"Why would he do this to me? Why would he let me think he's dead? Why would he abandon Talon—" Tears choked her words. "If you could've heard him. . . He wouldn't stop."

Cardinal pulled her into his arms, slamming a lid on the stirrings that erupted when she balled his shirt in her fist and clung tight to him. His pulse went haywire, holding her, comforting her. Not just out of attraction. But out of anger that Austin had hurt her like this.

Her body shook beneath the weight of her pain and tears. "Why? Why would Austin do this? Leave me, be here?" Tears soaking through his shirt, she pressed her forehead against his pecs.

"I don't know." And he truly didn't. Arm around her shoulders bouncing beneath her tears, Cardinal steeled himself. At least, he tried. *I'll drag those answers out of Austin Courtland if it's the last thing I do.*

Somehow, though it shook her to think of it, Aspen stood in Dane's arms. Warm, strong, capable arms. His words rumbled through his chest and poured like steel into her soul, strengthening her courage, infusing her with strength not her own.

She had totally lost it, listening to Talon crying for Austin. Because that's what she'd been doing for two years, hadn't she? Crying for her brother, the one the Marines had written off, declared dead.

Dead men tell no tales.

Well, this dead man would. Because dead men don't live in Djibouti with a missionary.

She looked up at Dane and cringed. "Wow, your eyes are really turning black."

He smirked. "First lovers' quarrel."

The admonishment was on her tongue when she saw Santos peeking at them through the door window. Panic punched her onto her toes. She curled a hand around the back of Dane's neck and tiptoed up. She pressed her lips to his.

Hands on her hips, Dane nudged her back. "What—?"

He'll see or hear us! She kissed him again, this time leaning into it, her mind on the man staring at them. Had to make it believable, right? This was the way they covered their tracks or something.

Dane pushed her away again. "Aspen."

"Santos," she muttered.

Dane snorted a laugh then ate it as he looked to the side.

"He's watching." The heat flared through her face, clutching her in a humiliating grip. "At the door."

"It's okay," he said to Santos and waved him onto the terrace. "Talon got a little excited, and it proved upsetting for them both. She was overcome."

What was he doing? Dismissing her? Confusion and anger coiled around her mind like a vise. How dare he relegate her revelation about Austin to nothing more than a hysterical outburst. Because that's what he was saying, wasn't he?

"I understand," Santos said, smiling. "When my Camille died, the littlest thing would make me hysterical."

"Hysterical." Aspen gulped the fury. Nodded. Great. Fine. They were writing her off as an emotional woman. And Dane. . .

He turned to her. "No, not hysterical. Concerned."

Platitudes. *That* she didn't need. She pushed him aside. "*Don't patronize me. I'm not an idiot.*" She snapped her fingers to call Talon and returned to the room, humiliation her only friend. Down the two steps to the upper level then into the room with the queen bed. Once inside with Talon, she clicked the lock. She shoved back her unruly curls, breathing a hard thing to do at the moment. He was making fun of her.

He pushed her away.

Her belly spasmed as she fought the tears. "He didn't want me."

That's ridiculous.

But it's true.

Arguing with herself only inflamed her shame. Made her feel even more stupid. This was insane. Absurd. This wasn't some romance novel where they played married then fell in love. This was real life. Capitalizing on a situation to get real answers.

But he didn't even seem to want the kiss. Or like it.

And that after they'd nearly kissed back at Lemonnier. Or was that her imagination?

On the terrace, he'd pushed her away. Like a petulant child. Like a silly girl with a crush on the high school senior.

"I don't have a crush!"

"It's good to hear."

Aspen spun, pulse thundering through her veins. "How did you get in? I locked it."

Shaking his head, Dane looked down and closed the door. He slid the bolt along the upper portion of the door then planted himself on a whicker chair in the corner. He sat, bent forward, elbows on his knees.

"What are you doing?" Now she *did* sound petulant. "Never mind." Aspen slumped on the bed and covered her face with her hands. Her head throbbed. So did her feet. And her back. And her pride.

Click.

She lifted her head and found him in front of her, sliding the pen back into his pocket. At this angle, his shoulders seemed broader. His chest bulkier. And his stubble just a shade darker. He had the ruffian thing going on real well.

Curse the man. Why did he have to be so gorgeous?

"Why did you kiss me?"

She tore her gaze from him and looked out the window behind him. "I—I saw Santos watching us. Why didn't you kiss me back?"

Amusement danced in his eyes, making her feel like she was fifteen

499

and had just kissed Tom Stanton, the prom king. "Did you want me to?"

"No!" A stampede thumped through her chest at the lie.

Dane stifled a laugh.

"Isn't that what you people do when others watch?"

His eyebrow winged up. " 'You people'?"

Aspen groaned. "Don't do this to me. I feel stupid enough as it is."

Dane took her hands in his and tugged her to her feet.

She resisted, at war with the way her heart beat like a bass drum at his touch and her determination to be angry with him.

On her feet, she swallowed and mustered a nonchalant stance.

Until his finger tilted her chin up and he frowned. "First, this isn't the movies. We don't have to kiss every time someone sees us alone together."

She tried to look away, but he redirected her gaze with a slight nudge of her chin.

"And let's be absolutely clear about one thing—our. . .*situation* is part of a mission. It's not a carte blanche for me to take advantage of you. I have no interest in crossing that line."

Aspen blinked and stepped out of his reach, still stinging from the words, *"No interest. . ."*

"Of course not." Had she been wrong at Lemonnier when they'd almost kissed? The shock of his words wore off about the time he said something about sleeping on the floor.

Sleep in the desert for all I care.

Why on earth was she so angry?

Because the wound was so familiar. Reminded her of growing up in the shadow of her twin brother. High school quarterback. Voted most popular, most handsome, most annoying—okay, that was her vote, but it counted. Homecoming king—both his junior and senior year, somehow. She was the one with the As, the scholarships to Ivy League colleges. But it was his dismissal of her as being nothing but a brain that drove her to prove him wrong. To join the Air Force instead. Good thing someone paid attention and landed her in the JAG offices, or she'd have been boots-on-ground deployed and possibly killed.

For that reason, despite the cutting words from Dane, she took the words in stride. Well, as much as she could. Why did she ever think she could come here, play spy, and find Austin? Everything in her was crumbling, falling apart. If they hadn't discovered that Austin had lived here, she'd have packed up and gone home already.

Since that wasn't an option, she'd settle for finding her brother. But tonight showed her she was way out of her league, both in the romance department and the military department. She just prayed she didn't get herself killed.

Seventeen

Darkness sneaked into the room, circled the bed that held Aspen, and circled around the wooden legs till it wrapped him in its black tendrils. Sleep evaded him. As it had so many times over far too many years. Arm stretched behind his head and one draped over the yellow Lab, Cardinal focused on the wood floor digging into his shoulder blades. A good, painful reminder of where he'd come from. Where he belonged—in the hard clutches of pain.

Eyes closed to the darkness, he still felt it surround his soul. Longed for a pew and some stained-glass windows. Flickering candles. Peace...

He'd done the right thing with Aspen. Though that look in her blue eyes haunted him even now, it was right. It was better. They'd focus on the mission, track Austin down, and then they'd go their separate ways. He'd never see her again.

He turned onto his side, his back to the bed. Talon shifted behind him with a loud sigh. *You and me both, buddy.*

The wood pressed against his shoulder. He stuffed the pillow beneath his head. Then lifted his head, folded the pillow in half, and jammed his head back down. As he relaxed, the pillow hissed and slid out.

Cardinal grunted, flattened the pillow, and dropped onto his back again. A pew with its too-thin-cushion would be more comfortable!

You'd still have to live with yourself.

He had no problem doing that. He'd done it all his life. His hard life. Which is why he belonged on the hard floor. He spent his life avoiding things that made him soft.

She had soft lips.

Augh! Dane thrust himself off the floor and reached for the door. Behind him, he heard the bed creak and pushed himself out the door, down the hall and stairs to the bathroom. He gripped the stand-alone sink. Arms behind his head, he stood facing the wall, eyes closed.

"Stand straight," the voice boomed. *"Never cower—even when you face punishment."*

He shoved a mental rod down his spine till he stood as tall as the man wielding the punishment. Braced.

Crack!

He flinched as leather met flesh. Scalded his back. The tip of the belt buckle caught him just below his shoulder the next time. Bit off a chunk. Fire tore down his spine. His knee buckled beneath the agony. His palm caught the wall.

But he jerked upright, knowing if he didn't, that one wouldn't count.

Cardinal shook his head to dislodge the stinging memory. Fifteen whips. He'd bled that day with each strike that had mirrored a year of his life.

"It'll make you stronger."

If only it had.

Maybe it was him. He was the failure. Where had he gone wrong? He'd disciplined himself. Had a healthy body. Kept his emotions in check. Even now, he drew into himself, hauled together all those elements that threatened his calm, his focus. He tied them in a virtual ball and lobbed it into the sea beyond the house. He had to.

"You cannot be broken if you don't let it."

He trained his mind on his pulse and coerced it into a slower pattern merely by breathing slower, more intentionally.

But like a needle ripping over a record, his mind jumped tracks.

Aspen.

No. Austin. Finding her brother. Putting the pieces together.

There were no pieces. He was stuck here, on a dead-end—

No.

"Master yourself or you will be mastered."

Frustration smothered him in the small box-of-a-bathroom. Cardinal removed himself to the terrace. Warm, balmy air lured him into the darkness. He removed his shirt, spread his legs shoulder-width apart, bent his knees, and glided through his tai-chi moves. Though he wished for a support bar to pull himself up and do something more strenuous, for tonight he'd settle on this. Bring his mind and body into submission through controlled exercises.

I hurt her.

He hung his head, tried to shrink from the thought. Stretched his neck. Straightened. Changed positions. Yes, he hurt her. She was innocent and a bit on the naive side. Easily pliable for those who went that route. He wouldn't. Neither would he go the other route. Allowing, encouraging, and fostering feelings he could not return.

She was emotionally compromised in this mission. If she did not create a fissure between her affection for her brother and the bald truth that Austin had lied to her, she would end up crushed. As such, he could not encourage any romantic notions. The appearance of a marriage between them served one purpose and one purpose only—to provide a cover while they were there. To hide his real identity. To protect her by having him with her at all times.

Burnett was right to arrange it.

Though Cardinal would use it to end the tepid relationship between him and the American government. They had dragged him along far enough. Once he returned their asset to them, it was time for them to give him the promised head on the silver platter.

His eyes popped open. Cardinal blinked, unmoving as he assessed his surroundings. Where was. . . ? Oh. Rooftop terrace. He'd dropped into one of the chairs, propped his head against the wall, and had fallen asleep. But what. . .

Voices skidded on the blue hues of dawn. Whispers. Fast.

Easing his legs onto the roof, he controlled his body in an extreme fashion. He scooted onto the edge of the chair, concealed and listening.

Santos could be heard. But somehow, the other voice proved too quiet to discern.

"I didn't tell them anything." Santos sounded frustrated.

A pause. At least thirty to forty-five seconds long. Water lapped. Inside and behind him, Cardinal heard quiet movement—Aspen and Talon, no doubt.

"Why would they bring the Army? She's merely looking for her brother."

Something about this conversation bugged him. To hear Santos, who spoke just below a normal voice at dawn. . .

Cardinal stood and casually walked to the edge. Looked around, as if he'd stepped out here just now, and glanced down. Santos stood near the back corner that abutted an abandoned shop talking with another man. Shadows deep and long concealed the man.

"Good morning," Cardinal called as he raised a hand.

Santos's gasp could probably be heard at Lemonnier. For show: "Ah, Mr. Markoski. You are up early."

"Guess jet lag is getting the best of me."

"Indeed. Are you hungry?"

"Starving." The shadows hadn't changed, and nobody flitted away in haste.

"I will put breakfast on right away." Santos vanished into the home.

Alone with the early morning, the lightening sky, and the stranger in the shadows, Cardinal perched on the hand-wide half wall, his gaze directed at the sea. Waiting for a sight of whoever found it necessary to be scampering around in the predawn hours to talk with a missionary.

The sun rose, and with it the shadows faded.

Laughter billowed from the house. Aspen's laugh. Talon's bark.

But strangest of all—nobody stood in the shadow.

Hustling back toward the house with Talon's lead firmly in her left hand, Aspen rounded a corner. A shape slipped past her. Aspen's heart rammed into her throat. She sucked in a breath. "Oh."

Talon tensed. Locked on to the stranger. Growled.

The other person gasped—a light, feminine one.

"Talon, out!" Aspen knew the tension she felt radiated down the lead and back up again between them both. "Heel! Sit!"

Surprisingly, he obeyed, returning to her side and sitting.

The slight figure darted around them, head ducked.

"Good boy, good boy," Aspen said, her heart still thundering from the encounter as she rubbed his head.

But. . .a woman? Out here at this hour?

Aspen glanced down the road. Rubble half-giants cowered beneath the rising sun. Scattered trees. Older cars. Dead cars. Men in trucks. But no woman.

After her fallout with Dane last night and then this creepy encounter this morning, she was ready to get answers and get back home. Talon looked up at her, those brown eyes asking if she was over the fright yet.

"C'mon, boy." She hurried back inside and found Santos in the kitchen. His smile wavered as he glanced toward the front then back to her. "You are both early risers."

"Both?" Her eyes betrayed her and drifted to the small hall.

"Yes, he just went in to shower." Santos nodded toward her. "Your hair is wet."

"Yeah, I showered before I took Talon for a walk."

"A walk." Nerves bounced in his face. "You should take someone with you next time. It's not so safe as one might expect. Especially not for a pretty woman like you." He turned back to the stove.

"Eggs?" she asked, trying to shift the awkwardness from the room.

"Yes. A local woman brings them to me from her chickens."

"Oh." She sat on the small sofa near the kitchen. "I think I bumped into her in the courtyard."

Clank! Thunk!

She looked over at him.

"Dropped the spoon," he said with a chuckle. He washed it then resumed cooking. "I hope this breakfast does not disappoint. Dane said you both had a long day planned, so I hope it holds you over."

"I'm sure it will." Why was he so jittery? She made her way back to the kitchen. "Can I help? Set the table maybe?"

"Oh, yes. I'm afraid we do not have much, but it is enough for the three of us."

After getting direction on where things were stored, Aspen set the table with mismatched plates, two forks, and a spoon. "How long have you been here in Djibouti?"

"Seven years." Santos worked a big cast-iron skillet, teeming with eggs, on the tiny stove.

"That's a long time for mission work." And not many dishes. Not even enough for a couple to sit down and eat with knives and forks.

"When you believe in what you're doing, time holds no boundaries."

Interesting philosophy. It'd be even more interesting if the man believed what he'd said. At least, she didn't think he did. There was no resolution in those words. "My parents sent me on a mission trip when

I was a senior. I went to Nepal. I fell in love with it, but I am so over eating half-cooked meat." She shuddered at the memory. "Okay, just need glasses." Hands on her hips, she turned—and froze.

Dane entered. "Smells wonderful." He'd shaved. Hair wet, it made his skin seem darker and his appearance more rugged.

Crazy thought.

"Glasses are in the cabinet there." Santos nodded to a narrow cupboard that hung a little crookedly and whose door sat off-center.

"Great." Aspen shifted her attention toward setting the table, toward feeling useful instead of like a decoration.

"We'll need to eat quickly. We're behind schedule."

We are? The thought lodged at the back of her throat, forbidden from escaping lest she undermine whatever Dane was up to. As far as she knew, there was no schedule other than to work the area, talking to locals and trying to find a scent Talon could track. With his million-receptor nose, he could track a scent that was weeks old. A fact she still grappled to believe.

"I was talking with Mr. Santos about his mission work." Aspen tucked herself in at the table, her back to the wall.

"Yeah?" Dane joined her, extending a hand toward Talon.

Aspen snapped a flat palm at him and shook her head. Unless he wanted to lose it, he'd better remember Talon wasn't a pet.

Dane gave a subtle nod and kept the conversation going. "What denomination are you? I didn't notice crucifixes in the rooms."

"None," Santos said quickly as he served them. "I mean—nondenominational. The focus here is to share God's love. Not religious mandates."

Aspen frowned. Was there as much venom in his words as butter on the eggs he heaped onto her plate? She eyed Dane over the table.

He dug into the eggs and let out a moan. "Wonderful. Thank you."

"It is a pleasure to cook for someone besides myself," Santos said as he started cleaning up. "Oh, I will be going out to a village later today. Some are coming down with sickness. I want to see what I can do."

"No problem. We'll be gone all day." He stuffed down the last of the eggs then took a sip of water and nodded to her. "Ready?"

Aspen ate a few bites, but the heavy butter and protein meal weighted her stomach. "Yeah."

RONIE KENDIG

"You did not finish," Santos objected.

"I'm sorry. I've always eaten like a mouse."

"Here in Djibouti, you will regret that. Drink like an elephant and eat like one. The heat will fry you if you don't."

"Thanks for the warning." Dane stood and held out a hand to her.

Right. Hold his hand. Because he wasn't interested.

Two could play at that game.

Aspen picked up Talon's lead and linked up. "Ready, boy?" Talon stood, tongue out and panting, as he flicked his tail. Keeping the lead slack so there was no tension like they'd shared earlier, she led him past Dane. "Bye, Mr. Santos."

The man nodded with a distant look.

Out in the sun, Dane slipped on a ball cap and started walking. Fast. Aspen had to double-time it to keep up. Down one street. Up another. Past a cluster of women walking with children.

Aspen smiled at a small child, maybe three or four years old, who stared back at her with wide, expressive eyes. So did the mothers. No doubt her fair skin and platinum hair stood out here. Though she expected Dane to try to talk to them, he didn't.

"Aren't we supposed to be talking to people?"

He kept walking. "Quiet."

Petulant now? Disappointment saturated her mood. She kept up, sweat trickling down her back and temples. It wasn't even noon and Djibouti felt like a sauna. Though Talon kept pace, even he seemed to be struggling in the heat.

About to protest his careless regard for them, she bit her tongue as he stepped into a building. She skidded and followed him in.

Darkness blanketed her. From behind, a hand clamped over her mouth.

Eighteen

Djibouti City, Djibouti

Eluding the National Army was one thing. Deceiving guerillas tough, but they'd managed. Escaping a tracking dog. . .

Hands on the table, Neil glanced at Lina in the old warehouse they'd taken shelter from the heat in. They'd survived two days without tipping off anyone. It'd been good. Reassuring. But the information—*augh!* What good did it do to have proof when he had nobody to show it to?

Lina folded her arms. She'd been impatient with him the last twenty-four hours. He couldn't blame her though. Not exactly ideal circumstances. "What are we going to do?"

"We go on."

Her blue eyes widened against her beautiful olive skin. "Go on?" She took a step forward, her hand on her stomach. "But they'll find us. I ran *right* into her. What if—?"

"No ifs. They won't. We won't let them."

"This isn't a small army we're talking about, Neil. The Americans are the best, the most highly trained." Her long black hair hung over her shoulders. "If we don't get out of here now, we'll never make it."

"Do you think I'm so weak I can't make this work?"

She came to him and held his arm. "No, I just don't want to lose you. Or die trying to get this information to the right people. It's not worth it."

He thrust his hands up, tossing off her grip. "Don't you get it? That's

509

just it!" He paced the abandoned warehouse. Dust bobbed on thin beams of light that poked through the slots and holes in the walls. So numerous, it reminded him of one of those orbs that cast constellations on ceilings. "If we don't finish this, if we don't make good—we're dead. Whether we're here or somewhere else, they will find us."

"Maybe they won't."

He fisted both hands and thumped them against his forehead. "How can you be so brilliant and so stupid at the same time?"

She drew back, her face awash with his crushing words.

He hated the way she looked at him, with that complete look of trust, believing he could do anything, including taking on world powers and dark, dangerous undergrounds. He'd stepped into a trap of a situation and had been fighting and on the run since. But how. . . *how* did they keep finding him? He hadn't been tagged, the way some operatives were. He'd been too new. His mentor told him to avoid it at all costs. Best advice he'd been given.

"Wait. . .make good?"

Neil wanted to curse himself.

"Make good on what?"

"Nothing. Let's just. . ."

That dog. . .that incredible, stupid dog. As long as they were in town, he'd be found. That had to be how they kept spotting him. Tracking him. Okay, that explained the Americans, but what about the other authorities? It didn't make sense.

What if he could eliminate the threat? Killing the dog nauseated him. But it was either the Lab or him.

"I need to put something into play." His mind whirred with the idea. "We'll hole up in one of the abandoned buildings. I think. . .I think I know how to get that handler off my scent."

It seemed there was only one way out: death.

But it wouldn't be his death. Or Lina's.

It'd be theirs. Starting with that dog.

A low rumble erupted into a snapping bark.

Cardinal's gut clinched. Talon had gone primal on Watterboy, who had a hand clamped around Aspen's mouth. Hackles raised, the dog lowered his front end—he'd pounce any second.

"Release her—the dog!" Cardinal shouted.

The danger must've registered because Watterboy released her and stepped back.

"Talon, out! Out!" Short of breath and a little pale, Aspen straightened her T-shirt as she let Talon sniff her hand. She met Cardinal's gaze and gave a short nod. "Thanks."

"That was some kind of muffed up. . . ," a lanky soldier said, his M4 propped over his chest, one hand on the butt. "That dog was going to take a chunk out of your—"

"Hey," Candyman slapped the guy in the gut, "watch your language."

"No harm intended." Watterboy shot an apologetic look at Aspen. "I was afraid you'd cry out. We didn't need that kind of attention."

Something twisted sideways in Cardinal when Watterboy manhandled Aspen into submission in the darkened building. The soldier whispered something to her, she nodded, then he released her. Also dressed in camo and a flak vest, Timbrel went to her friend.

But Cardinal saw the disquiet clouding Aspen's face. Saw the confusion that still clung to her. "Give her room," he said, feeling a surge of protectiveness. "Let her get her bearings." He touched her arm. "You okay?"

She swallowed and gave him a quick nod. "Surprised me, that's all."

"I couldn't warn you. When I spotted the signal, we were in the open. You did good." Cardinal turned to the captain. "What've you got?"

He waved a hand as he and five others headed to the rear and climbed a flight of stairs. "Burnett contacted and said things are still a go. But he said to be on our guard."

"About?" Cardinal hustled up the stairs pocked with bullet holes and peeling plaster. He rounded the rail, glancing down to the floor below. Hogan filled Aspen in on mundane things.

"Your missionary, Courtland, and this." Palms spread and arms stretched over the table that took up one side of a large open room, Watterboy stared up through his brow.

A political map of the area bore *X*s and a few circles. In his quick purview, Cardinal knew things were heating up. What worried him was the squiggly line separating Djibouti from Somalia. It'd been marked up with numbers and a series of hyphenated digits. Lat-long indicators.

"What's happening here?" He looked at Watterboy.

"That's what we're trying to figure out. There's been a buildup of fighters in recent months. DIA intercepted a phone conversation. . ." Droning on about the intelligence reports, Watterboy planted his hands on his belt. "But right now, Burnett wants us out here." He pressed his fingertip to a barren area about two klicks out.

"What's there?" Her voice had lost its quiver as Aspen came and stood beside him.

"It's a village. On familiar terms with your dear missionary friend."

"Why are we going there?" Aspen asked.

"Because," Watterboy said as he tugged out some photos from a manila envelope that sat beneath the map and spread them out, "UAV snapped these about two nights ago."

Leaning forward, Cardinal sorted through the photos from the unmanned aerial vehicle. Arranged them in an order that seemed to portray the layout of the village. A truck. Two men. A dozen villages. "Armed." That wasn't good. Not unusual in these parts where you negotiated a cup of goat's milk with an AK-47 on your back.

"DIA is working to ID the two men. The truck is driven by Somalis. We believe they're the same pirates who hijacked a shipping barge last week."

Cardinal met Watterboy's gaze. "And what was on that barge?"

"Weapons. Hundreds of them."

"Why would anyone be shipping weapons?"

"That's what we're going to find out." Watterboy grinned, his hazel eyes gleaming. "Right after we destroy the weapons."

"How's the honeymoon?" Candyman needed to be punched.

Aspen shifted. "So, we're headed to the village?"

"Roger," Watterboy said. "We're going to rendezvous with a medical detachment from Lemonnier and go in under the ruse of a welfare visit. They'll have a couple of nurses and doctors pass out goodies and deliver much-needed meds. Our contact there is Souleiman Hamadou, a Somali sultan—or at least he thinks he is. Most of the village sultans are overruled by the Djiboutian government, but out in the desert—"

"Out of sight, out of mind?" Having spent a little time there before things went south, Cardinal held a haunting awareness of the poverty that gripped the land.

"Pretty much." Watterboy shifted around, grabbed two bags, and tossed them over the table. "Suit up. We bug out in fifteen."

ACUs and body armor waited in the kit bag. "Weapons?"

Candyman shot another grin at him. "Right here." He pointed to a long box.

"Here, you can have some privacy in this room," Timbrel said to Aspen, and they headed off.

Waiting till he heard a door shut or their voices faded enough, he turned to Watterboy. "What aren't you telling me?"

The seasoned combat veteran betrayed nothing with his face or body language.

Muscles tightening, Cardinal eased closer. "Let me be painfully clear with you gentlemen. Nobody cares more about this mission than me."

"Aspen might disagree."

"If she knew what I did, no, she wouldn't." Lips tight, he glared at them. "If I so much as get a whiff that you're going to stiff me—"

"This isn't about stiffing you." Watterboy tucked his helmet on. "And the clock is ticking. We pull out with or without you. This is a favor, briefing you. Take it or leave it."

Cardinal ripped off his shirt, stuffed it in the bag, and lifted out the brown T-shirt. Threading his arms through it, he vowed to make sure he never let his guard down from now on.

A whistle carried through the battered room. "Those're some scars."

Ignoring Candyman, Cardinal slipped on the ACU jacket and body-armor vest. He strapped himself up with the knee and elbow guards.

"You do that like you know them."

Were they complete idiots? Or hadn't they read his files? No. . . they were just needling him. They knew very well he spent months in Afghanistan with Courtland. He may not have been career, his stint in the line of combat—officially—might have been short, but he was no stranger to playing this role. And part of that role meant knowing how.

Shirt tucked, he ran a hand through his hair and pivoted to ODA452, who were so tense, so alert to his every move, it was a wonder someone didn't accidentally shoot him. "Weapons."

"For your leg holster." Watterboy handed over a Glock. Then he passed an M4A1 and a mic/earpiece.

Tucking the piece in, he heard Talon returning.

Aspen came around the corner, adjusted her vest as she muttered something to Timbrel. The ring sparked on a beam of light.

"Take off the ring," Cardinal said. "You'll be a hot target with that."

"And without it, you'll be a hot target for every unsuspecting male." Timbrel glared at Candyman.

"Hey, I'm not unsuspecting."

Aspen tugged off the ring, slipped it into a pocket, and then her gaze lingered. . .on him. Traveled down his frame then back to his face. "You have weapons."

"So will you."

"Only a Glock," she said as she turned to Watterboy. "I can't handle anything bigger when I have Talon on lead, and I assume that's part of why we're going—so Talon can track. But you do know, he's not trained for explosives or weapons."

"That'd be Beo." Timbrel winked.

"Understood. No worries. Burnett wants you on-site, you're on-site." She had found her courage. And her groove.

And he liked it. "We should go."

At times, Dane stood like an impenetrable fortress. That was 98 percent of the time. The other 2 percent, she saw. . .something. Not quite vulnerability. The thought made her want to laugh. That man, vulnerable? Not in a million years. Scared? Of what? She had this feeling he could take care of himself—and anyone else who messed with him. And that whole thing when he'd intercepted the situation before Talon took a chunk out of Watters's arm or throat—brilliant. It made her heart swell because he'd been attuned to her, to Talon. Few had ever gotten to that place. It'd taken her months to get there with Talon as his handler.

"Let's do it." Watters pointed to two men. "Java, Pops, stay here with coms and maintain contact with base. Watch that feed from Aerial Two. We've got air support ready just in case."

Heart in her throat, Aspen realized this could be her first real op. And her last.

She fell into step behind Timbrel, the captain, and Candyman as they scurried down the stairs. Rock and dust dribbled around them as they moved. Behind her, she heard Cardinal and the other two members of the team—Rocket and Scrip—bringing up the rear. They buttonhooked out of the stairwell and hurried to a rear room.

Two beat-up Jeeps waited.

The doors flung open. Aspen held out her arm and showed her palm to Talon. "Talon, hup! Hup!" He leapt into the back, then she guided him over the seat into the rear.

"Hey."

The voice, so deep and masculine, drew her around. Cardinal stood close.

"Listen," he said, craning down, "don't trust your eyes out there."

She frowned. "Don't. . .what?"

"Trust your instincts"—he nodded to the rear—"and that trained warrior. Understood?"

Okay. Sure. That sounded good, but. . ."Why?"

"Because eyes are deceiving."

"Let's move!" Watters's bark carried across the makeshift garage.

They left through the rear of the building and jounced onto a side road that pushed through two buildings in a narrow alley. *Just breathe. Things are fine.* Even if she was sitting in a Jeep in Djibouti with a team of trained warriors and a man who was, legally, her husband.

Dane leaned forward, a hand clutching the seat. "How many in this village?"

"At least fifty, sixty skinnies," Watterboy called over his shoulder. The open window made the keffiyeh around his neck flap like crazy.

They talked up numbers and locals and warlords and terrorists.

Aspen's ears were going numb, and her back, thanks to the Kevlar vest, felt like a warming plate for hamburgers. With each jolt on the axles from the pothole-riddled roads, Aspen felt the heat rubbing her shoulder raw where the vest met flesh.

With the heat at 105, she would have to closely monitor Talon. She glanced back to him and found him panting. Thankfully, Timbrel had known to bring water for Talon. The others seemed oblivious to the needs of the working dog. They wanted him to work yet didn't know how to properly prep for the op. She dug a bottle of water out of the kit bag and reached over the seat. She uncapped it and drizzled some into his mouth. He smiled at her, his eyes nearly squeezed shut in thanks, then returned to panting.

Easing back into the seat, she tossed the empty bottle in the bag and sat back. Dane was still talking, laughing. He had the beginnings of laugh lines around his eyes. She'd noticed that the first time they met. It'd made her like him, like his smile. It was that, somehow, that told her she didn't have to fear him, even though there were times so unnerving she wanted to run away.

He'd been all business this morning and, well, even last night, when she'd made a fool out of herself. He hadn't exactly laughed at her, but it was close. *"Not interested."*

Why?

That was a stupid question. Aspen pushed her gaze out the window, watching the heartbreaking poverty as it slid by. And wasn't that just the way the world worked? People were starving here, dying of diseases easily cured in America, and the world just slid right on by. She'd known there were places like this, but being here, seeing it, experiencing it firsthand. . .she really had no clue how bad things could be for a people.

Was Austin out there somewhere? Walking among them? Did anyone know him? He'd stand out. Granted, there was a hefty French population, since this had been one of their territories, but Caucasians were still the minority here. As were Christians.

Laughter drew her attention back.

Dane slapped Candyman's shoulder. Something akin to jealousy squirmed through her stomach. She wasn't jealous of Candyman. That'd be crazy. But that he got Dane to laugh. . .a real laugh, a nice laugh, with his slightly chiseled jaw and that dark dusting of stubble. . .

"But this man? Is fine. *With a capital* F.*"*

Aspen tucked her chin as Brittain's words slipped through the hot Djibouti sun and straight into her heart. Yeah, her friend had been right. He was fine, though the word Aspen would've chosen started with an *h—hunky—*or a *g—gorgeous.*

"I'm not interested. . ." His words resounded like a gong against her pining.

Aspen pushed straight in the seat and shoved off the silliness. The Jeep jounced as it turned onto a strip of dirt that had ruts instead of lane markers. Nausea swirled as she saw the conditions—homes built with corrugated boxes, lean-tos draped with fabric and wobbly steel. That had to be hot during the day. But it'd provide shelter at night.

Beside her came a small whoosh, drawing her attention to the side.

Blue eyes made her stomach squirm. A grim expression stole through his normally stoic face. "This is one experience that never fades, no matter how long you're gone or how many times you see it."

Humanitarian, too? Aspen eyed him. With the headgear and camos, his features seemed amplified, stronger. And natural. "How long were you in the Army?"

"Not long enough." He winked. "And too long on the other hand."

The Jeep slowed and pulled to the side of the road.

Aspen peered through the front windshield as another vehicle bounded ahead. Only when she saw the uniforms did she remember Watterboy had said they were going in as a welfare mission—and that vehicle must have the medical staff.

A few more minutes delivered them into a village of four, maybe five huts, but dozens of people. Skin darkened by the sun and glistening with sweat, they were vibrant in their multicolored garb. Beyond the front bumper a cluster of Djiboutians stood with a handful of soldiers. "National Army?" But the vast majority of the soldiers were white.

Dane leaned forward. Said something to Watters she couldn't hear, then climbed out of the truck. "Stay," he said in a sharp tone.

"Bravo, Nightingale One this is Alpha One," Watters spoke into his coms. "Contact with French Army. Unknown intentions. Hold position." With that, Watters stepped into the heat. His body still protected by the armored door, he rested his hand on his leg-holstered Glock.

Talon shifted up, his head appearing over the seat as he panted almost in her ear. "What's wrong?"

"They're French." The snarl in Candyman's words made her hesitate.

"That's bad...why?"

"Don't you find the fact they're here when we show up a mighty big coincidence?" He huffed. "This stinks. Get ready to fight."

Nineteen

If it smelled like a trap and looked like a trap. . .

Fingers itching for the weapon holstered at his leg, Cardinal took in the scene. Though twenty or more villagers huddled in the background, it was the fear on their faces that warned him. Cardinal stood in front of the Jeep, praying he shielded Aspen from view. He wanted her presence made known when he deemed it safe. He scanned the foreign nationals. Next to the captain stood a man with no rank. Interesting.

"Hello." Watters said, as he came to the front. "Is there a problem here, Captain?" He seemed as tense as Cardinal felt. Scanning, checking, assessing—just like a good Special Forces soldier.

"No problem," came the slick-accented reply. "We are visiting the villages."

"Fancy that." Watters brought his gaze to the captain. "So are we." He waved to the secondary vehicle. Doors opened. Dirt crunched beneath boots. "Our doctors are here on a welfare check and visit."

"The generosity of the Americans is astounding." The captain shifted to the man on his right. *"As tu obtenu ce que tu voulais?"*

Mentally, Cardinal went on alert. Physically, he kept his posture detached, curious. Hand on his weapon, the other on his hip, he waited for the response from the one who stood a few inches shorter.

Only a quick nod served as the man's reply.

"Il semble que tes craintes n'étaient pas fondées. Ils sont aussi aveugles qu'ils sont stupides. Très bien. Je vous laisse à votre mission de miséricorde, les Américains."

Blind as we are stupid? And what unfounded fears are they hiding? But he had to play it cool. Play it off. With a quick look to Watters, who shrugged, Cardinal cocked his head. "Come again?" he asked.

The captain held his gaze for a few seconds longer than was necessary. "Forgive me."

Cardinal would if the request had been sincere.

"I forget myself." The captain didn't lie well. "We were just leaving. Enjoy your day, and stay hydrated." With that he waved to the men, who hustled toward a truck. The French soldiers climbed into the back.

At least, he heard them doing that. But Cardinal honed in on the captain's little minion, who ducked his head and looked into the Jeep.

Adrenaline buzzed through Cardinal's veins.

Barking erupted. The Jeep rocked. Inside, he heard Aspen giving commands to Talon, who whimpered, turned a circle, barked once more, then obeyed the command, but tension rippled through the Lab's coat.

Aspen turned back to Cardinal, and their gazes locked. He went to the door and crouched. "What happened?"

"I have no idea. That soldier looked in here, and Talon just came unglued." She swallowed, her cheeks flushed by the heat. "What did they say? Talon must've smelled or noticed something—were they aggressive?"

The rattle of a diesel clapped out conversation. Cardinal watched as the French made their hasty exit. Just like the French, though—quick to leave. "No, but that's the problem."

"We clear?" Watters called.

Looking over the top of the Jeep, Cardinal hesitated. The French wouldn't have hung around if they had rigged something. Wouldn't have let their faces be seen when an IED along the road would've taken out the Americans in a cleaner, hands-off situation. But something large and unsettling wafted on the hot winds. "Let's get this done and get out of here."

"So, it's safe?"

"It's never safe." The French were talking about something, and the stiff-necked response of the minion bothered him. And the words the captain spoke—something was off. But they had a job to do, and they'd better get under way.

He stalked to the rear of the Jeep and reached for the handle.

"No!" Aspen leapt out of the vehicle. "Please, don't open that. Talon might take it as an aggressive move." She brushed a curl from her face. "Sorry. I just don't want him to make strange or attack you."

Cardinal sniffed. "Neither do I." He stepped back and lifted his hands. "He's all yours."

"Nightingale, you have the all clear. ODA452, circle up."

Cardinal strode toward the much-shorter villager, the man who must be the sultan by the way the others deferred and hung back—and ironically, the way the bodies of the villagers were angled toward him. "You are Sultan Souleiman?"

Wire-rimmed glasses framed a weathered, sun-darkened face. He stood a little straighter with the acknowledgment. "I am. You are Mr. Dane?"

"It is an honor." Cardinal inclined his head to offer his submission to the man's position within the community. When he looked up, the sultan's eyes were wide and focused on something behind Cardinal. He glanced back.

Aspen. With Talon, who darted back and forth on the sixteen-foot lead, sniffing. Hauling in big, hard breaths through his nose. What had he hit on? He traced the path from the children—who squealed and jumped back but then burst into laughter when Talon nosed their legs—back toward Cardinal.

He shot a questioning look to Aspen, who shrugged.

A slew of Arabic flew from the sultan.

And that's when it hit Cardinal.

He needed to bridge this gap now. "Sultan Souleiman, this is Lieutenant Courtland. The dog is a working dog named Talon." Again, Cardinal inclined his head. "I hope his presence will not be offensive to you."

"They are not clean." He seemed aghast that they'd brought this animal into his village.

"Please, Sultan, do not be concerned. The dog will stay with his handler. Nobody should touch him. He's trained to protect the woman with his lead." *As am I.* Cardinal pointed to the village, away from Aspen. "Ready?"

With one last concerned glance to Aspen, or more specifically, Talon, Sultan Souleiman shifted around and headed toward a hut. It did not surprise Cardinal that the sultan of this village wasn't even old enough to be his own father. With the median age of twenty-two, most males had a life expectancy of only sixty or sixty-five. And of the entire population in Djibouti, only 3 percent were of that age. Daunting and haunting to know you wouldn't live long.

"Stay close," Cardinal said to Aspen. As the words sailed out of his mouth, he stiffened, praying she didn't take them wrong.

"She's not a dog that obeys your commands," Timbrel said.

"You're right. She's a smart woman who wants to stay alive." He glanced back, so proud of her unwavering resolve and grit-determination. "Ready?"

Aspen gave a nod. "I think he has a hit, but on what, I have no idea."

"Think it's your brother?"

"Out here?" The question wasn't one of information but one of confirmation. She'd thought the same thing and wanted him to confirm it.

"Keep your eyes out. You never know."

"Roger."

Already, the gaggle of children had crowded in around Aspen and Talon. She'd have her hands full keeping them away. Maybe he should offer. . .

"Talon, heel! Sit! Stay!"

The Lab trotted to her side, sat, and squinted up at her as if to say, "Yeah, okay, it's hot out here and I can smell something, but you're cute so I'll sit."

Cardinal felt a smirk tug up the side of his face. She'd read his mind. In that case, time to divert the sultan's attention. "It's so good of you to talk with me, Sultan." He pointed to a shady spot beneath the only two trees he'd seen for miles. No doubt the reason the nomadic villagers had set down stakes here. "Perhaps we could sit here and talk?"

The sultan lifted his chin a little higher. "Good, good."

As they walked, the sultan spoke of the poverty, of the search for jobs, of battling the refugees, and the effect not having rain had on the villagers. For a second, Cardinal worried about leaving Aspen alone. But when he glanced back and spotted the Lab with her—and Timbrel behind them—his fears were allayed. Talon would maul anyone who tried to hurt Aspen, and Timbrel would finish them off.

"He's dehydrated."

"I'll grab the water." Timbrel jogged off.

Whimpering, Talon panted and paced, his tail flicking, but Aspen kept a tight lead on him to keep him in the shade and from wearing himself out. "Talon, heel. Sit. Stay."

He complied, his belly jiggling in and out rapidly beneath the frenetic panting. She glanced back to the vehicles. Timbrel and Candyman were digging through a bag, searching. He must've made some comment because Timbrel shoved him. He grabbed the edge of the vehicle to catch himself. She was sure a smile hid beneath that gnarly beard.

Whimpering tugged her attention back to her partner. She smoothed a hand over his coat. "Easy, boy."

Talon had all the earmarks of dehydration or heat exhaustion. Jibril's sister, Khaterah, had warned her to watch for it.

Still whimpering, Talon lowered himself to the ground and lay on his side. His panting was ramping up. She checked his gums and cringed. Losing pigmentation. "C'mon," she called to Timbrel.

"Here, here." Timmy dropped the bottles.

Once she uncapped the bottle, Aspen doused Talon with the water, coaxing the liquid into his dense fur. Dogs only sweat through their bellies and the pads of their feet, which was why in this heat, she had avoided using the protective paw covers, though with the raw pad of his right foot, she feared they might have to use them.

They tugged out a collapsible waterproof nylon bowl and filled it so Talon could lap up the water. "It's okay, Talon. You're going to be fine." He fed off her emotions, so she worked to stay calm and confident— two things she wasn't feeling right now. As he drank, she doused him again. "It's too hot."

"I'd turn down the heat, but it seems the man upstairs likes it hot here." Candyman stood over them, his headgear, keffiyeh, and vest making him look forbidding. When he spoke she wasn't sure whether to laugh or what. She'd seen him in Afghanistan and the guy had been as cool and at ease as if he were back home at a barbecue—just like today.

Aspen poured another bottle over Talon and noted, with pleasure, that his panting had grown a little more regular and had slowed. "I knew you'd reset, buddy." She rubbed the spot between his eyes, and he slumped back, totally relaxed.

"Here they come," Candyman said.

Aspen swiped the sweat from her forehead as she looked toward the huts.

A group emerged with the sultan explaining something to Dane. The two had talked for more than thirty minutes beneath the shade of these trees. With one leg drawn close and the other hooked, Dane had seemed so at home. Was there anywhere he didn't manage to fit in? Fresh waves of respect and admiration sluiced through her. And, of course, the younger, unmarried women—at least she hoped they were unmarried, or maybe it would be better if they were married—trailed Dane like lovesick puppies.

His gaze slid across the open area and rammed right into hers. She felt it. All the way in the pit of her belly. She looked away and focused back on Talon, who stood on all fours now, as if to say, "Okay, I'm done with this heat stuff. Let's get outta Dodge."

Then he lifted his head and drew in a couple of big sniffs. More whimpering ensued. Talon trailed back and forth between the trees. Sniffing, whimpering, trotting. Blood blotted the sand.

She winced.

"Aspen, his paws."

"Get the protective booties."

Shouts and a loud bang exploded from somewhere.

Talon yelped and tore off.

Aspen held the lead, but it ripped out of her hands. "Talon, heel! Heel!"

He slowed, turned a circle, then scampered under the Jeep.

Disappointment and concern flooded Aspen. She trudged over to the truck, her head pounding from the stress of tending Talon and the unrelenting heat. Sweat streamed down her face and back as she went to her knees.

A soft touch on her arm. "You okay?" Dane asked.

"Yeah." Who was she kidding? "No. I don't know." Did she sound as psychotic as she felt? She gave a soft snort and wiped her forehead again. "Talon's been on edge for the last thirty minutes, whimpering. He got dehydrated, but I think it's under control. But now he's whimpering again, then that noise—" She stopped short. "What was it?"

"A couple of kids horsing around crashed into one of the metal walls."

"Oh." And the poor dog had lost his courage. So did she, knowing Talon still wasn't ready. It broke her heart. Tugged at her. Like that mother standing with the sultan beneath the shade tree now, with an infant strapped to her breast with a scarf-like sling, and another in another sling dangling against her hip. She held tiny little fingers of an older child. Three children. All skin and bones. All looking hungry, sad. Just like Talon.

Just like me.

Dane's hand rested on her shoulder. "Aspen?"

The tears were coming. She could feel them. Pushed them back. "It's all. . .wrong." Her eyes burned.

"Hey." Dane's hand slid to her neck, and he nudged her chin up with his thumb. "Aspen."

She shook her head, refusing to meet his gaze.

"Hey." He waited for her this time, but as soon as she looked into the eyes of iron, the squirming tangled up her stomach again. "It's good—good that you're feeling this way. It means it's changing you, that you won't forget. The worst thing we can do is walk out of here and forget."

She loved that he didn't want to forget, that the world around them impacted him. But more than those concerns plied at her. "It's not just that—Talon's not ready. If he can't even tolerate loud noises, how on earth can he find Austin? And the heat is getting to him, and he's injured his paw, so he has to rest for days if not a week, and—"

"Whoa."

She looked up at him and once again shook her head. "Why did I think I could do this? He was Austin's partner. His superior. They were inseparable. What am I doing out here?"

"Getting answers." Dane lowered his head and peered into her eyes. "Let's get him out from under there and get back to Lemonnier. We'll debrief."

Yanked out of her emotional collapse, she widened her eyes. "What'd you find out?"

He smirked. "A few things." He patted her shoulder. "C'mon. Let's get Talon and move out."

On her knees, she peered under the vehicle.

Talon sat beneath the Jeep, head up—as much as he could manage. He scooched forward on his belly and paws then dropped something at her feet.

Aspen gasped.

Twenty

Camp Lemonnier, Combined Joint Task Force—Horn of Africa
Republic of Djibouti, Africa

Y ou'll need to work her. Find out what she found. What it means."

Breathe. In. Out. "I will *not* work her." Pinching the bridge of his nose—and grateful it didn't hurt as bad as it did a week ago—Cardinal clamped down on his frustration.

"Cardinal, we don't have time. Understand this: General Payne went ballistic when he found out you were there."

"And how did he find that out?" Showered, he stuffed his arms in a clean shirt.

"No idea, but he's yelling and threatening to have you hauled back here and thrown in prison for the rest of your life."

"My job is to figure this out and find Courtland." Cardinal stuffed his feet in his boots as he talked. "Your job is to keep the hounds off my back." He huffed. "Don't worry. I'll find out what she knows, but I won't work her. I'll *ask* her."

Burnett laughed, and the slurping of a soda filled the line. "What's the difference?"

"Night and day."

Burnett cursed. "For the love of Pete." He muttered something. "Look, Payne's storming down the hall, obviously planning to be a pain in my backside." He grunted. "Listen, Cardinal—get Courtland and get back here before the dragon breathes fire down your neck."

"Understood."

Now to find Aspen. *Talk* to her. Give her the chance to be straight with him. So he could keep his conscience clear.

Feeling as if he'd been through a sauna after his shower, Cardinal made his way past the containerized living units, heat wafting off the cement. At least they'd been accommodated in the portable buildings rather than a tent—that, he knew, was for Talon to stay cool in the AC-regulated environment. When they'd arrived back at Lemonnier, Aspen and Timbrel went with the med staff to get Talon hydrated and cleaned up. They'd agreed to meet at the cantina after showers and a change of clothes.

The central path that snaked around "downtown" Lemonnier was known as Broadway and led Cardinal toward the cantina, theater, PX—and Aspen. At least, he hoped it did. She wasn't in her building. As he made his way through downtown, he spotted a group playing basketball down the road a bit. Candyman with his thick beard and thick build stuck out. And so did Timbrel, though she stood at least a head shorter. She had more spunk than most women—especially to play a game with men nearly twice her size.

Cardinal slipped into the cantina, scanning the area. No go. He stepped back into the heat and made his way to the gym.

Bag in hand, Watterboy strode toward him.

"Have you seen Aspen?"

"Saw her heading to the chapel on my way in." He shouldered past another soldier but called over his shoulder, "Hey. Briefing with Burnett in twenty."

"Thanks." Cardinal jogged toward the chapel, which looked more like something that belonged on the plains of America than in Eastern Africa.

Stepping inside stripped him of any preconceived notions as music rushed into him, drawing him deeper into its sanctuary. The door closed, and his eyes slowly adjusted to the Spartan interior. Certainly no St. Mary's Cathedral. With wood paneling, fluorescent bulbs on the sloped ceilings, and black vinyl chairs serving as pews, the chapel was functional at best.

Sitting at the black upright piano, Aspen had her back to him. Immersed in the music filling the air. Peaceful. The tune coiled around his chest and drew him to the front.

527

As he came up beside her, she jumped and lifted her fingers. Silence dropped like a bomb and felt just as destructive. Somehow, her playing soothed the savage atmosphere.

"Please," he said as he eased onto the bench with her. "Don't stop. It's beautiful."

"I'm a *closet* pianist. I don't play in front of others." Her embarrassment glowed through her cheeks and shy smile.

"Where'd you learn?"

"My mother was a concert pianist, and though I inherited her skill, I did not inherit her desire and ability to perform in front of others." She shrugged and flexed her hand. "It's easier on the knuckles than boxing."

Cardinal ran a hand along his face. "And jawbones."

Aspen laughed. "Blocking helps that."

"So, it's my fault?"

She wrinkled her nose. "You just need more practice."

The challenge sat in the quiet building like a warm blanket. Finally Aspen plunked a few keys, the higher notes tinkling through the cozy chapel. Then a heavy sigh. Her countenance was depressed, her song now somber.

"What's going on?"

Chewing her lower lip, she again dropped her hands into her lap and stared up at the framed print above the piano. "I came in here to try to think through it all—why would he leave me, be alive and never tell me? Let me think he's dead?" She bunched her shoulders. "I don't get it."

Considering he had something to do with all that, he had to tread lightly. "There are those who make sacrifices for their country most people will never understand."

She considered him, her pale eyes piercing. "Are you saying he's making a sacrifice?"

Whoa. Too close there. "What I'm saying is, unless you can talk to him, don't try to understand. Just go with your facts. Let them talk to you."

Aspen looked down at her hands. "They don't make sense, like they're speaking a different language."

He'd have to nudge her. "You found something at the village."

She whipped her face back to his. "How. . . ?"

"There's not much I miss."

Guilt crowded her soft, innocent features. She was so easy to read, so easy to. . . Cardinal fisted his hand. He would *not* work her. This had to be natural. But his curiosity was killing him. "If you hid it from us, I assume you had a reason. A good one. At the same time, you've separated yourself since finding it." He cocked his head and arched his eyebrow. "Those facts are talking to me."

Her expression shifted, but was it one of being caught with her hand in the proverbial cookie jar or one of genuine curiosity? "What are they saying?"

"That you don't trust me."

She opened her mouth to speak and drew back. "I—"

"Let me finish." He noticed her hand had moved to the pocket, probably where she hid the item. "Second, your seclusion and pensive disposition tell me whatever you found probably has personal meaning or evokes a memory. And somehow, it has pushed you into self-preservation mode."

Her gaze darted over the white and black keys, her mind seemingly somewhere else.

"And last. . .you don't trust anyone with what you're thinking, what you're considering, which is why you're here in the chapel." He lowered his voice because it just seemed appropriate. "Seeking the counsel of the divine."

Just rip her open and read her heart like a book! How on earth had he figured all that out?

A nervous tickle pushed out an equally nervous laugh. "Remind me never to ask you to evaluate me again." It was hard, sitting here next to him. Smelling the freshness of him after a shower. He hadn't shaved again, and a thin layer of dark stubble shadowed his mouth and jaw. His black hair dropped into his face, still a bit damp. Hard to think. Hard to hold her ground.

"So, I'm right?" Something shadowed his eyes.

It almost looked like disappointment. Why did that thought corkscrew through her chest, the thought of letting him down? She couldn't hurt him. Didn't want to lose the little connection they'd established, even though he'd shoved her away not two days ago.

Dane stood and walked away.

Was he leaving? She twisted around and pushed to her feet. "Dane. Wait."

He hesitated then planted himself on the first row of black chairs.

She didn't want him leaving mad. "Please." Panic clutched at her—she didn't want him to leave at all. "It wasn't my intention to hide this from you."

Okay, yeah, she was trying to hide the token. But only because she didn't know what it meant. And she hated that everything that had happened since arriving in Djibouti left her with that thought—she didn't know. She was sick of not knowing why her brother did this. Why he let her believe he was dead.

She brushed the curls from her face. "Okay. Look, I'm sorry. That's not true. I just..." She took the piece from her pocket and held it out to him.

Eyes on her, he took it. Turned it over. "A flattened penny?" Questions danced in his eyes. "I'm sorry, I..." He shrugged.

Taking it back, she lowered herself onto the vinyl padded seat next to him, rubbing her thumb along the smoothed surface. "After our parents' funeral, Austin and I went back to our grandparents' house." The memory made her ache. "The house was filling with church members bringing casseroles, telling us all these stories about Mom and Dad, how wonderful they were, how they were in a better place, that we shouldn't be sad."

An unbidden tear strolled down her cheek. She brushed it aside. "It was hard...so hard to sit there, thank them for coming, listen to them go on and on." More tears. The rawness felt new, fresh, not as if it'd been eight years.

"I always had a little more patience than Austin, but that day..." She tightened her lips as a tear rolled over them and bounced off her chin. "I just. Couldn't. Take. It." With the back of her hand, she dried the tears. "I went out back on the porch. Heard the train coming."

She blinked and looked at Dane through her tear-blurred vision. "Austin came out, grabbed my hand, and led me to the tracks. When we were kids visiting there, we'd put pennies on the track and wait for the train to flatten them." She held up the penny. "That's what we did that day. And we agreed to keep them with us—always." Aspen tugged a chain from beneath her shirt and revealed a second penny, equally flattened and smoothed.

His face remained impassive. As if he wasn't catching on, but she knew better than that. Dane didn't miss a thing—he even said so. In fact, he saw more than she could ever hope to notice.

"Austin's here, Dane. He's *here*." The tears and hurt squeezed past her will to hold them back. "Why? *Why* is he here? Why did he let them lie to us, let me believe he was dead?"

Dane's arms came around her and drew her close.

Clinging to him, Aspen cried, relishing the strength in his arms wrapped around her. His chest was firm and toned, yet comfortably soft. His heart boomed against her ear, regular, steady. Constant.

Dane. A veritable pillar of strength this whole time.

Clenching his shirt in her fist, she let the shudders smooth out her angst. But an epiphany stilled her. "He wants me to find him." Elation nudged her head off his chest but was quickly tempered with confusion.

"What are you thinking? Tell me." A smile seemed parked on his face, ready to flash.

She flicked her gaze to him and felt a giddy sensation thinking she might actually be on the right track, that Dane already knew what she was going to say. That he agreed with her. But the thought. . .it proved excruciating to voice. Her throat constricted. She hated feeling this way, feeling weak, betrayed. "Why. . . ?"

"Go on. Finish that thought."

"Why would he want me to find him when he's been hiding?"

"What answers haunt that question?"

She swallowed. "I'm not sure I want to go there."

"Explore every option."

Aspen gave a mental nod. "Either he's in danger and can't let me know he needs help."

"A bit far-fetched, considering his occupation."

"True, but not *completely* implausible."

"Agreed." Dane brushed the curls from her face. "Go on."

"Or he's. . ." Adrenaline squirted through her. "It's a trap."

"Let me guess," Dane said with a grin. "He got the brawn, you got the brains."

"That black eye says I have some brawn, too." Her heart spun in crazy circles as his hand slid along her cheek then down, cupping her neck.

"I deserved it." Steel eyes seemed molten as they traced her face.

Aspen's mind cartwheeled as it caught up with what was happening as his face came closer, his dark lashes fringing eyes that dropped to her mouth.

Oh man. They shouldn't be doing this. But she'd felt connected to him since they set boot here in Africa. She had to admit she'd wanted this. For a while. A long while.

"Hey!"

Aspen jolted at the shout from behind.

On his feet in a flash, Dane erupted in a storm. Brows tightly knit, fury rippled through his arms held to the side.

"You sorry son of a—"

"Timbrel!" Aspen shoved upward, planting herself between Dane and Timbrel, her hand on Dane's chest. His pulse hammered under her palm. Fists balled, jaw tight, he was ready to fight.

Candyman walked behind Timbrel, who trembled as she spoke, "I told you, *told* you to stay away from her or I would hurt you."

"Excuse me," Aspen snapped. "You don't speak for me."

"I do when you get played."

Candyman stood there, not speaking. Watching. As if. . .as if he knew something—they both knew something she didn't.

"What do you mean?"

Another man stepped from the back, only then noticeable.

Timbrel thumbed over her shoulder to the brawny man in ACUs. "This is Will Rankin."

Aspen's mind ricocheted off the name. "You're. . .you were Austin's fire buddy."

Twenty-One

What do you mean, you left it in the dirt for her to find?"

With a glowering look, he climbed into the truck. "I know what I'm doing. You take care of your responsibility, Admiral, and I'll take care of mine."

"What's wrong with you, leading her straight to you?"

He smirked. "How else do you kill a mouse than lure it out of its hole?"

"But she's with Burnett's pawn."

"Don't worry."

"Do you realize who he is?"

Seething, he stared across the room at the woman with raven hair and sky-blue eyes. "I know exactly who he is." He let himself smile. "And how to take care of him."

Camp Lemonnier, Combined Joint Task Force—Horn of Africa
Republic of Djibouti, Africa

Still reeling from the near collision of good sense and passion—*what got into him?*—Cardinal wasn't sure what this was about. And secretly, he was glad he'd been saved from caving to his carnal desires, to compromising himself, Aspen, and the mission with weakness.

Cardinal shifted everything in him to the man Aspen had just named as her brother's partner. "Lieutenant." He nodded to Rankin.

The man skirted a look to Timbrel.

She crossed her arms, defiance granitelike on what could be a pretty face without all that attitude. "He doesn't know you."

Cardinal inclined his head and cocked it. "Is he supposed to?" Why did it make his heart thump a million different ways that Aspen had hold of his forearm.

Timbrel frowned. "You said you were on Austin's team."

Ah. "Actually, no. I said I was with him in Kariz-e Sefid." He looked at Rankin. "You weren't there that day, were you?"

The man shrugged. "No, I was sick. Heat exhaustion or food poisoning. Docs weren't sure."

Cardinal returned his gaze to Timbrel. "Your point is. . . ?"

"He doesn't know you, and you claimed to be friends with Austin."

Aspen turned to Rankin. "Hi, I'm Aspen." She stuck out her hand and the L-T shook it, a blank expression glued to his face. "Do you know who I am?"

"Well, no, ma'am."

She smiled. "I'm Austin's twin sister, Aspen."

"He had a twin?"

With a rueful look to Timbrel, Aspen nodded.

Rankin's face reddened. "Well, Austin didn't talk much, so I'm not surprised I didn't know about you."

The man was covering his tracks—badly. Which worked well for Cardinal. Really well. He offered his hand. "We're sorry to have wasted your time, Lieutenant."

"Look," Rankin said, his deadpanned mask falling away, "I'm real sorry about Austin, but he was a good friend to me. A combat buddy, so I just—if I can help, I want to." He pointed to Cardinal's hand. "You two married?"

Cardinal slipped an arm around Aspen's waist. "Newlyweds."

The guy grinned. "Guess that's why we caught y'all lip-locked."

"Actually, we hadn't. . .he. . ." Embarrassment made Aspen all the more appealing. Even if their lips hadn't made contact yet, the accusation was enough to make her jittery.

"Guess so." Cardinal would not let Rankin think anything contrary about their cover story. It also served as a really good reminder to not slip up like that again. *Never work the women. No matter what you feel.*

The words left a hot streak down the back of his neck and into his shoulder, tightening like a noose.

They said their good-byes to the lieutenant and waited for the door to close. And that's when Cardinal turned on Timbrel. "If you have a problem with me—"

"Oh, I do."

"Then take it up with Burnett, but get off my back. And keep this between us. This op is top secret—you drag in everyone you think it takes to prove whatever whim you have against me, and we'll end up with no answers or dead." He pointed to Aspen. "We're trying to find her brother. Get with us or get off the team."

Eyes narrowed, Timbrel seemed to feed off his anger. "Don't you dare make yourself into a Boy Scout. I've seen the way you watch her, the way you ogle her." She waved a hand at Aspen. "I knew she'd fall for you with all your charm and good looks. You've been working her from day one, and I warned her."

Candyman gently rested a hand on Timbrel's arm.

"Get off me!" She flung her arm up, free of the touch. "Stay away from her. She's not a plaything."

"Enough!" Aspen snapped. "Timbrel, I get that you don't like him, that you don't like men in general, but that gives you no right to act like this. I am a grown woman. I can take care of myself."

"You're naive."

The words sliced through Aspen's anger, leaving a gaping wound that showed clearly on her face. "I may be less experienced than you when it comes to. . .relationships, but I think I know my own mind. I know when I like someone and he likes me."

Timbrel's nostrils flared. "He's got one thing on his mind—like all men. And when he's done here with this mission, he's done with you." Her lips flattened as she nailed Aspen with a piercing look. "Don't say I didn't warn you. I won't pick up the pieces when he proves me right." She stomped out of the building.

Candyman started after her. "Tim—"

"Bug off!" she shouted as she punched the door. As soon as she stepped into the blinding sun, she vanished.

Pulse ratcheting down, Cardinal hung his head. He'd lost it—really lost it with Hogan. "I'm sorry."

As he turned so did Aspen, and her hand came to rest on his side. Her fingers danced off then back on. "No, it's not your fault." Rubbing her forehead, she looked back to the door. "I'm tired of her attitude about men, especially when she tries to destroy something special in my life. I mean, I understand she's trying to protect me, but. . ." She smiled up at him. "There's nothing to protect me from. I feel safe with you."

Cardinal's breathing shallowed out.

Another smile, this one slow and coy. Aspen tugged his shirt and gave him a smirk. "I trust you."

The words detonated like a nuclear blast against his conscience. "Don't."

She almost laughed as her brows slid in and out in question. "What?"

God, help me! He was doing it—using her, manipulating her. Like he vowed not to do. She'd fallen for every play he'd dealt. Trust him? That would be the biggest mistake of her life. "Don't trust me."

This time, the smile lost its flirtation and became nervous. "What do you mean? Of course I trust you." She reached toward his face.

He grabbed her hand. Hated to do this. It had to be done. "Don't. Trust. Me." *Leave. Walk out. Sever this thing that's growing between you and her.* "Don't ever trust me." *Just tell her everything and get it over with.* It was a sarcastic thought, but it slingshot back at him. *Tell her.*

Cardinal stepped back. Stared at her. Studied her. Memorized her confusion. Thinly veiled fear speared his heart. She *didn't* trust him.

"I. . .I don't understand."

Of course she didn't. Couldn't. Because she only knew a small piece of the truth. "I have things to take care of."

"Dane."

As he walked away, he let his eyes slide shut briefly. It wasn't even his name, or even his identity. Dane was the man she married. Not Cardinal. Not the real man behind the religious moniker. She didn't know *him.* That was good—it meant she was safe from that man.

The truth wounded him. Strange, he thought as he pushed open the door, that he even cared. He shouldn't. It took only one small step to become the man he hated. To blur the ethical and moral lines between doing a job and abusing it.

Embroiled in the heat and dust that was distinctly Djibouti, he let the brilliance blind him. If only it could sear the image of Aspen Courtland's hurt from his mind.

But no, he wanted to remember that. To memorize it. So he'd never forget. And never make the mistake again.

"Girl, just come back."

Aspen cradled her head in her hand as she Skyped with Brittain, who was on the other side of the world. "I can't." She fought the urge to cry. There'd been enough tears lately, and she was through being weak. "Austin is here. I am not going home till I find him and figure out what's going on."

"Is that a ring on your finger?"

Aspen straightened, feeling the heat in her face. "Yeah." She slid it off. "It's part of our cover while we're here. In fact, we're supposed to be staying with some missionary in the city, not here on the base. But Talon's still recovering from a cut on his paw and the heat."

"What are you going to do about Mr. Don't Trust Me?"

Aspen groaned. "I have no idea." She raised her hands. "What does that mean?"

"Hello?" Brittain laughed. "It means don't trust him."

Rolling her eyes, Aspen sighed. "But why would he tell me that? It makes no sense—and it defies what I feel. When he said it, I just couldn't move. It wouldn't. . .process, especially after he almost kissed me."

"What?"

Shoot. "Um. . .never mind about that."

"Oh no." Brittain's face drew closer on the screen. "No, you can't do that to me, girl. You need to spill. Now."

"Look, it's. . .an unusual situation."

"Uh-huh."

No, she wasn't going to lie about this, wouldn't downplay what she felt. "I like him." She looked at the flat surface that held her friend's visage. "He's strong—internally and externally. He has helped *me* stay strong when I just wanted to puddle up. And even though he said not to trust him, there aren't many people I'd trust the way I trust him."

"Uh-oh."

"I know what you're going to say, so don't say it."

"All right. I won't. But you need to hear it anyway—I can smell what's happening from all the way over here. You're falling for him, hard. Be careful, Aspen. If this guy is warning you not to trust him"—she let out an "are you dumb" laugh—"then you probably need to be listening to the man. Ya know?"

Fingers digging in the curls at the back of her head, Aspen nodded. "I know, but. . ."

"Look, girl. The only time you've got a bigger *butt* than me is when you're trying to rationalize."

Aspen laughed. "Normally I'd agree. But this isn't rationalizing. I. . . it feels different."

"What does?"

"What I feel for him"—she knew Brittain would jump on that, so she leapt ahead—"*and* the motivation behind what he said."

"You have such a good heart. Always have."

Aspen cringed. She knew what would come next. "But. . ."

Silence stretched between them, and she watched her friend, who stared back unmoving. "Aspen?"

"Yeah?"

"Someone's at your door."

Lying on her bunk with the laptop, she glanced over her shoulder. Through the small filmy square window, she saw a shadowy form.

Two solid raps hit the metal door—and banged against her heart as she rolled off the bunk. "Hang on, I'll be right back."

"No!" Brittain said with a laugh. "What if it's him? I'll go so you two can talk."

After a quick good-bye, Aspen hurried and opened the door.

A man wearing ACUs saluted. "Aspen Courtland?"

"Yes?"

"Here, ma'am. This just arrived for you." He handed her a cream envelope.

Three-by-four inches, the envelope was small and only had her name written in all block lettering. "Weird." When she looked up, he'd already started away. "Thanks," she called after him.

Back in her room, she dropped onto the gray mattress and criss-crossed her legs. Opening the envelope, she wondered who'd written it. She plucked a single sheet of paper out. Opened it.

Did you find the coin?
Boys' orphanage, tomorrow, Djibouti City

Cardinal sat in the outdoor restaurant, the remains of his dinner in front of him. The weight of the band on his left ring finger anchored his mind to it. Elbow on the table, he stared down, rubbing his knuckles along his lip.

"*I trust you.*"

Three deadly words.

At least, they had been for his mom.

"*Do you trust me, Eliana?*"

"*Of course I do, but. . .*"

"*There is no but. Only yes or no.*" The colonel held her face in his large, powerful hands. "*You said you loved me.*"

"*I do! I swear it!*"

"*Then trust me!*"

Swiping a hand over his stubbly mouth and chin, Cardinal sat back. Pushed his gaze to the walkway, where seamen, airmen, and soldiers made their way to and from dinner.

"*You've always been a great lover.*"

Crack!

Nikol jerked.

A thousand tiny splinters snaked through the large pane of glass from the bullet.

"*And,*" the colonel hissed, "*a horrible liar.*"

Crack! *The fractured glass rushed down like a mighty waterfall.*

"*No more.*" *With a great thrust, he shoved her backward.*

Then the angel flew.

"Hey!" A clatter erupted.

Cardinal blinked. Someone stood in front of his table. Only as his mind emerged from the past and his brain aligned with his surroundings did he manage to respond. "No need to yell. I'm right here."

"When I have to call your name three times—"

He squinted up at the woman. "Maybe I was waiting for you to talk nicely."

Timbrel dropped into the chair, and next to her, Candyman joined them. "Listen, I might have been wrong about Rankin—"

"Might have been?" He couldn't believe how easy it was to annoy her. And keeping her unbalanced would make her do more stupid things. It'd keep the *balance* of power in his hands.

"But I'm not wrong about you." She leveled a gaze at him. "If you pull a stunt like that again, I'm going to Burnett and having him yank your sorry butt stateside."

Cardinal lifted his bottled water and sipped. "According to him, I'm married to Aspen and under orders to make it look authentic."

Anger exploded across her face.

"Wait," he said, an authoritative tone in his word. "First—you came in before we kissed. It didn't happen, thanks to you." It ticked him off how she seemed to gloat under that revelation. Ah, let her have this one. It worked better for him. "But if it had, it would've been real. I like her. She's a good woman. I'm not going to play her." His heart careened at the admission. "This isn't my first op. I know how to work the angles without messing with the heart." At least, he hoped he did. "Besides, it won't happen again."

"Why not?" Timbrel scowled. "You jumping ship on her that fast?"

"No." Man, she gave him no credit. "Thanks to your accusations, she doesn't trust me. And I don't want her to. Not here, not while her mind is wrapped around finding her brother. Her emotions are high, her adrenaline higher. What she's feeling can't be trusted."

Candyman grinned through his thick, mangy beard. "You're not sure she likes you for you or for the hero role you're in."

"Exactly."

"Markoski! Candyman!"

The shout from down the path drew their attention, Candyman coming out of his chair even before the sound of his name finished.

At the command building, Watterboy waved them down. "Move! Aspen's MIA!"

Twenty-Two

W hat do you mean, she's MIA?"

"Checked the base, the kennel, her temporary bunk, mess—everything." Captain Dean Watters stood, hands on hips, as he relayed the information. "She didn't sign out of the base, but she's not here."

Lance Burnett flung the Dr Pepper can in the trash can across his office. It hit the wall and clattered into the metal bin. "How in Sam Hill does a person go missing on a military base?" He stabbed his fingers through his hair and clenched his fist. "Look, you know what? I don't care *how* she got lost." Glaring into the webcam, he made his foul mood known. "Just get her *un*lost. I don't need any more gray hair than I already have."

"Yessir," Watters said, his grim expression betraying his displeasure. Whether that was for Lance's anger or Courtland's MIA status, Lance couldn't decipher. "You take that irritation, Captain, and you aim it at finding this young woman. She might be former Air Force, but she's not seen combat. Out there in a city that is ninety-something percent Muslim is *not* a recipe for Granny's homemade pudding. Got it?"

"Yessir."

"The last thing I need is for some beautiful former JAG assistant to go missing, end up in the hands of terrorists, and have that all over the news. Because the Good Lord knows that it will soon come out that her brother went missing, too. And how will *that* look?"

Via live video feed, Lance again surveyed those gathered. "And where in Sam Hill is my man?"

"He said he had a few ideas."

The pot of hot water that sat beneath Lance's backside—the one Payne and the others would use to scald him right down to private—began to boil. "Ideas? About what? I want him on this feed right now. VanAllen!"

"Sir." Candyman straightened.

"Drag his sorry carcass back in there. Now. I want words with that no-good—"

Light ballooned against a wall in the small conference room at Lemonnier. A dark shadow slid across it, then the explosion of light winked out.

"As you wish," VanAllen said with a smirk and motioned to someone.

Cardinal stepped into view and handed something to Candyman. "Send that to the general." He peered into the monitor. "General, I need you to get Hastings and Smith on this as we talk. Have them work the images. They'll know what to look for."

It took one call and the others were on their way. Lance would love to reach through the feed and strangle that cocky operative if he could. But he was too doggone valuable. "Well? What'd you find?"

He stretched to the credenza beside his desk and used it to pull himself to the small fridge then tugged out another maroon and white can. When he rolled back to the monitor, he found Cardinal, hands planted on the table, towering over the webcam. Lips tight, nostrils flared, he looked ticked.

Lance set the can aside, bracing himself. "That bad, eh?"

"Candyman's sending the key feed clips to you." Cardinal looked around the room. "The rest can crowd up and see on this monitor. Aspen retrieved Talon from the kennel at 2215 last night."

"That's normal," Timbrel added. "Handlers prefer to keep their dogs with them, and she has an air-conditioned CLU."

"Yes, but the kennel has a controlled environment as well," Cardinal countered.

"Getting her dog at ten fifteen at night is normal?" Lance wasn't buying it.

"I find it curious considering Talon was injured and dehydrated when she left him in the vet's care. I know she's protective and vigilant of the dog, but I also know she wanted him to get better. The only thing that would've made her compromise his recovery time and process would be something related to her brother."

Tolerance was being stretched in the way Lance viewed Cardinal. Though he hated the man's rogue methods, more times than not, Cardinal got his man. Or woman in this case.

"So?"

"Ran security tapes." Cardinal flicked a hand toward the monitor. "Traced Aspen into the kennel and out. She went to her CLU and came out with a pack." Cardinal mumbled something to VanAllen about the next image. "MP at the checkpoint said no woman and dog left through the gate. Inside the wire there are rows of cement barricades. There's no way she could've scaled that, not with the dog, and especially not with his paw injured."

"If you'd like to give me a tour of the base, you're wasting your time. I've been there. Get on with this."

Cardinal stared at him. Then pointed to Candyman. "So, I ran a few hunches. Tried a few tricks."

"Am I supposed to be impressed?" Why wouldn't the man just tell them what he found? Get on with it, so they could begin the search. If he knew where she was, wouldn't he. . . ? "You have no idea where she is, do you?"

"I searched the egress logs. Cross-referenced that with destinations and capacity."

"Capacity." Watters nodded. "She hitched a ride."

"In doing these and searching the security logs, I came across this." Again, Cardinal pointed to Candyman.

The image hogged over the screen. The motor pool. Jeeps. MRAPS. A medical team could be seen piling into a Land Rover.

"That looks routine." Lance lifted his Dr Pepper.

"Except that it's happening at four thirty in the morning. And the medical staff returned with us from their weekly rounds to the villages."

He squinted at the image. Not the best quality, but that was to be expected with the security cameras.

"Look at the airman, second left. When the person turns and says something—"

A dog trotted out from behind a container and hopped into the back of the SUV.

Lance sighed. "And why didn't the guards at the gate notice him leaving?"

"Sir, we had coms get into the computer Aspen had here. She had a Skype call last night with one"—Candyman read from his computer—"Brittain Larabie."

"On it," one of ODA452 said as keys started clicking.

"She's her best friend," Timbrel said.

"She's also the reporter who interviewed me," Cardinal added. "Get her on the horn."

"Yep," the ODA452 team member said, diverting his efforts to a phone. A few seconds later, he handed the device to Cardinal.

"Miss Larabie, Dane Markoski here. . .yeah. . .good, listen, we've got a situation here. Aspen is missing. . .calm down. We'll find her, but I can't do that without your help. Last night you Skyped with her. Did she mention anything that raised concern for you?"

Riveted to the monitor trying to gauge the conversation happening, Lance watched Cardinal. What was Larabie saying? Why had Cardinal gone silent? "Markoski?" Lance popped the top on the soda can, his mouth nearly watering at the *tssssssssk* that erupted from the depressurization of the can.

"But she said nothing about leaving or. . . ?" Cardinal nodded. "Okay, good. That helps. What time did your call end?" More nodding. "Thank you. It's very helpful. . .yes, of course. As soon as we can."

"Well?"

"Anyone here go to Aspen's CLU last night around eight?" When everyone responded to the negative, Cardinal sighed. "According to Larabie, while they were Skyping last night, someone knocked on Aspen's door."

"Who was it?"

"Larabie doesn't know because they ended it so Aspen could answer the door. I'm going to dig around and see if I can figure out who went to her and why. That might give us some indication of what provoked her to grab her dog and run."

"Got it," Lieutenant Hastings said. "I scrambled through the various video feeds. I found one that's really shady, but give our analysts a few hours—"

"Aspen's already out there. We don't have hours."

544

"Give us some time and we can have this guy's history. But he's about five eleven, brown hair, wearing ACUs. He has something in hand—looks like an envelope. We lose him when he steps under the CLU's walkway."

"Time stamp?"

"Twenty-oh-eight."

Finally. A break. "That's our guy. Find him." Cardinal fisted his hand. Something was going on here. A woman with a dog didn't just walk off a base. Or ride off in a Land Rover. There were too many security protocols. So, how'd she bypass them? Why did the man in the motor pool help her?

No sense. It made no sense at all.

"Hey." Timbrel dropped her booted foot to the floor and sat forward. "Whoever that was, he had to have something pretty important in that envelope. Aspen doesn't have adventure in her blood like some, so her leaving means something."

"Agreed. But what?"

Timbrel shrugged. "I'm not going to do your job for you."

"Markoski, that SUV you said she might've climbed into?" Lieutenant Hastings spoke up from the Pentagon. "I cross-checked gate logs. It went out with supplies for Peltier General at 0630."

"Who signed out?"

"Uhh. . .no name—oh wait, here we go. Lieutenant Will Rankin."

The idiot. He had no idea what he'd just done.

"Let's go." Timbrel punched to her feet.

"Hold up," Cardinal said. "We know where the truck was headed, but—"

"Talon got a hit there, so it makes sense she'd go there again. Maybe she thinks she can track down Austin. Since that SUV left at six thirty, that means she's been on her own for over six hours. We don't have time to—"

"That's right." Cardinal tempered his frustration with Timbrel's charge-first, think-later method. "We don't have time to rush out there with unknowns that cost us time. And if we all went out there as U.S. military, everyone would clam up."

"Then we break up into teams." Timbrel stuffed her hands on her hips. "I'll go with you."

"No way."

"Why not?" Timbrel had gone into confrontational mode.

"I need to go into town as a husband worried about his wife's disappearance. That will get me local sympathy and awareness—people will start talking. If I can suggest a reward, then that will spread like wildfire. They'll bring me word. It'll go faster. I'll book a room at the Sheraton. Brie," he said, talking to the Pentagon again. "Once I'm there, relay the phone so it will come to my sat phone."

"Roger that."

"Markoski," General Burnett spoke up, roughing a hand through his tightly cropped hair. "I have to get clearance on this change."

"Then get it." The general was trying to stall. Though he probably had a great reason, Cardinal didn't have time for them to work out all their theories and probabilities. Aspen was out there, with her dog, but utterly alone. She didn't know the language, probably didn't know customs. Forget that she was beautiful. "But cut me loose to do this, my way."

Burnett's rugged face glowered. "Now, listen—"

"You and I both know if we all go out there, if all these uniforms show up, we'll never find her." He leaned in. "I work better on my own, and I can do it faster. Let me find her and bring her back. Things are screwed up, and we need to move swiftly. I can do that better alone."

"What are you afraid of?" Timbrel challenged. "Afraid you ran her off with your sweet-talking and charm?"

Wrong button to push. Cardinal swung around. "If you want to play the blame game, fine. My interest is getting Aspen back—alive. What you aren't thinking about is that someone seems to have lured her off the base, alone, in the middle of the night. And I don't know where you come from, Hogan, but in most cities I grew up in, that was a death sentence. Now, do you want your friend and handler back alive, or do you want to bring her home in a casket?"

Timbrel swallowed, and in doing that, signaled her retreat.

"Burnett—"

"Sorry, son. I have to put my boot down. Payne's being the royal pain I warned you about, and if he found out—and no, I'm not hinting you should do anything rogue. If he found out, they'd rip these stars off my shoulders." He wagged a finger at Cardinal. "This is a direct order: Do not go out there alone. Things are hot. Something's off, and we need to figure it out before we go guns blazing after her, not to mention we need to get some things in place before it's too late."

Cardinal frowned. "It's already too late."

"Are you forgetting who's in charge here?"

Cardinal's heart pounded. It'd been a long time since he'd directly disobeyed an order. "I'll get back to you on that." He cut the live-feed transmission, stood, and saw the others coming to their feet, clearly ready to stop him. "I need twenty-four hours to find her. That's it."

No one moved. Good sign.

"Let's send two teams," Watterboy said. "I'll return to the base in the city, across from the missionary's home. Candyman and Timbrel can go to the hotel as well, posing as tourists—"

"No," Cardinal said. "Watterboy, you and Timbrel get a room at the hotel as well. Candyman's too noticeable with that beard and thick chest."

Candyman frowned, holding his hands up as if inspecting himself. "Yeah, guess this body is on America's Most Wanted list."

"Good plan change." Timbrel narrowed her eyes at Candyman. "His ego wouldn't fit in the hotel room anyway."

"Agreed." Cardinal focused. Trained his mind to quiet. "Candyman, make sure your team is ready to jump if we get a lead or eyes on target."

Candyman nodded. "Roger. But for the record, I'm not too happy with the captain here shacking up with my girl."

If only there was time to joke. "Listen, I won't kid you—Aspen out there is not good. It was foolish for her to go off on her own."

"Assuming she's on her own," Watterboy added.

"We have to assume that she wanted her brother back, and her one weakness pushed her to make a stupid move." Cardinal gave a nod. "If she's not alone, then once we find her, it could be a fight to the death to get her back."

The door banged open. Rocket burst in, his face flushed. "A team just got ambushed. Admiral Kuhn is locking down Lemonnier under McLellan's orders. Nobody in, nobody out."

Lance cursed. "Okay." He sat up, took a swig of his sugary addiction, and then focused on Cardinal, who stood waiting, glaring. "McLellan is the personal assistant to Colonel Hendricks."

Cardinal stilled. "Payne's Hendricks?"

"Yeah." Adrenaline spiraled through his system like a gusher. "So listen up—nobody tells anyone we know this." Another swig. Another. There was a lot of work to do. Even more to hide. Because if Payne had sent Hendricks' man to usher Aspen out of there. . .

Lord God—what does this mean?

Cardinal scowled at the man with an extra jowl. "Burnett, if this means what I think it means—"

"We don't know what it means, so I'm going to start digging. You get out there and find that girl."

God have mercy on her. Because if this trail was leading where he thought it might, Aspen Courtland could already be dead.

★ ★ Twenty-Three ★ ★

Boys' Orphanage, Djibouti

Sitting in the shade of the building, the warmed cement and plaster against her back, Aspen smoothed a hand along Talon's ribs. Lying on his side did little to ease the heat discomfort. But at least they had shade and water, thanks to the generosity of the orphanage director. She'd never been a good liar or pretender, so she'd just gone with a narrow version of the truth: she was waiting here to meet someone. That had been good enough for the director, who said he'd gladly welcome visitors, especially those who would give something to the children, whether laughter or treats.

A guilty knot tied in Aspen's stomach. She had nothing for the children. Muslims viewed dogs as unclean, so most of the adults were appalled that Aspen had brought Talon. The children, however, could not be dissuaded.

In fact, there had been peals of delight and laughter throughout the morning as she demonstrated some of Talon's simpler skills.

Back at Lemonnier she'd spotted Rankin gearing up, and intentionally plying on his guilt over Austin's death/disappearance, she convinced him to give her a lift into the city. She'd said she was going to the orphanage and let him assume what he wanted. He agreed to pick her back up on their return route. Two more hours.

Aspen blew the curls off her forehead. With an exhausted groan, Talon stretched then went limp as he drifted off to sleep. Though Aspen would love nothing more than to catch a few Zs, she couldn't risk missing whoever had sent the note.

A shadow slid out and touched her, drawing her gaze to the doorway. "You want eat?" Director Siddiqi asked.

Talon pulled off the ground, ears and attention perked. He let out a whimper, and his tail thumped twice. Peculiar. Had he understood the word *eat*, or was it something more? But here, Aspen knew the orphanage struggled to feed the dozens of boys. She'd seen the kitchen and the grill donated by the servicemen and women at Lemonnier. In a world where your next meal wasn't guaranteed, she wouldn't dare take from the mouths of children.

"No, thank you." She'd brought her pack with Talon's food and hers, knowing that anything could incapacitate Talon, and that meant he wouldn't be at the top of his game to track.

"You friend not come?"

She swatted away a fly and the discouragement that lingered over the contact not showing up. "Not yet." She squinted over the empty play yard, eyeing the cars that sped by. Surely whoever had gone through the trouble of getting her off the base wouldn't just leave her here. "Soon, though."

He smiled and nodded. "Soon." Director Siddiqi turned and let the building swallow him.

Had the note instructed her to meet somewhere less safe, less open and public, she wouldn't have risked everything—including Dane's anger and disapproval. She'd had several hours to attach a meaning to what he'd said: *"Don't trust me."* Though part of her railed at those instructions, a deeper part of her couldn't let go of one thought: her trust terrified Dane. Aspen shook her head as she pulled out a few treats.

Talon's ears and head perked up, and he cast those soulful eyes at her as he pushed himself into an attentive "sit" position.

"Focus," she gave the command that instructed him to look into her eyes, a confidence builder, the dog trainer had said.

His gaze bounced from the treat to her eyes almost instantly.

"Yes! Good boy." She gave him the treat and smoothed a hand over the top of his head. Now how was it he could do one-on-one moments so well, but add noise and he was a puddle of panic? Like with the children. Oh man, she'd gotten so worried. He'd started shrinking and looking for a place to hide as the children shrieked and squealed, running around the playground.

"We should've stayed in Texas." She rustled his fur, gave him another treat, then leaned against his thick shoulder. "And I shouldn't have rushed you back into working, but I am glad you're here." It almost felt like she had a piece of Austin with her. And a very good friend. "I wouldn't want to be here without you, Talon."

At his name, he flicked his gaze to hers and swiped his tongue along her cheek.

Aspen laughed and turned away to avoid a slobber-fest. As he nudged her hand, she noticed his nose wasn't quite the shiny black it should be. She pushed to her feet. "C'mon, boy. Let's get some water."

She led him into the building and made her way to the kitchen. There, she filled a water bottle, dropped in two tablets, tightened the lid back on, then shook it. Using his collapsible bowl, she dumped in the contents and let Talon lap it up.

Voices skated through the hall outside the kitchen. Stern, quick words. Probably one of the teen boys getting chewed out again. She'd seen it a few times, only because the boys were pushing their boundaries as expected. Lord knows, Austin did it enough back home. Mom and Dad were at their wit's end, then Austin up and asked them to sign for an early entry into the Marines. Dad was relieved, Mom terrified—*"There's a war going on. They'll ship out."*

Ironically, it wasn't Austin who died a few months later. It was Mom and Dad.

Talon consumed the water in what felt like two heartbeats. She opted not to give him more because they might be stuck here for a while. Especially if the mystery guest didn't show.

Call of nature came. She stood, dried out the bowl, then folded it and stuffed it back on her pack. Since she couldn't very well tie Talon off to a tree—there weren't any—she led him down the hall to the bathroom. A cozy little closet of a thing that stunk to high heaven. Aspen made quick work of relieving herself then used her own sanitizer to clean her hands as she made her way out of the bathroom.

Shouts stopped her. They were still arguing? Gran would've said to take a switch to his backside. Nowadays, if you did that, someone would call it abuse.

But then. . .something about the argument piqued her curiosity.

She ambled down the hall, back toward the kitchen.

"This has nothing to do with you, Nazir."

"But this my orphanage. Bad things happen here, they close doors. Where boys go?"

Bad things happen? What bad things? What was the director talking about? Was this man threatening him?

"Not my problem, old man. She has the dog with her?"

In the space of two heartbeats, Aspen's world upended. *He's asking about me! And Talon!* She took a step back.

Talon whimpered.

Aspen flinched and tensed. He must be reading her body language, smelling her fear. She lowered her hand and rubbed his ears, trying to reassure him—and her. This couldn't be what she thought it was.

"Yes." The answer had been so quiet. . .so resigned. . .

"Good." A laugh sounded. "Say, anyone here know how to make dog stew?"

Hand over her mouth, Aspen backstepped. Talon stayed with her. She spun and hurried down the hall. Out the door.

"There! Stop her!"

"If you go out there," Candyman stated, sounding perturbed, "and they kill you? Don't blame me, man."

"If they kill me, I doubt I'll be able to blame anyone." Cardinal grinned. Waited for the point to sink in.

"Hey, this isn't a joke. You're talking about exposing yourself, possibly getting peppered full of holes."

"I'd prefer to skip the peppered full of holes, but yes, I will be exposed." In more ways than one. Going after Aspen compromised every Cardinal rule that existed. But he'd already lost one Courtland. He wasn't about to lose another.

Timbrel fumed. "I should be going with you."

"What you should be doing," he said as he slid a black skull cap over his head, "is going over every log and surveillance video with Candyman. Find out who gave her that envelope. Find out what it said. Find out where Rankin went and why."

Watters entered the room and locked it behind himself. The way he lingered there, staring at the knob, then the floor, set off a dozen alarms in Cardinal's mind.

"What's on your mind?" Cardinal asked.

They shared a long look, one that told him Watters was surprised he'd been read that easily, but then the next, more lingering message became one of camaraderie. "It makes no sense."

"What's that?" Cardinal stilled, watching the captain. A man he'd grown to trust. A man whose instincts were crazy accurate.

Watters hiked up a leg and slumped against the table around which the rest of ODA452 had gathered. "Base is locked down due to a supposed ambush, right?"

Cardinal gave a slow nod as he continued gearing up.

"We can't find out who got ambushed." Watters held up a finger. "There's one team out right now—Rankin's team. On a supply run through the city. There's been no activity that Burnett or his people can find. No radio chatter for help, backup, nothin'."

Very interesting. "That non-chatter chats a lot, doesn't it?" He smirked.

"Something's going on."

"It's some kind of messed-up insanity. Wasn't this supposed to be an easy mission—get in here, find the man who'd been lost?" Candyman sat on the end of the table, his boots on a chair. "And now, we got ambushes with no personnel, a missing dog handler, and a spook about to go rogue."

"Spook?" Timbrel straightened and looked at Candyman. Then Cardinal.

"He's referencing your insinuation that I'm not who I say I am." Cardinal lifted the water bottle and took a nice long guzzle.

"I swear, Markoski, if you hurt her. . ."

"Hurt her?" Cardinal laughed. "Timbrel, I wouldn't be willing to get my head blown off if I wanted her hurt."

"I didn't say what you *wanted*." She jutted her jaw. "I know your type. And she's too sweet to get it."

"Okay." Candyman hopped off the table. "Let's get this show on the road."

"Agreed. Keep your eyes and ears open. See what you can figure out." Cardinal huffed.

"Don't worry. I intend to find answers." Watters had a rare type of steel running through his veins.

"Time to play decoy with the dummy." Candyman grinned, and how he didn't end up with a mouthful of facial hair, Cardinal didn't know. And right now, he didn't care. His only concern was Aspen.

"Ready?" Watters's eyes seemed to sparkle with the thrill of what they were about to do.

With a nod, Cardinal looked to the others. Adrenaline thrummed through his blood. Creating a diversion so he could slip through the barriers was risky. They didn't want anyone getting hurt, but they also had to make this significant enough to draw eyes off the perimeter fence on the southeastern side. He'd bolt to the water and swim his way to safety. Grab some dry duds from a street vendor then check in at the hotel. That should be high-profile enough to attract some attention. Get his name on radars. He just prayed—and if he could find a chapel he would pray, honestly and truly—he could get a location on Aspen before someone put lead between his eyes.

They left the room a few at a time, going in different directions. Two here, two that way, one on his way to the cinema. Nothing that attracted attention. . .that is, unless someone looked close. Bulk could be deceptive, but anyone who did a double-take would figure out he had a second layer of clothes on. They ducked behind the first row of stacked CLUs then scurried to the fence.

Squatting at the perimeter behind one of the cement dividers, Cardinal adjusted the flak vest. Choked back the memory of Aspen's frightened blue eyes when he'd told her not to trust him. A stupid move. Showing his hand. But the thought of her trusting him when he was nothing she believed him to be. . .

He shouldn't care. Shouldn't be concerned with what happened to her at the end of this mission. But he was. In fact, he couldn't get away from the thoughts of the moment she discovered he was not Dane Markoski. Watters crouched beside him with the wire cutters, setting up a rerouter for the electrical current so it wouldn't attract the attention of the MPs.

"If you find her, get word back to us."

Cardinal nodded.

"Hey."

The hesitation, the softer tone, pulled Cardinal's attention to the captain.

"Candyman told me...about you and Aspen." Watters held his gaze strong, firm. "I don't care if you have a thing going on, but don't let it get in the way. Because I'll come after you for compromising me and my team, and our target."

He'd never had someone be direct with him like that, in such a friendly but threatening way. Well, he'd had those who were going to cut his heart out if he double-crossed them. That was evil. This was... justified.

"I have one goal, Captain," he said, meeting the guy's intensity, "to get her and her brother back, even if I have to die to do it."

"Good to know." Watters smirked. "I think her friend would prefer it that way—with you dead."

"Good thing my fate's not in her hands."

Something flashed through the captain's face. "Whose is it in?"

Cardinal felt like this was one of those defining moments. One of those—admit you're weak and then you get killed moments—and he wasn't sure he wanted to face it. "I'd like to hope God's got it."

"He will if you let Him."

Cardinal gave a slow shake of his head. "Not sure it's quite that simple."

"Sure it is." Watters patted his shoulder. "We humans are the ones who make it difficult and complicated. Surrender is the only way."

Crack!

The first indication of their plan igniting—literally—pounded through his chest. He and Watters gave nods of affirmation that said *this is it.*

Boooom!

Just a little longer. . .

Sirens wailed.

Watters cut a hole in under fifteen seconds. "Go!"

Cardinal folded himself through the fence. Once he made it through clear, Watters should bolt back. Double-checking the base conditions and Watters, Cardinal turned. The spot Watters had occupied sat empty. As Cardinal whipped back around, he caught the hulking form of the captain in his periphery, skimming along the barriers back toward the CLUs.

On my own.

He eyed the guard hut and saw two guards pointing toward the explosion Timbrel and Candyman had created with a vehicle. He bolted across the road and over the field.

A crack of gunfire pierced the hot day.

Dirt spit up at him.

His pulse amped up. They'd spotted him. Ten seconds to the water. He pumped it hard, pushing to safety. Feet beating a quick path.

A blazing heat whipped across his ear. He sprinted, darting left. Then right, doing his best to make it impossible for them to get a bead on him.

Five seconds. He freed the first buckle of the vest.

Four.

Water erupted in several distinct spots.

Three.

He ripped an arm free of the vest.

Dove for the water.

Like a lead fist, a tremendous weight pounded into his back.

Twenty-Four

Djibouti City, Djibouti

Neil! Neil, hurry!"

He bolted out of the bathroom in the run-down apartment they'd rented with cash. "What?"

Lina stood at the window, peering through a razor-thin slit in the triple-layered cloth he'd nailed over the hole. "Look!"

At her side, he angled his head to see through the skinny space. The street bustled with the normal gaggle of women carrying infants and toddlers in slings, guiding other children down the streets as men hurried here and there. "I don't see anything. What?"

She extended her arm and pointed up the street. "Past the bank. Watch the shadows." Lina smelled fresh, even though the shower was anything but. Not for the first time did he consider her beauty, both inside and out. "Not me, out there."

He grinned and slipped an arm around her waist as he once again checked the ground from their second-story apartment. "I'm still not—"

Something moved, this time north of the bank. He leaned forward a little and shifted toward the window.

Lina held his shoulders as she peered over his left. "Is it. . . ?"

He spied blond curls and yellow fur running beneath the balcony of a two-story shop. "Crap!"

How had she found them? This was unbelievable!

A distant pop froze him.

She slipped into an alley.

His heart stalled. "Someone's chasing her."

"Doesn't that work better for us?"

"Yes, but what if they miss?" He grabbed a ball cap and started for the door. "Lock it. Don't let anyone in and don't go anywhere till I get back."

"What are you going to do?"

Neil hesitated. He knew. Knew beyond a shadow of a doubt but couldn't tell her. She wouldn't understand.

Aspen slid around the corner, hauling Talon with her.

Plaster from the arches spit at her. She ducked but kept moving. Talon had kept up with her, but he was limping. They needed a break. Needed rest. Had to find a place. A safe place.

Scanning doors and alleys, she didn't stop. Couldn't afford to. Her legs felt like pudding, heavy yet jiggly. Her heart pounded so hard, she struggled to breathe. And Talon, God bless him, continued without complaint.

Not that she could just let him keep going. The dog's heart was one of the most loyal, going and loving and doing whatever it was to make her happy, but he would let her run him straight into the ground. She had a responsibility to find a place to give him rest.

God, help me!

Feet pounded behind her. The men's shouts as unrelenting as their pace. Didn't they need to breathe? And who was it exactly? She didn't know the people chasing her. How did they know her? How had they known about the coin?

Why had she thought this was a good idea?

Because you always want to rescue people.

Plaster leapt at her.

She yelped, shielded her face, and banked right.

Two feet in, darkness dropped on her. About the time her mind registered the dead end, a form emerged from the shadows. "Back!" she snapped.

"Here," the man said in a hushed whisper. "Hide in here." He pointed to the side.

Aspen stopped. "You're helping me?"

With a nod, he lifted a panel and waved her into the spot. "Hurry!"

As he bent forward and waved, his dark hair dipped into the light.

Talon did his high-pitched whimper thing.

Aspen didn't have time to lose. She scuttled into the narrow space and tugged Talon in with her. "Talon, heel! Sit! Stay!" She said the commands rapid-fire.

Two large pieces of two-by-fours strung together dropped over the space, sealing them in.

Aspen sucked in a breath and placed a hand on the wood. "Wait!"

Thunk!

Though she thought it impossibly dark, Aspen could see through the slivers of light that the man had sat down in front of the wood. What was he doing? His head was down. He looked. . .asleep?

Feet pounded nearby.

"You got her?"

Head against the wall, Aspen closed her eyes and held her breath. *God. . .this would be a great time for Talon to be completely happy hiding.*

"Nothing—hey, you!"

The man flinched. "Hey, was—"

"Drunken fool. What are you doing back here?"

"I'm not drunk," the man, the hero who'd stepped into the line of fire to help her, stood tall.

"Then what are you doing back here?"

Her lungs were on fire from the exertion of slowing her breathing from a dead run to a quiet rhythm not detectable through the wood. Talon wasn't panting hard—or at all. Maybe he sensed the danger. When he was on alert, his jaw snapped shut. Was he doing that now? She traced her fingers along the top of his broad skull.

"Getting away from my boss for a nap."

"Did you see a girl run past here with a dog?"

"I didn't see anything—I was asleep. Besides, why would she run past here? It's a dead end." Her hero shifted away from the wood, toward the other side of the alley.

"Forget him," another man shouted. "We can't lose her."

"Can I help if you have lousy aim?"

The voices faded and with them, Aspen's alarm. Her muscles ached. She opened her mouth and expelled the fiery breath, slowly bringing her heartbeat to a normal rate. Quiet descended over the next several minutes, even though somewhere not too far, she heard the two men still shouting.

"Stay here till nightfall," the hero said.

"My dog needs water. He's dehydrated."

"You'll have to wait. If I bring water back, they might see."

And with that, he was gone.

Aspen nodded, not trusting herself to speak—to fall apart.

Time ticked by with the weight of an anvil, each second pummeling her courage. Wait until night? Panic thumped against her silent consent of his order. She couldn't wait till dark. Then she'd have no way to get back to Lemonnier. In fact, if she didn't find a way back soon, she'd be alone. All night.

Indecision rooted her to the hiding spot.

Letting herself slide down, Aspen wedged herself in the tiny space. Her knees grazed the plaster. This must be some kind of stoop. A steel door pressed against her spine, but the lock wouldn't budge. Trapped.

Then it registered—Talon's rapid breathing. His lethargy.

She couldn't look at his gums, but she'd bet the heat was getting to him again. *You are the most irresponsible handler ever. Austin would string you up.*

But Austin was gone. Or here. Or. . .whatever.

Had the coin simply been a coincidence? She thumped her head against the wall. Leaping without looking to help others. Good intentions—she always had good intentions, but they most often got her into a ton of trouble.

God, I need serious help. And I have no idea what to pray for. Just. . .get us out safely.

Quiet coiled around her as the city slowed and the traffic, both foot and vehicular, dulled from the roar it'd been when she was running for her life.

An urgency clutched her by the throat. *"Go, now."* She tried to quell the thought, not give in to panic. But then realized—it's not panic.

Just urgency.

That still, small voice. *"Go."*

Aspen pressed her hand against the wood. It budged, but barely. She straightened in the space and pressed both palms against the wood. When she gained an inch on the left side, she dug her fingers in and pulled it aside. A heavy crate sat in front of it. She hiked her leg over it then hopped out. "Talon, come."

Slow moving, he appeared, just his head.

Aspen sat on the crate, realizing this was what the hero had done, then wrapped her arms around Talon's chest and hindquarters. With a small grunt, she heaved him over the crate and set him down. He plopped his rear on the ground, panting, and turned those soulful brown eyes to her, as if to ask, "Do we have to?"

"Come on, boy. We need to find water."

She stood, noticing the aching burn in her thighs from her flight earlier. Her legs trembled, but she'd have to shove mental steel down them to hoof it back to the orphanage in order to get the ride back to Lemonnier.

"Hey."

Aspen spun around, fully expecting Talon to lunge at this person. "Talon—" But she froze. Tail wagging, Talon let out that pathetic whimper again.

"I told you to stay hidden till dark."

"My dog needs water, and I have to get back. . .home."

"You don't live here." His brown eyes seemed to enjoy knowing that.

"I didn't say I did."

"Look." He came closer, glancing over his shoulder then back to her. "You need to get out of here."

"That's what I intend to do."

"No, I mean out of Djibouti. Now." He stood closer and reached a hand toward Talon. "Hey there, buddy."

Talon whimpered more, wagged his tail so hard she thought he might break in two, then rubbed against the man's hand.

"Heel!"

"He's okay." The man looked at her. "Seriously—get out. There's some bad stuff going down. Those men who were after you—"

The man tripped. Only he hadn't been moving. But he pitched forward and rolled to the ground.

"Go! Run!" he grunted as he collapsed. Something dark spread over his chest.

"You're shot!"

"Go, now! Talon—seek, seek, seek!"

Talon tore off, Aspen hauled behind him.

★ ★ Twenty-Five ★ ★

"Where? Where?" Cardinal shouted into the phone as he drove the tiny import away from the Sheraton, barreling through traffic like a drunk.

"Last known reporting of shots fired is on Avenue Georges Clemenceau. A woman called the police and reported two men chasing a woman and dog through the alleys," Lieutenant Brie Hastings said. "You're about a mile from the address provided. Take the next right—Rue de Paris, north for about a half mile, then left on Rue de Bender."

"Thanks, Brie. Do we have a satellite monitoring the area?"

"Officially, no."

Then unofficially—yes. "Good. Get on it, find her. That area's pretty heavy with sidewalk vendors and market shops. I need an extra set of eyes."

"Okay, but you are so going to owe me."

Why couldn't Brie just let it go? He wasn't interested. Never would be. She knew his profile, knew his history. Knew he didn't date.

No, but you try to kiss cute blonds in chapels.

The pang of conscience clunked him over the head.

Cardinal concentrated on weaving through the tangle of pedestrians and traffic. If he didn't exert more restraint, he'd draw attention to himself. He'd been at the hotel not twenty minutes when he got the call that police were flooding the scene of an incident. By now, he'd be too late. Unless...somehow...by some miracle...Aspen had escaped.

He'd questioned God's existence, His power, since his mother's death, but he could not deny the strange draw he had to cathedrals.

All the same, putting his life in the hands of some greater power defied good sense. *Make your own destiny. Master your own life.*

He swung into the painted area of the street that divided the two lanes and stuffed the gear in PARK. "Going to foot."

"Satellite's coming online. . .now."

Running would draw attention. Walking would be too slow.

Cardinal would love to crawl out of his skin, break into wings like his moniker implied, and soar over this place. *C'mon, Aspen. Where are you?*

Large parasol umbrellas arched over wares. Tip to tip, the material shielded both the products and their sellers from the unrelenting heat. Even with the sun going down, there was almost no reprieve in the summer heat. It'd topped 113 today. And Aspen was out there with Talon, on foot, running for her life.

Something in his gut clinched. A dose of guilt sprinkled over his thoughts. Pushing her away, telling her not to trust him—had those words contributed to her willingness to fling herself into the arms of deadly danger?

"Okay, I've got a line on you."

"I need your eyes on the market, not on me."

"No duh, Sherlock, but I have to know where you are to tell you where to go, and right now, I have someplace *very* hot in mind."

"I'm already there." He wouldn't play into her irritation. He had enough of his own as he scanned the long stretch of street. Vegetables, fruit, rugs, clothes, sandals. . .

Barking slowed him. "A dog. I hear a dog barking."

"Hmm, might want to hurry before they turn it into dinner."

"Muslim, smart aleck. They consider them unclean."

"You spoiled all my—wait."

Cardinal slowed, turning a circle. "What d'you see?"

"Head toward that three-story apartment complex."

As he came around, Cardinal saw a building with three rows of windows. Another with balconies lining the front. Another that seemed abandoned. "Brie, which one?"

"The one with the dishes on top."

Cardinal sprinted in that direction.

"Yeah, I see two people with a dog. In an alley. Tell me that's not curious."

"Thanks." He stuffed the phone in his pocket and sprinted toward the buildings.

He hurdled over a mound of oriental rugs. The seller shouted at him with a raised fist. But Cardinal's eyes were locked on the building. On searching for any sign of Aspen.

Movement caught his attention at the top of another building. A man. . .up there. . .waiting. . .

Sniper!

"No!" Cardinal pumped his arms harder, faster. His feet felt like they'd tangle over each other. So heavy, so tired. But he couldn't stop. Wouldn't. Not till he had Aspen safe again.

He whipped around a porta potty. The door flashed open. Nailed him in the cheek. He grunted, spun around, and picked up where he'd left off.

Across the street. He saw the opening to the alley. Saw the laundry strung from balcony to balcony. The clothes draped the alley in darkness. No way to see if Aspen was there. Or still there. *Or alive.*

Oh man. He didn't need that thought.

Chest burning, legs rubbery, Cardinal pushed. Hard. Harder.

A car burst from the left.

Cardinal dove over it. Banged his knee. Cursed but didn't stop, despite the numbing pain. Couldn't slow. Couldn't stop. Aspen.

Weakness gripped him. Slowed him. His mind screamed not to slow. His body warred for supremacy.

A scream from the alley punched through his chest, ripped his heart out and bungeed it back to its owner.

"As—" Her name caught in his dried throat. He nearly choked on the gust of air and his parched esophagus.

Overhead the clothes danced like soulless ghouls hovering over the city.

Cardinal propelled himself the last dozen feet, the material flapping above. A fourth building behind the one with the satellites shielded the location from sun.

A blur exploded from that direction. Rammed into him. Knocked him backward, into the plaster wall of the satellite building. He clamped his arms around whatever barreled into him.

A scream blasted his ears. Another scream. Barking and tiny

punches against his leg warned him of the dog. His mind reengaged as the curls bounced in his face. The fist drove forward. He narrowly avoided another jolt with her fist. "Aspen!"

The writhing, flailing frame of Aspen Courtland slowed. Terrified eyes stared up at him. "Dane?" Her confusion bled into sheer panic. She fisted his shirt. "Dane!" She glanced back. "They shot him!"

He guided her out of the sniper's line of sight, his mind roaring at the sight of blood on her face and shoulder. "You're bleeding."

As if the words slowly brought reality into a violent collision with her nightmare, Aspen looked down at her clothes. "No. . ." She shook her head and swallowed. "It's not my blood. It's his. They shot him. He was right there helping me, and they shot him."

"Who?"

She bunched her shoulders, as if warding off the pain, the trauma. She swiveled around and pointed. Aspen jerked. Looked to the left, the right. "He. . ." She covered her mouth with her hand then lowered it, her eyes glossing. "He. . .he was right there. He collapsed." She slumped back against him, and he could tell she was about to lose it. "He was *right* there. Dead. He was *dead!*"

"Hey, it's okay."

She jerked to him. "No. It's not okay. They shot him. I saw it. Now he's gone. But I saw it, Dane. I did!"

"Hey." He tightened his hold very gently, just enough to give her some grounding, some reassurance. "Let's get out of here, get you and Talon to safety. We'll sort it out there. We have sat imaging, so we can scour to see what happened."

Her vacant expression warned him of the shock taking over.

"Aspen?"

Pools of pale blue looked up at him. Her chin trembled.

Cardinal wrapped his arm around her and tugged her close. "Just. . . hold on. I'll get us out of here." He couldn't let her fall apart till they were no longer in the open. He cupped her face, searching for recognition that she was with him. "Okay, Angel?"

He held her face. Did he know he held her heart?

Calling her Angel—the nickname her parents and grandparents

had given her as a little girl—it righted her universe. Enabled her to muster the minuscule drops of courage left after seeing that man shot right in front of her.

Aspen lifted her jaw. She would not be a teary, whiny basket case in his arms. She swallowed, coiled Talon's lead around her wrist once more, then gave Dane a nod.

Dane wrapped his hand around hers. "Okay, hold on. Don't let go. We're going to the safe house."

"Got it." And she did. She got it that Dane was there to help. That even though he said not to trust him, his actions demanded it of her time and again. And honestly, she had no problem giving it. No problem letting him shoulder the burden of this disaster. It was nice not having to carry the world on her back.

He stalked through the alleys at a pretty fast clip, eyes alert, tension radiating off his strong build. The moments before he showed up were like being on a Tilt-a-Whirl at a fair, where the lights, the images, the people all blurred into one frenetic mural of chaos. Then Dane stepped in, caught her, and made everything right again.

Darkness had descended by the time they made it out of the shops and tangle of street vendors into the dusty, abandoned section of Djibouti City. A million questions peppered her mind, but she stowed them. The night, the danger, the men—they all prompted her to follow his lead. If he wasn't talking, she wouldn't talk. If he walked fast, she walked fast. If he slowed, as he had now, then she slowed.

"Just a little more," he said, sounding as tired as she felt.

As they strolled up the street, she spotted Santos's home. Would Dane lead them there?

Almost as soon as the thought flickered through her exhausted mind, he crossed the street, slipping behind a row of crumbling buildings. "You don't trust him."

"I don't trust anyone."

The retort was so quick, so sharp, she wasn't sure if that included her. She prayed it didn't. But she was too exhausted to fight the sadness that encompassed her. What was keeping him locked up, his heart smothered?

She stumbled, her feet tripping over each other. She grunted—everything hurt. Her eyes burned, her feet ached, her back throbbed, her mind screamed. . .yet her soul was quiet.

I don't understand, Lord. She should be a cracked nut by now. But she wasn't. Why?

A verse from Psalm 23 drifted into her mind: *"Yea, though I walk through the valley of the shadow of death, I will fear no evil."* She had nothing to fear. Yet she had everything to fear—the man, whoever he was, warning her to get out before she got hurt. Austin—where was he? They were in this place, and it seemed everything was going wrong. Yet she had peace. The same peace that carried her into the dilapidated safe house.

Holding her hand, Dane shifted, bolted the door with all four dead bolts. Her shoes crunched over the dirt and debris. Talon padded along beside her, head down, shoulders drooping. In the middle of the building, a room had been walled in to prevent light from seeping out and giving away their position.

Dane gave a quick rap then eased into the room.

Two men dressed in ACUs stood with M4s aimed at the door—at them. Aspen remembered them from Candyman's team, which made her wonder where he and Timbrel were.

Inside, Dane engaged the locks as he said, "Evening, gentlemen."

Rocket let out a whistle. "You scared us. Nobody said you were coming."

"Sorry. Didn't tell anyone. Going to use the back rooms. You got motion detectors out there, right?"

Rocket nodded.

"Shoot to kill anyone else who shows up." Dane started for the back then stopped. "How'd you get off base?"

Rocket shrugged with a cheeky grin that Aspen didn't quite understand. "After that little diversion, word came down it was a false alarm."

"Huh. Well, glad you're here. She needs to rest and eat."

"Scrip here can get something cooked up." Rocket nodded to his partner.

"No," Aspen said, her objection much weaker than she'd intended, "it's okay."

"Bring her whatever you can." Dane strode toward the back with her in tow.

She peered up at him. Why had he countered her?

"You need the nourishment to rest well."

Only as he turned did she realize they were still holding hands. He hadn't let go. He hadn't surrendered his position of control. And he was still asking her to trust him. Did he realize that?

In the back he led them into the rear room. A bunk bed, a table, and chairs hunkered in one corner against a peeling and cracked wall. A makeshift shower stood in the other with a curtain pinned to the walls that stood at right angles.

"Here." Dane guided her onto the lower bunk and squatted in front of her, once again cupping her face. "Rest. I'll be here. So will Talon."

"Talon. . .he needs water."

"I'll see to it. Just rest." With that, he slipped out and returned in what felt like seconds later with a bowl of water. He set it in front of Talon, who splashed it around as he inhaled the liquid.

Dane smoothed a hand along her cheek again. "Aspen, rest."

Mutely, she obeyed. Curled on the gray mattress with the thin sheet wrapped around her shoulders, Aspen stared at the ground. At nothing in particular. Just something for her gaze to rest on. The replay of those terrifying seconds in the alley replayed over and over. She shuddered, her mind taking every element down to the microsecond. Talon had never hit or alerted to the danger. Strange.

She must've drifted off to sleep because when her eyes opened next, Dane was gone. Aspen drew herself off the mattress and sat propped against the wall, her knees pulled against her chest. She tugged the sheet around her. Not that she was cold. She wasn't. Couldn't be—not in one-hundred-plus-degree weather. But there a chill coiled around her bones. From the stress. The anxiety. The man calling Talon by name.

"You okay?"

She turned, feeling numb and out of touch with reality. Dane eased into a chair in front of a computer, the side door ajar. She pushed the curls from her face and drew in a long breath, her mind hung up on the man in the alley. "I think I knew him."

Dane sat back, expectation hovering in his handsome features. "Yeah?"

She shook her head and shrugged at the same time. "I don't know. It's ludicrous to think someone I might know or have met is here in

Djibouti, the armpit of the world."

"But. . ."

"There was just. . . something." She sighed. "I can't explain it." As she extended her legs so they draped over the edge of the mattress, Talon pushed himself upright and cast those soulful brown orbs her way. His gaze darted to the mattress then to her as if begging for permission. Like he needed to. "Hup," she said and held her palm out over the mattress.

He leapt up and slumped against her side. She wrapped her arms around him, finding familiar strength and warmth in his pure devotion and loyalty.

"So, he felt familiar? Or something?"

"Yeah." Aspen dug her fingers into Talon's fur and bent to kiss his head. "Even Talon never made strange with him."

"Is that unusual?"

"Think about when you first met him."

Dane nodded. "Noted."

"A total stranger, and Talon doesn't warn the guy off with a throaty growl?"

"Do you think it could've been Austin?"

"No. He didn't look anything like my brother."

"You're sure?"

She laughed. "Trust me, I know my brother."

"Disguised, maybe?"

Searching her memory banks, she scoured the mental notes of the man. "No," she said slowly. "He didn't look anything like my brother. Black hair—"

"Could be dye."

"Brown eyes—Austin had blue like mine."

"Contacts."

Aspen wrinkled her nose. "Wrong nose. Austin's was aquiline. This guy's nose was hooked."

"Broken nose?"

"No, it was wide and hooked—what is this? I told you I didn't know this guy."

"I know, but sometimes it's those things that feel familiar, that we can't quite finger, that are the biggest connectors. Can you think of anything else that seemed similar or familiar?"

She sought more differences, but it stopped there. "No." And thank goodness. She couldn't grapple with the thought that the man could have been Austin and now he was shot and killed, right in front of her eyes. A shudder wiggled through her spine.

Dane stood and came to the bed. He perched on the edge next to her, making her stomach squirm. "But you said he felt familiar."

She nodded as she traced his profile and frowned when his jaw muscle popped. "What are you thinking?"

His steel eyes rammed into hers, sending a silent, intense signal of warning. "I have to go back to the alley."

"No!" She shoved off the wall and scooted to the edge of the bunk bed. "Are you crazy? Someone was out there *sniping* at us, and you just want to walk back into the middle of that?"

"Not want, have to." He remained undeterred. "Two things need to be ascertained—whether the man is dead and who he is. Why he knew what he knew."

"Maybe he knew Santos. There are a thousand explanations. But you don't have to go." Her heart pounded at the thought of him out there, exposed and getting shot at. "Please."

He hesitated, watching her. A war seemed to erupt within him, dancing in his blue eyes. It was something deep, something. . .dark. "I *have* to do this."

Somehow Aspen knew that this moment was a new one for Dane. In all the times they'd been working on finding Austin, he had rarely taken the time to explain what he was doing or justify it.

He was opening up to her. Something told her to give him the room to do it. To give him another reason to trust her. She almost smiled as that word—*trust*—sneaked into their relationship again. "Okay."

Dane's eyebrows danced for a second. "That was easy."

She laughed. "I'm never easy."

"I knew there'd be a catch."

"Just help me understand what is going on in that mind of yours. You never smile."

"I just did."

"No, that wasn't a smile. It's a smirk. Now, what's the look that's haunting you?"

He drew back, surprise etched into his face.

Spurred by that reaction, she knew she'd somehow hit on something. Maybe even something close to home, close to his heart. "Please."

"Okay."

Her heart rapid-fired.

"When I get back."

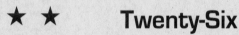

 Twenty-Six

Special Operations Safe House, Djibouti

Weren't we supposed to find something here?" Candyman glanced around, eyes shielded by his sunglasses and the bill of the baseball cap he wore low over his brow. The sun glinted off his thick, sandy blond beard. "Like a body?"

"Should've brought the dog." Watters walked to the end of the alley where the building abutted another.

"That dog don't go nowhere without his girl," Candyman countered. "And I don't like going nowhere without my girl."

"What girl?" Watterboy turned from his surveying and scowled at his buddy.

"Timbrel."

"Dude, you've got a long, hard road if you think she's going to be your girl."

"I got time. And hard roads—they're the best kind."

"You're begging for trouble."

"Nah, see, it's like this—the biggest trouble yields the best reward."

"That's some messed-up thinking." Watterboy patted his shoulder, a big grin ripping through his dark beard.

Ignoring their banter and honing his skills, Cardinal stood at the intersecting paths, examining, studying, thinking. They were both right—Talon would've been an asset in tracking down the man. Or the body. Considering the disruption of the molding cardboard, the stench wafting up from a freshly exposed patch of wet earth—no doubt caused

572

by the overturned cardboard—whoever went down, whoever terrified Aspen when he got shot, that person was still alive.

"Thinking we should bug out. Keep our heads and body parts where they belong."

Cardinal looked at Candyman. "What?"

"He doesn't want to get shot and lose his chance to win the woman whose head is as thick and stubborn as his." Watterboy started out of the alley.

Candyman grinned wide through that scraggly beard. "See? I knew you understood."

"Give me a minute." Cardinal stalked down the alley, searching the dirt, the cardboard. A rat scurried from one box to another, surprisingly nimble for its fat body. But it wasn't the rodent or the smell that drew him in. It was the trail of blood. Smeared up and over the seven-foot cement block wall that barred the exit.

Who are you?

Cardinal breathed out in frustration. He knew the answer. Didn't want to admit he did, but the gnawing in his gut told him he couldn't ignore this any longer.

Austin. Somehow and for some reason, the only man Cardinal had ever brought under his wing to train and mentor had turned on him.

Which meant when Austin cornered Aspen—the man *knew* she was his sister.

Yet he didn't tell her.

It was rare to have an agent go rogue and in such a super-expensive way like this. He couldn't be Austin. Not with the cost of plastic surgeons and experts it would take to create an entirely new identity. It meant Austin wasn't working alone—he had a handler.

A new handler.

Who was Cardinal's competition? Who had ripped his agent right out of his fingers?

You're really reaching with this one, Cardinal. This was all speculation. Trying to put the pieces together that were dangling in front of his nose. Options. . .options. What other options were there?

Austin wanted out.

No. He had thrived and excelled. Said he loved getting to take care of things that were otherwise undoable due to laws and such. Cardinal tried to remind him they weren't necessarily breaking laws. Just bending them. Really far.

Options. . .Austin. . .found. . .something. Or someone.

Okay, that made some sense. One of Austin's last communiqués mentioned meeting someone. Cardinal had taken it to mean a contact.

What if it was another agent? What if someone turned him, made him a double agent?

Cardinal ran a hand along the back of his neck. That thought had a ring of truth to it. Somehow.

"Hey, Spook."

Cardinal dragged his attention back to the two soldiers.

"We should get moving. Dark's coming." Watterboy thumbed over his shoulder. "And we have an audience."

Cardinal's gaze shifted to the narrow space between the two buildings. A small crowd had assembled at the corner of the northernmost building. He nodded and started back. The ride was made in relative quiet, affording him the time to sort out his thoughts. Anything was plausible at this point. Until they had some more facts. . .

"What're you thinking?"

Cardinal met the ironclad gaze of Watters just as Candyman slowed and turned into the alley behind the safe house. "Too much."

"You do remember we're on your side, right?"

"This isn't 'my' side—it's a mission." He flung open the door, agitated with the questions, the ones that had no answers, just more mystery. Inside, Rocket and Scrip pushed from their seats. Both lobbed questions at him.

Cardinal gritted his teeth and kept walking. Down the hall.

Growling announced Talon's presence seconds before the yellow Lab and Aspen stepped into view at the other end. The sight of her, those blond curls framing that beautiful face, slowed him. *I'm failing her.* The sidewinder of a thought spiraled through his chest and rammed into his heart.

Cardinal lowered his head and banked right. Flung back the door to the stairs. Climbed them three at a time, moving quicker with each advance until he jogged toward the door. Pushed through it. Agitation kept him moving, his mind warring that he had to corral his buzzing nerves.

Sticky, warm air coiled its arms around him. He paced. His nerves vibrated. Nothing was going right. Everything was wrong. The mission. Austin. Burnett. Payne. Aspen—especially Aspen. This wasn't supposed to happen. This—the way things had changed between them—was the reason he had Cardinal rules. Cardinal Rule #1—*Never work women.* He had others—never stay somewhere longer than you have to, always have an exit strategy, never engage the heart.

The door groaned and creaked behind him.

"Hey, you okay?" Aspen's sultry voice was as warm as the air. Her shoes crunched over the rooftop as she came closer, trailed by the soft padding of Talon's paws.

Just give her the facts. Get the game plan established. Move on it. That should be enough to keep his mind active and his heart inactive.

He pivoted and dropped against the half wall that served as a barrier against the two-story fall. Arms folded should send the message he wanted: he was closed to her. Had to be. "No body."

Aspen frowned. "I guess that's good."

"Good? No, it's not good. It means someone wants that person dead. And if that person tries to contact you again, it puts your life in jeopardy."

"*Our* lives."

He shoved off the wall and turned around. Had he really done that? Funneled down the danger to include only her? Is that where his mind had gone? Not good. Anger tingled through his chest, down into his arms. To avoid fisting his hands, he gripped the ledge. Stared out over the darkening sky.

A devastating realization spread through him. Aspen. He was worried about her. Austin he could sort out. The mission he could handle. Aspen. . .if anything happened to her. . .

And the angel flew.

No! He snapped his eyes closed against the image, against the face becoming Aspen's. *Oh merciful God! Help me. I can't go there. . . . I* can't *fall for her.*

"Dane?" Aspen came to his side and touched his oblique. "What's going on?"

"Nothing," he ground out. His mind reared, ordering him to pull away from her.

But he couldn't. Didn't want to. Her warm touch soothed the beast within. Made the sun shine in a storm-ridden life. Just as someone else in his life once had. "My mother."

Aspen gave him a quizzical look.

Worms. A can of worms. But. . . "She died when I was fifteen." He slumped against the wall and forced himself to straighten. Look at her. "There are very few amazing women in this world. When she died, the world was one less a beautiful, amazing woman." Torment smothered him. *Don't do this. Don't go there. Not with Aspen.* "I always wondered if I could've saved her, stopped her death." He looked at her. Knowing he was defeated having opened that cauldron of history. "I don't want to have that regret with you, Aspen."

No sweeter words could've moved her heart more. And yet anchored her life more firmly in his hands. He cared about her. A lot. That's what all this "don't trust me" stuff was about.

"Dane, you're not God."

The fight seemed to have drained out of him. "Trust me, I'm completely aware of that."

"But you're trying to be Him, trying to control the outcome." Emboldened by his openness, she reached out to brush away the hair from his face.

He caught her hand and held it in midair. "Please, Aspen." He shook his head. "I'm not. . .I can't do this." He lowered his gaze then tugged her hand to his face and kissed her palm.

Butterflies swarmed her stomach. "Then you shouldn't do things like that." She smiled as she inched closer to him. "Tell me about your mom."

The shift in his demeanor was swift and large. "No."

"Why do you think you could've saved her, stopped her death?"

"She was murdered." His breathing grew heavier, his eyes clouded. "Murdered right in front of me."

"Oh Dane, I'm so sorry." Less than a foot remained between them, but the romance dimmed beneath his words.

"I just stood there, watching, like I was disembodied." His words whispered his agony. "But I wasn't. I was there. *Right there.*" His brows rippled. "Why didn't I stop him?"

"You were only fifteen."

"But she was my life, the only good thing besides my sister."

Waves of grief and awe crashed through Aspen—first that he'd paralleled what he felt for her with what he felt for his mother, murdered. And he'd just told her he had a sister, too. "Is your sister still alive?"

Dane blinked. His grief washed away. "What?"

Oh no. She saw it. The vulnerable side of him blinked out, like darkness when a light is turned off, and in its place returned the formidable fortress that was Dane Markoski. Aspen cupped his face. The move surprised them both.

"Dane, don't shut me out." She leaned closer, just inches from him. "Please—I see what you feel for me. It's a reflection of my feelings for you. It's not wrong or bad."

"No, but I am." He stood, and she saw the move for what it was—his attempt to place distance between them.

"You're what? Bad?"

Though he stood at least a foot taller than her, he sagged beneath whatever weighted him. "That's an oversimplification. I'm just. . ."

"What?"

He cast a sidelong glance in her direction, the moon and city lights, sparse though they were, reflecting off his face and eyes. "This is upsetting you." He turned and stalked the three feet to the other ledge. More distance.

"No." She snorted off a laugh as she trailed him. "You are upsetting me by consistently pushing me away when I can see as plain as day you are attracted to me. Whatever it is, Dane, whatever is haunting you, you need to get out from under its power."

"I wish it were that simple."

Aspen didn't yield. "Why isn't it?"

He traced her cheek, tingling and shooting darts of heat down her neck and into her stomach. "You are sweet but nai—"

"Naive." She smiled up at him. "Yeah. It's not the first time that's been said about me. And it's not a bad thing, I'll have you know. Just because I believe in you, believe in the man you are—"

"You don't know who I am." Razor sharp, his words sliced through her heart.

577

Fear and uncertainty swooped in, striking at the essence of what she believed was happening—clearing the air, deepening their relationship. She wanted that. Wanted him to break free from whatever stopped him from accepting her.

"See? You aren't even sure. Is that what you want?" His words weren't as confident this time. Hurt glowed like a halo around them. "Doubts, fears—about me, being afraid of me?"

What was he saying? Why did he look at her with that loathing expression?

"So, you're not Dane Markoski, technically and legally my husband?" Man, she wanted to smack him, smack some sense into him. Or the cantankerous side out of him.

After a long, lingering look, he turned away. "Right now, he's the only person I want to be."

"How is it you can face untold terrors and dangers in the field, on missions, but when it comes to what you feel for me, you run scared?"

"I'm not scared."

Aspen nearly laughed. He sounded just like Austin in high school, when he gave his litany of reasons why he couldn't ask Amanda Blair to the homecoming dance.

"Baloney!" Aspen slapped the curl from her face that kept batting her cheek. "Fear is driving your campaign of misery. Fear is stopping you from what you feel for me. When will you man up and face whatever is eating you alive? If this isn't who you are, then *be* who you are. Show that man to me!"

Fire spewed from his eyes. "Be careful what you ask for."

"Why?" She stepped closer, furious. "Are you afraid I might actually like him better?"

Everything in him seemed to swell. His shoulders bunched. His fists balled as he curled in on himself, his chin tucked. "You will never see that man." He took a breath, and the fire gushed out of him. The difference reminded her of a balloon, deflated of helium. Shriveled. Used. Empty.

Though something in her wanted to quit, to walk away from this insane argument with him, she had a larger sense of dread that if she did, Dane would be lost to her forever.

Fight for him. The words boomed through her. So, he said she'd never see that man, huh? "Why? I'm not good enough?"

"Once you see that man, you'll beat the fastest path out of my life."

Oh no, no he wouldn't get away with that. Wouldn't blame her for walking away. "Give me more credit than that. I might be stupid and naive in your book, but at least I have a heart and give people a chance, believe in them—in you, Dane." How many times would she have to say it before he believed and accepted it?

"Then your belief is misplaced."

"No." Breathing through the pounding of her heart hurt. "No, it's not. Your fear is crippling you, Dane. Robbing you, stealing joy from your life. You sit in cathedrals longing for something you think you can never have because you're too afraid to reach for it."

Dane jerked toward her, scowling. But silent.

"That's the same thing happening right here, right now. I know that. I feel it deep"—she touched her fingers together and pressed them to her abdomen—"in the core of my being."

"Can't you see?" He took a step toward her but held himself tense. "You're angry. *I* made you angry. Do you think it ends there?"

"Dane, people fight. They argue. Get mad at each other. It's normal."

"No." He returned to the wall and stepped around her. "Not like—" He clamped his mouth shut. Lips in a thin line, he lowered his head.

There. There it was, whatever was haunting him, turning him into this stubborn, thickheaded oaf who wouldn't release whatever insanity held his mind and heart captive in a painful prison.

"Like what? Like you?"

He wouldn't look at her. Wouldn't talk. Wouldn't move.

Aspen went to him. "Dane. . . ?"

"The c"—he drew in a long breath—"the man who killed my mother."

Was that who Dane feared? Why? What did his mom's murderer have to do with him? The dots wouldn't connect. "Talk to me, please. I want to help." She touched his side, felt the deep rise and fall of his breathing. "I'm not going anywhere, Dane. I'm here. I love you." The words rang in her ears, startling. Exhilarating.

Locked on to her, Dane's eyes searched her face. "Don't say that. Please. . .don't. I don't want to hurt you."

She couldn't help the smile. His words warred with the longing, the aching resonating through his handsome face. "Well, I *do* love you, and you *will* hurt me. It's what people do, but it doesn't mean we shouldn't try."

"You are so beautiful, so pure. . ." His hand slid to the back of her neck as he captured her mouth with his, pulling her deeper beneath the swell of his strength and passion. It felt as if she tumbled into a hot tub, the warmth bubbling around her as his arms encircled her. Crushed her against his chest.

Abandoned Building, Djibouti

Neil Crane cursed. God forgive his Christian upbringing, but he did. That whopper of a kiss severely complicated things.

"You ready?"

He turned to Lina. "You kidding? That"—he pointed toward the building where Cardinal and the American team had holed up—"screws up everything."

"It changes nothing." She turned and lifted a phone from the windowsill. Eyes on him, she pressed a button then placed the phone to her ear.

"Who are you calling?" He drew his own phone out, surreptitiously hitting the record button.

With a rueful smile, she walked away from him. Out of the room. "*Privet. . . On v lyubvi.*"

Neil turned from the window. Russian? She was speaking Russian? Since when? He moved carefully, quietly, closer. He watched the screen as his phone received the words and translated them for him.

HELLO. HE'S IN LOVE.

Thank God for gadgets.

"*. . .da. . .nyet!* Nyet, *on slishkom khorosho. . .* Khorosho. *Prekrasno.* Da, *segodnya vecherom. . .*"

YES. NO! NO, HE'S TOO GOOD. . . OKAY. VERY WELL. YES, TONIGHT.

She stood by a wall, her head in her hand as she listened. "*Poka.*"

BYE.

Neil pocketed the phone and drew the Ruger from its holster. He eased into the room, aiming at her head.

★ ★ Twenty-Seven ★ ★

Special Operations Safe House, Djibouti

His universe tilted a degree. Cardinal felt the implosion of everything he'd carefully constructed to keep him safe, to stop him from perpetuating a curse. And Aspen Courtland had dismantled every trap, every barrier, every reason.

The way she fit in his arms amazed him. The kiss had been long enough to sear his conscience. Long enough to tell him he wanted more, so much more. Long enough to scare the living daylights out of him, too.

Perfect. She was perfect. Being with her was perfect.

A perfect formula for disaster.

Cardinal closed his eyes against the thought, swallowed and inhaled the sweet scent of her hair. Lavender. Maybe some vanilla. He hated that he knew those smells because they would forever be ingrained in his mind as belonging to her. He'd never be able to forget her. Forget what had just transpired.

"I love you."

She had no idea *who* she loved. She didn't even know his real name. The question burning against his conscience was, did he love her?

He'd do anything for her. Maybe that was the terror of it all—he'd kill for her. Kill anyone and anything, including his feelings for her, if he felt that would keep her safest. Because suddenly this woman, who was sweet and sensitive yet had an iron will, seemed like a glass rose in his large, clumsy hands.

Aspen drew back and looked up at him again.

Cardinal couldn't help himself. Or rather—he *did* help himself—to another kiss. So sweet. So willing. He liked the way she stiffened at first under the touch of their lips then relaxed into it. Her hands on his back, fingers pressing into him, deepening the kiss burned the last of his resolve.

Something bumped against his leg. Pushed between them—no, pushed them *apart*.

Giggling, Aspen drew back and looked down. "I think he's jealous." When she met Cardinal's gaze again, she wore a shy smile.

Talon plopped between them, panting as he peered up at them.

Cardinal eased against the half wall, hauling in his reeling thoughts, and petted the Lab. "I think it's me who should be jealous." Smart dog. Wedging in, planting himself solidly in a position as if to say, "Back off. She's mine." As he reached toward the dog, a low rumble carried through Talon's chest. His tail flicked.

"Hey. Sorry. That's normal—he's not a pet, and sometimes—"

Talon's bark severed her words.

Aspen ruffled his head and rubbed his ears. "It's okay, boy. I can handle having two handsome guys in my life."

In her life...

Didn't she realize that couldn't happen? Man, he'd never felt the urge to backpedal faster than he did right now. Fear. No, it was bigger, stronger. He could feel it. Aspen was right. He was afraid of this. Letting go of his strict Cardinal rules was like jumping off a cliff. Free fall. Straight to his death. Maybe even hers.

And the angel flew.

"Aspen, listen." Cardinal raked his hand through his hair, groping for some tendril of sanity. Some way to lower the boom. "I...I can't—"

Again, Talon's growl leapt into the night. Cardinal glanced at the dog, who pushed onto all fours and walked to the other side, sniffing the air. He barked. Whimpered. Sat down. Looked at her then scooted closer to the wall.

"That's...weird." Aspen turned toward the dog.

Cardinal stood, using the distraction to turn the conversation away from his weakness. "What?"

"That's...I think that's a hit." She looked at him with a frown. "But on what?"

The door flung open. Candyman leapt out. "Hey." He slowed for a second, his gaze taking in the scene. No doubt the entirely too observant grunt knew what was going on. "Downstairs. Burnett's on the line. We're moving." And just as quick the guy disappeared the way he'd come.

Downstairs, Cardinal, Aspen, and Talon gathered with the others. A full ensemble.

"Circle up." Watterboy motioned them around a laptop that sat on the table. "Go ahead, General. We're all present."

"Where's the happy couple?"

Cardinal arched his eyebrow as he planted a hand on the table and leaned in. "You're not funny."

Burnett roared, his broad shoulders bouncing. "Yeah, I keep telling my doctor that." He pounded a fist on the table. "Lousy, no-good—he put me on a diet! Said my blood pressure is too high." He wagged a finger at the camera. "That's your fault, you know. I'm not drinking no crappy Diet Dr Pepper, so get me some answers I can cram into this leak that's pouring dung into my lap."

"What leak?"

"Payne!"

Cardinal digested the news. "What do you have?"

"Show him," Burnett said as he stabbed a thick finger at the webcam.

Watterboy flattened a map between Cardinal's hand and the laptop's keyboard. "Here and here."

"What am I looking at?"

"Caravans."

Cardinal peered through his brow at the live-feed video. Was that word supposed to mean something? "There are caravans all over the place. I see them every day."

"Not like this."

"Why?"

"In and out," Watterboy said. "Same route. Twice a week."

"Where are they going?"

"Sliding right past our base to the docks."

"Cargo?"

"That's what you need to find out." Burnett popped the top on a DP can and took a slurp.

"It's muffed up," Candyman said, chomping into an apple. Juice dribbled down his beard.

"You're disgusting," Timbrel said, her lip curled.

"Hey, hazards of the beard." Candyman winked as he used his sleeve to clean up.

Cardinal waited for someone to elaborate. He hated being the last one in on the information.

"At first look," Watterboy said, "we thought maybe weapons."

"No way." Candyman pitched the apple into a metal bin. "Pardon me, General," he said as he leaned in, keyed in something, and drew up images. His thick, tanned finger jabbed toward the screen. "Check it. Those aren't weapons' crates, and though there is a butt-load of illegal weapons traipsing across this desert, that's not a known weapons' cache."

"Where was that image taken and when?"

"A half-dozen kilometers outside Omo National Park."

Pushing up, Cardinal frowned. "Sudan?" It made no sense. Clearly Burnett and Hastings had been busy, tracking the caravan from one place to the next. "Aren't there gold mines out there?"

"Yeah, but dude, c'mon." Candyman grinned. "They aren't smuggling gold. No reason to. Everyone knows that's what's there and that it's being mined. Besides—" Candyman traced a path on the map from Sudan, past the base and to another point. "FOB Kendall is funneling whatever it is through their little camp then giving them clear passage to the docks."

Cardinal stared at the information, at the maps, at the images. "What else is in that region? Minerals, I mean."

Watterboy shrugged. "Got me."

Though the man feigned ignorance, Cardinal had a gut instinct that he could wager a pretty accurate guess. "Gold mines." He rubbed his jaw, thinking. Actually, *not* liking what he was thinking.

"What is it?" Aspen stepped closer. "What's wrong?"

"There are gold mines there, just like Candyman said." He sighed. "Some uranium is also recovered as a by-product with copper, or as a by-product from the treatment of other ores, such as the gold-bearing ores of South Africa."

"Uranium?" Aspen scrunched her nose.

Candyman whistled. "Yeah, aka, yellowcake."

Curses flitted on the hot air and from the laptop.

"Hey, get me back on!" the general growled. At his command and a few clicks, Burnett's round face glared at them again. "Cardinal, if you really think that's what's happening out there, then we have to find that—"

"Should be easy. The uranium decay puts off radiation."

"Think I need you to tell me that, VanAllen?"

Contrite and smirking, Candyman lowered his head. "No, sir."

"Then shut up."

"General," Cardinal said, wanting to laugh, "your blood pressure."

"Get off my back. I know what I'm doing. And you bunch of girls are the ones blowing my pressure through the roof. Now, get down there and find those crates. I want this solved."

"Sir?" Cardinal eased into view again. "Think Payne is connected to this? Think that's why he wanted me out of here and the rest of us locked up on base so we couldn't catch wind of his little operation?"

"That's exactly what I'm thinking. But we don't have time for guesses. I need proof!"

Cardinal looked to Watters. "Where are the crates now?"

"Port of Djibouti."

"We need to move or we'll lose them."

"Gear up!"

Abandoned Apartment, Djibouti

Lina turned, her eyes widening as she lowered the phone.

"Hands up." He stared down the sights of his Ruger, shoving his mind away from the feelings that had strangled his good sense, stopped him from figuring this out sooner. "Where I can see them." He nodded as she turned, arms held out. His head pounded—why had he ever trusted her? "You've been working me."

She swallowed. Guilt. Nerves.

"Who are you?"

"It doesn't matter who I am. What matters is that we have the same goal."

Neil laughed. "I don't think so."

"You want Cardinal captured. So do we—I."

"No." He cocked his head. "Let's go with your first try—*we*. Who's we?"

"I cannot tell you that."

"Then let me put another hole in that pretty head of yours."

"Don't be stupid. You kill me, you don't get Cardinal."

"Hey, doll, if I don't kill you, then I *don't* get him—because you're going to take him right out from under me, isn't that right?"

She had a will of iron. "You will get your answers." She lifted her jaw. "Then I get mine."

"That sounds mighty tidy. Too tidy."

"We're out of time." She wasn't the Lina he'd been willing to spill his guts for two hours ago. The soft, innocent facade had evaporated with her seething anger. "We do this or we don't. What's it going to be, cowboy?" She tossed a look over her shoulder. "They're leaving."

Neil rose from the chair and walked to the window. He tugged back the dingy sheet and peered along the sliver between the material and the chipped plaster wall. Darkness inside and out made it easier to see without losing time for compensating as vision adjusted to the new light setting.

He was right. "They know." Then he'd been right not to trust Cardinal.

But he'd been wrong to trust the woman beside him. He'd been sucked into the old romance trap. Bought it. And the island in Arkansas.

Gah! Had he really been that stupid?

As he watched their vehicle lumber onto the road and speed off toward the docks, he heard something. To his right.

Tones.

Neil mastered his body. Forced himself not to betray what he'd detected—she was using a phone. Why couldn't he see the light from the display? Had she killed it somehow? What was she sending through that device?

What if. . .what if *she* was behind everything?

They're heading toward the port. Fury wormed through him. He'd been right! They had known. Cardinal. Burnett—they had to know. Why else would they make a run to the docks in the middle of the night? A dead weight plunked into his gut.

Cardinal had told him once: trust nobody. Not even yourself. And Neil had failed. He'd trusted himself, trusted his instincts. Believed that this demure woman was innocent. That she really cared about him and was in danger. Classic damsel-in-distress game. But....how? Why? Why would she target him? *I'm nobody.*

Yeah, a nobody with an arsenal of information and secrets.

Safe House, Djibouti

Cardinal. What did that mean? General Burnett had used it while talking to Dane. Was it some type of code?

Aspen shrugged off the questions, her mind still racing at the idea of going into a dockyard and sneaking around crates that potentially held yellowcake. She didn't know enough about the mineral to know if she'd end up with radiation poisoning, so she trusted that Dane wouldn't lead her into a situation that could potentially hurt her or the others.

Sitting between her feet, Talon panted and seemed to sense the thrumming adrenaline in the vehicle. Leaning into her touch, he whimpered. At least—she thought he did. With the high engine noise and the road chatter, sounds collided. He'd really been off lately. On the rooftop, in action. He'd been through a lot, and she wasn't sure he was weathering the storms very well.

Next to her, Timbrel bumped her knee against Aspen's. "You okay?"

Aspen nodded as her gaze made its way to Dane, who sat with his forearms on his legs. Decked out in an Interceptor vest and a weapon across his legs, he stared at a map using his small shoulder lamp. Intense. Direct. Strong. Being in his arms, that kiss. . .and just as swift, that regret.

Something bigger than herself compelled her to stand her ground and not let him slink away from their mutual attraction. She'd never been like that, confrontational. In fact, that type of behavior was Class-A Timbrel. Maybe her friend had rubbed off on her some.

"Go easy, Aspen," Timbrel said in her ear, soft but firm. "He's not who you think he is."

Aspen glanced at her friend, surprised. "What does that mean?" Her attention swung back to Dane.

Watterboy said something that pushed Dane upright, and he adjusted the weapon on the strap and stretched his neck. His gaze struck hers. The granite expression softened, a flicker of a smile wavering on his lips. But she must've had confusion still on her face because his brow knotted, then his gaze slid to Timbrel. The momentary softening vanished as the granite slammed back into place.

The vehicle lurched to a stop. "All quiet," Watterboy called.

Unloaded, they grouped up in the night-darkened alley behind a building that squatted in the dirt like a fat spider. Despite being a good seventy yards from the docks, port noises drifted loud and clear to their position.

Aspen lifted a ball from her pocket and let Talon nose it. It'd be his reward once they got back to the safe house and now served as an initiative to do a good, quick job.

With a Glock strapped to her thigh, Aspen had firepower, and with Talon at her side, she had dog power. But the power she found the greatest comfort in was her heavenly Father. He'd been her rock and fortress through every storm. Though she didn't have the answers she wanted, the comfort of His presence remained true and steadfast. More than any human ever had.

Aspen would be a liar, though, if she didn't admit to having an increased measure of comfort in the presence of someone else, too— Dane. She found herself looking to him even now as the team prepped to sneak onto the barge with the purported yellowcake.

Watterboy gave the signal that launched the mission.

The precision and stealth of the half-dozen men—Watterboy, Candyman, Scrip, Rocket, and two others whose names she couldn't remember—amazed her. She'd been in the Air Force, but sitting behind a desk at the JAG offices didn't compare to this in-your-face tactical stuff. She prayed for strength, prayed she could do her position as Talon's handler justice and make the guys proud. Make Dane proud.

She scurried along the wall, sandwiched between Timbrel and Candyman, keeping Talon at her side. Though the preferred method for a CTT dog was to be off-lead or on a long lead, until they got on the boat they had to stay close and quiet.

The team slowed at a juncture, and she watched as they gave silent signals. Two bolted away from the building, their boots thumping quietly—but it felt much louder at this hour with the emptied docks and port—as they beat a path to a smaller structure. A shack that probably served as an office of sorts. Or something.

The lineup shortened as each member made tracks to the other side until it was her turn. She reached down and touched Talon's head. "Go," she said in a hushed but firm voice.

Aspen rushed from the protection of one building, across the alley, to the next. Only as she and Talon stepped up with the others did she release the pent-up breath. Muttering praise to Talon, she checked the others, checked for Dane.

His strong back was to her. He faced front with Watterboy and Candyman, assuming a stance to cover as the other two hustled the last dozen feet to the ship. With all the swishing of tactical pants and thumping of boots, she marveled that they hadn't drawn attention. Then again, those not looking for trouble rarely found it.

From this position, if she peered out. . .just a little. . .she could see the barge that jutted beyond the lip of the harbor. Its red-and-white hull shone clearly. Water rippled and lapped, glittering. She glanced up at the moon, full in its brilliance, unfettered by clouds. Which meant the team could be seen just as clearly.

From her protective cover with Timbrel and Rocket, Aspen waited as the others did a close-up assessment of the barge. Candyman shifted and gave hand signals.

"Move," Rocket said as he darted toward the barge.

Aspen and Timbrel jogged toward the team, Talon working with grace and without hesitation. It gave her hope that he'd be okay.

Watterboy and Candyman leapt from the dock onto the deck of the self-propelled barge. A dark form moved out from a shadow. Watterboy wheeled around and aimed his weapon. A small muted spark exploded in the darkness. The form wilted, and Candyman dropped in behind to catch the man and lower him to the steel.

On the dock, next to a barrel that gave flimsy cover, Scrip knelt, eyes out as he scanned the dock down the barrel of his M4.

"Candyman wants the dog," Rocket said, hand on Aspen's shoulder. "Go."

Aspen's gaze bounced to the deck where Candyman stood, motioning her up. Stomach in her throat, she moved forward with Talon. Even as she made the climb, there was resistance on the lead. "Talon, seek, seek!"

He surged forward, but as his paw hit the metal plank up to the barge, he turned back.

"Talon, hup!" Aspen continued forward, keeping her fear smothered and her authority focused. If she let him know his actions distressed her, it'd only add to his confusion, his momentary panic. He needed her to lead, to express certainty about their mission.

As they jumped across, Candyman hooked her arm and tugged her aside, into the shadows. "That way." He pointed down a narrow steel catwalk that stretched over an open area filled with containers. Did he want her to cross it? Alone—she'd be completely exposed with the bow to her left and the stern with the wheelhouse to her right. Though she didn't *see* danger, this hot, humid night screamed it.

Great. Heights and danger. Didn't they know she wasn't a combat veteran?

Yeah, but you have a combat *tracking team dog.*

"Go!" Candyman prompted, his teeth gritted through the word.

Right. Okay. Talon was trained to protect her and the others by scouting ahead for danger, so she needed to let him do that. But they'd been through so much. He'd come a long way in their relatively short time together. Letting him go ahead of her, knowing there could be insurgents, Aspen knew how this could end.

She pushed that thought from her mind as she stepped onto the catwalk. It bounced a little beneath her feet. Talon's nails scratched on the steel as they hurried over it. Not much separated her and a twenty-foot fall to the well floor. And nothing protected her from being seen. Bent, she crouch-scurried toward safety.

"Hey!"

Aspen froze as a shape loomed ahead of her.

★ ★ Twenty-Eight ★ ★

Two shapes stood on the catwalk. One was Aspen. The other was trouble.

Cardinal threw himself around, bringing his weapon to bear. He aimed—but in that split second, he knew if he shot the guy they'd alert everyone within a couple of miles to their presence. Would Aspen know to catch the guy? If he didn't shoot, the guy would make a lot more noise.

Cardinal applied pressure to the trigger. Felt the kick of the weapon. Kept his eyes trained on the target, who jerked back—the impact of the bullet.

Like lightning, someone darted behind the guy. Caught him. Lowered him to the rail. Watterboy motioned Aspen and Talon onward. The breath that had lodged in the back of Cardinal's throat finally processed as he trailed Aspen hurrying to cover.

Squatting at the lip of the deck, she looked down and hesitated. In that move, he saw the dilemma—Talon. The jump was too high for him. She eyed the canisters. That'd be a big jump, but worse, it'd be loud. They'd wake the neighborhood. Or at least the men shacked up in the cramped living quarters below deck.

Talon jumped. Right over Cardinal's head and onto the first canister.

A metal thwunk resonated through the well.

Cardinal tensed, listening, alert. He flinched when he saw Aspen moving down the rungs of the wall-mounted ladder. Two more thwunks sounded by the time Aspen touched down.

Weapon pointed up, Cardinal's gaze traced the wheelhouse, waiting for a light. For a shout. For a sign that Talon's adventure had been heard.

He sensed something at his side and glanced there. Aspen stood next to him, coiling the lead around her arm, her expression tense, a mixture of relief and fear. She gave him a half smile that told him she felt safer with him, a smile that extended thanks for saving her from the guy on the catwalk.

"Phil? That you?" came a wary, groggy voice.

"Yeah." The voice came from Candyman. "Just tripped. Go back to bed."

"Bed? What the heck are you talking about?" Light flooded out from a side door and delivered a man into the middle of the team.

Cardinal grabbed Aspen and spun around, pinning her between himself and the crates stacked twenty feet up. From his location, he peered to the side, watching that door well.

Candyman slid up along the wall, hidden, as the man in overalls stepped into the open.

A scraggly, unkempt beard and hair framed a sea-bronzed face. Clearly the codger had seen years on the open waters. He looked around, scratching his head. "What are you tal—?"

An arm snaked around the back of the guy.

Old eyes bulged in fright. The man gripped the arm that encircled his neck.

A hand thrust a needle into the man's carotid. Old Man of the Sea went limp, and Candyman dragged him out of sight between two of the fifteen-foot-tall canisters.

"Frank?"

Candyman widened his eyes and held out his hands, as if to say, "Seriously?" then jumped back against the wall again. Seconds later, the last guy joined Frank. Someone took out the light, and they were back in motion.

Cardinal keyed his mic. "Intel has about a dozen more men. Let's *not* wake them."

Candyman nodded.

"You okay?" Cardinal asked Aspen, who seemed to wilt now that the immediate threat had been eliminated.

She gave a nod.

Lowering his gun, he bobbed his head toward Talon, who trotted toward them. "We'll find the crates. Keep him on guard."

Aspen nodded again, smoothing a hand along Talon's head.

About forty canisters sat in the well. Roughly a dozen of them could hold a small import with ease. But the smaller crates numbered close to thirty and resembled the images Burnett had shared with the team. If they had to search all of them, it'd be a long night. But that's why they had the radiation device.

Cardinal joined Rocket and Watterboy who walked the crates, waving the device over them. They rose to about shoulder height on the outside and at least twice that in the middle. Stacked carefully, the crates in the middle had the best chance of being their gold mine.

He watched, waited, all the while keeping tabs on Aspen and Talon. As the minutes ticked away, so did his patience. Those crates had been buried well within the center of this cluster. Intentionally.

Cardinal wouldn't surrender. Not yet. Not ever.

He climbed atop the crates and started shifting them. He motioned to Candyman to give him the device. Reader in hand, he wanded the wooden crates.

The thing squawked a positive reading. He grinned and tossed the reader back. Tapping the blade of his Ka-Bar knife between the lid and the rest, he worked it in then wedged it against the wood and lifted. A loud crack echoed through the well as he lifted the top.

Candyman climbed up next to him, his shoulder lamp hitting the packaging. "Vaults. Yellow vaults. That supposed to be a clue?"

His sarcasm only served to grate on Cardinal's nerves. Cardinal snapped the lock with a multitool and flipped the lid.

Candyman cursed. Several times really fast.

Couldn't have said it better. Cardinal slapped the lid closed, praying the radiation levels of the decaying uranium weren't strong enough to contaminate him. "Check the others," he said as he sheathed his knife. Knuckles against his lips, he watched as the others opened the other crates.

He eased back on another crate and drew out the camera and opened the live-feed connection to Burnett. Toeing the lid, he opened the vault and filmed the contents, then let the lens scrape over the rest, just enough to show Burnett that this shipment had to be intercepted before it got to wherever it was going.

This barge couldn't deliver its contents. Most barges were hired. So maybe the owner didn't realize what he carried. Or maybe he was being paid off—just like Admiral Kuhn? The shifting of the plot elements in this nightmare felt like tectonic plates colliding beneath the earth. There were bound to be seismic-scale responses.

Who was behind this? Where would the contents end up? Did that really matter when something like this being under the cover of darkness meant it wasn't on the up-and-up? That meant treaties or laws or embargoes were being violated.

What if this stuff was headed to Iran?

As if led to that thought via the divine, Cardinal's gaze fell on the canister across from him. More precisely, the markings on said canister. He climbed off the crates, squinting. Tried to aim the shoulder lamp at the stenciled marks as he moved.

"Whaddya got?" Candyman asked, his voice quiet and quick.

In a terrifying shift, the past surged over his barriers and rammed into the present. Heart backfiring, Cardinal traced the stenciled lettering.

Беларусь

Talon straightened, his keen eyes locked on one man. He rose and padded over to Dane, nosing the man's thigh. Talon had done that a thousand times to Aspen over the past year as she struggled with her brother's disappearance.

Sitting at Dane's feet, Talon gazed up at him perceptively. Whimpered. Inched closer.

Dane didn't move, his attention glued to the rusting red canister that loomed over him. Hand on painted letters that had once been white, he stared. As if he could see straight through it.

"Dane?" Aspen whispered to him as she joined him.

No response. What was wrong? She peeked around at his face.

Haunted. Stricken.

Something rumbled in the pit of her belly. Aspen touched his back. "Dane?"

Jaw tightened, he snapped out of it. Lowered his gaze to the side but did not look at her. "We need to clear out."

And that was it. He morphed back into the super soldier or whatever he was. "Cardinal." The word burst from her lips before she had time to consider what it might do. What it might mean.

Dane flinched. Started to look at her. But froze. He turned—away from her. "Candyman, get a picture." He tapped the canister. "Let's move out."

They were headed to the ladder when he strode past her.

She caught his arm. Held tight.

Though meaning flashed through his face, he seemed to harness it. Anger shifted and slid through his expression. His gaze went down. Then bounced to hers. "Can you get Talon topside or do you need help?"

Topside. Right. How *would* she get Talon out of there? Aspen felt disembodied from the events. Something happened back there. She wanted to know what it was. *"He's not who you think he is."* When she'd used that term—*Cardinal*—he'd responded. But it wasn't the response she'd expected, though she wasn't sure what she expected. Or why she'd even spoken the word. It'd made him angry.

Her gaze went to the hall where the ship's workers had come from. Would that work?

"No." Dane glared at her. "Too dangerous." He shifted to the ladder as he scooped Talon's lead from her hands. "Candyman, catch."

Dane took Talon's lead and tossed one end up. He clipped the other to Talon's vest. He pointed Aspen to the ladder. "Climb with him."

She started up the rungs, one arm hooked around Talon, who clamped his mouth shut, unsettled with the lifting method. " 'S okay, boy." Up. . .up. . .up.

Paws on deck, Talon sat. Huffed through a closed snout, letting his objection be known.

Aspen took his head and reassured him as she led him toward the catwalk, glancing back as Dane reached the top. He might have avoided the conversation for now, but he had some questions to answer. It wouldn't change her feelings. She'd known for a long time he hid things. He was a master at it, in fact.

He hooked a leg over the top and pushed to—he pitched forward.

Aspen sucked in a breath.

Sparks flew off the hull.

"Taking fire! Taking fire!" Candyman barreled into her and slammed her temple into the ship. "Down!"

Pain ricocheted through Aspen's head and down her neck, jarring. She yelped and reached for it. Hearing hollowed. Vision blurred. All from using her noggin to break her fall. Warmth slid down her face.

Spine to her, Candyman shoved her backward, using his boots to push them to cover. Talon whimpered and dug his snout beneath her arm. Poor guy. No doubt this was too familiar.

M4s pounded the night with their report. *Tsings* and cracks rattled the barge.

Aspen wiped the blood from her cheek and watched as Dane rolled to the side, to cover.

"Move!" Candyman shouted as he fired off several rounds. Suppressive fire.

Dane lunged toward them. Sidled up and plastered himself to the steel that protected them. She felt stupid. Out of her element. The mortal danger reminded her of what was important—living.

"Now!" Candyman hauled her up as he once again fired. He hook-thrusted her across the catwalk.

Dane was with them. Holding his side.

"You ok—?"

"Go!" He pushed her forward.

"Coming out," Candyman shouted as he keyed his mic. "Cover!"

Had the others made it out? Where was Timbrel? They reached the far side. A few more steps and they'd bound over the three-foot drop into the water and onto the dock. In reach. Talon jogged with them.

Aspen aimed for the jump that would put her on the dock. Her foot slipped. Heat seared down her leg. She cried out. Stumbled. Kept moving.

Deft hands carried her up. Over the drop.

Panic hammered erratically through her. Mind buzzing. Ears ringing. Leg burning. Vision blurring. Only as her feet left the deck of the ship did she feel the rush of adrenaline that carried her over the drop.

Her right knee buckled as she landed.

Again, a hand kept her moving. Threw her toward the barrels that lined the dock. She crashed into them. Gulping air. Choking on fear.

Someone landed on her.

Talon's yelp forced her mind from the fraying panic. "Talon!"

Another whimper. Behind. She twisted—and cried out.

"Stop moving," Dane hissed in her ear.

She stilled, realizing his hand had clamped onto her arm. She glanced down and saw moonlight glinting off something dark on her arm. "Blood?"

Their eyes snagged together.

Ping!

Dane ducked and pushed himself into her. "Candyman—get us out of here!"

"If you'd stop flirting and start shooting, we might get out of here," Candyman shouted back.

"You sound jealous."

Aspen glanced from one man to the next, aware they were both fully engaged in what they were doing. Dane—stopping her from bleeding. Candyman—stopping them from getting killed.

Wouldn't it be better if they all worked on that last one?

"I'm fine." Aspen dragged herself free and reached for the gun holstered at her thigh. Only. . .it wasn't there.

"Looking for this? You dropped it when they tagged your arm in that jump." Dane held up her Glock. "Can you walk?"

"My arm was shot, not my leg."

He arched an eyebrow.

"What?"

He nodded down. She looked and blanched. Where had that come from? A tear, not a hole. She must've sliced it on something. "It's just a cut."

"Okay, they're coming in for us."

"Where are the targets?"

"One in Blue Two." Candyman pointed to the northeastern side of the dock. "Who knows where else. I can't peg them."

A vehicle ripped around the corner. Tires squalled.

Even from here she saw the bullets pinging off the hull. Thank God for armor plating!

It whipped around. Rammed into reverse and roared toward them.

Tires screeched again as they skidded to a stop five feet to the left.

"C'mon, c'mon," Rocket shouted from inside.

Dane pulled Aspen up, propping his arm around her waist and shoulders. "Ready?"

Teeth clamped as fire tore through her leg, she nodded. They rushed forward.

Candyman used his weapon for cover fire and his broad shoulders and back to shield them. Talon leapt into the vehicle. Aspen jumped in after him.

"Go, go, go!" Candyman shouted, banging the hull.

"Wait." Aspen glanced back, knowing Dane hadn't climbed in. She saw him throw himself at her.

The vehicle lurched forward.

Dane landed with a thud. Right behind him came Candyman, crawling over both of them to get out of the way as the rear doors flapped closed. Rocket secured them.

Aspen laughed and extricated herself from Dane, pulling herself onto a seat. Relief swirled fierce and potent. That was close. She tried to shift her legs, but Dane—

"Dane?" She reached for him. "Why isn't he moving?"

Candyman cursed again. Grabbed Dane. Flipped him over.

Blood trailed down his temple. Gushed over his neck.

Twenty-Nine

$\mathbb{N}$eil Crane stuffed a wadded-up T-shirt against his chest, biting through the pain. "*What* was that?" Glowering at Lina, he waited for an answer.

Hatred spewed from her eyes. "I told you—leave Cardinal alone."

"No, you said I couldn't kill him." He flung the rag across the room and yanked off his soiled shirt to see his wound.

"And you just might've. If he's dead, then—"

"Then what?" he hollered. "Are you going to shoot me? Kill me?"

"I should."

Which meant she wouldn't. But he didn't care. He was too ticked off. Coupled with this Russian woman. Someone he thought he knew. Thought he loved. But didn't know the first thing about. When she ripped off the mask of innocence, he couldn't have been more shocked at the demon beneath.

Now he was totally screwed. Back to where he was eight months ago. Nobody to trust. No answers. Just a barge full of trouble.

He stomped to the back room and cranked the knob on the rusting sink. Water poured out of it, brown, then slowly cleared. He lapped water against the wound, hissing.

Soft, gentle hands touched his side.

He flinched and looked at her.

"I need to sew it up."

Why? Why wasn't he surprised she knew how to do that? "Why would you?"

Her blue eyes lingered on his, soft then razor sharp. "Because you're more useful alive than dead."

Neil grunted. "Thanks. Good to know."

"Come sit down."

Neil muttered a curse and gripped the edge of the sink. This was totally messed up. If he had *any* options, he'd ditch her. Vanish. Just disappear into the vast sea of people who populated this crazy planet and become a real nobody.

"Stop brooding."

"You've gotten sassy since you ditched the whole innocent-damsel-in-distress routine." He turned and stalked into what used to be a family room of the abandoned apartment.

"And you've gotten grumpy."

"Nah, I've always been that way."

"That's true." She pushed him into the chair and went to her knees, a small bowl and supplies set up on a towel on the floor. He grunted—cold. Her fingers had always been cold.

"You'd better hope Cardinal is not dead."

"Actually, I'm hoping he is."

She pinched her lips together as she cleaned the wound then used scissorlike tongs to reach into it.

Neil pulled his head up and clenched his eyes shut as pain burst through his abdomen. Fresh warmth oozed down his side. She dabbed. Probed. He thought he might vomit. A groan wormed through his chest.

"Sorry."

Clunk.

"There."

He glanced down and saw the fragment. They'd nailed him on their way out. But he'd landed a few of his own in them.

"What. . . ?" Lina's voice was whisper-quiet.

He looked at her, surprised at the sudden rush of innocence that flooded her expression and mentally pushed him back a foot or two.

"What if he didn't betray you?"

Neil watched her. Tried to read her. She looked. . .stricken. Could he believe her?

No.

But there was something different here. Something. . .weird. The change in her had been too drastic. Cardinal had taught him to pay attention to little things like that. Follow them to their logical conclusion or end. "If he didn't, then who did?"

She dropped her gaze. "Would it matter? Your vendetta has been against Cardinal. If he didn't shoot you, then. . ."

Why would she even bring this up? He'd already shot the guy. Killed him, if the fates were on his side. "I guess it doesn't matter now, huh?"

"You're stupid." She snatched up the supplies and pushed to her feet. "You deserve what's coming."

Pentagon, Arlington County, Virginia

"What part of 'stealth' don't you sorry excuses for soldiers understand?" Lance Burnett's pulse pounded against his temple warning him to calm down. Like he would. He banged a fist against his desk, glaring at the bearded face in the monitor.

"Sir, with all due respect—"

"Don't even go there."

"Sir, Cardinal's down."

Lance felt as if someone had dumped ice down his back. "How in Sam Hill did that happen?" He grabbed for his Dr Pepper and hit the top. The drink toppled over. He cursed as he leapt up to salvage the disaster. "What happened down there, VanAllen?"

"Unknown, sir. We encountered some unfriendlies while in the hold but neutralized them and continued. On our way out, we came under fire. Several were hit, Cardinal went down."

"Down? How down?"

"Unconscious, sir. Dr. Helverson came over from Lemonnier."

"Good." About time something went right. "Well, what'd you find down there?"

"Exactly what we expected to find, sir."

"God have mercy." He mopped his brow then used the napkin to mop up the spilled soda. Things were out of control. Someone was down there picking off his men. Uranium oxide sitting in the port.

"We could go down there," Lieutenant Hastings offered.

Lance chewed the idea. "VanAllen."

"Sir."

"Keep me posted."

"Yessir."

Ending the call, he leaned back in his chair. "What'd he send?"

Hastings handed the digital reader to him. "Video footage of the lockers. More than fifty of them. All marked dangerous. You'll see he opened one of them. Radiation readings are high."

"We'll need to force that ship not to leave port."

"Already done," Smith said from the chair beside Hastings. "Seems there's a problem with their permits."

Lance grunted. Man, he felt like crud. He reached for his DP, more carefully this time. "How soon can we be down there?" There were too many variables involved for him to manhandle this from another continent. And he had this twitching feeling that if he could dig deep enough or reach far enough, his fingers would coil around the neck of one General Payne.

Hastings smirked. "Flight leaves in an hour."

Lance laughed. "Got my suitcase packed?"

"On its way up from the front desk as we speak. Your wife says she'll miss you."

He laughed again. "More like she's partying now that she got rid of me for a while." He sighed and ran a hand over his face. He felt old. Old and out of shape. Maybe he should've listened to the doctors.

Well, too late for that. And now he had a brewing international disaster. Cardinal was done—that went beyond bad to the hellfire and damnation bad. That man simply could not die. Because with him went a bevy of information and contacts and resources. Not to mention that Lance's obligation to the man, long overdue, had yet to be paid. If the Grim Reaper came for Cardinal, he'd come for Lance. Sooner rather than later.

"Where's Payne?"

Smith lifted his chin. "Officially? Taking personal time with his family."

"Unofficially?"

"Security cameras at Lemonnier have a man who looks just like Payne." Hastings tapped another picture into view. "That's a mighty deep pocket, reaching all the way to the Dark Continent."

"Let's empty that pocket. Give Payne a little pain of his own."

Special Operations Safe House, Djibouti

Arms wrapped around her waist, Aspen stood as the doctor emerged from the room where he'd worked on Dane. "How is he?"

The doctor hesitated, glancing at Candyman.

What? Was it bad news, and he didn't think she could handle it?

Candyman gave the doctor a nod as Timbrel came to her side.

"He was hit twice—head and neck. And he lost a lot of blood." Dr. Helverson accepted a bottled water from Rocket, uncapped it, and guzzled. "He needs to rest, but the bullet did not nick his carotid, thank goodness. If it had, we'd be planning a burial."

"Two hits?"

Aspen closed her eyes and turned away.

"What about the head?"

Candyman's questions drew her back round.

"Just a graze. Head wounds are messy because they bleed a lot." His eyes seemed to bore into her. "How's your head?"

Her fingers went to the knot almost on their own will. "A headache, but I'm okay."

"Dizziness? Blurry vision?"

"No."

"Let's hope it stays that way," Helverson said as he started for the door. "If she becomes disoriented or she doesn't make sense when she talks or her speech slurs, call me. She could have brain swelling."

"I think she already does," Timbrel said. "She likes that guy in there."

Aspen couldn't resist the smile but shook her head at her friend. "At least I can admit when I like a guy." She rolled her gaze toward Candyman.

Timbrel stiffened.

"Night, folks." Helverson glanced at his watch. "Make that, morning."

"I'm going to go in with him." Aspen clicked her tongue at Talon, who lumbered out of his sleep and onto his feet to follow.

As she slipped into the next room, which was barren of furniture or decoration save a chair, a sink, and the table upon which Dane was stretched, she allowed Talon in. He curled up in a corner, apparently exhausted from the excitement an hour ago.

Feeling drawn like a flower to the sun, she went to Dane. A blanket draped over his legs and waist, his upper torso bare. Two white bandages glared against his olive skin, one on his neck, one just above his temple.

In the chair, Watterboy sat up and gave a sleepy "hey" then pulled to his feet. "Doc says he's going to make it."

At the table, Aspen took in the man she'd fallen in love with. So incredibly familiar, as if she'd known him all her life. Yet a stranger. A very handsome, rugged, brooding one. But handsome all the same.

"Thank God," Aspen said. "Hey, if you want a break, I'll stay with him now."

A small divot of his hair had been shaved near the graze at his temple. A shame. She'd liked the way the strands near his temple always dropped into his eyes. She brushed the hair back. He probably wouldn't let her do this if he was awake. He'd tell her she didn't know him, tell her not to trust him.

"He's a good man."

Her heart zigzagged. She'd almost forgotten Watterboy was in the room still. "Yeah, he is." But she sensed that the team leader was trying to tell her something else, something *more*.

She looked at the man with the dark hair, still garbed in his tactical gear, blood on his shoulder and chest from hauling Dane into the space that became the surgical bay. Candyman had radioed en route for a doc, and thankfully, Helverson had been at the hospital, just minutes away.

Watterboy was a stark contrast to Candyman, who was all play and games. The man before her took his job seriously and himself even more so. What was his hidden message?

"Do you. . .*know* him? I mean—really know him, Captain?"

"You care about him?"

Aspen couldn't hide the blush if she wanted to and let her focus return to Dane, still unconscious. Sedated. A beautiful face. She swiped her thumb over his cheek and rested her hand on his shoulder. Did she care about him? "Yeah."

Oh, it went way beyond that. Seeing him with all that blood, thinking of him being dead, leaving her alone—it terrified her. More than anything she'd experienced losing her parents. Losing Austin. They all seemed like the end of her world. But then Dane came, and she felt like the world was a good place to be again.

Watterboy's expression softened. "That look on your face. . ."

Aspen's cheeks heated even more as she met the man's hazel eyes. "You must think me silly."

"Hardly." He gave a quick shake of his head. "But. . .just remember what you're feeling now."

Remember? "When? What do you mean?"

"I should grab some rack time." Watterboy left the room without another word.

Confusion settled on her like a weight. Ominous words. She turned back to Dane, contemplating Watterboy's words. It left her unsettled, much like Timbrel's warning had. She studied Dane. The pads of her fingers tickled at the stubble on his jaw and chin. Such chiseled features. Everything about him was chiseled. With his chest bared, she couldn't help but notice, though she tried to keep her eyes on his face. His heart had even seemed chiseled—right out of granite—when she'd first met him. But little by little, that mask crumbled.

She brushed her fingers through his hair and bent down, planting a kiss on his left temple. "Father, bring him back to me. We'll figure it out. Whatever it is." She planted one more kiss, resolving to brave the coming storm. And there was definitely one coming. It made her stomach quaver. She'd been through a lot in her life, but nothing like this. And never had she felt the accompanying peace that quieted her panic. Gave her strength.

"I love you," she whispered against his ear. When she eased back, her heart jackhammered as a steel gaze bored into her. "Oh. Hi."

A smile wobbled on his lips, then his eye fluttered closed.

"Dane?"

Nothing but the quiet rise and fall of his toned chest.

Would he remember waking up to her whispered confessions of love? She moved to the side and dragged the chair Watterboy had occupied.

Without lifting his head, Talon peeked at her with one eye.

"You're a good boy."

His tail thumped twice, and he returned to chasing squirrels through the dream fields, just as Dane had returned to the drug-induced dreamland.

The side door creaked open. Candyman entered. He'd changed out of his combat duds into jeans. A circular tattoo of some sort dipped below the cuff of the black T-shirt that stretched tightly around his bicep. She'd not noticed with all the gear he wore how barrel-chested he was. His blond hair hung damp. She wasn't sure, but it looked like his beard might be wet, too.

"Watterboy isn't here."

"Yeah." He thumbed over his shoulder. "Headed to the showers." One hand rested over his other, which was balled into a fist. He looked tense. No, not tense. Uncomfortable.

Maybe he was nervous about losing Dane. No, he'd heard Helverson reassure them. . . "You okay?"

"Yeah." His gaze sparked. "Actually. . .can I talk to you?"

She hesitated. Wasn't that what they were doing?

"About Timbrel."

Smothering her smile, she nodded. "Sure."

"Good." He stuffed his hands in his jean pockets. "See, I'm crazy about her."

Aspen nodded again, not trusting herself to talk.

"But she's. . ." He held his hands out, waving them, clearly searching for the right word. "Unapproachable."

His shoulders slumped. Poor guy. "Yeah. I mean, I see it in her eyes that she digs me, ya know? But. . .just when things start to happen, or seem like they're going to happen—bam!" He pounded his fist into his hand.

Talon jumped.

"Sorry." Candyman held his hands out in a placating manner. "Sorry," he said to Aspen. "I just thought you might know. . .what am I doing wrong? How can I get her to give me the time of day?"

On her feet, Aspen smiled. "Stop wearing a watch."

Candyman shot her a blank stare. "Come again?"

"Look." She hated the truth she'd have to put into her words. She could do no less for the man who'd protected her, Talon, and Dane in that firefight. "Timbrel's. . .unique. She's been through a lot."

"Like what?"

Aspen shook her head. "Sorry, that's not my tale to tell. If you want to win her, it's going to take time. A *long* time. And honestly," she said with a heavy sigh, "I'm not even sure if it will ever work."

"Look, I get it. She's been wounded. Probably used and/or abused. I've seen it in the field and off the field." He scratched his beard. "But I can't figure out how to convince her that I want to give this a shot. I mean a real one, know what I mean?"

"No." She crossed her arms over her chest. "What do you mean, Sergeant?" Something protective and challenging rose up within her. "You just met her."

"Actually, no—remember in Afghanistan with the other handler, Ghost?"

Whoa, the guy had a killer smile. It really made her want to see Dane's even more. And suddenly, instead of this combat-hardened Special Forces soldier, she saw a nervous cowboy.

"I took her picture." He grinned bigger. "I wear it in my helmet. Have ever since. She's what keeps me coming home."

"Candyman, you haven't even—"

He held up his hands. "I know. It don't make sense to someone like you." He scratched his beard again. "Well, for most people for that fact, but I knew when I first met her out there in the desert that she was for me. Seeing her here on this mission, spending time with her—it sealed my fate."

Aspen laughed. "Don't tell her that."

His frown dropped. "Why not?"

"Timbrel doesn't believe in fate."

"What does she believe in?"

"Why don't you find out?"

He studied her, eyes narrowed. "Seriously? Just like that."

"Don't beat around the bush with Timmy. She doesn't play games, you've figured that out."

"No kidding."

"But let me give you one warning."

"Yeah?"

"You'd better love big, tough war dogs."

He hesitated, glancing at Talon. "She has a war dog?"

"Ghost calls him the Hound of Hell."

"Oh man." The man's face fell. "Those dogs hate me."

Thirty

Clothes floated like ghouls around her. Rising. Falling. Twirling. An eerie sky embraced them as they rose once again then fluttered down. So beautiful. So terrifying. A sheet dropped with a bang.

She jolted. Looked around. Turned a circle. Like blank walls, two sheets stood perfect and straight. A dark, bloodied form drifted through them.

Her feet wouldn't move. Her heart stopped. She couldn't breathe. Run! Hurry!

The man came forward. Closer.

He looked kind. Reached a hand out, extended in friendship. In kindness. Aspen saw her own arm stretched toward him.

A screech ripped through the air.

Lightning struck—struck the man.

Flames devoured the sheets.

She screamed. Tried to run. Her feet tangled. She dropped to the ground. Hand in front of her face, she watched the man, now singed and smoking, float toward her. His face. . .

No, it wasn't possible!

"No!" *It couldn't be.* "Austin!" *she howled.*

Aspen bolted upright. Drenched in sweat, she groped for light in the darkness. A dream. . . She hauled in a thick breath. One hand over her chest, she pressed the heel of her other hand to the bridge of her nose and stifled a sob.

A soft thump-thump-thump drew her gaze to the side.

Talon stared up at her with those gorgeous brown eyes. Tail wagging, he wanted to reassure her that everything was okay.

608

Aspen patted the cot, and that was enough for him. He leapt up next to her and stretched out. Arms around him, she buried her face in his fur. Where was Austin? What was wrong? What if. . .what if Dane had been right? What if that man *was* Austin?

Exhaustion pulled at her limbs. At her mind. Seeing Dane nearly die. Watching over him for four hours till Candyman relieved her. She wouldn't have left, but she could barely keep her eyes open.

She smoothed the dense fur of the Lab, his paws already kicking as he chased prey again through the field of dreams. He hadn't been himself lately. Could it be. . .that Talon knew what Dane suspected?

Crazy.

Only crazy in that it was entirely likely that if the man *was* Austin, Talon would know. Better than anyone else. The thought took root. The children's hospital—had Talon spotted that man? Is that why he took off then hid beneath the house, terrified by the bullets?

But Austin would never shoot at Talon. They were partners. That bond was thicker than blood.

That's what I thought—that the blood bond was thick. But if this was true, then Austin abandoned that bond.

The ramifications were heartrending.

No, there was no way Austin would do that. Not after what they went through with losing their parents. Their deaths had been brutal on Austin. He'd never knowingly do that to her.

Not even for some noble cause?

The question challenged her beliefs. Hadn't she done things she never thought she'd do—like climbing aboard a barge filled with radioactive material—in the name of national defense?

Was that the same?

She dug her fingers into Talon's fur and stroked it. So comforting, so warm, thinking. . .culling. . .formulating. . .remembering.

The man had Austin's build. Even—*oh my word!*—his walk! Austin was a toe-walker, using the balls of his feet to walk rather than hitting heel first.

She flopped onto her back, one arm under Talon's neck and the other propped over her head. Was it possible? Really possible that the man in the alley, the one who warned her and called Talon by name. . . was he Austin?

Possible.

But not probable. Aspen just couldn't let that be the truth. Austin loved her too much. They were twins. They'd often joked that when one got hurt, it was like hurting the other. They'd promised since they were kids to always—*always*—protect each other.

"Angel, they're gone now, but I will always be here. I'll do everything to protect you."

The words were sweet. They comforted—at the time. But even then, she'd wondered at those words. Austin was the rambunctious twin. The one who got in trouble. Her best friend had often called him the "evil twin" because of his sneaky side. How deft he was at—Aspen's pulse slowed as her thoughts powered down to that final word—*deception*.

Water rushed in, deluging the barge. "Aspen!"

She whirled, blue eyes wide with panic. "Talon, I can't find him."

"He'll be okay."

"No, I can't leave him. I'll never leave him."

Cardinal rushed to her, waters sloshing against his feet. He glanced down. Why was he barefoot? No time to figure it out. "Come!" He reached toward her. "Hurry!"

Her fingers thrust forward.

The ship canted right.

She wavered with a yelp.

"Aspen!"

Behind her, a wall of water dropped. Like a blanket.

Weird.

The spray blasted against her. Eyes wide, mouth open in a perfect O, she stared at him. Clanking reverberated through the air. Vibrations wormed through his very bones. He knew what would happen. He tried to lurch forward.

Feet wouldn't move. Legs hurt. Water swirled around him.

Then the angel flew.

She flew backward, straight through the water. Vanished.

Forever gone.

"No!" Cardinal lunged. Fire raked his neck and head. Booming thundered through his skull.

He raised his hand. . .or did he?

"Dane?"

Light seared his corneas. He moaned and looked away. Squinting and blinking at the same time, he stilled at the vision hovering over him. No, this couldn't be hell. There was an angel standing over him.

Man, that was crazy-corny. But it was true. With the light ringing her curls and her ivory-pale complexion and her white top. . . "Angel." His grin felt lopsided. So did his head. Sweet, swift relief staved off the panic as the dream rushed back to the front of his mind. Just like that squall that overtook her. Dropped like a blank—

No, not a blanket. A wall of glass. The dissonance of the dream alarmed him. His mind combining the past and present. Didn't like that his brain had shifted the "angel" in his dream to Aspen.

Fear. That was fear driving that. Worrying about her. That he couldn't protect her. That she'd be lost to him somehow.

But for now, she was here.

Groaning, he peeled himself off the table and sat with his legs dangling. He didn't care if he'd lost a limb. Aspen was alive. He couldn't take losing her. Not the way he'd lost his mom.

He caught her shoulder and pulled her into his arms. Held her tight. She was here. Aspen was okay. He tried to breathe without pain. But. . .there was so much. . .

The room spun. He closed his eyes and waited for the dizziness to pass. "How long have I been out?"

"It's lunchtime—eight or ten hours." She shrugged. "I don't know. I was. . .I don't know what time we got back." Aspen stood close, worry marring her beautiful face. "The doctor checked on you about ten minutes ago—you lost a lot of blood. He wanted you to rest." She smelled good. Looked good. Talked good.

He remembered. . ."You kissed me." He touched his temple. "Here." He smiled. A real one.

Aspen held the corner of her lip between her teeth as her gaze skidded to the floor.

He took her hand and drew her closer, noticing the red, angry scab on her forehead. "How's your head?"

"Apparently, my head's just as hard as yours."

"Good. Then we might just survive." He kissed her. Savored her warmth—*she's alive!* The docks. Seeing her getting shot. The blood. The dream. . . *Oh man. The dream.* His mind had tangled past and present. Twisted them up so tight, he'd been ready to slay a thousand demons to get her back.

Aspen curled into him. She was soft. Sweet. But then she pressed a hand to his chest and nudged him back. "You're awfully cheery—you even smiled. I think I need to call the doctor back in. That bullet might've grazed more than your hairline."

Cardinal tested his legs. Not quite solid, but they'd hold.

"Hey." Concern replaced Aspen's smile. "Should you be getting up yet? You're not even dressed." When that concern deepened, he knew she'd seen the scars on his back and shoulders.

Instinctively, he reached for his shirt. "Sorry."

Her cheeks rosied. "I just meant—"

"You said you loved me."

Her bright blue eyes came to his. She shifted, her arm around his waist, supporting him, though he didn't need it. "I told you I do."

He stared down at her. "I don't deserve you." But he wanted her. Wanted to never be separated from her. Even he knew that wasn't in his power. Just like the churches, just like the feeling that the universe righted as he sat on those pews, Aspen did the same thing for him. Why? How?

"That's sorta the point of love, isn't it? Something we can never earn but is freely given."

It felt like there was a chunk of cement in his chest as three words churned through his mind. He wanted to say them. But you didn't get to that point after a few weeks of running an op. But nearly dying sort of changes a man's mind. Yet. . . No matter how much the planets aligned or God—*are You there?*—set in motion. . .

She doesn't even know who I am. And in a way, without his career, without his identity as Cardinal, did *he* even know who he was anymore? "You need to know the truth. Everything."

She shifted. "When you're ready."

He let out a breathy snort of disbelief. "You may never speak to me again, but I want you to know the truth. All of it. You deserve that."

Clapping resounded through the room.

Aspen gasped.

Cardinal flung himself around. The room rebelled, spinning and twisting.

"Very moving," Neil Crane said as he produced a silenced weapon then dabbed a finger against his eye, as if drying a tear. "I almost cried. Really. And Cardinal, I'll take that wager."

Refusing to take his eyes off the man, Cardinal noted the door wasn't locked. Noted the man was entirely confident that he was in control. And that's what Cardinal needed to go along with. If the team was down—

The thought tightened the muscles in his shoulders. Fighting wouldn't do any good. Having been through surgery, losing blood, he would lose. Fast. And Aspen. . .

He moved his hand to her and tucked her behind him as he watched the man sidle up next to Talon, never showing them his back. He grinned at them then glanced at Talon, who sat up and panted, his tale thumping.

"Hello, boy." The man petted Talon then stood, wagging the gun at Cardinal. "I see you managed to get your shirt off."

"You shot me." It was a guess but one Cardinal didn't think was too outside the realm of possibilities.

"I couldn't let you undo what I'd orchestrated." He smiled as his gaze drifted to Cardinal's left. "Aspen, really? Falling in love with the world's most renown spy?"

"Talon, heel." Aspen moved forward a step, and Cardinal wanted to yank her back and whip out a weapon—but he didn't have one. And a sudden move could set off Crane.

Neil caught Talon's collar. "No, I think it's best he stay here."

"Who are you?" Aspen's voice wavered.

And in that hesitation and pitch of her voice Cardinal could tell she had accepted his theory. "His name is Neil Crane."

"Actually," Neil said as he shook his head and started forward, "that's the name you gave me, Cardinal." His gaze came back to him. "Tell her." He stabbed the weapon at him. And through gritted teeth demanded, "Tell her who I am!"

Thirty-One

Y ou did this to me!"

Had the world upended and dumped hell at her feet, Aspen could not have been more shocked. It was him. The voice. The mannerisms. All undeniably Austin. But the thought, the last two years of grieving whatever had happened to him, forbid her from fully embracing the thought.

"No!" Dane shifted, his expression dark. Angry. Frightening. "That is not my doing. You stepped out, you went your own way."

"No!" His voice scraped the walls with painful fury. His lips were tight. His mouth almost foaming.

Aspen shrunk at the rage and grief roiling through the man's reddening face. It was him. It was her brother. He still had the telltale temper. "Austin." She took a steadying breath.

The man's brown eyes bumped to hers.

A bubble of elation burst through her. A strangled cry. "Austin?" She took a step forward. "Is it really you?"

"Aspen." Dane's voice carried a measure of warning. "He's not—"

"Don't you dare!" Austin shuffled forward, waving the gun like a madman. "Don't you dare turn her against me. You've taken everything from me. *Everything!*"

Stumbling to mentally keep up, Aspen found herself moving away from Dane. Away from the security she'd felt two minutes ago. Away from the certainty. Dane? Dane had done this to Austin? But it didn't make sense. "Did he do something when he was with you in Kariz-e Sefid?"

Austin laughed. "With me?" He shook his head. "Oh, if only it'd been that. That's where he made sure Austin Courtland died. That's where he secured his latest pawn."

"You willingly joined DIA."

"Don't!" Austin snapped the weapon at Dane, who raised his hands in a gesture of peace. His soulful steel gaze hit hers. Telegraphed a message.

Aspen didn't know whether to hate Dane or trust him. To run *from* him or run *to* him. That was a fight for another hour. She focused back on her brother. "What. . .what happened to you, Austin?"

"Tell her," Austin said again.

"No, this is your story. Tell us. Tell both of us what happened."

"You *know* what happened."

"I know you vanished without a trace."

"Vanished because you betrayed me!"

"Enough!" Aspen turned to her brother. Her twin. Her mind tumbled through the questions, too many slamming her mind for her to even know where to start. And Dane—should she be mad at him? "Why. . .why don't you look like. . .like you used to?"

Austin grinned. "When Cardinal here betrayed me, I had to vanish—completely. A few surgeries and I became a new man."

"But your eyes are brown." Aspen couldn't wrap her mind around the transformation. He looked nothing like the brother she'd last seen at Amadore's.

"They'll be blue again eventually. The method wears off." He shrugged. "Keeps me hidden. And I need to stay hidden to bring Cardinal and his thugs down."

"You're wrong. This isn't my doing, but we can figure that out later," Dane said. "What are you doing here now? What do you want enough that you're willing to put your life on the line with that gun?"

Aspen heard the threat within the words. Dane knew how to take Austin down, even though Austin held a weapon and Dane didn't. Her nerves buzzed.

"No," Austin said with a half laugh as he moved to the side. "You don't get to dictate this. I'm here. I'm the one with the gun."

"Okay," Dane said. "Fine. You have the gun." Why did that sound like a challenge?

"Let's bring the testosterone down a level." Aspen had always mediated between Austin and their grandfather, both thickheaded mules. "Austin, if you want to talk, if you have questions, put the gun down and let's sort it out. I'd rather not get accidentally shot while you're ranting."

"He already shot me."

"Twice." Austin seethed. "I'd like to go for a third."

Dane huffed. "Then shoot me and get on with it!"

"No!" Aspen stepped between the two men, uncertain which one she would defend. Which man *deserved* being defended. Blood ties were stronger, right? "Austin, why are you here?"

"I want to know why he betrayed me."

Aspen stilled, a shudder of a blink swiveling her attention to Dane. What did that mean?

"Me?" Dane looked shocked. "How did *I* betray you? You're the one who abandoned the mission. Stopped responding. I spent two months down here looking for you."

"Looking for me?" Austin laughed. "Don't believe your own press, Cardinal. You aren't that good of a liar. You were down here working with them."

Silence drenched the room.

Dane drew up. "Working with whom?" His voice had lost its edge.

Austin pursed his lips. "Don't tell me you don't know!"

"Okay, I won't. Do you want me to tell you what I do know?"

Hesitation stretched between them. Aspen's heart thudded against the words. Did she want to know? Would Dane tell the truth? Could she handle the truth? *"You don't know me."* His words plunked in front of her like an anchor. *"Don't trust me."* Another anchor.

Austin finally said, "Let's hear it."

"Yes, I recruited you—in Afghanistan. I saw you were a stellar soldier. But I also saw the anger. That made you a prime candidate for covert operations because it drives you." Dane darted a look to Aspen, and she saw in his gaze the desperation. "I brought you in—but you came willingly."

"That's right. And then you had me killed." Austin arched an eyebrow. "Tell her about that."

"You're still alive."

"No. Killed me. MIA—that's the official report for a while, then the MIA is declared dead. Right, Cardinal?"

"You knew that when you signed. You can't claim ignorance or innocence. What is your point? Why are you so ticked at me?"

"Because—you told me something was happening in Sudan. You sent me there. But it was a trap."

"How?" Dane leaned forward, hands by his side. Very controlled. "How was it a trap?"

Austin's gaze bounced between them. "Don't listen to him, little sister. He's a master liar. He knows how to tell people what they want to hear to get his way. No doubt that's how you fell for him. He played your heartstrings like a prodigy."

Humiliation clotted Aspen's heart that had beat for Dane. Was it true? Had he worked her all this time?

"Aspen." Dane tucked his chin and met her gaze with those steely eyes. "I did not play you."

She could only look at him. Who should she believe? Her twin brother? Or the man she loved—thought she loved? Closing her eyes, she shook her head.

"Austin, you willingly joined. Nobody forced you. Remember, you agreed to become a spy for the American military. I sent you down here. There were rumblings about corruption. We couldn't get a finger on it."

"Oh, I got your finger—"

"Is it the yellowcake?"

Austin froze. "You do know!"

"Yes, we found it last night—you shot us trying to leave."

Austin frowned. "I. . .no. . .that was. . ." His voice trailed off. "Oh no."

"We found it last night. But I didn't know till then."

"How could you *not* know? The conspiracy goes all the way up!"

Even a master magician could not keep all the plates spinning forever.

Cardinal stilled at the words Austin Courtland, the man he'd remade into Neil Crane—precosmetic surgery—shouted. "What do you mean, all the way up?"

"Straight to the top." Austin glowered. "What? Feigning ignorance?" The weapon lowered toward Cardinal's leg.

Cement peppered his leg.

Lightning fast, Cardinal stepped forward. Sliced the bony part of his right hand against Austin's wrist and used his left hand to swipe the weapon. Flip it. Aim it back at Austin.

The man's grin turned greedy. He laughed.

This scenario was one Cardinal had faced a dozen times. The outcome the same—except this time, he wouldn't neutralize the threat the way he'd had to so many other times.

"Think you've won?" Austin sneered. "Think again—Talon, seek!"

The Lab looked at Austin as if the man had spoken Chinese.

"Talon," Aspen said, her voice calm. Way more calm than normal. "Heel."

With a flick of his tail, Talon moved to Aspen's side and sat on his haunches.

"When you left me, you left him," Aspen said. "He's not your dog anymore."

Finally! Something got through Austin's seek-and-destroy mentality. "Talon!" Austin nearly growled at the dog. "Seek, boy! Seek!"

Taking his eyes off Austin would be a mistake, but Cardinal wanted to see, to verify that the dog had not moved or even wanted to move. In his periphery, Cardinal noticed Aspen's arms dangling at her side in a loose manner. Her fingers rubbed Talon's ears.

Cardinal removed the magazine. Let it thunk against the ground. Ejected the chambered round. *Shink!* Released the slide. Dropped the frame and slide. His neck wound still burned. But what burned more was the way his world had just upended. "I'm not the enemy, Austin. I came to find you, find out what happened."

Anger whipping into fury, Austin launched at him like a tornado.

Mentally prepared for the impact, Cardinal tossed himself backward. Used the momentum to gain control. Flipped Austin onto his back. Rammed his fist into the man's face.

Though Austin worked to flip him, Cardinal maintained control. "Stand down!"

"Not on your life," Austin ground out, his face reddened as he struggled to push Cardinal.

Agitating him would only strengthen Austin's fight. "Let it go. Talk to Aspen."

"Don't use her!" Austin balled his fist and shot it into Cardinal's side.

White-hot, blinding pain exploded. His vision blurred.

Hollowed vision.

Searing agony.

Thud!

Cardinal blinked and found himself staring up at Austin, arms pinned by the man's knees. Pounding agony in his leg eroded his thoughts. Another blink and he stared down the barrel of a weapon.

"Eye for an eye, Cardinal?" Staggered breathing. A greedy gleam in his eye, Austin was poised to fill Cardinal's brain with lead.

"Austin, *no!*" Aspen screamed.

Snarling and snapping vaulted through the room.

"He took *everything.*"

"No!" Aspen snapped. "You gave it up!"

Austin's nostrils flared and stared down at Cardinal. In that second he knew the belief that consumed Austin's thinking—killing Cardinal would solve everything.

"Even if you kill me," Cardinal said, "you won't find what you're looking for."

Shifting, Austin planted a knee against Cardinal's throat.

Cardinal worked to wedge his arm between his trachea and Austin's knee. He grunted and strained against the deprivation. Rocks bit into the back of his head, his shoulders, but that had nothing on the still-thundering throb in his neck.

"How's it feel, Cardinal? Master Spy."

"Austin!" Aspen shouted over the snapping and snarling.

"Not so tough. You took everything away from me—"

"Austin!"

"—now I'm taking it away from you."

"Austin, so help me, God—get off him and drop that weapon or I'll release Talon."

Scritching forced Cardinal to glance to his right.

Aspen stood, her feet planted as she held tight to the harness Talon strained against. The powerful jaws clamped and chomped the air. Begging for a taste of flesh.

Cardinal's heart backed into his throat. If Aspen released Talon. . . against her own brother. . .against Talon's former handler. . .

"Austin!" Aspen's scream went primal.

Booom!

A gust of hot, dirt- and debris-laden air barreled across the room. Slammed against Cardinal. He winced and jerked away.

Light and dark mingled. Dust cocooned the room.

Grit dug into his eyes and mouth. Cardinal coughed.

"Stand down! Stand down!"

"On the ground!"

"Drop the weapon!"

Blinking rapidly, Cardinal saw a half-dozen shapes emerge from the dirt cloud. ODA452 had blown the door and stormed in, all business. Candyman—the guy looked downright ticked, blood staining his beard. A big welt on his right cheekbone. No hat. No sunglasses. Whoever had undressed the guy also unleashed the monster within.

Watterboy's hands were bloodied. The others were there—Rocket, Scrip, Pops. . .all roughed up, clearly having fought their way out of a mess. Now, all that adrenaline. All that fury, trained 100 percent on Austin Courtland.

Timbrel hurried to Aspen's side.

Slowly, Austin raised his hand, gun still held firmly.

"Drop. The. Gun," Watterboy said, taking a bead on Austin.

Talon's bark continued. Shouts.

Two seconds later, Candyman shuffle-stepped forward fast. "Give me a reason, you sorry piece of dirt."

"Talon, out," Aspen said. "Talon, heel!"

Quiet dropped on the room, but the silence proved deafening with Austin's unwillingness to yield.

A flicker of movement.

Cardinal tensed. And in the split-second camera lens of his life, he knew it was about to end. Austin would force it to end.

The guy snapped the weapon toward him.

Candyman fired.

Then whipped back and to the side. Flopped. Groaned. Cried out.

"Don't kill him!" Cardinal hauled himself out of the fray as Candyman and Rocket dropped on the guy.

Watterboy helped Cardinal to his feet. "You okay?"

With a nod, he kept his eyes trained as the others subdued the man who'd been willing to end his life. He'd seen it—the same agonizing guilt. Cardinal felt it. Lived it. But he'd mastered it. Stopped it from mastering him. Controlling him. The way it had taken over for Austin.

"All right," Watterboy said with a huff. "Clean up. I'm going to call this in. Burnett won't—"

Thump. Thump. Clink.

A meaty scream announced, "*Frag!*"

Red-hot air blasted the room.

Thirty-Two

Blinded, Cardinal felt himself falling.

Or was that the world?

Spinning...everything...He swung a hand out. Hit something. His knee collided. Dirt...

White. Blinding white.

Ringing. Hollow hearing. A vacuum had swallowed him.

"Augh!" Though he knew air passed over his vocal chords, he heard nothing.

White succumbed to gray...

Holding his head, Cardinal waited out the disorientation. They'd been hit. Someone threw a flash-bang into the room. The overpressure of the concussion knocked out his vision. Sucked out his hearing.

Though he knew it'd only last three to five seconds, it felt like an eternity. No way to defend yourself. No way to fight back.

He didn't even know who to fight.

Was this Austin's doing? If it was, he'd kill that punk.

Shapes took form like pillowy giants. Cardinal felt the dirt beneath his hands and slowly straightened. Searching for bearings.

The door...where was it? He turned his head.

The room tilted. "Augh!" Warbling noises hammered.

Movement...the doorway! Light bled through it, piercing against his corneas, which were still traumatized from the concussive explosion.

Two or three shapes hurried out the door. Who?

"Cardinal!" Though it sounded like someone spoke his name under water, he knew it was someone close by.

He turned. Saw a large shape looming beside him. He shook his head—the room whipped around. He groped to steady himself. A hand caught his. His vision, still vibrating, brought the image into focus. "Watterboy."

"You okay?" The man wiggled a finger in his ear.

"Yeah." Coordination returned. Hearing, mostly. Vision clear.

"Everyone okay?" Watterboy asked, turning a circle.

As the affirmatives came in, Cardinal hesitated. "Nobody's hurt?" That didn't make any sense. He searched the team for injuries. Timbrel sat against the wall, pinching the bridge of her nose. Candyman knelt beside her and offered a rag for her nosebleed. Rocket and Scrip were still shaking off the effects.

Wait. Cardinal jerked. Nearly fell. "Aspen." She'd been right there with Timbrel. He whipped around. Ignoring the way the room canted to the left. "Aspen!"

His mind ricocheted back to what he saw.

He sprinted for the door. *"Aspen!"*

A curse sailed through the air behind him. Boots pounded. He burst into the inner room. Two of the four men they'd caught were down. Cardinal threw himself at the rear cavernous area that served as a garage. How long? How long had it been? Ten, fifteen seconds?

He sprinted into the garage. Gaping open. Sunlight shatteringly bright. He flinched. Popping! He ducked then realized it wasn't gunfire. Tires! He bolted out. Saw a black SUV stirring up dust.

Cardinal plunged through the bay. Bore down on the vehicle spitting rocks as he scrambled for traction on the dirt road. The rear end fishtailed. Caught purchase on the paved road. Squealed and tore off.

He pushed himself. Hard.

Couldn't stop. That was Aspen in there. Someone had taken her. He'd kill them. Cut out their hearts and feed them to the dogs.

A high-pitched whistle shot through the day.

Trailing smoke careened past him. Hot. Wicked fast.

Grenade?

He spun. Candyman, kneeling at the corner of the building, an M203 propped against his shoulder, pulled the trigger again.

Boom!

Cardinal jerked around. A building rained down dirt and fire.

The vehicle swerved. Banked right.

Boom! The building in front of Cardinal exploded.

Tires squalled. The shriek of death.

And they were gone.

Teeth grinding, Cardinal stared at the fires that mottled the poverty-stricken street. Breathing hard and struggling not to allow the demons of his past, of his ancestry, to awaken, he dug himself out of the chaos. Aspen was gone.

And he knew exactly who was responsible.

"Sorry, man. I wasn't fast enough," came the empty words of Candyman.

Cardinal pivoted around, stalked toward the man decked out in gear, patted his chest, deftly swiping his thumb over the flap. "Thanks. You tried." And with one expert move, he extracted the Glock from Candyman's chest holster.

"Hey! Stop!"

Confirming a round was in the chamber, Cardinal stormed back into the building.

Thirty-Three

FOB Kendall, Djibouti

Trailed by a security force and his two senior officers, General Lance Burnett strode into the command building of the temporary forward operating base covered in dust and heat. The wake he and the others left as they stormed ahead shone on the faces of those serving under the command of Admiral Kuhn. The hushed whispers haunted his steps.

Banking right, Lance caught sight of two armed sentries guarding the offices of the commanding officer. The two snapped to attention, fingertips pressed to their temples.

Burnett returned the salute. "At ease." He slowed and hesitated, staring at the door handles. He shifted his gaze to the left. "How is he?"

"Quiet, sir."

With a nod, Lance entered the office.

A gray steel desk anchored a spot in front of a window. Behind it, the chair swiveled around. Admiral Kuhn rose and saluted. "General Burnett."

Lance gave a stiff response, lowered his hand, then huffed. "At ease." He strolled to the window where cheap plastic blinds served as a flimsy barrier against the miserable Djibouti sun and its heat. He'd been baking since he stepped off the aircraft.

And he wasn't the only thing baking. "For cryin' out loud, Mack." He turned to him. "Well? What do you have to say?"

"Shouldn't I have a lawyer?"

"Do you need one?"

Kuhn pointed to the doors, to Hastings, and the security team. "You brought yours." He grunted then dropped back into his chair. "Ya know, I'm glad."

Lance frowned.

"I'm glad it's over." He removed the stars from his uniform and thrust them on the table. "Hendricks put my nose to the fire, threatened me with punitive action if I didn't look the other way, then he vanishes."

"Vanishes?" Lance couldn't digest the information fast enough. "Punitive—so, you're willing to testify?"

"Absolutely. The man yanked my career out of my hands."

"I think you did that, sir," Hastings spoke up. "You are the one who acted."

"Tell you what, Lieutenant," Kuhn said, "when you're out here baking your assets off and nobody gives a rip if you live or die except one man willing to make you dead—well, lines get a little fuzzy."

Lance planted himself in the chair and mopped his sweaty brow. "You said Hendricks vanished?"

"Yeah. Nobody knows where he is. Haven't seen in him. . .well, since your man showed up."

"Cardinal."

"That's the one. Payne flew down here, and they rode off into the sunset together." Kuhn shrugged. "The people here are oppressed enough. They don't need American power mongers making it worse."

"Yet you helped make it worse." Lance pushed to his feet and motioned the security forces toward Kuhn. "While I clean up your mess, it's your turn to ride off into the sunset."

"Don't even move."

Shedding the Neil Crane persona and returning to his original identity, his birth identity, felt incredibly freeing. Head pounding like a bass drum still, Austin focused on the two men who held him at gunpoint. They had good reason. Anger vibrated through him.

"That's my sister, you moron!"

"Yeah. Well, this is my M4." The man with a dark blond beard hefted it a little higher, nearly blotting out the beard.

Austin growled. "If she dies—"

"Stop him! Somebody—stop him!"

Austin peered over the shoulders of the two men.

A storm swept in named Cardinal. Eerily calm. Striding straight toward—*Me!*

One of the nearby men swore. Took a step back.

So did Austin—when he saw the weapon Cardinal held low.

Fury darkened the man's face. Something inside Austin curled up and died. He'd never seen that expression on Cardinal. In the mirror—yeah, a lot. On others. But not on Cardinal, the guy calm as a tranquility pool.

"He's got a gun!"

Boots thudded as two men raced up behind Cardinal.

Austin's feet seemed to have turned to cement. He couldn't move. Saw it coming. Saw the future in one heartbeat—Cardinal was going to stuff that Glock in Austin's mouth and make him eat a bullet.

He's blaming me for Aspen.

"I didn't do this." Austin stepped between the two men who had shifted from guarding him to protecting his life. Not that he'd put his life in their hands. He wouldn't. Wouldn't trust anyone on that level. Never again. He held up his hands.

"Where is she?" Cardinal demanded. Two men hooked Cardinal's arms, hauling him backward. He wrestled against them, seemingly possessing supernatural strength because he came forward several paces. "Tell me!"

With the tangling and wrangling of arms and legs, it looked like an octopus writhing before him.

The Glock slid across the room.

Grab it. Maybe he should.

A brunette lifted it from the ground and stuffed it at the small of her back.

Austin let himself draw in a breath, steadying his nerves. This man had mentored him. Taught him so much. Then betrayed him. "Even if I knew," Austin injected as much disdain into his voice as possible, "I wouldn't trust *you* with that information."

Though Cardinal tried to wrest himself from the two men, their restraint held. Cardinal again attempted to jerk free before slumping back, looking defeated, as he said, "The gun's gone. What can I do?"

Watterboy gave a nod.

"No!" Austin's shout mixed with another. Apparently someone else saw what Austin did—Cardinal's body language belied the fury roiling off the man. Loose, Cardinal would kill him.

Seconds took on supernatural length. Cardinal shot forward. His foot swept Austin off his feet. He landed with a thud. Cardinal was on top of him, pinning him with his knee. His fist rammed like a ball-peen hammer. Right into Austin's face.

Shouts and a series of pops erupted.

Lance hesitated, glancing back to Hastings, whose eyes had widened. He shoved himself through the building. Through one door. Another. He burst into the safe house, drenched in sweat after the quick ride out from FOB Kendall.

Two men wrestled a third beneath them. Legs and arms thrashed.

Another was laid out cold, blood snaking out his nose and down his neck.

Scrip dug through a sack on the floor.

Suddenly, the writhing mass of bodies stilled.

"Get off me," came a familiar voice.

"Not liking that idea," Candyman countered.

"What in Sam Hill is going on?" Lance demanded.

Candyman and Watterboy shifted toward Lance. Slowly eased off the third—Cardinal. The man pushed back on his legs and stayed on the floor. Lance never fully realized how big that guy's shoulders and fists were.

"Cardinal?" He hated that name.

The man pushed onto his haunches. Then stood.

Watterboy and Candyman stepped back, and Lance noticed they seemed to be guarding the body on the floor. Watterboy's gaze skidded to Lance, and he gave a nod. "General."

"What's going on?" He sounded like a broken record, but considering nobody had answered, he didn't care.

Cardinal swung toward him.

Instinct pushed Lance back a step. He bumped into someone.

Hastings muttered an apology as she shifted aside, her gaze locked

628

on Cardinal. "Da—Markoski?"

Death lurked in that man's eyes as he stalked out of the room.

Lance took a step forward. "Hey—"

Cardinal held up a staying hand but didn't look back. "No." He hung his head. Took a breath then walked out.

Silence drenched the tension that seeped through every pore and crack in this crumbling former storefront. Hastings started after Dane.

"Leave him, Lieutenant." Lance had never seen that look on Cardinal before. And he had this feeling the guy just needed some time. "Watters—fill me in."

The man nodded, glanced to the man on the floor, then crossed the room. "We got hit not ten minutes ago. That guy showed up with a team, Russians. They put us in lockdown, while he came in here with Aspen and Markoski."

"Lockdown?"

Candyman muttered something as he paced.

"Yes, sir. They held us at gunpoint, but thanks to Scrip"—he nodded to the man on the floor, who now slumped against the wall—"we subdued the captors and blew out the door. When we got in here, he"—another indication, this time to the unconscious man—"had Aspen and Dane at gunpoint. Two minutes later, someone lobbed a flash-bang in here. By the time we were able to sort out what happened, Aspen was gone."

"Gone?"

Watters's expression tightened. "They took her. Markoski sprinted after them. Candyman went with him. Me and the team tried to hold the other guy down—we don't know who he is."

Lance strode over to the man and squatted in front of him. "Russian, huh? And nobody's ID'd him?"

"No, but Markoski came back in—"

"Took my Glock right out of my holster." Candyman grunted. Disgust shaded his features. "Did it so fast, I didn't know till I saw the gun in his hand."

"He came storming in here and was about to kill that guy."

"If Markoski says he's a threat, then he is. Hogtie the heck out of him." Lance straightened, his mind racing as Candyman and Rocket went to work zip-tying the man. "Pops, get on the horn. Notify the embassy that an American has been kidnapped. Leak her information to everyone."

He stormed out of the room, biting back curses. Hating that he didn't have a single Dr Pepper handy.

Hastings stood in the open area at the back, eyes on the upper level.

Lance took the cue and headed toward the stairs that lacked a banister or other support.

Behind him he heard steps. Over his shoulder he saw Hastings and Smith trailing him. "Stay with the team. Get a game plan. Wake that man up and find out who he is."

Hastings paused, her gaze tracing the upper level again. He'd have to be blind not to know she was smitten with Cardinal.

"Go on. Get it done, Lieutenant."

With a reluctant nod, she turned.

As he continued up, he wondered if the entire thing would collapse without a guardrail. Plaster dribbled. Three doors presented themselves. He pushed open the first door. His body swayed and swooped—straight toward the ten-foot drop. He grabbed the doorjamb and yanked himself back. His heart dropped with the gaping emptiness. Only half the room still existed. The other half, blown out with whatever relegated this building to abandonment. Hauling his stomach and courage back, he eased the door closed. Whispered a prayer of thanks to his maker.

As he made his way along the narrow ledge, he tried to avoid looking to the right, the drop to the lower level. The next door, he decided, sat too close to the previous one, so it most likely had its space missing, too. Lance tried the last door. Darkness spread its venom. He scanned the black void. Nothing.

As he turned away, a shape caught his eye.

He whipped back to it. Strained against the darkness to figure out what snagged his attention. There, in the corner. . . "Cardinal?"

Whispering wind was the only response.

Lance stepped in, embraced by the shadows as his eyes slowly adjusted. Sure enough. There sat Cardinal. In the corner, each shoulder blade pressed against an adjacent wall. Legs bent and pulled close, he rested his arms over his knees.

This wasn't the time for booming sarcasm. Nor for biting wit. What he'd seen down there, Cardinal completely unglued, required delicate and precise wording. An arrow to aim right at this man's steel-barricaded heart. Cardinal would like Lance to believe he didn't have a heart so he couldn't do any damage. But Lance held the firm belief that *every* person had a soft spot. The trick was finding it.

"I want you to know," Lance said, treading a thin line, "whatever's going on"—his mind ping-ponged over the facts, over the past, over his knowledge of this über-skilled operative he'd recruited right out from under the nose of the Russians, right out from under the man's father—"I've got your back."

"It is a nice sentiment but unrealistic and therefore false." Cardinal's sigh carried heavily through the dank room. "And if you knew the price of that statement, you'd backpedal so fast. . ."

There was entirely too much truth in that statement. Already, thanks to Payne, Cardinal's role within DIA hung in jeopardy. Lance's own position there could be compromised.

"I know what the price is," Lance said. "I also know you're probably the single best asset we've ever had."

"Again, nice sentiment, but it's not true."

"What's going on, Cardinal?" Ominous quiet rankled Lance. Something huge had shifted in the man before him. Left Lance with a bad taste in his mouth. He knew the whole marriage thing to Aspen would push the man, but he'd really thought it would make him work better, harder. Had he been wrong? "If this is about the marriage—"

"When you walk out of here, you'll never see me again."

Thirty-Four

Cardinal never thought this day would come. But that was foolhardy. Expecting to live this life—to actually have a life. To think his father would never find him...

"Cardinal—you can't."

"I can." He drew himself off the ground. "I should have done this a dozen years ago."

"Done what?" An edge had crept into Burnett's voice that marked him as angry.

"Vanished. Disappeared."

"You did that. Became Cardinal."

The man was trying to talk him out of it. "Good-bye, General."

"So, that's it? You walk out of here. What happens to Aspen? Someone took her."

"Then you should stop arguing with me and find her. You have the resources."

"You and I both know finding her is next to impossible without a lead."

Cardinal steadied his breathing. Was the general implying he didn't know where she was? That...surely he knew.

Wait. Of course he knew. Had to. "You're baiting me."

Darkness worked wonders to conceal facial expressions. The general hadn't had as much experience as he in detecting silent signals.

"She needs you, Cardinal."

"No." His heart ka-thumped through the next few beats. "She needs to be saved so she can live a long, happy, healthy life."

"Word has it, you and her hit it off."

He would *not* be goaded.

"Real well. In fact, someone suggested you made that marriage legitimate."

Guilt harangued him. He hadn't crossed ethical lines. Perhaps succumbed to weakness. Made a foolish error in judgment. Let his feelings get the better of him. "You're wasting breath and time, General."

Cardinal walked out of the room, across the lip, and down the stairs. He spotted Hastings.

"Dane."

He held up a hand, and apparently more of his foul mood showed in his body language because that slight signal was enough to stay her response.

"What's he doing?" someone—it sounded like Candyman—asked.

"Leaving." Burnett stomped down the steps.

"Hey!" Candyman shouted.

Cardinal kept walking. Reached the door.

Boots thudded behind him.

"Hey, you sorry piece of crap!"

The door squeaked closed. Cardinal let it. Let it shut on the guilt they wanted to heap on him. The weight that oppressed him.

Thap!

"You sorry son of a—"

Cardinal glanced back.

A fist collided with his jaw.

He stumbled back, but there was no fight left in him. Not after what happened. Not after feeling disembodied as he watched the demon of a man within him take over. The one that was so like his father he couldn't tell the difference between that man and the colonel.

Chin up, he swiped the blood from his lip. Eyed Candyman.

"She loved you!" Candyman's tension radiated a nuclear yield. "She gave you everything, trusted you. And this—*this!*—is how you repay that?"

Cardinal took the blow. Turned. Started walking.

"I see. It's only a game to you. You're a spook, so you screw people over and move on, is that it? All Aspen was to you was a warm body?"

The words twisted around his heart. He slowed. Hung his head.

"You're unbelievable. Walking away knowing full well she could be dead by nightfall."

"She won't be dead."

"That's right. Because she's already dead, thanks to you."

Cardinal stretched his neck. "If they wanted her dead, they wouldn't have kidnapped her. She won't die."

"That's right. She won't die," Candyman said, his nostrils flaring, "because some of us actually care about her. Some of us are willing to fight to the death for one of our own. Because some of us didn't play a beautiful, innocent woman's affections."

"I did not play her." *Can't go there. . .can't. . .open. . .that. . .*

Angel headstone. Glass shattering. Screaming. Flash. Bright light. The sickeningly hollow flap of her clothes as she fell to her death.

Cardinal flinched. Clenched his eyes. He raised a hand as if to ward off the jumbled thoughts. *What's happening to me?*

"Hey." Candyman's voice changed. "You okay, man?"

Cardinal met the ironclad gaze of the special operator. A man who'd been an ally. Cardinal glanced down the road where he'd seen that vehicle tear off with Aspen inside. He'd known then, hadn't he, what happened? Who took her? Even though he unleashed on Austin, he *knew.* The beating he'd given her brother was pent-up rage. He'd been found. He'd been cornered. Trapped. And they had bait.

"Look, whatever spooked you, I get it. But she needs you. And right now, you're the only one primed to do this." Candyman's left eyebrow dipped. "In fact, by that look on your face, I'm thinking you have a good guess about what happened."

Cardinal said nothing. Didn't want to give voice to the demons rising up from the past to consume him, his life, his soul.

"Who?" Candyman stood a couple inches shorter, but the man measured feet above the rest in courage. "Who did this?"

The second Cardinal's mind started to answer, he shut it down. He rerouted his thoughts to a solution. "Take the dog. Go to Russia." With that, he started walking.

"Dude, in case you missed the news flash, Russia's big. That's not helpful. And by the time we figure out where to go, she could be dead."

At the gate, Cardinal muttered, "She won't be dead."

Because he wants me to come for her. But he couldn't. Wouldn't go there, literally or mentally. Could *not* enter that psychological war zone again. He'd escaped it twenty years ago.

"Dude! Seriously?"

Cardinal turned. Eyed Candyman across the grounds. "If you want to find Aspen, find General Tselekova."

Burnett stepped into the open. Hands stuffed in his pant pockets, he frowned. A frown that said a lot. Said he knew what was happening.

Arms wide, Candyman shrugged. "Who the heck is that?"

"My father."

★ ★ Thirty-Five ★ ★

Warbling plucked at her hearing. A steady vibration wormed through her being, each microbounce jarring her further awake. Her head thundered. She swallowed, and her ears screamed in protest. She winced and curled in—at least tried. Only then did she realize she couldn't move her arms. She tugged but felt something holding her by the wrists.

She tried to open her eyes. . .but as she lifted from the fog of sleep, she felt her whole body rising. *What on earth?* Her eyes—she couldn't see. No. . .no, something covered her eyes. A dart of fear mingled with adrenaline as she remembered being in the safe house. Remembered her brother and Dane—Cardinal—going at it. The explosion. . .then. . .

Dizzying images. Being. . .

She grimaced as pain smacked her head.

Why couldn't she remember it clearly? Crazy wobbly. The world just seemed to be on fast-forward and reverse combined, images and memories shifting and colliding.

Being flung around.

She shook her head. If something was tied around her eyes, could she get it off? Aspen tried rubbing her head against whatever it was. Not the floor. Too soft. The swish of the fabric spoke of leather or vinyl. Her shoulder dug into something. Ached.

Again, she dragged her head over the material. Lifted and used her shoulder to— Light peeked in under the mask.

Aspen tensed and stilled.

Airplane. She knew that much instantly. How did she get on an airplane? And why?

Voices skidded into the cabin. Hurried footsteps.

Aspen dropped back, her stomach lurching at the sight of a man in black looming over her. He bent closer, a needle in his hand.

"No." Her voice faded out as she slumped back, feeling a strange warmth spiraling through her arm. Her muscles went limp. Again, her head swam in that thick ocean of confusion.

"Sir, I think you need to hear this."

Lance looked across the room where Hastings had been interrogating the previously unconscious man for information. Two hours. He'd been in country for two hours, and things had gone south in a handbasket. He hoisted himself off the chair and lumbered over to the room. It took every effort of mental energy not to just turn around and go home. He didn't have that luxury.

Neither did Cardinal, but he'd left. Curse that man! Handling him was like trying to contain a fire with your bare hands. He'd known that for years. But he'd been willing to put in the hours, the exhaustion, the aggravation. And it'd paid off. Until today.

As he crossed the room, Lance spotted Timbrel. She'd been working Candyman down for the last twenty minutes since Cardinal had beaten the path of least resistance out of here.

Lance entered the room.

Hastings stood beside the man handcuffed to a pipe that held no function other than being convenient for interrogations.

"My name," the man began, his face a little bloodied, "is Austin Courtland."

"Well crap." Lance wanted to curse. "You're an enemy of the state, Mr. Courtland."

"No, sir. I'm its patriot."

"Do tell, and while you're telling, explain why you no longer look like Austin Courtland. Ya know what? On second thought, I don't care."

"I went off the grid because I came upon the operation to hide the yellowcake. I couldn't ascertain who was involved and who wasn't, so I had to wait it out."

"And that took you eight months?"

"Yes, sir. But. . .the woman—"

"What woman?"

"My girlfriend—well, I thought she was. Discovered a couple of days ago that she's a Russian operative."

Lance muttered his mom's Catholic oaths. "Russian, so that's where you got those thugs that hit my men?"

Courtland stared hard. "Yes, sir."

"That is some seriously bad news, Courtland."

He gave a slow, contemplative nod. "And now, they have my sister."

Unswayed by the man's sudden surge of patriotism and familial duty, Lance shook his head. "Don't tell me what I already know. You left your mentor and handler in the lurch. You abandoned protocol. That tells me I can't trust you—"

"I saw Cardinal down here with Admiral Kuhn. I had to assume collusion."

"Assume." Lance grunted. "You know what assuming does, right, Courtland?"

The man gritted his teeth. "Let me help find her, General. I can do this."

Yeah, right. And Lance was a monkey's uncle. "Nothing doing." Like he would really put the lives of one of his best operatives and an innocent civilian woman on the line. "I can't trust you, and I have more experienced assets than you."

"The best bet you had walked out of here." Courtland jutted his jaw. "I'm the next bet."

"No, that dog is. And you're going back to Virginia like Kuhn." Lance pivoted and stalked out of the room. He'd managed to get Kuhn strung up on charges related to his obstruction of justice and collusion with the enemy to transport fissile material. He just had to make sure it stuck.

Man, he just didn't have time for anything. He just didn't care. Didn't want to stand in there and listen to that traitor spout off his puffed-up, vain-riddled reasons for dereliction of duty. An asset going rogue on shifty information told him the man couldn't be trusted. Told him the man was no longer fit for duty.

Demons had a way of sneaking up on you, especially ones from the past. If this was what was truly happening, then they were in deep kimchi.

Tselekova. Lance Burnett sat with his head in his hands. God have mercy on Aspen! But they had a chance—a prayer, if one liked to think along those lines, and right now he couldn't afford to offend—with the dog. If they could just rig a few favors, get over there with Talon, they might have a chance to get Aspen back. Cardinal gave them the name to go after. They had the dog. . .

"Talon, heel!" Hogan stood a few feet away. Her voice had been firm. Authoritative.

The yellow Lab hunkered and inched closer to the wall beneath the table. Head down, he trembled.

"It's no use," Hastings said.

"You're no use," Timbrel shot back, glowering.

"I could just kill that man," Candyman said, pacing and muttering. He'd been primed since Cardinal left an hour ago. In that time, they'd formulated a plan.

"What's with Kuhn?"

Lance checked his watch. "Should be en route, in protective custody, back to Virginia." Did he sound smug? That sorry excuse for an officer had put lives at risk—but worse, entire countries at the hands of brutal dictators. Lance couldn't wrap his mind around it. The very thing they were trained and seasoned to thwart and interrupt—corruption, crimes against humanity—Payne had perpetuated.

Lance dropped into the chair and focused on Hogan, a tough girl who approached animals with more consideration than she did people. Lance nearly grinned. He kinda liked this woman.

"Hogan." He motioned to the dog. "Do we have a prayer?"

She lowered herself to her knees. "I don't know. Clearly that percussion grenade affected him, but I am pretty sure he could detect Aspen's panic. Imagine being able to sense that but not being able to do anything about it, when he's trained to protect at all times?"

"Yeah." Candyman stomped closer. "I can relate to that *real well*."

"Why don't you come off your testosterone trip and help—"

Candyman pounded the pavement to Hastings. "You want to go there? Do you *really* want to go there?"

Lance sat up, knowing by the look in Candyman's face that things were about to get ugly. It wasn't personal—well, it was personal. Candyman had failed to protect an asset. The guy would go ballistic on anyone right now, Lance imagined.

Hogan darted between the two. "Hey." When Candyman tried to skirt her, she shoved him back. "Hey! Get a grip."

"I'll get a grip all right," he mumbled as he skulked away from the others, led off by Hogan like a dog on a lead. His eyes shot RPGs at Smith and Hastings, who took up sides with each other.

The two stood off to the side, and though Lance was no expert, he thought they acted a little cozy. A thought struck him. He stood. "Hogan."

Hand on Candyman's arm, she looked at Lance.

"What was the sitrep with Aspen and Cardinal?"

"He was a sleazy scumbag who deserv—"

"Hey!" Timbrel nudged Candyman's chest. "Stop." She looked back to Lance. "Well on their way to the altar if Aspen had any say about it."

Heat churned through Lance's gut. He came off the chair. "Oh man." He swiped a hand over his weary face. He angled toward Hogan again. "You're sure—the feelings were mutual?"

Candyman frowned, easing away from Hogan. "What's on your mind, General?"

"Trouble." He grinned. "A Russian storm named Nikol Tselekova."

Thirty-Six

Oppression.

Despite the late hour, the heat held its fist-hold oppression on the city, much the way this situation did on his heart and life. Cardinal sat on the beach, staring out over the night-darkened waters.

He had her. Cardinal *knew* that the colonel—wait. He's a general now. Cardinal smirked. Though the man had risen in rank, he would always sit at the lower rank in Cardinal's mind. Colonel. It'd been the only noun he'd been allowed to use in reference to the man. If he called him father, Cardinal got a beating.

But one didn't use a nice term such as that with a man like Colonel Vasily Tselekova.

I thought I escaped him.

There was no escape from a past like that. It shaped his life. More like *disfigured* his life. The same blood that drove his father to be a cruel, hard taskmaster pumped through Cardinal's veins. For the last two decades, he'd worked to master it. Master the anger. The rage.

He wanted nothing more than to become a better man than the colonel.

Tonight, he completely failed. The way he'd unleashed on Courtland.

Breathing hurt as the memories assailed him. How he felt the feeding frenzy off the pain and fear in the man's face. The bloody nose. The busted lip fed the demons chomping on the chains he'd wrapped them in.

Cardinal roughed a hand over his face and eyes. *I let him out. Let the beast out.* Failure. Weakness.

"You are weak, Nikol. I must do this. Can't you see? Weak men fail."

Cardinal tilted his head back and opened his mouth, searching for a clear breath. Not one stifled by the suffocating, brutal past that so often felt closer than his next breath. Head in his hands, Cardinal tried to block the barrage of memories. He allowed his mind to settle on one.

"Don't let them make you weak, Nikol. Show them who's in control. Show them who has the power. Make them obey you, or get rid of them." The colonel knelt in front of him. Held his shoulders. *"You are my son. Destined for great, great things. Great power! Just like me."* He shook Nikol. *"You see this, yes?"*

But Nikol's eyes drifted to the window. To the place where the angel flew.

"No!" The colonel jerked him. *"She is where she belongs. You are where you belong—with me. Da?"*

There was only one acceptable answer. "Da."

"I failed her, God." Completely. Utterly. Stood there while the colonel threw her to her death. *I could've stopped him.* But he hadn't.

Just like now.

No. It was different. There was no proof this was the colonel.

The devil was in the details—quite literally. He couldn't deny that this had the colonel written all over it. He'd taken Aspen. That's where she was. In Russia. It was the only plausible explanation with the presence of Austin's Russian girlfriend. The Russian lettering on the yellowcake crates. BELARUS.

Hand fisted and on his knee, he stared up at the stars. Let the fury build. Why? Why take Aspen? There were many more high-value targets there. Austin. Admiral Kuhn.

Why didn't he just take me?

Control. This was about control. About making Cardinal come crawling on his knees. Admit he'd been wrong. Made a mistake. Cower and show his weakness groveling over a woman.

No, he wouldn't grovel to that man. Never. He wouldn't give the colonel what he wanted. He wouldn't satisfy the sick need for control and power. That meant he couldn't go after Aspen. In his career, he'd made it a Cardinal rule to never, *ever* play into someone's hands. He'd walked and turned the tables. Turned the power.

God. . .I can't. . .go back there. I just can't.

Where were the stained-glass windows and peaceful flickering candles when he desperately needed them?

"I am here."

Warmth spread through his chest. "God. . . ?" What an idiot. *Do you think God cares about you? He has a universe to run.*

An image, searing and terrifying, of Aspen lying dead on a bed of springlike grass ripped through Cardinal's mind. He tensed, tucked his chin, waiting for the image to pass.

Blood. . .in her blond hair.

Lips dry, cracked.

He squeezed his eyes.

Her arm outstretched. To him.

"No," he ground out. The surreal tapestry spread out before him. Panned out. Not just the ground. The surroundings. Crosses. Stone houses. A wrought-iron fence. Headstones.

"The cemetery," he whispered. Fire wormed through his stomach and squirmed into his chest. No. . .no, he couldn't.

They aren't the same.

He pushed the thoughts back. Pushed the past into the great oblivion from which it'd escaped.

"And the angel flew," he heard himself say.

She had flown out that window. Terrifyingly eerie. Terrifyingly haunting. Watching her slide out of view. Frozen like marble to the spot in his bedroom. Staring at the hole in time and space that had held her not two seconds earlier. The thump—

Oh, God! Please. . .no. . .

He'd tried to forget. Tried to bury that memory. He'd stayed there. Right in his spot. Stared at the hole. Then the sharp glass glistening in the early morning light. And the colonel. . .

Cardinal tasted the bitter herb of vengeance. Yes, Colonel Tselekova took his mother from him. To make him stronger. So he wouldn't be weak. And it'd worked—just not in the way the colonel expected.

He'd failed his mother. And going after Aspen, having to face the colonel, the man who'd bred him through a mistress. . . "I can't. Don't ask this of me. Send someone." Anyone. *Just not me.*

"I do that all the time."

Cardinal jerked to his feet, stunned to find a smelly beggar squatting a few feet from him. Scraggly beard matched scraggly hair. "Talking to myself, ya know? Or maybe talking to God when no one's around. That way, I can ignore what I don't want to hear." A fisherman's jacket hung on bony shoulders. A jacket? In this heat?

The man smiled, the moonlight catching a hopscotch pattern of teeth.

"Don't worry, boy. I'm not going to hurt you." He reached for a makeshift spit where a fish sparkled under the moon's glow. "Say, can you hand me that plate?"

Cardinal frowned. "What pl—?"

A plate lay less than two feet from him.

Where did that come from?

"Couldja hurry?" The old man wagged his gnarly, dirty fingers. "It's burning."

Cardinal bent, retrieved the plate, and handed it to the homeless guy, then started to turn.

"You had dinner?" The man slid the fish from the spit and tugged the stick out. He patted himself down, each slap poofing a foul odor Cardinal's way.

"Not hungry." As if to defy him, his stomach growled. Loud.

The man cackled. "Sounds like your belly would disagree. C'mon." He waved Cardinal back to himself. "Pop a squat. I won't bite—and neither will this fella." Another cackle. "Say, you got a knife?"

With an annoyed yet amused snort, Cardinal tugged his butterfly knife out, worked it open, then handed it over. Why he sat down, he didn't know. Maybe it was the weariness. He just didn't care anymore. And he was too tired to fight. Didn't want to be alone with his thoughts. With the guilt.

The old man gave him a piece of wood on which half the fish waited.

"You look like you could take a load off your mind." The man chomped into the flesh.

Cardinal wondered for a second what it was like to chew with half your teeth missing.

"I knew this fella once, when I was younger." He waggled his eyebrows. "And had my looks about me still. He could talk a horse dead and never say a word." The man ate more fish, grinning as he did, and nodded toward Cardinal. "I'm thinking you're like that fella."

"Maybe he didn't have anything to say." The fish proved tasty.

Cardinal finished it off in just a couple of bites.

"Where you come from, Lone Stranger?"

Cardinal bunched his shoulders. "Everywhere, I guess."

The man laughed, lifted his leg, and slapped it. "If that ain't a sailor's answer, I don't know what is. I come from just beyond the horizon." His eyes snapped at him, keen and inquisitive. "So. Don't mean to pry— well, yes I do, I guess. I overheard you say you can't do it. Mind if I ask what that is?"

Cardinal looked out at the water.

"Eh, don't mind me. I get up in people's business and make 'em mad." He waved a hand around the beach. "It's why I'm out here." He laughed. "Can't help it if I care about people. You know? I mean, what else is there? People. . .and animals."

"Chaos. Corruption. Evil."

"You got the right of it there." The man clucked his tongue. Ate the last of his fish. "I seen a lot of that in my time." He shook his head.

Cardinal couldn't help but notice how the man suddenly seemed weighted. Man, he could relate.

"But you know, I seen good, too." The man nodded, his jaw jutted and lips pressed tight, almost as if he had no teeth at all now. "Sometimes, you have to look for it. Get out of where you are and look—really look for it."

Good? The only good in his life had been. . .Aspen.

"Sometimes," the man said, his voice bearing the burden of grief, "it gets taken from you."

Shooting a look to the old man, Cardinal tried to ignore the sudden electric dart through his gut.

"Sometimes, we got choices to make when that happens. And sometimes, we make a choice that hurts."

"The wrong choice," Cardinal said.

The man scowled, his bushy eyebrows pulling together like a snowdrift over blue eyes. "Son, jus' 'cause it hurts don't make it wrong." The man sniffled loudly then swiped a hand beneath his nose. "Takes a real man to fight that battle. Yes, sir."

Cardinal's stomach warmed. "Sometimes, a bigger battle is won by *not* fighting, not engaging the opponent."

"Yep, you're sure right." The man shrugged in a way that told

Cardinal there was more coming. Yet only the lapping of the nearby water whispered in the warm night.

The man had nearly stepped on Cardinal's toes—metaphorically. He wouldn't hand him a personal invitation.

"There was this man," the beggar spoke, leaning closer and spiraling his stench over the area. It was strong. Almost spicy. "He'd stolen something from his brother. Pretty much the entire inheritance. Right out from under his brother's nose."

The man swiped his thumb under his nose. "Decades went by, and he finally wanted to return home. Felt he was supposed to. So he starts heading home."

Something I won't do.

"He was so scared, he had his people go before him."

The man must've been rich to send people home with him.

"And he was still so scared, he sent his wife ahead of him. And the children." The man slapped his leg. "Ha! Can you imagine?"

"That's a coward."

Wise-beyond-their-years eyes came to him slowly. "Yeah, but he *went home.*"

The words sailed over the hot night and corkscrewed past Cardinal's every excuse, every defense, straight into his chest. Warmth spread. "I can't go home."

"That can't sounds a lot like won't, son." The man poked his shoulder. "Sometimes, we make a choice that hurts." He grinned his checkerboard grin. "But hurts heal when we face them. Leave them to fester, we have to chop off that limb or end up dying from the poison that infects our system."

Heady over the man's words, Cardinal felt a strange, alarming fear grip him. "Who are you?"

The man guffawed. "Shouldn't you have asked me that before you ate that fish?" He clapped a hand on Cardinal's shoulder. "Son, I think you know what you need to do." He grunted and strained as he pushed to his feet, wobbling.

Cardinal helped him, coming to his own feet as he did.

"Now, I'd better be gettin' back."

"You have a home?"

Laughing, the man patted his jacket as if looking for something.

"Nothin' like a fresh North African catfish to fill the belly."

Where were his manners? "Thanks." Cardinal touched his stomach. "I think I needed that more than I realized."

"Then finish it off."

"I did." Cardinal frowned when the man stared at him like he'd lost his mind then motioned with his arthritis-curled hand toward the wood. When Cardinal glanced at it, he was stumped to see several more bites. "Oh." But. . .he'd eaten it all.

He looked up.

The beach stretched and curled around the bay. Empty.

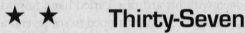

★ ★   **Thirty-Seven**   ★ ★

Safe House, Djibouti

W e need a game plan."

"No. Really, Sherlock?"

Austin skated a heated look to the only female left on the team. "Want to stow the sarcasm and actually contribute?"

"Hey." Candyman stepped up, his broad chest puffed. "Ease up there, chief."

"Let's all bring the tension down." Boots thudded across the open room as General Burnett joined them. "This entire thing stinks, but we've got to get a handle on it." He turned to Brie Hastings, an attractive late-twenties lieutenant who had as much spit and fire as Aspen. "What'd you find out about Hendricks and Payne?"

"Nothing yet, sir."

He wagged a meaty finger at her. "Keep working those channels—find Payne. He's the key. He went somewhere. I want to know where."

"Sorry," Austin said, his anger getting the best of him again, "but the bigger concern here is Aspen. We have to find her. She's not trained for this."

"She's stronger than you think," Timbrel Hogan said. Condemnation and accusation formed her venom-laced words. "She grew a lot after you abandoned her. Figured out where her priorities were." She smirked. "And she found a good man."

"Good?" Austin snapped. "He walked *out* on her and us!"

"Did he?" Hogan spat. "Or did he abandon dead weight, and right now he's out there hunting down whatever idiot took her from him?"

Austin wanted to curse at her ignorance. "If you believe that, then you don't know the first thing about the man who played my sister."

Arms folded, Hogan glowered back. "I bet Aspen's thinking the same thing about her twin brother right now."

"All right, all right." The big guy sidestepped in front of Hogan, facing her. His voice softened and quieted as he spoke with her, his words shielded from others in the room. The salve of his approach seemed to soothe her, calm her down.

"Hogan," Burnett spoke up, "how's Talon?"

"A basket case," she said, once again nailing Austin with a glare. "His first handler pretty much screwed him up."

"Look—"

Burnett slapped his hand against the table, ending the argument. "Can you get him back together?"

Hogan hesitated. "I. . .I don't know. He's pretty shot."

"What about that vet you people use?"

"Khat?" Her voice pitched. "She's in Texas!"

"Do we have time to get her over here?"

Hastings shook her head. "I think we should have something pinned down in the next hour or two. And if we get word on Payne, we have to leave immediately. The jet's already on standby. We should be airborne within a couple of hours, at the latest."

Burnett muttered something about a can of soda then scratched the back of his head. He again focused on Hogan. "So get that vet on the webcam. Talk to her. Find out how to help him."

"Sir," Hogan said, Candyman hovering close by, "even if we talked to her—he's psychologically traumatized, out to lunch." Her gaze went to the Lab, still sitting beneath the table.

Austin's heart chugged with guilt. Talon had been one of the best and smartest working dogs out there. When the time came for him to disappear, he'd expected Talon, tough dog that he was, to be fine. It hurt—a lot—to think that his commitment to serving his country in a deeper way had traumatized the poor fella. And now, with Aspen getting snatched. . .

"Let me try." Austin's heart vaulted into his throat. *What are you doing?* Talon had already shown that he wouldn't respond to him.

Not anymore. He remembered him, that was clear. But letting Austin handle him?

"What?" Hogan raised her arms. "Haven't you done enough already?"

"No." No, he hadn't. "Not for Aspen." He saw it now. Going under deep cover like he had wasn't supposed to work this way. When you made that commitment, rules dictated no further contact with family members. For this reason and a plethora of other reasons. And staying here arguing like middle schoolers would land him in an institution, a room with a cozy jacket.

"Hey," Burnett's voice boomed as he scowled at them. "We'll need Talon when we figure out where General Tselekova is hiding, so do what you can. Use what you need. Just—get him operational." He pivoted and glanced at the other end of the table where Smith sat at a bank of computers. "How's it going on Tselekova?"

"Last known location was Moscow, officially. He got in some trouble, but nobody's sure what." Smith stretched his arms and yawned.

"Should we just head to Moscow?" Hastings suggested. "The flight time would give us extra hours to keep hunting. Once in country, we can go where necessary."

"Get that working," Burnett said.

She nodded and gave Austin a look.

"Timbrel, you got—"

"Khaterah, hey there!" Hogan pointed to a screen where a video feed showed a grainy image of a beautiful Middle Eastern woman.

"Timbrel?" She squinted into the screen. A man hovered over her shoulder. "What—is something wrong?"

"Yeah, there is." Hands planted on either side of the screen, Hogan sighed. "Things have been pretty exciting here, and Talon's not weathering it so great."

"Define exciting," the man said.

Highlighted with a glow from the monitor, Hogan's face amplified her hesitation. "Aspen was snatched. Markoski is missing."

A flood of questions and comments rushed through the camera.

"Hey, hey!" Hogan said as she held out her hands to stem the bevy of questions. "Khat, listen. We're short on time. But I need help with Talon. He's not responding. What can I do?"

"Okay," Khaterah said. "Are you able to give him his own safe place?"

"Yeah. . .no, maybe." Hogan nudged up the rim of her baseball cap. "We're about to get on a plane. I can crate him."

"Okay, have the crate. He'll need a safe place to go. But in flight, stay near him, and every time he looks at you, give him a reward—whatever you can find. Hot dogs, chicken strips, something that is more alluring than his panic. You remember the 'focus' command, yes?"

Hogan nodded.

"Every time he looks at you, give him praise and a treat. Then introduce noises but keep that focus command going. Rapid-fire it till he's looking at you every time the noise comes. We've got to build his confidence back up."

The conversation continued over the next fifteen minutes. Austin listened hard and fast, determined to right this wrong he'd done to his partner. His superior officer. At Talon's side, he smoothed a hand down the thick chest of the Lab, over the harness. Rubbed the soft ears that flopped down near his face.

"They said I was handsome, but I knew it was you the ladies loved," Austin whispered to Talon as he inched closer.

His jaw snapped shut, the panting demanded by the heat ignored. Wary brown eyes gave furtive glances in Austin's direction. Cheeks puffed with a stifled pant.

Too stressed.

Austin leaned away. "Good boy."

Talon let his pink tongue dangle as he panted again.

Hogan walked toward him with a bag of treats.

"Let me do it." Austin held out his hand.

She shot fiery arrows from her eyes.

Enough already. "He was my dog, my partner."

"And you abandoned him."

He hauled himself up to face off, and in his periphery he noticed her bulldog-champion coming closer. "I sacrificed my relationship with him and Aspen to serve my country, but that doesn't mean I don't love them both very much." He snapped his hand out for the treats. "Talon knows me. You've never handled him. You're a handler, right?"

She gave a slow nod, her brown eyes sparking with fury.

"Then you know these dogs are fiercely loyal. They won't work with just anyone."

"Including you."

Man, this chick knew where to hit. *Give a guy a break, okay?* "I want to help him remember what we had." He put his hand on the treat bag. "Please. Just let me try. I have to. No matter what you think of me, I love my sister. And I love Talon."

She didn't release the bag.

"You need to grab gear to head out. Besides, if you see anything questionable, you and your bulldog can take me down."

She darted a glance to the side. "You think *he's* big?" She smirked. "Wait till you meet Beo."

Thirty-Eight

Murmuring drew Aspen from a sleep fog. She lifted her head—and winced at the pain that spiked through her neck and skull. Pounding forced her to squint against the pain. She searched for an explanation to wherever she was. However she'd gotten there.

Her head hurt. Her back. Pretty much everything. She lifted heavy eyelids to look around but kept the moans and groans begging for release to herself.

That's right—the girl. The plane. But. . .this wasn't a plane. *Where am I? Where's Talon? Is he okay? He doesn't take stress well. Especially not the kind with chaos.*

Light winked at her as she peeked across the sun-drenched room. Light streamed from high windows down onto the pale gray, cracked surface. On the floor. In a warehouse? A wild guess but the most probable considering her limited range of motion and ability to see her surroundings. She blinked against the sunlight as she strained backward to see behind her.

Crates in assorted sizes towered over her, like guardians.

Or captors.

Her mind scrambled back to the attack when she was yanked from the safe house. Talon's deafening barks swirled in the jarring bubble of memories. Was he alive? Had they killed him?

And Dane. Her eyes shuttered closed remembering Austin's accusations. Remembering that Dane wasn't who he said. But he'd told her that himself, hadn't he? Warned her not to look to him for affection or attention. Told her he couldn't, wouldn't get involved.

Who are you?

She couldn't worry about him right now.

Escape. Maybe she could escape.

Okay, while many people would say she should do that, it presented a whole shipment of new problems—getting to the American embassy and convincing them of her identity. Before that, she had to *find* the embassy. She remembered Dane pointing it out when they went to the hospital. Good grief—that felt like a lifetime past.

After another check of her location to verify she was alone, Aspen pushed up on her shoulder then propped herself on her elbow—and a strange tug came at her right arm. Her mind registered the tightness around her wrists. Tied up. She huffed. Another problem to solve. But she'd do it. She hurried, knowing her time alone was probably short. They'd come back and beat the snot out of her. Or worse.

Then shut it and get moving!

She had a brother to smack senseless. A. . .guy to riddle full of questions, and a dog to lovingly coerce back to healthdom. If that was a word.

Skating a look around, she slowly hauled herself upright, expecting at any second to hear shouting or feel bullets riddling her body.

When nothing happened, she swung her legs around. Ankles tied. Okay, another problem. *Augh! Really, Lord? Can't make this easy, huh?*

She shrugged and hopped over her bound hands, bringing them to the front, beneath her knees. Fingers nimble, she worked the plastic cord. It wouldn't fray, but it was the type of binding that if she worked it enough. . .

Aspen grunted. Felt a fingernail snap. Below the quick. She hissed but hurried, scissoring her legs back and forth the bare half inch the binding allowed. They must've found this stuff lying around the warehouse. Her gaze again skimmed the building. The high windows. A high-level catwalk-type thing that ran along the perimeter. . .straight into an office.

Her breath caught. Shadows moved behind the blinds.

She dug harder at the binding. Slid out of view. Yeah! Scooting back, she worked the binding. Felt it give. Her heart raced.

Voices carried through the building. She couldn't make out their words. Just upset. And getting closer.

She scurried backward. Her ankles sprung apart.

Aspen swung around. Came up on a knee. Pushed to her feet. Darted between the rows of boxes that stood twenty and thirty feet tall on pallets. Reminded her of the cargo on the boat. As she sprinted down the long line that seemed to stretch for a mile, she remembered Dane fingering some lettering. Cyrillic, wasn't it?

She clung to the right, hoping to avoid being spotted by whoever cast the shadow in the office.

A shout shot up.

Aspen pushed harder.

The door—she could see the door! Freedom's call yanked her onward. Hands still bound, she couldn't run her fastest. But she pumped her legs hard. A whimper climbed up her throat. *God, help me!*

Shouts erupted back in the warehouse.

She plunged forward. Reached for the door. Hit it at full throttle.

The door flew open. Hit the wall. Snapped back. Thudded against her shoulder.

She yelped as it spun her around. Tripped her. She went to a knee. Pushed back up. Panting. Choking—air! She couldn't breathe. Couldn't stop. Couldn't slow. She had to go. Keep going.

To her left, a canal-like stretch of water.

Buildings lined the street to her right, sentries against her escape.

Aspen sprinted toward the buildings, praying she could get lost in the dizzying menagerie of structures. There were enough. She could find some place. Hide till danger passed.

Talon. He'd never ventured far from her thoughts. But what could she do? Nothing, unless she could escape.

She sprinted, tugging against the bindings on her wrist. It'd be so much easier. . .if they were free. . .

Something loomed in the horizon to the left. By the time her mind registered it, another three-story warehouse blocked her view. At the next street, she shot a look left.

Skidded to a stop.

Heart in her throat, she stared at the distant specter.

"No. . ." Panic swirled a toxic potion in her chest.

Spires leapt toward the sky above bulbous protrusions. Gold ones. Turquoise ones. Swirls of gold tracing the bubble up to the spire. Cathedral. "Russia." She spun. Searched the surroundings for landmarks. Signs. Anything to verify what had her heart misfiring—so much that it hurt.

Tires squalled behind her.

She whirled, her hair whipping into her face. Blurring her vision. Not for long. But enough to cost precious time.

A black vehicle lurched toward her. Rubber screeched against cement. Doors clunked open.

She sprinted to the left, willing back tears.

Feet thumped behind her. Several.

Weight rammed into her back with a meaty grunt. Pitched her forward. Cement rushed up at her. Fire lit through her palms as she slammed into the street.

Almost as quickly, she was hauled to her feet. Two men held her, their grips on her arms brutal.

More men stalked toward her. The first sneered, his nostrils flared. He eyed her from top to bottom—a look that made her feel undressed and undone. He smirked. Muttered something in a language she didn't know but guessed to be Russian. That was where she was, right? He bobbed his head toward the warehouse.

Aspen wrestled against them, knowing if she went back in there, in that building, she may never be seen again. She let her legs go limp, but they merely hoisted her up. She screamed. Thrashed.

Almost without warning, she flew through the air. Onto the ground.

The girl who'd been on the flight with her stood there, her face hard as marble. She stared at the man who'd raped Aspen with those stormy eyes. She said something to the man, her expression impassive. Unreadable.

The man matched her stonelike mask. He muttered something to her, and his lip curled.

The girl's chin lifted ever so slightly—just like Timbrel when someone said something that challenged her. Her eyes glinted. She replied to the man.

What Aspen wouldn't do for a personal translator.

The man's voice rose, and his words flew as he whirled around and stalked off. The second man with him shot Aspen a sidelong glance that almost seemed to carry an apology.

Her heart skipped a beat. She pulled her gaze from the man who wielded power without a lot of brute force, unlike the brute squad behind him.

The girl—who couldn't be any more than twenty-one or -two—merely uttered two words, her gaze still on the men who left. "Do it."

Aspen's gut churned. "Do what?" *Kill me?*

The grunts who'd held Aspen moved toward her. She withdrew, but one held her. The other pinned her leg to the ground. Drove his large fist straight into her calf. Pain blinded her.

Thirty-Nine

Safe House, Djibouti

Lid down and door locked, the bathroom became a haven. When he thought of what took place—or rather, what got deposited—in this room, the irony couldn't be any greater that he found it to be a place of quiet, a place to think.

Austin cranked the knob on the shower then sat on the lid of the toilet, waiting as the pipes filtered the junk and turned the water clear. From his pocket, he retrieved the phone. Ran his thumb over the screen, swiping away the sweat that mottled the display.

Calling her could unleash trouble.

Not calling her. . .well, he'd never know.

Everything in him wanted to believe he hadn't been played.

You're grasping.

Yeah, he knew he was. But still. . .he had to know. He'd never felt this way about anyone, till Lina showed up. Finding her, connecting with her, sharing the journey—

That's what he thought he'd been doing.

Was it all an act? A way for her to bleed him of information?

Austin stepped from the still-functional bathroom after a quick shower. He grabbed his gear and stuffed it in a duffel Rocket loaned him. Back in his old duds, Austin realized the clothes were rank. But at least he'd scrubbed down.

He crossed the open bay and spotted the others loading gear. They were trying to load up the steel crate. He smirked. Knowing Talon was in good hands with Scrip, Austin headed over to help. He tossed in his bag then waved the guys off. With a few deft moves, he collapsed the crate.

"Thanks," Rocket said.

"No worries." He motioned to the SUV. "Is this everything? We ready to go?"

"Just about. Waiting on the general. He's on the line with HQ." Rocket closed the rear hatch. As they headed back toward the main room, he glanced toward him. "Can I ask you a question?"

"Sure."

"Why'd you do it? Ya know—the spook thing? Digging deep and leaving your family?" The guy shrugged, his lanky build and squared shoulders a dichotomy. "Not sure I could do that."

"It wasn't easy, but I believed I could help my country. Help others." Austin shook his head. "I just felt it was right." Memories slipped and slid through his mind. "I went back to Austin twice. To check on Aspen." A raw burning began at the back of his throat. "The last time, I just. . .I saw her and Talon. . .and I knew I couldn't visit them again. It haunted me. But I felt I was doing the right thing."

"Do you regret it?"

"Sure." Austin hated admitting it. "Yeah. I do—hate what it did to Aspen, to Talon. But would I do it again?" He shrugged and pursed his lips. "I probably would. What I did, leaving, working for the country, it was important. I was one of the few willing to do it."

They stepped into the mini operations room.

Awareness lit through his mind. Energy—*bad* energy. Not that he was into all that mysticism. But whatever happened—

And Timbrel. She was as angry as a wet cat as she railed at Burnett, who held a hand over his forehead. "Where's Courtland?" she demanded.

"Right here." Austin moved forward. "What's going on?"

"Where is he? What'd you do with him?"

"Do with whom? What are you talking about?"

"Talon's missing!"

Forty

Weakness.
Power.
Disgraced.
Honored.
Shoved down.
Raised up.

Bent forward, elbows on his knees, Cardinal rubbed the knuckles of his fist. Polar opposites had served to define his existence, growing up under the authoritarian rule of the colonel. Terror had shaped Cardinal's performance. Terror that should he fail, no matter how large or how much, he would pay. And severely. Beatings were as commonplace as the smiles and love other children received.

"You never smile."

Cardinal sat back with a thump against the pew. Aspen's soft words played over in his mind, tormenting him. If he could get her back—alive—he'd smile for her every day of the year. She'd be the reason for those smiles.

Which was why he had to do this. Why he had to accept that the fisher/beggar man, whoever—or whatever—he was, had delivered a message.

Much like the one who had lured him into his current profession. Sitting in this very cathedral, agony the only warmth in life during the hard, bitter winter that defined his life. It'd been ten winters since his mother's burial. And that's all—a burial. Outside a small church. No service. The colonel had refused. To do anything, including acknowledge that she had been his mistress. That she had given birth to his son.

Thanks to the man on the beach, Cardinal realized his inaction regarding Aspen mirrored that of his father's. Refusing to dip his baton into the cauldron he'd stirred. Refusing to accept responsibility for the mistress he'd used and the son he'd fathered.

The only reason Aspen got snatched was because of Cardinal.

No.

Not Cardinal. That moniker belonged to the man sitting here now. A man who'd built his life with strategic moves, building block upon block. Creating a fortress between himself and the past. The pain. The shame. The very name. . .Nikol.

Just hearing the name internally whipped him. Made him feel like he lay on the stripped mattress in the dark, icy room. Punishment came in forms of deprivation. No heat in his room. No bedding. No dinner. Things mattered little to him when he could conjure up images of his mom. *Or Kalyna.*

His father could rape his mind, but he would never touch Kalyna. That thought seed had dug deep roots, enabled him to endure just about everything. Especially after their mother died. But then, he'd had to stop visiting Kalyna. Things got dangerous. For her. For him. It was the greatest coup he pulled on the colonel, hiding her existence. A great victory his mother took to her grave.

He'd lost her. . .lost Kalyna in the years, in the distance that grew between them. Both physical and emotional.

He peeked up through his brows at the colorful glass sparkling in the high walls and the brilliant frescoes stretching across the domes. . . straight to the one that held his heart. The angel.

Then the angel flew.

Angel. . .his mom. . .Aspen. . .

Cardinal blew out a breath and closed his eyes. "I'm here. . ." Was he really talking to God? He'd never cemented his stance on that existence of the deity. Sitting in cathedral after cathedral soothed his soul. Used the time to think. To sort out whatever problem or situation he'd found himself in. But he'd stopped, every time, short of acknowledging God.

"But You didn't do that to me, did You?"

Thoughts flitted from the moment Burnett put Aspen in his path, knowing full well that had Cardinal known she was a woman, the mission would've ended before it started. Then seeing Aspen for the first time. Sunlight filtering through her halolike curls. Then he'd crumbled beneath the fear, the frantic possibility of losing control and hurting Aspen. Her finding him at St. Mary's in Austin. Then Burnett "marrying" them. Then Aspen's declaration of love. Something Cardinal didn't deserve. And at the time shunned her and the thought, though everything in him wanted to seize it. Then to the beggar. Who fed him. Not just fish but courage. Purpose. Fuel to the fire that simmered in his gut.

Acknowledge God.

He avoided that—out of fear. Afraid of being vulnerable. Afraid of letting go. . . Because then, what did he have to fuel him? Drive him? Keep him focused?

He wasn't sitting here because he was trying to talk himself out of this. He knew what he had to do. That was just it. Confronting the colonel—*general now.* . .

He sloughed his palms together, wishing he could slough off the past. Wished the lethal and cunning precision he'd exerted in his profession could bleed into this situation. But the terror that suffocated his character as a teen surged to the front of his mind. That man. . . nobody held power over him the way the colonel did.

The kid inside him, the one who never had a childhood but a strict, militaristic, authoritarian upbringing, screamed to run. Flee Mother Russia before the general could do something.

"God. . .he. . .I can't. . ." Cardinal pushed back and pressed his spine against the wood of the pew. Weak. Weak. Weak. Thirty-three years old and still as petrified as at ten.

Pathetic.

Weak.

"You sit in cathedrals longing for something you think you can never have because you're too afraid to reach for it."

He hung his head. Aspen was right. But there'd been no condemnation in her voice. Only hurt—for him. *She believes in me.*

Like my mother.

His eyes traced the stained glass, the relics that held symbolic power. "Like You." Something inside him heated. "You believed in me, didn't You? Drew me here, to Yourself?"

The thought solidified. Gave him purpose. "God, I'm not going to let Aspen down." He swallowed the swell of panic. Felt the acid roiling through his gut. "I ask nothing for myself—save this one guilty pleasure: Help me save her."

Knowing he could save her, knowing he could thwart the colonel one last time. . . Facing Vasily Tselekova. Confronting him. Bringing all Cardinal was and knew to bear on this man. . . He nodded. Yes, he would die in peace.

Resolve hardened in his chest. He glanced to the cross over the altar. "Help me do this. Please. If she lives, I can die in peace. I am willing to do that. For her." Conviction, a familiar yet entirely new agony boomed through him with adrenaline. "Please."

And that's exactly what would happen.

Cardinal pushed up from the pew and strode out the side door. Greedy sunlight rushed into him, momentarily blinded him. A soft, wet nose nudged his hand. A smile threatened his stiff composure. He paused and knelt.

Talon stepped in closer and sat.

Arms wrapped around the Lab's chest, Cardinal ran a hand across the broad skull. "Thank you, boy. For your trust. For your cooperation." Incredible that he didn't feel odd talking to a dog. "She loves you, and I know you love her. We'll find her soon. Just. . ." His gaze drifted over the stone sentries peppering the grounds. "Give me a minute." He patted Talon then stood.

Squinting against the sun, he strode down the bricked main path. Turned right then strolled down the square stone path. Trees loomed overhead, wooden guardians of the granite coffins, sarcophagi, grave sites fenced in wrought iron. . .

Cardinal walked on, feeling the chill of that day. The terrible time of aloneness that engulfed him. Mother was in a better place, where she would be loved and treasured as she should have been on this earth. His father was a different, crueler man from that day forward.

Could it be possible. . .had the colonel loved her?

Or was he simply furious that he'd been pushed beyond the bounds of his self-control?

Cardinal turned down a narrow alley, noting the vines snaking around the iron and soapstone crosses, angels, and plain headstones. At the pauper's section, he wove a few more rows down then slowed.

Warmth flooded him as the past assaulted his mind.

Beneath his boots snow crunched loud and obnoxious. As if heralding his presence.

Nikol pressed himself against the bare-limbed tree, holding the bark as if it could save him from this nightmare. As if it gave him hope.

The earth, not too hard for burial, mounded to the left. Concealing the hole. Two men dressed in old trousers, jackets, and hats wielded shovels with such skill, Nikol knew they'd performed the soulless tasks of burial many times.

But he hadn't. And the thought of trespassing over the bodies of those who'd walked these places before him poked at his courage.

He should be ashamed! To stand here when she. . .

Something tickled his cheek. He scratched it, his fingers cold and hurting. Wet. Tears? The colonel will kill me! He scrubbed his face—

Thunk! Thunk-thunk.

Nikol stilled. Stepped out from behind the tree.

Laughter carried on the icy wind as more thunks and thuds joined the voices. Taunting.

He punched his way across the snow. No, they couldn't bury her yet! He hadn't said good-bye. "Podozhdite." Oh, please wait. "Stop!"

One glanced over his shoulder, surprise etched in his face when his gaze hit Nikol. The man straightened.

"Podozhdite. Pozhaluĭsta." Please, he begged again. By the time he reached the mound, the sight on the other side of the large rectangle they'd dug, Nikol couldn't move. The box. . .so thin. So little to protect her. Heat and water ran down his cheeks. "Mama. . ." Seeing that coffin, that box. . .things became real. Hellish. He was alone. No strength, no hope to light his day, anxious to see her once more when his father felt "weak."

She was gone. Gone! No no no no! He launched over the mound, sliding over the dirt. He dropped to his knees next to the flimsy coffin. He threw himself over the top. Sobbing. "Nyet, ne ostavlyaĭ menya." No, please, please don't leave me.

But, of course, she had. Not of her own choice. She died in her attempt to free him. Irony at its best—worst?—she ultimately freed herself. Completely.

"You are predictable."

The soft, feminine voice drew Cardinal up. Around. He stumbled back. Blinked. Heart careening at the image before him. Waves of amber hair. Wide mahogany eyes. *Mama?* No, no it was impossible.

She smirked as two men joined her. "Predictable," she said, her words thickened by her Russian accent. "Just as he predicted."

Cardinal glanced back to the headstone. To the name engraved: Элиана Маркоски. The Cyrllic lettering that spelled ELIANA MARKOSKI. Checked the dates. Yes, she died. *Shake it off.* This girl, this young girl, whoever she was. . .

Her gaze skidded from his to the headstone. Blue eyes seemed to absorb the information on the plain stone. Something blinked in her eyes. Flashed through her expression as she slowly dragged her attention back to him. Her mouth parted.

He flashed back more than nearly two decades. To the young girl in the woods, watching him. Calling after him. Cardinal hauled in a breath and let it out with her name. "Kalyna?"

Forty-One

33,000 Feet Over the Middle East

W here do we stand?" Lance closed the shade to the portal of the great blue beyond and turned his focus to the huddle around his leather chair. Thank God, Payne's lackeys had splurged on the Lear to get down to Djibouti lickety-split, or Lance would be hoofing it for twenty-four hours to St. Petersburg on a commercial liner.

"Not much. We know Tselekova fell out of grace with his superiors about two years ago." Lieutenant Hastings set a picture on the low table between the four chairs.

Members of ODA452 and Timbrel leaned in to get a glimpse of the man.

"What happened?" Watters asked.

"His ideas were—"

"Radical?" Austin offered.

"No." Brie locked gazes with the man. "Familiar. He wants to help return Russia to its former glory, and he believes it's acceptable to do it on the backs and lives of anyone. Since he was merely a general and not a politician or cabinet member or president. . ." She shrugged. "They sent him away to work some obscure job on a frozen base."

Ah, a lead? "Where?"

"Doesn't matter," Smith said. "He never showed up. Went completely off-grid."

"Why?"

"Because," Smith said, laying out more photos, "while politicians and superiors didn't like him, he had a fist hold over the throats and hearts of many under him. Promises of wealth and power were served up at every meeting. He's formed a quiet little insurrection."

Lance scooted to the edge of the chair, thumbing his bottom lip as he considered the information.

"Why does he want Aspen?" Austin knelt at the table. "Why her? What does she have to do with anything?"

"Yeah, why her? The hit was pretty deliberate."

"They didn't want her," Lance finally said. "They wanted him." He pointed to the image of Cardinal.

"Why? Why Cardinal? Because of the yellowcake?"

"I think that just tipped the hat." Lance eased back in the seat and wished for a Dr Pepper for the millionth time. This was bloody torture to be under this much stress and not have one single can of liquid genius. "Things heated up down here—first with you."

Austin's eyes widened. "Me?"

"When you found the yellowcake—what happened?"

"They hunted me down."

Lance nodded. "Thought so." He shook his head. "Then we sent Cardinal down here looking for you. Kuhn must've mentioned it to his sources. News travels fast when protecting an illegal—and international—operation. No doubt the heat alerted someone—or Tselekova himself. He sent his little minion to do the job."

"You seriously believe Lina is behind all this?"

"Absolutely."

"Whatever happened to 'innocent till proven guilty'?"

"You seriously think you'll be able to drag her into a U.S. court and fry her there?" Lance snorted. "Russia wouldn't let you get that close. Remember the spies discovered in 2010? If you'll remember, they went back to their homeland. Good ol'-fashioned spy swap."

"She just didn't seem the type—"

"Then she did her job well." Lance pointed to the table. "Go on, Hast—"

"Got it!" Smith shot up from the laptop on his lap. "Payne's wife just received communication."

Good news. Tell me good news, Smith.

"St. Petersburg."

"That's a big city, Lieutenant Smith."

He grinned. "Yes, sir. Another hour or so and I can get you within a mile of where the e-mail was sent from."

"Good. Relay that to the pilot. Divert to Pulkovo."

Smith leapt up and hurried to the front.

It took a lot of political capital to get the clearance necessary to enter Russian airspace—without getting shot down. His stomach churned and threatened to toss the modest airplane meal he'd eaten an hour ago back up the way it'd come.

The dog missing.

Aspen missing.

Cardinal MIA. Vanishing like this. . . . *I ought to ring his ruddy neck!* This was *not* the time to go rogue. A lot of questions had been raised about Cardinal's loyalty and trustworthiness—all thanks to General Payne, who should be halfway to Langley and right into the arms of federal penitentiary guards.

Lance sipped a Dr Pepper and swallowed. He nudged the drink aside.

"You okay, sir?"

In the glass of the oval window, he saw Lieutenant Hastings's reflection. "No. Nothing is okay. The dog, Aspen—Cardinal! Even my Dr Pepper doesn't taste right."

"That's because it's a Perrier, sir."

Snickers sent a heated flush through his cheeks as he glanced at the bottle. Green bottle. He muttered an oath. Ran a hand over his face. "I think I need to retire." He glared at the others. "Don't you have work to do?"

"I thought you chipped your spies," Rocket said from his chair, where he sat with closed eyes.

"That's the movies, Rocket. If we can track them, so can anyone else."

Timbrel sucked in a hard breath. "Wait!"

"You okay?" Candyman asked.

"Better than that." She grinned—and wow, that girl was pretty when she smiled. She brushed bangs from her face. "I don't know why I didn't think of it before. I'm stupid. I mean—I'm a handler."

"Hogan!" Lance snapped. "Calm down and tell me—"

"Talon." She gulped air. "He's microchipped and has a tracking device. They tag all MWDs in case something happens and they get separated."

Lance snapped his fingers at Hastings. "Get on that. Get it tracked."

The air and space cleared as the others rushed to the table near the back where they went to work on getting them closer to stopping this nightmare.

As he pushed back in his chair, Lance eyed the men of ODA452. Two of them snored loudly, their heads cocked at odd angles against the seats and windows. Watterboy and Candyman were engaged with Timbrel, working to track Talon's chip. Weariness marked the faces of every last one. If he looked at his own, he was sure it'd show up there, too.

And after eight hours in flight, they were only halfway to Russia. He punched the seat as he sat down. Eight hours. *Eight!* Half a day. When Lance had given the pilot hay about the length of time, the man warned him that this was a good day. Sometimes, the flight took twenty hours.

Curses exploded from the back.

On his feet, Lance searched for the upset.

"Is it her? Can you verify it?"

Lance rushed to the back. "What's going on?"

"Sat imaging, sir. We piggybacked a satellite. I started checking locations connected to insurgents. After a few back-channel searches—"

"What'd you find?" Lance thought his head might explode.

"Aspen." Smith blinked. Looked at the screen. "At least. . .it looks like her. She appears to be running down a street. There's a black car. Four men." He dragged his finger along the screen. "Chasing her."

Austin swung around. Face red. Eyes enraged. He threw a punch.

Crack! Lance felt the world tumble.

"If she dies, you die!" Austin screamed.

Weapons snapped up. Hastings. Smith. ODA452. All aimed at Austin.

The man's chest heaved. "I swear—if she dies because of this, because of your agent—" He hauled in a breath, face tormented. "I swear I'll kill you."

"Why don't you stop wasting your energy on hate and venom, Mr. Courtland, and get to work helping us find your sister."

But the man's words. . .the rage. . .Lance could relate. And shared the fears that drove them. With eight hours—*hours!*—between them and Aspen. . .

Were they already too late?

BEAUTIFUL

"She's beautiful, isn't she?" He looked from the cherub to his mother's sweaty, glowing face.

"Yes, she is."

He heard something in his mother's voice and looked up. Red circled her eyes. "What? Why are you crying? She's beautiful and healthy!" But that wasn't the best. "And he doesn't know!"

Her brown eyes locked onto his. "But he will." Her chin trembled. "He always does." A sob punched its way out, and she clutched the newborn to her face, kissing her.

He watched them. His mother and new baby sister. Knew his mother was right. The colonel found out everything. He always did. Somehow. Someway. He just did. "We have to hide her."

"Give her up?" Panic clanked through his mother's words. "I can't! No, I can't."

Nikol stood, feeling every bit the eight-year-old he was. "We must. Just as we hid that you were pregnant."

"That's not the same, Nikol. He doesn't like me in his life, so it's easy to stay away. But you see what he's done with you."

"It's different." It hurt his heart to even think it. "I'm a boy. He won't want her."

Mother cried again. Slowly, she settled in the bed with his baby sister cuddled in her arms. Then she lifted her head. Lips slightly apart. Light settled in her eyes. She smiled.

"What?"

"There's a family. . .my brother knows a missionary family in Brno." She smiled through a still-wet face. "They're American."

"He'd never think to look there."

Forty-Two

Amazing the way a million things can happen in a microsecond. Cardinal noticed the blue eyes peering at him from over a headstone.

Kalyna's gleam, the thirst for him to hurt, that poured out of her eyes.

The way the weapon dipped.

Tiny explosion.

The report of her weapon registered a fraction too late.

Fire lit down his arm. Flung his arm back.

In the second it took him to recover, Cardinal lunged. Straight into one of the men who stepped into his path. Their collision barreled right into Kalyna. The second guy tripped trying to get out of the way.

As Cardinal went down, he saw a dark gray blur. Braced himself. *Crack!* Stars sprinkled across his vision, compliments of the gravestone he'd hit. He lifted but didn't release the guy. Flipped the man over. Cold-cocked him.

"Get up," Kalyna shouted. "I'll shoot if you try anything."

Cardinal fishtailed and scissored his legs, gauging where she stood, and ripped her feet out from under her. The gun flipped from her hand. She landed with a thud.

He dove for the weapon. Saw the second guy charging. Cardinal rolled, lifting the weapon and bringing it to bear. He fired, and the guy took one, center mass. Red bloomed over his blue shirt like a dark sun.

Cardinal came up. His mind registered Kalyna's movement, reaching for something. *Threat.* Quickly, he realigned. Fired again. This time winging Kalyna's firing arm.

The other man stopped, one hand clutching his chest, the other raised in surrender.

Cardinal pointed the gun at the man. *"Khod'by ot otelya."* Would the guy walk away as Cardinal ordered? Would he make this as easy as it could be?

The man shook his head. Muttered something about not being willing to die but then stumbled away. Down the path.

"Don't make any sudden moves," Cardinal said in Russian.

Kalyna shot him a look, holding her arm. Blood dribbled down it. "You shot my arm."

"I missed." Cardinal gave a slight nod to the man, telling him to keep going. As the distance grew, he shifted most of his attention to Kalyna.

"He has the girl," Kalyna said.

He would not, even though she was his sister, give her the benefit of seeing him squirm. "You delivered her to him." Disappointment churned through his veins. "How could you do this? Work for him?"

"Why not?" Defiant, she jutted her chin and raised her head. "You left me. My mother abandoned me."

"She gave you a life!" Cardinal growled. "Sacrificed *everything* for you."

"Sacrificed? A life? I was poor and the adopted child of a missionary family. Tell me, dear brother, do you know how shunned I was—raised by Christians, abandoned by my family?" She looked every bit like their mother. "He came to me, has given me *everything*."

Fury smothered him. "You foolish girl! *He* is the reason our mother lays there." Cardinal pointed to the grave. *"He killed her!"*

"You lie!"

"To you, never." His chest ached with the lies the colonel had fed her. Poisoned her with. And she'd bought right into them.

"I wanted nothing more than to know my family. You came to me, time and again. But never told me. Then—when I needed you most, you vanished. Never came back."

"I had to! He discovered you existed—that's why he killed Mama."

"No, it's not true. He's a good man."

"Only when compared to the devil!" He yanked up his shirt and bared his back to her. "Do these look like the marks a *good* man would give his son? To teach him to be *strong*?" He shoved down the shirt and looked back at her.

Fear quivered through her young, beautiful face. She could only be in her midtwenties. So impressionable. Had she really become what their father was? The spawn of the underworld? He could not believe it of her. She had always been sweet. Her nature gentle.

"She is my mother?" Kalyna looked to the grave marker.

"Yes." He held out his hands then motioned to her arm and took a step closer. "Once she discovered she carried his child again, she had to hide from the colonel. He'd beaten her bloody once before over an unwanted baby." He inched closer, slowly reaching for the lightweight jacket she wore.

She tensed, suspicious.

"Easy, just going to bind your arm." When she didn't object, he tore off a section of her jacket. Tore that into two strips. Tucked one in his pocket. Held the other as he lifted her arm. "She was so excited when you were born. I was so scared for her, for you. What I went through, I didn't want anyone else to endure." He wrapped, talking quietly, pleased with the way she hung on the words. Hungry, so very hungry for a connection. He understood. It was incredible to think this beautiful, vibrant girl was his *little* sister.

"She spent two months with you, making sure you grew strong and healthy before she could bring herself to release you to the Christians." He nodded to the cathedral over the hill. "This is where they met, where she delivered you to their safekeeping. It was the only place we thought the colonel would not think to look for you."

A sad smile shivered across her lips. "You were right."

He saw it. The uncertainty. The fear. Perhaps even the confirmation that what he'd told her gave credence to something she suspected. Time was short. The colonel had Aspen. "Where is he keeping her?"

Kalyna's expressive eyes came to his. "You care for this American?"

Cardinal felt his gaze start to dip but forced it to stay on her. "Very much."

"Do you love her?"

His heart thudded. "Yes, I think I do."

She gave him a weird look.

Feeling stupid, he shrugged. "It's never happened before. And it's happened fast this time. But yes. . .she means everything to me."

The sadness slid away. Tears pooling in her eyes blinked away. *"Vy prikhodili k nyeĭ, no ne dlya menya?"*

You would come for her but not for me? Dimples bounced in and out of her chin. Her accusation slashed his heart.

"No. It's not—"

"Tikho, Nikol!" She touched a finger to her lips, reinforcing her "quiet" command.

Not too far away, tires screeched.

She half smiled. "See? He always knows, yes?"

"Kalyna, come with me. Please. I could not find you."

"But you found her. When you love someone, you never give up."

"I did not give up!"

More squalling. This time closer.

"Kalyna, listen to me, *sestra*. . ."

"Sister." She nodded but fought tears and a grieved smile. "It is too late."

"Kalyna—I do love you. For your protection, I stopped coming. Sent money."

"Money?" Eyes blazed in outrage. "I wanted family! But you did not want me." She reached around to her back, her expression going hard. Her actions practiced. She produced another handgun. "If you want to live, you should run. Now."

"Kalyna, please!" His gaze darted to the black car barreling down the street. "Take me to her. Help me save her."

"If you got to her, he would kill her." Cold, hard eyes held his—no, that's what she wanted him to believe. Something in her expression betrayed her and filtered into her words. "Run, Nikol. Keep her alive until you can die trying to be heroic."

"I'm not running anymore."

"Sometimes. . .running does not have to be bad." A strange smile played over her lips. "Do svidaniya, Nikol." She aimed a gun at him.

Cardinal backpedaled. Saw the car screaming to a stop. "Please, Kalyna!"

She fired.

★ ★   Forty-Three   ★ ★

Y ou're sure?" Lance stepped from the van and glanced at the old church. It sure fit Cardinal's MO, but the place sat eerily quiet. It'd been entirely too many hours in the plane. "Watters, Hastings, Hogan, VanAllen—check inside. Scrip, Smith, Rocket—check the cemetery. Courtland, you're with me."

"You mean, you don't trust me."

"There is that."

"I'm not your enemy here."

"Perhaps, but you're also not my ally. You broke protocol because you felt something was important enough to do that. Your sister is involved, and I'd wager my career you'd sacrifice every one of us if you thought it'd save her."

"So wouldn't you want that type of determination behind this hunt? It is my sister's life. And the man she loves." Austin pounded the back of the front seat. "This is stupid! Let me help!"

"Calm down. You're not winning points with that behavior. Decision's been made." Lance squinted toward the cathedral. "What's taking them so long?"

"It's a cathedral." Austin raised his eyebrows. "It's big."

This mission was so insane. So hopeless. If they couldn't find them in time. . . Being here, in Cardinal's homeland, his territory, added a level of uncertainty Lance had never experienced before. There was a reason he'd taken the DIA job—and staying put in Virginia was one of them. He was out of practice with field work. Like pitting an admin against an athlete. And with the lives of an innocent woman and a spy—a man he'd admired and respected since their first meeting. Right here.

"Mother of God. . ." Why hadn't he recognized it before?

"Yeah, pretty sure you'd find *her* in there." Austin smirked then stopped. Frowned as he leaned out of the van.

"Keep your jokes to yourself, Courtland."

Austin stepped from the van.

"What are you doing? Don't go any farther."

Courtland held out a hand. "Shh." He scanned the trees that hemmed the perimeter of the churchyard. He stilled, cocked his head. "You hear that?"

"Your mouth running is all I hear."

"Shh!" He tilted his head the other way. "Listen!" He pivoted. "Talon!" Cupping his hands around his mouth, he shouted the name once more.

Lance's pulse sped. Was the dog really here?

A commotion near the doors caught his attention. Watters emerged, holding the door as laughter filtered out with Candyman. . .who carried Hogan on his back. Hastings rolled her eyes. "Nothing," she called.

Austin bolted toward the trees.

"Stop him!"

He knew that bark! Austin sprinted, knowing he had seconds at best to find Talon before the others pummeled him into oblivion. Even now he heard them closing in from behind.

"Courtland!" one shouted.

He plunged into the trees. "Talon!" He skidded to a stop so he could hear. Breathing hard and his heart hammering, he couldn't hear. "Talon!"

Leaves crunched. Shouts.

He dove to the right and kept moving. "Talon, heel!"

"Courtland, don't make me shoot you."

"He's here," Austin shouted back. "Talon's here. I heard him."

"Check it out." Watters. Had to be Watters. He was the only one the others yielded to. "Five minutes, Courtland, and then your number's up."

Jogging in a wide circle, he slowly narrowed the field. Iron fences, stone crypts—man, this place was creepy to the nth degree. "Talon, where are you boy?"

Barking to the left.

Austin plunged through the forest, around shrubs. Over headstones. Around a mausoleum.

Snarling and snapping lunged at him. Talon strained against a lead.

Austin scrabbled backward. "Good boy. Good Talon." He held his hands out.

Hackles raised, Talon growled and snapped again.

"Easy, boy. What's wrong?" The lead wrapped around a headstone. Austin reached for it then saw the hand. His lunch climbed up his throat. The fingers moved. "Out," came a raspy voice.

Talon whimpered as he slumped back on his haunches.

Austin shifted to the right three paces.

Propped against a crumbling marker, Cardinal looked up at him, his face beaded with sweat and blood. He held his side.

"You look good," Austin said as he knelt.

A crooked smile. "It's the fresh air." He pushed to his feet, grimacing as he did.

"Markoski!" Hastings rushed toward them, the others converging on their location.

Austin shifted his attention to Talon. "Good boy, Talon." He offered a treat. Talon wolfed it down as Austin freed the lead.

Candyman helped Cardinal to his feet as Austin straightened.

"Here." Cardinal tugged something from his pocket. A bloody rag.

"Thanks, but—"

"Scent." He waved it. "He's a tracking dog, right?"

"Why didn't you go after her if you had Talon and that?"

"After they shot me, I scrambled back here to get Talon. That's when I heard your shouts. Thought they'd come back." Cardinal knelt beside Talon. "I thought they'd come back to finish me off."

"Let's see if this works."

"Oh, it works." Austin joined Cardinal next to Talon. "The bigger question is—will Talon?"

★ ★ Forty-Four ★ ★

An hour. Talon had been sniffing and tracking for an hour. Cardinal kept him hydrated, and Austin proved a great help as the team trailed in the van. Talon hopped up on sidewalks but mostly trotted down the road. Cars honked and drivers shared one-finger salutes, but Cardinal didn't care as he jogged beside Talon. Fresh spurts of warmth slid down his hip and side. He still couldn't believe Kalyna clipped him. It wasn't a full wound. A graze, but a deep one.

Was she just a bad shot? She didn't have the training he did. The colonel had drilled into him how to fire, how to nail a target from a football-field length.

She'd tipped her hand. Maybe intentionally. He wasn't sure he'd ever know. But Kalyna could've killed him. Should've. But she'd run him off. Told him to save Aspen. Running wasn't always a bad thing. Because running away then meant he could find Aspen and save her.

If he walked into the trap with Kalyna, the colonel would implant a bullet or two in Aspen's head. The man showed no qualms throwing his mom from a five-story building, so he'd show none when it came to killing a woman he'd never met.

The woman his son loved. Was that what this was about?

"Want me to take over?" Austin asked from the van.

Cardinal saved his breath for running and continued on.

Talon trotted up onto a sidewalk. Sniffed then paused. Snout in the air, Talon puffed his cheeks with his mouth closed. Processing the scent, no doubt.

"Think he lost it?"

"No way. His snout isn't broken."

"No, but his heart is," Timbrel countered.

"Quiet," Cardinal said as he gave the Lab room to search for his girl. "Give me the water bowl."

Austin produced the collapsible bowl and dumped a bottle of water in it.

Cardinal set the bowl in front of the dog. "Good boy."

"Cardinal, switch with Austin," Burnett said from the front passenger seat.

"No."

"It's not a question."

"I don't care what it is."

"You two can take turns. You're gushing blood all over St. Petersburg. Rest. Let him track him for a couple of miles."

Lapping the water, Talon seemed to inhale the cool liquid then jerked his head up. Cheeks puffed, black nose bouncing. He moved to the curb. Sniffed again.

It made sense. It was right. But yielding, knowing Aspen was out there with his psycho father, and with Kalyna. . .whichever side she was on. . .he just—

With a loud bark, Talon tore off around the corner.

"Got it!" Austin exploded from the van and beat a path after Talon.

Cardinal gulped failure.

Hands grabbed him. "Get in, idiot!"

He fell back against the van. They hauled him up onto the bench seat as Watters floored it. Pain sluiced through his side and back as the van careened around other vehicles, even using the northbound lane for fifty yards.

"Watch it, watch it!" Burnett shouted.

"I'm good. I'm good," Watterboy responded as he navigated the tangled streets with the skill of a Russian familiar with the area.

But the only thing Cardinal cared about was Talon. He was the key. *Hang on, Aspen. I'm coming.* He would not—would *not*!—let the madman win this one. He wouldn't stand still while the colonel shoved the only person he loved into the afterlife.

The distance between the van and the dog-handler team lengthened.

"You're losing them," Cardinal said.

"No I'm not."

As they rounded a corner, Cardinal's pulse slowed to a painfully cruel rate. *Nevsky Prospekt*. No. He wouldn't have brought her here. There were too many people. Too many witnesses. His gaze locked on to the fifth-floor windows. The flat.

"Cardinal?"

That window. . .what had it looked like from the outside? Her falling. . .

The distance shortened. Slower at first then faster, until they caught up with them. The golden dog paced back and forth, sniffing. He leapt up the steps to the door. Then sat.

"I think he's got it."

Cardinal stepped out. Strode up the walk. Up to the door. Kicked it in.

Light reached across the floor. Its fingers traced the first step to the second level. Kalyna stretched over several steps at an odd angle.

"No!" Austin shouted as he darted toward the stairs. "Lina!"

Standing there, staring at his sister laid out, blood covering her chest and shirt, Cardinal realized he'd failed. One more time. The colonel *had* won.

"Lina, please talk to me." Austin lowered her to the floor, where her blood had puddled.

Cardinal drew in a short breath, blinked out of the dimension that had gouged out his thinking and ability to function. A dimension of the past.

"Make a hole." Scrip hurried to her side with a pack.

Candyman and Watters hurried up the steps, clearing as they went. Cardinal trailed them but climbed to the fifth floor. He kicked in the door.

A woman screamed.

Vision tunneled, hearing hollowed, he moved through the kitchen. The living room. Past the colonel's room.

"Nikol!"

"Mama, you are here?"

"Yes. It's a good surprise, yes?"

He wrapped his arms around her, savoring her touch.

Cardinal jerked to the hall. Strode down it. To the bedroom. *His bedroom.* He stood in front of the window. Lacy curtains draped the view. Lace? The colonel would've hated that.

But that. . .that is where it happened. Where his father threw his mother to her death. He backed up a step then glanced at the window. No, another foot or two. Yes. This was better. He stood here. Where he'd done nothing as his mother was murdered. Right before his eyes.

If Kalyna was here, killed, then that meant the colonel knew. Knew Kalyna had warned him, tried to help him. That meant Aspen's time was short, if not already gone.

Cardinal threw a punch into the wall. Roared against the failures. The defeat. He dropped against the wall. Gripped his knees. *She's dead.* Aspen was as good as dead. There was no way she could still be alive. How would they find her now? She wasn't there. Talon didn't have a scent. In a smog-infected city. . .there was no hope.

He banged his head against the wall. Squeezed his eyes against the pain. Ran his hands over his head and gripped the nape of his neck. "Augh!" Rammed his elbows into the wall.

Tears warming his cheeks, he stared at the window. "I'm sorry," he muttered, something he'd never allowed himself to say before. "I am so sorry I didn't stop him."

He cried.

God, I did nothing to save my mother. Help me—help me!—not make the same mistake now. Please, You sent me here. Now—show me!

Something wet nudged his hand.

He glanced down and found Talon at his side. "Good boy."

Talon had found Kalyna and maybe saved her life. He'd done exactly what Cardinal had asked him to do—to find the owner of the rag. That was Kalyna. But he'd expected Kalyna to be with Aspen. She probably would've been if she hadn't gone up against one of the most ruthless, cruelest men in Russia.

"Hey, man. You okay?"

Cardinal shot a sidelong look to the man hovering in the doorway. "He will kill her if he hasn't already. Just to teach me a lesson."

"So, what? You're giving up?"

"Don't you get it?"

"Don't you?" Candyman snapped. "You're wasting breath. We could be searching!"

"How? How are we supposed to find her?"

"The girl." Candyman hooked a thumb over his shoulder. "She told us where Aspen is."

Cardinal came off the wall. "Kalyna? She's still alive?"

"So far."

Sirens wailed through the afternoon.

"We need to bug out."

"We have to take her. They'll kill her if she's found."

"Already loaded up. Let's move!"

Downstairs, Cardinal stepped out into the afternoon. Candyman climbed in the van.

Talon turned a few circles. Sniffed a tree.

"Talon, heel."

Instead, Talon tore off.

In the split second it took for Talon's movement to register, Cardinal *knew* the dog had hit on Aspen's scent.

Yes! Cardinal sprinted after him, ignoring the fire in his side. The renewed pain in his neck from the injury in Djibouti. Down the street. Straight toward Ligovksy Prospekt. The roundabout. Beneath trolley lines. He pushed himself.

Talon vanished when he banked left. What street was that? He knew this city. Walked it. Worked it. Prospekt Bakunina?

He careened onto the street. With one last push, Cardinal shoved himself onward. Wove around cars caught in traffic. His mind warred, knowing the others were most likely stranded in traffic, too. Which meant. . .

I'm alone.

Forty-Five

Y ou promised me!"

"You are lucky to be alive, General Payne."

Despite the crippling pain from her broken leg, Aspen focused on the two men arguing within earshot. Kept still so the chains anchoring her to the table didn't rattle as she tried to do a little recon on her surroundings and captors.

There was no chance to escape with the chain and broken leg, but she wouldn't have a prayer anyway with the horde of men working in the warehouse.

The men thought she was unconscious, and that served her well. The man she'd seen with the cruel soldier was American—clear English gave him away. They'd worked diligently for the last two hours, barely a word spoken as trucks were loaded with crates marked in the same fashion as the ones on the boat in Djibouti.

As more trucks left and the emptiness reigned in the dingy warehouse, the voices rose again. This time, angrier.

"I've sacrificed everything. Done everything you've asked, Tselekova. I gave him to you."

"Yes, and now our business is at an end, General." Tselekova flicked a wrist toward a man in uniform.

He aimed at the American.

Aspen clenched her eyes. But closing her eyes could not prevent her from hearing the primal scream and the gunfire that silenced it.

As her hearing and thundering heart cleared, Aspen heard the boots.

Right next to her.

"Get up," he said in a thickly accented voice.

Aspen stared up at him as she slowly rose to a sitting position, chains clanking.

Snarling and snapping echoed through the warehouse. *Talon?* She looked to the side, and her stomach heaved. Three Dobermans strained against chain leads. Eyes trained on her as they vied for permission to devour her.

Lord. . .

"You are dog handler, yes?" Tselekova stuffed a key into the lock and twisted it. The chains dropped to the floor, tugging the rest off her like a slithering snake till they piled in a mound at her feet.

The question all but forced her to look at the dogs again. The handler's bulging muscles and face warned he had little control left. The Dobermans jerked him forward. His feet slipped and slid over the cement.

Swallowing, Aspen skated a sidelong glance to Tselekova. Gave a slow nod.

He hooked a hand beneath her arm. Hauled her up off the crate that had been her prison for the last. . .well, she had no idea how long she'd been out. When she woke after they broke her leg, the pain had punched her back into oblivion.

He yanked her to the front.

Her weight fell on her right leg. She cried out.

"Your foolishness," he said, his breath salty and warm against her cheek, "in trying to escape, to thwart my plans, will now serve to bring about your end. . .quicker."

Was that a threat?

He smiled as the handler shouted, now straining with both hands to hold back the dogs.

Aspen swallowed.

"You love my Nikol."

Nikol. Was that Dane's real name? There was no use denying it. Another sidelong glance churned her stomach. How could the man look like an older version of Dane yet look nothing like him? "Yes."

"As I thought." The man's gaze fixed on something. "And it seems he loves you, too."

A truck lumbered out of the warehouse. Sunlight bled across the cement and delivered into the chaos Dane.

Aspen sucked in a breath. Relief flooded her.

Rabid snapping and barking.

He leveled a gun at Tselekova as he closed the gap. "Let her go."

"Where are your friends?" Tselekova's grip on her arm tightened. "And your sister, Nikol?"

"You already took care of her, *Father*." Dane stopped. "Or am I still not allowed to call you that?"

"You never earned the right."

Dane smiled in disdain. "A son should not have to earn that right."

"I see you are already poisoned by this woman. You are weaker than you were before you left."

"No, Colonel, I am stronger than ever before." He nodded to Aspen. "Release her."

"If I release her, Anton will release them."

Both hands held the gun steady and sure. Aspen saw the pure determination in Dane's stance, his body language. The fear she'd seen before when he talked about the past, about the reasons he couldn't love her, were gone.

Dane held Tselekova's gaze. "I'm ready when you are."

Forty-Six

Calculated risks were always *risky*.

But the surreal confidence, peace, and laser-like focus on freeing Aspen from the colonel's clutches simmered in his gut. He spotted Aspen's nervous response.

"Do you know why I killed your sister?"

"I really don't care." Cardinal kept his breathing steady, his focus pure. Because he had the upper hand. Kalyna wasn't dead—she might die before the team got her some help. But for now, she was alive. The colonel didn't know that. But he did know that Cardinal *never* missed a shot. Because it was the colonel who taught him to shoot. Taught him to never miss lest he wanted raw, bloodied hands.

"You killed the one person who was on your side. Kalyna merely wanted your approval. Just like I did." Cardinal thrust his chin toward Aspen. "Release her. Without the dogs, and you walk out of here alive and intact."

"I believe you miscounted, Nikol."

"Dane!"

The sound of the shot hit him at the same time the bullet did. Winged him. He stumbled.

A flurry of insanity erupted. The colonel shoved Aspen forward. She screamed and dropped, holding her leg.

The colonel signaled the handler.

Free, the dogs vaulted.

On a knee, Cardinal took aim at the lead dog. The one headed straight for Aspen. Ignored the one that sailed over the air and cement toward him. He aimed a few seconds ahead. Fired. Let the dog catch up with the bullet.

He swung around. Saw the meaty jowls widen as the dog pawed air. Cardinal fired.

Searing pain chomped into his hand at the same time a yelp erupted. The weight of the dog barreled into him and knocked him backward. The teeth came loose. The dog yelped again as he flipped onto all fours. He walked a wide circle around, away from Dane before collapsing on the ground, panting hard. Wounded.

Cardinal rolled, holding his bitten hand close. Two men sprinted after another—the colonel. Candyman threw himself into the back of the colonel. The two went sprawling over the cement.

A primal scream seared Cardinal's mind. The third dog! Aspen!

Forty-Seven

The first dog slid to his death at her knees. Aspen fought the tears, watching as Dane went down beneath the second dog. It'd all happened in seconds.

But her focus was on the third. Horror gripped her as the beast tore up ground toward her. No way Dane could recover in time. No way he could save her. Not this time.

The Doberman sprinted. Front paws nailed the ground simultaneously with back paws, launching it forward. One bound. Muscles rippling. Eyes locked. Canines exposed. A second bound. A third. He went airborne.

Aspen curled in, as she'd been taught to protect her vital organs and leave the meatier—ugh!—parts of her arms to fend off the attack. No doubt this dog wanted all the meat he could get. She loved dogs, but stopping these killers pulled the plug on her nice tactics.

Weight rammed into her side. She braced. Pressure clamped onto her arm. Pain exploded. She cried out. Fought. Kicked the dog. Punched with her other hand. The dog snarled and caught Aspen's shoulder. She screamed. Punched him.

"Aspen!" Dane's shout was loud but not close.

A blur flashed in front of her.

Thud!

A yelp clapped through the air. Turned to snapping and snarling. Barking.

Aspen looked over her bloodied shoulder. Heart in her throat, she watched. "Talon!"

He tackled the Doberman. They rolled and flipped. Snapping. Biting. Barking. Vicious and primal. Terrifying. Aspen scooted back against the corner of the crate, keeping her right arm close to avoid jarring the bites in her forearm and shoulder.

On its feet, the Doberman paced. Snapped.

Talon unleashed one of the mightiest barks she'd ever heard from him. Then another. Front paws spread, head lowered, hind quarters up, he took an attack position. Another demonesque bark. The Doberman paced, trying to come around and flank Talon, but her guy matched him, step for step. Only then did she see the blood around his neck.

Tears sprung to her eyes. He saved her! All those months training, working with him. She wasn't sure he had it in him anymore. But there he stood. Facing off.

The dog turned and trotted to its wounded compatriot and slumped down.

Talon growled one last warning to the two dog-thugs then turned to Aspen.

Wrapping her arms around him, she buried her face in his fur. Cried. Sobbed. "Good boy," she said, over and over. "Good boy."

Dane slid to his knees beside them. "Aspen! You okay?"

With a laugh-cry, she nodded. "Yeah. He saved me!" She assessed his injuries and knew they were not terrible. A few bites, but they weren't bleeding much. "I'm so proud of him."

Talon swiped his tongue along her cheek then plopped over her legs, as if to say, "All in a hard day's work."

Epilogue

A Breed Apart Ranch, Texas Hill Country
Four Months Later

How long will it take, Aspen?"

Pulling her gaze from where Talon bounded after the ball, Aspen peeked around one of her curls at her brother. "I don't know, Austin. I'm trying."

He looked down and gave a nod. But thick frustration betrayed him. "I'm sorry."

"You've said that about a thousand times." She rubbed her shoulder, the visible injuries gone but the invisible ones, the aches in her bone and mended muscles, still hurting. "Finding you has helped Talon heal."

She smiled as Talon trotted to the water trough, dropped his ball on the ground, then lapped some water. With winter approaching, he wasn't worn out by heat. And the PTSD symptoms were diminishing.

"I think fighting for you is why he healed." Austin stuffed his hands in his pockets.

She eyed him. Quite a concession.

Leaves crunched and rocks popped in the drive, luring Aspen's gaze to the car sliding into view. Her heart tripped. Dane! The sun glinted off the windshield, stopping her from seeing him, but she waved all the same as she started that way. "Come on. He's finally here."

Talon trotted to her side and followed her out of the training yard.

Timbrel stepped out onto the porch. " 'Bout time you decided to show up," she shouted as soon as the car door opened. "Food's cold."

Dane glanced up at the house but said nothing. In fact, he looked. . . not pleased.

"Hey you," Aspen said, her breathing a little heavy as she hoofed it up the slight hill to his sedan. "You okay?"

A smile tugged at one side of his mouth. "Yeah." He stepped around the door and reached for her hand, drawing her closer. He kissed her. Swept a thumb along her cheek.

"That's definitely the type of greeting a girl could get used to."

"Can we talk?" His gaze bounced to Timbrel then back.

"Sure." Aspen motioned beyond the house. "What's wrong?"

"Hey, Cardinal."

Dane's jaw muscle popped as his eyes went to Austin, who made his way up the hill to the house. He gave a curt nod.

Aspen touched his face. "Hey, what's eating you?"

"He's dead."

She blinked. Her mind hopscotching over those two words. "Who?"

"The colonel."

She widened her gaze and drew back. "I thought he was in prison, in the pink of health."

"He apparently had a sudden decline." His lips flattened. *Livid* was the word that came to mind.

"Dane, what are you saying?"

"Everything that I'm *not* saying." He leaned back against the car.

"You think someone killed him."

"I *know* someone killed him. I just don't know who or why." He scratched the stubble along his jaw. "A man like the colonel. . .people wanted him dead."

"I mean no disrespect, but in the months since St. Petersburg, you've told me many times you were afraid he'd get free."

"But now. . .now I get no resolution."

Aspen tilted her head. "What kind of resolution?"

He frowned. "What does that mean?"

"Nothing. Just that. . ." She touched his folded arms. "Dane, his power over you is gone. He's gone."

"No, Aspen. He's right here." He tapped his temple. "I hear his words constantly."

She smiled at him. Tiptoed up and kissed the spot he'd just touched.

" 'Therefore, if anyone is in Christ, the new creation has come: the old has gone, the new is here!'" She wrapped her arm around his neck and grinned as his arms snaked around her waist. "I really like the new."

"Do me a favor?"

Aspen craned her neck back a bit to look at him without her eyes crossing. "What's that?"

"Call me Nikol."

He'd insisted in the last few months that she *not* call him that. "That's one giant leap for Danekind."

"Nikol is the name my mother gave me. It was her father's name. I'd forgotten that, shut out the good parts with the bad. I don't want to forget her."

"She sounds like she was an amazing woman."

His steely eyes traced her face. Gauging. Watching. Searching. . .

"What?" she asked with a nervous laugh.

"One more favor."

"Too many and you're going to need to start a tab."

He kissed her. Aspen melted into his arms. Talon barked. Aspen giggled in the middle of the kiss. "He's jealous."

"So am I." Dane—Nikol looked at her.

"So, what's the last favor?"

He tugged something from his pocket. Handed it to her.

Aspen eased out of his arms and unfolded the paper. Right above *Nikol Tselekova* and the name *Aspen Elizabeth Courtland* were the words *Certificate of Marriage.*

Her heart beat in tune to a new, partially erratic rhythm. "I. . .I thought General Burnett annulled it." She eased back, staring at the paper in confusion. "Wiped the slate clean. And. . .your name. That's not the name you used in Djibouti."

"I asked him not to annul but merely to amend the document."

Rapid-fire drumming of her heart pulsed against her lungs. She raised her eyebrows. Though she knew what meaning *she* would attach to that statement, she wanted to know his. "Why?"

"Because I want you to marry me." He touched her lips with a finger as she started to respond. "If it takes two more years to convince you that I'm the man for you, then I have nothing better to do."

"You know, you're pretty thickheaded."

His face fell. "Is that a no?"

"That's an 'I told you six months ago I loved you.' Just one problem."

"Yeah?"

"I can't pronounce your last name."

He grinned. And she loved the way it pinched his eyes with joy. "Better start practicing." Nikol leaned in for another kiss.

"Aspen!"

She growled as she rolled her shoulder to look up at the house. "What?"

"They're waiting on you." Austin looked at a watch he wasn't wearing. "And. . .might want to come talk to Timbrel."

"Why?"

Austin shrugged. "She just seems edgy to me."

"She's always edgy. All right," Aspen said as she turned. She called Talon then joined hands with Nikol as they made their way up onto the wraparound porch. She reached for the door just as it flew open.

Timbrel stormed out. Brow knitted and lips pinched tight, she swung around. Her face blanched. "Oh."

"Timbrel," a voice called from inside as the sound of feet drew close. "Hold up."

"I gotta go." Timbrel hustled down the steps.

Aspen watched, concerned.

Candyman burst out. Dressed in jeans and a T-shirt, the guy seemed to have as much bulk as when he had his tac vest and gear on. "Where—?" He spotted her and hurried after Timbrel. "Wait."

In her brown Jeep, Timbrel backed out, tires spitting rocks at Candyman. As she rammed it into DRIVE, she glared over the half door at him. "I don't kiss beards. Period!"

"I—"

Scrambling tires muffled his response.

Candyman swung around and pounded a fist into the side of a blue truck and let out a growl that rivaled Talon's when he'd defeated the demon dogs.

"I don't know what he sees in her," Nikol said.

"Most men don't." Aspen eyed him then shrugged. "Don't take it personally. I already told him he's got his work cut out for him."

"I think he should quit while he's ahead."

"If he's got it that bad for her, I think he should fight for her with his dying breath." She nodded to the driveway where Candyman had climbed into his truck and tore down the drive after Timbrel. Yeah. . . this was going to be interesting.

SGT Kowtko & MWD Igor M064

My name is Sgt Andrew Kowtko. I am currently the Military Working Dog Trainer aboard MCAS Yuma, Arizona. I moved from MCB Camp LeJeune, II MEF, II MHG, 2d Law Enforcement Battalion where I served as a Military Working Dog Handler for four years. I have two combat deployments with II MEF—one to Operation Iraqi Freedom and one to Operation Enduring Freedom. I deployed as a Patrol Explosive Detector Dog Handler to both Operations.

Out of several bedtime stories, this one in particular comes to mind. We were deployed in support of (ISO) Operation Enduring Freedom (OEF); Military Working Dog (MWD) Igor M064—a Patrol Explosive Detector Dog (P/EDD)—and myself were supporting 3rd Battalion, 8th Marines, Kilo Company. We dug into an area untouched by Coalition troops since the beginning of the war. After setting up our Combat Outpost, we constantly patrolled the "Green Zone" for Taliban fighters fleeing the heavy fighting to our north in Sangin. We were located on the west side of the Helmand River adjacent to Forward Outpost Robinson. On a routine patrol, we were pushing into the city of Qaleh Ye Gaz looking for Taliban activity and to impede the enemy's free movement. While we were pushing around a compound, MWD

Blade L612, along with handler Cpl Cory Bracy, showed a slight change of behavior on a possible improvised explosive device (IED). Upon our spotting the IED, a Taliban fighter detonated it by means of a command pull wire.

The blast threw me and the other handler back approximately 5 feet. Once we regained our senses, looking ourselves over making sure we had all limbs we walked in with, we immediately took contact from enemy fighters dug into compounds surrounding the IED. The small arms fire was extremely accurate with rounds impacting 1–2 feet around friendly positions. After about ten minutes, enemy guns were quickly silenced by our superior firepower. We utilized all means of firepower including tanks, mortars, and crew served weapons. We broke contact by pushing south. While crossing an open field, MWD Blade threw another change of behavior on an Afghan-built foot bridge; now, see, these can be extremely dangerous choke points to any patrol moving without the aid of a good dog team. Noticing wires protruding from the dirt, we quickly marked the location to push around. Within 30 feet, MWD Blade was sent to search a crossing into another field. MWD Blade showed a third change of behavior on a raised piece of dirt covered by poppy plants. Once again, we quickly marked the grid coordinates and kept pushing. We finished the patrol and returned to the COP.

If there had not been a Military Working Dog present on the patrol, multiple lives would have been lost. We train on a daily basis for the moment when we can save ourselves, other service members, and innocent civilians. Being an MWD handler, I have always sworn by utilizing MWDs on patrols in the relentless world of war. On that day, in the moments that we need MWDs the most, we proved ourselves to be true life-savers.

Sgt Andrew Kowtko enlisted in the Marine Corps in August 2007 and is currently stationed in Yuma, Arizona. He works as a Military Policeman, Patrol/Narcotics Detector Dog Handler. Sgt Kowtko has been awarded numerous decorations, including the Purple Heart.

Retired Military Working Dog Assistance Organization's goal is "To act and operate as a public benefit, educational, and charitable organization in (i) educating the public about the benefits to our Armed Forces of military working dogs, contractor working dogs and specialized search dogs; (ii) financially supporting active duty and retired military working dogs, contractor working dogs and specialized search dogs; (iii) preventing cruelty to retired military working dogs, contractor working dogs and specialized search dogs by helping financially with medical bills, transportation and any other necessary requirements for their health and well being; and (iv) facilitate the adoption of retired military, contractor, and specialized search dogs."

The Retired Military Working Dog Assistance Organization (RMWDAO) was founded in October of 2011 in Universal City, Texas. RMWDAO was formed after a push to get the military to reclassify Military Working Dogs from "excess equipment" to "canine service members" and to help get Military Working Dogs medical benefits after retirement. RMWDAO is a nonprofit organization that takes donations to help cover those medical costs after a MWD retires, so that tax dollars aren't used. RMWDAO is currently pending 501(c)(3) tax exempt status with the IRS.

Visit them online: http://www.rmwdao.org, and on Facebook: http://www.facebook.com/RMWDAO

BEOWULF

EXPLOSIVES DETECTION DOG

DEDICATION

To the four-legged military heroes who serve on the battlefields of war and the battlefields of therapy, helping save the lives of our military heroes.

ACKNOWLEDGMENTS

Special thanks to Dr. Brian Reid for help with chemicals and explosions. But also thanks to the way you so diligently serve the community through co-op classes and making science fun!

Many thanks to Erynn Newman and Bethany Kaczmarek who read Beo and made sure this dog had the stuff it takes to lunge into the loving arms of readers.

To the many bloggers & reviewers out there who have championed my books, written stellar reviews, and encouraged me and so many other authors: Rel Mollet, Linda Attaway, Deb Ogle Haggerty, Renee Chaw, Lydia Mazzei, Casey Herringshaw, "Rissi," Michelle Sutton, Julie Johnson, Lori Twichell, Melissa Willis, and so many more.

Thanks to my agent, Steve Laube, who remains steadfast and constant in an ever-changing industry. Thanks, Agent-Man!

Rel Mollet—Where would I be without you, dearest? You keep me encouraged and laughing when, really, I just want to puddle up and cry. You're one of the truest and most genuine friends I've ever had!

Friends who keep me on "this" side of sanity (okay, yes—that's debatable, but go with me on this): Jim Rubart, Shannon McNear, Kellie Coates Gilbert, Dineen Miller, Robin Miller, Margie Vawter, Kim Woodhouse, and Ian Acheson.

Thanks to the Barbour Fiction & Sales teams, relentless in their efforts to make our books successful: Shalyn Sattler, Annie Tipton, Rebecca Germany, Mary Burns, Elizabeth Shrider, Laura Young, Kelsey McConaha, Linda Hang, and Ashley Schrock.

Glossary of Terms/Acronyms

AAR—After-Action Report

ACUs—Army Combat Uniforms

AHOD—All Hands On Deck

Colt M1911—Semiautomatic pistol

DIA—Defense Intelligence Agency

EDD—Explosives Detection Dog

EOD—Explosive Ordnance Disposal

Glock—A semiautomatic handgun

HUMINT—Human Intelligence

IED—Improvised Explosive Device

ISAF—International Security Assistance Force

M4, M4A1, M16—Military assault rifles

MP—Military Police

MRAP—Mine-Resistant Ambush-Protected vehicle

MWD—Military War Dog

ODA452—Operational Detachment A (Special Forces A-Team)

RPG—Rocket-Propelled Grenade

SAS—Special Air Service (Foreign Special Operations Team)

SATINT—Satellite Intelligence

Sitrep—Situation report

SOCOM—Special Operations Command

STK—Shoot To Kill

SureFire—A tactical flashlight

TBI—Traumatic Brain Injury

UAV—Unmanned Aerial Vehicle

Prologue

April 9, 2003
Baghdad, Iraq

The ground rattled. Dust plumed and pushed aside the curtain, unveiling the specter of war that raged beyond. The bridge... The American Marines had already taken the bridge. The airport.

Boom! The concussion vibrated through the air and thumped against his chest. Wind gusted back the curtain again. He traced the curtain. She had been so proud of that find in the market. White and filled with tiny holes. He teased her that she could purchase any old cloth and in a few years it would have its own holes. She swatted his shoulder with a playful smile.

A guttural scream choked the air. Pulled him around.

He stared at the striped curtain that hung, separating him from his mother who helped his wife, struggling to usher their firstborn into the world.

Another shriek spun him back to the door. To the east, to Mecca. *Please, Allah...protect her. I will live in peace. Always. Just...*

The familiar *tat-tat-tat* of automatic weapons sounded close. AK-47s. His heart ka-thumped. They were closing in. *Please, Allah!*

Pebbles thunked against the ledge, dribbled onto the floor.

Steady and tickling, a vibration wormed through the house. Like some evil dance to an unheard song, the walls jounced rapidly. The bowl of olives and dates rattled across the wood table. He saved them and set them back. She had loved those olives. Her favorite. He brought them home for her last night. Anything to let her know how special she was.

His gaze traced the simple dwelling. He had not done so well in providing for her. But someday. . .someday he would. If only—

Something flickered. Through the window, he saw something. . . What? What was it?

Frowning, Ahmad moved to the window. Nudged aside the curtain. He peered out at the massive hulk of steel lumbering through the narrow streets. Cars and wagons beat into submission beneath its mammoth tracks. The M1A1 Abrams tank—a colossal giant of steel and destruction. Beyond it, in stark contrast to the dirty hull, the opulence and splendor of a dictator who had crushed his people, gassed thousands, and brutally beat others to death, mentally if not physically, towered over the city in defiance.

And here. . .here Ahmad sat with his wife and unborn child fighting to live, in squalor.

At least the Americans would stop Saddam. *Madman!*

A loud, lusty cry streaked through the day.

Ahmad jerked to the back of the home.

The cry strengthened.

He scurried three steps forward, his nose almost against the rough wool material. "What is it? What's happening? Can I see the babe? Freshta, are you well?"

The curtain swung aside. His mother stood before him, a babe wrapped in a blanket. "Your son!"

Awe spread through him. Spilled through his brain, stifling a response. Down through his chest until he felt as if the sun itself existed within him. *My son!* He reached for his son. "Siddiq. . . his name is—"

Boom! Boom!

BooooOOOOOOooooom!

Thrown upward. Then thrust aside by the maniacal claws of gravity, Ahmad screamed as his body slammed into a wall. Cement exploded. Collapsed on top of him. His hearing faded. His breathing shallowed. *My son! Where is my son!*

Darkness snuffed out his breath.

Six Months Ago
A Breed Apart Ranch, Outside Austin, Texas

"Go out with me."

"No."

"Why?" From behind, his hands came around her waist. He rested his chin on her shoulder, his beard tickling her chin and neck. He tugged her closer. "C'mon. I know you like me. And you know it."

Warmth and pleasure spun a heady cocktail numbing Timbrel Hogan, slowing her automatic responses, her sensibility. It felt good, so very good to be in his arms. To be held. To hear his voice, the teasing huskiness in her ear. The zinging and zipping through her arms and belly at his touch. She saw herself kissing him. Saw herself enjoying it.

Too much like Mom.

"You can't even give me a good reason."

She rolled out of his reach, stretching her neck to shake the lingering effects of *his* effect.

"Because I don't want to." Timbrel focused on setting out the trays of food Khaterah had provided.

Candyman palmed the counter, hung his head, then peered up through a knotted brow. "That's a lie."

With a mean sidelong glare, she gritted her teeth.

"I can see straight through you, Timbrel."

She snorted. He didn't even know her real name. "You don't know anything about me, so don't even pretend to. If there's something I can't stand, it's a liar."

"Then you must hate yourself a lot."

She snapped to him. Augh! Why had she left Beo in the yard? He'd so lunge at this arrogant jerk. The vault of anger thrust her past him.

"Timbrel, wait!"

Tears burned. She stuffed on sunglasses as she punched through the front door. Barreled around Aspen and Mr. SexyKillerBlueEyes, who stood frozen on the front porch. Ghost stood by the training yard.

"Beo, come!" Timbrel called, waving to Ghost and praying he didn't make her come over there to get her dog.

Thankfully, despite his frown, he released Beo, who bounded across the yard and leapt into the back of the Jeep. She climbed in, ignoring the blurring vision, cranked the engine, and ripped out of the yard.

"Timbrel!"

She wouldn't look in the rearview mirror. Wouldn't.

She checked.

Candyman stood, hands on his blue truck. Kicked the tires. Punched the side. Threw a fist in the air.

She swallowed. Good. He knew some of what she felt.

RONIE KENDIG

Her Jeep lumbered onto the paved road and leveled out at sixty. Dirt plumed behind, cocooning her. Protecting her—from trying to check to see if he followed. Of course he wouldn't. She'd ticked him off. It was her safety net. Making men angry so they'd go away. Safety and security in solitude.

Warm and wet, Beo's tongue swiped her cheek. She laughed and roughed his head, pressing her cheek against his skull as she angled onto the access road and aimed for the highway. Put as much distance between her and the ranch. Between her and James Anthony "Candyman" VanAllen.

She hit seventy mph and glanced in the mirror. A silver glint merging into traffic detonated the nervous jellies in her stomach.

"No," she breathed as she glanced over her shoulder.

Jerked back.

It was him!

He's chasing me.

But no. . .no, that wouldn't work. She couldn't go there. She couldn't become her mother. Wouldn't. Timbrel fished her cell phone from the console and pressed 911. He'd never forgive her for this, but it was the only way.

★ ★   One   ★ ★

Present Day
Bagram AFB, Afghanistan

Says here, bullmastiffs were originally bred in England. Supposed to be 40 percent bulldog, 60 percent English mastiff." Candyman stroked his beard as he stared at the monitor in the communications tent.

Team commander Captain Dean "Watterboy" Watters shrugged. "Yeah, but the handler is 80 percent bulldog."

"Hey."

"C'mon, Tony," Dean said. "Even you have to admit that—she called the cops on you, man. Or did you forget?"

Tony. The name that reminded him of who he was, who he wasn't. Only Dean had permission to use his middle name instead of his call sign or first name. They'd worked the last seven years together, affording them a larger berth than he gave to the rest of the ODA452 team.

"Didn't forget. I understood it." Which was why Tony should back down now. But why did it pour acid through his gut when Dean said that about Timbrel?

"Then I don't know if it makes you as crazy as her or worse. Right, Rocket?" Dean shot a grin to the sergeant first class who'd entered the briefing room, a closing arc of morning sun sliding across the floor, bringing with it a gust of warmth. August rated "too hot" here.

"What's that?" Rocket's black hair was mussed and the bags under his eyes bespoke the exhaustion he must be feeling from the last patrol. He lumbered to the coffee bar, fisting a hand against a yawn.

"Hogan—"

"Who?" Rocket slurped the black tar.

"Hogan," Dean repeated. "The handler from A Breed Apart."

Rocket turned back to the bar and applied a lid to his hot brew. "That tough-as-nails witch?"

Tony punched to his feet, straddling the metal folding chair. Drew back his arms. "Hey." He wouldn't let anyone talk about Timbrel that way. Not if he had a say in it. And he did. With two fists if necessary.

"That's the one." Though Dean wasn't smiling, it could be heard in his words. "I mentioned to Tony she was part bulldog."

"Part?" Rocket angled back to the table, cup to his mouth. "That woman is pure bulldog and 100 percent rabid."

"Rocket." Stabbing a finger at the man, Tony glared. "You better get a lock on that mouth before I do it for you."

Rocket and Dean laughed long and hard.

You've been played. Tony dropped into the chair. Stared at the monitor, hand balled against his lips. He felt ready to blow. Weird. So not like him. But just like Dad.

He sat up straight, feeling nauseated. He powered down the computer and his anger. No way he was going there. No way he would become like—

"You're right." Tony propelled himself on the wheeled chair to the briefing table, then scooted back and snatched the bag of candy his mom had sent. These sweet treats had gotten him branded with the call sign Candyman because he used them on patrol to ingratiate the team with the locals. "She's got attitude. It's what I like."

"Attitude? That's a nice word for it." Thumbing the side of his eye, Dean shook his head. "I've never seen you get so worked up."

"You and me both," Rocket said as he dug in the bag and withdrew a mini Butterfinger. "Why are we talking about her anyway?"

Tony popped Rocket's hand. "Stay out of my stash."

"Burnett tapped her for this mission."

"The good general taps a lot of people." Rocket then added, "And teams."

"His stars give him the right." Dean lifted a pack and set it on the chair. "Regardless, she's coming with her dog—a bullmastiff. He's EDD."

Calmed, Tony nodded mentally to himself. Better. In control. Focused.

"We have a whole kennel of bomb and drug sniffers out there."

"Not like this one." Dean checked his watch, then glanced out the window into the main hall of the subbase command building. "He's specially trained for WMD chemicals."

"That's reassuring that I won't die in a fallout like Chernobyl, but I'm still not getting it."

"You will—during the brief when the team gets here."

"Roger," Rocket nodded, "but I want it on record that I object to her presence here." He avoided looking at Tony.

Tony grinned at the thought of those brown eyes and the strike-first attitude. "We don't have *her* though."

"Her? Seriously?" Rocket leaned forward, his eyebrows pushed into his scalp. "She's unpredictable and volatile. If she were still in regs, she'd get thrown out on a psych discharge."

"Afternoon, boys," came a taunting, sultry voice.

Tony turned. "Be still my beating heart." Oh man. She looked better than ever. Hair pulled back, black A Breed Apart T-shirt that hugged all the right curves, dark brown hiking boots, and a ball cap shielding her eyes—all screamed tough mama. And *hot* mama!

On his feet, he held out his arms. "Hey, beautiful!" He couldn't resist. Knew it riled her. But she could use a little color in those cheeks.

She hesitated—clearly remembering the last time they saw each other at the ranch. And that she'd called the cops on him. She almost seemed to wilt. But she finally groaned. "They haven't killed you yet?"

Tony slapped his chest. "Too valuable." He stepped closer and reached for her.

In the split second it took for his brain to transmit the warning signal, Tony knew it was too late. The indicators snapped through his brain. The ominous rumble—growling. The blur of black.

From the shadow erupted a beast of a dog. Jowls snapping. Canines groping for flesh.

My flesh!

Something hit his cheek, the snout just inches away. Snapping, and with it a ravenous bark. A bark that shoved Tony back over the table and tumbling onto the other side. He came up, drawing his weapon.

Lip curled, sharp white teeth exposed, broad chest lowered, the dog growled his challenge.

Then without warning, the dog straightened. Heeled. His large pink tongue slopped the drool from his massive mouth.

Silence devoured the room.

Heaving breaths squeezed oxygen as Tony slowly straightened. Slowly realized he was staring down his weapon.

Lips thinned, nostrils flared, Timbrel glowered. "Aim that at my boy again, and it'll be the last thing you do."

"Next time your dog tries to take a piece of me. . ."

Her hand went to the broad skull of the dog at her side. No, not just a dog. A beast. A mountainous monster of canine muscle. Broad skull, perpetual pout—and teeth. Holy merciful God, that thing had huge teeth! A black-and-tan mural of a coat cloaked that dog in evil.

Demon dog.

Beowulf.

Nerves buzzing, Tony ran a hand over his thick beard—and felt something thick and slimy. A look at his hand made him recoil. Slobber.

"Just so we're clear"—Watters rested fingers on the utility belt, a smile toying at his lips—"you *can* keep that dog under control, right?"

Timbrel eyed the captain with his sun-bronzed skin and dark hair. "Rugged" came to mind. He looked older than Candyman's twenty-sevenish years, but she wasn't sure since they both had beards shielding their appearances. But there was also a kindness in his eyes she'd noted even while working with him and the team in Djibouti.

"He didn't kill anyone, did he?" Timbrel wouldn't get riled. It wasn't meant as a slam. Captain Watters's concern was for his team. "Yes, Beowulf obeys my commands. Would you like a demonstration?"

"Not necessary," the captain said.

The side door swung open and in filed a half-dozen men. Timbrel kept her posture relaxed, knowing her boy fed off her body language.

"Cool," a guy with wiry light brown hair and personality grinned—she'd met him in Djibouti, right? What was his name. . .Java? "A working dog." He high-fived another member. "Guess we get to live today."

Timbrel smirked. Most troops wanted MWDs with them because the dog's training and presence increased the probability that threats would be detected before anyone lost limb or life.

"You guys just missed the excitement." The lanky guy they called Rocket chuckled.

"Yeah?"

"Hogan's dog about ate Candyman's lunch." Rocket seemed far too pleased.

"Seriously?" Awe brightened Java's eyes. He nodded to Timbrel. "Sweet. Whatever you need, you got it."

The others—the older member with reddish-blond hair everyone called Pops, and the soldier who seemed to be an old guy in a young man's body with so much going on in those eyes—she couldn't remember his name—joined the laughter.

"I didn't know Tony could move that fast." Captain Watters didn't hide his smile.

"Hey, I like to keep my parts intact," Candyman said, his face red against the tanned skin and bushy beard. But his eyes. . .his green eyes came to her.

And she remembered. Man, did she remember—the tickle of his beard against her jaw, his fiery touch, his breath. . .

"Yeah, but his heart is another thing," muttered someone. And she couldn't tell who'd spoken the words—everyone suddenly seemed gun-shy as an awkward silence settled them in the chairs around the table.

Timbrel flinched at the comment referencing her and relocated herself away from his gaze and proximity. She swallowed and moved to the side wall, slid down it, and sat, legs stretched out and ankles crossed. Beo reclined against her. Chin on her thigh, he let out a huff.

Smoothing his beautiful coat, Timbrel kept her gaze down. So that "something" she felt a minute ago after humiliating Candyman in front of his team—it was familiar. She'd felt it on I-35 the night she hung him out to dry.

Guilt.

Crazy. She hadn't done anything wrong. Sure, she'd let Beo challenge Candyman, but they needed to understand what Beo could do. The other men needed to trust her boy. Besides, maybe Candyman needed another reminder that there was only one guy for her—Beowulf.

"Right, boy?" Using both hands, she massaged Beo's head, then bent forward and kissed the top of his skull, right along the indention that traced between his eyes, straight to his keen sniffer.

Beowulf slumped back, his head against her chest, legs spread and belly exposed.

"Big baby." She smiled as she rubbed his stomach.

Stomping boots yanked Beowulf upright. Head swiveled toward the door.

Six one, graying, take-the-bull-by-the-horns General Lance Burnett removed his cap and slapped a file on the table. "Take a seat, gentlemen." His gaze skidded to Timbrel. "Miss Hogan."

"General."

He sighed as another soldier entered. Brie Hastings. Timbrel had liked the lieutenant even though Brie had shown an affinity for Aspen's Russian hunk, Dane. Brie worked her way around the room handing out file folders to the team, then one to Timbrel.

"Now, why didn't that dog attack Hastings?" Rocket asked. "I was so waiting—"

"You'll notice," Timbrel said, "the obvious one—she's a woman. And second, Brie kept her movements small and respected Beo's space. She didn't make a move toward me."

"Listen up," Burnett groused. "Those folders have reports that have come in over the last six to eight months. We're trailing something we can't finger."

"How so?" Captain Watters asked.

"There are hints, indicators of some big trouble coming, but we can't seem to pull the pieces together."

"So. . ." Watters looked around the room. "What are we doing today?"

"You're going out with Hogan and her dog. See if he gets any hits."

"WMDs?" Rocket jerked forward. "That's what we're looking for, right? You're not saying it, but the commander said her dog is EDD, specialized in chemical weapons. That's why you brought her and that dog, right?"

"Beowulf. His name is Beowulf." Timbrel stood and dusted off her backside. She swallowed the adrenaline spiraling through her system. "General, you never said anything about WMDs when you asked for Beo and me."

He didn't flinch. "Thought it'd be obvious, Hogan. Think I wanted you out here to put my men in a bad mood?"

She ignored the jibe. "Beo's also trained for drugs and bombs."

He waved at her. "We got those dogs by the dozen."

Stay calm, stay calm.

"Isn't this what you're trained for, Hogan?" Burnett growled. "Or do you two want to head home with your tail between your legs and forfeit your contract? And your in-theater authorization and certification?"

The threat lifted her chin. It'd taken Jibril Khouri too long to get them cleared. He'd have her head if she messed things up. He'd warned her to hold it together, to set aside her agitation if she expected any more gigs.

And she didn't want to leave. She thrived on the chaos of danger. But the thought of hunting down weapons of mass destruction. . .chemical bombs. . .

"Well?" Burnett demanded.

"We're good, sir."

"Good." He shifted his attention back to the men. "We've narrowed down a radius, but we're flying blind. This is a recon mission. Do not engage. Don't think I have to explain the delicate nature of this situation, especially as our forces move toward a more advise-and-guide role here." He gave a nod. "You'll head out first thing. Dismissed."

Anger churned through Timbrel. She waited as the others cleared out then moved to Burnett's side. "Sir, with all due respect—"

"You're either in or you're not. And if you're not, I need you out of my way." He narrowed his eyes. "In fact, I can reactivate you."

"I was Navy, sir."

"I don't care. I can make your life a living hell right out of the Bible, Hogan, or you can lend me your expertise right here, right now. I need you, but I don't have time for you to get comfortable with the danger level. Think those men are happy about going out there?"

"But Beo—"

"I'm sure Watters has several 'buts' he'd like to add—in fact, probably six of them."

One for each member of ODA452. She got the point.

Heat plumed through her chest at that threat. She couldn't go back in. . .

"This isn't about you. In fact, it's bigger than you. Understand what I'm saying, Hogan? We've got a butt load of trouble coming down the pipe." He jabbed a finger toward Beo. "And I need that dog to find it before it's too late."

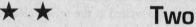

★ ★ TWO ★ ★

That is one ugly dog." Piled into the RG-33 MRAP, Tony grinned. He couldn't resist prodding Timbrel about her dog, panting hard in the Mine-Resistant Ambush-Protected vehicle.

She sat one man down and facing him, her left knee knocking his left. "Best-looking guy in here."

"You saying he's better looking than me?"

"Every day of the year."

"Ugly? I think he's beast." Java secured the rear hatch and the vehicle lurched into motion.

"A beast is right!" Scrip teased.

"More than right." Tony nodded. The dog nearly rearranged his face.

"No, beast. As in boss." Java shook his head at Scrip. "You are seriously lacking appreciation skills."

"I imagine you're right," Scrip said from the front of the MRAP as it barreled through one village after another. "We safe in here, with him?" Scrip had the most to lose since the bullmastiff sat directly in front of him.

"As long as I'm fine, you're fine."

"Baby," Tony said, "you are more than fine."

Timbrel rolled her eyes. He'd give her time, let her figure out how much she liked him. He'd been there the same day she had been when he made a move and she responded—then reacted. It'd been too fast. He figured that out. But she hadn't returned any of his calls, e-mails, or letters.

Tony held the UAV snapshot of the village, studying the buildings, the layout. They'd gone over it before gearing up, but this was some serious stuff. WMDs. Threat of that pushed Bush to war. Many people forgot the roughly six months the UN had given Saddam. Just enough time to clear out whatever he did have. And sat imaging hadn't caught anything.

Tony didn't think the guy was a complete idiot—the vast tunnels and underground facilities could easily have transported the material before the inspectors showed up.

But that was Iraq. This was Afghanistan. And if weapons capable of mass destruction existed here. . .plausible scenarios included the Taliban getting hold of it. Using it. Against the troops. Against Americans.

A hand, partially gloved, ran along the thick chest of the war dog. Tony flicked his attention to Beowulf. Right name, that's for sure. He sat between Timbrel's feet as she stroked his fur, her mouth against his ear as she talked to the EDD. A big pink tongue dangled from the wide mouth, which was pulled back as the dog panted.

Beowulf looked over, locked on to Tony. The tongue vanished amid a snarl.

Curse the luck. Dogs hated Tony. Always had. It'd never been mutual—until now. He hated that dog. Because he was one more barrier between Tony and Timbrel Hogan.

"Hey, Hogan," Java shouted over the noise of the engine and road noise, "anyone ever tell you that you look like that movie actress?"

Groans and laughter choked the dusty air. Someone ribbed him.

"Lay off, Java."

"No." The guy sat forward, too eager beaver. "I'm serious. She looks just like that actress who came here last month. The cougar lady, who wanted to sign Candyman's pec!"

Tony ground his molars. That had been one sick woman.

"Nina Laurens." When the others eyed him, Scrip shrugged. "Got her autograph for my dad."

"Yes!" Java sat straighter. "That's her!" He snapped his fingers and pointed at Timbrel, who shot fifty-calibers from her narrowed eyes. "You look just like her. Well, except you have brown hair. But your face—"

"We're here," Dean announced with two bangs on the hull of the MRAP.

The vehicle veered to the side and stopped. Tony lowered his Oakleys from atop his head as Java opened the hatch, but something in Timbrel's expression made him hesitate. Once they hustled down the deployed steel steps, he sidled up to her. "You okay?"

"Yeah." Her smile wasn't convincing. "You guys see a lot of Hollywood?"

"Only the ones who support us. Why?" He shifted his M4 to the front and adjusted the keffiyeh around his neck.

She shook her head and knelt beside her dog, but there wasn't any hiding that something bothered her. She just wouldn't talk.

"Sure is a hot mother," Rocket said.

"Hey," Tony said. "Check your language."

Rocket huffed, but his gaze skidded to Timbrel, who stood with her dog off to the side. She'd been issued the Glock strapped to her leg holster, the coms piece, and the body armor that wrapped her torso. But even with the CamelBak and boots, she looked petite. Which was downright funny because there was nothing small about that woman.

Around her were the rest of ODA452 and a half-dozen EOD guys, who'd followed in a second MRAP. Candyman couldn't help but notice the appreciative glances several of them shot at Timbrel. Made him want to punch their faces through the backs of their skulls.

"Okay," Dean said as he adjusted his weapon sling and slid down his sunglasses. "We work till the dog finds something."

Timbrel tugged on her ball cap. "What if he doesn't find anything?"

Dean considered her then Beowulf before he gave a cockeyed nod. "Then we go home late."

Meaning, they stayed till they found something.

"We'll take it building by building," Dean continued. "Insert, subdue the workers, split them up, and gather intel. Hogan, you and the dog wait till it's secure. Then Tony will bring you in."

Tony nodded. "Hooah." God was smiling on him today.

Stacked and ready, the team prepared to insert into the first building. Burnett had authorized use of deadly force if warranted. It gave the team the ability to operate more freely. To use the means they deemed necessary in the situation.

Candyman held his hand down and to the side, indicating that she should stay with him as they inserted. Her heart thumped. She hadn't been in combat for a while. Djibouti had been intense, but this was face-first real. Anything could go wrong. If bombs were in there, if the team rushed in and startled someone. . .

Crack!

Timbrel flinched, her mind snagged on explosives. But it'd only been the door that gave under the boot-first strike Rocket used to breach the entry.

Weapons ready. Tension high. Like a tidal wave, the team streamed inside.

"U.S. military! On your knees! On your knees!"

Timbrel waited with the EOD guys and HAZMAT by the armored vehicles.

"Get down, get down!"

"Don't shoot," a local begged.

"Down, down!"

Timbrel's pulse sped as she heard Candyman's voice. Knew he was in there working. Doing his thing. So sure. So confident.

One by one, they brought the workers out, cuffed, and separated them.

Candyman emerged, the sun glinting against the sandy blond beard, and stalked toward her. "Ready?"

Okay, no worries. Just do your thing. Timbrel moved toward the building.

A man lunged with a shout.

Timbrel jerked her head away from the man. Heard Beo growl.

Crack!

The man dropped in a heap as her mind registered that Candyman coldcocked the guy.

Rocket shouted something to rest of the villagers, who seemed especially rattled by what had just happened.

Shaking out his fist, Candyman scowled. "You okay?"

Shaken but unwilling to admit it, she gave him a nod. "Tell them I'm letting Beo off-lead. If anyone moves toward me, he will attack them."

A broad grin peeked between the beard. He rattled off the warning in Dari.

Java and Rocket snickered.

Timbrel hesitated.

"Might've embellished your words a little," Candyman said.

She shook her head as she unleashed Beowulf. "But they understand the threat he poses?"

"They know."

Inside, Timbrel glanced around, pausing to let her eyes adjust to the lighting. The captain came toward her. "It's clear. What do you need us to do?"

"Stay out of the way." Timbrel coiled the lead as Beowulf trotted around the room. "Beo, seek. *Seek*," she commanded.

With Beo trailing her, she moved her hand along the perimeter, around cabinets and shelves as he sniffed. "What is this place?"

"An office," Captain Watters said.

"No kidding." Eyeing him, Timbrel continued, allowing Beo to process the scents. If Watters had orders to keep her information limited, getting mad wouldn't do any good. Ten minutes of scenting and they had nothing. "It's clear."

Watters gave a small huff. "You're sure?"

"No." Timbrel let him sweat it for a minute, saw the uncertainty. "But Beo is. If he doesn't smell it, the chemicals aren't here."

The two Green Berets considered her 120-pound bullmastiff.

"Next," Candyman shouted as he started for the door.

At the next building, nothing. And the next. A dozen more. Nothing. The team swept all the buildings indicated on their map and came up with *nada*. Tension radiated off the men growing agitated at her and her beloved boy. She could almost hear their thoughts, that Beo didn't know what he was doing.

"Okay," Watters said, his expression grim as he considered Beowulf. "Let's call it a day."

"This was a total bust." Rocket shook his head.

"Thought he was supposed to be sniffing out trouble?" Java used his sleeve to swipe the sweat away.

"He only sniffs what's there." Timbrel wouldn't be goaded.

"You sure his nose isn't. . .I don't know, blocked or something?" Java tugged on his CamelBak bite valve and sipped, swished, then spit. "I mean, he's been inhaling a lot of dirt with that snout."

"Want him to sneeze on you to prove he's not clogged?" Timbrel asked.

"Hey, we've been out here for six hours clearing buildings, and what do we have to show for it?"

"Your attitude?"

"Hold up there." Candyman stepped up to Timbrel and touched her arm. "It's hot, we're all tired."

"Tell your guy that my dog can't sniff what isn't there. It's not his fault or mine if you have bad intel and we wasted a day."

"Nobody's blaming anyone." Candyman's voice was smooth as caramel, spreading over Timbrel's frustration. "It's just the way things work."

"Let's pack up and head back," Watters said.

"I told you bringing her and this dog in meant trouble." Rocket started back.

"What does that mean?"

"Timbrel—"

"No." She waved off Candyman and honed in on Rocket. "What does that mean? What trouble have we brought?"

"Timbrel!"

"What?"

"What's your dog doing?"

A quick look sent pinpricks of dread through her. Ten yards ahead, Beo sat, staring at a building. Then at her. Back to the building. "He's got a hit!"

Three

Hauling tail after Timbrel, Tony prayed this was it. For her sake. For the team's sake. They needed good news.

Timbrel slowed and cupped the dog's face. "Good seek! Good boy!" She showed him a ball with more praise. She considered the building. "What is it?"

Tony checked the script on the small sign. "Bookshop."

A small frown flicked across her face, but then she met his gaze with a short nod. "Ready."

What was that? "Sure?"

"Yep."

Dean joined them and pressed his shoulder to the wall next to the door. "Same routine. Once we clear, you search."

Another nod.

Be still my beating heart. He loved the way she found that inner courage to warrior on. He clapped a hand on Dean's shoulder, indicating his readiness.

Watterboy flung open the door.

"U.S. military! Hands in the air." Tony shouted in Dari, then Farsi as he threw himself into the open, cheek to his weapon as he stepped inside. Movement to the left. "Hands, hands!" He shouted as he swung that way.

A woman wearing a hijab yelped as she flashed her palms.

"Out, out!" He waved her out of the shop, knowing she could take anything with her under that garb, but relations were already delicate. Any of their men manhandling a woman would ignite things.

Two men appeared in the door.

"On your knees, on your knees," he ordered.

Scrip and Java cuffed them then led them out.

Tony checked the small office the men had been in. "Clear."

He came around. Dean and Rocket were clearing out the other rooms.

The process of rousting the workers, cuffing them, guiding them into the open road, and turning them over to the EOD guys, who were already logging and detailing information, proved tedious.

Inside, Tony cleared the second level that contained two offices and a small apartment with a torn and stained mattress pressed into the corner. A table and chair sat by a window guarded by a thin, holey sheet. He leaned out the window and eyed what was left of the wood stairs and landing. The walled-in backyard held a truck with the name of the shop and two other vehicles loaded with boxes.

Sighting down the scope, he trained his weapon on the vehicles. Two men were back there, loading more boxes. He'd need to get down there and secure them. But the stairs wouldn't hold his weight. Tony keyed his mic. "Java, two males in the back courtyard with a truck."

"On it," Java replied.

Tony kept a line of sight on the two till Java jogged into the back, shouting for the men to get their hands up. Wouldn't leave Java exposed and alone. Once the men were secured and escorted out, Tony trotted back into the shop. As he hustled down the steps, he called, "Clear."

"Clear." Rocket met him at the foot of the steps and thrust his chin toward a small hall where Dean stood. "Anything?" "A big storeroom." Light hit his face as he stepped back into the open.

"Sent Java after two men out back."

"We've got at least twenty out front."

Tony's gaze swept the small shop. Something felt. . .off. Six or seven shelves lined the rear wall and two more flanked the desk. He considered the building. The rooms. Two small offices down here, a bathroom, a hall with a storeroom, and. . .twenty men? Must've been cramped working conditions.

"Bring her in," Dean said.

The nagging wouldn't let him alone, but he couldn't finger the problem. He backtracked to the door and signaled to Timbrel. "Showtime."

Rocket, Scrip, and Dean stood out of the way as Timbrel walked Beowulf through the motions. Incredible animal. Large and butt-ugly, but the dog had a presence about him. The comments Timbrel made about Beowulf being the only guy for her and her constant referrals to the beast. . . What did she see in him?

At a wall of cabinets in the office, Beowulf reared up on his hind legs, sniffing the drawers. Timbrel pointed to the cracks, the crevices, the corners, leading and encouraging him.

He dropped onto all fours, turned, and trotted out. Considered Tony. A deep but quiet growl pushed Tony's breath into the back of his throat as pink gums trembled.

Tony cocked his head at the dog. *Feeling's mutual.* Holding his breath gave him little assurance the dog wouldn't try to snap his head off. Thing of it was, Beowulf somehow reminded him of an old, distinguished English professor. He had this stuffy, noble look to him.

Until he bared those fangs. Then it was all Beowulf, Hound of Hell.

Tony shifted his gaze to Dean and Rocket who had a mixture of amusement and concern on their faces. Smart guys, not to try to stare down that dog. Though he wasn't looking at the bullmastiff, Tony kept track of him in his periphery.

Challenge issued, Beowulf trotted down the hall. Sniffing. He scratched at a door.

"Storage room," Dean said.

Timbrel kept pace with her dog, and when she went into the narrow space, Tony followed. Behind him, he heard the boots of Rocket and Dean.

Timbrel opened the door and flipped on the light. A ten-by-ten room bore metal shelving and reams of paper.

"This is it?" Tony muttered as he peeked behind the door. "How did they fit twenty guys and a woman in here?"

"Good question."

Timbrel shifted to the side and watched, holding her hand out to them.

Beowulf sniffed the corner, then ran like a locomotive with his nose against where the floor and wall met. Switchback. Corner again. Two paces left. Crouched and sniffed. Waited. Sniffed again. He returned to the corner. Same thing.

Finally, he trotted back to the left. Sniffed. Then sat. Turned to Timbrel and wagged his tail.

She frowned. "He's got something."

Tony moved forward.

Beowulf snarled.

He shoved back and scowled at Timbrel.

"Beo, *out*," she said with an apologetic shrug, though not much of one. "Beo, heel."

Tony went to his knees and felt along the floor. No discernible difference in temperature. No breeze.

"Air?"

"Can't feel anything." Tony pressed his face against the dirt. "And no light." His gut churned. He believed in Timbrel and Beo. But there was nothing here. "No breeze, no light." On his knees, he checked with his commander.

"You're not looking hard enough," Timbrel said, going to her knees as well. "If Beo sniffed it, then it's there."

"It's not. Check for yourself."

Tony watched as the hardheaded woman did just that. He looked at Dean and shook his head.

Frustration darkened Dean's expression. "You're sure?"

"Certain." This wasn't his first rodeo, but Tony checked the floor again. "Yeah." His eyes traced the ninety-degree angle. . .saw the way the dirt seemed lined up. A well, of sorts. "Wait." He traced a finger along the spine. Felt the dirt give beneath his finger. "There's a groove or something here. Dirt's built up."

"It has to be a hidden room or something," Timbrel said. "It has to be there, whether behind or under us—Beo can smell something buried eight to ten feet."

"Java, get the owner in here," Dean ordered.

"Roger!"

Tony pushed onto his haunches and stood, then started rummaging through the stacks of paper, searching for an access panel or something.

"Rocket, look around for a switch or lever." Turning in a circle, Dean aimed his SureFire into the corners. Bright light scattered the shadows.

"Anything?" Dean asked.

"Nothing."

"Same here," Tony said with a huff. "Let me check something." He mentally tracked the distance from the wall to the corner then left the room. Eyed the opposite corner, traced it to the back door, then stepped into the rear courtyard. He measured it, felt along the wall, estimating.

"Candyman!" Timbrel shouted.

As Tony pulled the door closed, he spotted someone in the hall. With a weapon. Taking a bead on the storeroom.

Tony drew his Glock for close quarters. "Stop! Drop the weapon. Right. Now!"

The man swung the weapon at him.

Easing back the trigger, Tony fired. Ducked. Fired again. Fire lit down his forearm. He hissed through the pain but eyed it and figured the graze wouldn't even leave a scar. The man crumpled. Beyond him, Tony saw Java groaning and coming up.

Rocket rushed into the open and helped Java. "You okay?"

"Stupid guy head butted me."

"Yeah, well he shot me," Tony said.

"That tiny graze?" Java asked, the knot red and large on his forehead.

Tony grinned as he patted him on the shoulder but saw Timbrel watching him, her face. . .what was that look? "Everything okay?"

"Yeah. You?"

It almost seemed like she cared. *Right, keep dreaming.* "Never better."

"Did you get both men?"

"Both? There was only one."

She frowned but nodded.

He pointed into the storage room. "There's definitely more building there."

"Well, nobody's talking," Java said. "I had to practically drag him in here. And that's when things went haywire."

Stroking his beard, Tony grinned. "Sounds like they don't want us to find something."

Hands on his belt, Dean flashed a smile. "Then, let's take it down."

"Hooah."

Since the threat of WMDs existed, ODA452 couldn't blow it. Timbrel hung back as Tony and Rocket scooted the shelves out of the way. They brought in X-ray scanners to determine where they could cut and went to work dismantling the wall. Dust and tiny cement particles choked the air as the hole grew. Coughing, Timbrel struggled to see through the gray-filled air.

Candyman folded himself into the void they'd created. "There's a room!" he called from the other side. "Hands, hands!"

His shout from the other side sent Captain Watters and Java rushing through the narrow opening. Rocket stood guard on this side with her.

"Hands up, hands up!" Candyman ordered something in Dari and Farsi, his tone commanding and warning.

She waited in the corner, arms around Beo's chest. Watching. Anticipating the call.

A figure loomed in the dissipating fog. Then two more men. Cuffed. Escorted by Java.

Timbrel straightened to her full height, ready to enter the cleared room. As the two escorted nationals came toward her, she held Beo's collar. "Good boy."

Her shoulder jarred.

The Afghan man muttered something to her.

"Sorry." She frowned. *Wait. That wasn't my mistake.* The man had moved into her path. She glanced back, catching only his profile in the dusty and filmy air.

"Timbrel."

Right. Candyman, who didn't sound happy. "Let's go, Beo." She led him through the hole and straightened as she eyed the large space. Nearly the size of a warehouse, but not quite as high ceilings or as large in square footage. But not much smaller either.

Candyman, M4 cradled in one hand, keyed his mic and met her gaze as he spoke quietly into the mic. His words didn't come through her coms. Who was he talking to? Blond eyebrows pulled toward his nose. Not a happy camper.

What am I missing?

Candyman was at her side, caught her arm. "Tell me there's something here. Tell me Beowulf has a hit. A real hit."

The way he said that... Timbrel frowned, already feeling guilty. Or like a failure. But for what? She tugged out of his grip, stifling the adrenaline his words spiked. Gaze tracking the room, she hit the captain. Scowling until he dropped his gaze, which was filled with disappointment. Rocket.. .no disappointment there. Just outrage. Anger.

Another frown and she said, "Beowulf, seek." Her words didn't have the force she wanted them to have.

As Beo trotted around the room, their frustration, their anger coalesced into the big picture. Oh no. . .

She saw the printing press. The barrels of paper. The supplies of ink. Stacks of books on a conveyor. The little food in her stomach soured. Beowulf moved around the room, whimpering. Sniffing. Back and forth until he stopped at a far wall and sat. He looked at her as if to say, "Right here."

But right here wasn't WMDs. Right here, he'd found hydrogen cyanide.

A chemical used in the production of some books. Java and Scrip came in.

Curses flew through the air.

TAWHID—
THE ONENESS OF ALLAH

Eight Years Ago

With heaving breaths he stepped around the body and moved to the window. A lone, shabby curtain guarded the interior from an invasion of sunlight and hope.

There was no hope. Not for those who would set themselves against the will of Allah. As the infidels would die, so would those too weak to defend Islam. Those who bent their knees to Americans. They might believe they had good cause. They might be deluded and brainwashed by the Americans into believing the Western allies were occupying the country for the benefit of all people. But it was a lie. *A lie!*

He gulped, forcing his pulse to steady. His breathing to return to normal.

Closed his eyes. Quietly he recited the Qur'an, " 'Allah has borne witness that there is no God but Him—and the angels, and those with knowledge also witness this. He is always standing firm on justice. There is no God but Him, the Mighty, the Wise.' " He bowed his head. Then lifted his chin and spoke to the officers behind him. "It is good to be the sword of Allah."

Shouts erupted down the street.

He nudged aside the curtain and peered out. Directly in front of the dilapidated home that held him in quiet repose, a half-dozen ISAF soldiers waited. NATO forces helping with security here in Afghanistan. Though they held their weapons down, tension poured off them. The gazes of his men focused on the end of the street.

Craning to the side, he saw the cross street. Saw the American bulletproof, mine-resistant vehicle lumber across, heading north. Back to the base, no doubt. Children raced alongside, some begging candy and money.

But one lone boy pelted the vehicle with rocks.

727

Infused with pride over the youth's behavior, he smiled. He'd find that boy. Make sure he had a home, training. Allah had given the boy a warrior's spirit. *I will hone it.*

He let the curtain drop back into place, a dark smudge bright against the dingy white curtain. He glanced at his hand. Light poked through the curtain and glinted against the steel. As he rotated his wrist, examining the singular beauty of the sword, the glint vanished. Reappeared.

Smiling, he watched the life force glide along the silver surface. Two forces still competing. Steel and blood. One had surrendered a life as it chased the length of the blade.

Just as he would chase the Great Satan. Two forces competing. Islam and America.

They did not belong here. They did not belong in the lands of his fathers. They'd come under the ruse of peace and protecting freedom. But they'd brought death and destruction. Taken wives, mothers, fathers. . .children.

And one who had betrayed his people and breathed more death upon his own people would now never draw another breath.

"Sir," Irfael said quietly as he came to a stop at the door. "Americans coming this way."

"Good." They would find their spy—dead and unable to give them any more ammunition against the people of Islam. "Let's go." A tickle along the fleshy part of his hand drew his attention. A rivulet of blood slid down the side and vanished beneath the cuff of his sleeve.

Wiping it on his pant leg, he turned. Stepped over the body.

A sound resonated through the city. Call to prayer.

He paused. "My rug."

"Sir?"

He flashed a glare at his second. "My rug!"

The man gave a quick nod and bolted from the room. Within a minute, Irfael returned with the mat.

Peace. He needed peace within. Peace without. And if he had to bring all of hell to the world to do it, he would. Determining his position to the sun, he spread the mat on the floor. Watched as the threads greedily consumed the blood and drew the dark stain farther into itself. *As I will for you, Allah. I am your servant.*

And he knelt.

Four

"What in the name of all that's holy were you thinking?" Lance paced, feeling the thump of his blood pressure in his temple. Straining against his neck. "This is the mother of all screwups, gentlemen."

He shoved his hand through his short wavy hair, wanting to scream. Wanting to throttle each and every one of them. "That shop, the one where you killed a man and destroyed the wall, and therefore ruined the integrity of the entire building?"

Man, he needed a Dr Pepper.

Scratch that. A glycerin tablet.

"That building belongs to a family connected to our industrious humanitarian and who is a colonel in the ISAF!"

A curse split the tension.

Lance spun. "That's right. Curse, because that's exactly what you turned me into!" He stomped back to his desk. "How am I supposed to explain this to General Phillips?"

Watters lifted his chin and squared his shoulders. "Permission to speak, sir?"

Lance huffed. "Fine. Speak. Tell me something that I can pass to my superiors that will convince them not to discharge my sorry carcass. And if that happens, if they do, you can kiss your careers good-bye, because by golly, I will take you down, too."

"Sir," Watters began, his voice firm and calm, "Hogan and her dog found that scent."

"No kidding."

"It was a false positive, but through that we found the room."

"That's right. After you killed Colonel Karzai's right hand. After you blew up the wall of his shop."

729

"Sir," VanAllen interjected, "may I?"

Lance threw his hands up. "Why not? Watters sure isn't helping."

"Sir, the man I hit took a shot at me first. You authorized use of deadly force—"

"Don't you dare," Lance barked. "Don't throw this back in my face, VanAllen."

"Not my intention in the least, sir. My point is that this man had hostile intentions. If the wall and the printing press weren't a problem, then why attack us? Why hide the entrance?"

Lance couldn't fight it. The man had a point. It didn't make sense—none of it made sense. But it didn't matter. Karzai would grind him and the team up like hamburger.

"I'd like to make a request, sir," Russo said.

Lance glared at him. "Go on."

"I think Hogan is trouble. She and this dog—"

"Don't," VanAllen snapped, his face red beneath that sandy blond beard. "Do not blame her on this."

"That dog—"

"Did what he was trained to do. Cyanide is used in both printing and in WMDs. He's trained to find it and he did. He can't read the signs on the doors."

"No," Lance growled. "But you sure can."

VanAllen closed his mouth. His eyes screamed his fury.

Though Lance couldn't see the man's lips, he was sure they were thin and pulled tight. "VanAllen, trim up that rat's nest you call a beard." He grabbed a cold can from the fridge. "I want your after-action reports on my desk at 0800. Dismissed."

Tony stepped from the general's office in the subbase command center and got hit with a blast of hot, unrelenting Afghanistan heat.

A weight plowed into his shoulder from behind.

He stumbled and looked back.

Rocket stormed past him.

Tony grabbed the guy by the drag straps. Hauled him up against the building. Pressed his forearm into his throat. "I don't care if you are pissed off at me, I am still your superior officer."

Dark icy eyes hit his. "Noted. Sir."

"Hey." Dean came up beside them. "Let's ratchet it down. The whole mission was messed up. Placing blame doesn't do any good."

Taking in a breath, Tony released Rocket. Patted his shoulders. "I understand your anger."

"Don't do me any favors. I still think tasking our team with her is a mistake."

"Noted." Tony held the man's gaze.

"Russo," Dean said, moving in on Rocket, "you can check your attitude or your discharge papers."

Rocket's eyes widened.

"It's one thing to have a problem with something. It's another to let it get in the way." Dean looked to the side as if weighing his words. "We all need to put this behind us. The dog did what he was trained to do. And if we all think about it, though we can't prove a thing, there is something wrong with that shop. The hidden press. The guy who tried to off Candyman."

Dean's hazel eyes met the rest of the team. "Burnett's going to take some serious heat, but we need to be ready to go back and dig some more."

Java stepped forward. "Seriously? You think—?"

"Just be ready." Dean walked off.

Tony forced himself to turn and remove himself from the potential of a fight with Rocket. Tony went in, filled out his AAR, and submitted it. In the showers, he had to remind himself that he had feelings for Timbrel, so his actions were primed to protect her. To defend her. Not good. Team first. Had to be.

She didn't do anything wrong though.

Didn't matter. The team would come under a microscope. That could be messy. But again, they hadn't done anything wrong.

In the steamed-up mirror, he considered the general's warning to clean up his beard.

Trim. That's all. Not a full shave. With a groan, he trimmed it up. Wondered what Timbrel would think.

I don't do beards.

The first cut was the hardest. Cleaning it up and making sure the sides were even proved challenging. In the end, he appraised his work. Not bad. She couldn't object now. Right? Even David Beckham sported a beard now and then.

Toiletries packed up, he returned to his bunk. Stored the gear and headed to the chow hall. He stepped in and a bevy of odors assaulted him. Was that spaghetti or Alfredo? Or both? The scents nearly nauseated.

"Hey." Java slapped his gut. "You going tonight?"

"Where?"

"Concert—rock group's coming in. Eight Beatings or something like that."

Tony shrugged as he lifted a tray from the beginning of the line. "Yeah, sounds good." Downtime. Wouldn't have to think. Maybe Timbrel would come.

"D'you hear?" Java followed him to a table and sat down.

"No, but I'm guessing you're going to tell me."

"Burnett talked with Hogan."

Tony paused. Eyed Java.

"Apparently there was shouting—a lot."

The smile couldn't be hidden. He didn't imagine Timbrel would take the reprimand lying down. Or standing up. Or breathing.

"Speaking of. . ." Java spun out of the chair. "I'll be back."

Shoveling in a mouthful of Alfredo noodles, Tony bounced his attention to the door and spotted Hogan seconds before Java made it to her. The two talked for a moment, then she gave a slow nod before moving through the chow line. Hiking boots. Tactical pants. A clean tank. Long brown hair loose around her face. Man, she was more woman than most men could deal with. Including him.

But he was willing to brave the fight.

Bring it. That was, after she kenneled her MWD. The dog's withers reached Timbrel's thigh. Huge. Barrel-chested. Mean. *Hates me.*

Why did she have to bring that attack dog with her everywhere? It was as if she used him to ward off men and terrorists alike.

That's exactly what the hound of hell was. Her safety net.

Tony lowered his fork and rubbed his beard. His brain snagged on the shorter length. Would she notice?

Her gaze skipped around the hall, checking tables and chairs, then rammed into his eyes. A blink of recognition. Then another. Her lips quirked and an eyebrow arched.

Yep, she noticed.

And be still his beating heart, she was headed his way. Good, homegrown manners pushed him to his feet.

She strode right past him. "Hey!" She greeted a female officer—Brie Hastings.

Swallowing his pride and tending his bruised ego, Tony grabbed his tray. He stalked across the chow hall, her laughter tangling his mind and ticking him off.

Why? Why wouldn't she give him the time of day? He'd even shaved! Sort of. He slammed the tray onto the counter with the other dirty ones and stormed down the hall and into the night heat.

Growling exploded from the side. Jerked him up straight, ready to fight.

Laughter—her laughter wrapped around him. "You are so easy, Candyman." To his right, he found her leaning against the wall.

The smile that made it to his face lit through his whole being. "You. . ." He snorted. "You ignored me on purpose." To antagonize him. And though he wanted to turn and toss some smart-aleck comment in her face, Tony had this feeling. . . He started walking.

"Hey."

He smirked but didn't stop. "What do you want, Hogan?"

"Nothing." She sounded hurt. "Forget it."

Tony turned. "Look. I'm sorry. Things didn't go well with Burnett and I'm just eating a lot of stress right now."

"It seems that's all you're eating."

"Welcome to life in the Army."

"Look, I just wanted. . ." She puffed her cheeks and blew out a heavy breath as she looked around. "I'm sorry."

This conversation so wasn't going the way he thought it would. "For what?"

"What happened today. I know Burnett came down hard on you and the team."

"Heard you weren't exactly left out."

Hands in her back pockets, she tucked her chin. "No, but I'm used to getting yelled at."

Something about the way she said that twisted up his gut. "Sorry to hear that." But he started walking again. Playing it nice, playing soft, didn't win with the enigmatic woman. Besides, if he invited her along, she wouldn't come. So he hoped this ignoring her thing would keep working.

"I heard. . .I heard you stuck up for Beo and me."

He slowed his pace but not much. "Yeah, who told you that?"

"Doesn't matter. Just—thank you."

He stopped short. "Hold up." He cocked his head. "You think I backed you just because—?" He swiped a hand over his face. "Look, it's no secret I like you, but what I did in there, it wasn't because I was taking sides or because my thinking was compromised."

Her lips parted as she watched him.

"That wasn't about you, Timbrel." Was he coming off too strong? If he was, well, too bad. She needed to understand. "My team comes first. And if I ever think something you're doing will put them in danger—all bets are off, baby."

She raised her eyebrows. "Good to know." Took a step back.

He paced her. Touched her arm. "You also need to know that I believe in you."

She swallowed.

"And I trust you. That's not just because you're drop-dead gorgeous." Man, the heat had sure cranked. "You're good at what you do. You hold your own, and I respect that. What happened in that bookshop could've happened to anyone, anywhere. And I don't care what Burnett says, something's off."

Her face went slack.

What? What had he said now?

"Thank you, Candyman." Emotion thickened her words.

He huffed. Were they really still at square one? "Tony. Please. Call me Tony."

She wrinkled her brow. "But your name is James."

Great. They *were* at square one. Frustration knotted his muscles and he shoved his gaze to the surroundings. To the tan buildings, tents, and vehicles. Choppers thundering away. "It's also my dad's name so I go by my middle name—Anthony."

Her brown eyes sparkled as they traced his face. Could she feel that electric current humming between them? "You don't look like a Tony."

"Call me whatever you want as long as you're still talking to me."

She laughed. "You're slick."

"Does that mean you'll keep following me down to the market and get dinner at the same time?"

She squinted an eye at him. "Are you asking me out?"

"No way. I learned my lesson once." He grinned. "Just wanting to know if you're headed the same direction I am."

Trimmed beard. Loaded personality. Killer smile. Timbrel sat across the table from Candyman as he put away a meal from one of the local on-base vendors. She plucked apart some naan, a local bread, and tucked a piece in her mouth as he went on about his sister, niece, and nephew. Family life.

"Anyway, Stephanie was so mad when I helped Marlee grease up and gear up for their church's harvest festival."

Timbrel smiled. "Why? Because you dressed your niece like a soldier?"

He thumbed away a laugh-tear and shook his head. "No, Steph's not uptight about that stuff. It was because she'd just spent a hundred bucks on a Tinker Bell costume that Marlee demanded."

His family was way more domestic and. . .normal.

Beowulf stretched out by her feet, sound asleep and snoring.

"He always snore that bad?"

With a laugh, Timbrel rubbed her boot gently along Beo's belly. "Even worse on our bed back home."

Tony leaned forward, his eyebrows raised, chin lowered. " 'Our bed'?" He dropped back against the chair. "No way. He sleeps with you?"

"Where else?"

"On the floor? On a pallet or in a crate?"

Timbrel reached down and rubbed his triangular ears between her fingers. Relegating Beo to the floor meant he was far from her. He wouldn't be there for her to hold when the nightmares resurfaced.

Candyman went on. "My parents had a German shepherd, Patriot, who slept in a crate by their bed. I could deal with that, but no way I'd want a dog getting between my woman and me."

Now it was her turn to raise her eyebrows.

"Whoa. Hold up." He thumped his chest, belched, then cleared his throat. "I wasn't making a reference to you and me in that statement."

"Good to know."

Though Tony laughed it off, Timbrel wondered. . . No, she didn't wonder. She realized. Realized they could never have a future. Beowulf didn't like Tony. And Tony didn't like Beo. And if Tony didn't like dogs in beds. . .well, not that it would go that far, but what was the point of sitting here right now, talking, risking everything she'd protected if there was no point?

An acrid taste glanced along her tongue. Fire lit through her body, tugging her from the greedy claws of darkness. Rolling onto her side, she groaned. Dirt and rocks pressed against her arms. Panic edged into her body with a zipping dose of adrenaline.

Mentally, she dragged herself out. No. This wasn't Bahrain. It was Bagram. She was safe. With Candyman.

But the sticky perspiration made her antsy. The memory clung like a strong spiderweb to the fragments of her courage. To the small pieces that convinced her to sit, enjoy some downtime.

Timbrel dragged her booted feet under her and pushed to her feet.

Beowulf alerted and pounced upright at her side. "We'd better get back. Early morning."

Even though he still wore the beard, she saw his jaw stretch. Disappointment lurked in his eyes as he looked up at her and nodded. As if he'd known. Expected her to bail. He tossed down his napkin and stood. "Bedding down pretty early. There's a concert down at the USO rec center."

"Yeah, I'm not really into crowds."

"It'd be nice to see you there." He glanced at Beo then touched her shoulder. "Thanks for walking in the same direction as me."

She tried to kill the laugh, but it didn't work. She tucked her chin and gave a quiet snort. "Lucky coincidence."

Candyman grinned. "Then I hope my luck holds."

"I. . .I really don't think so, but thanks for asking." Timbrel stepped away from the table, but not before his expression reminded her of his disappointment, clinging to Candyman thicker than his trimmed beard. "Bye."

"Night, Timbrel."

She held up a hand in a small wave but trudged back toward the tent she shared with a couple dozen female soldiers. But that disappointment seemed to have attached a tether to her heart because she couldn't shake the image of his face.

No. . . Timbrel hesitated. She wasn't remembering his disappointment. She lifted her head and looked off at nothing in particular. It was her own disappointment. *I wanted to stay with him. But that. . .that can't happen.*

She dropped onto her cot and buried her face in her hands. *I'm so tired of hiding. Of being alone.*

A soft, wet snout nudged her hand.

Timbrel held Beo's head and kissed the divot between his eyes. "Thank you, boy." He knew. He always knew when she was down, when she needed a rescue.

Much like Candyman.

"Hey," a young female private said, stopping by her cot. "We're heading over to the concert. Want to join us?"

"Oh." Timbrel considered the group of three. "Thanks, but I think we'll just hang out here."

"You sure?" Cute, blond, and entirely too suited for the uniform she wore, the private smiled again. "It's a lot of fun. There are movies and pool tables, too."

"Thanks for asking, but I don't think so."

The other girls nudged their friend along, and soon Timbrel found herself alone. Her gaze roved the tent. The beds, crisply made with hospital corners. Lockers. A stray colorful scarf broke the monotony. She'd once found comfort in the drab scheme here. Now, it just felt. . .lonely.

She stretched out on the cot and crossed her ankles. Beo climbed up next to her and slumped down, almost immediately snoring. Timbrel stared up at the canvas covering, and with a thick, humid breeze, she felt the oncoming nightmare.

Heat radiated through Beowulf's brindle coat, soothing the cuts and dispersing the cold that wrapped her in the dark hour.

Not cold. It was summer. Not cold. Stop thinking about it.

Instinctively, she curled her arm around the neck of her 120-pound bullmastiff and dug her fingers into his fur.

Dark. It was still dark.

Why did her legs feel cold?

She glanced down—and froze.

In a violent, terrifying wave, she fell once again into the terror.

Five

Pounding thumped against his chest.

On any other day here in the desert, the source would've been a firefight. Tonight, it was a rockin' band with a mean bass. And they were killin' it.

She hadn't come. He knew she wouldn't. But he'd hoped. A sucker for a pretty face, that's what he was. She'd shoveled a heap of hope into his lap as they sat there in the market talking. As he watched her laugh. Man, what a sound.

She didn't fool him though. Tony had seen a lot of trauma in his life, and she wore it like a unit patch. They'd been sitting there, him doing most of the talking but that was fine. She seemed okay with it. Way he figured, it'd wear down that wall she had erected around her heart and life.

Though dusk descended, Tony couldn't miss the pallor that drained that pretty pink from her face. She'd remembered something, an awful something, as her gaze slid from his eyes to his chest, and with it went her smile and willingness to stick around.

That's when he knew he was dealing with more than a tough woman.

Timbrel Hogan wasn't just broken. She'd been shattered.

And if he ever met the person responsible. . .

Throngs of troops threw up their fists, shouting with the music, and some even danced. Tony sat on a table at the back of the building, nursing a Coke. He leaned back against the wall, hiking a leg up and resting his forearm over his knee. She made him want to be a better version of himself. And he'd trimmed his beard.

For cryin' out loud. Didn't she get that sacrifice?

Rocket pushed through a group of female soldiers and headed his way. He stuck out a hand. "Hey, no hard feelings?"

"Never." After a fist bump, Tony tossed his can in the receptacle.

"I'm surprised she showed up here."

Tony frowned. "She didn't. Too many people."

Rocket pointed toward the side entrance.

"You're just trying to make me look stupid."

"You do that all on your own, brother." Rocket patted his shoulder and vanished back into the crowd.

Seriously? Was she here? Shoving off the table, Tony searched the faces by the door. A handful of officers moved farther into the teeming audience, exposing a gap.

And there she was. Alluring with her uncertainty and long brown hair. Tony lumbered toward her.

Though he couldn't hear it, he knew the dog growled at him by the way Timbrel signaled him to stand down. Then she saw Tony and smiled sheepishly. "Hard to sleep with decibels like this pounding the base worse than mortars."

"This?" He shrugged. "I could sleep like a baby. It's like home to me."

"And you complained about my dog's snoring?"

Tony chuckled. She had her fight back. Good. "Let's head outside so we don't have to shout." He pushed open the door, and she and Beowulf exited. Outside, Timbrel tossed the ball and Beowulf tore off after it. "He's one tough dog."

"He's the only guy for me."

"Yeah, I think you said that a time or two already."

"You sound disappointed."

Tony said nothing. He just trudged over to a picnic table and sat atop it, his feet on the bench. "How long have you had him?"

"Five years. Nobody else was willing to work with him." She shrugged. "Actually, he wouldn't work with anyone else. The instructors were ready to retire him and he wasn't even a year old yet."

"Tough, thickheaded. . . Don't they pair handlers and dogs with similar personalities?"

The light overhead bathed her face, colored with surprise. "You did not just go there."

Tony chuckled.

"Oh wow, you did." She sat on the bench to his left, accepted the ball from Beowulf, and threw it again. It hit the wall. Beowulf didn't miss a beat, launching himself off the cement bricks and tearing after the ball.

Leaning back, she crossed her ankles. "So, what do you think will happen—with Burnett and this mission?"

"Mission's over." Tony rested his forearms on his knees. "With the way it ended, I wouldn't be surprised if the whole thing gets officially buried."

Her brow furrowed. "But he said he was looking for WMDs. How can it be over?"

He nudged her shoulder with his knee. "I said *officially*."

Casting him a sidelong glance, she nodded. Her dog returned and she praised him, rubbed his fur, then threw the ball a few more times. No dialogue. No idle chitchat. Just chilling with the music pulsing through the USO building. He liked this. Nothing special. No mission. No argument. Just being. With her, of course.

He didn't want it any other way. But. . .would they ever get past square one?

"How long do you stay out here?" She looked at him as a hot breeze tossed a loose strand of her hair into his face.

"Till the music stops, I guess."

"No, I meant your deployment—wasn't sure with you being Special Forces."

"Ah." Tony peered down at her, the top of her head catching the lamplight. "Another two weeks, then we'll head home for a few months."

"When you come out. . .?" Her words were almost lost in the chaos of the concert, especially when the door opened and out spilled a half-dozen soldiers. She waited as they greeted him with a sarcastic salute then moseyed away. Timbrel shifted, pulled a leg up to her chest, and rested her boot on the bench. "When you deploy, how long is it for?"

"Till the job's done."

She nodded, but he couldn't see her face. And that was annoying.

Tony hopped off the table.

Beowulf spun toward him and growled.

Timbrel smirked. "Beowulf, heel." She petted his sides as he sat down with a huff, his broad mouth pouting.

"He looks offended that you stopped him from taking a piece out of me."

"He is." Timbrel stroked the fur, hugged her dog, then looked up at Tony. "He's a lot like you—ugly, mean, but on the inside, he's a big ol' softie."

"You calling me soft?" Indignant that she'd compared him to her dog—he wasn't sure whether to be offended or feel complimented. He tugged up his sleeve and flexed his bicep. "Does this look soft?"

Timbrel gave him a playful smile. "That looks like you're compensating."

Oh, getting ruthless. He must be hitting home or reaching new places. "Compensating." He took a step closer. "What would I be compensating for?"

"Well, with that wall of muscle you call a chest and the tattoo—"

"Now what's wrong with my tattoo?" Tony eyed the ink sliding out from under his sleeve.

"How big is it?" Hands on her hips, she faced off with him.

He knew if she saw this thing, she'd draw a correlation to his manhood somehow. And he so wasn't going there. "It has meaning."

She laughed. "How big?"

She was so dang pretty. Did she know that? He'd do anything for her. Including this. Tony hiked up his shirt and tugged it off, angling his shoulder down toward her.

"Holy cow!" Timbrel's laugh echoed through the night as if they were the only two who existed. She touched the ink that traced up his bicep, over his shoulder, and swooped down around his left pectoral. "Wow. This is some piece of work."

Her touch set off emergency flares in his gut.

With one hand on his left shoulder and one on his right arm, she tilted him toward the light. "That's. . .amazing. It had to be painful to get inked that much."

He lowered his chin, bracing himself against her soft fingers tracing his bare chest. *Do not to react. Correction: stop reacting.*

"What is it?"

Think. *She's talking to you, moron.* "It's. . .uh, it's from the *Book of Kells.*"

She was still touching. Tracing.

Stay still. Don't. . .don't do it.

His hand went to her face. So soft. So. . .

Brown eyes snapped to his. He had no doubt she suddenly realized the power she held over him. That she knew what was blazing through his mind because her lips parted as his hand slipped to the back of her neck. Tugged her closer.

She resisted.

Tony stilled. Afraid to set her off. Set off her dog.

But he felt the tension collapse.

He craned his neck toward her face.

She looked up, watching as he honed in.

RPGs had nothing on the mess happening in his heart. He touched his lips to hers. Heard the whisper of a snatched-in breath. Tony kissed her again, this time lingering. Reveling in his victory. She hadn't pushed him away. Was it really possible. . .?

He slipped a hand around her waist. Felt the tickle of her hair against his other arm. He kissed her again, debating on deepening it.

Tension roiled through her shoulders. Knotted. She arched away.

No no no.

Her hands pushed against his chest. "Stop."

Just one more kiss.

"Let. Me. Go."

Growling erupted.

Veering off, Tony grunted. "Okay. Sorry."

Timbrel's chest heaved. Head down, she stepped back. Bumped into the table. Her breathing went shallow. Panicked.

"Tim?"

She raised a hand. Shook her head. Long, wavy hair shielded her face.

"I'm sorry. I didn't—"

"Don't." She pivoted. "Just. . .leave it. Forget it."

"Forget it? I don't want to forget it." He reached toward her.

Beo snapped at him.

Tony yanked back.

"Beo, *heel*." A volley of force punctured her words. "Look, I'm sorry. It's . . .it's not you. Okay? Just. . .it won't work. It just. . .won't. . ."

"No, no way are you getting off that easy." He narrowed his eyes. "Why? Why are you showing me the door? You wanted that kiss as much as I did."

"Yeah, and I want a million dollars, too, but it's not going to happen."

"That was lame. Even for you. If you wanted this thing with me, you could." Tony noticed two female officers checking him out and he remembered his shirt. "But you're walking away. No, you're running." He thrust his arms through the sleeves and tugged it down. "Why? At least give me that much respect."

"Because." She cocked her head then shook it as if to ward off something. She patted her chest. "I can't do this. Okay? I can't."

It sure sounded like there was more after that, but she choked it off.

"Then don't. This doesn't have to be anything but one day at a time."

She waved her hand and turned in a circle, a caustic laugh trailing her. "That doesn't work, Candyman."

Why was she still calling him that? *To keep me at a distance.* Was it really that simple to her? He stepped into her personal space again. Touched her arm. "I want to make this work, Timbrel."

Her eyebrows raised in question then she frowned. "Why?" Then blinked. "No." She touched her forehead. "Never mind. Just—let's forget this happened. Ya know, just forget me." Her words sounded raw, wounded, as she backed away. "Trust me. You'll be happier in the long run."

"You're the most *un*forgettable woman I know."

"You don't even know who I am."

"I've been on several lengthy missions with you, spent a total of about six months with you—the heat of combat sears relationships together." He held up a hand to stop her from interrupting. "But I hear what you're saying. Just. . .just don't say no to this, to us. We won't make plans about anything other than today. No expectations."

Cautiously, she reached up and touched his face. Something strange, tormented flickered through her expression. "I don't kiss beards."

If the fuzz was a problem, then, "The beard is gone." Tony inched in toward her. "Does that mean we can restart this?"

Her lip and chin seemed to tremble. "I never make promises I can't keep."

"Good, I wouldn't want you to." He smiled down at her, trying to soften the tension. Okay, she was still here, that counted for something. Still talking to him. Counted for more. He had to keep her engaged. "Listen, I'll be at mess at 0700." Hope lay pinned between her tortured expression and the banging of his heart. "Just going in the same direction, right?"

Timbrel lifted her chin. "See you, Candyman." With that, she turned, signaled to her dog, and walked into the night.

Why did that feel a lot like, "So long sucker"?

743

*C*owards *die many times before their deaths; the valiant never taste of death but once."*

Resting her head against the portal-style window, Timbrel ran her thumb along Beowulf's head as he stretched over the two seats beside her. She was a coward. Running and running. Even Candyman had seen that. Called her on it. He was the valiant Shakespeare had spoken of. . .she the coward. And how many times had she died inside?

She closed her eyes and let herself relive that moment when Candyman had stepped in, taken her heart hostage, and stolen that kiss. Was it her blind attraction to his well-muscled torso in the light of the evening? The tattoo that bordered on spectacular and inked his entire well-toned pec?

No, though she could appreciate the beauty of his body, she'd seen way too many men who were big on talk and muscles and small on brains and heart.

That was the difference with Candyman. He had heart. Somehow, they'd connected in the months they'd spent together on missions. Djibouti tilted her perception of him. Until then, he'd just been a hairy grunt with a lot of gear and personality.

Since then, Candyman had braved her storms. Met them with undeterred charm. Made her smile, laugh. Saw through her defenses. Made her want to lower them.

And therein lay the problem.

She'd opened up to a man once before. "Biggest mistake of my life."

Beowulf lifted his head and looked at her as if to say, "I'm the only guy you need."

She ruffled his head. "Right you are." She looked out the portal window. "And you won't let me down, will you?"

With a huff, he stretched across her lap again.

Timbrel dug through her pack and fished out two ibuprofen p.m. tablets. After swallowing them with some water, she leaned the seat back and let herself drift into the numbing blackness of a drug-induced sleep. Mom used to do that.

She readjusted and stretched her neck.

Zero seven hundred came early on most mornings.

But on this one, it had to be dragged from the cover of darkness by the sands of time. At least, that's how it felt since he hadn't been able to sleep. Tony pried himself off the bed, headed to the showers, took care of business, then strolled into the mess hall. After filling his tray with runny grits, burned sausage, and RPG-quality biscuits, he folded himself into a chair at a table. Each tick of his watch counting down the seconds felt like years slipping by.

She's not coming.

No, no. He'd give her the benefit of the doubt.

She gave you the royal kiss-off.

That kiss. It wasn't passionate. It'd taken every ounce of self-control to hold back, to be aware of her tendency toward flight. True, he didn't back off at the first hint of trouble. It'd been too good. But he'd been gentle. And still she bolted.

He rubbed his beard as soldiers streamed in and out.

A clock-check added a kink to his knotted muscles: 0730.

Grinding his teeth, he shifted on the metal chair. *Don't do this to me, Timbrel. Give me a chance.* But the whole thing wasn't about him. It was about her. She was scared. Afraid of feeling. The girl operated in "self-preservation" mode 24/7. Tony balled his fist and brought it to his mouth as he watched female soldiers make their way through the line.

What could he have done differently? Gone a little slower?

The guys here might think he'd been too fast, but they didn't know he'd spent a full month in Djibouti at her side. And while that might be fast back home—in a world where the biggest worry was the number of "likes" or friends on Facebook one had—in combat, a month measured as a lifetime.

Besides, going slower did nothing but give Timbrel more power. Power to say no. Power to control the not-happening romance.

No, he could've weighed anchor in the harbor of her soul and never gotten to shore.

The beard.

Right. She'd used that as an excuse, but he knew better.

Timbrel Hogan was like a frightened doe by a highway. He'd have to trap her to save her.

He shoved to his feet, eyed the clock once more—0800—and stomped out of the chow hall. He crossed the base and headed to her tent. Ducking beneath the cover, he already knew the answer. Just had to see it for himself.

Stripped of bedding, her designated bunk sat empty. He walked over to it, ignoring the others inside, and flipped open her locker. Empty. Tony punched it and cursed.

And that made him mad. He'd cursed more since she showed up a week ago than he had in a year. He just didn't talk that way, but that woman brought out the worst in him.

"Her flight left at four."

Shoulders tight, hands balled, Tony acknowledged the woman's voice with a curt nod and stomped out of the tent.

He'd wanted to be there for her. Wanted to protect her. Make a difference in her life. But she was so bullheaded and bent on protecting herself that she isolated herself. Cut herself off from anyone and everyone who got too close.

"Hey, Candyman!"

Teeth grinding, he shook his head. "Not in the mood, Java."

"I think you'll be in the mood for this." Java jogged up to him and thrust a paper in front of him. "What do you think?"

Repulsion that nearly made him want to vomit hit him as he stared at the photo. It was taken the night Nina Laurens had come. She manipulated him and Java into posing with her. She practically pressed herself against him. He hadn't had his skin crawl like that since sixth grade when he fell into a pit with a dead deer oozing maggots.

He slapped it back at Java. "Told you—"

"So you recognize her."

Tony grabbed Java's shirt by the collar. "Java—"

"Hold up, Sergeant." He shoved away. "Look. Just look at this."

Whoa! Get a grip. He patted his teammate. "Sorry."

"No worries. I know you're probably ticked she bailed." Java tapped the paper. "Taken ten years ago at the Oscars."

He pushed his gaze to the photo. In a leopard-print dress, Nina Laurens stood in the limelight, a leg curved out and exposing a lot of flesh and cleavage. Blond hair short and spiky, she exuded sensuality.

She's old enough to be my mother! Tony grunted. "So?" He held it out.

"No, no." Java shifted and stood beside him. "Look next to her."

Tony eyeballed the picture again. "What? I don't. . ." His words faded as he took in the brunette beside Nina. And he fell into the time warp that encapsulated the images before his eyes. "No way." His gaze dropped to the words at the bottom.

Nina Laurens and Audrey Laurens.

His mouth went dry as he took in the familiar face, a sultry, gorgeous one surrounded by curls from her pinned-up hair and sparkling diamond earrings and necklace. Timbrel—Audrey?—was drop-dead gorgeous. Curves. . . He'd never seen this side of her. He was a guy. A soldier in the desert. He could appreciate those curves. Though she didn't flash flesh the way Nina did, Timbrel Hogan exuded a sensuality all her own.

She gave the camera a look that could kill. He saw it, but did the paparazzi? Did they realize she was ticked off, even on the red carpet?

"It's her—Hogan." Java grinned like a schoolboy. Then peered at the page again. "I mean, it looks like her. A lot like her. Just as I said in the MRAP. She's the image of Nina Laurens. The article said she's her daughter." He slapped Tony's chest. "Dude, you have the hots for a Hollywood socialite!"

"Bug off, man." Tony pushed past him, clenching the page in his hand.

"Hey, can I have that back?"

Ignoring him, Tony stormed toward the SOCOM offices. He stepped in and removed his ball cap, nodded to the admin. "Hey, is—?"

Burnett's door opened and he emerged.

"Sir." Tony resisted the urge to toss the paper at the general's chest. Getting busted a rank or two wasn't worth the anger spiraling through him.

"VanAllen." Burnett considered him. "You look like you need to talk."

He took a heavy breath. "Yessir."

Already backing into his office, Burnett waved him in.

Inside, Tony eased the door shut. "Sir," he said as he turned and handed off the paper. "Did you know?"

One quick look. "Yep."

Tony felt so. . .stupid. "Why weren't we told?"

"Her relation to the actress is of no consequence to what we're doing here, that's why."

"No, sir. I guess not, but. . ."

"Look, you got yourself tangled up romantically with her. She bailed. Now you find out you didn't even know her. Get over it, and her!"

Tony studied the carpet, his teeth grinding.

"Timbrel Hogan is a darn good handler, but that's about where her 'plusses' stop."

"No, sir." Tony felt his pulse hammer against his ribs. "I have to disagree with that statement. She's tough, intelligent, funny. . ."

"If you want the trouble of pursuing her, do it later. Here, you're mine. And I need your mind here. Am I clear?"

Stiff, Tony hesitated. "Sir, has something happened?"

"Yes." Burnett stilled then shook his head. "No. Nothing I can mention. Not yet. Just. . ." Lips tight, he shook a meaty finger at him. "In fact, you know what—I'm sending the team home for some R & R."

Tony straightened. "Sir? That's two weeks early. I thought you just said you needed my head in the game."

"Consider it a gift of my generosity."

"I would, sir." Something wasn't right. "If you had any."

Burnett laughed. "Smart man."

Going home early wasn't a gift. It was a time to prepare, to get themselves together. But for what? "Sir, what's going on?"

"Don't ask."

"We'll need time to prep."

"Don't tell me what you'll need. I know what you need!" Burnett's snarl slithered through the room. "And if I say you're going home, you're going home. Don't look a gift horse in the mouth."

"What are we going to owe you later? Our lives?"

"I already got that—you signed on the dotted line years ago, VanAllen." He grunted. "Don't think about it. Just go home, get some downtime, but be ready for that call, Sergeant."

"Sir. Yes, sir."

"And Sergeant?"

Tony hesitated by the door, looking over his shoulder to the general.

"I'm not sure Timbrel Hogan is a fire you want to play with."

Straightening, he eyed the older man. Gray hair softened the face that lined blue eyes with age. "Is that an order, sir?"

Burnett gave him a "you're an idiot" smile. "Call it a suggestion. For your own good." The smile vanished. "Dismissed."

Pounding the dirt beneath his feet, Tony made his way back to his bunk. He could take a lot of heat, he could handle anger, but telling him what to do and with whom he could do it—that ticked him off. Especially since it related to Timbrel.

From his locker, he grabbed his duffel. Slammed his gear inside it.

"What's up?" Java asked from his bunk two over.

"Heading home."

"Says who? And why'd you get to go early?"

"Burnett." Tony tossed in his Bible, stared at it, then lifted it back out. "We're all going back." He peeked at the inscription from Exodus 14 his mother had added: *The LORD will fight for you; you need only to be still.*

That was just it. Sitting still defied his nature. Action. Taking the proverbial bull by the horns, that was his way.

"What'd he say?" Dean asked as he sat across from him on Rocket's bunk.

Fanning the super-thin pages, Tony looked up through his brow. "Nothing." He tucked the Bible in his bag and the rest of what little he'd brought over. "Said we're heading home and we're to rest up. But I could tell something was bothering him. He's working on something."

"Bet it's those WMDs." Dean rubbed his knuckles. "I have a feeling this will get ugly before it ends."

'ADL—
DIVINE JUSTICE

Seven Years Ago

Screams echoed through the village. The shout of injustice meeting the sword of Allah. The shriek of evil dying. The howl of penitence.

The voices fell on the deaf ears of a colonel who sought to right the way of his people, to restore to Allah the people who had once served him wholly. War and violence were the way of his people. Especially when injustice propagated itself in the hearts and minds of Allah's children.

"Colonel." Irfael strode toward him, hard lines gouged into his face by years of working in the unrelenting Afghan heat. Tall, beady-eyed, he could be trusted only in the way of violence. "We've gathered the men around back."

Shrieking, a young girl bolted from a house. Fist up, dagger in hand, she dove at him. "I'll kill you!"

Catching her wrist, the colonel sidestepped. Yanked her around in front. Arm around her throat. Hand struggling to control her more against that deadly blade. "Why do you do this?" His heart spun. Her fire. Her passion. Her willingness to throw herself on the coals of hell for something she believed in.

Brown eyes met his with hatred. "You killed my father."

"So you come to kill me? To deliver your own justice?"

Her nostrils flared, revealing a small gem embedded there. "Isn't that what you are doing?"

He grabbed her by the hair and jerked her toward the vehicles. "You want to see justice?"

She cried out, slapping at him, kicking. She even dropped to her knees, but he yanked her onward. Stumbling, she regained her feet.

Irfael stepped out from a plaster-and-thatched-roof hut, blood splattered across his face.

Around the corner, the colonel found his men guarding a half-dozen men. All dressed in international uniforms. All on their knees.

One of the younger men looked up, and his gaze widened at the prize the colonel dragged with him. "Leave her!" He lunged upward.

A single shot rang out.

The man crumpled to the ground, a plume of dirt the last applause of his life.

The girl screamed. "No!" She wrested herself from the colonel and threw herself at the man's body.

"Please," the village elder begged, spittle clinging to his beard as thickly as the man's betrayal. "Do not do this thing. They are innocent."

"They are *not innocent*!" Sword in hand, he walked around him. "You have tainted them, Shamil, when you helped the Americans."

"No, no. I did not help." Tears marked beige paths down the man's dirty cheeks. Knuckles white from clenching his hands so hard, he continued to beg.

"Colonel." Irfael nodded to the end of the street.

He turned and saw two of his guards assaulting a young girl. "See what it is you have done, Shamil? *You* have done this. Your sin."

"No, no, no," the man cried as he hung his head. "Please stop this, Colonel. You have the power. I beg you. I will do anything. Just do not do this."

"I have the power because it is given by Allah." He lifted the sword and let it ring along Shamil's neck. Once the head rolled from its body, the colonel marched over to the girl. Hauled her up and away from the body.

"A prize, Colonel?" A sneer on Irfael's face infuriated him.

He held her up before the men. "Shamil was a fool. He believed working with the Americans and British would bring peace. But only Allah can bring peace, and I am an instrument of peace. Through violence. We must not work with the devil! Did not the Prophet Muhammad—peace be upon him—"

"Peace be upon him."

"—say: 'My Lord has enjoined upon me justice.' Then we must be that justice." He swept his arm around the village. The smoke fleeing the sins of the people. The fire searing away their evil ways. "This, *this*, is what happens when one is not faithful to Allah!

"You wear the uniforms of the Infidels. A year ago, I would have shot each of you dead in the street. But today"—he drew in an impassioned breath—"today I give you a chance to redeem yourselves. Wage war on the Americans. You have access to the

RONIE KENDIG

bases. Wipe them out!"

Uncertainty flickered through the men's gazes. Some slid sideways glances to the others. Others refused to look at him.

Cries of women rose and grew.

"If you do not follow this way, Allah will bring death upon you. And I pray with all my heart that it is me who will deliver that justice." He gripped the face of the young girl with his right hand, resting his other on her shoulder. "If you do not, then this"—he snapped her neck—"is what will become of your families."

She fell onto the dirty earth.

The colonel walked over to his armored vehicle and opened the door. He knelt against the running board and cupped the face of a ten-year-old boy. "Did you see?"

Wide brown eyes held his. The boy nodded.

"Do you understand, my son?" The two months he'd had with the street urchin transformed the youth, but doubt still lingered in his eyes.

He nodded.

The colonel smiled.

"No." The boy shook his head. "Why did you harm them? The women, the children—"

"Oh, Dehqan." He motioned the boy over, climbed into the warmed seat, and closed the door. "What does the Qur'an say, son?"

Uncertainty flickered where confidence should rest.

Nudging aside the disappointment, he gave the boy a hint. Instruction would take time, to convert the boy, to have him consumed with a passion for Islam. But it was time well spent. More of the sons of Islam needed to be raised up, trained, equipped both mentally and psychologically. " 'We did not wrong them, but they wronged themselves.' "

A crack of a smile. "Surah 16, verse 118."

The colonel hugged the boy. "Well done, my son."

Seven

Austin, Texas

Y‍ou're serious? Black-tie formal?" Staring past her booted feet propped on the table, Timbrel ignored the way her stomach squirmed over wearing a dress again.

"Absolutely." Khaterah Khouri's smile gleamed as she sat at the conference table at the back of the ranch house. "We're bringing in some very distinguished dignitaries and holding it at the National in New York."

"New York," Timbrel balked. "Do you know how expensive that will be?"

Khat nodded. "I'm aware, but most of the investors are in that area, and we want to make a good impression."

"You mean, you want to empty their pockets into ABA's coffers."

Khat's smile went wicked. "Is there a difference?"

Timbrel shoved her hands through her hair. "But seriously, Khat. Dresses?"

"It's one night. It won't kill you."

"You have no idea."

"Well, this isn't about you."

"Tell me how you really feel," Timbrel snapped.

"I see your people skills are as good as ever," Heath "Ghost" Daniels said as he entered.

Timbrel glared.

Folding her arms over her chest, Khaterah held her ground. "This benefit gala is crucial for A Breed Apart. My brother has worked very hard to make this facility a success, to give back where he saw a way. After all he's

753

gone through, I won't let him down." Large mahogany eyes glossed. "And I won't let anyone else ruin the night for him. Not over a dress. He believed in you, Timbrel. The least you can do for him is this small thing."

Chastised, Timbrel hung her head. "Okay." She couldn't hide from this. "You're right." Jibril had sacrificed more than most of them—he'd come back from Afghanistan minus a leg. And yet he fought on.

But a dress—nobody here could understand what that meant. Broke beyond broke, she would have to use one of her old gowns.

"Do you need help with a gown. . .I mean, financially?"

Timbrel snorted and let her boots thud against the ground. "No." She needed to redirect this conversation and deflect the attention. She tugged a spreadsheet closer and scanned the numbers and names. "How far are we from our goal?"

"Well, we've really stretched our faith out there, believing for a million dollars. We're about halfway." Khaterah blew a stream of air from puffed cheeks. "I can't lie to you—we'll really be hurting if we don't make it."

"Hurting? What are you doing with the money? I just did a mission—"

"Are you accusing me of stealing?"

"If the boots—"

"Whoa!" Ghost shouted. "Stop. Both of you. Nobody's going there. This business is expensive. Jibril is growing the organization. He's just invested in a stud for breeding."

"Why are we holding it at the hotel? Host it here—"

"It's the middle of August. In Central Texas. Want to offer ice-cube baths with their champagne?"

"We're serving champagne?"

Khat huffed. "It was a figure of speech."

"I say dump the hotel and liquor—"

"The hotel has been donated by—"

"Hogan," Ghost snapped. He looked down then at Timbrel. "She doesn't have to justify every decision to you. Trust her to get the job done. She didn't go over to A-stan with you and Beowulf, second-guessing your every move. That new harness, that new vest you got for Beo—that's Khat working her backside off to get the best at the lowest prices. Get over yourself."

Timbrel swallowed the baseball-sized lump of humble pie.

Khaterah sighed. "A lot happened in the month you were gone. Vet bills—"

"You're the vet!"

"Yes," Khat hissed. "But I am not a specialist. One of the donated dogs got hurt."

Timbrel's heart and head thudded. What was she doing? *Shut up and sit down.*

Khaterah sighed again. "I'm interviewing for a kennel master and. . ." She shook her head.

"So we still need a lot," Ghost said.

"Yes," Khaterah said. "I've spent the day sending out invitations, e-mailing others, and phoning."

"Oh, speaking of phone lists. . ." Ghost tugged a folded paper from his back pocket. "Darci gave me this. She said this list should prove lucrative and to use her name when calling."

Leave it to Heath's spy wife to have connections that would be lucrative.

"Brilliant!" Khat had cornered the market on gorgeous. Those exotic features and the fiery personality, a brother who cared, parents who loved them. . . Khat loved animals, devoted her life to taking care of them, giving back. She deserved to be loved and loved completely.

So, why hadn't a guy tripped over his tongue regarding her? Why didn't she have a man like Candyman pounding down her door? Khaterah deserved that.

I don't.

"I'm heading out. Hogan, do something productive." Ghost gave her a warning look. "Khat, thanks for your hard work."

Draped in heat and silence, the room seemed to throb. Timbrel tugged a sheet closer and aimed her gaze at it with the pretense of studying it.

"So what happened over there?"

Timbrel flinched. "What?"

Khat's laugh proved hollow. "While you and I haven't exactly been BFFs"—she hooked her fingers in air quotes—"you've never treated me like. . .this. You're very agitated, more so than normal."

Was she that obvious? Candyman had yanked her chain. Called her number. "Nothing." Her gaze leapfrogged over the gala-planning pages, yet she saw nothing but her own humiliation.

"Timbrel." Soft and pliable, Khaterah's chiding tone also exuded warmth and caring.

Hard to breathe. Hard to function. "Look, I'm sorry I bit your head off. You don't deserve that, and I was wrong to do it." Timbrel shoved the chair back and stood.

A firm but gentle hand on her arms stilled her.

Timbrel froze. Felt the morbid drill of panic boring holes in her steel-reinforced cage that kept her from drowning in life.

"He called."

Her heart crashed into her ribs, her gaze pulled by some unseen force to Khaterah. "He did?" Why were her eyes burning?

"He thought he might have the wrong phone number for you. Said you hadn't called him back."

She swallowed the gush of adrenaline. When she sensed Khaterah step closer, Timbrel turned away. "I. . .I think I'll. . .take some names to call." She scrunched a paper between her fingers.

Khat's hand covered hers. "What happened?"

Timbrel shoved the emotion, the fright, the embarrassment over the cliff of denial. She mustered the smile her mother had perfected and taught her. "I'm not sure what you're talking about." She strode from the room. "I'll make some calls."

"Timbrel."

She stopped cold.

"Ghost told me not to tell you, but I think you should know."

Okay, that didn't sound good. She slowly looked over her shoulder.

"I did not want you to think I was mishandling the money or accounts here. I am very dedicated and loyal to my brother, but also to you handlers. For that reason, I think you should know."

"What?"

"We had a benefactor for the hotel."

"Right. You'd said it was do. . .nate. . .ed." Oh curse her foolish brain! Why hadn't she thought of it before? She swung her head side to side, pained. "Please. Tell me you didn't. . ."

"It was an accident. Elysian Evangelos Industries is known for donations, so I called and talked to the chairman of the board of directors, who agreed to cover the cost of the hotel and a sizeable donation."

Timbrel groaned.

"I promise, I had no idea she was your mother!"

Leesburg, Virginia

Tony dropped the rucksack by the washer and dryer, then eased the back door closed. He stepped through the mudroom. In the gourmet kitchen, he spotted his mother at the Viking stove, stirring a pot. From behind, in a T-shirt and capris, she could easily be taken for a twentysomething.

He slipped up behind her and covered her eyes. "Guess who?"

"Oh!" She yelped and jerked around. "Tony, you're home!" She threw her arms around him and hugged him tight.

Wrapping her in his arms, he held on. Man, there was nothing like a "mom" hug, no matter how old he got. And it seemed every mission that kept him away made her hugs all the sweeter.

She pulled back and rested her hands on his shoulders. "Why didn't you call? I could've picked you up."

"Eh, I knew you were busy." He took in the nearly pristine granite countertops and cherrywood cabinets. Not a thing out of place. He'd never forget her face that day. "Still enjoying your kitchen?"

"Immensely." She planted a kiss on his cheek. "I still can't believe you did this. It's too much."

"No such thing as 'too much' for you." He'd surprised her for her sixtieth birthday with the complete kitchen remodel, done just as she'd always dreamed.

Her manicured nails scratched over his beard. "All these years, and I still don't like the fuzz."

He groaned. "Not you, too." At the fridge, he tugged it open and scanned the contents before choosing a pitcher of sweet tea and pouring himself a glass.

"Oh? Who else commented on your beard?"

"My CO and Timbrel."

Her eyebrow arched.

"What?"

"Nothing, just. . .she keeps popping up in your conversations."

"So? Is that unusual?"

"Yes, actually, it is."

He grinned as he lifted the drink and held her gaze. "How are things?"

Her smile flickered, but true to her nature, Irene VanAllen remained composed. "Fine. Not much has changed."

Tony dumped a big mouthful back—then gagged. Spit it in the sink. "What is this?"

Mischief sparked in her eyes. "Tea."

"No, this isn't tea. This is some kind of nasty."

She laughed. "It's not sweetened."

"Why would you do that—*not* do that? Are you trying to kill me?"

"Because I'm watching blood sugars for your father."

Tony hauled himself back in line. "Oh." He should've been paying attention—she'd said not much had changed, but how many little things like this had changed? "Where is he?"

"Sleeping." The vibrancy washed out of her, and it seemed she had aged years in those seconds. But then it changed again. She snapped the towel at him. "As much as I love my son, he smells like a jungle and looks like one. Go on with you. Get showered and changed. I'll call Stephanie and text Grady to let them know you're home."

"Don't bother with Grady," Tony said as headed down the hall. "He won't come."

"Doesn't mean he shouldn't be invited."

"Maybe it does," he called as he plopped on the bed. He shed his boots, yanked off his shirt, and tossed it in the laundry bin. Armed with a pair of jeans and a shirt, he headed to the shower.

Fifteen minutes later, wrapped in a towel, he stood before the mirror and wiped away the condensation.

So. Beard. He ran his hand over it, his stomach tight. This would hurt, in more ways than one. Using scissors, he cut the beard down then used his razor to remove the rest. Rinsing his razor, he caught his reflection. . .and hesitated.

She'd better like this. He'd spent the last five years with that wiry mess for added camo in protecting his identity. Now he'd have to grow it back out. And those first few weeks of fuzzies drove him nuts.

Tony donned his jeans, snatched his shirt, and emerged from the room. Heading back to the kitchen, he heard voices. Children's voices! He quickened his pace.

"Uncle Tony!" Bright blue eyes went wide as four-year-old Hayden lunged.

He caught his nephew and, in a fluid move, flipped him up and over his shoulder with a shout. "How's my buddy?"

Hayden climbed onto his shoulders like a monkey. "Great! Mom, look how tall I am."

His sister, Stephanie, smiled. "So I see."

Tony inched over, shirt clutched in his hand, and kissed his sister. "Hey." He flipped her blond hair, the front much longer than the back. "Nice cut."

"You don't like it?"

"It's short."

"It's easier to manage with two children."

"It's short," he said again. A tug at his jeans alerted him to his niece and he tossed aside his shirt. "Marlee!" He lifted her into his arms, careful to keep Hayden balanced. "How's my little angel?"

"Did you get me a necklace?" Marlee asked.

"Yes, I did." He'd nearly forgotten. "Okay, deploy, soldiers." He knelt and waited for them both to scramble off him. "I'll be right back bearing gifts." Their cheers sent him jogging toward the laundry room, where he retrieved the items from his rucksack. Now. . .which one was Marlee's? The smaller was the necklace, right? He rounded the corner, eyeballing the simple brown paper.

A blur came from the side. A hand swung at him.

Instincts flared.

Tony arched his spine backward, narrowly missing a collision with the experienced fist.

Dad!

"James, no!" his mother cried out.

"What's Grandpa doing?"

"Get them out of here," Tony shouted as he deflected another punch.

"James, please," his mom said as Steph hurried the children to the living room. "It's Tony!"

Heart in his throat, Tony responded to the attack. Cursed what happened to his dad. Cursed the way his father had been tossed aside, written off. The accident made everything worse.

"Dad, it's me." Tony kept his moves smooth, fluid. Nothing aggressive. Nothing that would make his dad feel any more threatened than he already did. That state of mind threw his father back to 'Nam, to confidential conflicts in the years thereafter that his father wasn't allowed to talk about. Conflicts that shattered his mind.

"Don't give me any of your lies! You killed my team!"

"Dad, I'm Tony. Your son." Don't know why he said it. The dialogue never made a difference. It had in the early days, but not anymore.

"Get away from me, you piece of—"

"James!"

The fist came at him again. Adrenaline and grief strangled Tony. But it wasn't time to think about it. Knew what he had to do.

Tony stepped in. Caught his father's fingers. Locked his grip. Pushed down, bending the wrist backward. His other hand went to his father's shoulder, giving him the needed leverage. He swung the arm up and pinned it behind his father's back, then he used his free hand to turn his father's head away, thereby blocking any punches and gaining control. He pressed his thumb into the carotid, blocking the flow of blood to the brain.

Four seconds later, his father went limp.

Tony caught him. Held him the way he would a child. Slid along the wall to the floor, cradling his unconscious dad in his arms. Tears begged to be freed. Anger resisted. Frustration pushed them out. *Oh, Dad. . .* He touched his father's cheek. Stubbled but shaven. The scar along his cheekbone, the only evidence of what had happened. The only proof that something changed his father.

Tony held him close, burying his face against his father's cheek. *Dad. . . God! Why?*

"Let me give him the sedative. Then hurry him to the bedroom, won't you?" His mother knelt beside him and slid the needle into the meaty part of his father's thigh. "Before the children see him again."

"He didn't know me."

Her brown eyes held his. "You weren't expected. I didn't have time to try to prepare him." She sniffled. "Though I'm not sure that matters anymore."

Tony frowned, the tears drying on his cheek but not in his heart. "Is it that bad, Mom? Has he gotten that bad?"

Her tears slipped free. "Worse."

Pushing himself up, careful not to bang his father's head or legs, Tony tried to pick up the pieces of his heart, too. His mom guided him through the house and into the room they'd converted for his father. Tony knelt and gently laid his father on the bed.

Mom went to work, covering him with the blanket and checking his pulse. "He'll only be out a short while. Hopefully, when he wakes, he won't still be in his fight-or-flight mode."

There was nothing like staring down at the man he'd just had to incapacitate, knowing he'd been a hero, earned a Purple Heart, several Bronze Stars. . . And yet there were days James VanAllen had no idea what planet he was on.

Tony's confliction went deep. He'd gone into the Army to be like his father. And he lived with the terror every day of knowing one wrong incident and he could be just like him.

I'd eat a bullet before I became a burden.

Eight

Steam rose from the mug he cradled between both hands, forearms propped on his knees as Tony sat on the back patio, staring at the trees. He took a sip and cringed at the stinging the hot liquid created against his split lip.

Steps sounded from the right and he turned. Came to his feet. "Grady."

His big brother, who was shorter by four inches and heftier by twenty pounds, stalked toward him. His gaze struck Tony's lip, sporting the telltale evidence of having to subdue their father, then lowered. "We weren't expecting you for a couple of weeks."

Tony nodded as he returned to his cushioned seat. "Change of plans."

"Mom told me what happened."

Tony stared into his coffee.

"I'm sorry."

He slurped some of the hot liquid, careful to avoid his injury, and swallowed. "Nobody's fault."

Grady rubbed his long, thin hands together. "I feel like it's mine. He's getting more unpredictable. I just can't seem to talk Mom into putting him into managed care."

"Give her time." Tony hated this conversation.

"Another stint like that—I mean, what if he went after Mom like that? She doesn't have your training. He'd have killed her."

He swirled his coffee. Grady seemed overly eager to put their father away. But even now, Tony had to admit his brother was right. "I'll put in for an extended leave." He threw back the rest of the brew and savored the heat of it searing his esophagus. "We'll get him moved then."

He didn't like it. Didn't like the idea of relegating his father to a soldier's home, of abandoning the man who'd given everything he had, including

761

his mind, to fight for his country. Putting him away felt like the ultimate betrayal of one of the nation's finest.

"When's that, Jimmy?"

The only time his brother used that name card was when he wanted the upper hand. "As soon as I can."

"Mom said you have a girlfriend."

Tony smirked and let out a breathy laugh. "Mom wants me married. She thinks that will tame me."

"Will it?"

Tony eyed his brother. "Don't go there, Grady. Not today. Not this time."

"Look, you know I think—"

"Yes." Tony stomped to his feet. "I do know. But I joined, it's who I am. And quite honestly, I'm pretty dang good at what I do. It's an honor to serve."

"You mean, to escape *this*. To escape watching Dad fall apart."

"Escape? Grady, I was here the first time he went haywire. The last two years of high school were spent wondering when I walked through the door after football practice, if Dad would be here or in wherever he was when things went bad." He stabbed a finger at his lip. "Serving in the Special Forces doesn't mean I'm escaping."

"No, you just went from one hell to another."

Tony laughed, despite his frustration. His brother had a valid point. "It sure ain't heaven." Unless one counted meeting certain beautiful dog handlers.

"What's her name, the girl you mentioned to Mom?"

Another laugh escaped as he let his eyes close. "Timbrel." Or should he say Audrey? No. . .no, he didn't want to arm his brother with that information, that he'd taken a shining to the daughter of a Hollywood socialite.

"How'd you meet her? Or can't you tell me?"

"She's a dog handler."

"So, she's military, too?"

"No, not anymore."

"When do we get to meet her?"

That's where it hurt. "Probably never." He looked at Grady, at the brother who was his opposite in so many ways, right down to the black hair and brown eyes. "She stood me up. We had a great night then she bolted."

"Sounds just like your type."

Tony frowned at his brother.

Grady laughed. "Sorry. I just meant she's a challenge. That's your type."

"She's wounded."

"No surprise there."

"Don't." Tony scowled. Though he could take Grady's antimilitary talk when it came to himself, Tony wouldn't tolerate his talking about Timbrel that way. "Don't do that. Keep your poison to yourself."

Stomping her foot on the vinyl floor, Timbrel gritted her teeth. "Okay." She banged her foot against the cabinet. "Bye." She jammed her thumb against the END button and threw her phone on the counter. Holding the edges, she kicked the cabinet again.

Clicking nails alerted her to Beo's entrance into her tiny kitchen.

Bent, she clawed her fingers through her hair and balled her hands into fists. Elbows on the Formica, she resisted the urge to scream. This was just like her mom. Nina Laurens knew exactly the organization she'd donated to. She was inserting herself into Timbrel's life once again.

No. Not again. Not this time. Handling was one thing her mom hadn't been able to touch or contaminate. Timbrel sure wasn't going to let her start now. She snatched her phone and hit the AUTODIAL.

"Hello, darling."

The Indy 500 had nothing on the rate of Timbrel's pulse. "I want you to back out of the fund-raiser."

"Which one, sweetie? There are—"

"You know exactly which one." The growl in her voice matched the one Beo threw at squirrels scampering up the tree outside her tiny cottage.

"Ah." Her mom's voice dipped. "That one. Well, I'm sorry—it's not possible."

"It is possible. You find a way to do it. I don't want you in this. I don't want you meddling in my life." Timbrel's lungs struggled to expand.

"Think past yourself for once, Audrey." The first edge of frustration bled into her mother's voice.

"Timbrel."

"Listen, darling, I've got to run. But if you want to talk about this, then come to dinner Friday night at seven."

"No."

"I am willing to hear you out, hear your reasons for asking me to go back on my word, but you have to do it here, to my face, in my house. If not, then my answer is the same—no."

"Mom, just—please. Stay out of this."

"Gotta run. Dinner. Adios!"

Dead silence rang in Timbrel's ear. She turned and flung her phone across the room. It hit the wall and dropped. Pieces splintered and spun across her floor.

Timbrel dropped her head into her hands again and groaned. "Why won't she just stay out of my life?" She slid along the cabinets onto the floor.

A soft nudge at her arm made her grunt.

"Beo, stop." She wrapped her arms around her knees and rested her forehead on a knee.

Another nudge.

Timbrel ignored him.

Beo charged in, shoving his head beneath her arm, then lifting it, forcing her to let him in. Timbrel laughed as he swiped a drool-laden tongue along her face. "All right, you big bully."

Another slop.

Timbrel laughed again.

Another. Timbrel pushed back.

He pushed into her, effectively pinning her as he went to town, slathering her with kisses. Trying to shield herself against his uncanny ability to lick her when her mouth was open, Timbrel wrapped her arms around his broad chest. "Okay, okay. I give!"

He slumped against her, panting. Completely pleased with himself.

She smoothed a hand along his skull. "Thank you." Planted a kiss there. He always knew how to make her feel better. Cheek against his head, she sighed and petted him. "What am I going to do?"

She'd left LA, left her mother to get away. To have a life—her *own* life. A real life. To be. . .safe. But every time she turned around, her mother somehow managed to inject herself. Timbrel's becoming a handler was something her mom couldn't touch, couldn't understand, since she hated dogs. To have her now dropping zeroes in the bank account of A Breed Apart—her mom was being the diva once again.

Timbrel pushed Beo off her lap. Grabbed her phone, reassembled it, cringing at the broken plastic on the corner. She powered it up. . .and waited. Had she broken another phone? She snatched her keys from the counter and whistled. "C'mon, boy. Let's go for a ride."

If she couldn't convince Khat, maybe Jibril would listen. Or maybe Heath. He was usually at the training yard at this time of day. The forty-minute drive out to the ranch gave her time to formulate her plan. Because the last thing she would do was ask her mom. Showing up for dinner wasn't just dinner. It'd be a social event with at least thirty "close friends." Not family, because Nina Laurens didn't have family. Both parents dead, husband—well, which of her five ex-husbands did one invite?—and her siblings wouldn't speak to her. Surprise. Surprise.

Timbrel cleared the security gate, and her Jeep bounded down the road toward the house. As she broke through the trees into the clearing, she nailed her brakes. What on earth?

A half-dozen cars crowded the makeshift parking area.

She pulled up to the main house and parked. Climbing out, she searched the training yard. She could hear voices but couldn't see who was down there. No worries. She'd just talk to Jibril and hope for the best.

She knocked on the door and entered. "Hello?"

The conference room door near the back opened. Aspen appeared, surprise etching her pretty face. "Timmy? What are you doing here?"

"Looking for Jibril. Or Heath." She pointed in the direction of the parking lot. "What's with all the cars?"

"General Burnett is here talking with potential handlers."

"Burnett?" Why did her stomach squeeze tight and bring to mind a pair of green eyes belonging to a Special Forces soldier?

Heath appeared behind her. "Asp—oh. Hey, Timbrel."

"Heath," Timbrel said as she started toward him, "I need to talk to you."

"Yeah, sure. But it'll have to be later." He turned to Aspen. "He wants the files."

"Right. Excuse me." Aspen hurried toward the office.

"Hogan, that you?"

At the general's booming voice, Timbrel smirked. "Probably wants to chew me out again."

"It's his way of showing affection."

Timbrel laughed as she stepped forward with Beo at her heels. She entered the conference room. A quick look delivered four recruits sitting around the table. A Hispanic male, a blond, and a brown-haired soldier, both in camo, and a woman with nearly white hair. Timbrel then locked on to her target. Familiar blue eyes, framed by salt-and-pepper hair, smiled at her.

"Hello, General."

"That's a lot more civil than last time."

"Likewise."

He guffawed. Wiping his eyes with his thumbs, he pointed to the corner. "You remember this guy, don't you?"

Timbrel checked over her shoulder as a large shape rose over her.

Beo growled.

Giving him the signal to heel, Timbrel shrugged—the man was gorgeous! Mussed sandy blond hair. Clean shaven. A straight nose, defined jaw. Built well, in shape—but no, she'd *know* if she'd met him before. The eyes.

"Sorry. . .I don't—"

A hand to his jaw, the man rubbed his face, as if that should mean something. Green eyes telegraphed some strange message, and his eyebrows bounced as if to say, "See?"

The eyes. She knew those eyes!

The little things that pinged at the back of her mind collided. His build. His smirk. The way he moved his hand over his face. Beard. . .less.

"What are you doing here?"

The chemistry between the two was undeniable. And unforgivable. Lance couldn't afford to lose Hogan or VanAllen on the upcoming mission. So they needed to get over whatever had happened.

"I'm working."

"Working whom?"

"Hey," VanAllen said with a little too much cheek, "I'm not the one who kissed and ran."

"Easy, you two. The rest of you, take a break. Back here in ten." Lance lowered himself to the chair. "Hogan, I hear you're giving Khat trouble about the donors."

"No, not about donors. About *a* donor."

Lance slumped back against the chair. "Nina Laurens."

Lips tight, Timbrel darted a look at VanAllen but gave a sharp nod at the same time. "I'd rather not discuss this here, sir."

"Well, too bad. And don't worry about VanAllen. He's got more clearance than you. Besides, he already knows about Nina."

Timbrel's facade shattered like a glass pane. In each sliver, he saw pieces of a broken childhood and upbringing, all mixing into a massive ball of insecurity and uncertainty.

"Listen, Hogan. I'm sorry for the way things are between you and your mom, but your demands, your little fit here, are making things worse. Just leave it alone. While I am utilizing this organization, I cannot keep you fully funded. Khouri needs the money."

"It's not a *fit*, sir," she spat out. "And how could I make it worse on them? They're getting their money."

"Not on them." Burnett tugged his wire-rimmed glasses from his face. Man he hated the readers, but getting old did that to a fella. "On yourself. Nina called about an hour ago. She'll give the other half of the donation. . ."

She looked like she was about to hurl. "But?"

"But you have to retrieve it."

Nine

Can't you do something about her?"

Tony saw the angst in Timbrel's face, the borderline panic lurking beneath her frustration. Even in shorts and a T-shirt, she made a formidable impression.

General Burnett laughed. "What am I supposed to do about a movie star? I'm not a superhero." He tossed his Dr Pepper can in the trash. "A woman like her has more power than me, I think."

"Look," Timbrel said, leaning across the table, "you know that woman is just yanking my chain."

"Yes, I'm afraid I do, but that doesn't mean I can stop her."

"Is it so bad?" Tony put in, curious about the mother-daughter hatred. "To just go get the check from her?"

"Yes, it's bad," Timbrel hissed at him. "This isn't some quaint little family dinner. She wants me there Friday night."

Tony looked to the general, who shrugged.

"She has a social every Friday night with close friends—a hundred *close* friends. It's not dinner, it's an event."

Tony shrugged. "It's one night."

Timbrel jerked away.

"One night," Tony repeated, "and ABA is set up for the rest of the year."

"It's not just one night!" Timbrel shouted. "Forget it." With that, she snapped her fingers and Beowulf was at her side as she left the room.

"Timbrel," Tony said as he followed her.

The dog swung around, snarling.

"Timbrel, wait."

She didn't. Instead, she stomped out the front door with her hound right on her heels.

768

"What's she mad about this time?" Ghost Daniels asked.

Tony looked at him and snorted. "Her mom."

"You brought up her mom and she left you alive?"

Tony eyed him.

"Sorry. A little sarcasm, but not much. Her mom is a nuclear area for her."

"What happened?"

Ghost bounced his shoulders. "Nobody knows. She won't talk about it."

"Any way around taking that money?"

"Afraid not," Ghost said as he headed back to the conference room. "We're already behind, and if we don't get her donation, we may not survive the next year in operation."

"But you're taking on new handlers." Tony nodded to the others milling around the living room.

"Contingent upon that money from Elysian—Nina's company." Ghost paused in the doorway. "What's the story with you and Timbrel?"

"No story, in case you didn't just see that arctic blast she threw my way."

"That's not what Aspen told me. She said you two seemed to hit it off in Djibouti."

Tony laughed, not surprised that Talon's handler would've said that. "She also warned me I might as well play with fire."

"Less painful."

Tony nodded.

"But. . .?"

Tony considered Ghost. They'd worked together once. Until Ghost went down in an op gone bad. "I can't stop thinking about her. When she yells at me, I hear the hurt that's making her feel threatened. I don't see a bitter, angry woman. I see a raw, hurting, beautiful, incredible woman."

"Is this a mission for you, soldier?"

"Mission?"

"Are you trying to fix her?"

Tony frowned.

"Because if you are, it'll backfire. I promise."

"I just want a chance."

"What if she never gives it?"

Tony looked at Ghost, sandy blond hair trimmed short, dressed in a black shirt and black jeans. "I know what you're trying to do."

"Which is?"

"Same thing Aspen did—trying to get me to see the futility."

"No, I'm trying to make you understand that Timbrel won't give you that chance. She's been hurt. You pose a threat. She's had enough training through hard life experiences to know not to let anyone in, that even if she wants to, she can't take that risk. So like I said, Timbrel won't give you the chance you want."

Jaw set, Tony refused to back down. "Then I'll take it."

"Take it, how?" Ghost scowled. "You hurt her and I'll—"

"No, I mean. . . Listen, I've got a dad at home who doesn't recognize me half the time. I work some of the most dangerous missions in some of the darkest places on earth. I don't scare easily. I'll do what I do in the field with the candy bars, gaining the trust of the people."

"You're going to give her candy bars?"

Tony grinned. "I'm going to make her life sweet."

How? How did her mom always get her way?

Timbrel swatted the bag-draped dresses at the back of her small closet. She stepped back and dropped on the bed then threw herself backward. "Augh! Give me jeans, a T-shirt, and hiking boots any day!" Not the glitz and glamour that defined her mother's life and friends. Fake, artificial people that they were.

The twangy roar of a sport bike raced down the street, the sound hesitating, it seemed, in front of her home. Pulling off the mattress, she muttered, "Who. . .?"

A low rumble trilled through Beo's throat and chest as he hopped off the bed and trotted out of the room.

Timbrel peered down the hall and through the front window curtain. A rider in a black leather jacket and silver helmet turned a circle in front of the house then backed in against the curb. He set the stand and dismounted.

Pinpricks of dread filtered through her for a couple of reasons: One— she'd left the door open during the rain, and now the screen provided the only protection against her boy. Two—she'd *never* let anyone into her private space. She'd done that once before. . .

"Beo, easy," Timbrel said as he stood guard at the screen door. "Do we know someone who owns a bike?" Halfway down the hall, she paused as the rider swung his helmeted head toward the house.

Maybe once he took that shiny dome off, she'd recognize him. He had a big build, but. . .

The rider shed his helmet and ruffled his hair and turned toward the house.

Beowulf's growl increased.

"Candyman," she whispered. The shock that registered at A Breed Apart when she realized who the gorgeous man was in jeans and a black T-shirt. . .the concussive boom from that moment vibrated through her again.

But she didn't want him here. Didn't want him in her life.

That's a lie.

She did want him. Did want to experiment, see if they could stay alive beyond one date, but she'd played Russian roulette once before.

When Candyman started for the four-foot fence that encompassed her front yard, Timbrel noticed the hook on the door dangling free. "No!"

Beowulf bolted.

The screen's wood frame hit the wall with a loud crack. Beo's "out" command lodged in her throat.

Candyman reacted, his face ashen as he spotted her bullmastiff charging him. "Timbrel!" Scrambling, he threw himself back.

It wasn't funny. It really wasn't, but she couldn't stop laughing.

He launched over the fence.

The chain-link ensnared his pant leg. He tipped over and down, thudding against the cracked cement sidewalk. "Timbrel! Call him off!"

He looked like a slab of beef hanging on a hook. Arms on the sidewalk, he supported himself. Kicked at the fence.

Beowulf snapped.

Candyman kicked again. "Get back. Timbrel," he called, a warning growl in his tone.

Beowulf went up on his hind legs, chomping at Tony's boots.

"I swear, if he—" Finally freed, he swung his leg away and vaulted to his feet. Legs apart, he drew his fists. Probably would've drawn a gun if he'd had it on him. And yet, he didn't move.

Neither did Beo.

"My dog knows his boundaries. Beo, sit." As her dog complied, sitting right in front of the fence with his "stiff-upper-lip" snout giving him a *hmph!* look, Timbrel folded her arms over her chest. She snickered at the way Beo acted all gangsta. "You don't."

He looked up at her. "Timbrel, call him off."

"What do you want?" She'd stood him up. Flown away without a word. Then seeing him at the ranch. . .

Unzipping his safety jacket with one hand, he spread his other hand. "What do you think? To see you."

He'd come all the way out here? Which, come to think of it— "How'd you find me?"

Mr. GorgeousCockyGreenBeret shrugged. "Just asked everyone where the meanest, ugliest dog lived."

"But wouldn't that lead you home?"

"You didn't seem to think I was ugly back at Bagram."

Tanned, toned legs stretched in the morning sunlight, one on the porch step above. Ready to bolt again. In shorts and a tank top, she seemed far less intimidating and much more. . .sexy. The woman had him wrapped around that cat-o'-nine-tails heart of hers. Chasing a parked rig would be easier and less painful than the pursuit of the woman standing on her porch. And right now those eyes, her guarded expression, and that look that could eat the lunch of lesser men, shouted her warning that she'd take down anyone who dared to enter her sanctuary.

"I couldn't see your true colors there." She jutted her chin toward him. "You've shaved since then."

He'd seen the shock when she realized who he was. He'd gotten a little nervous, wondering if she suffered some form of PTSD like his father when she didn't recognize him. But when that grit zapped back into her posture, he knew the game was on again.

"I wasn't sure you'd notice," he said with a half smile as he reached for the gate latch.

Gnashing teeth nearly took off his fingers. Tony pushed his gaze to Timbrel. "Call him off." She was as much a tough mama as the last time he'd seen her. "Please?"

Without a word, she started up the steps. He heard two snaps.

Beowulf's attack mode morphed into just plain ugly. The monstrous-sized dog gave another growl, then trotted up. Tony made his way across the path and up the three wooden steps.

He stood over Timbrel as she opened the door. Held her gaze. "Good to see you, Hogan."

Her cheeks brightened. Score!

"Do you want me to release my dog to chase you back to your bike, or are you coming in?"

He smiled and entered the cramped cottage. Scanning his surroundings, he stilled. Never would he have guessed this place belonged to Timbrel Hogan. Immaculate. Like it was right out of a brochure. "This is your place?"

She scowled. "Yeah. Why?"

Tony set down his helmet, gloves, and safety jacket on an overstuffed chair. "Just didn't imagine your place like this."

Timbrel went into the kitchen and stood behind the counter. "What did you expect?"

Was it his imagination or was she taking up position to defend herself? He'd already put her on edge. Good. That's what she got for standing him up.

"Guess something simpler, less. . .crowded."

"The cottage came furnished."

"Ah." He gave another sweep of the room. A short hall dumped into a bedroom, the door wide open. There, he spied a low platform bed, a simple white down comforter, and green walls. "Now that—that's you, right? You decorated the bedroom."

Timbrel stomped down the hall, pulled the door shut, and turned to him, arms folded. "Why are you here?"

"Thought we should talk."

Her left eyebrow winged up. "Talk. You haven't heard of the phone?"

"Funny you should mention that." He rubbed his jaw. So weird not to have the beard. "You know the number that keeps showing up on your caller ID at least once every other day? Yeah, that's me trying to call you." He gave a shrug and held up his hands as he walked the house, pretending to size up her digs. But each step was strategic, putting him in closer proximity to her. "So I thought I'd try face-to-face."

"Didn't think you'd be this dense." The words didn't have the bite they normally had. "Me not answering is me not wanting to talk to you."

He strolled around the island and came to her side. Waited for her to look up at him. Man, she was beautiful. Brown eyes with flecks of green and gold. And right now, those eyes were singing a whole different song than what made it past her windpipe. "I don't think so."

She huffed and turned away, wandering toward the kitchenette, where she grabbed the finial that poked up from one of the chairs. "What do you know about me?"

"Not enough." Tony leaned back against the Formica counter, crossed his ankles, and tucked his hands under his armpits. "I'd like to remedy that."

"Forget it."

"To quote one of my favorite movies, 'You keep using that word. I do not think it means what you think it means.'"

Timbrel tried to hide her smile but it cracked. *Princess Bride.*

He inclined his head. "You're a fan?"

She looked down, her hands twisting the wood as if a towel she wanted to wring. " 'Miners, not minors.'"

Shock rippled through him. "*Galaxy Quest*? You're quoting *Galaxy Quest*?" Tony laughed and placed a hand over his left pec. "Be still my beating heart—a girl who watches sci-fi."

Timbrel laughed and eased into the chair. She now worried one of the fabric napkins set out and waiting for guests who probably never came. Timbrel was too guarded and isolated to entertain. The napkins, like the house, were another element for the "got it together" facade.

She tugged the elastic from her ponytail and let her hair fall, digging her fingernails into her scalp.

Tony joined her at the table. "Hey, you okay?"

She lifted her face and he saw her torment.

"Your mom?"

She sagged. "She wins. Every time, she gets her way."

"This about the money she's giving ABA?"

A solemn nod. "The only reason she's donating is to wiggle her way into my life."

Elbow on the table, he sat sideways in the chair. "I'm not playing with all the pieces, so help me understand what's so bad about her giving money to the organization."

Her face twisted. "I don't even know why I'm talking to you about this." She rolled out of the chair and moved back to the kitchen island. To her barrier.

"Timbrel, listen—I am *not* defending her. I'm trying to understand. I don't know the whole story." He closed the distance.

"This is her way of controlling me, of keeping me under her thumb. I've been her little puppet, her little doll since I was born. An adornment to make her look good. This isn't about her doing something good. This is about her trying to insert herself into my world, and make herself look good doing it." Timbrel let out a growl-shriek. "I am *so* sick of it. I won't play her games anymore. There is no way I'm going out there again and—"

"Out where?"

"LA." She rounded to the other side. "LA ruined me. . ."

Tony held up a hand. "Timbrel, stop moving."

She looked at him with a frown. "What?"

"Do you see what you're doing?" He indicated to the island, the space between them. "Are you doing it on purpose?"

Innocence wreathed her face. "Doing what?"

He rapped his knuckles against the Formica. "Using this as a barrier to keep me away."

"No." Her gaze dropped to the cream surface. Her pretty brown eyes came back to him. "Yes."

He tilted his head.

"I mean—yes, that's what I'm doing." She seemed to be searching for something, her gaze skittering around the kitchen, then came back to him. "But it wasn't on purpose."

Whoa. This was a whole lot of honesty, especially for Timbrel. "I'm not a threat. Hurting you is the last thing I want to do."

"I know." Her voice was small, the realization apparently dawning on her at the same time she spoke.

Heady admission. It unnerved even him. All this time chasing her, and she was here, being open, honest. Wouldn't last long. Better to leap back before she slammed the door again. "Okay, back to your mom."

Timbrel groaned.

"Let me go with you."

Lips parted, she stared. "What?"

"Let me go with you to get the check. You said it was a dinner, right?"

"Candyman, listen—"

"Tony. I want you to call me Tony."

"This isn't dinner like you and I might go out—"

"Which we will, right?"

"This is a fancy event. Dresses, suits."

Okay, now it was his turn to blanch. "Suit?"

"Yeah." She swept her hair from her face. "So, it was a sweet offer, but—"

"I'm in."

Disbelief rushed through her expression.

"Hey," he said with a shrug, "I dress up in a beard, keffiyeh, and smelly gear for terrorists, why not a suit and goop for your mom?"

"Because the moment she sets eyes on your gorgeous self, she's going to go all cougar on you."

Tony grinned. "You think I'm gorgeous? Does that mean you're going to fight her for me?"

"More like throw you to the wolves—or in this case, the cougar."

"That's mean." Tony winked at her. "But for you, I'm in. I'll just tell her we're dating." He walked around behind her. In her ear, he breathed, "Intimately."

Nubuwwa—
Prophethood

Last Year

Ten long years he'd been fighting,. working, toiling to find a way to stop the infidels. To prevent the influence of the West upon the people of Islam. Time and again he'd come close. But failed.

Why, Allah? Why have you set me to failure? The scripture that came to mind gave him no peace: *"Allah does what He wills."*

He slammed his fist against the edge of the sofa then held it against his forehead.

A quiet presence tugged at his mind, and he turned to the side. Dehqan stood, hands behind his back. He'd grown a lot the last two years.

"What can I do for you, Father?"

He warmed at the endearment Dehqan had adopted of late. Even the way the boy said it and the way his shoulders drew back in pride stirred something deep in him. An empty place he'd not visited in many, many years. Not since Baghdad.

"Come. Tell me of your studies."

Having just turned seventeen, Dehqan had filled out. Strength lurked in his arms, maturity in his young face—as much as could be said of a teenager—and an awareness of the dark forces they warred glimmered in his brown-green eyes. Little remained of the street urchin he'd found almost eight years ago except the unusual iris color.

"They go well enough. I was told that I could apply for a scholarship."

He raised his eyebrow. "Scholarship?"

Dehqan nodded. "For university." There was that hunger he'd seen so early in the boy's eyes.

"What of the army? I've taught you everything so you can follow."

"Yes." Dehqan tucked his chin. "I do not want university. You asked of my studies, and I report what is told to me."

Was it truly humility that brought those words to the air? He was not certain of the boy's motives. He'd learned well how to hide his feelings. Dark and brooding, Dehqan did very well.

"What is it you want, Dehqan?"

Uncertainty flickered through his features many had called handsome. "Sir?"

On his feet, the colonel moved to the gilded desk that sat in a swatch of sunlight. He set down his crystal glass and poured more water into it. "What do you want to do with your future?"

Irfael had suggested arranging a marriage for the boy. It should be done. It was normal. "A wife? A family?" Watching the boy's reaction carefully gave the colonel the answer. "So, is there someone you have set your sight upon?"

Dehqan again studied the marble floor.

"What is her name?"

Then swift as an eagle, Dehqan lifted his chin. "No, sir. I seek no woman."

"Do women not please you?"

His face went red. "They please me quite well." Bashful? Dehqan? It did not seem possible. "Some more than others."

The colonel laughed and clapped his hands once. "I see. Is she pretty?"

Stretching his jaw, Dehqan would not meet his gaze. "I do not speak of one girl. And this is of no consequence. I believe Allah placed me in your capable hands for a purpose."

"And what is that?"

"To train me, to equip me. That I would not be among the lost."

Ah, here they were on the correct path. His chest swelled as he smiled upon the boy who had become his family. "Equip you to what end, Dehqan?"

Dehqan squared his shoulders. "To be a servant of Allah." He frowned. "To avenge those who killed my father and mother."

"Very good. Very good." Squeezing the boy's shoulder, the colonel raised his eyebrows and laughed. "You are already taller than me!"

"Yes, sir."

He laughed. "Irfael thinks you should take a bride."

Eyes wide, mouth open, Dehqan drew back.

Was it fear? Shock? "But I am not convinced the time is right.

You have much to learn and you are young."

A loud rap severed whatever response sat poised on the edge of Dehqan's tongue.

"Enter." The colonel returned to his desk and eased into the chair as the door groaned and issued Irfael into the study. "Ah, we were just speaking of you."

His lieutenant rushed across the richly detailed Persian rug and snapped a salute. "Sir, we've captured al Dossari."

Fire exploded through his gut. "Two years we have chased this snake." He pointed to Dehqan. "We will talk later." Hustling across the room, the colonel followed Irfael into the marbled hall, past the massive pillars, and down the sweeping staircase. "Where did you find him?"

"He and his family were crossing the border into Turkey. They were brought by helicopter to the base and delivered here minutes ago." Irfael rushed around the corner, sunlight chasing him as he took the stairs to the basement.

Allah be praised!

Down another flight of stairs and through a long, anemic cement brick hall, he tried to push back the thrum of excitement. So many months, tracking, tracing. . .

Irfael threw back a steel door and the colonel swept past him.

Huddled in the corner like a pack of rats stood the al Dossari family. Sweat rings darkened the father's shirt. Mussed, matted hair suggested the doctor's head had been covered with a hood. Two boys and a girl hid behind their father. As if that would protect them.

"Altair," he began as he strode toward the foursome, "a man of your character and reputation. . .I would've expected more. But you've condemned your children to death by taking them with you."

"Please, this does not have to happen," Altair al Dossari said. "Try me for my crimes, but my children are innocent."

"Ah." The colonel shoved his hands behind his back and nodded. "A father would, of course, say that to protect the ones he loves. But that is not true."

Fierce fire and light beamed through the man's eyes. "The Qur'an, which you are no doubt familiar with, states that when ones goes astray, he does so to his *own* loss.",

His fist flew. Straight into the man's face. *Crack!*

Altair al Dossari stumbled back and collapsed.

The girl yelped and caught her father, her brothers aiding her.

Blood spurted and dripped down al Dossari's face as the man coughed and grunted. His eyes fluttered.

"Do not quote to me from the holy scriptures when you yourself have abandoned it for the way of the infidels."

"No, not infidels. I have found Truth."

The colonel lifted his Webley and aimed it. Fired.

"No!" al Dossari shouted as he lunged to his fallen son.

"The *truth* you found is that you have waged war against Allah and Islam by bedding with the Great Satan." Huffing, he holstered his weapon and paced. "I will rout those like you who are deceiving innocent minds."

"You have lost your mind," al Dossari cried as he closed his now-dead son's eyes. "Abdul was prepared to lose his life for—"

Knowing where this was going, the colonel drew his weapon again.

Altair shielded his children. "No more! What do you want with me?"

"You are to be made an example of." The colonel dragged a chair to the center of the room then straddled it, staring down at the cowering family. "Your cooperation will buy the lives of your children."

"No," the daughter growled as she turned to her father. "Do not do it. Please. Stay true to God, Father. Do not—"

"Quiet, Nafisa." Al Dossari brushed her long, black hair from her face. "Remember, 'no weapon formed against us. . .' "

She gave a slow nod as if reprimanded.

A bond here could be used.

The colonel eyed Irfael and gave a lone nod.

His lieutenant stomped in and hauled the girl off her father.

She shrieked and screamed.

"Stop this, Colonel!"

"Father!"

"Dispose of her."

The girl spun to her father. "I am at peace, Father. I will die for Him, if I must."

"No, release her!"

Irfael drove her to her knees.

Tears streamed down her face as she looked to her father. "Please, Father. Do not abandon God. He said call to Him in your hour of need—"

"This is why you are doomed, Altair. You have taught your children wicked things."

"The holy scripture," a voice from behind said loud and true, "says, 'the soul certainly incites evil, unless my lord do bestow His mercy.' Also, 'O My servants who have transgressed to your own hurt, despair not of Allah's mercy, for all sins doth Allah forgive. Gracious, Merciful is He.' Surah Az-Zumar 39:53." Dehqan smiled at the colonel.

Rage squeezed through the colonel's chest. "You would suggest this woman deserves mercy?"

With a smirk, Dehqan took two more steps into the room. Casual, calm—an almost deadly calm—lurked in his gaze. "If she deserved it, would it be mercy?"

"Should I kill her?" Irfael asked, his weapon now against her temple.

The girl's eyes pleaded—not with the colonel but with Dehqan.

"No," the colonel said, an idea taking hold. He turned to Dehqan. "You seem a bit taken with the girl."

Dehqan shrugged. "As I said earlier, some more than others."

"I will do what you ask," al Dossari yielded, desperation choking his voice. "Please. Nafisa is a child. She is young."

"Father, be at peace," the girl said.

"Peace is only found in Allah," Dehqan said.

When the other brother lunged, the colonel watched in awe as his son's training took over. He moved to the side, deflected the punch. Came around, and with one well-placed strike, dropped the traitor.

★ ★ Ten ★ ★

Los Angeles, California
Embassy Suites, Glendale

A two-room suite wasn't enough to separate Timbrel from the gnawing dread in her stomach. Candyman—Tony—*whatever*—was here. They'd flown out using the credit card her mother had given her years ago. One she'd used only to pay for the flights back to LA, and since her mom was blackmailing her into coming, she might as well foot the bill for Candyman's ticket, too.

But here, in the hotel, just an hour before the dinner, Timbrel had major reservations. Not just about the slacks and silk top, though they were conservative by all accounts, but facing Candyman in them. And having her mom meet Candyman. Her mom would assume all the wrong things, and he'd made it clear he intended to milk this trip for all it's worth.

But the biggest knot in the dread was walking out of her room and into the adjoining living area—and watching Candyman's reaction.

Oh, curse it all. She had to admit, she wanted to see approval in his eyes.

But she also didn't.

She knew where that could lead. That yearning had gotten her in trouble before.

Candyman—*"Tony. I want you to call me Tony."*—had nailed her about the counter. Even though she hadn't done it on purpose, she felt safer behind it. Which was crazy. She'd never trusted anyone the way she did Candyman. . .Tony.

She wrinkled her nose. He so didn't seem like a Tony.

Thud! Thud!

Timbrel flinched.

Beo barked.

She flung around. "Heel, boy."

He came to her side and licked her hand. Staring down at his big, brown eyes, she sighed and petted him. "Why can't he be like you, Beo?"

"Timbrel," Candyman called from the other side, "it's six twenty."

"Shoot!" Timbrel snatched her black beaded bag from the vanity and drew in a measured breath. She opened the door.

Candyman's eyebrows winged up. "Whoa."

Had her tongue not been dried up by the total package of gorgeousness in a tux standing before her, hair stylishly gooped, as he'd put it, Timbrel would've snapped at him. Instead she found herself appreciating his appearance. Too much. Far too much. The threads of the sleeves seemed to strain against his bulk. In seventy pounds of gear, a do-rag, goggles, ACUs, and a beard, his good looks had truly been camouflaged.

Unabashed, he held his jacket and strutted from side to side. "Not bad, eh?"

Her nerves crashed. He was a very beautiful man, and her mom and every female there tonight would be all over him. "You need to change."

He frowned. "What? Why?"

"You look too good."

He hesitated, holding her gaze. Then a broad smile split his lips. "Yeah?" Insufferable flirt. Did he just puff out his chest?

"And don't smile." Why did she suddenly feel sick to her stomach?

"Why?"

"Because she's a cougar."

Now came a cocky smile that she wanted to punch off his face. "You're jealous."

"I'm not jealous. I—" Timbrel clamped her mouth shut. What was she then? Why did it upset her that her mom would fawn over Candyman? That her mom's girlfriends—and maybe some guy friends—would be all over him, too? Why did it matter? She vowed long ago not to care about another man. To not get involved. "Forget it. Just put on a suit."

With a disbelieving laugh, he shook his head. "You saw my pack. It has exactly one pair of jeans and a T-shirt." He thumbed toward the slick threads he wore. "I rented this, remember?"

Her phone rang. She glanced at the screen. "We're out of time. Limo's here."

"Limo?"

"Don't do that," Timbrel said, a groan working its way up her throat. "It's just a car."

"A really long one."

She shot him a look. "Right."

He offered his arm. "My lady."

"This is the twenty-first century. Not the fifteen hundreds." She stalked to the door and whistled to her dog.

Beowulf trotted across the room and snapped a growl Candyman's way as he came to heel.

"Wait, you're bringing him?"

"Of course."

"Your mom's okay with that?"

Timbrel smiled. "Nope."

His frustration scratched into his face. "Finally, she and I have something in common."

"Another reason to throw you to the cougars." Timbrel locked the door and headed to the elevator. The doors slid open and Timbrel entered with Beo and Candyman on her heels.

A woman in a mink stole and gown recoiled.

"Don't worry. His drool just adds character." Timbrel wanted to laugh at the way the woman's lips slithered like a snake as she drew away, pressing her back into the mirrored walls.

Tony choked back the laugh and nearly made Timbrel give away hers. Thankfully the doors slid open and delivered them into the lobby. Even from the doors, Timbrel spotted the limo and a friendly face.

She hurried out to the one "thing"—the driver—her mom had gotten right. "Hey, Rocky."

The midsixties gentleman smiled as he held the door. "Hello, Miss Audrey. You look beautiful."

Oh, she hadn't really thought about how that name would be used, how Candyman would react to it. Too late to do anything now. She pushed up on her tiptoes and kissed his cheek. "And you still look as handsome as ever."

He chuckled, a blush coloring his ruddy face. "See you brought your beau again."

Beowulf let out a happy bark as he lunged into the car. "Better than American Express."

He laughed. "Never leave home without him."

"I knew you loved me." She bent to step into the car.

"And this gentleman?" His face like granite, Rocky eyed Candyman.

"Oh." Timbrel turned. "This—"

"Tony VanAllen, sir." He stuck out a hand.

Granite softened to putty. *Nice, SexySoldierBoy—putting the driver at ease.* Pleased, no doubt, by the use of the term "sir," Rocky gave a nod. "Mr. VanAllen." He slanted a look at her. "Ms. Nina doesn't know about your. . . *guest.*"

Timbrel gave a lazy shrug. "Last-minute decision." She tucked herself into the car and spotted Beo stretched out over the backseat. Her mind did the math—with the seating capacity, if Beo didn't sit next to her, Tony would. Timbrel wedged in and lifted Beo's head onto her lap.

Tony's bulk blotted the light as he slipped into the darkened interior, eyeballed her and Beo, then sighed as he lowered himself onto the seat, his back to the driver. "I meant what I said."

Scratching Beo's belly, she withheld her gaze. "What's that?"

"I'm no threat to you."

If he only knew. . . He threatened everything. Especially her heart. She smiled at Beo, ignoring the conversation, savoring the minutes that stretched between them.

Tony scooted to the edge of the seat, his hands close. But he apparently didn't plan to let it go.

Beo popped up, snarling.

Candyman glowered.

"Beo, out," Timbrel whispered.

"Timbrel, what's with the space?"

She lowered her head, pretended to adjust something on Beo's collar.

"Look, if I intended to hurt you, if I wanted to. . .*take* something from you, I could—I have the training." He held her gaze. "Do you understand what I'm saying?"

The car slowed and angled up a shrub-lined drive.

Saved once again! "We're here."

At the top a wrought-iron gate forbade entry. Hot and cold traced down her spine as the limo came around the fountain. Breathing grew more difficult with each second.

Candyman whistled. "This is some place."

"Sure is," Timbrel said as the door opened. Rocky held out his hand, and she placed hers in his and climbed from the car.

Timbrel stared at the house. So many memories. So many nightmares. All rolled up into one mansion-sized building. *I swore I'd never come back. . .* Oh man. What was she doing here? This was a mistake. She had to—

"Remember," Tony whispered, his words warm against her ear.

The surprise, the shock of having him so close forced her to draw in a breath. She held it then slowly let it out.

"I've got your six."

His words almost made her giddy. She gave a nod. How could one man exude gorgeous and dangerous so perfectly? In those few words, he'd given her a reassurance nobody else could. Because she knew without a shadow of a doubt that this Green Beret could deliver. Smiling at him was the worst thing she could do. It'd encourage him. But she couldn't stop it. Didn't want to.

"And a flash-bang."

She hesitated. "Seriously?"

He shrugged sheepishly. "In case we need a stealthy exit."

"Audrey, darling!"

As soon as the shrill reception crackled the air, Tony drew back. Watched as Nina Laurens sashayed—*never thought anyone really did that*—down the path toward them. She caught Timbrel's shoulders and pulled her into a hug. Tony prayed she didn't mention meeting him, that she'd have forgotten her offer of seduction back at Bagram. And he'd begged God a thousand times that she hadn't gotten a copy of that picture they took.

A low growl rumbled through the night as Nina dragged Timbrel toward the house.

Tony grinned at Beowulf whose massive jowls tremored with rejection. "Me too, buddy. Me too." Beo licked his chops and growled even louder.

"Oh, Audrey," came words filled with disgust. "Tell me you didn't bring that beast."

"Depends on which one you mean." There was entirely too much amusement in Timbrel's voice, but Tony knew his place. Not moving till her hound of hell went first if he wanted to keep all his body parts intact.

Her mother took a step back in her umpteen-inch stilettos, and her gaze finally hit him. "Oh. Hello, handsome!"

Timbrel looked as frustrated as Tony felt. "Mother, this is Candyman."

Still? She was still calling him that? He extended his hand. "Most people call me Tony." Why he gave only part of his name, he didn't know. Maybe he didn't want her finding him. Or blackmailing him. Or whatever. He just didn't want this woman having information on him.

Nina stepped to the side and placed a hand over her heart. "Oh, Audrey." Stroking Tony's arm, she sent her daughter a conspiratorial grin. "Very well done, daughter." She let out this hideous giggle-laugh thing.

Pardon me while I hurl in your thousand-dollar shrubs.

Then her eyebrows knotted. "You seem familiar. Have we met before?"

It would've been a bad line from a B-rated movie if she wasn't right. *Please don't remember where. . .please don't remember.*

"Sorry, ma'am. I don't normally attend gigs like this."

"Mom," Timbrel huffed, "can we go inside?"

"Oh." Her mother shot Tony an appraising look loaded with question. "Of course. Yes." She linked arms with Timbrel. "I want you to meet someone."

"Again?"

"Be nice, Audrey." Nina cast another glance at Tony as she led her daughter into the three-story home.

Flowers spilled over the sidewalk as if someone had painted them in a perfect pattern. Not a weed or thorn in sight. Trimmed and shaped bushes stood proud like a woman on a runway—why did that thought not surprise him?

Because this is Nina Laurens we're talking about.

Tugging at the bow tie strapped to his neck, Tony trailed the ladies up the walk. He could just hope for some entertainment, compliments of the bullmastiff trotting alongside Timbrel. Wait—that entertainment would probably include Tony's backside and very large teeth.

Maybe he should just wait outside. Or in the bushes. He could recon with a long gun and scope. In the dirt. Safer, away from the claws of Nina Laurens.

Tony eyed the columns that held point at the outdoor foyer, or whatever it was called. A glint blinded him. What was that? He squinted up and found a dozen more sparks shooting at him. A chandelier? Seriously? Who has a chandelier *outside* their home?

As he passed beneath it, he couldn't help but wonder if the thing was rigged to nail him. Tony hurried his steps. Cool air brushed against his skin as he stepped into the marbled foyer. A grand staircase swept right and left, up and over the main foyer, forming a catwalk. All marble. All gorgeous. Glass, crystal, wood—elements he'd been known to break, shatter, and obliterate. He tucked his elbows as years-past admonishments from his mother roared their ugly heads. *"Careful or you'll break that."* Which he invariably did. *"Don't bump that, you'll knock it over."* Yup. That too. He was the veritable bull in the crystal shop. At least, his mom had said that a thousand times.

Tony hustled down five steps thinking he'd take a foxhole and desert heat over stiff-shirted events like this any day. A din of voices and fancy music filtered out of a large room filled with sparkly dresses, cleavage, testosterone, and full-of-themselves guests. And more crystal. He resisted the groan lodged in his throat and stuffed his hands in his pockets.

Yeah, he belonged out in the dirt.

Immersed in the opulence and ridiculous extravagance that defined most of Hollywood, Tony slowed and pulled to the side. His combat-trained mind went to work, plotting out exit strategies. The entire south wall offered a half-dozen open doors that led outside. A side panel, used by the waitstaff, offered another exit. Tables draped in white linen and adorned with silver already hosted a few guests. Most were mingling, apparently waiting to be called to dinner.

A chorus of laughter bobbed above the surface of the heavy chatter, drawing his gaze to Timbrel again. Another roar of laughter erupted—from Nina. She leaned into a man in a slick olive suit. Probably Italian or something. *Not a tux though.* South Asian features defined his appearance, but his actions, his behavior, felt distinctly American. Laughing, carrying on, intermingling. The man was comfortable in this setting.

Timbrel averted her gaze, lips flattening. Clearly not happy with the display of affection her mother gave the guest.

"Hey."

Tony turned to his right where a platinum-blond bombshell slunk closer.

"I haven't seen you at one of Nina's soirees before."

"That's probably because I haven't been to one." Tony had to admit she was pretty. And young, but not inexperienced by the way she posed.

"Are you in the guild? It seems everyone's in the guild or wants to be."

"No." Tony wished he had something to deaden his ears.

"Good, I hate meeting men who are in. They're all about positioning and posturing, looking out for themselves." She nodded toward Nina. "As you can see."

Tony's gaze skidded across the room to the ever-growing huddle. The girl was right—Nina Laurens had the crowd around her. "Is it always the same people?" Simpering women, fawning men, but it seemed Nina had eyes only for her Indian hunk.

Brown eyes struck his.

Timbrel.

"No, not always," the girl said. "Some of us are regulars because we're *friends* with Nina, but there are the others. . ." The curl in her lips carried into her words. He didn't need to look at her face to see it. Nor did he want to look away when he had Timbrel's undivided attention.

Long, delicate fingers, jammed with so many diamonds he needed his Oakleys, wiggled in front of his eyes. Tony blinked and drew back.

"Simone Bergren." The girl gave a coy smile and waited for him.

Did she expect him to kiss her hand or shake it? He gripped it tight. "Tony VanAllen."

Her electric blue eyes, encircled in black, widened. "Wow, that's some grip."

Groan.

"So, you're not an actor—"

Was Timbrel still watching? His gaze flipped across the room. Head cocked, Timbrel arched an eyebrow and jutted her jaw in question. He just wasn't sure what that question was.

Maybe it was jealousy. But that'd be too much to hope for.

The chick tugged his arm, snapping his attention back to her as she pulled him out of his self-imposed corner of isolation.

"What. . .what are we doing?"

"I want you to meet someone."

Oh man. Just give me a double-tap now.

"Hey, Carla," Simone said as she touched the shoulder of a woman who stood with her back to them. "Have you met Tony?"

Petite, curvaceous, she probably turned a lot of heads. Smooth black hair cascaded in waves down her spine—and only then did Tony realize half her dress was missing. He shoved his gaze away, but not before the woman turned.

Holy plastic cougars, Batman! The woman had to be at least twice his age. As her gaze raked him, Tony felt buck naked. Her eyebrows, which looked like someone took a Sharpie to them, arced. Her lips looked stitched on. Her skin pulled tight like some freak-show mannequin or something. And he thought the carnage after an IED was bad? A shudder ripped through Tony.

"Oohhh."

Did she really just purr?

Where is my emergency evac?

Eleven

"Timbrel, this is Sajjan Takkar. He's a philanthropist."

Yet another gold digger, she guessed. But keeping her mask of gentility, Timbrel shook his hand. "Nice to meet you, Mr.—" What was his last name?

"Mr. Takkar, but please—call me Sajjan."

"Why would I do that?"

His smile faltered on that handsome mug of his. He had this older Indian prince thing going on with the olive skin, black hair with smatterings of gray, and a turban. "Forgive me. I meant—"

"No," her mom said quickly, "it's not you, Sajjan. Audrey's a little out of sorts."

"Actually, I'm quite fine, Mother. Thank you." Timbrel searched the crowd for Candyman. He'd left the corner. So cute to watch him hunkering down to weather the storm of this party. But then Simone had shown up.

Where did they go?

Timbrel turned her head, searching the partygoers for him. She'd really thought he'd stick out. Probably because in her mind, he was Candyman—bearded, geared-up, and carrying a military-grade assault rifle. But that's not who stood in this ballroom. The man didn't *wear* that tux. He personified it. It amplified every good attribute—his size, his good looks. And she wasn't the only one who'd noticed.

He stood laughing in the middle of a crowd of women.

She liked the way his eyes crinkled when he smiled. A light came to his face then. Her stomach lurched when she realized he was staring back at her.

Timbrel jerked her attention back to Sajjan and her mother, rambling about some organization they were planning to help. "Do you two do this a lot?"

"Do what, darling?" Mom asked, her arm hooked around his elbow.

What's that about? "Helping causes."

"Well, baby," her mom said, as if surprised she would ask. "That's what Sajjan does."

Sajjan, ever the gentleman and apparently not one to brag, inclined his head. "It is true. My family is very wealthy, my father a very shrewd investor. Takkar Corporation is known worldwide for our endeavors with worthy causes."

"Sajjan is why I wanted you to come tonight, darling. I think he could help your dog people."

Timbrel laughed. "Dog people?"

Her mother waved a hand at her. "Don't exert yourself, Audrey. You know what I mean."

"Nina tells me you are a dog handler. And that"—he nodded at Beowulf—"I suppose, is your partner."

Timbrel lifted her chin. "He's more than a partner."

Sajjan smiled and gave a short nod. "My brother handled dogs—he was a police officer in San Jose."

Surprise cartwheeled through her. "Yeah? What breed?" "A black Lab."

Timbrel nodded, her hand smoothing over Beo's skull. "I almost got paired with a yellow Lab, but once I met Beo, it was all she wrote."

"The bond," he said with a really nice smile, "is undeniable between you two."

Hold up. I'm not supposed to like this guy.

A hyena shrieked from behind.

Timbrel shifted, scowling at the noise.

"Carla Santana," Mom whispered in her ear. Then nudged Timbrel's shoulder. "Why don't you rescue him and bring him to our table."

"He's fine." Timbrel's stomach churned at the way the women hung on Tony. And he didn't seem to mind.

Not true. He looked positively ticked.

Her mom nudged her. "Go on. Poor guy looks like a cornered rabbit."

"Rabbit?" Timbrel scoffed. "That man could bring any woman to her knees if he wanted."

"I think he already has." Her mom laughed. "You'd better hurry before you lose your grip on him."

"My grip?" Timbrel frowned at her mom.

"Carla looks pretty intrigued by your rogue soldier."

"Oh, come on—wait." Timbrel's heart tripped. "How'd you know he was a soldier?"

"It's written all over him, and let me tell you, a woman knows a warrior when she meets one." Her mother gave that shrewd, eyebrow-raised/nostril-flaring look Timbrel hated. "A man who's seen combat, killed people, been in the desert for too long, isn't going to resist feminine wiles for very long." She gave a knowing nod. "Especially when they're being handed to him on a silver platter."

Heart hammering at the insinuation, Timbrel stiffened. "You clearly don't know him." She took in the sight of him with Simone dangling off his arm. Carla fawning. Surely, he wouldn't. . . A strange surge of heat rushed through her. Was he enjoying the attention the floozies were all too willing to lavish on him?

"But I'd like to."

"Ugh. Mom, that's disgusting. He's almost young enough to be your son."

"That's *not* what I meant." Her mom's face reddened, and she shot Sajjan a nervous look mixed with a weak, apologetic smile. "Just seat him at the head table, dear."

Clearly her mother was already involved enough with Sajjan that she worried what he thought about her. This would make, what, her sixth husband?

Arm in arm with the turban-wearing man, her mother sauntered through the room, greeting guests and smiling. Ever the diva. Sajjan seated her mother then joined her at the table, his arm spilling across the back of her seat as they talked quietly. Ya know. . .it almost seemed like the man truly had interest in her mother beyond the money and fame.

"Right. You've heard that before," Timbrel muttered to herself. Though she wanted to be frustrated or disgusted, there was something. . . off about this relationship.

A sickening cackle spun her around.

Candyman, now standing in profile, ducked his head. His neck and face had gone crimson. The ladies were howling. He shook his head. Ticked. He was ticked off.

Scratching the top of Beo's head, Timbrel said, "C'mon, boy. Let's save the rogue in distress."

Every step toward Candyman smacked her with a realization: Carla Santana was determined to dig her claws into him—*Well, good luck with that. Candyman wears tough armor*—and if it wasn't Carla, it'd be Simone. Timbrel had lost to the loose girl way too many times. But she'd never cared. . .before. . .

Weird. I do care this time.

A lot.

She just wasn't sure how to tame the beast of jealousy before it ruined what little of a friendship she had with this man. *"A woman knows a warrior when she meets one."*

Yeah. . .Timbrel could relate.

At his side, she smiled. "Having fun?"

He glowered. "Loads."

Man, she wanted to laugh, and she could feel the shade of it tugging at her lips.

A bell resounded through the ballroom.

She raised an eyebrow. "Saved by the bell. Mom wants us at her table." When she turned, her hand caught.

Tony's large paw wrapped around hers, and he leaned down, his mouth near her ear. "You leave me to the cougars again"—his warm breath skated down her neck, goose bumps racing through her spine—"and I can't be responsible for what happens."

"Like them that much?"

He grunted. "I'd probably make a sizable donation to some charity looking for plastic containers for impoverished children."

Timbrel burst out laughing but quickly scaled it back. She frowned at him. "That was terrible."

"Yeah?" His irritation seemed to have a sharp edge to it. "Well, consider yourself warned."

Timbrel couldn't help laughing again as she moved to the seat catty-corner from her mom. She reached for the chair, only to have it slide out for her. Candyman. "What's this?" Timbrel asked as she tucked herself into the spot. "A gentleman, too?"

"My mama didn't raise no hick, ma'am," he drawled out.

Saying it that way. . .Timbrel heard her own giggle and wanted to cut her throat out. Had she really resorted to that? As Tony took his place at the table, Timbrel's gaze snagged on a man making a beeline toward the table. Who. . .?

Something. . .familiar. . .

She sucked in a breath. "Can't be."

Quiet descended as the plates of food glided to rest in front of the guests.

Utensils clanked delicately in the room, the chatter fading as everyone dug into their food. Tony stared down at the top sirloin atop a bed of mashed potatoes with a brown mushroom sauce. Taste buds popping, he quickly tucked his chin and prayed, asking God's blessing on the meal and that he could make it out of this dinner intact and alive.

Timbrel eyed him, question begging for answers.

"What?"

"You pray at every meal?"

"Every time I can." He sawed through the meat and stabbed it with his fork. He lifted it to his mouth.

Beowulf wedged between their chairs, noisily sniffing the air.

Tony arched an eyebrow at the brindled dog. "Sorry, champ. This is mine." He chomped into the meat and tried to ignore the way the hound whiffed at the food. "You don't pray?"

Timbrel ducked. "Mom wouldn't let me. She is fiercely antiorganized religion."

"What about you?"

"What?"

"Where do you stand regarding religion—or better yet, faith?"

She sighed, chewing the edge of her lip. "Undecided."

"What's undecided—believing He exists?"

"No. . .I just—"

"C'mon. Don't give me the whole 'I've seen too many things' line."

She adjusted her position, leaning closer, an elbow on the table. "Haven't you? What about what you see out there every time you get deployed?"

Tony took a gulp of his drink. "What I *see* is the corruption and greed of *man*. We live in a fallen world."

"Why doesn't God do something?"

"Well, therein lies the dichotomy. First—if He *made* us do anything, then we'd be puppets to a puppet master. God wants a relationship." He winked at her. "Just like me."

Timbrel ignored him and went on, her brow tightly knit. "But there are innocent children out there. Children raised without fathers."

Those words sounded seriously personal. Was this more about innocent children or Timbrel? It slammed him from out of left field that she'd never mentioned her father. He'd have to ask her about that later.

She turned a little more so her right knee almost rested against his thigh. There, she rubbed the side of Beo's head. "I struggle that God could leave them defenseless and unprotected."

As he cut away another piece of steak, Tony grinned at her. "Unprotected? Babe, why do you think God put me here?"

Her brown eyes, framed by those bouncy curls, held his gaze. "You really believe God put you out there, in danger?"

"He gave me a choice, but He's the One who put the drive in me to join up, so I went with it. Wanted to serve the greater good the way my father did. But yes, I believe without a doubt He wired me to want to protect those who can't and won't protect themselves. I *know* it." He stuffed the bite into his mouth. "What about you? Where do you stand with God?"

Timbrel lifted a shoulder lazily. "I grew up in the Catholic Church, and I believe in God, but I haven't been terribly close to Him." She met his gaze. "Not the way you seem to be."

Tony winked. "Stick around, babe. Maybe He sent me to help you find Him in a better, stronger way."

Something washed over her face that he couldn't make out. It was that thing again—that thing that made him think she admired him. Instead of saying it, instead of denying it with words that might come next, Timbrel went silent. Nibbled at her salad.

She had both legs turned now. As much as he'd like to believe her interest in the conversation—which was legit—focused her attention on him, a shadow lurking beneath her eyes warned him something was wrong.

Over the next hour, ice clinked. People chatted. Divas cackled. Men acted like stupid peacocks trying to show their colors for the women around them.

Tony gritted his teeth and chomped into the last piece of his steak. Here a hundred people dined on caviar, sushi, and drank wine and champagne and, by the look of the bar across the room, mixed drinks. Yet on the other side of the world, troops would bed down on canvas cots and thin mattresses with only memories, dust, and the threat of bombings to keep them warm. It didn't sour his food. It actually made it sweeter because he knew it'd be a long time before he got something of this quality again.

A bubble of conversation rose and fell at the other side of the table. Tony polished off his meal, listening and watching. Timbrel's mother seemed enthralled with the gentleman to her left, who sported a dark tailored suit that bespoke his wealth. That and the way he carried himself— or maybe that mighty attitude was about the gray-blue turban atop the man's head. How well did the man's deeply held religious beliefs fit with Nina Laurens's lavish lifestyle? The values seemed opposed at the least.

Interesting match: Ms. Hollywood Socialite and her Sikh boyfriend.

Timbrel looked that way then shoved herself back against the chair, craning her neck toward Tony.

He frowned and rested his chin on his shoulder. "What's going on?"

"His name is Sajjan Takkar," Timbrel spoke, her voice low, her spine pushed into the back of the chair, almost like she wanted to hide from someone. "He's a philanthropist according to my mother. But that other man..."

Sajjan Takkar turned to the person on his left. He lacked the turban, so he either wasn't a devout Sikh, or he wasn't a Sikh at all. But definitely Middle Eastern. Ten years, give or take a year or two, older than Tony. Whereas Takkar sported smiles and a nice presence, his friend was trouble. Tony could smell it. The hard lines around his mouth. Irritation while dealing with the waitstaff as they served the first course...

"That is trouble."

When Timbrel read his mind, Tony skidded his gaze to her. "Yeah?" What'd she see? "Tell me."

"Dunno," she said with a lazy shrug. "I just have this feeling I've met him before. I can't place where. Just that I have a really sick feeling in my stomach when I look into his eyes."

Beo's nose worked the edge of the table, and eventually he went up on his hind legs, searching for a meaty morsel.

"Down, Beo."

"Audrey, dear—must that beast of yours really be in here during the meal?"

"He's a working dog. He doesn't leave my side." Timbrel angled her body away from her mother. "What do you think about Sajjan?"

"The Sikh? He's...tall."

Timbrel frowned.

"Handsome?"

"That's not what I meant."

Tony laughed. "I know. Just trying to relieve some of that tension knotting your neck." He eased back and reached back to massage her shoulders.

Beo growled.

Tony growled back.

Beo snapped.

"Really, Audrey!"

Timbrel swatted his arm with a laugh. "Stop antagonizing him."

"No, this dog and I need to come to terms."

"With what?"

"That I'm here to stay." Tony rested his hand on her shoulder. Pressed his thumb into her shoulder-blade muscles, massaging. "Why'd you ask about your mom's boyfriend?"

"I don't know. Just. . .honestly?" Timbrel seemed to struggle with her words. Or with what she was about to say. "I can't make out whether I like him or not. Usually, I hate all of her flings."

"Flings or boyfriends?"

"There's a difference?"

He laughed. "I guess not."

Nina Laurens stood, and like a pop-up game, men around the room came to their feet as she made her way out of the room on the arm of Sajjan. The other guy had vanished.

Nina walked to Timbrel, bent down, and whispered something.

Timbrel's eyes closed and her lips went flat.

Nina straightened. "Join us on the veranda, Mr. VanAllen?"

"Um. . ." Tony gauged Timbrel. "Sure. I'll be there in a minute."

Timbrel pinched the bridge of her nose as the din in the room rose. "She said she wants to talk and get to know you better."

"But you don't want to go out there."

"I don't want to do anything my mom wants me to do, especially not where it comes to my love life."

"Love life?"

"*Not* what I meant."

"But it's what you said."

She groaned and rolled her eyes. "Let's just get this over with. You can interrogate me later."

Tony grinned without remorse. "You promise?"

"If you can get past Beo."

Timbrel emerged from the restroom and spotted Tony sitting on the stairs, Beo next to him. Raptly, Beo stared at Tony. Heart in her throat, she thought he was growling. No, Candyman had a chunk of steak in his hand.

"Now, you're going to back off and give me room to figure this out," Candyman said. He tossed a piece and produced another from his pocket.

Timbrel covered her mouth, afraid she'd give her presence away.

"I know you were here first, but this time, you have to learn to share."

Beo growled.

"Just give me a chance." Candyman held out the steak on his palm. "Give *her* a chance to figure out she likes me."

Beo wolfed down the meat.

Candyman tugged back his hand a little reticent.

Timbrel stepped in. "Ready?"

Jerked upright, Candyman's gaze flickered with uncertainty. "D'you just hear all that?"

"Yep."

He glanced down at Beo. "Traitor."

"Him?" Timbrel laughed. "Why is he a traitor?"

"He has superhuman hearing. He knew you were there." He huffed. "He just wanted me for my steak."

Laughter trickled through Timbrel's chest and seized her. She laughed more. Teared up. And couldn't stop.

Until she saw him. The man. He crossed the foyer, oblivious to her presence. Thank goodness.

Do I know him? No, she couldn't. Yet a distinct chill and a thick fog of fear dropped over her. She'd done her best to stay out of the man's sight, but his identity hounded her all through the meal. And now—now he'd vanished. How and when?

"Tell me about the guy."

Timbrel looked up at Candyman, her mind and heart still racing. *Something's not. . .right.*

"Tim?" Tony's touch at her elbow yanked her back to the present. *Wrong. It's wrong. He's wrong. Doesn't belong. . .*

"Timbrel." The terse crack of her name snapped her gaze to Candyman. "Timbrel, you with me? Beo's growling."

"What?" She pulled away. "Yeah. I. . ." Yanked from the hollowness of that moment, she looked at Beo. On all fours, he faced the direction in which the man had disappeared and growled.

"Is that a hit?" Candyman asked. "Or does he hate all men, like you?"

She eyed him. "I don't hate *all* men."

"Since when?"

Since you. The thought speared her with virulent fear. Yet it. . .did strange things to her stomach, too. She shrugged. "He's trained for passive hits—meaning, sitting when he spots something. Not growling." She wrinkled her nose. "I just don't know why Beo reacted that way to him. He's not easily bothered."

"Except by me."

"There is that. C'mon," she said, hurrying after the guy. "Let's find out what's going on."

Twelve

Did Timbrel realize she was still holding his hand?

Okay. Technically not his hand, just two fingers. He didn't care. She'd done it so casually, so without thinking, which he liked. Because it meant it was a natural gesture. One that implied trust.

The moment ended as they stepped between two marble columns and out onto the veranda. A clear pool the length of the house featured a wall of earth and rock that banked out and up at a rapid rise. Tucked into it, amid the picture-perfect vegetation, a fountain spewed its content into a smaller pool.

String lights stretched over the seating areas offered little light but plenty of ambience. Romantic. Some couples cuddled and talked with others, while a group at the back appeared to play a game of cards, their laughter and shouts echoed through the night.

Hand on Beowulf's head, Timbrel took a deep breath.

Tony touched the small of her back. "You okay?"

"Not when I'm around her." Timbrel moved down the tier of three stone steps and crossed the veranda to the intimate seating group beneath a covered area on the opposite side of the fountain.

"Ah, Audrey, darling. We were just talking about you."

Timbrel's fingers trailed a repetitive path along the indentation of Beowulf's broad skull. Her jaw was set, and the fire of determination brightened her eyes.

"Mr. VanAllen, please—have a seat. You remember Sajjan from dinner."

Tony offered his hand. "Of course." Even as they shook hands, Tony felt the presence of someone behind him.

"And this," Sajjan said as he stood and indicated over Tony's shoulder, "is Bashir Bijan."

Two things stood out to Tony—that Sajjan did not refer to the man as a friend, and the way Timbrel stiffened at his presence.

"Ah, Bashir," Nina said. "This is my daughter, Audrey, and her boyfriend, Tony."

Boyfriend. He liked the sound of that. No need to correct the uninitiated to the fact he only served one purpose here—to be Timbrel's backup as she got the check. And hooah! Timbrel hadn't corrected her mother.

"Please, everyone, let's relax and talk." Nina situated herself next to Sajjan and caught Timbrel's wrist, tugging her into the chair to the right.

Beowulf objected at the woman touching his girl, but Timbrel gave a hand signal and the dog ceased aggression. So. . .that meant that while Timbrel hated her mom, she wasn't willing to inflict bodily harm.

But as they sat and an awkward silence ensued, Beo didn't sit. He wove in and around the seats and people, nose to the ground, furniture, and eventually pant legs.

"Timbrel, your dog."

"Relax, he won't bite their legs off," Timbrel said with a rueful smile. "Unless I tell him to."

"She's quite obstinate, isn't she, Tony?"

He considered Timbrel, gauging whether he'd live to see tomorrow if he answered. But in her eyes, he found a challenge. "She's determined and focused."

"Oh, Audrey." Nina's words were almost a laugh. "You've hooked a good one, darling."

Timbrel didn't say anything.

Odd. He couldn't remember a time she didn't have a retort ready.

"She was smart, Tony. Smart to leave this craziness." Nina waved a bejeweled hand in the air, apparently indicating her life. "I am addicted to the life, and I find it can be useful and helpful so I can give to causes I'd otherwise be unable to support."

A blatant reference to A Breed Apart.

Again, no Timbrel comeback. Tony eyed her and found her staring. He followed her line of sight. Why was she locked on to Bijan hotter than a heat-seeking missile?

He placed his hand on her knee.

"And I can host important dignitaries like Mr. Bijan."

"I appreciate your generosity, Ms. Laurens." The guy was slicker than snot, even Tony could see that, but apparently Nina either had her blinders on or she was much more practiced than Tony at schooling expressions.

Nina laughed. "Anything for a friend of Sajjan's."

Takkar lowered his head.

"Mr. Bijan," Nina began, "you've been with me a week, but I hardly know anything about you. Sajjan says you are a businessman."

"Indeed." The man's beady eyes were made more sinister by the firepit shadows that leapt and danced over his face. "I make books."

"Do not be modest, Bashir," Sajjan said with a laugh. "He is a publisher, but what you should know is that he publishes books and textbooks and donates them to the schools in Iraq and Afghanistan. He's quite the philanthropist."

"Books."

A light touch against Tony's hand caught his attention. Timbrel had tapped him. Why? The way she sat forward on her seat, the spark in her voice and eyes smacked Tony and told him to pay attention.

"Imagine that, *books*." She met his gaze with a meaningful look. "He's a big reader," she said as she tore her gaze from Tony. "Is there a shop nearby? We'd love to visit."

"I am so sorry, but they are not here. They are in Iraq and Afghanistan."

Tony's nerve endings buzzed. Somehow, Timbrel had known the guy was a book publisher. How, he didn't know, but he would be paying a lot of attention, especially now that the man admitted he had shops in Afghanistan.

All the same, they must be very careful taking leaps like that. There were plenty of men named Bashir and enough bookmakers and bookshops in Afghanistan to make the leap unrealistic that this guy had a connection to the shop they'd raided on their last mission.

Timbrel gave a subtle nod toward Beo and then gave a smile to the others. "Wow! That's amazing." Quite the actress, Timbrel plowed ahead. "Where are they?"

Bijan stilled. "Why do you ask?" A hollow laugh did nothing to hide the sudden nerves the guy exhibited. "Are you planning to visit and buy a book? Or does book publishing interest you?"

"Of course she's not," Nina injected, her face pale.

"No, not at all," Timbrel said. "There are places in Afghanistan—"

With a stealthy hand on her knee, Tony gave a soft squeeze. He knew exactly where she was headed with this, and it was so not a good idea.

A wary glance bounced from him to the two men. Timbrel gave a shrug. "I don't know. I just heard on the news they aren't letting girls go to school."

Nice cover. Tony let himself expel the breath he'd held. He leaned back and draped his arm around her back in an effort to look calm.

"What about you, Tony?" Nina curled her feet up on the sofa she shared with Sajjan. "What do you do for a living?"

"Security." Safe, nonlying answer. "I look out for those who can't or won't do it for themselves." Plot thickening, Tony determined to keep this conversation steered in a direction he could handle.

Timbrel turned her head, her lips brushing the lobe of his ear. It took every ounce of self-control to steel his response and hear her three whispered words, "Keep him here."

Tony touched her face, keeping it close. In her irises he saw the fires of determination brewing. *What are you up to?*

She telegraphed the message, *"Don't ask."*

So Tony kissed her. He needed an excuse for them to be staring into each other's eyes, right?

And it flustered her—the pinked cheeks and half smile betrayed her. She scooted to the edge of her seat.

"Oh, look! I think Audrey's dog likes you, Bashir."

"Actually, he might need to take care of business." On her feet, Timbrel exited their private grouping. "If you'll excuse me for a moment. Beo, come."

Nerves on fire, he watched her leave. Should he go after her? The girl he knew as Timbrel Hogan didn't want help with anything. And most often, he'd agree that she didn't need the help. But there were times, with that bullheaded nature, that she got herself in deep.

"Tony." Nina set in as soon as Timbrel disappeared into the house. "Something's bothering me."

Great. He met her gaze.

"We've met before, I just know it."

"Is that right?"

"Yes." She squinted and looked down and to the left.

Oh man. Here it comes. . .

"Oh, I remember—"

With the late hour and dim lighting, he couldn't be sure, but it seemed she blanched.

"Yes?" Sajjan asked. "Where is it you met?"

Nervous was a new emotion for Nina Laurens. "Oh, I think on one of my tours. I've been all over." She met Tony's stare. "You said you worked security. It's with one of those contractors, right?"

So Nina remembered but didn't want her new beau to hear about her behavior. *That's interesting.* "Something like that." Her need to conceal that racy moment would benefit him. Tony didn't need Bijan to find out he was a Green Beret because the guy might connect some loosely hanging dots in this picture.

Annnnd. . .too late. The silence that dropped over them felt as dense as the concussive hearing loss from a flash-bang.

"So, you were there in Afghanistan fighting?"

Some people believed it was wrong to lie. And so did Tony. Except when it came to protecting lives, to competing harms. Like during the Holocaust when Germans hid Jews. This wasn't a situation of that caliber— at least he hoped not—but discretion was priority one here. "My group delivered food, supplies, and medical help to the poor." Completely true.

"But you said security." Bijan narrowed his eyes.

"I did. When delivering food and supplies, we make sure the villages are secure."

It wasn't a lie. He just omitted facts. And by the look in Bijan's eyes, Tony had a deep, dark feeling the gig was up. Bijan knew.

Shadows and voices flickered through the dark room. Timbrel moved quickly, using her hand to guide Beo's search. His snout trailed her. Along the bed, below it, at the foot, then the luggage sitting on the ottoman. "Good boy," she said as she led him to the closet.

He strutted in, rotated, his nose pressed to the carpet as he traced the floorboards.

Timbrel didn't care what General Burnett or Tony or anyone else said. That so-called book publisher had something going on under the table. She recognized him. Somehow. Some way. The whole picture just wouldn't click together.

Bathroom and bedroom cleared, she and Beo snuck out and made their way to the next room. The east wing sported her mother's typical extravagant tastes with the hardwood floors, rich mahogany doors and trim, imported Persian rugs, and antiques accented with floral arrangements that reached into the hundreds of dollars. Timbrel eyed the four doors, grateful her mom only had four guest rooms. She pivoted and peered across the catwalk-style landing that led to another hall where you needed a code to enter the family wing. To a lavish master suit that could easily be a middle-class family's entire home.

And right next door—a similar setup. *My room.* She hadn't been there since. . .

Timbrel shuddered, her stomach churning.

She covered her mouth with the back of her hand. Jerked back to the guest wing. Refused to entertain or be tormented by what had driven her away. He hadn't lasted. The thing was—he lasted *too* long in her mom's life.

Beo whimpered.

"Yeah, me too, boy." Timbrel took a knee, encircling his broad chest with her arms. She inhaled and let his unique scent steady her heart, mind, and stomach. Face buried in his neck, she mumbled, "You'd have ripped his throat out if you'd been around."

As if to agree, he licked her.

She laughed, her sense of safety back, and let her attention return to the hall. "Okay, let's finish this, find Candyman, and get out of here."

After a gentle rap on the nearest door yielded no response, Timbrel eased into the room. "Beo, seek." He trotted around the room, sniffing, moving, working.

She'd half expected Candyman to follow her up here, but he'd understood her message. The one she didn't have to speak, the one that said she needed to check something out and Bijan had to stay put. Tony held her face. Then the rat stole a kiss.

That was the third one. The first happened because she'd lost her mind at the base. She was tired, stressed, and weak. Then he'd stolen one earlier tonight. Was it wrong to admit she liked his kisses? They were soft, gentle, yet indicated a restrained passion.

Unlike—

Darkness rushed in like a plague. Timbrel blinked, feeling a distinct chill. *Beo.* Where was he? She strained to see through the blackness that engulfed the room. "Beo?"

Movement a dozen feet in front pinpointed him.

By the fireplace, he sat in front of a cozy armchair. A large suitcase stretched across the heavily padded arms. With a look at her then at the case, Beowulf remained resolute with an expression that said, "Wake up and smell the coffee."

Her heart surged. He'd alerted!

Pulse pounding, Timbrel hurried across the shadow-ridden space, resisting the urge to flip a light. Normally, this would be where she notified EOD and they took care of whatever Beo hit on. But since there wasn't a reason for Bijan to have a bomb here. . .

Okay, I'm hoping *he doesn't.*

Better to exercise caution than initiate her will. Thoughts ran wild as she examined the suitcase to make sure it wasn't rigged to blow upon opening.

Ugh. The thought of dying, of not being here for Beo. . . Who would take him?

Candyman.

Timbrel almost laughed out loud. Right. Candyman and Beo. The two would have each other for lunch. Leftovers for dessert.

She traced the zipper with her fingers. A man like Bijan, if he was trouble the way she believed, would use extra precautions—

Her fingers hit. . .something. On her knees, she tucked a loose curl back and angled for a better view of the side. A silver pin glinted. She grinned. A way for him to know if someone opened it. The unwitting thief would either ruin the zipper opening it or prick herself. Timbrel eased back the pin, half expecting a click that would signal her impending death. Instead it came free without a hitch. A nervous, breathy laugh sifted through her body. She stuck the pin just below the zipper, marking its spot.

On her feet, she lifted the lid and peered inside.

So a chemical residue didn't necessarily have to be visible. It could be invisible and odorless—at least to humans. But good ol' Beowulf had a sniffer that could ferret out something hidden six to ten feet belowground.

Timbrel rustled his head. "That's my boy. Good boy. You'll get a big treat on the way home." She rifled through the contents, searching for something, anything that would put him on the scene in that bookshop they'd raided.

Eyes. . .nose. . .that profile. A wash of warm fear poured through her veins. *It's him—the guy from the shop!* The one who'd banged her shoulder as ODA452 led him from the hidden room at the back of the shop. If he owned the shops, then why was he dressed like a worker?

To escape.

Escape what?

An icy finger traced her spine. That was about ten days ago. But the residue would still be on his clothes. Right?

"Long shot," she muttered, frustrated that there wasn't anything suspicious in the suitcase.

Voices carried through the house. Close. Timbrel let out a low growl. Too close. She rummaged once more. A white lab coat glared back at her. Timbrel held her breath, fingers hovering over the material. No logo, no name, but it was just like the one the guys at the bookshop had worn. She snatched it up, careful not to upend the rest of his clothes. Crap! Where would she hide it? No way she could hide the coat on her person. Nervous jellies swarmed her stomach as she groped for a solution.

Beowulf stared back at her. Reflection of the yard light through the window caught in his eye.

Window! She rushed to the window and peeked beyond the sheer curtain. Yikes! Pool veranda. Timbrel darted to the other side, spotted shrubs directly below. Once she opened the window, she balled up the coat and flung it into the bushes. With a whoosh, it rustled the leaves and hit with a gentle *thwat* against the bed of mulch.

As she closed the window and locked it, the sound echoed through the room.

Wait. Not an echo—a door!

Beowulf growled and lunged as Timbrel came around. "Beo, stay."

Rooted, legs spread, chest down and back-end up, Beowulf issued his challenge.

The barrel of a weapon stared back at her, dipped to Beo, then back to Timbrel. Bashir Bijan couldn't determine who his biggest threat was.

"I am walking out this door in five seconds or you're going to be carried out—in a bag," Timbrel said, her gaze boring holes through the man's head.

"Not if I shoot you first."

"It'll be the last thing you do."

"It was you—you were the woman in my shop." Sweat beaded his brow.

Folding her arms, Timbrel noticed the door opening behind Bijan. She needed to keep him distracted. "Here's the funny thing, Mr. Bijan—the Americans didn't find anything at your shop. In fact, the mission, as far as Central Command is concerned, was a bust." She shrugged. "So right now, I'm wondering why you're threatening to kill me."

"What are you doing in my room?"

"Oh." Timbrel feigned ignorance as the door came full open.

Candyman loomed behind the man.

"Sorry, I thought this was his room."

Bijan froze.

With incredible skill and speed that belied his size, Candyman knocked the gun from Bijan's hand and noosed his neck with his arm. "Grab the gun." He held tight and waited as the guy thrashed.

"You can't kill him!"

Lips flat, bicep bulging around the man's throat, Candyman went to a knee as Bijan lost consciousness. "Go! I'll meet you downstairs." He lifted the publisher and placed him on the bed.

As she watched Candyman carrying Bashir to the bed, Timbrel moved to the door with Beo. She slipped into the hall and made her way downstairs.

Halfway down, she slowed, letting her pulse that had run away with the adrenaline catch up with her. She blew out a shaky breath, stealing a glance across the rotunda to the party. At only ten o'clock, it wouldn't wind down for another three hours. On a bad night.

Candyman. . .he'd. . .he'd been amazing up there. How he'd known to come. . . She thought of his mussed hair, that flexing bicep. . .sexy. There. She admitted it—Candyman was sexy. In a warrior way. Not a pretty-boy way like the men prancing around her mom's home right now. Tony had power, raw power. But more than that, he had restraint. Incredible, gorgeous restraint.

He appeared at her side, taking her elbow. A little hard. She glanced down just as his words hissed in her ear. "*What* were you doing?"

Timbrel yanked free. "Research." Which was stuffed behind the shrub. How was she supposed to get that without attracting attention?

"He could've killed you."

"But he didn't."

"Do not do that with me."

Timbrel frowned just as an idea formed. "I'll be right back." Spinning on her heels, she ignored the fury in his handsome mug and hurried up the stairs.

"Tim—no!" His words were quiet but harsh. And then his feet pounded the marble behind her. "You foolish, pigheaded. . ."

She ignored him. But his words nailed her heart. How many times had she been called that? Treated as if she couldn't think for herself?

"He could wake up," Candyman said as he trailed her, his hard abs jarring her elbow. "Our window of opportunity is very small."

She rolled her gaze to his. "I told you to keep him downstairs." Palming the panel, she tried to steady the heart rate that ricocheted off her panic. She punched in the code. "But you couldn't do that."

"Not without putting the man in a body bag."

She hustled through the secured family wing, not even enjoying Candyman's bewilderment at another entire wing where he thought there was only a wall.

"Timbrel, I'm not kidding. I don't want any more tours of this place. I am compromised. I need to get out of here and report in to Burnett." He grunted. "I may not have a career anymore."

Thirteen

"Why would you not have a career?"

"Doesn't matter. Never mind." This was an exercise in futility, trying to make a point to pigheaded Timbrel. Right now, he wanted to strangle her. "We need to get out of here—now!"

"Look," Timbrel said as she trotted into a bedroom, crossed the wood floor, and threw open two french doors. "I'll explain to Burnett what happened."

Right. Just like she did with the bookshop? "Please." Tony pinched the bridge of his nose. "Don't. The last thing I need is for Burnett to end up ticked at you and taking that anger out on my butt. At least right now, I think I can still get an honorable discharge." He scrubbed his fingernails against his scalp and paced. "Maybe."

He turned back to the room. Creepy. But pretty. Creepy pretty. Because the dichotomy made sludge of his brain. What was creepy about floral curtains and a massive bed with what looked like a very expensive down comforter? He tried to pinpoint what hung up his brain. Same kind his mom liked? No, that wasn't it.

Slowly it came to him. . .the floral pattern. . .the *feel* of the room—it matched Timbrel's home on Prevost Drive. The one that hadn't really felt like her. But. . .maybe. . .it *was* her. And maybe the girl standing in the walk-in closet wasn't the real Timbrel.

Heady thought. Especially considering the realization he wasn't sure who she was. What she wanted. One minute he thought she wanted him. The next, she'd jettison him with the waste. With his career. This was muffed up.

"Just calm down and listen," she said from the closet as things clunked and thumped.

Tony paced, just daring her to come up with some legitimate reason for getting herself nearly killed. "What were you even doing in his room?" What was he doing with a gun? It didn't track.

"Looking for something."

"Wow," he said with a snort and dropped against the bed. "I couldn't have figured that out on my own. Thanks."

"Grow up, Candyman. I recognized him from the bookshop, so I wanted to have fibers of his clothes tested."

Tony hung his head back. Fell back against the bed. "Please! Tell me you're kidding."

"Listen, you pigheaded—"

"Me!" He launched onto his feet. "That's you. Look it up online. I put your picture there!" His anger catapulted through the roof. He rubbed both hands over his face, trying to scrub off the frustration. The fear of seeing Bijan step beyond that mahogany door, and just having this *gut* feeling that's exactly where Timbrel had vanished to. Nothing like that feeling.

"I guess that makes two of us."

Eyes raised to the curtained canopy, Tony prayed silently, *Lord, why did You make me fall for her? At this point, I would've taken her dog over her!*

Feeling like he was being watched, Tony tilted his head. A painting leapt from the curtains tucked behind the headboard. He swung his torso sideways and stared at it.

He pushed himself off the bed—gaze still locked on to the framed oil painting. A young woman and a little girl reclining on a chaise. The background a blanket of flowers. But the girl—those eyes!

"This is your room?" Tony jerked toward the closet. "Tim, is this your—?"

Beowulf went to all fours, growling at him. His canines exposed.

"Hey." Tony jabbed a finger at the dog. "You and me, we need to have words. Or bites."

Beowulf snapped.

"Bring it," Tony warned.

"You're adorable." A backpack flew out at him.

He caught it. "Adorable? This isn't adorable. This is ticked!"

Timbrel gave him a coy smile. "Is there a difference?"

He looked through the backpack. Jeans. T-shirt. Another shirt. "What? D'you run out of clothes at home?"

"I hid one of Bijan's jackets in the bushes. Needed a way to get it without drawing attention."

"That's what this is all about?"

"Yeah."

"You stupid. . ." He tightened his jaw and refused to let any more words out.

"It's a sound method."

"It's not. We were there, in the bookshop. We didn't find anything, remember?"

"Oh, I remember. And what I also remember is that Beowulf got a hit. He doesn't make mistakes like you or me. And Bashir escaped as a worker, dressed in a lab coat. So what's on that lab coat? What will those fibers tell us?"

Unable to fight her logic, he slung the bag messenger-style over his shoulder and chest. "Fine." He huffed through an angry breath. "But when we get out of here, you and I are going to talk."

"I already promised you an interrogation." Timbrel led them out of the room and to the left, darting to the servants' passage at the back of the 1920s home. It'd take them down to the lower level and out the side—right by the window.

The look on Tony's face, the distinct impression of failing him, sat like anchors in the pit of her stomach. Yet she railed against the way he talked to her, the way he chewed her out. Her mother was the same way. Carson, Don. . .all took the same tone.

She scrambled down the hall and through the kitchen. At the lower lounge area, she located Rocky. "Hey."

He peeked over a newspaper, his eyes widening. "Audrey!"

"If you wouldn't mind, I'm ready."

With a knowing huff, he snapped the paper closed. "That bad?"

"Worse." He'd always understood. More than her mother. More than Candyman. Okay, that wasn't a fair assessment since he only had about a third of the information Rocky held. "I'm going to let Beo do his duty. Meet you out front?"

"On my way."

Down the hall and up a half flight of stairs, she pushed into the evening. A cool breeze tugged at her curls. Freeing her hair of the bun, she trudged across the grass. Beo trotted off to relieve himself as Timbrel scurried along the wall into the bushes. Double-checking her location, she looked up at the room.

A light shone through the latticed window.

Wrong one. She crawled on all fours another dozen feet. Looked up. No window. Wait. She attempted to get her bearings by taking in the shrubs, the trees. . . She'd passed it. Had to have. She went back. Again peered up at the window.

Oh no. The light—it was Bijan's room. She groped in the dark for the jacket. If he was awake. . . Frantically patting the ground beneath the waxy leaves, she let out a yelp.

"What's wrong?"

"He's awake."

Candyman cursed.

"I thought you were a Christian."

"Yeah, well, sometimes my mouth isn't."

Her fingers snagged material. "Got it." She pushed to her feet.

Voices came from the other side of the house.

Timbrel broke into a sprint toward the front. With a quick look, she confirmed the guys were behind her. She just prayed Beo didn't bark. Once they hit the gravel drive, Timbrel slowed and braved another glance back.

Candyman almost barreled into her. "Don't stop. Keep moving." He propelled her toward the waiting car and Rocky.

They dove into the backseat and Beowulf right behind. As the car pulled away from the front, she handed the jacket over.

Tony shook his head. "All that, and for nothing."

"What do you mean?"

"We wasted time in the house. You didn't get the check, for one."

Timbrel grunted and banged her head on the back of the seat.

"And two, we could've been long gone. Getting the bag. . ." He unhooked it from around his neck. "Didn't even use it. Taking the back stairs, down through the servants' passage—no need for the bag." He dropped it at her feet. "So, what'd you go back for? What was worth risking your life—my life for?"

IMAMA—
SUCCESSION TO MUHAMMAD

Five Months Ago

It soothed and restored the soul to be with his brothers at the mosque. To kneel and surrender his thoughts and troubles for a time of prayer. On his knees, he bent and pressed his face to the mat, silently reciting the Asr.

Allah is the Greatest.
In the Name of Allah, Most Gracious, Most Merciful
All praise is due to Allah,
Lord of all that exists
Most Gracious, Most Merciful
Master of the Day of Judgment

He went through the entire *salat* four times, standing when appropriate, bowing at other times, and kneeling and pressing his face to the floor, then squatting and looking to his left.

Once the prayer ended, he rose and moved into the outer foyer, trailed closely by Dehqan, Irfael, and two of the guards. As he moved through the small crowd of faithful, he noted the whisperings of the imam and his advisers.

"Colonel." Irfael leaned in close. "They have requested a meeting."

Excellent. Just as he'd hoped. Just as he'd planned. "When?"

"They will come to the house tonight, after dark."

He strode to the armored car and climbed in. Dehqan took his seat at his side. "Do you feel better now?"

"I did not feel bad before." Dehqan adjusted his jacket.

"What of your girl?"

Dehqan's jaw muscle bounced. He drove his gaze to the blurring roads as they raced back to town. "She is willful."

The boy might have taken the wrong approach to the girl, lulling her mind just like the incessant rocking over the ruts of the roads heading back to the compound. "She has gone astray—her father brainwashed her into believing the Christian's twisted truth. You

812

must break her. Make her see."

"I am working on it." His head lazily bobbed as it came back to him. "What meeting is this they have called?"

"A most important one." The colonel settled against the leather seat. "If all goes as planned, then I begin the final mission." He grinned at the boy.

"The bombs."

He nodded. "You and I will both see the justice of Allah. Finally."

Dehqan's gaze drifted past him to the dusty road beyond the windows, thoughts seemingly lost. "I had begun to doubt Allah remembered my pain."

The colonel gripped the teen's neck and leaned in close. "Never doubt, Dehqan. Never!"

BooooOOOOOOoooooom!

Up flew down. Sideways went crossways. Down became up. Pain wracked his body.

His head hit the window. Something struck his temple. Blackness ate the day.

Warbling noises pervaded his senses.

The colonel groaned and forced his eyes open. *What. . .?* He turned and gained his bearings. Belly up, the vehicle sat in a ditch.

Shouts from outside warned him of an attack.

He scrambled for Dehqan, who was bent over, his head down and his back end up. "Dehqan! Dehqan!"

His son groaned and turned. Blood slid down his temple.

"Was he shot?"

The colonel glanced up where Irfael peered down through the open window.

"No," Dehqan grunted, "just. . ."

"Move, get out!" Irfael shouted. "They're coming!"

Climbing out, the colonel had his weapon drawn and ready. Perched on the side of the vehicle that faced the sky, he reached down. "Dehqan, hurry!"

The boy clutched his arm. He dragged him up onto the hull, and together they scuttled over the side and dropped to the ditch.

"Who has done this?" he demanded as he crouched there.

"Americans, probably," one of the guards shouted.

"Where?" the colonel demanded. He would wipe them out.

"I. . .I don't know."

Shots peppered the armor.

Dehqan pointed across the street to a building. "The rooftop. Sniper."

"Irfael—put that RPG to use."

"Yes, sir!"

He waited for his lieutenant to hoist the launcher from the vehicle then take aim. Bullets ripped through the air. Pinged off the armor plating. Seared along his face, so close he could smell its path. Once he did, the colonel grabbed Dehqan's shirt. "Go. Move!"

Only, Dehqan wasn't moving.

At all.

The colonel stopped. Knelt. Froze at the blossoming dark stain on the boy's shirt. The hand clutching his chest, blood spurting between his fingers. At the pain squeezing his eyes shut.

Another well-placed RPG bought them the time to scurry to an alley, two guards carrying Dehqan with them. His men radioed for backup, and within minutes an armored SUV leapt into the confined space. Then another and another as the sky rained ash, cement, and bullets.

Irfael and the guard loaded Dehqan into the back of the middle one. "Mahmud, have the doctor ready. Dehqan has been shot. Chest wound," he spoke into his phone then ended the call and turned around. "They're waiting. They got word minutes ago about the attack."

Fury had no name like his right now. "They will pay for this." He pushed his gaze to the darkening day outside and braced against the bumpy roads. "We are sure it was the Americans?"

"Yes. I saw the sniper's team hustling toward the SUVs."

"Then they have targeted me."

"They have targeted the colonel." Irfael grinned. "They do not know who *you* are."

"It must stay this way. Especially with the imams' arrival tonight." He cut his gaze back to the lieutenant. "Make sure they're still coming."

Another grin. "Mahmud said they're waiting for you now."

Good. Good. Allah be praised! No matter how many times the enemy attempted to thwart his plans, to remove him from the map, Allah protected him. He shifted and looked back at the guard acting as medic. Now, if Allah would extend that protection to Dehqan. Allow him to live.

I have given you everything, Allah. Please—save my son. Every step has been made to follow your word.

The gate flew open and the SUV caravan launched into the compound. Seeing the urgency with which everyone moved did nothing to soothe his fears. Especially when they rushed Dehqan on the stretcher into the house. The blood. . .he'd lost so much blood.

A dozen guards surrounded him as he moved into the house. "Get away! Guard the gates. Guard the roads. Not me, you fools. I'm here. I'm safe." Light attacked his eyes as he stepped into the house.

And stopped short.

Twelve men waited in the foyer.

"*Assalamu alayikum*," he forced himself to say, though he did not want or seek peace at all. But for now. . .for now he must abide the talk. The flat, meaningless talk.

"*Wa alayikum assalam.*"

"Colonel," one said as he emerged from among them. His white kufi stirred the icy shards of the colonel's blood.

"*Salaam.*"

"And peace be upon you," they muttered almost in unison.

"Forgive me for the delay. We came under attack, as you know." He managed a half bow/nod to the imam. "I am surprised to see you here, Imam Abdul Razaaq."

"We would like to speak to you. But it seems you are injured." He motioned to the colonel's head. "Would you like time for the doctor to tend it?"

"I am well, praise Allah."

"It has come to our attention, Colonel, that you have worked hard and long to purge the country of ways contrary to that of Allah."

His heart hiked into his throat. "It is my greatest honor."

"All speak of your devotion to scripture, to our people." The imam turned, the hem of his gold cloak spinning as he did so. "And you have done well in raising Dehqan in the way of Islam."

A surge of protection spiraled through him. "He is as my own son."

"Which is why it is agreed you should be named an imam."

"I am. . .humbled. Are you sure?"

"Yes," Abdul Razaaq said. "It would be necessary for you to renounce your position within the ISAF, but you would be allowed and even encouraged to continue. . .defending Islam, instructing others."

"It would be my honor." As he embraced his new calling, he was reminded of the words of the Prophet—peace be upon him—"*And we appointed Imams from among them who should guide after our command when they had themselves endured with constancy, and had firmly believed in our signs.*"

Mashallah. Just as Allah has willed. Now, if Allah would clear his path for the big event.

Fourteen

The evening went nothing like she expected. Bad, she expected—*anticipated*—but coming out of it feeling like she'd betrayed Candyman . . . She wasn't ready for that, nor did she want it. After Rocky pulled away from the hotel, they made their way up to the suite. Tony had only spoken a handful of words the entire time. Even now, tension wove a thick band around their awkward pseudosilence.

In the room, Timbrel hesitated, watching but not really *watching* him. He went straight to his gear, lifted it from the bed, and started for the bathroom.

"We need to clear out. *Now*," Candyman said.

"Our flight's not until tomorrow."

"We leave *tonight*. If this man is trouble, the way you believe, then we are in danger."

Timbrel quickly changed and packed her overnight bag. When she emerged, Candyman was ending a call. He stood and grabbed his pack.

"You got the flights changed?" Timbrel felt like she'd been caught red-handed—but at what?

"Yep." That was the last word he spoke for the next four hours. Even the evening cicadas and humidity spoke louder than him. Their cab pulled to the curb and Timbrel shoved open the door. Beowulf leapt out and surged over the fence. Clearly, he had a job to do. Timbrel emerged from the taxi, exhausted, but pushed herself onto the sidewalk.

Keys jangled.

Over her shoulder, she saw Tony palming his keys as she let them into the yard.

Her heart fell. *What's wrong? What'd I do?* Yelling she could handle. His razor-sharp wit, sure. But this icy silence. . .

Beo raced the circuit, checking, sniffing, detecting whoever had been in his territory while he was away. She stepped up on the wood steps and unlocked the house. A beeping alarm shoved her to the security keypad. She punched in the code and cleared the intrusion from the system.

When she turned around, Candyman headed for the door. Holding his helmet, he shouldered into his jacket as he pushed open the screen.

"Hey," Timbrel said as she hurried after him. "Where are you going?"

"Home." Candyman stalked toward his bike and donned the helmet.

Out in the night, Timbrel stumped after him. "Why?" Her voice felt small and her heart heavy. "It's nearly five—we've been traveling all night. You need to rest."

He threw open the gate, zipping his jacket. "I'm fine." As he put on the helmet, he stood at the bike, staring at the street.

"Candyman, please. Just. . .come back inside."

"No need. If you want to kill yourself or put yourself in danger. . ." His hands dropped from fastening the helmet strap, and he hung his head. "I'm wasting my time. This is useless."

Panic and hurt stabbed her. "I'm *not* useless!" Her words echoed down the street illuminated by lamps.

"No," he said, his voice thick and the word forced. He yanked off the helmet. "That's not what I said, and I would *never* say that about you. But talking to you, waiting till you figure out I'm here for you, that I will help— it's like talking into the engine of a C-130. All noise."

"What are you talking about?" Timbrel's pulse pounded against her breast. She was finally making headway with him and they were already having a fight?

"You. I'm talking about you going into that man's room and snooping."

"So?"

Tony ducked, raised a hand to his head, but then lowered it. "You don't get it. You seriously don't get it?"

"If you want to make me feel stupid, you're excelling."

"Timbrel, that man—what did you suspect him of doing in Afghanistan?"

"WMDs."

"Right. And now that you exposed yourself by going through his things, what does he know about you?"

Oh. She licked her lips.

"Let me fill in the pieces for you. He knows you're Nina Laurens's daughter. And not only that, he also now knows who I am. And that means

I'm compromised—the entire *team* is compromised. You drew attention to yourself when you should've left it alone. *Then* you go back and say you have to get the bag." He snorted. "Do I really look that stupid to you?"

From her pocket she lifted a small gold necklace. Held it up. "This is why I went back."

Tony covered his eyes then scruffed his face. "It doesn't matter why."

"I don't understand."

A sad smile tugged at his handsome face. "I know." He shook his head. "I know. God help me, I know."

Was he laughing at her? Mocking her? She took a step back. "I'm not stupid, Candyman."

Like a tornado, he spun toward her. "Candyman? Timbrel, why can't you call me Tony?"

She shrugged. "I'm just used to it. You don't look like a Tony." She took another step back. Breathing hurt.

"Bullpucky! You want to know why? Because using my first name makes me human. It makes me a person—and you can't do that, can you?" His voice wasn't loud, yet his words hollered through her head. "Being a man, being a guy who's crazy about you makes *you* crazy, terrifies you!"

"You don't know what you're talking about," she screamed, her pulse straining in her throat.

"Don't I?" He angled his shoulder toward her. "Why is it every time a little light manages to creep into your world through me, you snuff it out?"

"Just because I don't throw myself at you like other women, like Simone and Carla—"

"*Don't* go there." He stabbed a finger at her. "You *know* I don't give a rat's behind about those women. You're the one I want. You're the only one I think of, the one I want to be there for. I'd risk everything for you—and I did. Tonight."

She tucked her chin as he ripped open her soul, her secrets, her fears. She traced the gold star that dangled from the chain. It blurred.

"You know why I'm here, Timbrel. Why I keep coming back, and if it's too much for you, if you can't go there, then tell me now." In the blue glow of the street lamp, his chest heaved. "Because God knows I can't keep doing this. It's been a year. Four missions—I'm cemented to you more than I am many of my ODA brothers. But if you won't let me in, if you throw away every peace offering—"

She turned, her throat tight and her vision awash with tears. "I can't do this."

He caught her elbow and pulled her around.

Beo barked and charged, his weight rattling the fence.

Timbrel gave him a silent hand signal, and only by that small gesture did she prevent the beast from scaling the fence. She stood toe-to-toe with Can—Tony. Her chin trembled, threatening more emotion. Tears. She hated weak-kneed women who cried at the drop of a hat. Lifting shaking fingers from the chain, she warred with the shifting of the universe happening right under her feet.

She touched Tony's chest. Folding the chain in her fist, she pressed that too against his chest. "I. . .it's. . .scary." She sounded like a five-year-old. Braving a look up at him, she saw the reflection of her own torture in his gorgeous features.

"Let me in, or let me go, Tim," he said, his soft words filled with a raw ache.

Let him in? There was only one way to let him in—right through the front door: truth. Her past, her nightmares, her failings. . . But if she did that, she might as well place grenades in his hands to blow any chance they had for a future.

But this was what he wanted. And she knew she had to go there. Had to open that vault. She could do this—for him. After all he'd done for her . . .Timbrel dropped her gaze, afraid if she looked into his pale green eyes, she wouldn't be able to tell him.

She had to do this. Cross this line. Break the molds.

Timbrel eyed the line of his jacket zipper up to his neck. Thick. Strong. Tanned. His jaw. Muscle popping—was he ever *not* intense? To his mouth.

Timbrel slid her hand up the same path her eyes had taken. A fire erupted through her belly and chest as she angled her head toward him.

Tony closed the distance. Captured her mouth with his.

Her hand touched his face. Exhilaration raced through her.

Yet so did a terrible dark fear.

No. I can do this. I can.

She pushed her arm up. . .elbow over his shoulder. A strange type of surrender enveloped her as her fingers curled into his short-cropped hair.

Tony crushed her to himself, deepening the kiss. His large hands held her tight. Melted into his passion, she let herself enjoy it. His strength. His raw power that had attracted Simone and Carla. *But he chose me. He believes in me.*

Carson Diehl believed in her, too.

Timbrel shuddered.

No. She couldn't go there. Couldn't think of him.

Tony was better, stronger, had more character.

Carson had said he loved her.

"No," she mouthed around the kiss.

Kisses were warm and tender.

Carson's were demanding. More. . .more, till he pinned her.

"No!" she squeaked.

Tony broke off. Breathing heavy, he froze. "Timbrel, what's wrong?"

She dropped her forehead against his chest. "I'm sorry." She ruined it. She *was* useless. "I'm sorry. I can't do this." Never. She couldn't even kiss the one man she might be able to love without thinking of Carson. Or Don Stephens.

Her stomach heaved at the thought of her stepfather.

Frozen tundra had nothing on the drastic shift that occurred. "Tim, what is it?"

She shook her head and swallowed. She'd tasted sweet, felt incredible in his arms. Like the mystery to the universe had been solved right here. Right now. With her.

It took two seconds longer than it should have for her plea to make it through the fog of passion. But when it did, Tony had broken off.

"Okay. It's okay." Tony hesitated before holding her upper arms.

This fear, this panic that intruded on every quiet moment had to be a demon from her past. Or some jerk from her past. It infuriated him to think that someone had hurt her so badly and put her in this kind of shape.

When he drew away, she grabbed his jacket.

"Please. . ." Her voice almost didn't register, but her fingers digging into his jacket sure did. She had a death grip on him. "Don't. . .go."

He didn't move, afraid he'd scared her off. There'd been a lot of passion flying between them, but nothing he regretted. He hadn't crossed lines. He'd kissed her long and hard, but it wasn't out of control. Which was a minor miracle in and of itself. He could easily go too far when it came to her.

She shook against him.

Tony craned his neck trying to see her. But with her hair down and her face buried in his chest, he couldn't see her. Sure felt like she was crying. "Hey." He cupped the back of her head and wrapped an arm around her. "It's okay."

The tears grew harder.

Man, he'd kill whoever did this to her. "Easy there, babe. It's okay."

She wrapped her arms around his waist and held on tight. Stomped her foot. "It's not. They ruined me. *I* ruin everything!"

He bounced his pec in an attempt to get her to look at him. "Hey. Don't talk about my girlfriend like that. Okay? She's the best thing that ever happened to this sorry world."

Coming off his chest, she laughed. "You are a sap." Swiped at her tears.

"As long as I'm your sap, I don't care."

Her smile squished into agony. "I can't... I don't..." Her voice squeaked. She stomped her foot again. Threw back her head and stared at the sky, inhaling deeply. Using both hands, she pushed the hair from her face. "I'm okay. Really."

Tony quirked a brow at her.

She smiled. "All right, maybe not—but..." She bunched her shoulders. "Come and talk for a few minutes?"

He looked to the house, thinking of kissing her, and he knew there was a risk being alone with her. He'd had control a minute ago, but what would happen...? Especially at this hour. *God, give me strength.*

Though he gave her a nod, he made a resolution not to cross that threshold. So when he reached the stairs, he plopped down.

Beowulf was in his face. Sniffing. Snorting. And then he sneezed.

"Ugh!"

Timbrel laughed. "Sorry. I think he's a little upset that you kissed me in front of him."

Tony swiped the dog's drool and snot from his face with his sleeve. "Well, he needs to get used to it."

"Yeah?" Timbrel stared down at him. "Aren't you coming in?"

"No, I think..." Yeah, so much for that control he'd been proud of a few seconds ago. "This is probably better."

"Tony—"

He grinned. She'd used his name.

"It's nearly five in the morning. People will be driving by."

"You afraid they might see they have competition now?"

She swiped at his head. Then slowly eased down next to him, her expression serious. "Look, I want you to know..."

He wouldn't give her an out by saying he didn't have to know. If their relationship was going to progress, they had to get some things on the table.

Beowulf lumbered between them and kept going. Good. Maybe the hound of hell would go inside. Nope. Too much to hope for. The bullmastiff thrust himself into the middle and slumped down, a lot disgruntled. His eyebrows bobbed at Tony, as if to say, "What're you looking at?"

"He's jealous." Timbrel rubbed Beo's back.

"He's not the only one."

She laughed then hugged her knees. "Carson Diehl is the reason I left the Navy."

The swift change of topic pulled his gaze to hers, but he veered off so she'd have the room to talk openly.

"I thought he hung the moon. My friends warned me, but I didn't want to listen. I wanted to believe he liked me, for me." She snorted and did this half-shrug thing he found adorable. "You'd think after being raped by my stepfather, I'd have learned."

Tony stilled. Fought not to fist his hands. To stay still. Not stir her emotional pot.

And failed.

He pushed to his feet. Paced.

"Don't go all Chuck Norris on me, Tony."

"I won't. I'm better—a Green Beret. He'll never know what hit him."

"Sit." Timbrel reached out and caught his hand, tugged him back to the steps. "Don—that's my stepfather—is why I left home, why I left the glamour world my mom thrust me into from birth. He wouldn't stop. After the third time and his constantly telling me I was useless for anything else . . .I found a way out."

She ran her hands through her hair, looking out at the sky rimmed in dark blue as dawn made its approach. "Ya know, I actually used to love that lifestyle. The money, the designer labels. But when I realized my friends were only there for the money and props, that my mother preferred that to being a mom, to protecting me. . ." She looked at him with a sad smile. "She refused to believe me that he'd forced himself on me. I was seventeen. He. . ." Her head went down again. Then a shuddering breath. "He got me pregnant—but I miscarried. Only when I was in the hospital did my mom somehow believe me. But that whole ordeal left a pretty big hole in our relationship. I was so glad. . ."

Sitting quiet, sitting still, *listening* was the hardest thing he had ever done.

"Back then, I was so glad the baby died. Now, I have a greater appreciation for life, and I can't help but wonder. . .what he might be like today. He would've been ten this year."

822

"He?"

With a sardonic smile, she shrugged. "The doctor could tell after. . ."

"Timbrel. . .I am so sorry."

She had every right and more to hate men. To push and lock them out of her life.

"Yeah, me too. Carson—he was my fault. I went in determined I could change him." Another hollow laugh. "He changed me. I finally saw how stupid I'd been and broke it off before things got out of hand. Maybe I was too late. That bugger was smart—he penned Beo then ambushed me in the dark."

Tony couldn't harness his thoughts. They bled red. Murderously red. He'd kill those men if he ever met them. Rip the life from them that they stole from her.

"Tony?"

He blinked and looked at her.

"Did I say too much?" Vulnerability and fear swirled through her brown eyes.

"No." He reached over Beowulf, praying the bullmastiff didn't rip out the soft tissue under his arm, and took her hand. "No, I want to know. But you know me—I'm a protector. It's in my blood. And I just. . ." He fisted a hand and squeezed hard.

"Yeah, me too." Her gaze softened. "That's why I like you so much."

He leaned over the dog and kissed her.

Forehead against his, she smiled. "You make me crazy."

He cracked a grin.

"I can't promise I'll be an open book, but. . .I'll give it my best shot."

"That's all I ask, and knowing about those men explains a few things to me."

"Like what?"

"Like your lack of faith in God—I mean, it's not like you hate Him, but letting Him have control can be crazy-scary sometimes."

"Right?" she said with a grin.

Tony bounced his shoulders. "Sometimes, I think if it's not scary, it's not real faith. It means you're trusting someone else."

"Myself."

Tony beamed. "That's my girl. But maybe letting go of what you can't control will help you release your hatred of men, stop you from closing people out, walling-off, so to speak." He rubbed her back as a little more space sifted them. "You've been to hell and back, Timbrel. It's understandable for you to have some trust issues, but God never gave up on me, so if I see you trying, that's enough."

She nodded. "I'll try."

He went in for another kiss—and planted one solidly on Beowulf's slobbery mug.

My name is Aazim. It means "determined." I think my parents were right in giving me this name, but my name changed when a man altered my life. The colonel has told my story, but now. . .now I'd like to tell my own story. I miss my mother and father, even though they died when I was only three. In truth, they did not just die. They were killed. Not by the Taliban. Not by the Americans. They were killed on a bus by a suicide bomber.

The old men of my village said it was the Americans.

Americans said it was terrorists—the Taliban.

I did not care who caused my parents to leave me. I only cared that I was alone now. Angry and scared, I hated everyone and everything. My anger protected me and pushed me to do things I would not have otherwise done. My aunts and uncles would not let me in their homes because I would punch, spit, and kick. I hurt many. And each time, a piece of the old me, the safe me, broke off, until all that was left of the little boy my parents left behind was a ghost.

As a youth, one of my favorite things to do was throw rocks at every car and bus that passed. Drivers might curse at me for denting or scratching their cars, and a few men would get out and chase me, but it never discouraged me enough to stop. I even pelted the big trucks Americans drove through our town.

That was when he found me, the man who took me off the street, gave me good food and a warm bed. He did many good things for me, but still my anger simmered. Brewed hot and angry within my chest. At first the things he did, the things he allowed me to see, were so shocking and so awful that my heart would beat wildly, ready to escape. My fiery spirit fed off his violence. For a time.

But then, the way a father might give his child a toy, he gave me *her*. Nafisa.

I think he wanted to make me feel better after I'd been shot—bullets meant for him. But taken through my chest. I still have the scars, and moving quickly stirs fire in my lungs.

"What about Isa?"

I blinked as she said the words and darted my gaze to the heavy doors that closed out the rest of the compound. Wetting my lips, I leaned on the mound of books and papers strewn between us. "I have told you of Isa before." If *he* heard her ask about the Christian Messiah, he would become irate.

Hair black as night, lips the same color as a poppy, she stared back at me. A brightly colored hijab of blues and golds wrapped her heart-shaped face. So pretty. So sweet. She is a Christian, which does not make sense to me. I have been told they are mean, intolerant people. But Nafisa had never shown me that. Which I did not understand either because I was there the day her father had been shot. How could she be so nice to me? As far as she knew, I was the son of the man who murdered her father so cruelly. I wanted her to know the truth, to know who I really was.

But who am I?

Aazim? Dehqan? Or someone else?

She gave me a coy smile. "No, you've avoided Him before." She shifted and lifted a text.

Voices in the hall warned me. I slapped a hand over the book she held. "No. Enough." If Father—it was the only name I was allowed to use— heard this conversation, he would kill her. "I am hungry."

Laughing, Nafisa slumped back. "What scares you, Dehqan?"

That, too, was the only name I was allowed to use. It was my own fault, though. The day he had pulled me aside, I thought I was in trouble again so I lied. Told him my name was Dehqan. Maybe. . .maybe I was now that boy I so hated who had beaten me up more times than I could count.

"I am not afraid of anything!"

The doors flung open. "Dehqan!"

Jumping to my feet, I felt my heart pounding. My father. He was back. I'd grown lazy while he traveled for business. Now he returned—had he heard her forbidden question about Isa? As my father stepped into sight, I heard Nafisa's intake of breath, and something in me, something very deep that I could not fight or understand, surged to the front of my mind screaming: *Protect her!*

Scowling, he looked from me to Nafisa then to the table of books. "Stop wasting your breath talking to her. Beat the truth into her if you must."

Nothing hurt me as much as to hear him treat her as if she were a dog to be trained and taught to beg. But I had spent enough time with him, at his side, to learn his ways. "Father, it is good to see you. Was your meeting well?"

His wrath returned with a vengeance. "Come with me!" He whirled and stomped out of the room.

I gave Nafisa a look that I hope told her I was sorry for leaving. "Soon, I will return."

She smiled, but then one of the guards roughly dragged her to her feet. "Do not—"

"Dehqan, now!"

I turned to stop the guard, but Nafisa's warm brown eyes hit mine. She gave me a frantic shake of her head. As if to warn me not to say anything, not to worry about her. Because she, too, knew my father's anger would burn against her if I appeared soft. But I do. How could I not? She is mine. Given to me to protect.

Then why did *she* protect *me*?

Rushing into the hall, I feared how the guards would treat her. But I feared more what my father would do to me in a state if I was not obedient. Only by the shaken expressions on the guards' faces in the marble-lined halls did I find him in the main library.

He threw a book across the room. "We must crush them!" He slammed his fist against the counter then flung his arms along the surface, sweeping glass, flowers, books to the floor. Palms on the wood, he drew in ragged breaths.

I started forward. "Father—"

He sliced a hand at me, silencing me. He looked to Irfael. "I still don't know how—*how*—they knew where to look. It won't leave my mind. I think there is something to this." He straightened, staring at Irfael then at me. With a pointed finger, he aimed his accusations at his first officer. "You have worked that store more than anyone, staffed its workers. Did you know th—?"

"No, Colonel! No, of course not." My father's officer looked paler than I've ever seen him. Sweat ringed his forehead and underarms, darkening his tan uniform. "You know I would have warned you."

"They are too close." Father ducked his head, thinking, pacing. "Much too close."

"The dog, Colonel."

"I saw the beast," he spat out, then curled his lip as he looked at me. "They had tracking dogs. Led them right to the hidden factory. We barely had time to conceal our work." He spun to his first officer again. "But how did the American soldiers know to even come looking? What tipped them off?"

"We are looking into that," Irfael said. "Have you. . .have you considered—?"

"Sir!" a guard shouted as he burst into the library and stopped short.

My father whipped around, and in that fluid motion, I could sense things were collapsing around the man who had worked so hard, for so many years, crafting a great plan against the Americans.

"He's—"

Another man walked into the room now. One I had seen before, one who had stolen the courage of every man—including myself—with a single glance. I could feel my muscles and stomach tightening as he moved into the room without a word.

Father was quiet. Unmoving. Watching.

The man walked to the eastern wall of windows and stared out through the thin sheer curtains over the town. He turned, and the sun silhouetted his broad shoulders draped in an expensive suit. This man had a silent strength that both repelled and drew me. He always wore dark suits that looked tailored and expensive, but since I wore a perahan tunban and waistcoat, what would I know about the cost? Besides, a long tunic had to be more comfortable than a tight-fitting suit. I could not deny, though, that I would like to wear a suit. Just once. Like the stranger. To have the impact he had when he walked into a room. But it was not the clothes that gave the man his confidence, nor the white turban atop his head.

It is fear. He held their hearts in his hand because of a silent power he wielded. *Maahir.* That was the name they gave this man for it meant "skilled."

"Ah, friend." When Father spoke, it jolted the room as if wakened from a slumber. Father took two steps closer, but no more. And the smile did not make it to his words. "You are come at last!"

"Forgive my delay," Maahir said with a slight nod. "What has happened?"

"My shop—have you already forgotten what they did to my shop?" That was Father. Right down to business, as Maahir demanded. And I doubted Father wanted to spend more time in this man's presence than he must. "If they are allowed to continue invasive actions like this, we will be discovered. The bombs, the nukes—"

"What do you expect from me?"

My father swallowed but did not waver. "Put pressure on them. You have the contacts, the connections."

Maahir shrugged. "And because I have these connections, you expect me to use them to help you." When the man's probing eyes hit me, I felt dread and excitement at the same time. Excitement that he had noticed me—never before had he acknowledged I even existed. Yet having this man's attention was not something one wanted to have too often.

"Your loyalty—"

"Is it in question?" The speculating arch of Maahir's eyebrow held its own warning. "What you forget, Colonel, is that I *do* have the means, but I also have the means to shut down someone who is out of control."

"Out of—"

"One who does not know how to hold his tongue when it's good for him." Amazing how the man's words never raised, yet his message was conveyed.

Father's face grew red. His jaw muscle flexed, as if a stealthy punch. But he said nothing. Hands fisted at his sides, he lifted his jaw.

"I will look into the problem," Maahir said as he started across the room. "Remember, Colonel, not everyone is of the same mind that violence of action is the only way to succeed."

Fifteen

Nasty!"

Laughing so hard she could barely breathe, Timbrel leaned back against the porch post. "You so deserved that."

Hunched over, Tony spit several times into the flower bed. "He and I are going to have to have it out."

"But I'm not ready to lose you yet."

Tony looked at her and stilled.

More laughter.

His eyes narrowed.

Oh snap! Timbrel leapt up with a shriek, shoved herself over the cement porch, and ripped open the screen. Beo barked and was on her heels.

The screen door never clattered.

She glanced back—

Tony was right there.

With a scream, she darted to the kitchen island. Took cover, Beo at her side, panting.

With a greedy grin, Tony threw himself over the counter. His left thigh slid over the Formica and he flew at her.

If she could make it—Timbrel lunged to her right.

Tony snagged her arm. Tugged her back. She resisted, straining to get her finger around the jamb to the hall. Meaty hands captured her waist. Pulled her, right off her feet.

Beowulf snapped and barked.

Timbrel, in the midst of a hard laugh that came out more like a snort, signaled Beo that all was well. But her boy was playing, too!

Tony whirled her around into his arms—which released her. She threw herself toward the door jamb again.

Groaning, he caught her again.

Lights on the road captured her attention. Through the screen she saw a dark-colored sedan slow in front of the house. Eh, probably a neighbor heading to work. A bit early, but hey, not everyone slept till noon like she did.

But. . .hold up. Timbrel felt a chill chase away the fun warmth as Tony tugged her against himself. "Wait. . . Stop."

Red lights—brakes—lit the night as the car paused in front of the house.

"What is it?" His words skidded along her neck and ear.

The car revved. Pulled away. Fast.

"They just stopped—right in front."

"I was afraid this might happen." He rubbed a hand over his jaw. "Okay, get your stuff—enough for a week. We need to clear out."

"What—wait. Why?" Timbrel looked at him. "You don't seriously think Bijan—"

"Whether him or someone else, you're being watched. Time to go. Now, Hogan."

" 'No power in the 'verse. . .can stop me!'"

Tony shook his head and smiled. "*Firefly*—nice. But those guys *will* stop you. Now, do I need to pack for you?"

"Like I'd let you touch my stuff."

"You have five." He set his watch timer.

"You're a pain in my backside, Candyman."

"Right back atcha, baby."

Timbrel muffled a laugh as she hurried back to her room. She emptied the backpack she'd taken to LA with her then repacked. Being a tomboy and dressing in jeans and T-shirts made packing easy and light. "Where exactly are we going?"

"Virginia."

Timbrel stilled, stepped back, and glanced down the hall. "You realize that's a two-day drive?"

"Three minutes."

She rolled her eyes. Then it hit her—he'd ridden his bike from Virginia to Texas earlier in the week to find her. Dude.

Don't think. Don't think.

Throwing herself back into the packing, she added a lightweight jacket on top of her unmentionables and toiletries. With her gear, she headed back to the kitchen. Dropped the bag and knelt at the pantry. Beo pushed in beside her. No doubt wanting some treats.

"That all you're taking?" Tony's form shadowed her.

"Half. Get out of my light." She grabbed the pack she used for Beo, filled fourteen plastic pouches with dog food, and loaded them up. Couldn't go without his treats or his balls. Or his shampoo, extra collar, and lead. Packed, she fed Beo a peanut-butter treat then kissed his head. "That's my boy."

On her feet, she noticed Tony had shouldered her first pack. "Ready."

"I'll lead on my bike, if you're cool with that."

"Okay, but why don't we stop and get a trailer? My Jeep has a hitch."

He smiled. "Cool."

After four hours, a hitch, and a pit stop at what Tony called Four Bucks for coffee and pastries, they were en route to Virginia. "Tell me why we're going to Virginia." She said as she waited for Beo to jump up into the Jeep. Getting behind the wheel, she looked at Tony.

"That's where I live. Me and my family."

"Family?" She arched an eyebrow.

"Parents."

She nearly choked on her warmed bear-claw pastry. "You still live with your parents?"

Tony chomped into one of two cinnamon rolls he got and shrugged. But something else flashed through his expression, and the way he did that shrug told her to leave it alone.

She hadn't even hit the Texas-Arkansas border and Tony's head was bobbing, eyes drifting shut. He pushed himself straight and scrubbed at his face.

"Dude," Timbrel said with a laugh, glancing over at him. "Lay your seat back and crash. I'm good."

Uncertainty tugged at his exhausted features. "You sure?"

"Yeah. I got first watch. I slept on the plane."

"It was a three-hour flight."

Beo let out a long-suffering sigh and shifted so his face was between theirs.

"I think Beo just ended this conversation."

"Fine." Tony let the seat down and stretched an arm over his face. Then eased back up. "Wake me if you need me to take over. I can go on twenty-minute spurts when necessary."

She patted his stomach—man, his abs were solid!—and laughed.

"Nighty night, Mr. Knight in Shining Armor."

When Tony slumped back down with a grunt, it caught Beo's attention. Timbrel tried not to laugh as Beo sniffed and inspected Tony's hair—

Tony cleared his throat.

—then his arm—

"Hey," Tony warned quietly.

—then his underarm.

"Hey!" Tony folded his arms and stuffed his hands in his pits. "Can't a guy get some privacy here?"

Beo sneezed.

"Augh!" Tony flung upward, tugging his shirt up to wipe his face. "I swear he does that on purpose." He angled toward her. "And you prefer this snotty, drool-blathering beast to me?"

"Well," Timbrel said trying to bite back the laugh, "since you put it that way. . ." She hooked her arm up and rubbed Beo's ears.

Cleaned, Tony turned toward the passenger window and lay on his side, one arm under his head and one over—protecting himself from Beo.

Timbrel giggled. That posture would only egg on her beloved beast. It was one of their favorite ways to play. Instead of letting him pursue Tony, she gave him the signal to lie down. With a defeated grunt and sigh that sounded a lot like exasperation, Beo stretched over the backseat.

Quiet settled as the miles stretched before her. So, Virginia. That's awfully close to DC. Clogged streets, endless traffic. . .rapist ex-boyfriends.

Carson Diehl.

Timbrel pushed herself straight in the driver's seat. Rolled her hand over the steering wheel. It'd been years since she'd even seen him. But he lived there.

In DC.

Not Virginia.

It'd be okay.

Right. *You just told Tony every deep, dark secret and you're going to hole up with him?*

With his parents.

Acid poured through her stomach. What if he told them everything?

You're stupid, Timbrel. Telling him. Handing him a get-out-of-jail-free card from this relationship. And what guy in his right mind would stick around for a girl who couldn't even make out without freaking out?

Tony might think he wanted or knew her. But he didn't. He had no idea. And once he realized his mistake. . .

He wasn't the type to spill stuff. He understood sensitive material, but...

Okay, here's the plan. Virginia, home of the Pentagon, gave her the perfect opportunity to find Burnett and get him to test that lab coat. It was a legit reason not to stay with Tony. Not be exposed to humiliation or have to open the vault up more. He thought he knew her secrets. And he did.

Just not all of them.

Slowing movement tugged Tony from a sound sleep. Still on his side, he shifted. But something had wedged against his back.

"You can sleep anywhere."

Looking over his shoulder, he realized the big brindled mutt had stretched over the console and laid his head in Timbrel's lap.

Beo—hind paws in Tony's side—stretched and rolled onto his back, exposing his manhood to the world.

"You gotta be kidding me." He shoved the dog. "Dude. Stop sharing the family jewels."

Beo flipped upright, bringing his ugly mug right into Tony's face.

"Hey, c'mon, move!" Tony pushed against the bullmastiff. They needed to establish a few things—as in Tony wasn't Beo's stool or stooge.

Beo growled.

With a growl of his own, Tony pushed harder.

Beo snapped but hopped into the back.

"Right where you belong." Tony pulled up his seat and huffed.

"You know," Timbrel said as she directed the car into a gas station. "He was here before you."

Tony hesitated, hearing a weird twinge in her words that got hung up in his mind. The words were off somehow.

Nah. Probably just him. Lying in that position with Beo cramping his back and shoulders, he'd woken up a bit grumpy.

Timbrel climbed out, holding the door as her dog vacated the Jeep, then she started for the gas nozzle. She had to be dog tired. He snickered at his own joke as he peeled himself out of the vehicle, muscles seizing and aching. "I can take over driving from here." Arms over his head, he stretched. "Where are we?"

"Little Rock." Timbrel stuffed the nozzle into the Jeep and set it then headed into the store, her lumbering beast with her.

Whoa—she'd driven for over six hours! Which meant he'd slept for that long. Maybe that's why she was short with him. The hose clicked, and

Tony returned it to the pump then secured her vehicle. Trotting inside, he heard someone inside the store shouting, "No dogs."

"He's a working dog," Timbrel said as she waited on the side for her food.

"I don't care. He's not allowed in a place that serves food."

"Wrong. Check the laws." Arms crossed, Timbrel stood steadfast with her canine buddy.

Tony stood on the opposite side, posing as a stranger, and nodded. "She's right. I know a really great handler and she's telling the truth." He looked at Timbrel, but she kept her attention on the counter. By the way she held her lips in a tight line, she was ticked off.

"Whatever." The food guy walked away from the counter.

Tony tried to catch Timbrel's gaze again, but she remained focused on the bag another employee filled and handed to her. She thanked the lady, took the bag, and headed out the side door.

Okay, just keeping up the pretense that they weren't together. Cool.

After making use of the facilities, Tony washed up and splashed the lukewarm water on his face. He checked himself in the mirror, did a breath check, then returned to the food counter to order.

Tony hung back as his burgers and peach milkshake were prepared. Bag in hand, he stepped outside. The smack of humidity pulled his gaze to the sky. A bit gray, but nothing threatening.

He started crossing toward the pump, tugging some fries from the bag, when he realized Timbrel's Jeep wasn't in that stall. Wrong one. Munching fries, he angled left. Then stilled. What the—? He lowered the bag, straining to see all the pumps. He turned a circle, checking the spots lining the front of the convenience store.

A knot formed in the pit of his stomach.

Lightning snaked through the afternoon, crackling.

Tony spotted the car wash. Hey, maybe. . . He trotted toward the cement structure and peered into the bay where a black sedan sat.

Nope.

Tony strode back. "She did *not* just leave me." Disbelief wove a tight band around his chest and mind.

A white SUV pulled away from the pump and the knot tightened. The trailer with his bike sat at the edge of the parking lot. Unhitched. Abandoned.

Sixteen

Thunder boomed and cracked, vibrating through him. Rain doused him.

Tony cursed. "Un-friggin'-believable." He had no helmet, no safety jacket. Unless... He jogged over to the trailer and found his pack, helmet, and safety jacket. He fished his phone out of his pocket and hit her speed-dial number.

Grabbing his gear, he pressed the phone to his ear. It rang...and rang. He hustled back into the convenience store restaurant. He deposited his gear and food on the table and ran a hand through his hair to wipe away the rain. The phone still rang.

He'd hound the tar out of her backside. No way would she get away with this.

Pushing himself into the seat, he stared out the window mottled with raindrops, creating a blurry mural. He ended the call and tossed the phone on the table with the rest of his stuff. Fingers threaded, elbows on the grimy surface, he stared.

Why would she do this? They were fine. He'd even started contemplating the words "long-term" when it came to their relationship. Though hadn't he always thought that way about her? He wanted her—not sexually—well okay, yes, there was that—but Tony had "for the rest of our lives" in mind while pursuing Timbrel.

And she'd played him. Right up to the predawn sob story.

No. Now he was just reacting out of the hurt of her yet-again rejection. *God, I do not know what to do.*

He'd chased her. From the very beginning. Nothing could fend him off, not even that toothy, ugly mutt of hers.

But in his line of work, Tony knew there were some people you just couldn't sway, and forcing them might get immediate results, but the net product would be resentment.

Is that what happened? He'd pushed too hard?

Fingers threaded, he rested his forehead in his palms. *What do I do, God? I've tried everything I know.* Despite the overall sense of futility where prayer was concerned—God certainly hadn't answered the pleas regarding his dad—Tony had no options left. Add to that, he wasn't ready to give up on Timbrel. That felt a lot like giving up on his dad.

He groaned and tugged a burger from the bag, unfolded the wrapper, caught a whiff, and tossed it back down. Why couldn't she just try to make things work? They'd made some great headway. He'd always known great pain buffered her from letting anyone in. But she pushed away anyone who got too close or knew too much.

You were two for two, genius.

I love her, God. Man. He did. He'd never voiced it before nor even gone there with the "L" word, but the truth was like a double-tap. Burnett had warned him off, so had the entire ODA452 team.

Tony snatched up the burger. Chomped into it, watching the downpour. *But you had to go and try to prove them wrong.*

He grabbed his shake and took a drag on the straw.

He was Class A certifiably stupid. Because loving her was more painful than a bullet to the brain.

What would it take to win her over, completely?

Him taking a bullet for her?

Loving her dog?

I'd rather take the bullet.

Two Days Later
The Pentagon, Virginia

"What have ya got?" Lance Burnett crumpled his Dr Pepper can, let out a belch, then tossed it in the recycle bin. It clanked and nestled among the rest of the burgundy cans.

Lieutenant Brie Hastings handed him a grainy black-and-white aerial shot. "SATINT shows some unusual activity going on in a small village an hour south of Kabul. Nothing airtight but enough to keep our interest."

Burnett nodded.

"Internet chatter seems to indicate something big is developing, but again, nothing airtight."

Things never came as simple as "airtight" in this day and age. The enemy was swiftly gaining access to the same high-tech methods. They had to stay one step ahead or they'd lose—equipment, troops, and the whole bloody war.

But chatter and grainy pictures wouldn't cut it. "What about boots on ground?"

Hastings nodded. "Yes, sir." She handed over a report. "This is the reason I suggested we meet. HUMINT is humming, but we haven't been able to sort it."

Chair squeaking as he dropped forward, Lance flung the paper back at her. "For cryin' out loud, Hastings!"

She held up another page.

He pinched the bridge of his nose. "What is that?"

Pushing up but not standing, she leaned closer and slid it onto his desk. "You realize we are in the doghouse with all this, right? After that bookshop fiasco. . ."

"Yes, sir, but I think that will help our situation."

Issuing an exaggerated sigh, Lance shifted his attention to the eight-and-a-half-by-eleven page. The first thing to settle the nerves in his stomach—besides the Dr Pepper fix—were the nearly half-dozen stamps at the top. Terah Jeffries, the field officer whose signature scrawled along the bottom. Ahmed Khan, the information center employee who collected the letter and sent it on up to DIA.

Nothing really to get his knickers in a knot considering the source of origination: Terah Jeffries. She'd been responsible for losing one of the single most important assets the United States ever had.

"What's Jeffries up to?"

"Finally some good."

The channels had been verified and the report passed to Hastings. Sent her running into his office.

Lance lifted his glasses, slid them on, and started reading. "In light of buzzing activity and rumors of an unprecedented attack against the West and her allies. . .after numerous attempts have been made over the last six months to secure definitive information. . .escalation of our intelligence efforts alerted counterintelligence. . .despite years of silence and unanswered requests for help, contact made with Vari—" His breath backed into his throat as his mind processed the code name typed on the page. Lance stopped and peered over the rim of his glasses, disbelief doing a number on his high blood pressure. "Is this—?"

"Yes, sir."

"Variable's back?"

A knock sounded at the door.

"What now?" Lance groused. "Enter!"

Lieutenant Smith poked his head in. "Sorry, sir. I tried to buzz you—"

"We're busy."

He nodded. "Yes, sir. But you have a visitor."

"I don't care who it is. He can wait." He waved Smith out and returned his energy to the news Hastings had delivered. "So. . .how in Sam Hill did Jeffries get Variable to come back?"

Hastings smiled. "She didn't. According to the report"—Hastings indicated to the paper—"he came to her."

Lance scanned the rest of the page. "He wants a meeting—but why? And with whom?"

"Unknown. Specifics are also unknown at this time. We haven't relayed authorization to reengage the asset."

"Bull." Lance tapped the communiqué. "If I know Jeffries, she's already engaged him. And we verified that Jeffries submitted this?"

"Sir," Lieutenant Hastings said, "it has her official seal."

"Yeah," Lance said, but it still didn't convince him. "I'll look over this stuff and we'll talk this afternoon."

What was all this about? Why now? Maybe he should be asking a bigger question.

What pulled Variable out of retirement?

Sitting still with a guilty conscience proved monumentally impossible. But Timbrel steeled herself and Beo alerted, lifting his head from the carpeted area and looking in the direction from which footsteps echoed.

She followed his lead and spotted a man in uniform approaching. Lieutenant Smith—they'd met once before during Heath's first mission as an ABA handler.

"Miss Hogan." The man smiled—flirted, really.

"Hi."

"It's good to see you on safe ground."

"Thanks." Why did the thought of flirting with anyone or vice versa churn violently in her stomach?

He shifted on his feet and motioned toward the elevators. "The general is ready for you."

After waiting for more than an hour, she wasn't sure he'd see her. Burnett had always ushered her into the facility with an almost air of mystery and urgency. But today he hadn't. Maybe Tony had already told him.

Then again, the delay could've been that she didn't have an appointment and therefore had no clearance to enter the secure offices. Lieutenant Smith escorted her to the DIA offices without commentary on her weekend, nor did he ask the whereabouts of a certain hunky, green-eyed Special Forces soldier.

Then again, they probably had Candyman's status recorded down to his number of heartbeats per minute. A guy with that level of security clearance and operating on "eyes only" missions—yeah, he was probably tagged and logged hourly.

Timbrel held Beo's lead tight as they made their way down the narrow hall. She couldn't help but think about Neo in the movie *The Matrix* being led to the corner office where his life forever changed.

As gypsum walls gave way to half-glass and carpeted cubicles, Timbrel took a long draught of the cool air that swirled through this place. It helped. A little. She just hoped Burnett would listen to her. Their last conversation had been. . .well, loud.

Smith gripped the handle, his shoulder blade to the wood as he turned to her. "Good luck."

With a nod, she stepped into the inner sanctum of the man who worked night and day to keep the world at peace through violence of action.

"Why are you in my neck of the woods, Miss Hogan?" The booming voice wrapped itself around her and tugged her into the unusually cold office.

"Good afternoon, sir. Nice to see you, too." Timbrel didn't want him in a foul mood when she was about to throw one major wrench in the war game.

His phone rang and he held a finger up at her as he answered.

His chair creaked as he pushed back and stared at her over the rim of his glasses. Ensconced by a library that no doubt rivaled the National Archives, Burnett had this air about him. One that bespoke power and presence. The gilded frames on the wall portrayed him with a number of dignitaries, and one—whoa! The dude was quite the looker in his younger days—captured his wedding day. Jet-black wavy hair, a killer smile, and clearly had eyes only for the blond wrapped in his arms. Now at sixtyish, she'd call him distinguished. But she couldn't be nicer than that. He treated her like a daughter, and yelled at her like one, too.

"Don't give me any of your cheek, young lady." He stood and shuffled to a side cabinet, where he opened a door and then another. Burnett held up a Dr Pepper. "Drink?"

"No, thank you."

He shut the doors and straightened, the *tssssk* hissing through the room. After a slurp, he moved back to his desk. "I've got an AHOD in fifteen, so you'd better get on with what you want." Then he hesitated. "This doesn't have anything to do with your mom, does it?"

Timbrel smirked. "No, sir. Well, not directly."

"Then how, *indirectly*?" He motioned her to one of the two leather chairs in front of his massive mahogany desk as he clanked down in his.

Where to start? Mom's house. . .Sajjan. . . "Remember the op we had some difficulty with—the bookshop one?"

After another slurp, he scowled.

Yeah. Right. "Remember that I mentioned one of the men who was escorted out of the hidden publishing area?"

Burnett said nothing. Only stared. He had some seriously fierce eyes.

"Well, I think that man was at my mother's dinner last Friday night."

"Hogan."

Timbrel gritted her teeth against the condescension that thickened the way he said her name. She unzipped her pack. "I got his jacket." She held it out. "I was thinking—"

"No! No, you weren't thinking." Burnett's red face matched his neck. "Of all the—what do you think you were doing?"

"Sir, I am convinced Beo had a positive hit in that bookshop—"

"Yes, on—" He shoved to his feet. "We already had this conversation. I won't repeat myself. That operation is over. There was nothing there except dadgum books! And you and I both know the chemicals used to make books are also used for bombs. It's an honest mistake, but one I'm not even going to attempt to make again. Your dog won't know the difference."

"I disagree."

Burnett growled. "Hogan, I'm not doing this again. I had to take heart meds the last time you and I talked."

"Sir, will you please just test the fabrics of this coat? Lab analysis will prove whether it's simple bookmaking chemicals or. . .more."

"No. Now listen—you were once an MP and it was your job to investigate. But not anymore. You're a dog handler."

"And if you won't listen to me when I say my dog has a hit—"

"That's not in question. I listened. You were wrong. End of story."

"But—"

"End. Of. Story!"

"Is everyone in the Army pigheaded like you?"

"Absolutely. We've been bred and trained." His lips pressed tight told her the story. Burnett knew what she'd done in Arkansas, to his soldier. "Now, I have an appointment."

Timbrel slam-dunked the lab coat on his desk. "Prove me wrong. I dare you. That man knew who I was, and there was something in his expression that warned me we'd hit close to a very raw nerve. He pulled a gun on me. Tony had to incapacitate him. If that doesn't tell you something, if you won't explore it—"

"So help me God—and I do mean that I will need the help of God not to bring everything down your neck if you go out there and stir up any more trouble." He jabbed a thick finger at her. "I will have your hardheaded butt on so many charges, you won't see straight." He grabbed his jacket and stuffed his fists through the sleeves. "You'd do well to mind your own business over the next few weeks while my teams work to quiet this storm you've stirred up. By the way, VanAllen was right."

Heat flared down Timbrel's spine and coiled around her stomach at the mention of his name. "What?"

"You might want to check the news. I don't think you have a home anymore. Seems someone didn't take kindly to you stealing that lab coat."

The world spun beneath her feet. "What?" She steeled herself, and in some vague, peripheral way felt Beo nudge her hand. No home? What did he mean no home? "But you see, that means my point is valid."

"No, it means you've stirred a hornet's nest that has me in some seriously deep kimchi. I mean it—stay out of it or you'll find yourself in jail. And remember this, Hogan. VanAllen saved your behind—again. What's it going to take after your home burning to the ground?"

Like a video powering down or freezing, Timbrel heard the general's words melted over the mental image of her home. *My home. . .* "Were you serious that I have no home?"

He quieted then clicked his tongue. "I'd say I'm sorry, and in a way I am. I see you like a daughter in some twisted way, but you did this to yourself."

Her eyes stung. "So, really—I have no home."

Burnett lowered his gaze for a moment. He blurred like a nightmarish image. "Too bad you walked away from the only person willing to give you the time of day." He grabbed a stack of files, his hat, and started for the door. "Good day, Miss Hogan." Down the narrow hall that separated the offices from cubicles, he could be heard saying, "Hastings, escort her out."

Hot, wet drops slipped down her face. She had nothing left. What did he mean? Her gaze hit a TV and she shoved herself across the office and jabbed the POWER button.

She stabbed the channel nub till she found a news source.

"Miss Hogan. . . May I help you?"

Timbrel spun. "What happened to my home?"

Crestfallen, Hastings gave her a sympathetic look. "Come here. I'll show you." She held the knob as Timbrel stumbled past her and wrapped her arms around her waist. She led her back to her cubicle, and after few keystrokes, she leaned back. Nudged her monitor toward her as Timbrel stood numb and mute.

There, a photo caption from the *Austin American-Statesman* read: HOME BURNS TO GROUND—OWNER MISSING.

Hauling in a painful breath, Timbrel covered her mouth.

"Burnett notified the authorities that you're okay and requested all future information about this be reported directly to him. It won't be in the media again."

As if that mattered or could make anything better. *"You did this to yourself."* Tears swirled and blurred the office into an impressionistic painting.

An arm came around her shoulder. "I'm sorry."

Timbrel burrowed out of the hold, smashing the tears from her face. "Thanks. I'm okay."

"Hey." A soft voice from behind turned her around.

Lieutenant Smith stood there, a small piece of paper in his hand. "Here."

Blinking against the tears she'd held back, Timbrel struggled to make out the lettering. "What. . .?"

"He said if you asked about him, to give you this." Smith shrugged. "But he didn't know about your house, so. . .I think he would want you to have it, especially now that you have no home."

Hastings slapped his gut. "Ignore him. He's a man—he's insensitive."

Timbrel glanced down as she unfolded the torn paper. An address scrawled in block letters filled the small ragged piece. "Tony?" Her voice squeaked. She cleared her throat. "He was here?"

Smith nodded. "Yesterday with his team. Go see him."

A squall of guilt and a burning ache churned through her chest.

Timbrel shoved it back at him. "I. . .I can't." Strangled by the thought of facing Tony after abandoning him, she knew she didn't have any right to see him, to want to see him. And she did. Everything in her wanted to run to him. But she'd closed that door by leaving him in Little Rock.

The rain. Oh man, the downpour that unleashed haunted her—it almost felt like the earth cried over her betrayal—and nearly made her turn back, ate her up with condemnation for leaving him there in the storm. Did he try to drive home then? Or. . .

Tormenting herself wouldn't help. "I can't." A hollow laugh climbed her throat. "He hates me. There's no way he'd see me now."

Hastings folded her hand over Timbrel's that held the note. "He wouldn't have left this if he hated you."

Timbrel wouldn't buy into false hopes. She'd known where to hit Tony and had nailed her mark. She wasn't as stupid as to think he'd just welcome her back with open arms. She crumpled the note into her pocket. On her way out, she'd pitch it in the lobby. Mustering her courage took what little she had left, but she met their gazes—*ugh, the sympathy!*—and plastered on a smile. "Thanks. I need to go."

Had to get out. *"You're useless. You ruin everything."*

The voices from the past came screaming back as she dragged herself and her beaten pride from the Pentagon. *Had to get out. Gotta breathe.* She aimed out of Arlington, Virginia, and just drove. But the torrent threatened.

She'd betrayed him. Abandoned him. Ran like a scared little girl— *which, I am*—and left him in the rain. And still—*still*—he left his address.

A sob leapt from her throat.

She shook her head. Steeled herself.

No, it had to be this way. It'd hurt for a while, but she'd get over it.

The lie tasted bitter and salty.

Air ruffled her hair as she crossed a bridge. Water sparkled from below, taunting and inviting. She glanced to the side and saw the Tidal Basin. She yanked the steering wheel right, narrowly avoiding a white SUV as she beelined for the exit.

Beo shifted in the passenger seat, then swung his head out the window, sniffing as she slowed and made her way onto Iowa, the street running along the basin. A car pulled away from the curb and Timbrel swung into the open spot. She hopped out and trudged over to the water's edge, her legs becoming leaden as she grew closer. Freeing her hair, she felt tendrils of control loosening. Control of her life. Control of her very being.

Control. What an illusion. She remembered when Tony said letting

God have control was crazy-scary. He had that right. The thought of *not* trying to protect herself when she'd had to do it her whole life. . . *Just not ready to go there yet.*

She sat on the grassy knoll, Potomac waters glistening like diamonds in the setting sun, and hugged her knees to her chest.

Beo trotted to her side and plopped his backside down. Chest puffed, snout in that pout that made him seem like an old Englishman staring at her, he faced her as if to say, "Go ahead, the doctor is in."

Timbrel rubbed the side of his face then his ear between her thumb and forefinger. "I did it, Beo. I ran him off." She managed a smile. "Just like all the other guys."

He sighed as if to say, "Finally."

"I know you're happy he's gone, but. . ." Her chin bounced. She fought it. "I'm not."

She hadn't been. Not in a long time. Hate, the heaping dose of family medicine that had been doled out since childhood, poisoned her to accepting love. Forbid her from even taking antidotal portions. Hate she could deal with.

This. . .this acceptance, this—what was it? Tony seemed completely unaffected by the attitude she'd delivered with a baseball bat and power swing. A sob wracked her. Add to all that, she'd lost her home. All her possessions went up in flames. Photo albums, computers, clothes, rings. . .

Now she'd also ruined a vital relationship—Burnett. As a handler, she depended on those gigs. Lately, the only ones coming her way were with DIA. If he saw her as reckless and incompetent, he wouldn't request her again. She'd be jobless.

You're useless.

Arms wrapped around her knees, she hugged them tighter and cried onto her jeans. *How do I always screw it up?* Without handling, without Tony. . .what did she have to live for? Carson had been right all those years ago. She'd fought it. Hated that he'd said it. But he was right.

I'm useless.

She stared at the water, felt the undulating invitation to sink to its depths.

"Life isn't worth doing."

AL-QIYAMA—
THE DAY OF JUDGMENT AND THE RESURRECTION

Present Day

"Raze it."

Karzai stood in the middle of the pothole-laden road, hands behind his back as he stared down the main route into the village. All looked innocent and quiet, but within her borders reeked a foul disease.

"Is it necessary?" Dehqan asked, his question quiet, contemplative. Not defiant. Or angry.

"Allah puts us on this earth to test us," he said to the boy who had become a man. "Trials are presented to us to determine our loyalty to Allah. It is of the utmost importance that we consider the al-Qiyama." He eyed Dehqan.

"The day of Judgment and the Resurrection." Dehqan's gaze hopped around the small, crude buildings.

"There are twelve-hundred verses in the Qur'an that speak of this." Karzai gave the signal to Irfael, who waved the men into the village. Fires were lit. Weapons discharged. Screams spiraled.

Karzai breathed in the smoke, the sacrifice of the impure, the evil. "These people lurk like serpents in the desert, and with their smooth talk and their adulterous words, they brainwash our friends, our loved ones, into believing in Isa."

A boy darted from a house, quick as a mouse, and started straight toward them. "Please, Imam Karzai, help us!" His mouth opened, but the scream that seemed ready to leap from his lips morphed into the sound of a gunshot. The boy dropped like a wet blanket.

Karzai nodded to his captain but noted the absence of his son and protégé.

Dehqan turned and slumped against the armored vehicle. Head tucked, arms folded, he seemed shaken. The popping jaw muscle spoke of his anger.

"What troubles you?"

Wide, expressive eyes shot to his. "That boy—how: . .how could he have done anything that warranted being shot in the back?"

Were he not certain the boy before him, the one who had witnessed far greater things, would not normally be affected by this cleansing of the unfaithful, Karzai would not mentally search to understand this reaction. Was it the age?

All at once, he understood. Yes. The age. "You see yourself in that boy." He went to the one he'd raised for the last decade. "Dehqan, come."

"No, I'm through. I want to leave." His panicked expression gave way to a wild frenzy. "This. . . I can't—"

"You will obey me!" Karzai snapped each word out. Breathing hard, he drew himself together. Held out a hand. "Come. I would show you something." He took him by the upper arm, only now realizing the boy stood several inches taller. His bicep, too, had filled out. It stirred pride in Karzai to know that Dehqan had become a man under his tutelage. But the mind—the mind must be molded like clay. And if he must break that clay and start over, he would do it.

Hauling Dehqan down the pocked road, Karzai led him to the boy. He motioned Irfael to his side. "Turn him over."

"No, please!" Dehqan's voice pitched. "Leave the dead in peace."

Fire lit through Karzai's soul as the body made a soft thump as the boy rolled onto his back. "You must look at him."

"No." That wild frenzy returned. "I have seen death. There is no need—"

"Look. At. Him!"

Nostrils flaring, shoulders squared, Dehqan stared back unabashedly at Karzai without complying. Then he sagged. His eyes dropped to the body.

Despite the processional of gunshots, crackling fire, and screams that mingled into a day of sacrifice, Karzai took in the boy. Black hair hung in his face, matted by the blood that had soaked the ground and his shirt from the chest wound. Even with the dark stain, the lettering was still visible.

"What is on his shirt?"

Dehqan wilted even more. "A cross."

"That is right. A gift to him, no doubt from Christian missionaries. A shirt that is paraded around this village. The people see it, accept it, grow *used* to it until the symbol itself is acceptable." Karzai felt the cauldron of fury bubbling up through his chest. "But it is *not* acceptable. We cannot allow the Christians to spread their lies! Not here. Not in our land. Not with our people."

His spittle struck Dehqan and made him flinch. Good. Something needed to make the boy snap out of his stupor.

"It can *never* be acceptable. Do you see this? We cannot tolerate this. Surah 3:18 says, 'There is no God but He, the Mighty, the Wise.'" Vindicated and awash with a sense of victory as the words from the Qur'an spilled over his tongue, Karzai let himself breathe a little deeper. A little slower. "As imam, it is my duty to administer this justice. It is your duty as a follower of Allah."

Dehqan lowered his head and bobbed it twice. Defeated.

"This boy, if he is by some miracle innocent, Allah will judge that. His life does not end here. Remember that, Dehqan. What is here is fleeting. He is in a better place." Karzai gave a smile. "We have done him a service to deliver him from the influence of the Great Satan before he could be pulled away by their tainted and perverted ways. Remember, some go to Paradise. Others go the fire."

"You are right," Dehqan finally said, standing taller. Swiped a hand over his face. "Yes. You are right. Forgive me for being weak, sir."

"No, no." Karzai clapped a hand on his son's shoulder. "Not weak. You value life, and that is good. You value our people—that is better. This—*this* is my mission. To protect our people. To rout the Great Satan from these lands." He swept his hand around the village and extended it toward the mountains in the distance. "This is our land, Dehqan." He wanted to turn this around, show Dehqan that he was strong. He patted his chest. "Surah 9:5."

With a small snort and smile, Dehqan nodded as he took one more look at the boy, then turned back to the car as he recited the words, " 'Fight and kill the disbelievers wherever you find them, take them captive, harass them, lie in wait and ambush them using every stratagem of war.' "

Seventeen

Leesburg, Virginia

S he's been missing for three days."

Tony pinched the bridge of his nose as he stood in his bedroom in jeans, a shirt dangling from his hand that held the phone. "What do you mean?"

"Look, I just need you to find her."

"Sir." Tony's chest tightened as he thought of Timbrel. Thought of her missing. Thought of how she'd just left him there in Little Rock. No, she fled.

"She came here, heard about her home, and then she and I had words over that lab coat."

Tony ground his teeth. Unbelievable. She'd ditch him but not the coat or her belief that Bashir Karzai was up to no good. Why couldn't she be that dogged about their relationship? "What kind of words?"

"I told her to quit playing detective and left. I had a meeting."

"Look, I'm sorry, sir, but Timbrel severed ties with me a week ago. I haven't heard from her since."

"I don't care what she did. Find her."

"Why?"

"Because. . .I think she may be right."

A firm knock banged on the door and his head.

"Tony?"

"I think this is a futile mission, sir. If Timbrel took off, and I know personally she has a tendency to do that, we can't find her. Because she doesn't want to be found." At another knock on the door, he called over his shoulder. "I'll be out in a minute."

"Um. . .okay," his mom said, but her voice. . . "But—"

"Two minutes."

"There's. . . Oh, Tony, please hurry."

Frustration strangled him. He yanked open the door—and froze.

Face knotted, she was wringing her hands.

"What's wrong? Is it Dad?"

"No." Her face was alive yet tormented. "Well, sort of."

"VanAllen." Burnett's voice boomed through the cell phone. "Find her and get back here. Tomorrow morning with the team."

"Yes, sir." It was the expected answer. "You know my feel—"

The line went dead. Tony flung the phone.

"Hurry, son," his mom prompted quietly then hesitated. Looked at his chest. "Might want to put on that shirt."

He couldn't help the laugh as her form retreated down the hall but pawed his way through the sleeves and made his way to the living room. Empty. He headed for the kitchen. "Mom?"

"Shh." She stood by the door to the back deck and placed a finger against her lips, then pointed to the seating group.

Tony's heart powered down.

His father sat on the wicker sofa laughing. Talking. Patting the knee of the person to his right. Timbrel!

A dozen questions peppered his mind—Where had she been? How did she find him? What was she doing here?—but he clenched his teeth.

"That's when I realized we were in trouble," Timbrel said.

"Ha! I got one better than that," his father said, a thick heaping of pride in his words. "Once, we slipped out to find a team that had been captured. They were elite soldiers, so how they got ambushed is beyond me, but we went in there under the cover of darkness. I tell you, that was one messed-up mission from the word 'go.' Halfway in, we start coming across bodies. . ."

"Dad never told me this one." Tony felt his frown but couldn't shake it. He looked to his mom. "You?"

Hand over her mouth, tears in her eyes, she shook her head.

Tony touched her shoulder but didn't move from the spot. He wanted to rush out there and light into Timbrel, but. . .

"We got in there, Timmy. But we were too late." His father grunted and went silent. He looked down. "Oh. Hello, fella." Hand out, he chuckled as Timbrel's dog leaned into the touch. "Bet she hasn't given you an ounce of love."

Timbrel laughed. "Definitely not. He's too mean."

Bending forward, his father whispered conspiratorially, "I won't betray your secrets, old fella." Then he looked out at the yard. "Sure is heatin' up. Could you get me a glass of water?"

"Um, sure." Timbrel was on her feet and coming straight toward where Tony stood before his mind could reengage.

Her gaze lifted.

Eyes locked.

Timbrel stilled.

Tony couldn't move. Could barely swallow that squirt of adrenaline that hit the back of his throat, forcing him to process it.

"Well, what happened? Your shoes stuck, pretty little lady?" His father laughed and stroked Beo's head. Weird that the dog hadn't tried to take off his dad's hand yet. "Nothing to be afraid of around here. You should meet my son. He's not married."

Timbrel balled her hands, wiping her fingers. Nervous.

Oh he wanted to be mad. Very mad. Beyond mad.

But he couldn't. Understanding her plight severed that tension cord.

"I'll get the water," his mother's voice came from somewhere in the middle of this black hole of he didn't know what. Just knew he couldn't get his brain to order his mouth to speak.

After a pause, Timbrel came forward. "I'm..."

Tony didn't trust himself to speak. He might not be ticked off, but the hurt she'd inflicted left a crater-sized hole in his ability to be reasonable. But the way she stood, rubbing her palms, looking contrite—no, scared.

Another uncertain step forward. He could tell by the way she wouldn't hold his gaze for longer than two seconds that she was no longer confident of his feelings for her.

Good thing. Neither was he.

Less than a foot stood between them. "Tony, I..." Their eyes met and froze. Her brows knotted.

"Excuse me," his mother said as she slipped out the door. "Here you go, Jimmy. You wanted some water?"

"Where'd that pretty girl go?"

"Why, James VanAllen, don't tell me you're flirting with younger women."

His father laughed.

Tony's heart caught.

"Can we talk?"

Without a word, he stepped aside and motioned her into the house. And for the first time in . . .well, forever, Beowulf stayed with his father, who still stroked the bullmastiff's head.

"Tony," his dad called, "don't keep her to yourself for long. I like that girl."

Silent, Tony led her to the family den where cozy furniture and built-ins gave the room a warm glow with the evening sun poking through the wood blinds. Hands tucked into his underarms, Tony stood at the fireplace, legs apart. Ready for a fight.

It'd been five years since she'd been without Beowulf. Not having him now. . . Timbrel instinctively wanted to retrieve the purple and green afghan draped over the leather sofa to cover herself. She felt naked standing before Tony VanAllen right now. Crazy since she was fully dressed and it was only autumn.

Her gaze trolled the pictures, the frames, the trophies—Tony had been quite the jock.

Not that it surprised her. There wasn't anything he couldn't do, including getting her to come to him after she'd given him the shaft. Timbrel felt more out of place than any place she'd ever visited before.

The family photo of five—Tony and a brother and sister. Timbrel couldn't tear herself from the young girl stuffed between her two big brothers. What must it have been like to be protected? Teased? With blond bangs and freckles, the sister looked like an all-American girl. And by the picture on the mantel, she apparently had a family of her own now. Strange that Timbrel could envy someone she'd never met, but she did.

Only as the quiet wrapped around her could Timbrel pull herself from the quicksand of lost dreams. She hugged herself, much like she had at the basin, and wet her lips as she forced herself to look at him.

He stood there, arms folded, legs spread. Did he realize how intimidating he was?

Yes. Yes, he absolutely did. Might as well get on with it.

"I. . ." She tugged the note from her pocket. Smoothed the crinkles out as best she could. "Thank you."

Tony said nothing. His green eyes yielding no hint of his feelings.

She let her finger trace the blurred blue ink. "I'm sorry."

"If you're going to apologize, have the decency to look me in the eye."

Startled at his tone, she drew up straight. And did just as he asked. No guessing now how he felt. Everything in her swelled to a pique, ready to lash out at him. But Timbrel quelled it. "I'm sorry"—the confession pushed her onward—"for everything. For Little Rock, for not talking to you, for not answering your calls."

Seconds felt like minutes. Finally, he gave a curt nod, lowering his arms and resting his hands on his jeans belt.

Talk about awkward. She fidgeted with the paper, unsure where to go from this point. "I've never done this before."

"What? Apologize?"

A snappy retort dangled at the tip of her tongue, begging for release. Instead, Timbrel eyed him, gauging him for anger. "No, come back. I've never. . .come back." She shifted on her feet. "I'm not. . .I'm not really sure what else to say."

"Where have you been? How'd you get here?"

"Everywhere. Drove." It was supposed to be funny, but his deadpan expression warned her of the fail. Holy cow, he wasn't going to make this easy, was he? "After spending some really cold, wet hours at the Tidal Basin, I drove till I found somewhere to sleep. A motel"—she waved her hand then scratched her forehead—"I don't remember where. Crashed there."

"It hasn't rained in several days. Why were you wet?"

Timbrel wet her lips and squeezed out that answer. "Decided to"—her throat burned—"to um, take a swim, but uh. . .Beo wasn't up for it." She tried to smile, but it quivered and collapsed just as quick.

Admitting she tried to commit suicide didn't rank real high on the "smart" scale, and she just didn't have the emotional capital to go there with Tony. She wanted things fixed between them. She'd do anything to have him crack a joke. Make her laugh. Tell her things would be okay. To have him hold her, fix this mess she'd created.

"Burnett said your home is gone."

Timbrel ducked. "Don't worry about me. I'll be fine. My mom has called my cell nine times begging me to let her help."

"Running back to your mother?"

Defiance plucked at her attempt to remain humble. "No, I've never run back to her, but this time, I may not have a choice."

"We have a brief at 0800. Burnett wants you there." Tony stepped off the bricks and crossed the room. "You can crash here for the night." He stalked toward the door, sweeping around her without a glance. "I'll have my mom get you set up in Steph's old room."

"Tony, please." Timbrel whirled around, stopping him. "I'm sorry. I really am. What I did to you in Little Rock—" She couldn't even say the words. But she had to. He deserved that. "Leaving you. . ."

"Yeah, what about that, Timbrel?"

"Look, it was stupid."

"Score one for Hogan."

"You know things—things about me nobody else does. And I just. . . I got scared you'd tell someone. That you'd—"

"Hold up." His brows nose-dived toward blazing green eyes. Like a fast-moving storm, he swooped in. "You're going to stand there and tell me this is my fault? You're questioning *my* integrity when I've shown nothing but absolute and 100 percent belief in you? When I've taken your snide comments, your razor-sharp words. . . And you thought *I* would be a problem? Tell me one time"—his chest heaved—*"one time"*—the words were deafening, his temples bulging with the effort of shouting before he took a long, ragged breath—"when I didn't act with the utmost honor regarding you."

Timbrel closed her eyes. He was right. He was always right. And it hurt. *God of heaven, it hurts.* Not the reprimand but knowing he had a point. She would do anything for Tony VanAllen, anything to make him proud of her, to make him see that she wasn't the loser she'd proven herself to be time and again.

But. . .what did his anger mean? Was he saying they were over? Not that they ever really got *started*, but. . .

She looked into his eyes, saw the fury, noted his shallow breaths. "You're right." She slipped around him. "I'll leave. I should've known coming here—"

Tony hooked her arm. Silenced her.

Eager to mend this rift, this giant chasm she'd created between them, Timbrel turned to him. What she saw there—the rage rising and falling through his facial features like a mighty storm, the torment, the way he closed his eyes for a second and looked to the side—kneaded a ball of dread in her stomach.

What have I done? The one man worth fighting for. . .

Tony huffed out a breath. "You'll stay here tonight."

"I don't—"

"Tomorrow we meet up with the team." His voice was almost normal. "After that. . . I don't know." Anguish poured through his green eyes that held her captive. "If there is such a thing."

Relief felt like someone hit the OFF valve on the toxin pouring into the container of her life.

"What you did, Timbrel. . . It wasn't just about ditching me. What you did told me I can't depend on you to be there when things get tough." His eyes narrowed with meaning. "Do you get me?"

As much as it pained her. . . "Yeah."

"It also tells me fear is controlling you. That whatever you think you're protecting is more important than me." He held her gaze. "That's no basis for a relationship. Right there in Little Rock, you ended what we had. That can't be fixed."

"But what of Isa?"

After watching my father raze the village of Christians, I tensed at her question. It burned against my conscience. "No more of that question." I shut the book, pushed to my feet, then trudged over to the sitting area. There, I dropped onto a chair and gripped my head in my hands. If only I could sear those images, those screams from my mind.

Watching the guilty die was one thing. Witnessing the murder of innocent children. . .

The scent of roses swirled around my face. A soft presence pressed against my awareness, and I opened my eyes.

Nafisa's brown eyes held my gaze, mere inches from my face. Green. I see flecks of green in the brown eyes. Why hadn't I noticed that before? She's so beautiful. So sweet.

"What is wrong, Dehqan?"

Lowering my gaze, I wrestled with telling her of the brutality. Part of me was afraid to speak of it, to give voice to the evil lurking beneath the surface. But if I did not, the evil would consume me. Already, I felt a strange anger toward her. I did not want her to talk to me. Did not want her to bring up Isa again. Ever! What if my father heard her?

A shudder shook my body.

Nafisa's expression clouded. "Did something happen?"

"He. . .he has a plan," I managed. The words were so far from what I wished to tell her. I felt repelled from the truth. And as the words rang in my own ears, I realized they were also filled with what ailed me. Father had a plan. A vicious, brutal plan to kill Americans. Many people would die. Innocent?

Father says the Great Satan is not innocent.

But how could *all* of them be guilty? How could all the children in that village have been guilty?

"What kind of plan?" Her eyes were thoughtful, words soft. But they angered me. I pushed to my feet and moved away from her.

Why? Why am I angry?

"I will pray for Isa to help you."

Whirling around with a mind full of rage, I growled, "No! No *Isa!*" I stomped toward her. Though I felt the demons of rage and violence whirring through my veins, it was as though I couldn't stop myself. "No more Isa. *No more!*"

Nafisa came to her feet.

Though I expected to see anger in her face, maybe hurt, all I saw was sadness.

"You believe in the ways of Allah, Dehqan, but I believe in Isa, that He was *more* than just a prophet. That He is God triune."

Allah forgive me, but I cursed at her.

"Not anger, not threats, not death can change my mind or my heart." A smile, genuine and full, lit her beautiful face. "Isa said, 'I am come that they might have life, and that they might have it more abundantly.'"

"Ha! Life," I scoffed and tossed my hands at her. "Where was that life when those children were cut down and killed? Where was Isa?"

Nafisa stilled. "What children?"

I hung my head. "Never mind." Turning away from her did not quiet my mind. With one arm around my midsection and one bracing my head, I warded off the. . . I don't know what it was. It just. . .*pounded*. Not a headache. It's inside me. "But you must stop talking about Isa. I do not want to hear about Him anymore. No more of your lies."

"I only quote what is written, Dehqan, and as much as I care for you, I will not quiet my voice even for you."

"How can you say that? Don't you know I can have you killed?"

Her eyes widened and she drew back a little—but then quick as a mouse, her strength returned. "You could cut off my voice, but you cannot cut off the voice of God, Dehqan. He is calling to you." Hurt pinched her delicate brows together. "Can't you see it, feel it?"

"I see and feel nothing!" The lie clumped in my throat. I coughed. Thumped my chest—regretted it as a fresh wave of pain from the bullet wound gripped me—and planted myself in the chair at the head of the table we'd used for studying. She could not sit close to me then. "You should leave."

"Something eats at your soul, my friend," Nafisa said as she crouched at my side, thin, long fingers holding the carved arm of the chair. "It wrestles within you, seeking solace. Seeking comfort. What you seek is Isa."

"No!"

"It is!" Vehemence coated her words as thickly as my own. "He has His hand on you. He is calling you out, just as He called me to be here, to be your friend, to help you see the truth."

"What is truth, Nafisa? Is it the colonel's truth? Is it the Qur'an? The Bible? The guard's truth? How do I know which one is right?"

Her full, rosy lips twisted in a conspiratorial smile. " 'I am the way, the truth, and the life.' " Her eyes were alive. "Isa said that in the book of John when Thomas asked how he could know the way." She touched my arm, and it felt like a current of electricity. "You can know the way, too, Dehqan. You feel alone, yes?"

How she knew this, I couldn't understand. Heat rose to my cheeks.

"Isa said He will not leave us as orphans but will come to us—"

My heart stuttered. "Orphans?"

Eighteen

Nasty!" Four-year-old Hayden wrinkled his nose and jumped up from his seat.

Tony sat at the end of the table, his father at the head, and refused to acknowledge what was happening. Refused to take another breath. He looked at his second helping of lasagna. Was it his imagination or was it wilting?

"I'm so sorry," Timbrel whispered.

"What's that smell?" Marlee waved her hand in front of her face. "Eww!"

The breath forced itself from his lungs. And in flooded a noxious, rancid smell he was sure burned his nose hairs.

Okay, nope. He couldn't take it anymore. Tony punched to his feet.

His mom stood. "Why don't we go out onto the patio?"

"It's still ninety degrees out there," Stephanie objected.

"Yeah," her husband said, "but at least you'll be able to breathe."

"Who cut one?" Hayden asked, laughing as his parents hauled him outside.

"Hayden Anthony!" Stephanie scowled at her son.

"Aw, that isn't anything," his dad said. "Try breathing in tear-gas training!"

His mother smiled politely. Fakely. "I'll bring dessert and the bowls."

Out in the yard, Tony stifled his laugh as his brother-in-law, Chad, stomped down the porch laughing. "That was something awful."

"Sorry," Timbrel managed as she sat on the wide steps with her Beowulf, the culprit of the stench that chased them from the house. "He tends to have room-clearing flatulence."

The fresh air, though hot and upward of eighty-five according to the outdoor thermometer, also helped Tony with the choked feeling he had around Timbrel. He just didn't know where to go. Letting her off easy, forgiving her—he wasn't sure that'd get through to her. He'd gone all out for her, been willing to do anything. . .

He wasn't mad. Not like he was three hours ago when he didn't know if she'd delivered herself from this world or not. But he just didn't know how to move beyond the fact she'd been able to walk away from him so easily.

Okay, maybe it hadn't been so easy. It'd taken a toll on her—she'd all but admitted to trying to drown herself. *Drowning herself.* An ache kinked his gut. Did she really think so little of herself? She had to get some serious grounding on her worth. He knew firsthand that if you didn't ground that identity first in Christ, then you would forever be searching for identity, for approval, for recognition.

She now sat next to his father, talking and laughing. Beo lounged between them. What a strange connection between those two. And odd that his father had been lucid and calm for most of the afternoon.

Since Timbrel arrived.

Yeah, that was a total coincidence since the only thing Timbrel Hogan excelled at was agitating people. What was it about her that drove people like his sister to catty, petulant words and activity?

She's perfect.

The words sifted through his frustration. Yeah. She was.

But she was also dogheaded and fiercely independent. Too afraid to let anyone in. But she'd let him in and it'd unglued her entire compass.

If he let her back in—and he knew he would because he loved that girl like crazy—he had to do it with the knowledge that she'd break his heart again. Because there sure wasn't an easy fix or remedy to the deep-seated fear that controlled her.

Maybe if he set conditions. . .

Love has no conditions.

He rubbed his jaw. He wasn't sure he had it in him to leap off the cliff for her. No—he would. He'd had a warrior's heart since kindergarten, but what weighted him now was wondering if Timbrel would even care if he jumped.

"Nana!" Five-year-old Marlee rushed over to his mom as she delivered the pie and plates to the table outside. "Did you see the necklace Uncle Tony got me?"

"Oh, so pretty." His mom served the first slice to his father. "That stone matches your pretty green eyes."

The back door swung open and Grady joined them. Finally. "What happened in there? Food's still on the table."

"Timbrel's dog farted," Hayden announced as he braced the soccer ball under his foot. "We had to escape. Boy did that stink." Nose scrunched, he waved a hand in front of his face. "It's better out here."

"Hayden, you apologize," Stephanie said.

"No, he's right," Timbrel said.

When Stephanie shot a look at Timbrel, apparently for going against her, Timbrel redirected her attention to the pie his mom offered.

"Pie, Grady?" Mom asked as she cut more slices, clearly wanting to divert the conversation.

"Marlee gave Beowulf some cheese," Hayden announced.

Batting blond hair from her face, Marlee fumed. "It wasn't my fault he farted!"

"Shh." Mom tugged the little girl closer. "That's enough, now." She turned her attention to Grady. "Did you want pie?"

"Sounds great." Grady cocked his head and made eye contact with Timbrel. Something went primal in Tony at the way his brother sized her up and made his way over to her. "Grady VanAllen."

She shook his hand. "Timbrel Hogan."

"She's Uncle Tony's girlfriend," Marlee said in a sweet voice as she spooned her dessert. "You can't have her, Uncle Grady."

"Marlee!" Stephanie gaped and offered an apologetic look to Tony.

In his periphery, Tony noted Timbrel jerked her head toward him. He ducked, not wanting to betray himself with his eyes. She needed to figure out a few things before she could know what he felt. What he fully felt. And God help him, because these feelings wouldn't go away just because of a fight between them. However, he wouldn't take this thing any further until she did understand.

"That so?" Grady gave her an appraising look as he eased into the seat next to her. "Never known Tony to bring a girl home." He nodded thanks as Mom gave him a plate of pie à la mode.

"He didn't... We're not..."

Yeah, let's see her dig herself out of this one. She wouldn't dare admit to anyone what she'd done. She almost hadn't admitted it to him. Timbrel wet her lips, apparently uncomfortable with the tension that had exploded through the quiet, awkward evening. "I..."

Totally wrecked everything? Ran off with another guy—a 120-pound furry, four-legged guy?

Nothing like being beaten by a drooling, flatulent hound of hell.

"You telling me my little brother finally decided he loved a woman more than war?"

Teeth gritted against Grady's penchant for direct-hitting conversation, Tony shifted in the chair but kept himself seated so his brother wouldn't know how close to "center mass" he'd come this time. "Timbrel's here because her home burned to the ground three nights ago."

"And what? She doesn't have family to stay with?" Surprise of all surprises, Stephanie teamed up with Grady this time. This had to be a record.

"My mother and I aren't close."

"What about your father?" Stephanie was going for the throat tonight.

"Look," Tony said, knowing this line of conversation would unglue Tim eventually. "She's here. I invited her." He eased back against the porch rail, crossed his ankles, and went to work on the pie. "We work together." He wouldn't look at her because that was like men looking at Medusa. Not that he'd turn to stone. The opposite—he'd be putty. She had a power over him no other woman had even come close to. And her stunt in Little Rock told him that was definitely *not* a good thing.

"So, how long are you staying?" Grady sounded too interested.

Would it be uncool to take out his brother with an RPG? "We head out in the morning for a mission." Tony set his plate down and folded his arms, doing his best to drive home his point for Grady to back off.

"Military? Never would've guessed." When Grady's gaze raked her again, it brought a chill then his big brother smiled.

"Why's that?" The edge in Timbrel's voice warned Tony this discussion was heading toward dangerous territory.

Grady, acting all cavalier and suave, gave a one-shouldered shrug. "Just too sweet." He grinned. "And pretty."

Tony sat on the small padded sofa next to Timbrel. "Prior Navy. She's a handler." He pointed to Beowulf, who trotted toward them. "That's her working dog. He can kill you with one bite."

Timbrel frowned at him. "I can talk."

Gaze shifting between her and Tony, amusement tugging at lips, Grady finally gave a slow nod. "Okay, little brother. No need to get riled." He smiled at Timbrel.

"So, you've seen combat?" his father asked.

The concussive boom of that question left a hollowness in Tony's gut. His mom slowed in her tidying, and he gave her a subtle nod to keep moving, keep things normal. Combat was *not* a good conversation topic with his father. In fact, it was one of his triggers.

Timbrel felt the dread tighten as she met Mr. VanAllen's steady, probing gaze. "A little." Was this appropriate talk in front of the children? Though she couldn't put her finger on it, something here on the deck had shifted.

"And your dog works with you?" Mr. VanAllen smiled.

"Yes, sir." *Don't look at Tony. Don't look at him.* "Beo and I did sweeps before high-profile events, but other than that, we patrolled."

"And you're working with Tony—does that go well?" A strange twinkle lit his green eyes—just like Tony's.

"Dad," Tony said, a warning in his tone.

Unsure whether to answer or not, Timbrel gave a slow nod. "Yes, sir. Most times."

He smiled. "Manners, pretty face"—he grinned at Tony—"I like this one. Good job, son."

Heat infused her cheeks. Timbrel cut into the pie sitting on her lap. Tony had as much said their relationship ended in Little Rock, and he'd been distant and aloof. Still, the baiting of his father embarrassed her. She'd come here seeking shelter.

No. . .not true. She came seeking resolution with Tony, though she had no right to ask for it. Though he clearly wasn't going to give it.

"Timbrel," Irene spoke up. "How long have you and Beowulf been partnered?"

"Five years. Since he was a year old." Timbrel rubbed her hand over Beowulf's head. The bullmastiff's eyes drooped in pleasure, panting lightly.

"You two have a strong bond."

Timbrel glanced to the side where Beo sat like a gentleman. "He's the best. Saved a lot of lives, including mine."

"Really?"

"Regarding the military," Stephanie Kowalski said, "I'm not convinced women should be in combat."

Timbrel heard the unspoken jibe. She'd detected cold vibes from the woman since she and her family walked in. "I patrol and that's not technically combat, although it can quickly escalate from a passive scenario to an active engagement."

A blond, her hair in a stylish inverted bob, she had it all. A husband, two children, a career as a teacher, and family. "I just don't know that I could do that. I'd prefer to take care of my family and husband."

Was this Stephanie's way of pointing out that Timbrel had neither of those?

"Or be with my family."

"Then it's not your calling," Tony said, his voice flat as he moved up onto a cushioned lawn chair. "And being in a classroom with twenty second graders isn't for Timbrel."

"Yeah, that's pretty obvious."

"Steph," Tony chided.

"No," Timbrel said, "it's okay. She's right. I'm not teacher material."

"Hey, Gunny. How's that coming?"

Confusion stilled Timbrel as she looked around to see who Mr. VanAllen was talking to. As she searched for the so-called Gunny, she noticed Tony come forward in his chair, movements controlled and intentional.

"Gunny, I asked you a question." Mr. VanAllen's voice held a rigidity she hadn't heard before. His salt-and-pepper hair glinted beneath the patio light as he scowled, his weathered features twisted in frustration.

"Get the kids inside," Tony said.

Stephanie and her husband gathered the children and hustled them into the house.

"Gunny, report." His father's eyes were on her. . .yet. . .not. A blank stare.

"Clear out," Tony's firm, tight words sliced through her confusion as he eased forward, moving between her and his father's line of sight. With a hand on her knee, he nudged her out of the space.

Timbrel complied, sensing Tony's "mission" mode. She stepped down the deck stairs and into the yard where Beowulf trotted up to her with his ball.

"Colonel, what's the sitrep?" Tony crouched by his father, eyeing the door where his mother hurried into the house.

"Not good, Lieutenant. Not good."

"I'm listening, sir."

Hand over her mouth, Timbrel watched the exchange. Watched Tony's skill with his father. Obviously not the first time this had happened—Tony had been prepared. His mother as well.

"If you'd just kept your tales of woe to yourself," Stephanie came up behind her and muttered the hateful words.

I thought she went inside.

Stephanie brushed past with one of Hayden's shoes in hand and slipped into the house without another word or scathing rebuke.

The words couldn't be dislodged and tightened like a poisonous vine around Timbrel's throat and heart. Whatever she did to Tony's sister to make her hate her, Timbrel wished she could undo that mistake. But being the daughter of a socialite, she also had people hate her just for existing. She didn't want to believe the latter of Stephanie, but she'd done nothing but be polite and quiet since they met right before dinner.

Grady eased into the seat on his father's left. Tony on the right. Tense. Alert. Both guys seemed ready to take down their father. Timbrel's heart ached and pushed her farther into the yard, away from the family stuff happening she didn't belong in.

"Dad—"

"Who is that out there?"

Timbrel's pulse slowed. *Oh no. He's looking right at me.*

"Johnson, you got a bead on that?"

In the dark, amid a few trees, she probably looked like a threat.

"Dad," Tony said, speaking softly, "that's just Timbrel. Remember— the girl you liked? Said she was pretty?"

"Gunny," his dad yelled, "get in here before they rip your head off! Johnson, take out that target before they get us!"

Timbrel guessed this to be some flashback, even though she hadn't witnessed one firsthand before. It was creepy and terrifying. He was there, normal and laughing. Then the next minute, he was in some perceived deadly situation.

"Dad, you're okay. You're at home."

"Now! Before we lose them!" Mr. VanAllen lunged between Tony and Grady.

The sons caught their father, hauling him back. Arms flailed. Shouting erupted.

Timbrel fought the tears. Seeing a grown man, a respectable grown man fighting his own sons. . .

An all-out brawl exploded. Fists. Grunts.

The hollow painful thud of a punch connecting.

Mortified, Timbrel backstepped.

Beowulf leapt forward.

She sucked in a breath. "Beo, heel!"

But he went unheeding. Shot up the steps. Right into the middle of the fray.

Nineteen

A fist flew.

Tony caught it and turned Dad's hand back as he and Grady wrestled Dad to the deck. "Easy there, Colonel," he said in a calm, firm voice, hopefully filled with reassurance.

Dad thrashed. "Get away from me you piece of—"

It wasn't the first time his dad, a Baptist-bred and -raised boy, spouted expletives at Tony during an episode.

"All clear!" Tony shouted. "Colonel, threat neutralized. Just me and the private here trying to help you out."

"Don't give me that! I know when I'm being manipulated." Dad's voice growled worse than Tim's dog. "It won't work this time. I'm not an idiot!"

Meaty jowls slopped into Dad's face.

Caught off guard, Tony flinched away. Nothing like finding a 120-pound dog staring you down. Beo pushed in closer, his weight against Tony's shoulder and arm pinning Dad to the deck. "Timbrel!" Man, the beast was heavy. "Call him off!"

Beo's tongue swiped Dad's cheek.

"What on earth?" Grady muttered as their father strained forward.

As drool slopped Tony's face, he cringed and pushed his father back down. "Timbrel, now!" A fist jabbed toward him. Tony dodged it as he scrabbled for purchase on the decking.

Panting, Beo stared at his father, their faces only inches apart. Head tilted, Beo watched. Licked. Watched. Licked again.

"I swear, if you don't get him out—"

Dad laughed.

Tony stilled. Laughed? His dad *laughed*?

Tension leeched out of his father. The arms hooked over Tony's shoulders in an attempt to flee insurgents who didn't exist relaxed. More laughter.

"What the heck?" Grady said, shifting aside to avoid getting nailed by the slobbering mouth.

With a happy bark that punched against Tony's chest, Beo moved in for another lick. Nailed it.

Hooting, Dad tried to swing away from the dog.

With a furtive glance to Grady, Tony eased onto his haunches, disbelieving the sight before him. His father had curled onto his side, shielding his face. Beowulf went into full attack—play attack—mode. Licking, barking, drooling.

His brother backed off, sitting in one of the Cracker Barrel rockers. Tony, legs and arms weak from the explosion of adrenaline in trying to protect his father from himself, dropped into a rocker. Bent forward, elbows on his knees, he watched, disbelieving the way the dog who'd always been so willing to rip off Tony's head, licked—*kissed*—his father out of a flashback.

Arms wrapped around the dog, his father laughed and wrestled himself free of the drool-bath.

"I've never seen anything like that," Grady mumbled.

"Pretty unbelievable." Tony couldn't wrap his mind around it.

Paws on Dad's shoulders and tail wagging, Beo pinned him and went to town dousing him in slobber. Barked at him.

"All right, all right," Dad laughed. "I surrender, you beast!"

Beo's head snapped up and swiveled around. He pushed off Dad and trotted over to Timbrel, who stood at the top of the deck steps. She cast a nervous glance to Tony but then moved into a chair near his father.

She patted the side of his shoulder with the back of her hand. "Trying to steal my dog, Mr. VanAllen?"

Wiping his face with the hem of his shirt, Dad laughed as he moved back onto his glider sofa. "Be warned, Miss Hogan, if you turn your back, that dog might disappear." Stroking the brindled fur, his dad seemed more at peace and more himself than Tony had seen him in a long while. But not only that, there was this look, this awareness, that hinted. . .perhaps, just perhaps, his father had some inkling of what this dog had just done for him.

Timbrel laughed. "I'd have to fight you."

"I reckon so." A laughing sigh settled through his father's chest, followed by a sigh of contentment, relief. "Reckon so. But what do you need him for when you've got a mean, ugly dog in my son?"

The words pulled Tony straight. "Now hold up."

With a chuckle, his dad slumped back. Beo hopped up next to Dad, eliciting more laughter. "You are one handsome fella, Beowulf."

"Handsome?" Tony said. "He's butt-ugly."

"Takes one to know one, son."

Retort on his tongue, Tony was ready to unleash it when his mom rushed out of the house onto the deck with a needle. And stopped short.

Bad—if his father saw the needle, he'd come unglued knowing he'd lost it in front of Timbrel, in front of anyone else.

Tony stood and walked to her. "Better save me, Mom. Dad's saying I'm as ugly as Timbrel's dog." In front of her, he took the needle and lightly patted her shoulder as he pocketed it. "He might need a rest," he whispered.

"What—?"

"Later." He wrapped his arm around his mom. "See? Mom knows I'm better looking."

His dad grunted, still focused on Beowulf. Might as well build a statue considering the way his father idolized the dog.

"Watch out, Dad," Tony said. "That thing knows how to take down a man in seconds flat."

"And clear a room in less time." His dad yawned.

After that adrenaline spike, his father's energy levels would deplete, just as they had many times before. Time to clear out.

"This is true." Tony met Timbrel's gaze and bobbed his head to the side, indicating toward the yard, hoping she'd get the hint that they needed to bug out so his father wouldn't feel obligated to stay up.

"I need to feed Beo and walk him before bedding down."

"How much you want for him?" His dad said with a laugh.

"No price."

"He's free?"

Timbrel smiled and stood. "Ha. Ha. Nice try." She leaned in closer. "No sale. He's mine." She started for the steps, using her hand to signal her dog.

Beo hesitated then leapt down and trotted after her into the yard.

"Traitor!" his dad called. "But I don't blame you. She's a pretty thing and needs protecting."

Tony walked the yard with Timbrel, keeping a keen eye on his family.

Arms folded, Timbrel hunched her shoulders. She cast him a furtive glance as she kicked the toe of her boot against a rock. He frowned. Timidity wasn't a coat Timbrel wore well. Or ever.

"I'm sorry about Beo." Timbrel tucked her long, wavy brown hair behind her ear. "I've never seen him do that—break behavior or lick a guy down. Sorry he got in the middle of it."

"No, no it was good. Probably one of the better endings for that scenario." He couldn't deny it. "Never seen anything like that. Is he trained to do that?"

Timbrel shook her head. "No. But he's always been keyed into my feelings. Can anticipate when I need help. I think it comes from. . ." She tucked her chin. Then straightened. "Anyway. . ."

There. She did it again. Shut down. Shut him out. Why was he surprised? Yeah, he'd jump off that cliff for her. Thing was, nobody would be waiting at the bottom.

Time to bail. "I need to check some things."

Like the slipping and colliding of arctic shelves, the frigid tension between her and Tony left Timbrel cold and jarred. Standing in the kitchen, she watched him through the back door. With a soda in hand, he trudged over to where his father sat on the steps and joined him, forearms on his knees.

"There now." Irene's soothing voice pulled Timbrel's attention to the kitchen where Tony's mom set the last glass she'd cleaned in the cupboard.

Tony's laughter lured her focus back to him. Would he ever forgive her? She'd apologized and asked to go back to where they were. Why was he so unwilling to give her a second chance?

Funny how she didn't really understand the degree of her future she'd pinned on him, pinned on facing with him. In fact, only as she studied his broad, strong back and broad shoulders did she realize how much she could lose, how much of what she wanted for her future, if she didn't find some way to fix this.

"Go talk to him." Irene's warm, soft voice spilled over Timbrel.

"What?" She blinked, tried to feign ignorance.

Irene, with her short blond hair stylishly groomed, leaned against the counter and smiled. "He's so much like his father, it's crazy. Good looking, dedicated, laid back—takes a lot to knock those two down. They just take the hits and keep going."

Timbrel nodded. His resolute character was one thing she loved about Tony.

"And their wit." Irene laughed and shook her head. "It's something else when they're both in the house."

"He makes me laugh," Timbrel thought out loud then felt a bit embarrassed for mentioning it. She shifted and crossed her arms over her chest. "There wasn't a lot of laughter for me growing up." Good night! Why on earth did she say that?

"When you first came to the door earlier, I wasn't sure what to make of you." Irene folded the tea towel and set it on the edge of the porcelain sink.

Okay, here it comes. Shouldn't be surprised since Tony's sister hated her that his mom would try to give her the send-off. And yet this strange, squirrelly feeling wouldn't leave Timbrel alone. The yearning to be liked, to be accepted. Why? She'd never cared before about what people thought.

Because Irene VanAllen was. . .different. *I respect and admire her.*

Laugh lines pinched the corners of her eyes as she smiled. "Last week, Tony came home in a tear. It was surprising." She rested the heels of her hands on the counter behind her. "He's normally so easygoing, nothing riles him. I asked what was wrong." She pursed her lower lip and shrugged. "He told me not to worry, said he'd be fine. Then left the room."

Sucker punch straight to her gut. Tony hadn't told his mom that she'd left him at the gas station in Arkansas?

Even Irene didn't seem ignorant of what was happening. Yet there was no anger. No hate. Just. . .amusement.

Timbrel dared to eye the woman. Soft skin, ivory complexion defined the woman with grace and elegance. Ironic how much she looked like Timbrel's mom, yet looked nothing like her. Both had white blond hair, though Irene's was a natural, beautiful silver and her mom's chemically processed, both had that ivory complexion—something Timbrel had inherited. Yet something in Irene drew Timbrel, while her mom repelled her.

"You're the first girl he's mentioned to me in about five years."

Surprise spiraled through Timbrel, dragging a faint hope with it. "He mentioned me?"

"Just casual conversation, but. . ." She smiled and nodded. "Don't get me wrong. Girls like him. He likes girls. He's a charmer and a flirt, but that's just who he is. But to bring that conversation home, with me. . ." A thickness settled into her voice. "That told me to pay attention."

Timbrel tried a caustic laugh. "He probably wanted to warn you about the girl with the big mouth, bad attitude, and bullmastiff."

"No," Irene said softly. "Tony hasn't spoken an ill word about you. Not even when you showed up, and I know things are not good between the two of you right now, but. . ." She bumped her left hip against the granite island. "You've been on missions with my son, and I know you have seen some of what he does. He's been doing that for a very long time. He's a warrior—that took shape when he was three. The charmer part, too." She smiled, her skin looking like angora. "But you need to understand, it's remarkable not what he said but that you were important enough for my son to have your name at the front of his mind."

"I ruined things." The confession felt good but awful as well. Her eyes burned. "I don't know how much you know about me. . ."

"Enough."

Timbrel met her tender gaze. "I didn't have the best family life. In fact, I was taught to perform—to win approval, to stay above the rest, to get what I wanted. Emotions weren't addressed. Things. . .happened to me that left me unwilling to brave relationships ever again."

Irene's pretty brown eyes glossed. "I'm sorry, Timbrel."

"It's okay."

Clasping her by the shoulders, Irene peered into her eyes. "No, it's not, sweetie. Being wronged is never okay."

Tears threatened. But Timbrel shoved them back. Took a step back. Immediately felt guilty for removing herself from Irene's touch and concern. "I'm sorry." Could she ever get this right? "I. . ." She checked her fingernails. Glanced at Beowulf curled up on the back-door rug.

Her gaze hopped to Tony. "I left him." Why was her throat burning again? "He was there for me, told me. . .told me he loved me." Her blurring vision sought Irene's face as Timbrel squeaked out, "I left him without a word. Just got in my Jeep and drove off."

When she saw the knotted brows and hurt scratched across his mother's face, Timbrel felt the guilt anew. What on earth was she doing telling this perfect woman with her perfect family that she'd just abandoned her son.

I've got to get out of here—now!

"He scared you off."

Sucking a breath, she tried to pull back the tears that had freed themselves. How did she know?

"Tony is an all-or-nothing kind of guy. Another reason I knew when he mentioned you, it wasn't just some girl."

"Yeah. He was so intense, so. . .serious." She bunched up her shoulders. "I just knew I'd mess it up. Every time Tony kissed me"—*dude, what are you doing saying this to his* mother?!—"all those fears swelled to the front and I just freaked." She shoved her fingers through her hair. "He deserves someone without baggage. Someone who can. . ."

"Love him?"

She tried a smile, but it tripped and fell off the ledge of her fears.

"But I think you already do. It's why you're here tonight. You wouldn't have come—"

"I came because someone burned down my house." Her chest pounded. When she saw the surprise on Irene's face, Timbrel accepted the condemnation. "I'm not a hero. Don't make me into one."

Irene touched her shoulder. "You could've gone to your mom. If you'd called her, she would've taken care of you. No matter the bad blood between a mom and daughter, we will always be there."

Timbrel gave a slight nod.

"You didn't want your mom. . ."

She knew where this open-ended statement was leading. And Timbrel wouldn't go there.

"You wanted Tony."

"When I was ten, I saw this crystal glass in a shop with my mom. I insisted I wanted it for my birthday." Timbrel worked to slow her racing pulse. "I got one." She shifted then bounced her knee. "I shattered it within a week playing football in the house with some of my friends."

Irene laughed and covered her mouth.

"At that age, I couldn't understand the value of what I had." Without turning her head, she peeked out at Tony. "This time, I do. . .and I'm terrified of shattering what little we have left of a friendship."

Tony stepped into the house, his expression taut. "We need to go."

"What? Now?" Switching gears from intense emotional to tense mission mode felt like stepping from an ice box into a hot tub.

He looked between her and his mom cautiously then nodded. "Now. Burnett moved up the AHOD." Tony kissed his mother on the cheek then stalked down the hall.

Timbrel whispered her good-bye and hurried after him. "Look, we should talk before we do this."

"Do what?" In his room, he grabbed his rucksack from the closet. No doubt he cleaned and prepped the bag and its contents first thing each time he returned from deployment.

"Talk, Tony."

He rounded on her. "I tried that. You left me standing in the rain."

"I've already apologized."

"Yes, you did."

What did she do with that? How could she respond?

"What?" He frowned. "Just because you spout pretty words, that makes everything go away?"

"No." Timbrel's chest constricted. "And I never implied that. But you're a Christian. So am I—you're probably a better one, so you should know that if you forgive someone, you let go."

"I do let go. But then there's the old saying, Fool me once, shame on you. Fool me twice, shame on me. Fool me three times—it's over."

Hurt and surprise mingled in a toxic potion. "I think that's a rather modern version."

"Yeah, written by James Anthony VanAllen about twenty seconds ago." He rubbed his temples. "Listen, I'm not saying it's over. I'm saying we need time, especially you."

"What for? I already told you I want this to go away. I want to go back to where we were."

"That's just it!" Lips taut, jaw jutted, he flexed his biceps and flashed his hands. "We can't go there, Timbrel. And I don't want to. What we have, what we go through—defines us. Makes us. Changes us, whether for better or worse, it crafts who we are." He inched forward. "You and I, we have history. That night in Arkansas is a part of who we are. And right now, I have to figure out how far I'm willing to go, how much of your self-imposed isolation and protective barbs I can take."

Timbrel widened her eyes to ward off the tears. She swallowed, hard.

"Look." His shoulders drooped. "I'd tilt the world upside down if I thought it would convince you to take a chance with me. I'd do anything—*anything* for you." He shrugged into his ruck. "But you're not willing to make that sacrifice for me, to risk it."

He stalked to the door, where Beo stood guard and gave a low growl. "Maybe that right there is my answer."

JIHAD

Qur'an: 8:39 "Fight them until all
opposition ends and all submit to Allah."

Early morning light flooded the office and swept away the slumber of night as Bashir and his twenty elite guards surrendered their wills once more to Allah. Facing Mecca, they offered the Fajr prayers, two rakats. All seeking nearness to God in obedience to Him.

After the prayers were offered, Bashir left the hall quietly with the others. He'd been taught the prayers would give him peace, that he'd have a clearer mind once he surrendered and obeyed. Yet as he walked the hall to his private quarters, anger devoured him.

The others dissipated in various directions, and he could not help but notice Dehqan slip quietly through a side door that led to his quarters. What of the girl? Had he molded a submissive spirit in her yet?

Insufferable Americans. They'd demolished his shop. Destroyed countless weeks of laborious care put into the work. It must stop.

Two of his elite slipped into place on either side of the double doors that led to his private quarters. As Bashir approached, the two immediately snapped a salute. Yes, they should show their respect.

One opened the door, allowing Bashir to enter uninhibited. He strode across the marble floors in the large room. Yellow curtains hung between the windows that flanked the entire eastern wall. Just as the prayer hall did. Always facing Mecca. Always seeking inspiration.

But why. . .why had Allah allowed these infidels to thwart him? To gain a foothold? He would not let them win. He would not fail in chasing them from the land, the hills, the mountains, the waters.

He went to the massive mahogany cabinet on the northern wall. Carved with a fig tree, the cabinet offered his choice of drinks. Bashir opened the twin doors and stared at the crystal decanters.

Even now he could taste the fruity warmth against his tongue. "No." He slammed it closed. Held the knobs. Gripped them tight. "Indeed, he succeeds who purifies his soul, and indeed, he fails who corrupts his soul."

Bashir spun away from the temptation. Away from the dark forces that sought to disrupt his mission. "I will not fail."

"Very good."

He jerked to the side. Anger barreled out of him as he found Imam Abdul Razaaq. It would not do him good to throw the imam out of his quarters. Or to shoot him for invading his privacy. "Imam." He gave a conciliatory nod, the barest recognition of his authority and position. "I was not aware you had arrived."

"I joined you for prayers, brother."

Bashir stopped. Considered the man. The graying splotches in the man's beard belied his forty-something age. But there was an ancient hatred that boiled in the man's eyes. Hatred for the infidels. Hatred for Americans and the ways of the West. "I am very busy, Razaaq. Could we meet another time? I will have Dehqan—"

Shouts from the hall pulled him around. What could be—? The door swung open and in rushed Irfael. "Sir." He snapped a salute but did not enter any farther.

Ah, a man who knew his place. Finally. But by Razaaq's rigid stance and furrowed brow, this wasn't the time to demand piety or the respect owed to him or the failed recognition of those by the man who stood before him in the kufi.

Grinding his teeth, Bashir gave a curt nod, allowing his second in command access to him. "What is happening?"

"Sir, the Americans entered the city."

Bashir flung himself around. Stormed to the windows. Placed a hand on the glass. Allah, please. . . No, no more prayers. He'd said enough. "The shop?"

"They've left."

"The supplies?"

"Nothing can be directly traced back to you, sir."

"But it is." Bashir felt as if all the fires of hell raged in his being. "If it were not, they would not be there. They would not be performing these so-called inspections. They are looking for evidence."

"Will they find it?"

Bashir flared his nostrils at the imam's question.

"No," Irfael spoke. "But we must stop them. If they keep digging—"

"I will call a friend. He is closely connected."

"If he is connected," Razaaq joined him at the windows, "can he be trusted?" Bashir must bury this contempt. It was too early to lose the backing of the imams. Eventually he would control them. Push them. Drive them. But for now. . .

"As much as any of us can be trusted." He must follow up with Maahir. Whether the man was an assassin, a spy, or what, nobody knew for sure. Just that he could get jobs done. Make connections where none existed. And his allegiance was not to a faith or a religion but to the Arab lands of his fathers.

"Brother," Razaaq said, the edge in his voice hardening, "do not mistake my favor of you for weakness. We chose you, Bashir."

Had he flames in his hands, Bashir would've singed the kufi right off the man's face and let his body burn with it. But Bashir swallowed back the demon within. "Of course. And I am grateful." He pushed his gaze to the window. Stared out over the compound. The green, green grass cultivated by the gardener he'd hired to provide a piece of Paradise on this side of heaven. And all of it, the grass, the plaster, the elite—all in jeopardy because the Americans invaded his country. Killed his people.

Razaaq gripped the top of Bashir's shoulder. He shook him then clamped a hand on Bashir's other side. "My brother." Pride mingled with a ferocity Bashir had not before noticed. "It is time, do you not think, to funnel that outrage at the infidels?"

"Beyond time."

Laughter snapped his attention to the corner.

Dehqan strode beneath the veranda onto the grass with the girl, who wore a veil. But not a burka. Why was she not concealed? Why was she not covered so the men would not be tempted? She should burn!

"Your protégé seems smitten." The rumble of the imam's voice unseated Bashir's control.

"I let him keep her."

"Then they are married?" The imam's question held both accusation and contempt. "Was she not from that Christian sect? And you allowed her to marry your adopted son?"

"Never." Bashir fisted his hands. "I would not allow him to take such a whore as his bride." Bashir stared down from on high at the two. "He will use her, take his pleasure as he sees fit, then I will kill her."

Twenty

You're on the next jet out of here." Lance Burnett peered over the top of his readers at the manifest Lieutenant Hastings handed him as he headed to meeting with ODA452. "There's a C-17 Globemaster waiting for you at Andrews."

Dean Watters stood beside him. "Sir, what changed?"

Lance frowned.

"No disrespect, sir, but you told us to bury our mistake out there a month ago and forget it happened. Now, we're going back?"

"That's right." Lance eyeballed Timbrel Hogan. "I said to bury it, but for someone in this room, that didn't happen."

"I'm sorry," Timbrel said. "I thought we were looking for chemical or biological weapons, not sticking our butts in the air and our heads in the sand. If there's something there—"

"Your problem—"

"I don't need your analysis, Rocket."

"Too bad because this is my team and you're screwing with it."

"If you want to talk—"

"Hogan," VanAllen barked as he turned to her. "Stand down."

"The last thing I'm doing is taking orders from you."

"Dang, Candyman," Java said. "What'd you do to piss her off?"

Hogan whirled on the Green Beret. "This has nothing to do with him!"

And if Lance believed that, he was a hairy monkey's uncle. "Hogan, VanAllen. In my office." And by office, he meant the dank closet of a space that held a single desk, a phone, and some other paraphernalia in the warehouse. Metal desk, metal chair—everything standard government issue, right along with the moldy smell.

Nails clicked as the handler entered with her beast and VanAllen.

RONIE KENDIG

"Shut the door." Hand on his belt, he waited. Ran his knuckles over his lips. The door clicked. "What in Sam Hill is going on? Hogan, you've always been a pain in a donkey's backside with me, but VanAllen. . ." He wagged a pointing finger at him. "You said you'd straighten her out."

"Did no such thing, sir. You said talk to her. I did." Green eyes sat weighted in their sockets.

"It went that good, huh?" Lance cursed. He scratched his head then raised his hands in surrender. "I don't care if you're sleeping with each other or hating each other. But I need both of you to get your heads in this game." His finger veered to Hogan. "Young lady, you have good instincts. But with that attitude of yours, I wouldn't care if you could read minds. Get that fixed or stow it. That team out there, they're mine. And I'd cut my own throat before I let you get them all riled up just before they head into the nastiest hornet's nest of a situation."

Contrition. He saw it all over her face but couldn't believe it. Was it an act?

"I'm—" She lifted her head and looked him in the eye. "You're right. I'm sorry, sir."

Her dog whimpered.

He almost cursed again. Since when had Hogan *ever* backed down. What did it mean? Was the fight in her gone? No, he'd seen and heard it not two minutes ago. But what could he do at this point? He needed that dog on-site. Needed him to sniff out the trouble they were hunting.

With a heavy sigh, Lance nodded, gathering his wits from the floor where her response had knocked them. "That's a good start." He looked at VanAllen. "I warned you to keep your head in the game. I see anything like this again and I'm pulling your sorry butt back here. You'll have desk duty till your eyes bleed."

"Understood." VanAllen, hands behind his back, gave a curt nod. "Not going to be a problem, sir. I'm in. One hundred percent."

"May I ask a question?" Timbrel didn't do the whole submissive-contrition thing very well, but he could appreciate her effort.

"Only one."

Timbrel wet her lips and shot VanAllen a sidelong glance. "So, the lab coat—"

"Gave us critical proof that what you found in that bookshop wasn't just bookmaking chemicals."

Exultation leapt through her expression.

He went on before she could say anything. "The levels were too highly concentrated. Although they had broken down some—the techs think the coat might've been washed—but there was enough for plausible concern." Lance suddenly understood how painful it was for her to be humble right now because he had to muster his own humility from the dregs of his foul mood. "You did good work, Hogan."

She seemed to breathe in and savor the praise.

"But don't go off half cocked again, or you'll be cleaning dog kennels for the rest of your life."

Timbrel smirked. "Already do, sir." She tussled Beo's fur.

Bagram AFB, Afghanistan

Warbling across the flat terrain, heat plumes warned of the unseasonably hot day. Sweat slid in sheets down Tony's face and trailed tickling fingers down his spine. He grunted as he lifted his gear and headed away from the Globemaster. His gaze hit Timbrel, who jogged along the runway with Beowulf. The dog had gone ape after nearly a full day airborne. He didn't want to think about how the bullmastiff took care of business. That's a nasty job he was glad didn't fall into his obligations.

Shouldering his ruck, he strode across the tarmac toward the tent that would be their home for the next however long it would take to finish this mission. According to the general, the mission should be pretty cut and dried. Get in. Get the intel. Get out.

But that was assuming a lot.

And Tony never assumed.

Another bead of sweat slipped from his hat and raced down his temple, skidding right into his eye. He grunted and tossed his gear onto a gray mattress.

"Hey," Java asked as he took the bunk next to him. "What happened with you and Hogan?"

Tony glared at him.

"Might wanna leave that one alone," Pops said in his low country drawl. Sitting on the edge of the bunk, he held a book in his hands. No, not a book. The Bible.

Tony faced the guy whose reddish-blond hair had gotten him a lot of ribbing. . .and a lot of flirting by female personnel. Though the big guy never flirted back. He was married. He took that commitment seriously. "Pops, you okay?"

Gray-blue eyes rose from the whisper-thin pages. "Just searching. . ."

Tony felt the frown. "For what?"

"Answers." The guy with brawny shoulders and stout heart closed the Book, stowed it in his locker, then started suiting up, donning his plate-carrier vest and standard issue Colt M1911.

Catching the guy's shoulder, Tony squeezed. "Todd. Seriously—you okay?"

Somber eyes held his then lowered slowly. He whispered, "Amy has cancer."

Drawn up short by the revelation, Tony took a step back. "Man, I'm sorry." He glanced around, suddenly irritated with himself for forcing the subject. "Do you want to go home, be with her?"

A weak smile wove through his face and faded out. "Can't let my team down."

Tony scowled. "Dude—she's your wife." He pointed to the locker where the Bible lay concealed. "God first, family second, country third."

Pops held up a hand. "I appreciate that, but she had surgery to remove the tumor. Chemo starts next week. She told me my hovering was driving her crazy." His snicker of a laugh had no humor to it, then he gave another nod. "I talked to Burnett. As soon as this mission is over, I'm heading home."

"Good." Relief swirled sweet and yet bitter. Tony patted his shoulder. "You'll be missed. You're doing the right thing. But don't think you can slack off."

Pops laughed, understanding Tony's attempt to not make light of his wife's situation but to let him know they had his back. "Wouldn't dream of it."

"Circle up," Dean said as he entered the tent armed with a couple of tubes—rolled-up maps, no doubt.

The team gathered, and it felt good to get out of the domestic element, to set aside relational challenges with his father, his brother, and even his sister, who took exception to Timbrel's presence.

Speaking of, Timbrel and Beowulf stepped into the tent, the dog panting against the 110 degrees dousing them in sweat and body odor. Even Timbrel had sweat rings around her black tank. But she hadn't said a word about the heat. That's one of the things he liked about her—she wasn't afraid to do hard work, to get down and gritty. In fact, she looked good with a little dirt caked on her face and a heat-flush in her cheeks.

He liked everything about her except her unwillingness to risk her heart, to be *real* and unafraid to embrace mistakes so she could grow. So their relationship could grow.

Java and Scrip made a hole for Timbrel to join them for the mission brief.

"Okay." Dean rolled out a political map. "Our mission is twofold." He held up a thumb. "Confirm or deny the presence of WMD or chemicals used in the construction of said weapons." He held up his pointer finger so his hand looked like a gun. "Snatch-and-grab."

Tony frowned. "Who?"

Dean laid out three photographs. "Any of these men. They're purportedly top tier with Bashir's organization—same Bashir we've been looking at. We just didn't put two and two together. Bashir Bijan is Bashir Karzai."

"Shoulda guessed," Java said. "These Muslim guys adopt a new name for every big event in life, it seems."

"Not quite that often, but yeah." Dean fingered an image. "This guy is Lieutenant Irfael Azizi, Bashir's right hand. It'd be ideal if we hauled him back here for a little one-on-one."

"Hooah," Scrip muttered.

"But we have STK orders if they engage us. The other is Altair al Dossari. He's a scientist who went missing about fifteen months ago. Chatter suggests Bashir has him."

"Why aren't we going after Bashir?" Timbrel asked. "He's the reason this is happening."

"Too hot," Java said with a wink.

Tony's bicep flinched. His buddy better stow that flirting unless he wanted a dent in his pretty mug.

"Java's right—Bashir is a high-profile humanitarian." Dean sighed. "The world believes him to be a saint, producing books for children and schools. We suspect differently, but we can't string him up yet. And until we can nail his nuke-making butt with one-hundred-proof evidence, he's hands off."

Timbrel digested the information with a slow bob of her head, eyes tracking the images.

"What's the plan?" Tony asked.

Squatting, Dean unfurled a large rendering of a fenced-in area. "The property is Bashir's largest book factory, so we're going in to check things out. We have to keep this under wraps, so we'll head out at 0300."

Java whistled. "Early bird catches the terrorist."

"Structure B-4 is a two-story warehouse at the center of the compound."

Dean pointed to large rectangular building attached to another smaller one. A U-shaped road wrapped back to the gate in front of the warehouse. "This building is our concern. It's been leased out by the same company that owned the bookshop." He slid the map aside and unrolled another. This one a blueprint. "Four offices upstairs, two on either side of this catwalk that stretches over the entire warehouse floor. One way up, one way down— these stairs. Now the place should be empty, but we need to expect trouble if what we suspect to be happening is really going on there."

"Hold up," Java said. "At the bookshop, the dog"—he pointed to Beowulf—"detected the chemicals hidden behind a wall. Think that could happen there? We lost some serious time there and ended up with our pants down."

Dean shook his head. "Sources have mapped out the building. No extra room."

"What about a basement or lower level like a tunnel? Terrorists tend to like those," Tony threw in, exploring all contingencies.

"Possible." Dean rubbed his jaw. "But unknown."

"Doesn't matter," Timbrel threw over her shoulder as her brown eyes struck him. "Beowulf can detect buried cache. Shouldn't be a problem."

"What *shouldn't* be a problem and what *becomes* a problem are usually two very different things," Tony countered.

"If it's there, Beo will find it." Timbrel's defense mechanisms were in full swing. Just like the first time he met her. She was primed and ready for a fight.

Thought we got past that.

"Good," Tony said, not willing to be baited.

"Still need to be prepared." Pops lifted the photographs, studied the faces one by one, then passed them around. "From what I hear, he got tipped off that we were curious about him."

Timbrel's chin dipped then lifted. "Unfortunately, he's right. But it was necessary to getting some proof."

"Might want to backtrack on that," Tony said. "We'll find out today if it was worth the risk."

Surprise and hurt washed through Timbrel's face. She'd taken his response personally. Of course. Great. He wouldn't be able to think tactically without worrying about her getting all up in arms.

Clearing his throat, Dean regrouped. "We'll search the warehouse once we clear the other structures. The two on the northeast side are both residences. We have mixed intel on who's living there. Either Bashir's family—"

"Thought this dude was single. The lone Jesus to the masses?" Java said irreverently.

Pops speared him with a wicked glare.

"What?" Java lifted his hands. "I'm right—they treat him like a freakin' messiah. Just became an imam. I'm surprised they don't lay palm branches at this guy's feet."

"He's greatly respected, it's true," Dean said, cutting through the tension with his mission focus. "That's why for now, we need to steer clear of him. He might not be married, but rumors have it that he's managed a mistress or two and an eighteen-year-old male he's taken under his wing named Dehqan." He held up a picture of an older teen. "If Bashir is there, you can count on Dehqan being there, too. He's to remain unharmed. He's off limits."

"Why?" Timbrel bounced her shoulders. "If the teen is always with Bashir, then he has the most access to the man who's creating WMDs. He probably knows what his father wants to do. Seems we'd want him here. Besides, kids are easier to persuade to talk."

"He's *off* limits." Dean's tone and expression severed a counterresponse. "You touch him, you'll answer to Burnett."

Now, that's interesting. Why would the boy be blacked out? The only targets they didn't touch were assets. But even assets could be dragged back to command for questioning, at least to give the appearance of being arrested.

"The residences might also be Azizi's—Bashir's right hand." He traced two lines connecting the buildings. "There's a makeshift balcony joining the buildings, creating a breezeway. Definite danger spot—perfect for armed guards to hide." Meeting each member of ODA452's eyes, Dean grew much more serious. "We had a fiasco last time. This has to go right or we're dog meat. The general wants this clean and black so nobody can point the finger at him, or us."

"So," Java said with a shrug, "what are we supposed to do if we find the stuff?"

"If we confirm the presence of WMDs, SOCOM sends in a SEAL team to take out the factory and secure the weapons for appropriate and safe disposal. Our job is to confirm and snatch." Dean stood, hands on his tactical belt. "Questions so far?"

Tony shook his head. The plan was pretty straightforward.

"Okay, Java, you'll hit the power and communication lines." Dean waited for the guy to acknowledge his role. "Rocket, you and Scrip will secure the residences. Pops, I'll need your eye high. Get set up on the roof, if you can, to cover me, Tony, and the dog team."

Pops nodded, his gaze studying the maps with his sniper skills roaring, no doubt.

"So again: residences first, then the warehouse." Dean nodded. "Meet on the tarmac at 0300."

The minutes that fell off the clock thudded like anvils against Tony's heart. He stretched out over his unmade bed, crossed his ankles, and folded his hands behind his head. Eyes closed, he trained his mind to quiet. Thought of the verse that said God trained his hands to war.

Even with Timbrel, it seemed.

He roughed a hand over his face. Sick of the fighting, he just wanted to make peace with her. But not if she could so easily throw away what little they already had together. He needed to be able to trust her.

I didn't wait till you could be trusted before giving My love.

Not fair, Lord.

It was true. He might not have had the bad-boy reputation like Java, but Tony had put his parents through some pretty crazy nights until he surrendered his life to God. Only through that loving draw did he find the courage to be what he could be.

Was it possible that by surrendering his expectations, his fear—yeah, there was that—of her running off, Timbrel would be better able to let go of whatever it was she held on to with Super-Glued fingers?

She doesn't trust me, though I've done everything to win her trust.

Except surrender these demands.

Demands on her person pushed her away.

Surrender. . . Could it draw her in?

The sound of water splattering against something nearby pulled Tony out of his self-talk. He snapped his arm down and pushed up on his bunk, leaning on his forearm.

A dark shadow moved near the foot of his bed.

"Dude!" Java laughed hard. "Beowulf just relieved himself on your bed!"

★ ★ Twenty-One ★ ★

Four hours later and after bleaching Tony's bunk, Timbrel sat on the Black Hawk with shriveled hands that smelled like she'd taken up janitorial duties. In a way she had, thanks to Beowulf. Her guy had a mile-wide stubborn streak and he didn't like Tony. If only she could clean up the mess *she* had made of their relationship with some bleach and elbow grease.

But that'd be too easy. Though it'd be something she understood— working hard, performing on life's stage the way her mother had taught her. When she'd messed up before, she found ways to fix things. Make them right. She knew how to the play the game. No, she'd mastered the game.

Then Tony stormed into her life.

Knocked all her skills to the ground. Left her empty-handed. Confused. What did he want?

Risk.

She didn't do risk. Not like that. Had to know the outcome, weigh the pros and cons.

What cons were there in being with him?

He knows too much. . .knows *everything*.

Well, no. Not everything. She hadn't told *anyone every*thing. But he sure knew more than most. And with friends like these guys, soldiers so much like Carson. . .

Forget the cons. Figure out the pros.

Pros: He made her laugh. He was a warrior, a fighter—in other words, not weak. He had a strong, stable family. Even though his father had some psychological problems thanks to invisible wounds, Tony took care of him. Respected him.

The way he treated his mom. With love and respect.

She'd heard once that a girl could tell the way a man would treat her by the way he treated his mother. In that case, Tony VanAllen was a perfect candidate.

"You're not willing to make that sacrifice for me, to risk it."

The scary thing? She was. She totally was willing to risk it. But if she told him now, he'd say the words were empty. Somehow, she had to show him. Prove it to him.

Or maybe I'm too late.

Augh! What could she do? Desperation plowed through her. She shifted on the seat, rousing Beo, who'd settled his chin on her knee. He looked up at her as if to ask why she'd interrupted his nap. She smoothed a hand over his head and he went back to his nap. *Give him a chance, Beo. I want this. . . I want to make this thing work.* But if her dog kept peeing on his bed and growling at him. . .

A paper flickered to her left. She glanced over at the small laminated card Pops held. Her gaze flicked to his moving lips, whether in silent or whispered recitation, she couldn't tell in the chopper.

Pops must've noticed her questioning glance. He rotated his wrist, allowing her to see the card. Her heart quickened as she read the words printed there. Psalm 91 marked the top of the well-used card. A stream of verses followed, reassurances of God's protection and love.

Timbrel nodded, unsure of what to say. She hadn't really pegged Pops as a Christian. But it made sense, she guessed. She hadn't had a mentor or anything, but the idea of a Jesus who loved children appealed to Timbrel's bruised soul. She'd been raised by her mother to attend mass and take communion, and she loved the formality, the safe haven of the sanctuary. How Timbrel had managed to keep her head on straight—for the most part—she couldn't explain. Still, what Pops had seemed a little deeper. He always seemed calm. In control.

Unlike me.

Just like Tony.

She'd really made him angry with the whole "go back to the beginning" idea. It wasn't what she meant, at least not consciously, but maybe she did.

"I'd do anything for you."

She wanted to say those words to him, but something held her back.

A touch against her hand snapped her attention back to Pops. He slid the card into her hand, closed her fingers around it, then patted her hand. He leaned toward her, their helmets bumping as he shouted, "I've got it memorized!"

Would God watch out for her? She'd like to think He would. . .that somebody would.

Watters gave a signal and the team prepped for their arrival at the compound. Pulse ramping, Timbrel tucked the card into her leg pocket and secured it. Beo lifted his head and sniffed the air. He pushed to his feet, crammed between everyone's legs.

Timbrel ran her hand along his back, detecting the tension. "Easy boy," she said, not sure if he'd hear her over the roar of the wind. His ears twitched, so maybe he had.

They set down a mile outside of the remote village, and the team scurried for cover. Timbrel kept pace with Tony, sensing safety in his presence. She always had. Even when he'd been cocky and playful.

Man, she missed that. Missed him.

Put it away. Focus on the mission.

A vehemence gripped her. Fine. She could do that. But just like he said—they'd figure "us" out after the mission. She'd make sure it ended right. Together.

Tucked into a ditch with ODA452, Timbrel struggled for her bearings as the din of the helo faded. Dirt crunched beneath her as she shifted against the dirt and rocks. A shrub thrust up defiantly from the rocks and reached toward the clear half moon hanging in the blanket of twinkling stars. So clear and beautiful.

"Let's go," Watters rasped. As the team filed out of the hiding position, Timbrel caught his arm and motioned to Beowulf, asking to take point.

Watters hesitated, shot a visual check to Tony.

Timbrel's heart stumbled. What if he held their fight against her, wouldn't let them—?

No. Tony wasn't vengeful that way. Timbrel strangled the doubt that once again exerted itself and tried to stamp out her belief in Tony. Her belief that he was a good man, that he had her best interests at heart.

Tony nodded.

She breathed a smile. Yeah, Tony believed in her. She believed in him. She'd never met anyone like him. Like that. Everyone in her life had befriended her for a reason. Her first taste of real friendship came from Aspen. But that was different. She was a *girl*friend. Tony was a guy, and he wanted to be her boyfriend.

The revelation spun her compass, and for once, she felt like he was her true north.

Stalking through the early morning, heat already stifling and mean, Timbrel kept Beowulf on a long lead so he could alert them to trouble and not give away the rest of the team. Heat pushed sweat beads down her neck and back, tickling and slick. Her shirt stuck to her chest beneath the heavy protective vest. She cradled the M4 with her right hand, the lead with her left. Darkness rushed in, taunting.

Timbrel glanced up, watching as a lone cloud sneaked in front of the moon. She slowed, feeling. . .off. Looking around, she tried to figure out what had unseated her confidence.

"Keep moving," Watters mumbled. "Almost there."

A building seemed to leap out of nowhere as they traced the road to the village. A hand caught her arm. "Hold up." Tony's voice was tense and had shifted into command mode.

He had the experience.

Timbrel plucked the sonic whistle from around her neck and gave the signal to Beo to heel. Seconds later, he trotted toward her, his tongue wagging.

Java and Rocket rushed the building and covered as the rest of the team hurried past it. Down the road on the left, the iron and wood gate barred the compound. Two floodlights, one at the gate and one inside the compound, glared through the darkness.

As they squatted amid a grove of fig trees, Timbrel watched Java, Rocket, and Scrip hurry to the compound. Heart climbing into her throat, she found herself whispering a prayer that Java would quickly disable the power and communications lines. The faster he did that, the sooner they could slip inside and not be exposed.

Then again, once inside those gates, all bets were off regarding safety. Beowulf could die.

I could die.

Tony. . .

Timbrel could die and he'd be responsible.

The thought sucked his brains dry, hollowed out his heart, and left him a shell of himself. Tony shook off the thought and watched through his thermals as Java worked the power grid. He ignored the desire to look at Timbrel, to reassure himself that she'd be okay. But he'd seen her gaze snap to him thirty seconds ago.

Tension rolled and thickened as irritating at the sweat that rubbed the back of his neck and other spots raw.

What if she got in there and didn't listen?

What if someone had a bead on her and took it?

Those are things I can't control.

But it'd eat him alive to watch her die.

A slap against his shoulder jerked him back to the situation. Dean snapped his hand toward the compound, the signal for Tony to get moving. *God, help me. My attention is divided.* He sprinted toward the gate and crouched beside the cement brick wall that had been plastered over. From his pack, he drew out the protective padding so they could scale the wall and crawl over the barbed wire without incident.

Yet even as he worked, his mind slithered back to Timbrel. Man, he hoped she played by the rules. When she got an idea in her head. . .

No, she's smart. She knows the dangers.

Set, he turned and nodded to Rocket. The spry guy sprang up over the wall, followed closely by Scrip. A few seconds later, the gate unlatched. Tony pivoted in his crouched position and signaled Dean. Even as he did, Timbrel, Beowulf, and Dean trotted toward them.

He patted Dean and guided him into the yard, Timbrel behind him.

A crack shattered the quiet.

Another.

Tony grabbed Timbrel's shoulder and jerked her back. She stumbled and they both went down.

Growling erupted.

"Beo, out!" Timbrel hissed. Shot him an apologetic glance.

But Tony moved around her, bringing his M16 to bear as he eased into the yard. On a knee, he peeked around the corner.

"Move," Dean hissed from the side.

Tony spotted him two yards in, next to the shack—apparently a guard hut. A man lay sprawled in the dirt. Monitoring for muzzle flash, Tony angled back and reached for Timbrel. When he saw the tiny explosive burst, he nudged her toward Dean. "Go!"

He covered her as she and Beowulf sprinted to safety. Tony shoved himself after them, firing in the direction of the shooter. He scuttled up to the structure, throwing himself against the wall.

"Entering now," Rocket whispered into the coms.

Tony eyed the windows and alleys with his scope, anxious as their men worked to clear the residence. In person, structure B-4 loomed like a demon with a gaping maw.

A series of "clear" came through quickly followed by Java's report, "All clear, lower level. Moving to second level."

Tony rolled to the left and scampered around the back of the guard hut. He hustled up along the other side and knelt, scoping the house. Not as tall as the warehouse, but the place had some serious outfitting going on. He eyed the satellite dish and prayed Java had stripped that of its communicating power.

A noise crept up on his six.

Chills tracing his spine, Tony glanced down and to the side. Prepped himself. Then flipped around, staring down his sights at the target. His fingers easing back to the trigger.

A gasp stabbed the air as his mind registered Timbrel's wide eyes.

Grunting, Tony turned back to watch the windows and exits. "I could've killed you."

"Watters wanted Beo sniffing, said to follow you." Her pitched words spoke of her fear, her adrenaline rush.

"House clear. Four civvies secured—two women and kids," Rocket announced quietly through the coms. "They say no one else is here. Bringing them down now."

"Go!" Dean grunted.

Four? Only four people for a compound that employed a hundred? That was said to have bunks for that many and more? It didn't make sense.

As Tony hustled along the perimeter, he wondered that the women were here alone. Timbrel let Beo's lead out and the giant dog trotted forward, his nose dusting the ground as he moved. Tony had to admit, if he saw that beast coming for him, he'd probably wet his pants.

Beside him, Timbrel kept pace as he moved forward, sweeping side to side as he gained the warehouse entrance, watching shadows. Probing alleys.

"At the door. Clear." Tony took a knee and stayed alert, noting Dean and Rocket coming his way. The four prisoners knelt in front of the house, and Tony spotted Pops on the rooftop. Beo sniffed in a corner beneath a window. He scratched. Sniffed. Scratched again.

"What's he doing?" Tony whispered.

"That's a hit," she said as the dog sat down.

"Out here?" Tony scowled. That didn't make sense. They were here to capitalize on intelligence that the warehouse had chemical weapons hidden inside.

"Let me check it."

Tony slapped out a hand. "No." He nudged her back. "Not yet." He nodded to the others who joined them.

"Something seem wrong to you about this place?" Dean asked as he squatted next to him.

So his commander felt it, too. "Yeah." He indicated to Beowulf. "Dog's got a hit on something."

"Check it," Dean said. "We're going in."

Pushing to his feet, Tony noticed Timbrel moved without him handing out instructions. They stalked the fifteen feet to where Beowulf sat. With that old-man pout and soulful brown eyes beneath the moon, Beo looked up at Timbrel, the whites of his eyes thin slivers.

"Good boy," she said as she went to one knee.

"Careful," Tony's heart pitched into his throat. "You're not EOD."

Timbrel bent and assessed the spot. Her fingers gently probed the area. On both knees, she leaned into the spot.

Tony swallowed hard—he'd seen enough to anticipate the worst. Like her head getting blown off. "Okay, get—"

After a deep intake, she blew on the spot.

Tony wanted to curse. He couldn't take this.

"What the. . .?" Timbrel dusted something. Then lifted a piece of paper from the ground. She held it up. Looked at him. "I don't get it."

"Neither do I." He wagged his hand at her. "Get up. Something's wrong." His gaze probed the darkness. The silence. No. . .no. . . He keyed his mic. "Watterboy, something's not right."

"You're telling me," Dean muttered. "This place is empty!"

Tony turned a slow circle. *God, what's going on here?*

"Tony." Timbrel's voice held warning.

He shifted toward her. Four people. In a compound with WMDs—supposedly. No men. No trucks. No. . .trash. . . "Pops, you got eyes on any people in here? Thermals show anything?"

"Negative."

"In the warehouse?"

A brief pause ensued as Tony imagined Pops scanning the interior with his thermal scope. "Negative."

"What about outside the fence? Anywhere?" His heart thundered as he stalked to the other side of the warehouse where a large garage-style door forbade entrance.

"Tony!"

He pivoted.

Timbrel's eyes were wide. She stabbed a finger toward him.

"What?"

"Behind you!"

He jerked around, expecting a combatant. Instead he saw Beowulf, sitting, staring at the door.

Tony spun around.

Fire pierced his shoulder. Threw him back. He hit the garage door. Heard *thunks* and *tinks* against the metal.

Gunfire!

"Pops, find that shooter!" Dean shouted through the coms. "Candyman, get out of there!"

Tony threw himself forward.

Felt the world *whoosh*. His hearing went.

A scream shrieked through his mind. Something slammed him forward. White hot fury exploded!

Twenty-Two

Massive and powerful, a concussive fist punched her backward. Airborne. Her back arched, vertebrae popping. Her neck snapped forward then backward. Flipped her over.

Her head hit the ground.

Teeth jarred. Something popped. Pain flashed through her neck and spine. But nothing like the frenetic pace of her heart. Tony! Beo! She rolled onto all fours, her entire being devoured in pain. Aches. She tasted blood. Timbrel spit, dirt grinding into her palms as she pushed to her feet. Whirling around, she tripped. Went to a knee.

The world spun.

Vision blurred, she blinked. Where. . .where was he and—? "Beo!" She pushed herself back onto her feet. Stumbled. Coughed against the smoke snaking down her throat and into her lungs. Covering her mouth with the crook of her elbow, she coughed again.

And saw him! Both of them.

Horror movies had nothing on the way her brain slowed down. Adrenaline exploded through her system. Racing, surging through her veins, drenching her in an eerie chill. Screaming that what her eyes told her was there couldn't be real.

Beowulf barked at her, standing guard. Over Tony, laid out on his back. Face bloodied and charred. The left sleeve of his ACU burned off. His leg bloodied.

Beo barked again. As if to say, "Get it together!"

Tears wormed through her body, pulling a wracking sob out of her. The sound shoved her toward them. She stumbled forward and dropped at Tony's side. She looked up at her loyal guardian. "Good boy," she said—and noticed the wounds on his back legs. She sucked in a breath. She traced his body visually. His hind legs were scratched up. A sizeable cut and some burns. Hurt, but he'd be okay.

But Tony's injuries screamed critical. As Beo slumped onto the ground with a moan, she turned her attention to Tony. His face covered in dirt and blood. Her stomach heaved as she saw the mangled mess the explosion had made of Tony's leg. The sickeningly sweet scent of blood doused the wind and mingled with the smoke and ash, forcing another cough. Trembling hands didn't know where to place. . . His leg.

Oh, sweet Jesus, his leg! The lower half was so mangled and gushing blood.

He'll bleed out! Do something!

Tourniquet. He needed a tourniquet. But she couldn't take her hands off the injury without freeing him to bleed out.

She clamped her hand just above his knee. "Help!" she screamed, looking around for the others. Her gaze roamed the compound. Searched for help.

At the spot where the entrance once stood, hulking metal and steel hunkered over three of the team. Watters pumped someone's chest. Java drove a needle into the arm.

"Help me!" she shouted again, her voice lost amid the howling blaze. She twisted and looked up where she'd seen Pops. The rooftop sat empty. *God, not him, too.* Timbrel's panic reached a fevered pitch.

Fire shot into the sky, its roar deafening and scalding. Timbrel leaned over Tony's body, shielding both of them from the angry claws of the fire. Crackling and popping debris floated through the air. Hissed against her cheek as another volley shot into the sky.

She ducked and found herself looking at Tony's chest. Was he even breathing? Her gaze flipped to his mouth. His throat. Blood squished between her fingers. She whimpered and tightened her grip. "Tony!" she shouted, though their faces were only inches apart. "Tony! Tony, wake up!"

He groaned, his head lolling from side to side.

"Tony!" Hope surged as she touched his shoulders.

Eyes fluttering, he let out another groan.

Oh man, those beautiful green eyes. So beautiful. "Tony, can you hear me? Please say you can."

He pried himself off the ground with a grunt.

"No, stay down!" She pinned his shoulders but he fought her.

"Get off!" He coughed, his personality combative. He came off the ground. "We need"—pain corkscrewed through his face—"augh!" The injury must have caught up with his adrenaline rush that tried to throw him back into the fray. Agony twisted his words and expression. He curled onto his side as he reached toward the injury.

"Don't," Timbrel snapped as she tried to hold him off. "Watters, help!"

"Get me out of here," Tony grunted, spittle sliding down his chin as he ground out the words. "It's not safe." He pushed up—threw himself backward, howling as he reached down. His head bounced off the ground. He writhed. Face red, he cried out. Gritted his teeth. "Crap, crap, crap!" The veins in his temples bulged. "My leg!"

"Stop it, Tony. Just keep still or you'll make it worse."

"I can't—it. . ." He groaned again.

I need help! Tony had to get a tourniquet or he'd bleed out with the artery chewed up by the bomb. She checked over her shoulder. Java and Watters were shaking their heads.

Someone had died. But if that man was dead, they needed to divert their attention to Tony. "Help!" she shouted again. "Tony's bleeding out!"

A thud beside her yanked her from the quicksand of grief that threatened to devour her. She flinched and found Pops at her side. He whipped a kit from his pack.

"I can't stop the bleeding."

"Pops, just get me out of here," Tony begged.

"Working on it, Candyman." Hands already bloodied, Pops ripped open a velcroed strap. He lifted Tony's knee and tucked the strap under it then tightened the strap.

A demonic howl roared from Tony. He dropped back, his eyes rolling.

"Tony!" Timbrel choked on her panic. "Tony, don't leave me. Hang in there, you hear me?"

"He's better unconscious." Using a straight bar secured to the top, Pops twisted it. Over and over, his hands slipping in the blood and fatty tissue. Bones exposed, broken.

Timbrel pressed her fingers to Tony's carotid. Where. . .where was his pulse?

"Is he breathing?" Pops asked as he cranked the tourniquet tighter and tighter.

But she saw his chest rise and drop quickly.

"Barely! His pulse is weak."

"Halo 1, this is Raptor 6, we need immediate evac," Watters demanded into his mic. "We have one man down, another critical." He knelt so he kept Tony's head between his knees while Java slipped in and set Tony's neck in

893

a brace. "Halo 1, this is Raptor 6. Repeat, we have sustained serious injuries and need immediate evac!" Watters slid an oxygen mask over Tony's face.

Timbrel scooted aside, letting the elite warriors do what they did best. She shifted her attention to Beo, tugging her first-aid kit from her pack. She gently cleaned his cuts and bandaged them. Darts of sympathy pain raced through her. The pads of his paws were burned off! And he'd stood there over Tony, protecting him.

Wrapping her arms around his chest, she gave Beowulf a hug. Held on to him. The only constant. The only reliable force.

Except Tony. . . Timbrel shifted her gaze to him. She wanted to cup his face, tell him to hang in there. But she would be in the way of their life-saving attempts. And she was not going to put Tony's life at risk.

Risk. He'd wanted her to risk love for him.

Something tickled her cheek.

"I'd do that and more," she whispered into Beo's fur.

"He's not going to make it!" Pops's grim face and shout startled Timbrel. She watched as he slid a needle into Tony's arm. "Where's that chopper?"

"En route. Two minutes."

"He's bad. Lost too much blood. He doesn't have two minutes!"

The words pounded Timbrel's conscience. Her hands felt funny. She looked down at them, surreal nightmare enveloping her. Tony's blood covered her hands. The realization bounced her gaze to his face.

With the fire and darkness in a death dance around them, she couldn't tell if he was pale. What she didn't like was that he was still. And silent.

"I'm losing him, Commander!"

★ ★ Twenty-Three ★ ★

Tony never woke up. The twenty-minute flight back to base had only served to heighten Timbrel's fears. He'd lost way too much blood. Face gray, lips pale, he lay lifeless on that stretcher, a strap securing his chest and thighs as the landscape blurred beneath them. The medics worked nonstop en route to Bagram's medical facility. Even as the skids touched down, the doctors were transferring Tony to a gurney. They rolled him away, two medical staff riding on the sides as they hurried him to surgery.

But she heard them—not their words so much, but their tone. Their hopelessness as they rushed him into the building.

Timbrel climbed down and stood there, watching as the hospital doors closed.

Something bumped her. She inched aside, feeling distanced from her own body. From this nightmare. As she turned, she saw the man they'd called Scrip now tucked in a body bag as they wheeled him toward the same doors.

What if they couldn't stop Tony's bleeding? What if they. . .they couldn't save him?

Her knees jellied. Wobbled.

He can't die. "He can't," she muttered.

"Hogan, your dog."

The barked words seemed to blast the hair from the back of her neck. She spun and spotted Beowulf. He hopped down from the chopper then hunkered as if in pain. He went down. Onto the ground. Looked up at her with those soulful eyes.

She rushed to his side. Her mind jarred from the thick cesspool of grief to the frantic fight-for-her-life—her dog's life—adrenaline burst.

Timbrel scooped him into her arms. Jerked toward Watters. "Where's the vet?"

"Get in," someone shouted.

Timbrel came around and found Rocket with a Jeep. "Thank you!" She climbed in, Beo's head resting against her shoulder. She hoisted him into a better hold, her boot pressed into the side of the Jeep's foot well as Rocket spun the steering wheel to round a corner. Timbrel strained against the pull of gravity as they shot toward the kennels.

Light exploded as the front door flew open. Timbrel saw a familiar face. "Harry," she whispered as she pressed her cheek against Beo's head. "It's okay, boy. Almost there."

Tires squealed as Rocket swung the Jeep around, almost throwing Timbrel and Beo from the vehicle.

Before she could set boot on ground, Harry was there. "What happened?"

"An explosion," Timbrel said as she hurried toward the building, Beo still coddled in her arms. It was safest to keep him in her arms until they could muzzle him, the grump and wimp he was when it came to pain. "He has cuts on his hind legs, and I think his paws were burned pretty bad."

"Here," Harry said as they raced through a door and into a bay. "Right there." He pointed to a table.

Timbrel eased Beo down, and two techs quickly slipped a muzzle on him. Her boy grew skittish, his claws scraping over the steel as he scrambled for safety from a danger that didn't exist.

"See he still hates doctor visits," Harry said with a note of amusement as he lifted a syringe from the tray sitting on the counter.

"You would too if someone stuck one of those in your butt every time you came." Timbrel stretched over Beo's abdomen and shoulder as Harry slid the needle into the fatty part of his hip.

With a grunt and long-suffering sigh—*I can't believe you did this to me again*—Beo slumped against the cold examination table. His brown eyes sought hers, but the focus quickly faded.

The techs moved in and Timbrel took a step back as Harry bent over her boy. "How's it look?"

"Timbrel," Harry said with a warning.

"Don't do that to me, Harry."

"Your hands are bloody. You're an unsanitary mess. Do you want to risk your dog's life?"

As if she'd been smacked, Timbrel took another step back, her gaze sliding to her hands.

"Wash up." Harry pointed to the sink. "Use the soap. Scrub hard."

Water rushed over her hands, the blood running in crimson rivulets down the industrial-sized sink. Tony's blood. . .his howls. The guy who went with the flow. The guy who'd stolen her heart. The guy who'd taken her to task for wimping out on a real commitment to him.

"He's bad. Lost too much blood."

A tool clattered, steel against steel, jarring her.

Timbrel sniffed, only then aware of the tears threatening. Using her elbow, she pumped several squirts of soap into her other hand. The strong scent of antiseptic filled her nostrils. Timbrel rubbed her palms together. Scrubbed and scrubbed. Stole a glance at the surgery happening behind her. Doused her hands with more cleanser, sloughed off the dirt. . .the memories. Oh, if only she could slough those off.

What if she had to live with the truth that she'd watched him die tonight?

He couldn't die. Beowulf had saved his life. Almost sacrificed his own to make sure Tony had a chance to live.

I could've lost them both!

Her knees went weak. She gripped the edge of the sink. *They're all I've got.* Timbrel pressed a wet hand against her mouth and stood there, water running and spiraling down the drain just like her thoughts.

He braved her mom. Handled it like a pro. He even put up with Beo's grumpiness. If Tony was gone. . .

Life would be empty.

No, not true. She had Beo.

A dog, she thought with a snort.

She loved Beo. More than life itself. But now. . .now. . .was it possible she felt that way about a man? About Tony? A knot of dread—no, not dread. What was swirling through her stomach as she watched the water rushing down the drain? She placed a hand over the spot where the crazy warmth emanated.

Maybe I'm sick.

Too much violence. Too much blood. Too much chaos.

"Go get something to drink." Harry's voice invaded her thoughts.

Timbrel slapped off the water, yanked a paper towel from the dispenser, and turned as she dried her hands.

Harry didn't look up, but he seemed unusually aware of what was happening as he shaved Beo's side near the hip joint. "There's food in the break room."

"No way I could eat right now."

897

"You're pale. Did you get hurt?"

Timbrel frowned as she pitched the used towels in the trash. "No. I wasn't close to the building when it. . ." Her mind shifted to the blast. To being thrown across the courtyard. Slamming into a shack.

"Timbrel?" Harry was watching her.

"I. . . The blast threw me."

"You should go to the hospital. Get checked."

"No, I'm not leaving Beo." Thumbnail between her teeth, Timbrel watched her boy. Watched the rhythmic rise and fall of his chest.

Saw the similar motion with Tony. Laid out. Injured. Bleeding out.

"Okay," Harry said. "Once we're done here, I'll drive you over."

Timbrel gave a short nod. She was fine. And she wasn't leaving Beo until she knew he'd be okay, that there wasn't any permanent damage. She might not be able to be there for Tony, but she sure wasn't going to leave the one guy who'd protected her for the last five years. Rather than pacing, she planted herself in the corner, leaning against a counter.

Twenty minutes in, Timbrel shifted. Sighed.

Harry shook his head.

Okay, so she wasn't a very patient patient. Especially when it came to Beo. "Thoughts?"

"That you need rest." Harry worked quietly over the next hour, cleaning, stitching, bandaging, until finally he straightened. Stretched his back and plucked off a glove.

Timbrel straightened, too. "Well?"

"Cuts are minor, mostly. One took a dozen stitches, another three. Removed a couple of pieces of shrapnel. We'll do X-rays and make sure he doesn't have any internal injuries." His voice lowered as he crouched and angled his head to the side, seized the opportunity while Beo was unconscious to give him a quick physical. "His pads will need fresh bandages and cleaning regularly. Afraid he needs to get home and rest. I want to keep him here for a few days to make sure no infection sets and that he can get up and move around before I release him."

Timbrel drew up her head. Swallowed. "That bad?"

"He's a tough dog, Timbrel, so I doubt much will keep him down." He shifted to the sink and scrubbed his hands while the techs took X-rays. "He's going to need treatments for a few weeks, but"—Harry's features softened—"I think he'll be fine." He ran a hand over Beo's abdomen. "Not hurting for food."

Once the techs cleared the room, Timbrel eased toward the table.

"Never has." She rubbed Beo's ear. Though he wasn't awake, she knew it was his favorite spot to be rubbed, next to his chest. But only those he let into his personal space ever figured that out. The others, he just bit their heads—or hands—off. Not literally. Unless the person was too slow.

Timbrel kissed his broad skull.

"What happened out there?" Harry asked as he relocated Beo to a rear kennel and laid him out comfortably.

What *did* happen out there? Timbrel couldn't help but wonder. Tony and Beo had been mortal enemies. But Beo. . .Beowulf had knocked Tony to safety. Well, as much as he could. And he'd taken some shrapnel and singed off the pads of his paws in the process.

"My furry hero." She squatted by his kennel, rubbing his fur. "You big softie." Tears burned her eyes. "Thank you."

"How is he?"

Timbrel pivoted on her haunches toward the strong voice from behind. There stood Watters, helmet in hand. Face still dirty but hands clean, he nodded to Beowulf. "Is he going to be okay?"

"Captain." Harry folded his arms. "The dog will recover. Hopefully 100 percent."

"Hopefully?" Timbrel punched to her feet.

The world washed gray, squeezing hard against her abdomen. A warbling din exploded in her mind then vanished.

Twenty-Four

Lance stood in the hall, arms folded, anger rippling. He glowered through the glass at the surgeons working to save the leg of one of the best operatives he'd ever met. VanAllen's father had an exemplary service record, the part anyone could access. It made him want to kill someone for almost taking out the son of one of the country's most valiant and unrecognized heroes. Nobody could know what James VanAllen Sr. had done, what he'd sacrificed. But his family suffered through the repercussions.

Lifting his chin, Lance tried to shake the fog of doom. He wanted to wring someone's ruddy neck. That op should've been clean. His source. . .

Doors flapped open.

"I need a doctor!" Watters sprinted in, Hogan limp in his arms.

Lance hurried toward them, his pulse skyrocketing at the sight of the woman. "What in blazes? She was fine!"

Two nurses shot forward and ushered Watters to a room with a gurney.

"She just collapsed." Out of breath, Watters laid her down gently then stepped back. "Out cold. Vet said she blanked a couple of times, looked pale, then when she stood—"

"Who is she?"

"Timbrel Hogan," Watters said. "Dog handler."

"I'll get her records transferred." Lance hurried toward the nurse's desk. He filled out a form and handed it off to an orderly then jerked around.

Watters, shoulders still rising and falling from the exertion of carrying Hogan, dropped against the wall. Farther down, Lance spotted Russo with the others, apparently still waiting on word about VanAllen. "Watters, get Russo. In my office in five."

He spun on his heels and stormed out of the hospital. Phone in hand, he punched in his code. Authenticated. Then dialed.

"This is risky—"

"I want your butt here tomorrow night."

Silence. Then, "You know that is not possible."

"What I know is you screwed us over."

"No. I did—"

"Tomorrow, or I'm floating your name to every server I can access. I'll rip your cover so wide open, you'll feel a draft halfway across the world." Lance stabbed the phone with a finger, ending the call. Stuffed the device back in his pocket and hopped into his Jeep. The driver delivered him to the SOCOM subbase command center.

Inside, Lance made it to his office, yanked out a can of Texas bliss, and popped the top. He guzzled the Dr Pepper, emptying it. With a heavy intake of breath, he arched his back and neck as a wiggling made its way up his esophagus. Then let out a long belch. As he reached for another can, he heard voices in the hall.

A light rap on the door preceded the entrance of Watters and Russo, who'd showered, it seemed, by the wet hair, clean pants, and black T-shirt. They closed the door and stood, hands at their sides, full attention.

With a wave of his hand, he growled, "At ease." He grunted, slammed down the can, then planted his hands on his belt. "What in Sam Hill happened out there, Watters?"

Captain Dean Watters tucked his chin at the verbal assault. "Sir, the explosion"—he shook his head—"it wasn't accidental."

Firm, hazel eyes held his own. "What are you saying?"

Jaw set, Watters scowled. "I think you know what I'm saying, sir."

"Then you know that what you're suggesting incriminates a half-dozen key intelligence sources." Including the one Lance had just threatened to expose.

"What I know," Watters said, his eyes ablaze, "is one of my men died, another is fighting for his life, the dog had his feet burned off, and the girl is in surgery to relieve cranial bleeding." Chest heaving, the man held his ground. "With all due respect, sir, someone wanted us dead. I want to know why."

"You and me both, son." Lance collapsed into his chair and waved them into the others opposite where he sat. Head in his hands, he gave a long sigh. "Give it to me. Play by play. I want to know everything."

Bleep. . .bleep. . .bleep. . .

Annoying and grating, the incessant noise hauled Timbrel from a deep sleep. Her eyes felt as though sandbags sat on them. She groaned and reached for her alarm clock, determined to silence its shrieking.

Her fingers hit something.

That something clattered.

A glass. She must've knocked over a glass. She yanked open her eyes—and slammed them shut with another loud groan. Too bright!

"Timbrel, please," a soft voice whispered. "Keep still. Don't move yet."

She frowned and squinted around the blinding light exploding around her. "Who. . .?"

An oval face came into view. Well, not perfectly. A bit distorted. As Timbrel blinked quickly, the blurred visage slowly came into focus. Large, almond-shaped brown eyes. Rich dark brown hair. Exotic beauty. "Khat?" Timbrel reached to push herself up. "What are you doing in my room?" Something pinched at the top of her hand. "Ow." She glanced down and spotted the needle and the tube taped to her skin. "Where. . .?"

Her gaze skidded around the room. Curtain. Gray-white walls. Stinging antiseptic smells. Someone came toward her room, a white coat over ACUs.

Bleeping accelerated. Snapping Timbrel's attention to the machine where her BP rushed across the screen. "Khat, what's going on? Why are you here?"

"Easy," Khat said, her face wobbling. "You have to relax or you'll pass out again."

"Again?" Panic stabbed her. "What happened to me? I was okay, with Beo—" She sucked in a hard breath. "How is he? Did something happen?" She grabbed the sheet and flung it back. "Where is he? Take me to him!"

"Whoa whoa whoa!" The medical staff member rushed into the room. "Easy there, Miss Hogan. I need you back in that bed."

The floor canted.

Oh wait. That's me. Timbrel flopped back down, hand going to her head. "What's wrong with me?" Her fingers met scratchy material. She traced it, trying to look up at whatever wrapped her head. "What is this? What did you do to me?"

Khaterah had the nerve to laugh. "Timbrel, calm down." She came to the other side of the bed and bent toward Timbrel's legs. "Back under the blanket."

"Not until someone tells me what's going on. And where is my dog!" And Tony! She gulped back the adrenaline, her gaze skipping around the medical ward where several beds were occupied, separated by curtains.

"You had intracranial bleeding." The name patch on the doctor's uniform read: HOLLISTER. He had youth on his side—maybe a little too much. Was he even a doctor? "The other members of the team said you were thrown a good fifteen feet by the blast. Yes?"

The blast. Right. Yeah. Timbrel gave a slow nod. "But I was fine. I made it back here, watched Harry fix Beo."

"It's a miracle," the doctor said. "You could've died had Captain Watters not rushed you here."

The words pushed her back. Only remotely aware of Khaterah tucking her into the bed, Timbrel eased against the mattress. "Am I. . .am I going to be okay?"

He smiled. Again, looking probably like he was maybe fifteen. *Or I am getting old?*

"You're up, talking, lucid—all very good signs. We'll run some tests over the next twenty-four hours and monitor your recovery. But so far"—he shrugged—"things are looking good. I would suggest you lie on your side until the incision where we drained the fluid has a chance to heal over."

With a half nod, Timbrel took her first normal breath and readjusted on the bed, which faced her toward Khaterah. "Beowulf—how is he?"

Dr. Hollister began taking her vitals, listening to her heart and so on.

"He is well. Harry said to let him know as soon as you woke up. Apparently, your dog is as bad a patient as you are."

Timbrel laughed but then frowned at the A Breed Apart vet. "Why are you here?"

Tilting her head, Khat gave a very soft smile. "You listed me as your next of kin, so they contacted me and I flew out immediately."

"Ah. I forgot about that." Timbrel worried the blanket as a nurse came in and adjusted a dial. Slid a needle into a tube, wrote something down, muttered to the doctor, then vanished.

"Why would you do that?" Khat shrugged. "Do not take that wrong—I am touched, but—"

"I knew if they had to notify next of kin, whatever happened to me would be bad." She licked her lips and found them to be parched. "And I needed to make sure Beo was taken care of. I knew you'd do that."

Khat beamed. "You are right. I got in last night and after checking on you, I went directly to his kennel." She lifted a jug with iced water and raised it toward Timbrel. "Thirsty?"

"Please." As Timbrel took the hefty container, something flittered across her mind. "Wait." She frowned at Khat. "The flight out here is nearly a full day." She turned her gaze to the doc. "How long have I been out?"

"Today makes two days," Dr. Hollister said as he stood in front of her, clipboard clasped between his hands. "But one of those, we had you sedated." He gave a mock salute then stepped toward the door. "I'll be back in a few hours. They'll be here within the hour to take you down for an MRI and some tests."

"Great." Timbrel waited till the door closed then nudged her gaze to Khat. "Sneak me out of here."

Laughter filled the room. "Not on your life—or mine."

"You're too good for your own good." Timbrel wrinkled her nose. "That sounded better in my head."

More laughter.

Holding the inside of her lower lip between her teeth, Timbrel let her mind go where she had avoided since waking up. Tony. He had been pretty messed up. Unconscious. Bleeding like crazy.

"Hey." Khat touched her hand. "Is everything okay?"

"Yeah." Timbrel blinked. She couldn't just pretend. "No." But it scared her—what if he'd died? She searched for some feeling, some indication in the intangible air around her that indicated Tony was alive. That he was here. But that was only what happened in romance novels. Or science fiction.

Something squeezed her hand. She flinched. Looked at Khat. "Do you know what happened to the rest of the team I was with?" Oh, why couldn't she just ask about him?

"Timbrel, do you think you're ready to talk about these things?"

"If he's gone, then no. I'm not. But. . .how can I not? It's going to hurt either way."

"He?" Khat angled her head. "Are we talking about Candyman?"

Heat flushed her cheeks.

"I am sad to say that I have no news for you, Timbrel. He was flown out before I got here."

"Flown out?"

Khat nodded. "To Landstuhl."

Her heart tripped. "That. . .that's where they send the most critical patients."

The armored SUV lumbered through the narrow alleys of the village. The heat baked through the inadequate insulation and left Lance feeling like a sardine. Another turn and they aimed for an archway with a colorful rug hanging from its arc. Despite the graceful architecture, the structure's plaster had been pocked and streaked from years of the owner's lack of care. Run-down, dilapidated. . .perfect cover for the asset.

"Nice and easy," Lance muttered as Watters guided the vehicle straight toward it, then slowed to ensure it didn't snag on something and rip the fabric off.

The tapestry thrummed its tattered fingers along the hood. . .along the windshield.

Light winked out.

Watters eased the Jeep into the anemic space, his gaze tracing the roof, the upper windows, the doors, and lower windows that surrounded them. "Perfect for an ambush," Watters said as he cut the engine.

Lance climbed out and shut the door. Hands on his belt, he let his gaze make the same trek Watters's had.

A figure appeared, wreathed in shadows and secrecy. "General Burnett, it is good of you to meet me here."

"Don't flatter yourself. I called this meeting." He wouldn't give this guy an inch. Not after what happened. "I've got one man dead, another laid up and with a missing leg, and another soldier"—no need to mention that one had four legs—"with bad burns."

The man came forward. Variable had always been an impressive and forbidding character in settings like this, but Lance wasn't going to show any fear.

"There are few people I trust and am willing to take information from. At one time you rated high on that list."

"But no longer."

"Not so much," Lance said, ignoring the way his heartbeat thudded against his temples. He could feel that blood pressure rising. "See, I tend to have a problem when someone poses as an ally, giving and receiving key intelligence facts, then goes and throws my people under the bus—or in front of a bomb."

"That would be a problem."

"You betrayed my team. Betrayed their location and plans."

"No." Variable took a step forward, fingertips together and held down.

In his periphery, Lance noted Watters stiffening, his elbows drawn back and hands poised.

"What happened was necessary."

"Want to explain 'necessary'?" Watters's shoulders were straight, squared.

RONIE KENDIG

"You're tracking a very sneaky sand spider. And because of certain impetuous and arrogant moves made by members of your team"—unyielding, he held Watters's gaze—"that spider has been alerted to your presence, your intention."

Lance peered at ODA452's commander. Raw intensity and power rolled off the guy's shoulders as he stared back, unyielding. "So, you're saying it's our fault."

With a shrug and pursed lips, the asset turned to rest against a window ledge. "What is the purpose of placing blame except to extract vengeance?" Arms folded over his tan tunic, Variable eyed them both. "Surely, that is not why you are here."

"No." Lance felt Watters jerk his gaze toward him. "I need to know you're not compromised, that from this point forward, I can trust what you say."

The asset raised his hands up and out with a smile. "And how am I to reassure you of that?"

"Say it."

Laughing, the man pushed off the wall. "I cannot do that because for me"—he planted a large hand over his heart—"my word is of greater value than your politics."

Watters took a step forward, his hand on his holstered weapon. "My team got ambushed. Your word means *nothing* to me now."

"For your losses, I am sorry. But to this accusation that because your team sustained injuries and a fatality I am untrustworthy, what proof have you?" He pointed to Lance. "I could just as easily say this man is to blame for not better securing a volatile area, or for even sending you in there."

"We went in there because you said they'd be there, the proof we needed would be there."

"It is troubling, yes." Variable shook his head. "You never can tell who your enemies are."

"Are you saying you're our enemy now?" Lance wanted to yank out his Glock and—

"Let's settle this, friend." The asset's expression had never shifted or reflected the anger Lance and Watters were struggling to contain. "Did I tell you to go to the warehouse? Yes, I did. Did I know you would find trouble there?"

Lance held his breath.

"Yes, I did."

Watters lunged.

The asset produced a silenced weapon and held it toward Watters. "Be slow to anger, Captain. It will keep you alive longer."

Trembling with fury, Watters stood frozen.

"Captain, stand down," Lance said as he moved forward. "You're talking in circles."

Variable lowered the weapon as Watters backed up several paces. "So I am." Another smile. "What you must understand is that we have the same goal, Lance. This game. . .it is deadly, and there is no way around that. Bashir is aware you are trying to stop him, to bring him down. So this is not a case of who will get one up on the other, but who will do it first."

The man should be a politician. Nobody would know his position and yet they'd follow him like lost puppies. *Just like Watters and me.*

"If I lose more men, you'd better start looking over your shoulder." Lance's pulse thumped against his temples. "Because if I find out you betrayed us and are playing us, I will out you so fast to every network, you won't have time to smirk."

The asset seemed to grow several inches. Stood a good five or six inches taller than Lance. "Do not mistake me for some nobody begging for scraps from your table!" The man's voice rang across the hood of the SUV and bounced back. Fierce eyes blazed at Lance. "I have more connections than your little war-fogged brain."

That was better. At least the guy could get riled. "We understand each other."

He smirked again. "If only you truly understood." Variable shook his head. "I would be on guard, General."

"Against what?"

Walking back into the shadows, he said, "We would not want America to go to the dogs."

Twenty-Five

*T*ony, don't leave me."

The voice thickened with panic and fright tugged at his mind. He reached for it with his thoughts, searching for her. For Timbrel.

He opened his eyes and stilled as the setting rushed in at him like an RPG that had acquired its target: The sheets on the bed. The curtain sectioning off half the room. The monitors. The heaviness in his limbs— *I'm drugged.* The Spartan furniture. A hospital. He was in a hospital.

Crap. Not again. Tony slumped back and stared at the ceiling. Then he let out a laugh. "I'm alive." He coughed against a dry, parched throat. But hey, he'd beaten whatever tried to take him out.

What was it this time? He searched his memory banks. Timbrel and Beo. He smiled at the slobbery, flatulent beast. A bark, garbled in a warped memory, sailed through his mind.

Tony hesitated.

Images flashed. Snapped. Explo—

"Explosion." There'd been an explosion. Tony raised a tubed-up hand to his head, trying to remember. He'd figured out what Timbrel screamed about. Threw himself—

Hot. Man, it'd been so hot.

But that. . .that was all he remembered. The explosion had seared his backside. But. . .if he was here in the hospital. . .lying on his backside, he must not've been burned. If he'd sustained burns, they'd have him prostrate on the bed.

Okay, so rule out burns.

The door opened. Tony braced himself. Prepped himself to find out what he was doing laid up in a hospital when his team was out there fighting. He felt fine. A little. . .fuzzy. . .but otherwise fine. He lifted his

908

hands. Yep, two hands. Lifting his shoulders off—

Whoa.

His vision went ghostlike.

Hearing hollowed.

Tony dropped against the bed. Okay, so. . .something whacked his head. He touched his forehead. . .ran his hand over his skull. Weird. No bandages.

Why else would he nearly pass out if he hadn't taken a head injury?

Blood loss.

Okay, but he had his fingers. He lifted himself—more slowly this time—and gazed down at his legs.

But. . .something. . .

Tony's brain wouldn't compute what his neurons relayed to his brain. There was a disconnect. Had to be.

Why. . .?

"No," he mouthed, but the air never crossed his voice pipe as he stared, disbelieving.

What on earth?

That wasn't. . .that wasn't possible.

He ordered his toes to wiggle. Both sets—the right and the left. Felt them. Felt the sheet tickle them.

Yet. . .the sheet didn't move. In fact. . .

Tony frowned. "No."

Closed his eyes. Squeezed them tight.

God. . .please. . .

He pinched the bridge of his nose as he propped himself up, feeling a heavy pull on his body to collapse. Leaning on his left forearm, he lowered his other hand. Eyes still closed, he forced himself to accept whatever was there. . .whatever. . . He tilted his head. Looked.

Breathing proved impossible.

"No," he gritted out between clenched teeth.

Right leg fully intact. Toes propped up the sheet.

But the left. . .below his knee. . .it dropped perilously flat.

Heat flashed through his arms. Chest.

Walls of gray closed in on his vision.

Tony thrust aside the sheet. It defied him. The sides tucked in, it didn't move the way he demanded. Fisting the cold material in his hand, he yanked hard. Fell back against the mattress. He tried to pull himself back up.

His body refused.

His fingers traced down his leg to the bandage. He couldn't feel the end. Tony gripped the side bed rail with his right hand, searching farther with his left. Dragged himself up and to the side, his gaze locked on to the place where the sheet lay depressed.

No. It couldn't be. His leg was there. It had to be.

He groped for purchase on his leg. His shin—

A gentle whoosh proved what his mind wouldn't believe.

His left leg. . .*it's not there.*

"No, no." He pulled and pulled on the sheet. His nostrils flared. His breathing laboring. "No," he ground out as the sheet finally came free. Slithered over the bed. Exposed the nightmare.

"No!" he shouted.

Tony dropped back against the bed. "No no no!" He stared at the ceiling, unblinking. "No, God." He gulped the fear that drowned his ability to breathe. To think. To fight. "Please, no!" He smashed his arm against the rail. "Please!" His hearing hollowed out. "I'll do anything!" He arched his back. Cried out. "Give me back my leg!"

Sobs wracked him.

Please. . .

Can't breathe.

Can't see.

"Jimmy? Oh son, I'm so sorry." His mother's voice filtered into his subconscious from somewhere. "Just rest, my sweet boy. I'm here. God's here."

Bright white blasted against his corneas.

Tony jerked. *Explosion!*

"Good morning, Sergeant VanAllen," a guy in scrub pants and a T-shirt yanked open the other curtain, sending shocks of sunlight into the dingy room. He turned and Tony wondered if the guy had even hit puberty yet. "So, my name is Corporal Jennings and I'm your physical therapist."

Tony turned his head toward the door and stilled. "Mom?"

She smiled and stepped closer. "Hey, handsome."

"What're you doing here?" He frowned, feeling vulnerable. Crazy. But this was his mom. The woman who had changed his diapers, changed his Band-Aids, and ushered him to the emergency room three times before he hit basic training. She understood him. Understood how he was wired. And if she was here, then that meant they'd notified next of kin. That meant. . .

The amputation is real.

It wasn't a dream.

Of course not. That'd be too easy.

No, it's a freakin' nightmare.

Something akin to a heavy blanket dropped over him.

"So," the corporal said as he lowered the security rail on the side of the bed. "You ready to get out of this bed?"

Tony eyeballed the all-too-chipper kid.

"Ah, strong silent type, huh?" Hair buzzed but enough there to see the dark color, Jennings grinned. "'S'okay. I'm used to it. And I promise—you'll hate my guts. And if you don't, then I'm doing something wrong."

· Tony pressed his lips together. Stared down at the bed. Could not believe rather than two whole legs he had one-point-five. His breathing chugged.

"Okay," Jennings said as he extended his arm, hand poised to accept Tony's.

What did the kid want?

"Your only job for the next twelve hours is to sit up till you pass out."

Tony frowned.

"What? Is that too hard for you?"

Tony stretched his jaw. His mom was here. She'd smack him if he said what he was thinking.

"C'mon, big guy." Jennings bounced his hand.

Tony closed his eyes. He did not want to mess with this kid. He didn't want to face this sick joke of a future God had slapped him with. Couldn't even give him time to accept what happened and this punk shows up acting like nothing happened, nothing was wrong.

"What? Don't think you can do it?"

"I'm tired." Tony rolled his gaze to his mom. "How—?"

"Hey, I get it. You don't want to face the music, but ya know," Jennings said, "it's gone. Your leg is gone." He shrugged. "You can't change that. Deal with it."

Tony grabbed the kid's collar. Hauled him to his face. "Say that to my face!"

"It's gone." Placid blue eyes held his. A hollow sound rapped to the side. "Just like mine."

Tony slanted a look.

The kid shrugged up his pant leg, showed the prosthesis attached to a nub just below his right hip.

"Hey," Tony said, his throat raw, "I'm—"

"Don't." Jennings slid the pant leg back down. "Don't apologize, dude." His face went hard. "Just promise me you won't become a bitter, old, sorry son-of-a-gun. Promise me, you'll honor that." He pointed to Tony's right bicep.

His unit patch tattoo.

"And that." Jennings wrinkled his nose as he eyed the pectoral inkwork. "Whatever that is."

"A family crest, of sorts," Tony said as he eyed his mom.

God. Country. Family. He and God would have to sort out later why He'd let this happen. His country. . .where there was the bugger of it all. He couldn't do anything laid up in this bed. And family. . .he was *not* going to be a burden like his father. He was not going to put his family in that position.

He was letting down all three with his attitude. Losing a leg. . .not even a whole leg. He'd seen worse. The last time their unit returned, there sitting under the shade of a sycamore was Sergeant Major Winthrop, a quadriplegic. That was the closest Tony had come to seeing someone he knew survived like that.

With a sidelong glance to the corporal, Tony stuck out his hand.

One Week Later
Walter Reed National Military Medical Center
Bethesda, Maryland

"Headache again?"

Timbrel straightened as the doctor eased the door to the hospital room closed, which pulled Beowulf to his feet. And started his growling. Though his hind paws were still wrapped in gauze that needed daily changing, he was on his feet and ready for action. Starting with a piece of the doctor, apparently. They'd been shipped Stateside two days ago and delivered to Walter Reed for observation and evaluation. Khaterah had secured a hotel room until the doctors released Timbrel from their care.

She'd been reunited with Beo. But she hadn't heard anything about Tony. How was it possible that nobody knew where he was or what his condition was?

"Beo, out." Timbrel winced beneath the weight of pain that pinched her shoulders into a knot, making the pounding worse. "A small one." She'd battled them, small and large, since landing back in DC two days ago.

He went to a screen and stuffed up some black-and-white film then flipped a switch on the side. The negative images sprang to life. As he eyed them, Timbrel shifted on the edge of the bed. *C'mon already. Discharge me. I gotta find Tony.*

"Mm," he muttered and traced his finger over the blackish lines of her brain. "There's no more bleeding, but it will take time for your head to recover from all the trauma, for all of the swelling to go down."

Timbrel nodded. Good. Right. "Then I'm cleared for duty?" On her feet, she stood ready to grab her bag, change, and get to Burnett's office. Stinker hadn't shown his face since they shipped her over here. And she knew he came back because Khat verified that information.

The doctor snorted. "No."

With a groan, Timbrel whirled around and slumped back onto the bed. "Are you serious?"

Despite the sympathetic smile, the doctor wasn't giving in. It was clear by the way he lowered himself onto the wheeled stool and almost couldn't bring himself to look at her. "That's not going to happen for at least a couple of weeks, if not *months*."

Timbrel gaped. "Months?"

He held up a placating hand. "Your scans are clear but the headaches are a concern, especially the frequency you indicated on your chart." He tapped the file with his pen then started writing. "Brain injuries are very delicate, and we want to make sure there is no further aggravation to the affected areas."

"You're kidding, right? I've spent all day on patrol with headaches worse than this."

"Yes, but those would be due to late nights partying or dehydration." He gave her a look that told her not to argue. "This is injury related." He pointed to Beo. "He has bandages. How would you feel if he just ripped them off and trotted off because he felt he'd braved worse days?"

Hitting below the belt there, Doc.

"So," he said, apparently convinced he'd made his point, "my orders are for you to continue to rest, take it easy. Your chart says you're returning to Texas, so you'll need to check in at BAMC in a week for a follow-up." He scribbled on her chart. "If you feel any pain, have any blackouts, I want you back immediately."

With puffy cheeks, she blew out a breath with a long-suffering sigh.

Her hands went to either side of Beo's head, where she massaged the spot just under his ears.

"Are you okay on painkillers and anti-inflammatories?"

"A regular pharmacy," Timbrel said with a nod to the bottles lining the small table next to the hospital bed. "So, not cleared for duty but cleared to return home?"

"Correct." He straightened and started for the door. "The nurses will get your discharge papers ready. You can go ahead and get dressed."

"Great." Yet. . .not.

After he left, Timbrel grabbed her duffel and stepped into the bathroom. Retrieving her cell phone, she figured it couldn't hurt to try one more time. She scrolled to Tony's name, opened a text screen, and typed up a message. PLEASE CALL WHEN YOU CAN. BEO MISSES GROWLING AT YOU.

She stared at the letters. *Why can't you just say it?*

Jabbing her thumb against the back arrow, she deleted the last line. She typed in:

I MISS. . .

BEO AND I MISS YOU. . .

She deleted the second sentence altogether.

Coward.

Yeah, well, he hadn't given her any indication that he'd let her back into his life.

Timbrel tossed aside the phone, showered and changed, then slid into her own clothes—real clothes. Not pajamas. It'd been ridiculous that she'd had to stay in lockup for so long. She was fine. And it'd prevented her from finding Tony.

"Hello?"

"In here," Timbrel called as she brushed out her long hair, wincing as it tugged on the scar site. "I'm being discharged."

"Yeah, the nurse is here with the papers."

"Oh!" Timbrel tugged open the door and pivoted around the corner. Finally a ray of sunshine. She went to the mobile tray where the nurse laid out the forms. She pointed to the first page and in a monotone voice explained the importance of—

" 'S'okay." Timbrel grabbed the stack, thumbed through each one, then signed. "I've been through this enough times to know the spiel." She held them between her hands, tapped the papers against the surface to straighten them out, then returned them. "There. Am I free to go?"

"One more?" The nurse handed Timbrel a card. A blank card.

"What's that?"

A sheepish grin spread over her face. "An autograph, please?" Her face went pink. "I mean, I know what the papers say, but. . .you're Audrey Laurens, right?"

Timbrel huffed and looked own, chewing the inside of her lip.

Beo rose onto all fours.

Irritation clawed through her that she just couldn't shed that part of her. *No, but you can make it work for you.* Timbrel smiled at the twentysomething nurse. "Tell you what, I'll sign that on one condition."

"What's that?"

"Tell me if you have a patient here."

"I—"

"Just tell me if he's here." Timbrel took a step closer even as the woman went back one. "I don't want to know anything else. Just his location. That's not violating anything, right?"

"Timbrel," Khaterah said. "You—"

"Khat, I just want to know if he's alive. If he's here or still there." She shrugged and looked at the girl. Then took the card, scratched a note and her signature, and handed it back. "His name's Tony VanAllen—oh, it might be under James Anthony VanAllen."

Without a word, she left the room.

Timbrel frowned. Checked Khat. "Is she going to help?"

"I can't believe you'd put her in that position."

"What position? It's not illegal." Shrugging into her pack, she reached for her phone and checked. No response. Though her stomach squeezed at the possible reasons why he wouldn't reply to her text, she went with the easiest to believe: His phone was dead, he didn't have it with him, or maybe he just hadn't turned it back on yet. "And it's not protected by HIPPA laws. Besides, since nobody is going to tell me, then I have to—"

"He's here."

Timbrel's entire world felt as if it powered down. "What?"

"He's here." Khat shrugged. "But he's not good, and the family has requested no visitors."

"Not good? What does that mean?"

"I don't know. I didn't want to ask. It seems inappropriate."

"Of course." Timbrel deflated against the bed. "I'm. . . Am I a visitor?" *Is that how he sees me? How his family sees me?* "His dad said he loved me. His mom—" Timbrel frowned as she snapped her gaze to Khat. "Who told you that?"

"The duty nurse." Khaterah took Timbrel's bag and put it on her own shoulder.

After another sweep of the room to ensure she hadn't left anything behind, Timbrel followed Khaterah into the hall. With Beo on a short lead, they made their way down to the first floor. Surprisingly, Timbrel felt winded, her head thundering. Annoying injury. She'd never been one to be sidelined by headaches or anything else. But the warning was there—it wasn't *just* a headache.

"Hey," Khat said in a quiet voice, "have a seat here. I had to park way out there. I'll get the car—."

"No, I'm fine."

"Timbrel. Sit there." Determination lit through Khat's gorgeous features.

With a huff, Timbrel sat. "Happy?"

"Immensely." Khat smiled and headed out the door.

Timbrel fought the frustration. Elbow propped on the arm of the chair, she ruffled Beo's fur. "They think I'm a visitor." The way that hurt she couldn't even describe.

"Timbrel?"

She jerked to the side, tensing at the dart of pain that spiraled up her neck and exploded in her head. More slowly, she looked in the direction of the voice. Her heart climbed into her throat as she made the connection and came out of her chair. "Irene."

Closing the door, I stood inside the library. Nafisa was there, head down, as she pored over a book. Her red and pink hijab complemented her olive skin and traditional Muslim features. I'd been so angry with her that day after the village had been razed. So afraid my father would find out she'd been proselytizing. But she had not cowered, had not yielded when I said I could even have her killed. I'd never do that, of course. I wanted to marry her.

Father would not allow it, but I would find a way. I had to. I love her. She shone as a light in a dark world. So fair, so strong.

"I don't understand you." The confession sounded as juvenile as if I'd handed Nafisa a toy doll and asked her to play.

Nafisa's face brightened as she looked up at me. "I believe many men say that of women they know, Dehqan."

I gave a nod. "I think you women enjoy being mysterious." At the table, I slid into the chair next to her.

She laughed. "I am no mystery. I will tell you what you want to know."

A bold proposition. I could not drink in enough of her. But beyond that beauty and that draw. . . "How do you know so much about the Christian's Bible?"

With a small shrug, she said, "My father." Her voice wavered. "He was a pastor and held church. I went with him everywhere he went."

"This was allowed because he did not have sons?"

"Oh, he had those, too." Again, grief came over her, but she pushed it aside and managed a smile. "But I had a hunger. I saw the miracles God brought about through my father, the healings done in the name of Isa. . ." Wonder sparkled in her brown-green eyes. "I could not get enough of the Isa's love."

"Love."

She nodded. "Yes, His love. It says in John 3:16, 'For God so loved the world that he gave his one and only Son, that whoever believes in him shall not perish but have eternal life.'"

Questions had turned in my mind since last she and I had time to speak. Since I'd wrestled violently with her persuasion about *al-Masihu Isa.* Her insistence that Isa was Messiah and yet God.

"What you quote speaks of Isa? God's Son—but that is blasphemy."

"No. It's not. Being a triune being does not make God any less God." She tilted her head at me thoughtfully. "You. . .you are Dehqan, a young man, yes?"

She was laying a trap. But I trusted her and nodded.

"But you are also Dehqan, my friend, yes?"

Again, I nodded.

"And you are Dehqan, the son. And yet—none of those make you any less *you.*"

"That is not my name." My heart thundered. Why did I voice that thought? I had told no one.

"What. . .what is your name?"

"Aazim. My parents were killed. The colonel took me in."

"That's why you gasped when I spoke of orphans!" Her eyes were wide with amazement. "I had no idea, and yet Isa wanted you to know that *He* knew your real identity, that He had not left you nor would He, if you seek Him."

He knows me?

"My analogy was a poor one—we are mere humans with various aspects to our persons, but God is three in one, Father, Son—Isa—and Holy Spirit."

"You mean, God the Mother?"

Nafisa blinked. "No. The Virgin Mary was blessed, favored of God, but not part of God Himself. And it is only through Isa that we can get to heaven, not through works or anything. The beautiful thing is that we do not have to prove our love—though He appreciates it when our actions match our words because it is tangible evidence of His love to people—through performance of the five pillars."

"You are saying they are wrong? But I have seen you pray when we pray!" I blushed as I realized this was something I shouldn't have seen. "I was not prying—but as I slipped in late one day, I saw you on your knees."

"I pray to God, but my salvation is already guaranteed by Isa." Her laugh was almost a giggle. "He wants your heart, not your performance. Isa loves you, like I do."

My heart skipped a beat. Then a second. I couldn't breathe as her words reverberated through my mind. "You. . .you love me?"

Her cheeks were a deep red, and she tucked her chin. "Isa loves you, He died so you could be with Him, but I love you. . .in another way."

I let out the breath that stuck in my throat. "Nafisa. . .I did not think you felt the same way."

Only as I sat there staring into her gorgeous eyes, did I realize how close we were. Though my mind screamed that this was forbidden, I moved in all the same. Exhilarated when she did not pull away, I kissed her.

She tucked her head even more. "I do not want to shame myself or God, Dehqan. Our love is different, fleeting. His love is real."

"It is not fleeting. I love you!" My heart thundered with my words, and I heard them bounce off the ceiling. I dropped my gaze, with a smile. They say love makes you do stupid things. I guess they were right.

I shifted my mind, my thoughts back to the talk about Isa. It's treacherous territory here. But I could not deny the tug they had on my heart. "I do not know what to think of these things about *al-Masihu Isa* and Allah—God. They seem. . .wrong."

"Perhaps because you have been taught they are wrong. Often, we grow up in a world that does not accept us, who we really are. Instead, there are demands on how we act, how we talk, what we believe, or we will not have the love we crave." Her eyes resonated with meaning.

And I felt as if she was reading my entire life from a book or something.

"God put that craving in us so we would seek Him. Isa is God, and God loves you."

A loud noise cracked our quiet conversation. I jumped and twisted toward the sound.

Father stood in the middle of the room, a black weapon extending from his hand. His face contorted in rage.

My mind spun a million directions, yanking my heart with it. As the world shifted into a terrifyingly slow pace, I turned. . .turned. . .to Nafisa.

Eyes glossing, she was slumped in the chair. A crimson stain blossomed across her right breast. She whimpered.

"Nafisa!" I lunged at her.

Sirens screamed through the compound. Shouts mingled with the agony ripping through my chest.

"Nafisa!" I shoved back her chair as she gasped and gurgled. "Help! Help me!" I yelled, but nobody could hear me over the shrieking alarms and the pounding of boots as guards approached from the main floor.

Her fingers clawed into my shoulder. Her lower lip trembled.

"Oh God," I cried out. "Don't die, Nafisa!" I lowered her to the floor, hoping it would help her breathe, that it might stop the bleeding. I ripped off my waistcoat and pressed it to the wound. "I'm sorry. I'm so sorry!" Tears made it hard to see if she was alive still.

Her fingers gripped my wrist that tried to staunch the flow.

Using my sleeve, I smeared away the hot tears.

"Dehqan," she breathed in a gurgling away. She was dying. I could tell. She was going to leave me, just like *moor* and *plaar*.

"Quiet, Nafisa. I will get help. I will not let you die." I applied more pressure to her chest. "I won't. Let. You. Die!"

" 'My peace. . .' " A tear slipped from her eye and slid down her cheek, right through a splotch of blood, turning the rivulet pink. Her back arched, and she hauled in what sounded like a painful, ragged breath. " 'P–peace I leave with you; my peace I give you.' " She struggled for a breath, writhing in my arms.

I clutched her to myself, not caring who would see. Not caring if her blood stained my clothes. "I'm so sorry, Nafisa. I'm sorry. This is my fault."

She smiled.

How could she smile—she was dying! "No. You can't leave me. Nafisa!"

But her face was the picture of serenity. Beauty. Love. Trembling fingers reached for my face. " 'I do not give to you as the world gives.' " A sob ripped my heart out. "Oh, Dehqan. . . 'Do not let your hearts be troubled and do not be afraid.' " Her fingers traced my face. "I love you." Another tear unleashed a flood. "Love Isa. . .for me." She shook her head. "For *you*."

And she breathed no more.

Twenty-Six

She hadn't come to see him. And it bugged him. Royally.

Tony worked through another rep of exercises Jennings had given him before they made the flight from Landstuhl to Walter Reed. Burnett made arrangements for his mom to fly with him and the others on the C-17 Globemaster III that returned him and thirty other wounded back to U.S. soil.

It was his own fault. He'd allowed his pride to dictate his actions. God hadn't put conditions on His love for Tony, and yet Tony had done just that to Timbrel.

But if the girl wasn't willing to face the good, bad, and ugly with him, to work through it rather than running from it. If she—

Forget it. Forget everything.

Tony released the handle dangling over the bed and let himself fall back against the bed, a bead of sweat rolling down his neck and chest. He just had to let her go. That's what she wanted. Obviously. Or she would've talked to him, visited him. Everyone else had. The guys. Burnett. But not her.

She knows. Is that it? Did she know about his amputation?

Tony's gaze dropped to the bandage that coiled around the stump just below his knee. He remembered coming to after the explosion, agony drilling through his body from the damage the blast did to his leg.

She doesn't want me now. Was that it? With his leg missing, he was a burden. *Just like Dad.*

She was right to leave. To ditch him. No woman needed to be saddled with someone in his condition.

The team. . . Could he get back into action?

No. He'd been off his game that night. It's why he'd missed the triggers.

Missed the telltale signs that something was off. He'd messed up and it cost him half a leg.

Teeth grinding, Tony fisted a hand. *My leg is gone.* The thought still hadn't connected. *It's gone. It's gone. It's gone.*

I'm handicapped.

A cripple.

A burden.

He let his head drop back against the pillow and stared up. Hand over his eyes, he fought the despair. Fought the anger. *God. . .where are You? Why? Why did it happen to me?*

The door pushed open.

Tony tensed.

Grady peeked in. "Hey." Hands in his pockets, he came to the side of the bed.

Tony caught his brother's hand and pulled him into a one-shouldered hug.

"How you doing?" Tension radiated from his brother.

He couldn't miss the way Grady's gaze kept bouncing to and from Tony's missing leg. "How d'you think I'm doing?"

"Like crap."

Tony gave a soft snort. "Something like that." He looked up at him. "Thanks for coming over."

"No worries." Grady tugged a chair closer. "I've been going bat-crazy since Mom caught that flight and left."

Tony eyed his brother. "Does Dad know?"

Grady shook his head. "Nah, we thought it better not to tell him yet. He'd just be agitated. You know he can't do hospitals."

"Too many memories." Tony remembered the many times his father refused to enter the hospital doors. Funny that. He'd resented it before. Wished his father would just gut it up, especially when Tony broke his leg—the leg that was now gone—during soccer championships.

"Has Steph come by?"

Tony nodded. "Left about an hour ago. I asked her not to bring the kids."

Grady nodded.

Silence blanketed the room thicker than the antiseptic smell permeating it. Tony knew. . .*knew* what his brother was thinking. What he wanted to say but wouldn't.

"Go ahead and say it." Tony wished the words hadn't come out so angry. "I know you want to."

Eyebrows knotted, Grady peered up at him. "Um, okay. . . Did Timbrel get hurt?"

Tony scowled. "Why are you asking about her?"

Grady gave a halfhearted shrug. "You said she'd worked with you." He motioned to the room. "She's not here now. . .so it made me wonder if she was with you when you got hurt."

"Tony, don't leave me. Please."

Had he pushed her too hard? Was that why she hadn't come? And he hadn't thought about whether or not she got hurt. "No, she was fine." They would've told him if she got hurt. "Why are you worrying about her anyway?"

"Because she's nice." Grady bobbed his head. "Pretty, too. Dad liked her, so did Mom."

Tony's blood hurled through his veins. His hearing whooshed. "Just forget it, forget *her*."

Grady winged an eyebrow at him. "Hey, from what I saw that night, you weren't exactly fawning over her. So what? Now that I'm interested—"

"Back off, Grady. I mean it."

"What? Are you afraid she'd want me?" Grady snickered. "That'd be a first. The girl wants me, not my all-American hero brother."

"Grady, leave her alone. She's—" Tony bit off his words. *She's mine.* That's what he'd almost said. But she wasn't. Things went south between them. Now, the rift seemed enormous.

On his feet, Grady held on to the side rails. "She's what, little brother?"

"She's been through a lot." There. That worked. It was true. Didn't breach a trust.

"You're pathetic." His lip curled.

"What does that mean?"

"It means—"

A light rap severed the terse words.

"Morning." His mom entered, her cheeks a bit red. "Sorry I'm late."

"Nah, it's great. You can put Grady in the corner," Tony said, his heart still hammering from the conversation.

"Well, I have a surprise." Pushing the door open wider, she nodded to someone.

Clicking preceded the beast of a dog.

Tony held his breath.

Timbrel.

Sure enough, she rounded the corner. Dressed in her typical jeans, boots, and black T-shirt, she didn't have her ball cap on this time. Instead her hair hung loose past her shoulders. A cinnamon color. Man, she looked good. But also a little. . .strained.

Tony steeled himself for her reaction. For her to burst into tears—and he knew they were coming because he saw his own torment in her eyes. The one that said he was messed up. A burden. That she couldn't face a future of taking care of someone like him. Someone like his father. No longer the model-perfect guy her mom had declared him to be, Tony probably had little value to her. He'd served her purpose.

He said nothing. Couldn't if he'd wanted to—his pulse chased the hope that she'd be different. She wouldn't. . .

"Timbrel," Grady said. "Good to see you. Man, you look good." His brother went to the side of the bed where she stood back and hugged her. "Came to check on Tony, huh?"

Tony's fury went through the roof as his brother hugged Timbrel. But more so that Timbrel let him.

Her smile wobbled unevenly as she tucked a strand of hair behind her ear. "Yeah." She looked at Tony then back at his brother. Arms crossed, she hugged herself, but her gaze kept bouncing as if unsure of where to settle.

It's my leg—the missing *leg. She can't bring herself to look at it.*

"Were you there when it happened?" Grady asked her, standing close. Too close.

"Yeah." Timbrel seemed to hold herself tighter.

Beowulf trotted to a corner and laid down. Only then did Tony notice the bandages. "What happened to Beo?"

Finally, Timbrel closed the distance. "He. . ." She smiled down at him, but it wasn't a "so glad to see you" smile. It screamed pity. "The pads of his paws got burned off in the explosion. He's recovering though." Her gaze traced his face. "How are you?"

"Recovering." The venom sluiced through that word so much it hurt Tony. Though he stared at her, he noticed his mom and Grady slip out. But with that poisonous explosion came agony to hold her in his arms. To pull her close and never let go.

"Did they"—his voice cracked. He cleared his throat—"did they tell you about Scrip?"

Timbrel twisted her mouth to one side. "When we were trying to evac you, I saw him." She shook her head, fighting emotion it seemed. "It wasn't pretty." She wet her lips, but her chin dimpled in and out. Eyes went glossy again. She shook her head. Ducked.

Without thinking, Tony reached for her hand.

"Seeing him like that—dead, I. . .was so scared"—her lips trembled—"you wouldn't make it." She held his hand.

Tony tugged her toward himself.

She rested against the bed and dropped her forehead against his shoulder.

Sweet relief swept through him as he held her. Slipped his fingers in her hair, cupped the back of her head.

Timbrel whimpered. Pulled back, her gaze locked on his.

Hesitation slowed but didn't stop him from kissing her. Luring her closer again.

Another whimper.

Hunger. . .a hunger unlike he'd ever known wove through his chest as he deepened the kiss. The only right thing, the only good thing left in his life. He wanted her to want him, to accept him. . .

His reason caught up with his hunger for her. The reminder of their first kiss. Then the way she completely walked away from him. Without any compunction.

Timbrel eased back, forehead against his. "I'm sorry."

"For what?"

"Your leg—"

Tony drew back. "I still have half of it."

"That's not what I meant."

Anger punctured the moment. "I know what you meant!"

Timbrel straightened. Frowned.

"I don't need pity."

"That's not—"

"Ya know what?" Why did he think she could do it? "Just. . .just leave."

"Tony." Her pretty face knotted up. "You're misunderstanding—"

"No, actually, I think I'm understanding just fine. You couldn't bring yourself to accept me, to risk it for me before I lost my leg, but now. . . *now* you'll do it?" He raised his hands, stomach cinched. "Forget it. I don't need your sympathy. I don't need your pity."

"Are you out of your mind? That is not—"

"Stop." He speared her with a glare. "Get out."

Timbrel shook her head rapidly. "Tony, no. Let me finish a sentence."

"Out!"

Twenty-Seven

One Week Later
A Breed Apart Ranch

Timbrel threw her duffel into the back of the Jeep and turned back to the front porch. She lifted the plastic tub that held Beo's gear, including bandages, medicine, food, treats, Kongs, etcetera, and set it in the back with her bag.

"Are you sure this is a good idea?"

Timbrel eyed Jibril, who stood at the door. "I have to try."

"Just be. . .gentle."

She smiled. "When am I not?"

"Most of the time," Jibril teased as he joined her. "Remember, he is wounded. As much inside"—he thumbed his chest—"as here"—tapped his temple—"and here." He rapped on his prosthesis. "I've been there."

"Yes, but he's also not a quitter. And I'm not going to be shoved out of his life without a fight. He's going to hear my side if it kills us both."

"What if it does, Timbrel?" Jibril's amazing blue-green eyes twinkled at her. "What if you say things you regret, that sever the thin cord of hope you are clinging to?"

Her heart thunked against his question. She did have a tendency to mouth off. For her defenses to come screaming to the surface and shove off any threat. That's pretty much what she'd done that day, leaving Tony in Arkansas. He'd never fully forgiven her for that. She'd wanted him to forgive and forget. But he said no.

She still didn't know why, and it bugged her.

Timbrel looked away, across the training yard and the new training building Jibril'd constructed recently. What if Tony didn't want her?

Then he sure shouldn't have kissed her the way he did. "I can't *not* try, Jibril." She pushed her hands through her hair, formed a ponytail with the long strands, then slid her black baseball cap on and tugged her hair through the opening at the back.

"Why?"

She slapped her hands against her thighs. "What do you mean? He needs to listen to me, hear me out. Tony believes I was there for sympathy, to feel sorry for him, but that couldn't be further from the truth. He needs to know that."

"Why?"

Timbrel jutted her jaw. "I'm not going to defend myself—"

"Is this for you or for him?"

Timbrel whirled on him. "I hope it's for *us*." She signaled Beo closer, lifted him in a cradle hold, and set him in the front seat, attentive to his still-bandaged paws. "I have to get going."

"I will be praying."

"Good. I have a feeling I'm going to need it." Timbrel hopped in the Jeep and started the two-day trek to Northern Virginia armed with her guy and a ton of anxiety. The first night they rested up at a pet-friendly hotel outside of Nashville, then headed out before dawn the next morning, so she pulled into Leesburg around dusk. She hit Route 7 and sweat coated her palms despite the forty-something temperature outside. It wasn't the weather that slickened her skin. It was the proximity to a certain medical center and the most powerful force in her life—Tony.

A glance at the in-dash clock told her it was too late for visiting hours. She GPS-mapped the nearest hotel and aimed in that direction. Stretched out over the bed, boots on and fully clothed, Timbrel wrapped her arms around Beo, who lay on his side, long legs and bandaged paws dangling off the bed.

Eyes closed, Timbrel willed herself to rest. To sleep so she'd be fresh faced in the morning. With an exaggerated sigh, Beowulf rolled onto his back, paws poised in the air, right along with his belly. Timbrel scratched his belly and wished she could doze off as easily as he did.

Funny how "quiet" wasn't really quiet in a place like this. Take for instance the thrumming mini fridge. And the vending machine that sat in a small alcove two doors down. Or the whine of traffic. And Beo's snoring.

Timbrel willed her mind to quiet, to shut out the other noises and just rest.

What if Tony really didn't want her there? Would he yell and throw her out again?

The thought pinched her nerves. She didn't want to upset him. If he really was through with her, then she could accept that. Just walk out. Never look back.

Never see him again. Never hear his voice.

Swinging her legs over the side of the bed, Timbrel sat on the edge of the mattress. She couldn't sit here all night thinking. Worrying. She had to talk to Tony. To be so close. . .to not know. . .

She wanted to believe he was just upset, still in shock at losing his leg.

Rubbing her forehead, she tried to imagine what he'd gone through, waking up with no leg. How terrifying! She thought of his father, how Tony had been there for his dad. Faithful, loyal, resolute.

Timbrel pushed off the bed. Grabbed her jacket and keys. Slinking through the night toward Walter Reed, her mind buzzed. Or was that the TBI she'd incurred? Traumatic brain injury had a way of messing with her. She pulled into the parking lot then trotted toward the front doors.

With Beo at her side, she entered and slunk through the halls. With Beo wearing his harness and paws bandaged, maybe they wouldn't get stopped. She made it to Tony's floor and slowed, trying to bring her pulse and nerves under control.

Beo trotted onward as if this were a walk in the park. He angled to the left, and Timbrel realized he was leading her. Then he nosed a door. Timbrel eyed the number. "Good boy," she said, a little in awe of his ability to find Tony in this maze.

Timbrel gave a soft rap on the laminate door before pushing it open.

Sitting with the upper portion of his bed inclined, Tony stared up at a wall-mounted television screen. The wash of blue on his face made him look pale. No, he wasn't watching TV. He was . . .was he crying? Tony took a hard breath and looked down. At his legs. Probably at the portion that wasn't there anymore.

Again he looked up.

Dear God, why. . .why did You do this to him*?* He didn't deserve this. The best there was in the world came in packages like Tony. Protecting innocents. Protecting the not-so-innocent. Timbrel would give just about anything to undo what happened to him. To return what had been ripped from him.

Snap. Bad timing.

Beo charged ahead.

She tried a signal.

Beo must've missed it. He raised up and planted his paws on the bed's edge and gave a low growl.

Tony started and jerked toward her. Yanked the blanket over his leg and glowered.

Stomach in her throat, Timbrel moved forward. Dropped her bag into a chair. Then before her mind could register her own actions, Timbrel yanked the blanket back.

"Hey!"

"Hey, nothing." She pointed to his leg. "That's nothing to hide or be ashamed of." She jabbed her hands on her hips. "And if you think I'm here out of pity, you're giving me more credit than I deserve. I'm not that good."

"Thought I told you—"

"Yeah, yeah. I know. You're going for grump of the year."

"Just leave." Tony tugged the blanket back over his legs and aimed the remote at the television.

"No, I'm here. And you're going to hear me out."

He cranked the volume on the television.

Timbrel turned, eyed the monitor and the cables that ran into the ceiling. She whipped the extra chair over, climbed up on it, straddling the arms, and reached for the cord.

"Hey!"

She yanked it free. The power cut. She hopped back down.

"Timbrel."

Back at his side, she bent over the bed. "Tony, listen to me. I am here because—"

"I don't care why you're here. I just want you to leave."

"No, you're going to listen."

"I'm not. You had a week to figure out a defense. I'm not interested in your rehearsed lies." He shook his head and touched his temple.

Had someone smacked her, she wouldn't have been so surprised. But to hear Tony accuse her of not only lying, but *rehearsing*. . . "Why you self-absorbed—"

"I'm not doing this." Tony reached for a cable attached to the bed.

"I expected juvenile behavior from the other soldiers on your team, but not from you. Not like this."

"Just leave."

"When I'm ready. And I won't be ready until I tell you that I'm *not leaving you*." Timbrel huffed. "You can be a Class A jerk—which you do very well, in case you were wondering—but I am not going to let that determine what I do."

"Whatever."

Bereft at his lackluster responses, Timbrel eased closer. "Tony, please." She swallowed the frustration that pushed her to get angry, to get loud. He was in a bad place. A really bad place. *Give him room to breathe and figure things out.*

"I'm not leaving, Tony. I'm here for you the way you were always there for me, even—*especially*—when I didn't want you to be." She smiled through the emotion clogging her veins. "I didn't realize until after it all how much that meant to me. And I will not abandon you in your time of need."

"Need?" Tony slapped the bed. "This isn't *need*. This is—" Tony pinched the bridge of his nose. Took several long breaths. Then glared at her. "What will it take for you to get it through your thick skull that I don't want you here?"

"More than loud words and a ticked-off attitude." Timbrel folded her arms over her chest. "You forget, I grew up with that. I'm impervious."

A stonelike transformation slid over his face. "I'm over you, Timbrel." Tony just held her gaze, his expression flat. His tone flat. "I want you to leave. I never want to see you again."

The words rang like a shriek of bats in a cave, terrifying yet pinning her to her spot, unable to move. He didn't mean those words. They were spoken out of trauma.

He's trying to protect you.

From what?

Himself.

The words swirled heady and strong like a crosscurrent in a storm. "I'm not leaving you, Tony."

"Can I help you, Sergeant?"

Timbrel shifted and looked toward the door where a nurse stood.

Eyes still on Timbrel, Tony said, "I'd like this woman removed, please."

"Tony—"

"Ma'am. I'm afraid you shouldn't be in here anyway." The nurse was at her side. "I need you to come with me." When she reached for Timbrel, Beo growled and went into aggression mode, causing the nurse to yelp. She darted out of the room.

"You'd better go." Tony closed his eyes. "She's probably bringing security."

"Tony, stop this. Please, I know you're upset about your leg, about being like your father—"

"You have no idea"—his voice roared through the night—"*no idea* what you're saying."

"I do, actually. I can see it in your eyes and hear it in your voice. You're not a burden—"

"Get out!"

"Where is the man who could stand up to my sharpest word, the man who loved me when nobody else saw anything worth caring about?"

"He's dead! *Dead!*"

Timbrel poked his chest. "This isn't the man I fell in love with. That man wouldn't sit here feeling sorry for himself and shoving everyone into dark corners of his life until all that's left are shadows and death."

"It's fitting," he said, his eyes ablaze. "I'm a soldier. All I do is kill."

"You *protect*."

The door flung open.

Two MPs stood there, weapons at the ready, not aimed at Beo, who stood with his legs apart, shoulders rolled forward, and his canines exposed. "Ma'am, I need you to call off your dog or I'll have to do it for you."

"Beo, out," Timbrel said as she locked gazes with Tony. "Please." He was serious. Dead serious about this. "Please, don't do this. I want to be here. I was wrong before. I apologized. Let me—"

"Good-bye, Timbrel." Tony nodded to the MPs. "Please remove her."

★ ★　Twenty-Eight　★ ★

Two Months Later
Leesburg, Virginia

Stairs loomed up the hall lined with decades of family portraits. Tony stood on the landing, eyeing the unlit corridor. Crutches in one hand, he hopped up the steps the way he might've as a kid to mess around. Make it harder. Have a challenge. But now. . .now everything was a challenge.

He aimed for the last step and miscalculated. With a grunt, he collided with the step. His shin took the worst. Tony rolled onto his hip and sat. Huffing, he stared at the crutches that had clattered back down to the basement floor. Frustration coiled around his heart and squeezed an iron fist around it.

Teeth gritted, he returned to the bottom. Yanked up the walking aids and faced the steps once more.

"Tony," his mom called then her head appeared at the top of the stairs. "Ah. There you are. I made your father some clam chowder. Want some?"

"No thanks." He hopped up a step, holding on to the rail.

"Here, dear. Let me help you." She started down—

"Mom." Tony held up his hand.

She stopped, one sneakered foot on a step higher than the other. "Tony, what is wrong with me helping you?"

"Because I have to do it myself."

"There is nothing wrong with accepting help or me offering. Don't treat me like a criminal for being your mother." She pivoted and disappeared around the corner.

Head on his forearm, Tony groaned. Would he ever be treated like a normal person again? It was true—his mother was Suzy Homemaker. A good, strong woman who loved helping people. Her motive was always borne out of her desire to be a blessing, not to make anyone feel inferior. But she was so doggone good at it—both the helping and the making one feel inferior. . .

Just like Timbrel.

Tony straightened and pressed his back against the wall. *"This isn't the man I fell in love with."* Her words still poked at him. He knew she'd come back. Knew she'd try to make him see her side. It was how she was wired. How she coped. That knowledge prepared him for her appearance.

Okay, not fully prepared. She'd been more beautiful than ever. So confident and strong.

"You're doing a good job holding up that wall."

Tony rolled his gaze to the side and saw his brother sitting on the landing.

"Why don't you sit outside in the cold and hold up the deck next so Mom and Dad don't have to pay for its repairs?" Grady slurped some white liquid from a bowl. Chowder, no doubt.

"Have you started paying rent yet?" Tony hopped up two steps. "You're here enough."

"I think with all the whining and brooding you're doing, Mom has forgotten I exist. I could probably clear out their bank account and she'd never notice."

Tony made it up two more, tempering his anger at Grady. "Dad would, and then he'd take you out back and do us all a favor."

"Tsk, tsk, Jimmy. Where's your brotherly love?"

"At the bottom of these stairs." Tony stabbed the crutch at Grady, pushing him out of the way. "Move."

"Man, did the bomb blow up your manners, too?"

"Shut up."

"Aha, I see. That's why Timbrel hasn't been here." Grady slurped from the spoon as he stood in the hall, watching Tony clamber.

"You don't know what you're talking about."

"Actually, I do."

Tony eyed him as he readjusted the crutches.

"Ya know," Grady said as he moved into the kitchen, set the bowl in the sink, then slid his hands into the pockets of his slick gray slacks, "I never thought I'd see the day my brother resorted to threats and wife-beating tactics to break up with a girl."

The rubber stopper of the right crutch slipped. Tony whooshed forward. Grabbed the granite counter. His brother saw that? Saw the fight with Timbrel?

Disappointment colored Grady's face. Where Tony had the sandy blond hair and green eyes, Grady sported the tall-dark-and-handsome genes. And brains. Grady had inherited the near-genius level intellect that had him soaring to the top of a computer security company. Had him driving a BMW 320i.

"Since you're done with her, since you shattered her heart, I'm going to see what I can do to pick up the pieces."

"Tss," Tony said with a smirk. "Threatening me?"

"Oh no, little brother." Grady guzzled a glass of water, rinsed it, and placed it in the dishwasher. "No threats." He walked toward the back door and opened it as their mother reappeared with a tray of empty dishes. "Remember, you walked away—or should I say hobbled?" He planted a kiss on their mother's cheek. "I like her. Mom likes her. I think it's time to introduce her to the way an incredible woman like her *should* be treated."

"*Grady.*" Tony's jaw muscles hurt from grinding them so much.

His brother walked out the door.

"Grady!" Tony swung his crutches and carried himself toward the garage.

The sound of a powerful engine roared to life and peeled away.

Slamming his hand against the jamb gave him little relief. He punched the wall. Again. Again.

"Tony." His mom's voice filtered through his fury. "Let me get you some water. Or do you need some pills?"

"Leave it!" He jerked around. "I'm sick of your pity. I'm not him. I'm not Dad!" He stabbed a finger toward the back porch where she'd served his father lunch. "Don't treat me like a cripple. Got it?"

Something slammed against his chest. Pinned him to the wall.

Breath knocked out of him, he blinked. His mind whiplashed. He found himself staring down at his father, whose arm pressed into this throat. "Dad," Tony croaked. Great. His father was having an episode again.

"Don't. Ever. Talk. To my wife like that again." His father's nose pushed against Tony's cheek, breath puffing in hot blasts. "Ever. Am I clear, boy?" Perfect clarity shimmered in his father's eyes. No, this wasn't a flashback. His father had hauled him up just as he had when Tony was twelve and mouthed off to his mother.

"Yes, sir," Tony choked out.

His father released him. Patted his shoulder. "I don't care if half your body is missing, you won't treat your mother like that again."

Tony gave a nod. Felt the world crumbling. Assaulted by his own actions, by the shock and grief on his mom's face, he lowered his gaze. Pulled it back up and met hers. "I'm sorry, Mom."

When she reached for him, tears glistening on her cheeks, he shook his head. Hobbled down the hall. To his room. He hopped inside, swung the rubber-tipped crutch at the door. And flung himself around.

The crutch caught.

Tony pitched forward, jerked off his foot. He went down. His face smacked into his footboard. Snapped back his head. Pain exploded. He slumped.

As he sat there, disgusted with himself, his gaze hit the shelf behind the door. Trophies. Team photos. Footballs. An autographed baseball that held the signatures of his team when they won state. Hockey. Prom. Sorority balls. Military balls. All things he'd never do, play, or be. Ever. Again.

Fury whipped him over. He grabbed the crutch. "Augh!" Swung it around. Aimed it at the shelf. Raked the trophies off. Smashed the photos.

Hobbling around, he spied himself. Spied the rage in his face. Hated himself more. He threw the crutch discus-style at the mirror.

The motion pulled him off balance. He landed hard against the desk. Footing lost, he flipped. Rolled. Swung out his hand to catch his balance. No good. The narrow casing that held his DVDs and Blu-rays tipped. Pushing him backward. He hopped to avoid the avalanche. The small desk chair clipped the back of his knee. Tony pitched backward.

His head thunked against the wood floor. The case chased him.

Arms over his head, Tony cried out as it battered him. Pinned, he growled. Shouted at God.

As the dust settled, the broken pieces of his grief and shame lay amid the ruins of his room. Instinctively, he shot out his leg to push off the shelf, but it was his left. And there wasn't enough leg to reach.

"Augh!" Weakened and defeated, Tony slumped down, then onto his back. He lay there, staring straight through his ceiling as if he could see the God of heaven and earth. The God who had rewritten Tony's life by stripping away his pride right along with his left tibia and fibula.

Tony surrendered to the agony that gripped his soul and cried. Sobbed.

Twenty-Nine

A Breed Apart Ranch
Texas Hill Country

A rich, thick, spiced scent coiled up the stairs and lured Timbrel from her loft bedroom at the A Breed Apart ranch. She lay across the bed and wrapped her arms around her barrel-chested bullmastiff. Beo threw his head back, slinging a line of drool with him.

Timbrel ducked and rubbed his side. "How's my favorite guy?"

He swiped his tongue along her cheek as she reached for his rear paw. Checked the pad by thumbing over the surface. Healed. "Lookin' much better, Beo." She placed a kiss on the top of his broad skull and scooted to the edge of the bed.

After stuffing her feet into her boots, she grabbed a black hoodie. Together with Beo, she headed downstairs. As they descended the wood stairs, her heart did a dance at hearing Beo's nails on the wood. He'd been given his all-clear two weeks ago, but the sound still made her heart happy.

"Khat, something smells wonderful!" They rounded the corner into the kitchen and drew up short. "Mother."

Her mom stood with her boyfriend—*interesting, still with the same guy*—at the kitchen island with Khaterah, who pored over some pastries laid out on the counter. Her mom sauntered toward her. "Hello, darling."

"What are you doing here?" This felt like the ultimate betrayal.

"I invited them," Khaterah said without looking up from her work, which, if Timbrel had guessed right, was homemade baklava.

"Why?" Timbrel hated to sound petulant, but having her mom here was the last thing she wanted.

935

"Well, first," Khat said as she laid down another ultrathin sheet of phyllo dough, brushed butter on it, then repeated the process, "it's Thanksgiving."

"You said you don't celebrate it."

"No, I said we don't make a big deal of it. But we do celebrate. Only my father was Iranian. Not our mother." She delivered a tray to the oven. "But second, Ms. Laurens, Mr. Takkar, and I have some final details to put together for the gala, and she brought over the check."

The check. Right. But still. "The gala's two more months away." Really, Timbrel wasn't sure any day would've been a *good* day to see her mother in her own home—or rather, the home in which Timbrel rented a room.

"I know," her mother said with almost a touch of glee. "It's so close. We can't afford to waste any time." Her mom came closer and touched Timbrel's face. "Please don't be mad, Audrey, darling. I've been so worried about you."

Suppressing the temptation to blast her mom for intruding in her life yet again, Timbrel stilled. Remembering acutely the way Tony had cut her out of his life, she suddenly had a new perspective on how much that hurt. Was that what her mom felt? No wonder she'd been obsessive about communication. While they weren't close, they didn't have anyone else.

"I'm okay." She gave a smile then moved out of her mother's touch. "Where's Jibril?"

"Outside. Emory brought over the female GSD and he's been working with her nonstop."

Timbrel paused. "A German shepherd? Is Emory a new MWD handler?"

"Trainer. I thought you knew." Khat cleaned up the counter and washed her hands. "This dog is for therapy. Possibly security as well."

"What kind of therapy?" Takkar asked.

My, what a handsome specimen. Timbrel couldn't believe her thoughts, but she suddenly understood the power this guy held over her mother. Dark eyes. Dark hair with a debonair touch of gray and a mysterious air that would leave any girl reeling. Though she had met him that night in LA, Timbrel hadn't really been able to assess him in a casual setting. No doubt he stood out on the red carpet as an exotic addition to Nina Laurens's fashion trends.

But even as much as Timbrel wanted to relegate this man to a "fling," she could see there was something different about this guy.

Yeah, it's called "terrorist."

"Wounded soldiers," Khat said. "They can train dogs to intervene when the person is getting upset or agitated. The dogs can detect when their handler is afraid. They can also train them to detect abnormal body chemicals, hopefully to prevent seizures or the like. I've encouraged Jibril for years to explore that option." Khat smiled at her handiwork. "Not bad. It won't last the day once Jibril knows they're here."

She waved a hand and started for the hall leading to the offices. "Okay, let's get to work. Hopefully we can finish before the turkey is done."

"Since when has he used ABA money to train dogs that won't bring us a profit?" Timbrel followed the trio into the back, Beo on her heels.

"Timbrel, I'm surprised at you."

She frowned at her mom. "What?"

"I'd think you'd show more concern after—"

Her defenses flared. "*What?*"

"After that bomb killed someone you worked with and hurt your boyfriend."

"He's not my boyfriend."

"Oh?" Her mom's expression wasn't flat or amused. This time, she genuinely seemed concerned. "You broke up with him?"

Shaken by this shift in the love-hate relationship with her mom, Timbrel turned to her friend. "Khat, seriously? We're having to do a fund-raiser to stay afloat"—she motioned to her mother and Takkar—"so why is ABA training therapy dogs? That's a massive investment, and once the dogs are adequately paired, they're gone. They can't be hired out, no ROI. Don't get me wrong, I'm all for canine therapy, but here with ABA?"

"It's Jibril's pet project, if you will. You will have to talk with him about it." She handed out folders to Timbrel's mom and Takkar. "I'm very excited. The fund-raiser is turning into an international event. We've had handlers from Britain, Australia, and Switzerland agree to send representatives to speak on the benefits of working dogs within the armed forces. Okay, here's what we have so far. . ."

Something in Timbrel wanted to strike out. Too many things she didn't know. Too many things that made her feel left out. Off kilter. "Mr. Takkar, where is your friend?"

He paused. "Excuse me? Which friend?"

"The one I met at my mother's home. He seemed especially glued to your hip."

"Timbrel," her mother reproached.

"What?" She shrugged. "I just thought. . ."

"Bashir is back in Afghanistan," Takkar said, his voice smooth as a serpent's movement. "His publishing business just received a large grant to help get the schools stocked with books." He gave a cocked nod. "He does much for the people of Afghanistan. And this meeting about the gala would not be in the best interest of his time."

"But it is in yours. Why? Surely my mom's fame doesn't add *that* much to your life or position."

Her mother swarmed forward. "Timbrel." She took hold of her arm. "Stop this. Please." The hurt in her mom's eyes surprised her.

Timbrel suddenly understood with astonishing clarity. "You really like him," she whispered.

Her mother lowered her head and looked to the side as if it pained her to admit it. "Yes." Brown eyes pleaded with her. "He's important to me. I care for him very much."

An explosion detonated in Timbrel's chest. What if. . .what if this man was like his friend Bashir? "Just be careful, Mom." She eyed Takkar, who watched them closely. "I don't want you hurt again." The words she didn't say had no need to be voiced, *Or drowning in the bottom of a bottle of Grey Goose.*

As had been her mother's way with every boyfriend breakup.

That was what Timbrel would've said, would've warned, if there hadn't been a much-greater concern—that Takkar was a terrorist.

"Don't hurt her," Timbrel said, backing out. "Or I'll make sure you die begging for mercy."

"Timbrel!"

She spun and stomped out of the room. Down the hall. Drove her fingers through her hair as another headache threatened. She thought about the three of them gathered around the conference table, pretending things were normal and good. Khat and her mom buying that guy's lies like charmed snakes.

With the gala coming up two weeks after Christmas—

Timbrel stopped short of the first trail. Christmas. Several months ago, she thought she'd be spending Christmas differently. *With Tony.* But that wouldn't happen. Now. . .now, she'd be alone. Single. No hope of ever changing that.

Shaking off the suffocation, Timbrel and Beo headed into the trails snaking around the ABA property and made their way to the overlook, which provided a gorgeous view of the property, and right into the training field.

From here, she spotted Jibril working with the female German shepherd. A gorgeous red-and-black plush-coat, it looked like. The girl had some pep to her.

Beo alerted on the dog. Panting stopped, he watched, his entire presence—shoulders, eyebrows, ears—seeming to point to her.

"She's a pretty thing, eh, big guy?"

But again, it didn't make sense when the organization needed money to stay in operation that he'd take on a charity case. Okay maybe that was a wrong attitude. She knew the amazing work those therapy dogs did, the life-and-death difference they made in the lives of their handlers, and she certainly could not ever begrudge that.

But. . .something felt off.

Dressed, Tony grabbed his gear and crutches then made his way out to the living room where Stephanie waited. He'd asked her to drive him out to Nashville, where Scrip's parents lived. It had killed Tony to miss the funeral, but being laid up in a hospital made it impossible. Still, he couldn't let it go any longer without paying his respects to his friend's family.

They streaked down 81 and made it to Nashville by evening. Then he rapped on the door.

A short, gray-haired woman frowned, her confusion from an "out of context" scenario. "Mrs. Barker?"

She tugged her sweater closed beneath her chin. "Yes?"

"I'm Sergeant First Class VanAllen." He gritted his teeth. "I served with your son, ma'am."

Her face brightened. "Oh! You knew Matt? Come in, come in!" She waved him in then saw someone behind him. "Oh, is this your wife?"

"No," Stephanie said. "I'm his sister."

"Oh, well come on in." She shifted aside for them to enter and called out, "Ted, one of Matt's friends is here."

A weathered man appeared at the end of the hall, jaw jutted about like Timbrel's bullmastiff. "A little late, aren't you?"

"Yes, sir. I am. Sorry." Tony lowered his gaze. "I came as soon as I could."

"Whaddya mean?" The man acted like a drill sergeant. "It's been over three months. My son is dead and buried."

Tony let the man rail. No justification existed in the world of pain for losing a loved one to combat.

"Ted, quiet. You'll scare him."

"I ain't going to scare him." He pointed a gnarled finger at Tony. "This boy has seen combat."

"I apologize I could not make the funeral. I would have been there if I could have."

"Why weren't you, then?"

"I was in the hospital, sir."

Mrs. Barker offered him a seat at the table. "Were you there, when Matt was hurt?"

"Yes, ma'am."

"So you got hurt, too?"

"I did." Tony shifted and looked at the flag in the triangular-shaped box. Above it, a shadow box of medals. "I just wanted you both to know Scrip always operated with 100 percent. He was truly one of the best."

His father lifted his jaw. "Yes, he was."

"I just wanted to come, apologize for your loss, thank you for raising a fine son, and apologize. . ." Tony's throat constricted. "Apologize for not bringing him back to you alive."

Mr. Barker's eyes glossed. "I know you would've if you could have."

"Absolutely, sir."

Two Months Later

"Look, I appreciate the. . .interest," Tony said as he sat on the sofa in his parents' living room. He pushed up, his balance equally divided between his right foot and his prosthesis. He steadied himself, the artificial limb a vast improvement but still awkward. "But I just don't think I'm up to that yet."

The relief was still powerful, swift, and sweet that he didn't need the crutches to maintain his balance anymore. His fingers coiled around the cane, but he refused to use it. It'd taken laser focus and endless hours of physical therapy, but he'd made it. Those walking down the street wouldn't notice the bit of a gimp he still had.

Dean Watters sat across from him with his black Army baseball hat tugged low. "Why?" The man might have an a lanky six-three height, but his thick chest and arms belied that. "Your physical therapist signed off. You're in great physical shape. A little training will put you on the road to passing the PFT. Then we can get back out there and—"

"No." Tony clamped down, jaw tight, lips tighter. "Forget it." He pushed himself off the couch, using the arm for leverage until he found his balance on the prosthesis. "As soon as Burnett signs off on my DD214—"

"Sorry, son." Burnett came to his feet. "I'm not signing off on it. I need you in the game."

"What part of 'I can't!' don't you get?" Tony stuck out his titanium leg.

"The *can't*," Dean said, squaring off with Tony. "Because you *can*. I've known you for seven long years, and I've never once seen you lie down— until now. What made you roll over and show your belly, Tony?"

"Losing half my leg."

"What are you really afraid of?"

Tony balled his fists. "I worked too freakin' hard to be a good soldier, a Green Beret. The last thing I want is them looking at me as an amputee."

"Then you need to stop thinking of yourself that way. Get over yourself, Tony. Get back in the game, where you belong."

"Bring her in," General Burnett said.

Tony frowned and looked around.

A man with a slight limp came through the door holding the lead of a dog. He wasn't sure what kind—looked like German shepherd but furrier. Then it hit him. "Wait. You own the ranch." The one that brought Timbrel into his life.

The man extended his arm. "Jibril Khouri."

Tony shook his hand. "Tony VanAllen." His gaze slid from the man with Middle Eastern features to the dog who sniffed the room. "What's this?"

"This is Rika." Jibril squatted. "She's a therapy dog."

Tony bit back the curse. "No." He shook his head and speared the two men he knew to be behind this. "I'm not taking a dog. I'm not screwed up. There are people out there who can't tell day from night." He threw a finger toward the back porch where his father spent most of his days. "My dad for one."

A cold, wet nose nudged his hand.

Tony snapped back to the gorgeous dog. She nudged his hand until it rested on her head.

Instinct moved his hand over her silky head. Panting in pleasure, she smiled up at him. Something in him oozed out.

"Would you excuse us, please?" Jibril nodded to the general and Dean.

"What is this, an ambush?" Tony said, but the dog had inched closer. He couldn't help but smile. His mind skipped to Beowulf. The hound of hell.

"I will not pretend with you, my friend." Jibril handed the lead to Tony and moved to the other side of the room. "Rika was trained for you."

"You mean for amputees. I get it—I've seen them at work at Walter Reed. But I'm not interested. I'm doing fine."

"No. I mean she was trained for *you*." Jibril's blue-green eyes bored into him. "Only you. I have spent the last two months perfecting her training, learning to work with an amputee, learning to detect stress and depression."

"I don't need pity or a dog that'll announce to the world that I'm screwed up."

Jibril held up a hand. Then, slowly, he lowered that same hand to his pant leg. Hiked it up. Metal and plastic gleamed beneath the light of the ceiling fan.

Tony felt the world heave. He lowered himself to the sofa with a quiet snort. Tugged up his own and revealed the airbrushed leg. "Had them paint the flag and eagle on mine."

Jibril smiled. "It's beautiful."

"What's beautiful," Tony said, feeling the rawness, the constricting of his throat as he thought of it, "is walking down the street and nobody really noticing me anymore. No more pity. No more shame."

"That piece of titanium and the sensors that anticipate your movement do not make the pity go away." Jibril's gaze was alive. "*You* hold that power. *You* determine what there is to be ashamed of." He shrugged. "Or not ashamed of. Rika is just"—another bounce of his shoulders as he pursed his lips—"your new girlfriend, who can surreptitiously let you know when things are messed up before they get more messed up."

Rika trotted to Jibril, took something from his hand, then returned to Tony. She dropped it in his lap and sat at his foot. Eyed the red Kong. Then him. Kong. Him.

"At eighteen months, she still has a lot of puppy in her," Jibril said with a laugh. "But I promise you, she will be keyed in to you 100 percent of the time."

"How do you know?" Tony lifted the rubber toy and tossed it out the door and down the hall.

She tore off after it.

"Because with me, she refused to surrender the toy."

Trotting into the living room, giant red Kong in her mouth, the yellow rope dangling to the side, Rika seemed to be grinning. She deposited her toy in his lap again. She still had pretty sharp canines and flashed those things at him as she waited for him to get with the game, literally. He eyed her harness. Pity. They'd ask about her, know she was a working dog. Know he couldn't get it together. *Just like Dad.*

"Nah." He held out the lead. "I can't do this. Give her to someone who will appreciate her more. Who needs her more."

"Sorry." Jibril slid his hands into his pant pockets. "I cannot do that. She was bought for you, trained for you. And since she has bonded to you, I will not remove her just because you are too stubborn to accept this beautiful gift."

Tony frowned. "Look—" He went to pull himself up.

Rika hopped up on the sofa with him. Dangling her front legs over his. Retrieved her toy. Gnawed on it then leaned back against him, playing with it and oblivious to his rejection.

Hesitating, arms out as if he were afraid to touch her, Tony couldn't help but laugh. Slowly, he rubbed her belly. Smoothed a hand over her strong shoulders and the fluffy sides of her face, all while she chomped the toy. Teeth squeaking over the rubber, she pawed at it.

"What breed is she?"

"Purebred long-coat German shepherd. Champion bloodline. The breeder donates one dog from each litter to therapy programs." Jibril lowered himself into the La-Z-Boy chair across from him.

The strangest awe came over Tony as he watched the dog playing on his lap as if they'd been best friends for life. Ya know. . .he remembered how Beo had brought his dad out of that flashback. Could Rika do that, too?

"Tony."

Rubbing her belly, Tony chuckled. Looked up. Met a strong gaze.

"I don't think she'll ever give up on you."

"I. . .I think she could be really good. Not only for me, but for my dad." He nodded. "Yeah, I could use a dog like her to get my mind off things."

Palms pressed together, Jibril touched his fingertips to his nose. "I did not mean Rika."

Tony's heart powered down. He drew in a long, shallow breath.

Rika flipped onto her belly. Sat up. Nudged her nose against his cheek.

The wetness made him breathe a laugh. He hooked Rika in a hug, suddenly ashamed yet relieved. Arms wrapped around her, he could make no sense of either. What was he ashamed of? What about the relief? Drawing in another long, uneven breath, he detected an unusual scent in her fur. What was that?

"What—?" When he looked up, he sat alone.

With Rika.

★ ★　　Thirty　　★ ★

Austin, Texas

Bundled against the frigid January weather, Timbrel entered the steak house in downtown Austin. Christmas had come and gone without a word from Tony. Without even so much as a "Merry Christmas." She didn't know what she expected, but what she *hadn't* imagined was that he would truly cut her off so resolutely.

With Beo on his lead and wearing his harness that marked him as a working/service dog, she glanced around but didn't see him. She checked her phone to make sure she hadn't misread the time. Confirmed, she tucked it away then searched the bar area.

"Sorry I'm late," came a deep, masculine voice.

Timbrel turned and smiled at Grady VanAllen. "I just got here a few minutes ago."

Beo growled at him then sniffed.

"Beo, out." Timbrel smiled at him. "Don't worry. He doesn't like anyone."

"Except my dad."

She couldn't argue that. Beo had known Mr. VanAllen was in trouble, and for her guy, that took precedence over personal dislike. And Beowulf hated all men.

"Table for two?" the hostess asked, her blond hair pulled back and her all-black attire making her appear much younger than her whole nineteen years.

"Please." Grady smiled and motioned Timbrel to lead the way into the

944

more formal seating area of the steak house. "Have you been here before?"

In her boots, jeans, black T-shirt and jacket, she quickly realized she'd underdressed. The white linen tablecloths, candles, and wineglasses had nothing on the dimmed lights, the crystal chandeliers, and the waitstaff in tux shirts. Whoa. Her mind had her swinging around and stomping right back out of there. This place had too much "romance" scrawled into the atmosphere. Her fingers automatically went to Beo's head. He nudged her hand and stood there, jaw jutted and ready to take down the testosterone.

As the hostess elegantly pointed to a table by a roaring fire, Timbrel checked Grady. In a sports coat, slacks, and a whole lot of gorgeous going on, he didn't seem to mind the setting. He held out her seat.

Teeth gritted, Timbrel forced herself onto the cushioned chair. The hostess offered wine, but Timbrel waved her off, but not before the petite Latina draped the white napkin across Timbrel's lap.

Once the woman repeated the move with Grady, she rambled off their specialties then said she'd give them a moment to *peruse* the menu.

I'd like to peruse the exit.

Timbrel stared at the black-and-white text of the gilded, leather-bound menu, her breathing growing more shallow as the words blurred. A shock of terror rippled through her as she realized—this was a lot like a date. And a whole lot *unlike* a "meet me?"—as in for coffee or dessert—invitation.

Surely. . .*surely* Grady knew better than to ask Timbrel on a date. A legitimate date. Everyone in the world knew she was Superman's kryptonite. Snow White's red apple. An addict's fatal overdose. She was poison, and if Grady seriously thought this. . .this. . .*evening* was anything but two friends talking—talking about Tony. . . That's what she thought this would be about.

But she'd been so hungry, so very desperate for word from Tony, that she'd not just leapt but donned a jet pack and rocketed right into this one.

"How was your Christmas?"

Timbrel so wasn't going to waste two hours like this, but maybe this was a good segue. "Pretty quiet. But I'm used to that. What about you? Did your parents have a good Christmas?"

"Definitely. Watching the kids play made it worthwhile."

So much for a segue. "How's Tony?" Timbrel set aside the burgundy binder and the waitress was there, ready to take their orders. That out of the way, Timbrel repeated the question because Grady acted as if he hadn't heard.

"I'm sorry?" Grady with his wavy black hair and impeccable manners seriously could not be that stupid.

"Tony." Timbrel swallowed and lowered her gaze. "Your brother."

Grady swirled the bourbon around his glass. "He's Tony." He took a sip and shook his head. "But let's not ruin tonight talking about him."

"What else are we supposed to talk about?" She had no tact—it'd been battered into oblivion after years of hangers-on and leeches.

Reaching into the bread basket, Grady smiled at her. "You. Tell me how you met Beowulf." He wagged the bread at her buddy—and nearly lost it and the hand.

Atta boy. "Sorry, he doesn't like being treated like a dog. And we met at Lackland a little more than five years ago. I was an MP and had gotten accepted into the working-dog program."

She gave a shrug, not really interested in sharing the long version. The one she'd shared with Tony.

"Why'd you get out of the Navy?"

She needed to sever the questions before he dragged them into the weak hours of the morning. "I was raped. Didn't want to hang around."

Grady stared at her, his face a bit gray.

"But I'd dare anyone to try anything nowadays," she said, indicating to Beo, who stared undoubting at Grady.

"No doubt." Something flickered through his expression, and Timbrel chided herself for priming that C4 cake. "Wait—you had him in the service, right?"

Timbrel stared at him. *Do not be an idiot and go there.*

"How'd the rapist get past him?"

Timbrel looked away, her pulse rapid-firing. What on earth was wrong with men? And she thought *she* lacked tact.

"Sorry." Grady tossed down the bread. "Forget I asked that."

"I will." Timbrel took a couple of steadying breaths. Ran her fingers over Beo's short, dense fur, but it did not deter her guy from protecting her.

Grady's phone buzzed and he withdrew it from his interior jacket pocket. "Excuse me." He glanced at the screen that lit his face. She had to give it to him—he was handsome. In a slick-guy sort of way. Not a rugged, all-you-can-stare-at type like Tony.

"Look." He leaned toward the table. "He just texted me."

"Who?" Timbrel knew the tactic was to get close to her and she wasn't playing.

"Tony." He wagged the phone. "I'd told him I wanted to meet up for coffee—"

"Coffee." Timbrel indicated with her eyes to his steak delivered to the spot in front of him.

He shrugged. "He texted me the next day."

Wary, Timbrel eased forward and tilted her head to read the display.

A bright flash exploded, blinding her.

Beo's barking pervaded the restaurant.

Timbrel blinked furiously trying to clear her vision.

"Audrey Laurens, who's your mystery man?"

As if someone sat on her chest, her lungs would not function. She hauled in a breath, stumbling out of her chair. Reached for Beowulf.

Someone shouted at the photographer.

Timbrel shoved her hand in the camera and ducked her head to prevent them from capturing any more images as she stalked out of the restaurant.

"Timbrel, wait!"

She barreled out of the place, shielding herself from the openmouthed stares, the humiliation, the anger. . . *Oh, sweet Jesus, help—the anger!* How in all that was wrong in this world did the paparazzo find her? Even know she was down here?

A man in a suit grabbed the door for her. "I am so sorry. We've secured the photographer."

Timbrel shook her head and hand at him. She rushed across the parking lot and headed for her Jeep. Beo leapt ahead of her into their vehicle.

"Wait. We should go this way," Grady said as he caught up with her.

"What?" Timbrel stopped. "Why?" Heart in her throat, she didn't want to encounter any more paparazzi. "My Jeep's right there."

"But the guy parked over there."

Timbrel stared at him. "He parked over there?" Did he really just say that? Did he seriously know. . .?

Grady closed his eyes.

"How do you know?"

"Just listen to me," Grady pleaded.

"You did this."

"I—"

"No!" Swirling thoughts left her sick to her stomach yet so angry she almost couldn't think straight. "You set this up?" No, that was ridiculous. But the thought gained momentum. "You told the press I'd be here."

"It was a harmless date. I just figured. . ." He shrugged.

Timbrel turned away from him. Shook her head. The biggest hurdle for her mind to leap over was that Tony's brother would do this. Amazing how all that trust she'd placed in Tony had inadvertently transferred to his family. "You wanted them to see me with you."

Grady said nothing.

Timbrel shook her head again. "You have *no idea* what you've just done." Unbelievable. She'd hidden at his home after her house had been torched. How much common sense would it take to figure out she didn't want a high profile? Tears stung her eyeballs, but he ticked her off too much to let those drops fall.

"I wanted Tony to see us. I wanted him to—"

"Augh!" Timbrel took a step away. Leaned to her left, arms bent and raised in a defense posture, hands fisted. And thrust her boot upward. Right into his chest.

A flash exploded.

Emerging from the shower after physical therapy, Tony grinned at his new girlfriend. "Hey, sexy." He scruffed the top of her head as he passed to the lockers, where he changed before heading out of Walter Reed. Rika trotted right along with him as if they'd been paired years ago.

Snow coated Route 7, but Christmas had come and gone quietly—save for the squealing of his niece and nephew who'd made out better than bandits. It was good to watch them get things they'd wished and dreamed for. Not too much to spoil them. Well...not much. That BB gun for Hayden might've gone over the top. Steph hadn't been too thrilled with that, not even when Tony promised to take the little man out and teach him gun safety and then how to shoot. Mom had made her infamous pineapple-ham and turkey.

But with all the happiness, with all the good, it felt empty.

Tony knew why. But dealing with it, facing what he feared...

Not yet.

As he pulled up to his parents' house, Tony slowed. Though he'd paid his respects to Scrip's family, thoughts still haunted him. Why had he survived and Scrip hadn't? Why had he only lost a leg when Scrip lost his life?

He headed to the backyard to let Rika take care of business and planted himself in a chair. Tony stared into the roaring fire, feeling the heat, seeing the sparkle and pops, yet feeling chilled to the bone.

I should've died.

His mind slipped into the past, into the agony of waking up in the compound and finding his leg mangled. Of Timbrel worrying over him.

He'd never forget her panic. Her screams. Her crying. Begging him not to leave her.

Which was why he couldn't reinitiate that relationship. Timbrel did not need to be shackled with a burden. She deserved better. And if he did somehow get back into shape enough to past the PFT, he didn't want to be involved with someone he had to leave behind. Leave to worry that he might not come back intact or at all.

Something plopped into his lap. Tony glanced down and found a newspaper as his brother stepped around him and dropped into a side chair, rubbing his forehead.

"I don't read the. . ." Tony pushed to his feet and tossed the paper onto the large wooden table that straddled the space directly in front of the fireplace. As he did, the name caught his attention. A tabloid?

"I always thought I was smarter than you."

His brother's words pulled his attention that way.

Grady, knuckles rimming his lips, slouched. Staring into the fire. "You had the brawns. I had the brains. It was like this unwritten code or something."

"More like an unintelligent, mistaken belief *you* had."

On his feet, Grady shoved his hands in his pockets. "I didn't mean. . . I. . ." The hesitation in his words, his actions seemed to expect something—no, not something. A fight.

What? Tony considered his brother then glanced at the paper again. His gaze fell to the headline. Screamed at him. His gut seized, twisted, knotted. The pictures. Timbrel and Grady cozied up at dinner. Then one of Grady taking a boot to his chest—Timbrel's, to be exact.

Tony threw a hard right cross.

Nailed Grady.

Barking ensued.

His brother stumbled back but came up like a punching bag, ready for a fight. But as he did, the wide eyes and gaping mouth gave way to slumped shoulders and a lowered head. "I deserved that."

"It's not half of what you deserve." Tony stalked back and forth, ignoring the rubbing of his prosthesis, the weight of it he still hadn't adjusted to but eventually would. "You *stupid* idiot!"

"Yeah, don't bother." Heel of his hand to the side of his mouth, Grady stalked toward the kitchen. "I already went through a list of expletives to call myself."

"You haven't even hit the bottom of my list yet." Tony stalked after him, ignoring the pulse of pain through his thigh and the low growl rumbling through Rika's belly as she trotted after them. "What were you thinking?"

"I just. . ." Grady spit into the sink and ran the water. He grabbed a chunk of ice and a paper towel for a makeshift ice pack. "I thought if you could see that she wasn't pining after you, if you saw her out with me—"

"You put her in danger!"

"She's not in danger. I am—she cracked one of my ribs."

"You selfish piece of crap!" Tony lumbered toward his brother. "She's been in hiding. Someone burned down her home. That's why she crashed here before. . ." Tony couldn't finish that sentence. "Remember that, genius?"

"Look, it was stupid."

"You can say that again. In fact, why don't you tattoo it on your forehead so everyone can see you coming and run?"

"Hey, back off! You're getting awfully riled for a guy who doesn't care about her."

"You have no idea." Something massive writhed within Tony. He searched for it, searched to finger what it was that coiled tight, poised to detonate. "You just don't get it, do you?" Tony flattened his palms against the counter, drawing in a ragged, uneven breath.

He tried to work through the bevy of feelings this fiasco unleashed, but he couldn't get past two points: One, Timbrel went on a date with his brother. Actually went out. On a date. When she wouldn't give him the time of day for months. And two, if Bashir found out where she was. . . "I have to call Burnett. Warn them."

"Tony, I'm sorry. My interest in her was genuine."

"So was your pride." He grunted. "Trying to make me jealous."

"For nothing, too."

Phone in hand, Tony eyed his brother.

"She showed up, but I could tell pretty quick she thought it was just a casual thing." Grady sighed. "I mean, that's the way I invited her, not wanting to scare her off. But I just got ahead of myself when she agreed without a fight." He smiled. "I saw the hard time she gave you, so I figured if she was willing to come. . ." Grady shrugged. "She's beautiful. You threw her away without a care. I didn't think she deserved that."

"For a man who rates Mensa, you're really stupid."

"Yeah? Well, who walked away from her, idiot?"

"Hey," their mom said as she set a plate in the sink and left, speaking over her shoulder. "No need for name-calling in this family."

"Yes, ma'am." Tony drew up Burnett's number.

"She got mad at me." Grady sounded a bit like a lost puppy.

Tony waved the paper that had a shot of Timbrel kicking him into the bushes. "Ya think?"

"No, I mean before. When she realized it was meant to be a date. She was ticked." Grady huffed a laugh. "I actually got scared for a second that she'd sic her dog on me. But then she just shifted. Asked about you."

She did?

"I was so ticked when she did that. You throw her aside and she still wants you."

Guilt harangued Tony even as he felt a strange warmth sliding in under his anger, but he turned his back and pressed TALK. "General, you might have a situation."

"Already talked to Hogan."

"Oh."

"Say, talked to your torture therapist this morning, too."

Tony's stomach churned, but he said nothing. Clicking on the tile alerted him to Rika closing in on him. Her head peeked up over the island, those gorgeous gold eyes locked on him.

"Says you are on track."

What track would that be? He leaned back against the counter and welcomed Rika's presence beside him.

"Five months since the amputation and you're doing very well with that bionic leg."

Tony snorted. Bionic. He rubbed Rika's silky ear between his fingers, already noticing the comfort that came with simply touching her. No wonder Timbrel had a crush on her dog. "I just called to make sure Hogan was okay, taken care of."

"I want you to consider coming back, VanAllen." The rough edges that normally defined the general's words bent and angled in, right toward Tony's heart.

"General—"

"You wouldn't be the first amputee to return to active duty, or the first to return to a special operations team."

Silence. Expectation. Frustration. They all swarmed Tony. They'd lost Scrip and Tony lost a part of himself—not just his leg.

"All I ask is that you think about it."

Slowly, hesitantly, Tony gave a nod the general couldn't see. "I can do that." He sat on the edge of the bar stool and scratched the spot below Rika's ears that was one of her favorites. Despite his own words, Tony knew the general wasn't asking, that the man could call him up at any minute, reactivate him, and throw him back into the fray. But it'd be stupid to put a man down on his luck into combat.

"Look, I'll be straight. I think. . .I think I wasn't at the top of my game. You were right—she distracted me."

"Are you blaming her now?"

"No." Tony drew up straight, cringing at the pinch of pain from the prosthetic sock. "No, sir. Just trying to explain what happened out there that morning."

"I'll tell you what happened, VanAllen—a terrorist ambushed your team. If you want to play pin the tail on the Taliban, stick it on his butt."

"You sound pretty sure."

"Why d'you think I want you back? You know what—here's one better. Since you called concerned about Miss Hogan—"

"For her safety."

"Exactly, son." Burnett sounded very pleased with himself. "I want you down there at the ranch. Keep an eye on her."

"Sir. . ." His gaze automatically dropped to his half leg.

"You have eyes, a mouth, and fingers to pull the trigger. Get down there."

Tony knew this would come, knew the general would call his number. "Sir—"

"And you need to know we've had a lot of chatter lately. She was right. Bashir Karzai is trouble, and I've got an asset who verifies that. And thanks to your brother and that little publicity stunt, now the bad guys know Timbrel's location. He tried to kill her and that dog once."

"The fire."

"He might just try a second time—and succeed. Is that something you could live with on your conscience, son?"

Thirty-One

At the ranch, things often smelled like wet dogs or. . .deposits made by said dogs.

But this moment was tender. His large hand touched her cheek. Sunlight, poised over her shoulder, sparkled against her white blond hair, as if accenting her beauty and goodness. She leaned into his touch. Their lips met.

"For the first time in my life," she said, pressing her cheek against his hand, "I feel like things are right."

"Puh-leez!" Timbrel stomped past her mom and beau, who stood on the ranch-house patio, and headed out for a jog. "Good grief. Did you get that from a script?"

The two split apart like atoms.

"Audrey." Her mom's voice, filled with remonstration and hurt, chased her. "Wait."

She shouldn't stop. She really shouldn't. But she did.

Her mom came to her. "Please." Those big eyes, which had men swooning at her feet and women hitting their plastic surgeons, pleaded. As her mom took her hands, Timbrel noted Takkar slipping out of sight around the house, phone in hand. "Please, Audrey—"

"Timbrel."

Her mom looked up, then seemed to gather herself and met her gaze. "Timbrel." Conceding wasn't something Nina Laurens did often. In fact, when Timbrel had made the demand about the name before, her mom had either scoffed or ignored her. "I know I've done wrong by you."

Timbrel snorted.

"A lot." Those eyes held her hostage again. "But I'm trying. Please try to see that. And. . .I know—" Her mom's lips twisted as she tried to cut off the torrent of emotions that flooded her face. "I don't have a good track record with men."

The retort about not having a *good* track record but a very long one with many men lurked behind Timbrel's teeth. And she held it there. Things had shifted. Whether it was quicksand beneath her feet or an honest-to-goodness change, she wasn't sure.

"But I love Sajjan. I'm working very hard to do this right." She squeezed Timbrel's fingers. "Please give him a chance."

"A chance to what? Break your heart? That's what men do, Mom."

Her mom's expression shifted. "What about that guy you brought to the house? What was his name—Teddy? Tony?"

A spear through the heart would've hurt less than that question. "Nothing." Timbrel tried to tug away, but her mom's grip went lethal, stopping her short.

"What happened?"

"Just what I said—nothing. He got injured"—wow, understatement of the year—"and. . .well, it doesn't matter. Don't worry. You won't see him again." Again, she pulled away.

Nina Laurens always had control. Always. Today was no different. "It does matter."

Timbrel's facade slipped.

"A lot, if I am reading my darling girl's face right."

"How would you know?"

"Because I see that face every day in the mirror." She traced Timbrel's cheek. "I've never seen you so affected. You loved him."

Love.

She'd just begun to believe she did. But he'd ripped the belief right out from under her. "It doesn't matter. He ended it."

"Did you fight for it?"

"*Fight?*" Her voice hitched. "You can't fight someone who tells you to get out of his life, someone who calls you names and accuses you of things that aren't true."

A smile Timbrel couldn't comprehend spread across her mother's pretty features. "That's when you fight all the harder, baby." Her words sounded raw, wounded. "That's when you know the heart is screaming out in pain."

Tony in pain? The man might as well be Hercules with his strength, inside and out. To think of him in pain, it just. . . Was it possible?

"He said I was just there because I felt sorry for him."

"Were you?"

"No." Timbrel felt the agony surging. "No! Yes, I hurt for him that he'd lost his leg, that he'd been injured—seeing him like that just shattered me. But only because I know the strength in him. I know what drew me and convinced me that maybe someone could love me, that I wasn't bad."

"Bad?" Her mother captured her face. "Baby, you're not bad."

"Then why do bad things keep happening to me? I tried, God knows I tried, when I was young to do the right thing, make you happy, make Don like me. But it just. . .it just got worse. And now? Now Tony believes these horrible things about me and won't talk to me." The tears were coming.

She pulled her mother's hands from her face. "Forget it. I don't know why. . ."

"I'm your mother."

"And you've never been there for me unless it benefitted you." Timbrel pushed out toward the trail and snapped her fingers twice for Beowulf to follow.

Even as she beat a path through the trails, the emotional energy beat her heart to dust. Where had she gone wrong? Why couldn't she do it right?

Cold, crisp air smacked her cheeks as she wound her way through the rocky trail that circled the A Breed Apart ranch. Timbrel jogged around a cedar tree and ducked to avoid a scraggly limb. As she came up, another caught her cheek. She hissed as it seared a path along her face, but she kept running.

Timbrel pushed on, the fire from the workout reminding her she was alive. That she had survived. Survived rape. Survived combat. Survived the night that had killed one man and taken Tony's leg.

And Tony.

She rounded a corner and swerved to avoid a blur of blue. Shoulders collided. "Sorry!" Timbrel whirled around to the man she'd about toppled. "Jibril," she breathed raggedly. "Sorry, you okay?"

"Of course." His hand went to his leg, but his smile never faded.

"Can I ask you a question?"

"Of course."

"How do I get through to Tony?"

Jibril blinked.

And she realized how stupid her question was. And that she'd only asked Jibril because he had lost his leg, too. Which was idiotic to think he would know Tony's inner workings just because of the common injury.

"Ya know what? Never mind." She pivoted and started running again.

"Timbrel!"

No, she really didn't want to talk about it. Didn't want to admit her foolishness, admit that she couldn't get over Tony. She was as pathetic as her mother.

Only Mom is now gaga over an Indian.

Weird. Totally weird. Not that he was Indian, but the sincerity with which her mom approached the relationship. Not lighthearted and flirtatious. Something. . .different. And mercy, she had to admit it ate her insides thinking that her mom had found someone special when Timbrel's someone special—at least she thought Tony was special—wasn't happening.

It was stupid. Pathetic. Idiotic.

This was why she didn't date. This was why she wrote off men two years ago.

They just brought hurt and heartache. As she returned to the house, Timbrel slowed her jogging pace. Swallowed against her dry throat and lifted Beo's Kong. "Ready, boy?"

He barked.

She flung it back the way they'd come.

He tore off after it, and she could not help but stand there and admire his strength and agility. *That* guy had never let her down. Not once. Seconds later, he tore around the corner, Kong in mouth, and bounded right up to her, skidding to a stop.

Timbrel thumped his sides and praised him. She flung it toward the training yard and sent him running. She'd grab the jacket she'd shed to run and would run him through some training maneuvers. As he tore off, she made her way up the slope to the terraced pool area.

"Yes, the National."

The male voice slowed her. Slinking along the sun-warmed bricks of the south wall, she eyed around the corner.

Takkar stood by a tree, talking into his cell phone. "Yes. They will all be there. Bashir, this is your one chance. . .yes, of course. . .no, I can make no guarantees, save one. If you do these things, if you bring them, you will never have such a prime opportunity to strike at the heart of the Great Satan."

"You can start," Timbrel stepped into the open, "with this demon right here."

Returning to the A Breed Apart ranch wasn't part of his plan.

But God had a sense of humor. His father had once told him, "If you want to make God laugh, tell Him your plans." But sure as fire, God would show you why your plans didn't work or would send you spiraling in the opposite direction.

Avowed to stay away from this place, away from Timbrel and her pity, this was the last place Tony wanted to be. Rika jumped out of the truck and bounded toward the yard. She obviously remembered the place. Tony had no sooner opened the gate to the yard than he heard shouts up the hill.

He turned and eyed the brick patio, the lip of it just discernible from this angle.

Shouts. *Timbrel.*

Tony let the gate shut, assured Rika would be fine in the pen, and hustled up the incline. His prosthesis wasn't as fluid as his natural leg, but he'd learned how to compensate and run with it. He reached the top and found Timbrel in a loud argument with—wait! Was that the guy from her mom's house?

Tony rushed forward. Where was her dog? No way Beowulf wouldn't be standing guard, snapping his challenge at the guy. "Timbrel!"

She spun, her face washing from fury to shock. She took a step back. Her gaze struck his leg, and he gritted his teeth. "Tony."

A sliding noise delivered Khaterah, Nina, and Jibril to the shouting match.

"Mr. VanAllen," the guy said as he wrapped an arm around Nina. So, things hadn't changed much there.

"What's going on here?" Tony slowed his walk, noting the sweat rubbing his prosthetic sock against his knee stub. He moved next to Timbrel and eyed her. "You okay?"

"I heard Takkar making threats against the gala, against all of us."

"I did no such thing." Calm and poised, Takkar made a powerful statement for his position just in the way he presented himself.

Tim, on the other hand, looked erratic and sounded worse. "Who were you talking to? It was Bashir Karzai, wasn't it?"

Tony couldn't help but check Takkar's response. But the guy was an impenetrable fortress. Information behind that face didn't get out easily, Tony had a feeling.

"Audrey, that's none of your business," Nina said.

"It's absolutely my business when he's telling whoever he talked to that our gala would be the perfect opportunity to strike at the heart of the Great Satan."

Whoa. Hold up, chief. "Timbrel." Tony caught her arm. "Can I talk to you?"

"No." Her irises flared with fury. "No, I want to—"

"Now." He didn't mean to order her, but Timbrel had no idea the cauldron she might've stepped into. But she should've. She knew how delicate things like this were. "Sorry, Mr. Takkar. Miss Laurens." He turned to Timbrel. "Where's Beowulf?"

Her gaze whipped around the pool. "Beo!" She pointed at Takkar. "We need to talk." She hurried off, calling her dog.

Tony eyed Jibril, trying to convey there was some serious trouble but that he'd isolate Timbrel, try to find out what happened. Jibril gave a slow nod.

"Mr. VanAllen," Nina called as Tony started after Timbrel.

He turned and looked over his shoulder at her.

"She's had a rough time. Especially today—go easy on her."

"Ma'am," Tony said, a little annoyed at her words. "Timbrel's a grown woman. I'm not looking to do anything but talk to her."

Tony's gaze hit Takkar's. Injected a heavy dose of "eyes on you" into that second, then went after Timbrel. As he banked right around the back of the house, she stepped from among a cluster of bushes.

And man. She still had that killer attitude and confidence. "Where is he?"

"Haven't seen Beo since I got here."

"No," she said as he closed the gap. "Takkar. He's planning—"

Tony caught her arm. "Hold up."

She swung toward him. Used her other hand to break his hold. "Get off me."

Hands up, Tony paused. "Timbrel, you can't do anything about this."

"Wanna bet? I am not going to stand idly by when the person who ripped off your leg—" She clamped her mouth shut. Eyes wide. She swallowed. "I'm sorry."

Ironically, he found guilty pleasure in the way she'd gotten so riled up on his behalf. "It's okay."

"Tony, I am not going to stand by while that man makes another attempt on people I love"—again, she clamped her mouth shut as those gorgeous brown eyes gauged him—"people I care about."

Nah, I kinda liked the first try. Did she really still feel that way? After what he'd done?

"They're planning something for the gala. I can't just let that happen.

I have to stop him."

"Not like this." Tony nodded toward the terrace where the A Breed Apart members stood with Takkar. "They like him. He's got allies here. If you go in there making accusations. . ."

"They aren't accusations. I *heard* him."

"Timbrel, come down to the training yard with me."

She scowled. "Why?"

Man, she had attitude. "Because they can hear you."

"So?"

"Who does it look like they're listening to? Your shouts or his soft words?"

Her eyes worked the scene. Came to his. Hurt marched across her face, but she shoved it aside. "Fine. Training yard."

That's my girl.

Tony tucked aside the thought. "Did you find Beo?"

"Yeah." Timbrel flipped her hand toward the fenced-in area. "Saw him trot into the yard a few minutes ago."

Tony stopped. "The training yard?" He eyed the area.

"Yeah." Timbrel glanced at him then frowned. "Why?"

Heart in his throat, Tony sprinted to the yard. "Call him. Call your dog," he shouted as he ripped open the gate.

"Beo, heel."

Dear God! That hound of hell was mean as all get-out and was in the yard with his girl. Tony rushed into the center of the obstacle area. He'd taken four steps when Beowulf came trotting toward them, looking a little sly.

Tony surveyed the equipment. Where was she? "Rika. Come, girl."

"What are you so—?"

A shadow broke from one of the mock houses. Rika scurried to his side. "Good, girl." Tony rewarded her with a treat.

"Who is that?" Timbrel asked.

"This is Rika, my girl."

"Your girl? Since when?"

"Since Jibril brought her to me a month ago." Tony smirked at her. "You sound jealous."

Timbrel rolled her eyes. "I have him"—she pointed to her stud—"and you seriously think I'll be jealous of that ball of fluff?"

Ruffling Rika's long coat, Tony nodded. "With this dark hair and gorgeous red highlights, she's stunning. Sweet. Sleeps with me." He

959

grinned, enjoying the taunts. "So, absolutely."

"Sleeps with you? Says the man who vowed a dog would never do that." Timbrel almost smiled. "Look, I don't have time for this. Takkar is plotting something, and I'm not going to let it happen."

"What're you going to do? Go up there and subdue him?"

Timbrel spun on him. "Don't—"

"What proof do you have?"

"I heard him!"

Tony shrugged. She had to see that rushing into this would be disastrous. "That's hearsay. Not proof."

Her anger exploded over her face. "Just because you don't like me anymore doesn't mean my thoughts are invalid."

Tony stuck out his jaw. "No, I'm the invalid."

Shock made her mouth gape. "How in the name of all that's holy did you go from my invalid thoughts to your injury?"

"Your actions shout it, just as they did in the hospital."

"Don't you dare put this off on me, Tony VanAllen. I'm not the one feeling sorry for you. Never have. Yes, it broke my heart to see you wounded, to watch you bleeding out that morning in Afghanistan. But I never—*never*—treated you less than the hero I know you to be. Yes, it took my thick head a little longer than most to figure out how I felt, but it wasn't pity that pushed me. It was the thought of not having you that did."

Tony's gut churned.

"So, if you want an excuse to fail, then do it on your own. Because the man I fell in love with doesn't play the coward."

A vicious warning bark sailed through the yard. One of those that happened among dogs when one exerted its alpha role and demanded the other "back off!"

Tony jerked to the side.

Beowulf, tail between his legs, head down, slunk back toward Timbrel. In the middle of the yard with her head up and withers spread in dominance, Rika stood as if daring Beowulf to come back. Beowulf stopped halfway across the yard, glanced back at Rika, then hurried his little brindled rear toward Timbrel.

Disbelief corkscrewed Tony. "I think we both just got our manhood handed to us."

An eternity had passed since she left me, or so it seemed. Taken to God

Himself because she was an angel. The world felt colder, darker without her smile and laughter. And yet. . .

A breeze pushed the curtains aside, giving me a glimpse of the clouds that shielded the moon from my eyes. Just as death had shielded Nafisa from my touch.

As I lay on my back, staring up at the sky, thoughts drenched in her blood. *Me* drenched in her blood. I'll never forget the warmth that seeped through my waistcoast and tunic as I held her tight. Cried. Growled for help that never came. I knew he would kill her. I always knew that's how it would end. But I had hoped.

Like a stupid, lovesick dog.

I could not help but wonder where she was up there. The angel who defied convention and stood resolute for her Christian faith. She told me she did not fear dying, and she would not let fear of death stop her from voicing the truth.

"I am the way, the truth, and the life. . .'"

I could still hear her melodious voice, the words from the Bible drifting through my mind. Light sliced through the shadows. Pulled my head to the side for a better view. Clouds slid aside and revealed the full moon, glowing like a beacon. Beckoning me.

To what?

A fiery thought scorched my dull mood.

With a quick look to my door, I verified it was locked. I'd done that since the day they dragged her away from me. The colonel—I would no longer call him Father as; he was no such a thing to me—had heard Nafisa talking of Isa. I think the colonel feared I believed her words. Believed what she said.

I slid my hand beneath the mattress and retrieved the small book. As I slipped to the wood floor, back against the bed, I traced the gold script on the cover. Reading from her Bible helped me feel like she was here, right in this room with me. Talking to me. Teaching me. *Loving me.*

The last words she spoke to me had locked into my soul. She said she left her peace with me. Oh, that it could be so. I felt no peace. I felt hunger—to be free. Free of the colonel. Free of the fear that he would kill me, too, when he found me unworthy.

I flipped through the pages, still surprised even these many days later, to find that she had marked up the holy text with her own notes. In this way, she *was* still here. Sitting beneath the moonlight, I angled my shoulder so I could better see the thin pages. Reading, I wondered what Nafisa would say, what story she would tell me about her father teaching this story or that one at their small gatherings.

It wasn't till I heard voices in the courtyard that I realized the blanket of night was being pushed back by dawn's deep blues. I hadn't slept. Quickly, I slid the Bible beneath the mattress and slipped into the cold comfort of the bed and blanket. Getting only two or three hours barely prepared me for the arrival of some daunting news.

"Get up!"

Dragging myself from the weight of sleep, I sat up on the bed. Squinted at the light that exploded through the room. "What. . .what is it?"

"Pack a bag. We fly out in two hours."

"Fly? Where?"

But the colonel was already out the door before my questions were finished. He had not treated me the same since he killed Nafisa. I was not sure whether it was my grieving that repulsed him or the thought that I might actually believe in the Christian God.

I was not sure I did. But if I weighed the actions of Nafisa on a good scale with the colonel's. . .I know whose side I would choose.

And the Bible. It was not that much different from the Qur'an, but there was something about it that kept me reading. After a shower and packing my bag as ordered, I stood outside my room. The compound was buzzing with noise.

Irfael stormed toward me. The man had never liked me, and now that the colonel seemed to share that feeling, Irfael was rougher with me than ever. "Outside, Dehqan. In the car. Now."

"Where is my father?"

"Do as you were told!"

As I moved toward the door, I knew that the time was upon us. The plan my father—the colonel—had plotted all these long years was happening. He would attack the Great Satan. America. And I was suddenly wondering if the colonel was wrong about that, too.

I was convinced as I climbed into the armored vehicle that a way would present itself for me to escape. To be who I should be. Whoever that was. Dehqan. Aazim. *Nafisa's love.* Peering through the dark, bulletproof side window, I gazed up at the still-lightening sky. A stirring in my chest seemed to betray where my thoughts were heading.

If You are the true God, help me stop him. For her. For me.

Thirty-Two

The National Hotel
New York City, New York

Would you like a walker for your dog?" Timbrel looked up from her phone at the bellhop. "What?"

"Your dog." He pointed toward Beowulf. "We have a service that will retrieve your pet and take him for a walk."

Avoiding the laugh that crept up her throat at the thought of some little high schooler even trying to put a lead on Beo, Timbrel shook her head. "No, thanks. We'll be fine. In fact, he's a working dog. Is there a way to note on our room that nobody should enter without our express permission, unless they want to lose a hand or other body part?"

Beo grunted and sat at her feet, staring the bellhop down.

The guy shifted. "Um, sure." He cast a look at Beo then whipped around and closed the door.

"You are wretched, darling," her mom said as she sailed through the room in a satin robe. "That poor boy is probably scared stiff."

"Well, it keeps nosy people out of our room, and will, for those who recognized you, keep the paps out of here, too." Timbrel retuned her attention to her phone. She pulled up General Burnett's office number and hit TALK. Phone to ear, she waited as the call connected.

"Offices of Generals Burnett, Holland, Reagan, and Whiting. How may I help you?"

"This is Timbrel Hogan. I'd like General Burnett's office, please."

"Let me transfer you to his admin. He's in a meeting right now."

Deflated, Timbrel agreed and held her breath as the call was transferred.

"Lieutenant Hastings."

Timbrel's hopes perked. "Brie, this is Timbrel Hogan."

"Hello." That didn't sound friendly the way she remembered the lieutenant. "What can I do for you?"

"I wanted to talk with General Burnett—"

"Sorry, he's tied up for the day."

"Again?"

"I'll be glad to give him a message though."

Frustration soaked her tired muscles. "Okay." Timbrel sat on the edge of the settee and peered out the floor-to-ceiling bank of windows that overlooked the city. "I needed to talk to him about a conversation I overheard with Sajjan Takkar. I'm pretty sure it's trouble, an attack."

"Okay, I'll give it to him. Thanks for calling."

"Brie—don't blow me off."

"Wouldn't dream of it."

If that wasn't a kiss-off, she didn't know a better one. "Right."

"Thanks for calling. Bye." Brie ended the conversation. Severed Timbrel's tiny thread of hope that she could get an audience with the one man who could stop this impending avalanche.

Why wouldn't he listen? Tony hadn't brushed her off, but he sure didn't give her the time of day. He'd given her a piece of his mind, and she shoved hers right back at him. After his comment about his manhood and Beo's, he'd gone into the new building to work with his new *girlfriend* Rika.

Timbrel resisted the green envy flooding her veins. He'd really seemed enthralled with that dog.

Wait. If he was. . . That dog. . . Timbrel recalled Khaterah talking about a therapy dog. She pivoted and looked at Beo. Was that who Rika was? A therapy dog? Was she the plush coat Timbrel has seen Jibril with?

Timbrel's heart broke a little more for Tony. And for a moment, she understood a little deeper that his terse words, his pushing her away, probably had more internal wounds than external wounds driving it.

"Okay. I'm ready to head down to help with decorations."

Timbrel smirked as she peeked over her shoulder. "You mean over—" Her words fell flat at the sight. Her mom in jeans, a T-shirt, and her hair pinned up. "You're seriously going to *work*?"

Her mom bristled. "Of course, I'm going to work." Her mom angled her head. "I actually enjoy decorating for parties." She strutted to the door, and Timbrel had to admit—Nina Laurens still had it going on. No wonder

Sajjan Takkar had turned his head.

Timbrel just wished he'd keep turning—and twist right off. The man was trouble with a capital *T*. But nobody would listen. And trying to tell her mom that was even harder.

Well, if she couldn't convince her mom, maybe she could protect her. "Right, Beo?" Timbrel brought him to his feet with that question. As they entered the elevator at the end of the hall, Timbrel stepped in and pressed the button for the first floor where the ballrooms were located. "I'm surprised you didn't have Rocky and Terrin."

"Rocky's here," her mom said. "His daughter lives here, so I gave him the day off. And Terrin, well, he fell ill last night. Sajjan and I agreed it'd be okay for him to stay back."

"Your head of security and you left him behind?"

"I have Sajjan."

"Oh, and there's some reassurance," Timbrel muttered.

Elevator doors slid open at the same time her mother flashed Timbrel a glare. "You might think I can't take care of myself, but I'm almost fifty years old, and I raised you, didn't I?"

The verbal smack made Timbrel draw back. She touched her mom's arm. "I don't think that, Mom."

Brown eyes framed by that platinum-blond hair gave her mom a youthful, playful look. "You don't?"

"It's not your fault I'm as messed up as I am," Timbrel admitted as they entered the grand ballroom.

"Good morning, ladies!"

Timbrel turned toward the voice and smiled. "Aspen! I didn't know you were coming."

White blond curls sprang from a lazy updo as Aspen Courtland hooked Timbrel in a hug. "You didn't? But we're all getting together tonight for a semireunion. I thought you knew."

"Who's we?"

"A Breed Apart."

"Oh!" Her mom spun to her. "I completely forgot to tell you. We're doing this private little soiree tonight for the handlers and dogs, to honor them."

"Heath and Darci will be here." Aspen smiled. "Dane's flying in. And Jibril has invited the two new handlers. It'll be fun."

Right. Fun. That she hadn't been invited to.

Khaterah came toward them. "Hey. You ready to get to work? We have

965

a lot to get done before tomorrow night."

"Walk me through the setup," Timbrel said, glad to get away from Aspen and her mom who immediately launched into colors, flowers, and dresses. Topics that just made her want to break out into hives.

Khaterah smiled. "Sure. Okay, well, as you can probably guess from the columns, we're doing a Greek-Roman theme because of the first guardian dogs, the Molossus, mentioned in Aristotle's works."

Sure enough, white columns mirrored each other and formed a line down each side. Gauzy, sheer material draped elegantly between the outer flanks. "We'll repeat the look on the stage once it's done."

Timbrel eyed the stage where she saw a curtain. "What's behind the curtain?"

"Oh, just more doors. They'll be locked. We'll have security here"—she indicated to where two banquet-length tables sat as sentries before the main access doors—"where everyone will check in. On their way out, they can pick up a small gift." Wide mahogany eyes held hers. "I know you don't like your mom—"

"No, it's not that. Please, just tell me about the gala."

"Your mom has been very generous. She's donated all the gifts and door prizes."

"Door prizes?"

Khaterah nodded. "She is so proud of you and the work you do with Beowulf."

Stunned stupid, Timbrel found herself staring at her mom. *She's proud of me? Since when?*

"Anyway, I can't think of anything else. Ready to help blow up balloons?"

Speaking of blowing up. . .what if this location was where Takkar and his friend were planning to use their weapon of mass destruction? What would they blow up here?

Nothing, she decided resolutely. Not as long as Beo's sniffer was on the job.

Light jazz notes drifted along the clean lines of the modern furniture with its sleek leather, glass, and steel. Timbrel shifted in the slacks and black scoop-neck blouse. Her mom had wrinkled her nose at the getup, but Timbrel sure wasn't putting on a dress. Wearing one twice in a weekend surely unseated the balance of nature or something. She railed. Insisted she be allowed to wear what she wanted.

Now, with Aspen and her cute athletic figure in a short black dress with Dane, her HunkyRussianGuy, lurking. . .and Heath's wife, Darci. Man, that chick commanded attention in a natural but powerful way that Timbrel envied. But even she had on a slinky black dress. Khaterah—same thing. Not quite as "sexy," but it definitely had drawn a look or two from the two new handlers, Jared Kendall and Eric Pena, both midthirties, prior Army, and single.

Definitely one of those should've-listened-to-my-mother moments. But Timbrel wouldn't voice that to anyone in this room.

Instead she made a beeline for Mr. HunkyRussianGuy. Dane Markoski, or whatever his real name was—he had this sordid past that never quite caught up with him or vice versa, and he had a personal "in" with General Burnett. So did Darci. But Timbrel was far less intimidated with Dane than Ms. Thang over in the corner laughing.

He saw her coming. Probably a mile out. And man, if Aspen hadn't snagged this guy and if Timbrel's heart weren't firmly wrapped up in the tangled mess of Tony VanAllen's life, she'd totally be into this guy.

"Timbrel."

"Hey, can I talk to you?"

Slick and smooth, the guy smiled in a way that made the old movie legends' smolder seem amateurish. "Sure." He aimed her toward a quieter corner, away from the others.

"I overheard a conversation, one that has given me considerable concern about the safety of everyone during the gala tomorrow night."

A lethal seriousness knifed through his expression. "Here?"

"Yes."

"What have you done?"

"Nothing. Nobody will listen to me. He's my mother's boyfriend, and—"

"What did you hear?"

"He said something to the effect that they'd all be there, and that if this person wanted to strike a blow against the Great Satan, this was the way to do it." Timbrel looked at Dane earnestly. "I've tried to contact General Burnett, but he won't speak to me or return my calls."

"Mm," he said, eyes working the room, taking in everything and processing.

"What does that mean?"

His gaze slid to hers. "It means exactly what it is." He straightened and looked at her directly. "What do you expect me to say, Timbrel?"

"I'd hoped you'd have an idea. And if not, I just. . ." She fought the urge to release the updo twist that tugged at her very nerves. "I'm afraid something will happen tomorrow. And I feel powerless against it."

He nodded. "I understand."

"Do you?"

Appraising her, he smiled. "Confrontation is often a front for insecurity."

He didn't hold any punches, but neither did she. "It's also one of the best ways to let someone know you're annoyed." Timbrel gave a cockeyed nod. "If you'll excuse me." She stalked off to the bar where she ordered a virgin strawberry daiquiri. She glanced down at Beo. "Why are you *still* the only guy I can stand being with?" She patted the vinyl chair beside her.

Without an ounce of hesitation, Beowulf leapt into the spot. Paws on the bar, he huffed.

The bartender's eyes came to Timbrel without turning his head.

"Can I get him a puppy latte?"

The bartender's eyebrow winged up.

"A cup with whipped cream."

"Seriously?"

"You want to tell him no?"

Beowulf growled.

Blinking, the bartender drew back. Gave a "whatever" shake of his head, filled a cup with whipped cream, then slid it down the counter. As if afraid to get too close to her dog's mouth.

"Thanks."

Beo went to town licking out the cream, making Timbrel laugh.

"*That* is disgusting," came the familiar, taunting voice of Heath "Ghost" Daniels as he slid onto the bar stool to Timbrel's left.

Timbrel laughed again.

"I think you about gave your mom a heart attack with this." He waved toward Beo slobbering and flinging drool and whipped cream around.

"Eh, gotta stir up some fun sometime. And don't tell me you don't give Trinity a puppy latte."

"Not a chance. Want to keep her lean and mean."

"Like you."

"We're a matched set."

"Where is she? I'm surprised you didn't bring her out."

"She's here." He nodded toward a corner.

Timbrel spun around and bobbed her gaze around the crowd till she found the corner where the Belgian Malinois lay at the feet of her handler's bride. Darci's eyebrows bounced as she watched the partygoers from the comfort of the floor. "Wow, she looks. . .bored."

"She's ticked."

Timbrel eyed him. "Why?"

Heath stared into his water glass. "Darci's pregnant. Thing of it is, Trin knew before us. She became überprotective of Darci, wouldn't let her out of her sight."

"Wow. Pregnant." Timbrel tried not to say it, but the words tumbled past her lazy mouth guard. "That was fast."

Heath lifted the glass to his mouth and paused. "You have no idea." After he gulped down the water, he turned to her. "So, what's going on with you—besides trouble?"

Timbrel tried to laugh off the jab. "What else is there?" But it hurt. She was sick of being trouble. Of it finding her. Of nobody believing her because of how often trouble and Timbrel seemed to pair up.

"Hey, Hogan." His use of her name pulled her gaze up. "You okay, kiddo?"

"Yeah." She didn't need to be a killjoy. She bumped Heath's shoulder with her own. "Besides, you need to get back over there and take care of your wife."

"Please don't make me. They're talking nursery colors." He roughed a hand over his face. "This is where I think I should've married someone like you."

"Someone like me?" Timbrel swallowed the way that hurt.

"Yeah, you're not all domestic. You wouldn't be there talking colors and animals, and. . .then again." Heath paused and scratched the back of his head. "I didn't think Darci would be doing that either." He playfully punched her shoulder. "But you're cast-iron tomboy. I think that's why Candyman had a thing for you."

Had. As in past tense?

She eyed the former Special Forces handler.

"Too bad this isn't happening down in Helmand Province, or even Bagram."

"Why's that?"

"Because the team would be here. For security." Heath grinned like a banshee. "You'd get to see him again. He could play the wounded soldier."

Timbrel forced her gaze away from him. Away from the way those words scalded. Tony was the wounded soldier, and he wanted nothing to do with her. "I bit his head off the other day. I doubt he'd want to give me the time of day."

Maybe. . .maybe if she'd been more domestic, more pliable, Tony wouldn't have walked away from her yesterday.

"Yeah?" Heath shrugged. "Seems you always gave him whatnot. He seemed to like that, that you weren't afraid of him and stood up to him."

"Well, like everything else, I messed it up."

"There he is," Heath muttered, his attention elsewhere.

Stung that he hadn't even heard her comment, Timbrel looked up as a commotion of noise and laughter ensued. As she did, her gaze struck Dane. Like a flicker of light that exploded and vanished in a second, something shifted in his expression. But he schooled it. Yet not fast enough for Timbrel not to see.

Dane's gaze was locked on to Sajjan Takkar. Like a missile.

Then he looked to Aspen beside him. Smiled at her. Excused himself.

As he strode away from the group toward the restrooms, he looked at Sajjan. The two shared the briefest of glances. But it was there.

Dane recognized him. He knows him. Dane knows Sajjan.

What did that mean? Timbrel started after Dane. If the guy thought Sajjan was trouble the way she did, then no way would she let this go.

"If I may please have your attention." Sajjan's voice rose over the din and pulled Timbrel around. Wearing his turban and a cloak of humility, he lifted his chin to talk so everyone could hear. Her mom, clinging sap that she was, stood nearby, fawning. No. . .not the right word. Staring at the guy in complete adoration.

"In the last couple of months," Sajjan continued, "my Nina has come to look upon you, especially Khaterah, as her friends. Family."

He did not just go there.

His gaze hit Timbrel's.

You are trouble, and I'm going to expose you.

"And since my family is not here in America, it just seemed appropriate that you would be my witnesses."

He's going to blow us up! That's why Dane left.

Timbrel's heart pounded.

She snapped her fingers. Beowulf leapt off the chair.

Trinity's ears swiveled and she lifted her head from the floor.

Sajjan reached into his pocket.

"Stop!"

He was already on a knee.

Several shot her a confused glance.

Then Timbrel's world seemed to grind to a halt as Sajjan produced a radiant ring with a large emerald surrounded by diamonds.

Attention returned to the couple. Not just a couple. Her mom. And her boyfriend. Her terrorist boyfriend. Mortified, Timbrel heard Tony's words as she watched. *What are you going to do?*

"Nina, would you do me the great honor of becoming my wife?"

★ ★ Thirty-Three ★ ★

Dripping with sweat and exhaustion, Tony walked a lap around the track. Hands on his hips, he gulped the air his lungs could barely take in before squeezing shut. Sweat had also dripped down his prosthesis and made the sock sweaty, rubbing him raw. But he didn't care. He wanted—*needed*—to know he could do this. Could pass the physical fitness test.

The push-ups and sit-ups were a breeze. As soon as he'd been able to sit up without passing out after the amputation, he'd started working out the parts of his body that hadn't been severely traumatized. In fact, his chest and bicep measurements were larger than before.

A black vehicle pulled to a stop just a few feet from the track.

Tony ignored the car. Didn't surprise him he'd come. Didn't want to talk to the man. Didn't want to hear what he had to say.

"Candyman."

Tony closed his eyes. No, he didn't want to engage in conversation. But he also knew he couldn't ignore them. He made one last circuit, glad when Rika lifted herself from the grass and joined him.

Decked out in his ACUs, Dean Watters offered a hand. "Sharp leg."

"Thanks." The man had been like a brother to him. They'd worked together for years. So, why were things so weird now?

"You passed the PFT." General Burnett sidled up next to him.

"I passed phase one," Tony said with a nod.

"That's all I need to see to want you back in the game."

Tony shook his head. "Not sure I'm ready for that." He had to voice his thoughts. Had to let them know what to expect. "I'm not sure I want to go back, sirs. I mean, I love being a soldier. It's an honor to serve, but. . . something about that last mission just really. . .changed me."

"It altered your physical appearance, but you're still the same die-hard

972

soldier I put in the field." Burnett wasn't softening.

"No, sir. I'm not convinced I am that soldier anymore." Tony held up his hands. "Look, don't ask for a firm answer right now, because if you do— it's no. I'm not going back."

"Will you come listen to what's happening?" Dean asked. "Something's going down, but honestly, Tony? I don't want to face this one without your know-how."

"Will you come have a look-see?" Burnett started backing toward the car.

Dean gave Burnett a wave-off. "Can I ride with you, Tony?"

"I can't be pushed into this, Dean."

"No pushing. Just talking. You've been isolated for a while. Thought maybe we could talk it out." Dean stood before him, his solid ways and personality firm. Impenetrable. "Tony, just hear us out. Listen to the mission brief. If you decide you can't do it, then. . ." His buddy nodded. "As much as I won't like it, I'll back you."

Only then did Tony notice he was rubbing Rika's ear. "All right. I'll listen. Let me shower up first."

A half hour later, they headed to the truck and he beeped the key fob. "Gotta warn you, Rika's a window hog."

Dean eyeballed him. "That mean I'm about to get drooled on?"

"Nah, that'd be Timbrel's hound." He laughed as he climbed into the cab. With the quad cab, Rika hopped in the back, and he let down the rear passenger pane so she could window surf as they headed toward Joint Base Myer-Henderson Hall.

"Has Hogan met her yet?" Dean looked over his shoulder at Rika.

"Yeah." Tony snorted. "Would you believe Rika sent Beowulf running, tail between his legs?"

Dean laughed. "I think I would've paid money to see that."

"It was pretty awesome." Tony rubbed Rika's withers.

"Is she helping you sort things?"

"Yeah. Even when I don't realize it." Tony didn't want this dialogue to go this way, but he knew Dean needed information on him. Knew this was as much a personal briefing as it was old friends catching up.

"Saw you do the run." Dean shook his head, not in disgust but in awe. "I'm impressed, Tony. You shot back from a place I don't know I could've come back from."

"Sure you could've. You've got the same mettle."

"Burnett mentioned having you talk to the troops, encourage them."

"Not happening." Tony already had that conversation with himself.

"Why?"

"I worked too hard to become a good soldier. A Green Beret. An amputee with a story is not how I want to be remembered." He stopped at the gate and showed his ID, as did Dean. Granted access, he drove through the secure checkpoint. "Look, I need to be straight with you. I can't see myself going back, ya know? I just. . . It's not working for me."

"Well, make it work for you, Tony."

"Not that easy." He stared out the window. "That moment, the explosion that sheared off my leg—it's right there at the front of my mind. I got out easy this time, only missing a leg, but next time. . ." He shook his head. "Timbrel came at me with a lot of the attitude you're throwing at me, too. I get it. You want me to rally. But that's just it—I'm rallied. Just toward another cause."

"What's that?"

Tony snorted. "Haven't figured it out. It's just not this." He waved his hand around the base, the soldiers.

"Never thought you'd say that. You are the guy who nothing affects. You let it roll off your shoulders and keep going."

"Yeah, well, the rolling just fell off a cliff, I guess."

"What about Hogan?"

"Don't go there."

"How'd you mess that up?"

Tony glared at him. "I didn't want her pity."

Dean laughed. "Pity? That woman? I don't think she has it in her. She's too hard-driving. I'd have thought she would've been all over your lazy butt with drills and demands."

Yeah, that was Timbrel. One hundred percent. "She tried." Tony swallowed and looked out of the truck, away from Dean and his all-too-accurate arrows. "I told her to get out." *And I've regretted it ever since.*

Needed to change this dialogue now. He cleared his throat and reached for Rika, who panted over his shoulder. "So, you know what this is about? Or am I new-meat status now?"

"Not at all." Dean shifted in the seat as they headed toward a white two-story structure. "Look, I just have to say, this. . .this is unlike anything we've seen or faced before. It's one of the slickest, stealthiest terrorists. Come in. Listen and then give us your answer. But one thing I know you'll like. . ."

Timbrel? Was she going to be there? "What?"

"It's full black."

Oh. Right. Not Timbrel. Full black—so far off the grid, only those involved would know about it.

"And here."

Tony jerked at the words. "Here? As in. . .?"

"U.S. soil."

They were some of the best of the best. Warriors at heart. Soldiers. They'd been through numerous missions. Many of which wouldn't ever have ears outside their gathering. And if they could just do this mission, if they could prove their mettle here, Lance had a prime gig waiting on the sidelines for the members of ODA452.

As the men filtered into the room, Lance mentally shifted his attention and annoyance from the man who stood to his left in silence. Then Staff Sergeant Todd "Pops" Archer lumbered in, his expression drawn. He'd spent the last two weeks with his wife, supporting her through chemo treatments. The journey was taking its toll.

"General." Archer stuffed his hand in Lance's.

"You sure you—?"

"All the way, sir." Resolute to the end.

Archer settled into a chair at the far end as Sergeant First Class Salvatore "Rocket" Russo made his way in. He clapped his hand on Archer's shoulder and took the seat next to him. Laughter preceded Brian "Java" Bledsoe, who entered and started a constant stream of dialogue that never ended until Watters and VanAllen arrived.

"Dude." Bledsoe punched to his feet. "Glad you're back."

"I'm here," VanAllen clarified.

"So, who's the new guy?" Bledsoe threw his chin toward the man who'd removed himself to the corner window and sat against the ledge.

Lance would address that question when the time came. "Okay, let's get this under way. We are short on time and long on expectations."

The team fell into a quiet, firm focus as Lance closed the door and flipped the lock. "Don't need any unexpected visitors." He clapped his hands and rubbed them together. "As you know, we've been tracking Bashir Karzai for the last umpteen months, and DIA, CIA, DOD have had their eyes on him for a lot longer."

"The dude's an imam, right?" Bledsoe asked.

"He is. But not always," Lance said. "His name was once Ahmad

Bijan." He held up a photograph of a younger version of their target. "He was there in 2003 when Baghdad fell. And we've recently discovered that his wife and son were killed as our troops routed Saddam loyalists. We believe these deaths have fueled his fury against us."

"You mean Americans." Bledsoe bounced his leg as he sat cockeyed in the seat.

"No." Lance drew in a breath. "I mean American *troops*. We have a source close to the target who says the vengeance Bashir Karzai wants to extract is with the blood of American soldiers. And that's why we believe he'll attempt something at the gala in New York."

VanAllen sat a little straighter. "A Breed Apart's fund-raiser."

"Yes." Lance removed his hat and smoothed his hair.

"Why them?"

"The guest list," Watters muttered.

Over his readers, Burnett eyed Dean and pointed. "Watters hit it on the head. ABA has unwittingly invited the very man in charge of operations that led to the death of Karzai's family. In addition, this thing has blown into a full-scale-brass shindig. Not only will our top officials and handlers be there, but so will foreign teams."

"But. . .why?" VanAllen asked. "What are they planning?"

"This whole thing with Karzai hasn't made a lick of sense," Russo said, elbow on the table as he rubbed his chin. "We've chased this guy up and down Afghanistan."

"He killed Scrip and nearly took out Tony." Watters sat forward, his forearms resting on his knees as he straddled the chair off to the side. "I want to bring a very swift justice to this man."

"Which is what we're going to do," Lance said. "To do that, you'll be joined by Straider." He eyed the man leaning back against the windowsill. Six two, a wall of muscle and power, the Australian SAS soldier could pass as an American any day of the year—until he opened his mouth.

"Who's he again?" The dark scowl that smeared over Bledsoe's brow pretty much hit the face of every man in this room.

"My name's Eamon Straider—"

"Whoa. Wait." Bledsoe slowly rose to his feet. "Hold up. First off, is it A-man or—"

"Java."

"No, seriously. And what's with the accent? Is that British?"

Black hair cropped close, Straider held his ground. No smile. No irritation, which was exactly what Bledsoe had tried to yank out of him with the comment.

"Australian SAS," Russo said as he sat back. "This is dangerous." He tossed a pen on the table. "Bringing an unknown element into the team right before a mission." He shook his head and looked around at the others. "I don't like this or him."

"Your job is not to like me." Straider joined Lance at the head of the conference table. "I'll insert with you. My purpose here is one part tactical, one part technological."

"Why you?" Archer asked, his expression unreadable. "Why not any other SAS flunkie?"

Jaw stretching, Straider took his time answering. "There is a company out of Sydney that is working with leading scientists around the world in developing a new technology." He bent forward, his large hand splayed and his upper body supported by the tips of his fingers on the table. "This technology will superheat anything in its vicinity. Normally, an accelerant takes a solid through the phases: solid, liquid, gas. This technology bypasses the liquid phase." His eyes bored into the gazes of the men.

"Basically, what a microwave does," Archer said, chair sideways, arm resting across the table.

"Precisely like that." Straider straightened. "Two weeks ago, one of these devices went missing from the lab. It is our belief that Bashir Karzai then bought it."

"Again," Bledsoe said, arms out wide, "I'm not getting the part where you're important."

"One of the dignitaries," Lance said as he rejoined the conversation, "is General Donaldson."

"My boss," Straider said.

"So basically," Bledsoe said, not an ounce of respect or acceptance in his tone or actions, "you're here because Big Daddy of Oz said so."

Lance almost smiled. He knew the men wouldn't readily accept a new team member. And he could not refuse when the Australians explained the possible technology Bashir could have acquired. "Straider knows the device. He can recognize it. That's his importance."

"It's imperative I retrieve that device. At all costs."

"As you can imagine," Lance said, "Bashir with chemical weapons and this pseudomicrowave technology—he could do some serious damage."

VanAllen whistled. "Turning WMDs from solid to gas. . .he could poison the air in minutes."

Straider stood tall, arms folded and exposing a line of dark ink on his upper forearm. "And murder not only the three hundred military and civilian personnel, but what happens when that gas leaks out past the hotel room?" He eyed them each. "Like me or not, we need to stop this man or a lot of people will die tomorrow."

VanAllen Residence, Leesburg, Virginia

"You and I need to talk."

Sitting on the back porch with Rika wedged between his feet, Tony rubbed her sides as he met his father's frown. "Okay."

"Nah, it's not okay. It's pretty messed up." Dad stood, arms folded over his still-thick chest, looking every bit the drill sergeant he'd once been. Was this a flashback? Awful early in the morning to start an argument. It didn't feel one, but it sure had the intensity of those moments.

"What're you doing sitting around here like a boy who got beat up by the school bully?"

Great. Him, too. Tony adjusted his gaze and focused on Rika. Petting her, smoothing her fur did wonders for him when stress unloaded on him. Like right now.

"I thought you liked that girl."

No way around this fight. "Dad, sometimes things just don't work out."

"You mean, sometimes you are a wuss and walk out?"

Heat blazed down Tony's neck and spine. Getting pinned to the wall by him not too long ago was enough to remind Tony the man still had enough strength to take him down. Knock him down a few notches. Not only that, but he was his father. Tony wanted to respect him. Honor him.

"What happened?"

He smoothed his hand along Rika's withers, her spine, then her haunches. "Things just changed after. . .after I lost my leg."

"You didn't *lose* it, son. People lose keys, cell phones, rings." His father pursed his lips and shook his head. "Your leg was ripped from you."

Tony eyed his father, surprised at this conversation. Combat and war were taboo topics because they were prone to set his father into a tailspin.

"Just like my mind was ripped from me."

Tony slowed. Didn't dare look at his father, didn't dare alert his dad to the fact he was actually talking about the forbidden subjects.

"Don't think I don't know what's happening when it happens. I do, and that's what kills me. . .*every time*." His father ran a hand over his head. "I see it. See you and your mother. But it's like there's two of me in there. And

I just can't. . .find the right one to fight it."

"Dad, I—"

"Nope." He held up a hand that had seen combat, killed people, saved his platoon, patted Tony on the back. "Don't do it. Just listen."

Reluctantly, Tony nodded. Returned his attention to Rika.

"Look, I know it changed me. Knowing I lose my good mind, that I am on the cusp of nearly killing you all—I can't tell you how many times I've sat on the bed, gun in hand, trying to figure out the quickest, best way to shoot myself." He drew in a heavy breath and let it out, slowly. "What had happened, I'd be breaking a dozen laws by telling you," his dad said, voice raw, "but Tony. . ."

God, help me.

"Don't let it do to you what it's done to me. Don't become bitter and angry, so much that you're alone. Isolated." His dad swatted his arm. "I stay here alone with your mother because it's physically safer for everyone. I don't have a choice. *You* do."

"Timbrel said pretty much the same thing."

"Dang, I knew I liked that girl."

Tony's smile didn't make it past his heavy heart.

"You have no reason to hide here, son. And if you sit here while your team is out there on an op, you'll never forgive yourself if they get hurt and you could've done something. You're letting them down. You're letting me down."

Surprise pushed Tony's gaze to his father. "I never want to let you down, Dad. You're my hero."

"Then get on with life. And get back in the game."

"I'm not sure I want to anymore. It wears on me, on my. . .soul."

"What's wearing on your soul is that you left something undone."

Again, he considered his father. "What?"

"That girl. The mission." The sunlight stretched through the branches of the oak trees, casting their amber glow on his face.

"How do you know there's a mission?"

His father snorted. "Son, I was running combat ops before you were in diapers. You hauled out of here. Passed that PFT."

"How do you know about that?"

"Never you mind. Never thought I'd see you take the bench on a mission. You're putting everyone's lives in danger, not to mention screwing up what you could've had with that girl and her dog."

Tony laughed. "I have no relationship with that dog."

"But I do, and I want him back here. She might as well come, too. God didn't intend for us to be alone."

Thirty-Four

Timbrel rapped three times on the hotel-room door. She glanced down at Beowulf, who sat attentive and expectant. Calm.

She tilted her head, listening to the other side of the wood barrier. Then knocked again.

The door behind her opened. Aspen peeked out, her hair in curlers.

Timbrel frowned. "I thought those curls were natural."

"Mostly. These tame them." She must've noticed Timbrel's eyebrow wing upward. "Okay, somewhat." Aspen nodded toward the door. "You looking for Dane?"

Worms slithered through Timbrel's belly. "Yeah, I just had a question. You know where he is?"

Aspen shrugged. "No, I thought he was getting ready." She checked her watch. "Speaking of—less than an hour. You should get ready yourself."

"No worries. I'm low maintenance." As in, if she changed out of her jeans, they should count themselves blessed.

Aspen chewed her lower lip. "If I were you, I'd change."

"Why?" Timbrel said as she pointed the toe of her boot. "You have something against glass slippers?"

"No." Aspen checked up one end of the hall then the other. "But if certain. . .*guests* show up, I'm sure you'd hate to be severely underdressed."

"Don't worry. I'll be fine. Besides, I'm going to be working."

"Working? How?"

"Beo and I just finished a walk-through of the ballroom and rooms."

Aspen gaped. "Wait—Beo's trained for bombs."

Timbrel nodded.

"Why would you have him sniffing out the ballroom? The only people coming are moneybags."

"And a few others." Timbrel bunched her shoulders, warding off the disdain she detected from Aspen. "Just trust me on this one. It won't hurt for Beo to work and. . .well, I just have this feeling. I don't trust Sajjan."

"But he's marrying your mom!"

"Which alone is enough reason to question the guy." Timbrel tried to joke, but it fell flat. "Look, I overheard him talking on the phone last week. Talking to this guy I believe to be responsible for the explosion that injured Tony and Beowulf."

"Why on earth didn't you tell anyone sooner?"

"I tried! Nobody would listen. I tried calling Burnett, but he wouldn't answer or return the calls." Timbrel sucked up the adrenaline, the surging memories of Tony bleeding out. Of him at the training yard. So gorgeous. So commanding. "I can't let it happen again."

Aspen touched her arm. "You won't be the only one there tonight who'll be watching." Meaning coursed through Aspen's gaze.

"Thank you," Timbrel said. But did Aspen mean something else? Or *someone* else? She scrutinized the woman's expression. "Wait. Who do you mean. . .?"

Tucking her chin, Aspen withdrew into the room. Used the door as a shield. She smiled. "Hope you have a killer dress."

The door closed. Timbrel hesitated before ruffling Beo's fur. "I wish I talked girl code." Because Aspen sure couldn't be implying what Timbrel thought she was. That *someone special* would be there tonight.

Tony.

He was the only someone Timbrel would want to see. "And Lord knows that's not happening." She stepped into the elevator and pressed the button. They rode up a floor, and the elevator stopped and the doors slid open.

Box tucked under her arm, Khaterah entered and frowned as her gaze struck Timbrel's. "Please tell me you're planning to change."

"I could say the same of you." Timbrel smiled. "I'm on my way up now." But she noticed her friend was a bundle of happy energy. "You okay?"

Practically bouncing, Khaterah covered her mouth. "I am so excited." She touched Timbrel's arm. "I just returned from the ballroom. We just got a wonderful surprise for all the sponsors tonight. A gift from one of Sajjan's friends."

Timbrel's tummy coiled. Takkar. She restrained the groan over that man.

"You'll see." Khaterah smiled. "It's going to be fantastic tonight. I cannot wait! We are gaining so much support, we might be set for several years."

"Wow, that's amazing." Timbrel couldn't deny the truth. She glanced down. And froze. "Khat." Timbrel stared at Beo, who had sat at Khaterah's side and stared up at her. "Don't move."

Her friend glanced down. "Wh. . .what's wrong?"

Timbrel punched the emergency button. "Beo has a hit."

Eyes bulging, Khaterah went rigid. "How?"

"That box." Timbrel nodded to the one perched on Khat's hip. "What's in it?"

"Nothing," Khat whimpered. "I used it to bring up my purse, water, and notebook."

"Beo, heel," Timbrel said and waited for her loyal guy to move to the side. "Okay, Khat, set down the box—*very* carefully."

Despite her fried nerve endings, Timbrel knew it didn't make sense. Why now? Why would they put the bomb in Khat's bag? An elevator explosion wouldn't do enough damage. If they wanted to strike a blow, it'd be tonight. With all the dignitaries, politicians, officers.

Still, as she knelt and peered into the box, Timbrel used a pen lying on the bottom to nudge the purse open. Nothing. Of course, some bombs were small.

"Timbrel, this is insane. There's nothing in there. Everything in there is what I brought. Nothing new." Khaterah retrieved her box. "And I don't have time to let you call in the cavalry."

Releasing her breath, Timbrel nodded. "But Beo never gets a false hit. He's got a perfect record."

Khaterah freed the elevator and winked. "I promise not to tell. Maybe he's just tired. You worked him pretty hard down there earlier."

Timbrel cupped Beo's face. "What was that, boy?"

Beo swiped his tongue along her face. She laughed and patted his broad chest. "C'mon. We both need to get cleaned up a bit."

She let herself into the suite, and—

"Oh, hello, darling!" Her mom sauntered toward her, dolled to the nines in a stunning navy number with enough bling to light the city. "Look. I just have to say this. You were abominable to Sajjan last night." Her eyes skittered around the suite. "But you didn't pursue it, and for that I'm thankful."

Timbrel said nothing because, for one, she saw the hurt plastered all over her mom's face. Nina Laurens truly cared about this man. And that angered Timbrel all the more because she could not win in this conversation—she'd only hurt her mother further. Her only hope would be proving that man's guilt resolutely.

Her mom motioned with her engagement-ring hand toward the plastic-shrouded garment hanging from the armoire. "And I've brought up a dress for you."

Timbrel grunted. "Thank you, but I've got my slacks and top."

"But it's from Caroline. Asymmetrical, one-shouldered—your favorite design. A modest number, down to the knees. No fluff or frills." Her mom gave an all-too-innocent shrug. "It has this darling flounce that drapes the left shoulder and arm—simple but elegant. Just the way you like it."

The cursed woman knew how to strike a low blow. "Not fair, Mom." Timbrel had been close to Caroline Whittington before she launched her runaway fashion line. And because of that, Timbrel had often worn Caroline's numbers whenever she could. "I'm sorry, but I have to be comfortable tonight because Beowulf will be there with me. I have to be sure I can move without restraint."

She lifted the pant ensemble from the closet. Not too casual, but it'd give her enough freedom to work Beo and the room.

"Darling, you can't. It's the organization's big night, and Caro will be so hurt."

"I'm sorry. Besides, nobody will notice or remember if I'm in slacks or some skimpy number."

Her mother deflated. "I'm not going to argue with you." She stared for the door. "Just remember, this evening isn't about you. It's about your friends. About your dog."

Low blow. Timbrel watched her mom leave then pushed herself into the shower. All the same, she had to wear the slacks. She had to be ready to stop whatever Sajjan Takkar and Bashir Karzai had up their Middle Eastern sleeves.

Wrapped in a towel, Timbrel cut off the water. Bent over to dry her hair, she heard a noise in the suite. She paused, head angled toward the door and holding the towel.

Riiiiiiiiiip. Rip. Riiiipp.

Timbrel lunged out of the bathroom. "No!"

Like rose petals strewn across the floor, shredded fabric graced the carpet and led to the bed. Amid strips of fabric—black palazzo pant fabric to be exact—Beo looked up at her, a black strip dangling from his mouth. His wiggling butt thumped against the bed as he pulled to his feet. Tugging one more piece free, he seemed to grin at her.

"You beast!"

His tail thumped harder.

The dress, the heels, the attitude—so reminiscent of days long past that Timbrel felt like a ghost haunting the hall of the hotel. She glided down the industrial-grade carpet as she aimed toward the elevator with Beowulf on his lead. The hotel manager made sure Timbrel had a clear awareness that city ordinance required all dogs to be on a lead. She understood their point of view, but really, Beo could do more damage with his flatulence and drool.

But tonight was the night. If Bashir was going to make his move, it'd happen tonight. Intestines wound tighter than a detonation cord, Timbrel crouched—ladylike, of course—beside her loyal guy. Wrapped her arms around his chest. Kissed the top of his brindled head. "You better strut your stuff since you made me wear this number," she whispered and stroked his ear, imagining what Ghost and the others would have to say about her attire. And considering she had on a dress that cost her several months' wages, she couldn't exactly just go sans makeup and hair updo. So here she stood. Dolled up more than Prom Date Barbie.

"You're going to sleep on the floor. For a *month!*"

He panted contentedly, seemingly oblivious to her threat.

"I know better." She roughed his ears. "That dumb-dog trick doesn't work on me. And there's no cat to blame this time."

The counterbalance of the elevator shifted, indicating they'd arrived. Timbrel straightened, drew in a breath. She knew to expect ribbing and taunting from Ghost, and probably Dane, though the latter was less prone to brotherly torment.

After a ding, the doors slid open.

Gripping Beo's lead, Timbrel stepped from the elevator and strode across the hotel's lobby. Harp music floated down the highly glossed corridor, luring Timbrel toward the gala. *Nice touch.*

Outside the doors, two massive dog statues stood guard. Timbrel plucked her ticket from the small pocketbook and passed beneath an arc of black and white balloons stretching over the guests from one side of the door to other.

"Good eve—" Khat's eyes went wide. "Timbrel!"

Already the heat tempted her cheeks to redden. Timbrel pushed her gaze away. "Something wrong?"

"No." Khat shook her head. "You're wearing—"

"A dress. Don't collapse, Khaterah." She handed the ticket to her friend and let her gaze surf the perimeter. "There must be fifty or sixty guests already."

"Great balls of fire," came a familiar voice. "Wait till Candyman gets an eyeful of this!"

Timbrel's face burned. "He's coming?"

Ghost pointed to the check-in table. "He was invited."

She shot Khaterah a look, but her friend was already talking with another guest.

"You really clean up good, Hogan."

Poking a finger in Beo's direction, she sighed. "It's his fault. He ate my slacks."

Ghost held out his hand to Beo. "Good boy."

Timbrel gave him a playful slap. "Hey."

Ghost laughed. "All kidding aside, Timbrel, you look amazing."

"You'd better be careful or your wife will get jealous."

"Hardly," Darci Kintz-Daniels said as she slid her arm around Ghost's shoulder. "I am supremely confident he loves me."

Timbrel eyed them. "Seriously?"

Darci also had that exotic thing going on with her Asian features subdued, but only a little, by her half-Caucasian side. "Of course. Because I know Heath wants to keep breathing."

The teasing threat hung between their laughter. Ghost tugged Darci in closer and kissed her.

"Wow, get a room, okay?" Timbrel laughed off their mushy romance stuff, but she could not deny the hurt that spiraled through her veins. What must it be like to be so free in love? What did it—?

Timbrel stopped dead in her tracks. What on earth? In the center of the room, at least two hundred books sat on the floor forming a cone shape, wide at the base and growing narrow at the top. Where did that come from? It wasn't there this morning.

Timbrel hurried back to the check-in table to ask Khaterah, but her friend was engrossed in helping a sponsor find her badge. Once the lady moved on, Timbrel edged in. "Khat, what's with the books?"

Sparkling eyes met hers. "Isn't it great? Sajjan's friend donated them— that's what I was talking about in the elevator. Everyone can take one home as they leave. He's very generous to do that. I know the books aren't cheap."

"What friend?"

"And he gave a sizeable contribution to A Breed Apart, so he'll get time to address the crowd tonight."

"Khaterah," Timbrel said, her heart rate ratcheting. "His name."

Khaterah greeted another guest then turned back. "What? Oh. Bashir Bijan."

Timbrel whirled toward the books. Bashir. Books. They had to be trouble. Had to be chemical weapons—that's what Burnett suspected. That's what Beo had hit on at the warehouse, yet it'd gotten shrugged off. She spun back to Khaterah. "Where did those books come from?"

Khaterah shot her a sidelong glance as she helped more guests. "I told you."

"No, I mean who put them up? Bashir's trouble, Khat. I'm afraid he might've set up—"

"Timbrel," she said with a huff. "The books are fine. I'm the one who set them up in the room."

"You. . .you did?" Timbrel reconsidered the mound. Okay, so if Khat set them up, then there couldn't be a bomb lurking in the middle. Right? Unless Bashir slipped in afterward. There was one way to find out if there was a bomb or chemical weapons. She tightened her hold on Beo's lead.

"Time to start," Khaterah said. In her long burgundy gown, Khat glided to the dais at the front of the ballroom.

Jibril, all decked out in his tux and slicked-back hair—the dude cleaned up nice—joined her, and together they took the stage. "Good evening," he spoke into the microphone that stood like a lone sentry in the middle.

The crowds quieted and took their seats at the tables around the perimeter. Leaving the dance floor and the mound of books alone. Which meant Timbrel couldn't just go up and lead Beo through a search. She'd have to wait. . .or be sneaky.

With a smirk, Timbrel eased along the edges of the room, working her way to the middle. Her mom and Sajjan sat toward the front with none other than Bashir Bijan. Timbrel had to admit the guy's presence alone struck her with a preternatural fear. She drew in a sharp breath. Beo looked up at her as if to ask if she was okay.

Applause erupted across the room as Jibril turned the microphone over to Khaterah, who looked tiny next to her brother.

Timbrel kept moving, knowing her bullmastiff would feed off her nervous energy that flowed to him in the form of scents, so she paused as the applause died down. No need to rush.

A waiter approached her, and she stepped back to give him a clear path. But he moved into her path. She frowned, and her gaze tracked down his outfit then back to his face and stilled. Heat splashed her stomach. *Rocket!*

Eyebrow arched, he let his gaze roam her dress, legs, and back to her face. "No wonder Candyman went nuts for you," he whispered around a smirk as he leaned toward her with the tray, hiding his conversation with his actions. "A drink, ma'am?"

"Thank you." She made her movements slow, strategic to buy some time. "What are you doing here? Dressed like *that*?"

"I could ask the same thing."

Timbrel glowered.

"We're probably here for the same reason you are skulking about the ballroom while your friends are onstage."

"We?" Timbrel's heart tripped. "Who. . .who's here?"

"Sorry. Not nim."

Disappointment chugged through her heart. When he navigated around her, she caught his arm. "The books." Timbrel sipped the drink then replaced the glass. "The books were a last-minute addition."

Rocket hesitated. Then bowed. "Enjoy your evening, ma'am."

Futility strangled her. There was no joy in the knowledge that she'd been right. In fact, she was a little peeved that she'd tried to warn them and gotten blown off. And now—she was here, the team was here, but Tony wasn't.

She just had to accept he'd walked out on her.

You know what they say about payback. . .

So. Focus. On tonight. Stopping whatever it was Bashir Bijan had planned. Burnett wouldn't have ODA452 here if this was just a nice evening to make money and new friends. Timbrel guided Beowulf up the middle, clinging to the columns when she could. Trying to act normal. A man in a tux next to a woman—

Timbrel stilled. Wait. Her gaze flipped back to the man. Captain Watters. And Brie Hastings!

Brie's eyes widened at Timbrel. Then dropped to Beo.

Timbrel glanced at her dog.

He sat. Right next to the books. *A hit.*

★ ★ Thirty-Five ★ ★

The girl and the dog must die. Now, before the rest of the plan became mutilated because of their interference.

Bashir slid his phone from his pocket and sent a text to Sajjan, who sat across the table with his arm around his American fiancée. A tidy and effective ruse that gave Sajjan the access and explanation for his whereabouts, movements, and requests. Nobody had even batted an eye at the sudden arrival of the books.

THE GIRL IS A PROBLEM THAT NEEDS TO BE ELIMINATED. THE DOG TOO. Now.

Bashir smiled. Even though the girl and her dog had detected the chemical, they would not be able to stop what was happening. They were too late. She had been too slow. She'd nearly toppled his plan eight months ago, but now she would pay for her meddling. With her life.

Laughter filtered through the crowd at something Miss Khouri said. It was a shame. To waste such a beautiful woman, a woman with Arab blood. But her allegiances were in question, and therefore of no consequence to him.

Sajjan reached into his breast pocket. A subtle blue glow on his face betrayed the text he read. The actress glanced over her shoulder and at his phone. She said something. Sajjan shook his head and whispered in her ear. Then he kissed her cheek, rose, and swept past Bashir without a glance as the first speech ended. Music saturated the glitz and glamour. Suits and uniforms mingled, danced.

It was easy, really. Incredibly and stupidly easy.

Enjoying their drinks, their slow dancing, their debauchery, a momentary respite from their politicking. Oh, he knew the high-ranking officials in this room would rebuff the notion that there were politics in what they did. But how could one remove the spine and still have a whole, functioning body? The motive and still have the mission?

He moved through the crowds, insignificant—to them. A step on a ladder in which they climbed to the top. But soon there would be no top to attain. The rungs would be removed. Their *ascent* would become *descent*.

Laughter billowed out from the corner. American military officers laughed, crystal snifters in hand, as they paraded their latest trophy wife, girlfriend, or indulgence.

So easily the mighty fall.

They would drive them out of the country, out of the Middle East.

Thirty-Six

Nothing like last minute.

Tony grabbed his bow tie and slid from the truck. He paused, and it took a second for him to realize he'd hesitated to allow Rika to follow him out of the cab. But she wasn't with him tonight. She was *dad-sitting* for him. Weird that he already missed the seventy-five pound German shepherd. Missed her presence. Missed her confidence.

Tony tossed the keys to the valet, took the ticket, and hurried into the hotel, hooking the tie around the back of his neck. He wrangled it into a knot as he rushed toward the ballrooms. Crap. Knot wasn't right. He tried again. The left side poked into the soft part under his chin. He yanked it off. Caught the arm of a waiter. "Restrooms?"

The guy pointed toward the far end of the dimly lit corridor. "Down there, to the left. At the end of that hall."

"Great." Tony stormed that way, savoring the fact that so far tonight nobody had even given him a second glance. No questioning looks about the slight limp that betrayed his prosthesis. The more he got used to it, the more he walked better. People accepted him more wholly. And speaking of more wholly, Timbrel had given him whatnot at the ranch. She hadn't backed down to protect his feelings.

Man, he missed her. Missed that mouth and snark. The attitude willing to face down any demon.

After the briefing, he'd had no peace. Only a very empty sense of failure. Failing the team. Failing Timbrel. If there was a real-and-present danger, he could not sit on his backside by the fire, petting his dog and sipping cider.

He'd fought it. Fought the urge to rush into this night and face whatever was coming. He'd faced it once. Lost a leg. Timbrel had been right—he was hiding from this. It wasn't about her. Wasn't about the military. It was about Tony VanAllen and the grudge he'd allowed into his heart. Bitterness had come in small, lethal injections till he took that fatal dose. Convinced himself he didn't need her or her pity. Really, he was terrified of that. Didn't want her to start treating him the way his mother did his father. Not when what they had had been so strong, so powerful.

Through that briefing, ODA452 went dark, covert—to walk the halls here as waiters, security guards, and Dean should be seated in the gala as a guest with Brie Hastings. The Aussie should be here as an attaché to the Australian SAS commander inside.

And Tony was supposed to be on-site, too, but he'd bailed. Sat at home, mulling the mission, the probability that Bashir Karzai would be stupid enough to attempt an attack against some of the highest-ranking military officers in the U.S. Armed Forces.

Okay, okay. He was pouting. Feeling sorry for himself. Until his conscience caught up with him and threw him out the door and into his truck.

Tony shouldered his way into the bathroom. Stomped to the mirror. Tied the bow. He wanted to see Timbrel. Wanted to know she was okay.

Tell her he was sorry.

Hauling in a breath, Tony eyed himself in the mirror. Let out the breath. Oh the irony. She'd walked out on him in Arkansas, and he'd basically returned the favor by not signing on to the mission at the get-go. When he'd realized that, he grabbed his tux and sped down Route 7.

Desperation bolted through his veins. He recognized it and closed his eyes. *God, please. . .help me. Give me a chance to talk to her. And protect us if Bashir is here to unleash some evil.* Tony couldn't help grin. *And if he is, help me send him back to his master in hell.*

Tony gave himself one last appraisal then left the bathroom. Double-checked the weapon he'd strapped to the lower portion of his prosthesis. When he set off the sensors, he'd tap his leg and expose enough for them to let him pass without a pat-down. Tugging his cuffs, he rounded the corner and headed to the ballroom. He strode toward the music and chatter that drifted out of the large room. A dense crowd. *Bigger body count.*

He couldn't believe this. Bashir seriously was going to try to wipe out key military personnel. If the guy was angry with the military for his family's deaths, he'd have more than enough motive to want to deal a lethal blow to the American military command structure.

Tony hurried his steps.

Someone yelped.

He glanced to the side as he moved. Saw a group hurrying toward an exit. His heart jacked into his throat as he registered what he saw: three armed men herding Timbrel through a door.

It took every ounce of training not to shout her name. Not to tip off the men. Tony bolted down the corridor, his mind scrambling to remember what he saw. The men—one man wrangling her out the door as another led the way. She fought them, hands free, flailing.

Wait. . .

Tony slowed as he came up on the door, pressed his shoulder against the wall, listening. Chaos beyond, but what. . .what had Timbrel been doing with her hands?

Signal.

That's...crazy. What would she be signaling? He'd seen her do that with— Low and ominous, a deep rumble spirited through the dark hall. Tony flung back, his eyes probing the darkness. Shadows shifted and collided. Took shape. Drew closer.

Tony reached for the weapon taped to his leg.

Yellow glinted.

His pulse sped as he watched the darkness birth the massive dog.

Head down, canines exposed as he continued his demonic growl, Beowulf stalked toward him. Mouth flaps quavered as Beo sucked in a breath and instantly resumed his growling. Legs spread, shoulders down, he exposed his spine from the shadows—and his raised hackles that added inches to the already massive beast.

Snapped.

Tony threw himself backward. Debated whether he could get his gun before the dog ripped out his throat.

Beo barked. Lunged a few places. Snarled.

He's going to eat me alive.

★ ★ Thirty-Seven ★ ★

After another demonlike bark, Beo paced back and forth. Turned on Tony and snarled again.

"Stupid, piece of. . ." Tony bit back his curses. He'd given up that life, but this hound of hell had put the fear of God into him in a new way. "We have to get her. Shut up and stand down."

Beo snapped, his front paws coming off the ground.

Tony flinched back, but then. . .

Pacing back and forth like a caged lion, Beowulf snarled. . .paced and snarled. . .

Tony eyed the door the men had hauled Timbrel through. The handle. Beo. Was he. . .? "If you take my hand, I'll shoot you," Tony hissed. With a breath for courage, he threw himself at the door and slapped the handle.

The door swung open.

With a bark, Beowulf launched through the opening.

Despite having the NYPD SWAT team on standby, Lance knew as the doors thudded shut and armed gunmen took up positions, help would be too late. He made eye contact with Watters, who stood next to Hastings. Casually, so he didn't tip off the guy lumbering to the stage with an air of determination, Lance shifted his eyes to Straider. The guy stood at the back of the gala in a tux. Something about that guy made Lance suddenly very happy he'd been tapped for this mission. Silently, he telegraphed the message, asking about the device. Had anyone seen it?

Straider gave an almost imperceptible shake of his head.

"Let's dispense with the formalities," Bashir Karzai said as he took the microphone. "You will all be here for a very long time, so please—make yourselves comfortable."

As some began to sit, he laughed.

"You thought I meant in chairs." Dressed like the imam he'd been elected as, Bashir spoke with a piety he did not possess. "No, no. Your lives of comfort and fattening are over. Please—to the floor."

Lance moved with the others, sitting around the stack of books. Of the seven men tasked with this assignment, only four were visible to him. Which left him with a boatload of panic. What happened to the others? VanAllen had said he hadn't decided, but if he showed, it'd be his last mission. *Great. Fine. Just show.*

But that would be too "god in the box" for VanAllen to appear out of nowhere and save the day. No, things never went down that smoothly or cooperatively. No, this would get really ugly. Bashir had too much confidence, which meant things were going as planned.

Which meant, they were in deep kimchi.

Surreptitiously, Lance shifted closer to Watters.

"We do not need heroes to die. . .yet."

Lance checked the stage. Sure enough, the guy was looking right at him.

"Please, General Burnett, have a seat."

Something about the man's words pulled Lance's gaze to his hand. To the chair Bashir had planted a hand on.

Mother of God. . . The prayer died on his lips as he realized what the man wanted.

"Not interested?" Bashir nodded. "Then you doom another man's life." He motioned to one of his men.

The guy slung his weapon over his shoulder and stomped across the room. He hauled a man in military dress uniform upward. A woman cried out as he was shoved toward the front of the room.

Lieutenant Colonel Bradley Abrams.

Lance wanted to curse. This was it—this was the man Bashir had come to kill. How he knew, Lance didn't know. There was just a fierce fury coursing through the black eyes in the pits of that man's face.

Abrams took the seat. And in his face, Lance saw the same determination resonating through his own chest.

"Tell us, Colonel, where you were in April 2003."

Surprise danced across the sun-bronzed face of the colonel. "I. . .I was in Baghdad." He braved a glance to their captor.

"What was your role there, Colonel?"

What is this? The mutterings of the crowd rose, echoing the question plaguing Lance's mind.

"I was a tank driver."

Oh no.

Crack!

The simultaneous explosion of the weapon and Lance's word pounded against his conscience as Abrams tumbled from the chair with a thud.

Merciful God! They had to stop this. He rammed his gaze into Straider. Then Watters. Archer and Russo sat near the back in waitstaff getup. Lance pummeled meaning into his expression. And they returned the fury.

And the desperate frustration. If they intervened, they would show their hands. They didn't know the location of the device. Which meant *everyone* could die. Not just one. Or two. It'd be three hundred if his men didn't make up some ground *now*.

Thirty-Eight

*R*iddle me this, Batman: *Why's the dog running full speed at a steel door?*

And how many more doors or turns would they make? How could the terrorists get this far with Timbrel?

"Beowulf," Tony hissed as he hurried after the dog on the hunt.

The bullmastiff threw himself at the door.

Thud.

Beo yelped but spun around and paced. Started snarling.

Not winning, not saving his girl, put Beowulf in a seriously bad mood.

I can relate. Tony kicked the door. It flung open. Before it could snap back, Beowulf shot through it. Skidded on the cement floor. His back end swung around as he headed in the opposite direction.

Tony paused. Worked to get his bearings. If he followed the dog, wouldn't they end up heading back to the ballroom? Or had he miscalculated the turns? Probably.

Back in motion, he caught up with Beowulf as he scratched at a door. Sniffed. Whimpered.

Sidling up by the door, Tony still had the fear of dog in him. Beo, if caught off guard, could easily take a chunk out of Tony's flesh. But they were both working toward the same goal—saving Timbrel. He'd just have to trust this beast. Tony thumped a boot against the wall.

Beo shifted his gaze for a second then went back to digging out the scent.

Tony tried the handle. Locked. Weird.

He looked around. A little wider than the halls, the area seemed a juncture between four possible routes. Yet Beowulf chose this door. Could he be wrong?

With Timbrel's life in the balance, Tony couldn't imagine that.

A noise ricocheted through the cement and steel corridors, working its way toward them. The first thought was a slamming door. But at the exact same moment Beo went into overdrive trying to dig through the cement—and the dog would probably wear his paws bloody trying—Tony knew it was the report of a weapon.

Timbrel!

He spun in front of the door. Drove his heel just above the handle.

Pain jarred his leg. Threw him off balance. He grunted as he swung wildly, trying to catch himself. Hit hard. Pain exploded up his back and spine, radiating from his hip. Tony jerked back up, ignoring the pain. Ignoring the way his nerves vibrated. He shot his foot into the door again.

It surrendered.

Beowulf barked and barreled onward.

Tony gave chase, only remotely aware of the pain shooting darts up his back and shoulders. He didn't care about discomfort. Timbrel was in danger!

Beo skidded around the corner, clawing for purchase on the cement floor. He caught and hauled tail out of sight. Tony did a bouncing slow down to keep from colliding with the opposite wall. He slapped the wall and pushed himself on.

Slipping and sliding around another bend, Beo struggled. Then vanished.

Tony sprinted after him, his heart in his throat. This stupid place felt worse than a labyrinth. Exhaustion gripped him but he couldn't stop. Had to find her. He stumbled and slowed as he realized Beo hadn't rounded a corner. He'd entered a room.

Tony drew up his weapon and hugged the wall. He whipped around the corner, weapon pieing out—

Beo stood beside Timbrel, who lay in the middle of the floor. Bloodied. Unconscious. Beo nudged her face and whimpered.

Tony threw himself toward them. "Timbrel!" On his knees, he reached for her.

Beo snarled and snapped at him.

Tony snapped back, "Out!"

Without warning, Beo's face punched at Tony. He tensed a second too late. Wet slobber swiped his face. A pathetic, high-pitched whimper issued from Beo's chest. With his snout, he bumped Timbrel's face again. His brown eyes bounced to Tony as if to say, "Fix her."

Blood streaked her face and neck.

How do I fix dead?

★ ★ Thirty-Nine ★ ★

*T*imbrel!" The garbled voice reached down into the depth of the black hole that had swallowed her.

A jolt against her face.

She groaned.

"Timbrel, c'mon, baby. Show me those brown eyes."

She swallowed hard. Groaned.

Warm snot blasted her face.

With a half laugh at Beo's slick insistence she wake up, she pried open her eyes. And found the most gorgeous green orbs staring back. "Tony?"

"Hey, beautiful."

She dragged herself upright and wrapped an arm around Beo, who pushed into her lap. "What. . .?"

"I was hoping you could tell us. Beo was about to rip this place apart to find you."

She wrapped her arms around him and hugged him tight. "That's my boy."

"What happened?"

Rubbing her shoulder, she shook her head. "It was. . .weird. I was screaming and yelling at Sajjan, kicking and screaming—"

"So you went along easy, huh?"

She glared at him. "They were going to kill me. I wasn't going to make it easy." Timbrel pushed to her feet. "The other guy started arguing with Sajjan, and he led me in here. He held me against his chest, aimed the gun at the guy, then all at once there's this explosion, a bright flash, a"—she clapped a hand over a spot on her neck—"he pinched me or something. Then you're over me crying like a baby."

Tony stepped closer. "Baby, I'll do a lot more than cry if someone hurts you again."

Her features went crazy soft. Tender. "You almost sound like you care."

The cadence of his heart in his chest rivaled the ramming speed of a warship's drums. "I would love to show you how much, but right now... Are you injured? There's blood all over your neck."

Her hand went to her throat. She touched it. "It's slick—not like blood."

"Fake blood?" Tony's mind knotted. "Why would he fake your death?"

"I. . .I don't know. He's as guilty as Bashir."

Tony nodded. "Speaking of, the team's here because Bashir has some device that is supposed to superheat something or the other."

"Wow, that's some impressive military intelligence."

He arched his eyebrow. "We all know he has chemical weapons and intends to use them to hurt Americans, we just don't know—"

"The books."

"What books?"

"Khaterah set up these books in the middle of the ballroom. Said they were a donation from one of Sajjan's friends—I'd bet my life it was Bashir. He sent the books over." Fingers to her forehead, she paced. "That's it. . . that's gotta be it. That's why Beowulf got a hit on Khaterah earlier—she handled the books so she had trace elements of the chemicals."

"Who, slow down, chief. I'm not tracking."

"Earlier, I met Khat in the elevator. Beo got a hit on her, but there was nothing that was dangerous. Then when I went to the gala, there's this stack of books in the middle of the room. Khat said she set them up, but when I took Beo over there—"

"Another hit."

Timbrel nodded. "The books must have a chemical in them or something."

"Wait—the books are in the middle of the room?"

"I just said that. And it's so weird—they're not Arabic books or Afghan. They looked American. Like a novel or something. I thought it was so strange."

"He's going to use that device to superheat them. Burn the books— very poetic. Burn those books and it releases whatever chemical is in them."

"If he does that, that room will turn into a gas chamber. Nobody will have a prayer."

RONIE KENDIG

tabarri min a'daa Allah—Turning Away from the Enemies of Allah

Three hundred Americans on their knees. Just as it should be. *Freshta and Sidiq will be avenged.* Infused with the thought, Bashir traced the room with a slow, casual glance. Closed his mind to the past, to the devastation of that April morning so many years ago. His wife, his son. . .they would have justice.

He met the gaze of Dehqan. Steady eyes. Sure, so very sure. Bashir had trained him well. Perhaps one day, he would wage his own holy war against the infidels. The thought pushed a smile into his face, and Dehqan mirrored it. Bashir offered a nod of appreciation to the boy who was no longer a boy.

"General Lance Burnett," Bashir spoke into the microphone.

The older man's head popped up. Rage and terror struck his ruddy complexion as those around him reacted to his name being announced.

Bashir set his hand on the steel-framed chair that now bore a dark stain. "Would you have a seat, General?"

"No," came a woman's cry—the fiancée of Sajjan. She shook her head, sorrow weighting her as she pushed her gaze to the carpet.

Ah, see? They already knew what would happen. They knew who held the power. So many here, rich, dressed like kings and queens in their diamonds, beaded gowns that cost more than most of his people saw in a year, and their tuxes that could feed an entire village for months. The women with their colored hair and luxurious makeup. . .the military with their shiny buttons that belied the rust in their hearts. . .the dignitaries with their bellies bloated from excess and indulgence, not starvation.

"You are probably wondering, each one of you, why I singled these men out. Why, if I am going to kill you"—Bashir paused as the whimpers of fear rippled through the crowd, around the pillars, gauzy material, and lights—"do I take time to bring an individual before you."

Dehqan, who stood at the back, gave him a solemn nod.

Good. Very good. "You see, beyond those doors guarded by my friends and brothers, the authorities are out there, trying to coerce me to talk to them, convince me to release you safely." His heart tremored. "But I want you Americans to know how close hope can come, how close freedom can be—so very close that you can taste it in the air."

For Freshta.

"Then experience the shattering of that hope."

Sidiq.

"The devastation thereafter."

As Burnett worked his way to the stage, escorted by Dehqan, Bashir supplied one last quote from the Qur'an. "Surah 60 says, 'Allah does not forbid you to deal justly and kindly with those who fought not against you on account of religion and did not drive you out of your homes. Verily, Allah loves those who deal with equity. It is regarding those who fought against you on account of religion and have driven you out of your homes and helped to drive you out that Allah forbids you to befriend them, and whoever will befriend them, then such are the wrongdoers.'"

Dehqan helped General Lance Burnett into the chair. Defeat had long ago stomped its imprint into the man's face. "This has to end," Burnett said.

Bashir smiled. "You are very right." He stepped to the side, hugged Dehqan, and then whispered in his ear, "It is time. Remember what to do?"

Dehqan nodded and slipped behind the curtains that draped the wall abutting the stage.

Microphone to his mouth, Bashir asked, "General Lance Burnett, tell these people, the men and women of the United States Armed Forces, where you were on April 9, 2003."

As if drawing in a breath of courage—for he would need that to confess his sins. To confess the wrong he had done—he said, "I was in Baghdad, much like Colonel Abrams."

"No," Bashir said, outrage pounding through his chest. "Not *like* Colonel Abrams." Control. Control it. "But that was a day of victory, was it not? You Americans played the video of that statue of Saddam being pulled down over and over again."

"We helped liberate people."

"No!" Bashir swung out with the microphone and whacked the sixty-something man over the head with it. A shriek pinged through the speakers as a rivulet of dark red sped down the general's temple and fed Bashir's fury. "That victory may have happened for the Iraqi people, but what were *you* doing?"

Burnett's gaze bounced to him then back to the floor.

"Or are you ashamed?"

Head up, chin out, Burnett seethed. "I'm not ashamed." The man had too much pride. "My team was engaged in an intense firefight on the other side of the city. Saddam loyalists weren't happy to see us there. They fought us—hard. We fought back."

Bashir waited. Waited for him to tell the rest of the story. To admit what he'd done. "What else?"

The general shrugged. "I'm not sure what you want me to say."

"That you killed my family—my wife just minutes after she gave birth to my son! You ordered Abrams to fire that tank. And that round decimated my house!"

Burnett's expression shifted from confusion to one of stunned awareness. "I'm sorry your wife and child died, but that wasn't at my hand."

"It was!" Rage boiled through his veins. Thumping. Whooshing. Hurting. Aching. "And now I will make you hurt the way I hurt!"

Forty

Bashir!" Sajjan Takkar stepped forward.

Effectively cutting off Tony's line of sight. He grunted and shifted to the side, his shoulder bumping Timbrel. Weapon trained on the guy, Tony watched from between the heavy black velvet as Takkar intruded on the violent end Bashir Karzai intended to give General Burnett.

Timbrel hovered at Tony's right with Beo.

"Get ready," he said, air barely passing over his vocal cords.

She nodded.

"What is this?" Bashir shouted. "You dare to defy me?"

"I would not dream of it, brother. But our time is short, is it not?"

"I will have justice."

"Will that not happen with the plan?" Sajjan motioned toward the books. "Whether you shoot him now or he dies with the rest of them, he *will* die. And remember, brother, jihad is also against the flesh. Dying to our desires. Does your thirst for vengeance cloud your mission from Allah?"

Wild fury detonated on Bashir's face.

C'mon, c'mon. Where's the device? Who has it?

"What does he think he's doing?" Timbrel hissed in his ear. "It'll push him over the edge taunting him like that."

"Challenging," Tony corrected. And saving the life of Lance Burnett. Or maybe just extending it by two minutes. Tony couldn't help but wonder whose side Takkar had taken with his slick words and jockeying.

"I begin to wonder, brother, if you even have the accelerator."

Nice. Draw the guy out.

A flicker of movement. Tony's attention fastened on the Aussie, kneeling at the back amid a cluster of other soldiers, including his superior. Shifting his position, he was locked on to something. No, some*one*. A

1003

woman. No, no. The man.

In the second Tony realized the SAS commando was going for the rogue terrorist, Tony noticed Bashir aim his weapon.

"Beo, seek!"

The dog bolted between the thick black velvet curtains. With one of his world-famous demon growl-barks, Beowulf sailed through the air.

Bashir spun around.

With the weapon.

Aimed at Beo!

Crack!

Chaos erupted.

All Timbrel could see, all she could process was the split-second explosion from Bashir's gun. The yelp of her dog.

And his dogged determination. Beo latched on to the man's arm.

Bashir screamed like a little girl.

The weapon thudded across the makeshift stage.

Burnett dove.

"Beo, out!" Timbrel shouted, afraid Beo would get hurt or hurt the wrong person. She rushed from cover seconds behind Tony, who broke right. Off the stage. Into the clogged ballroom, where the people sat huddled around the cone of books.

Screams echoed.

Like a bad horror movie, Timbrel spotted a man tossing a flashlight-like thing toward the books. It thumped against the stack.

A tendril of smoke spiraled up.

"Get out, get out," someone shouted.

Timbrel dragged her attention toward the warning and found Watters pushing people out the doors.

Fights ensued. Shots. Fists. Utter chaos.

Timbrel sprinted forward to stop the device. If she could just get it away from the books, maybe she could stop it.

But a body sailed into the air. Straight through her path. A giant of a guy dove into the books. They erupted like a volcano around him. Shots peppered the pages, tattering them as if a thousand years rushed through the pages, leaving them yellowed and the edges eaten.

"The device!" Timbrel shouted.

It felt like minutes that turned into hours. But in seconds, the guy rolled onto his back with the thing cradled in his hands.

She double-checked Bashir. A tangle of bodies writhed on the stage, and she spotted his face among them. Someone walked toward them with a gun. Maybe someone could stop this insanity.

But the bomb, or whatever it was—Timbrel whipped back to the tendrils snaking into the air. Dare she take a breath? What if once the device was activated there was no way to stop it? Her gaze surfed the books. Searched for the chemical. If it was cyanide or such, there wouldn't be an odor.

Except to bomb-sniffing dogs—Beo!

Timbrel whirled around, her mind catching up with the eruption of chaos, noise, and insanity. Where was her dog? "Beo?"

A whimper sounded behind her. Timbrel pivoted. Beo, head down, limped toward her. Stumbled. Collapsed. Darkness stained his coat. Glistened.

"No!" Timbrel leapt toward him. "Beo!" She planted a hand over the bloody spot. Tears blurred her vision before she could stop them. "Beo!"

A loud thud and crack erupted near the front. "Everyone, on your knees. Hands in the air!"

SWAT. *About time.*

But she had to tend Beo. He panted hard, his tongue dangling out of his mouth. On her knees, she assessed the spot where he'd been shot. In the shoulder. Good, that was good. It wasn't the chest or lungs. Thank the Lord every handler had to have basic life-saving skills for their dog, to be able to treat them in theater for a variety of injuries, or Beo. . . *No no no. Don't go there.*

But she had no supplies. Only panic. And fear. She could *not* lose him after all they'd been through. A table whooshed to the side, the stark-white fabric billowing like a ghost under the controlling fingers of death.

She reached for the cloth, for anything to staunch the blood.

Jibril scrambled toward her. "What can I do?"

"I need something to stop the bleeding," Timbrel said.

Hair akimbo, Jibril snatched the tablecloth and looked over Timbrel's shoulder. "Khaterah, hurry!"

Khat. Of course. A vet. Timbrel felt the edges of her panic begin to fade as Jibril's sister rushed toward them and dropped to her knees without hesitation. In Beo's blood.

"Khaterah!"

"I'm here, I'm here."

"Please, don't let him die."

"No, he's going to be fine. Too tough to die."

"Sort of like his handler."

Timbrel glanced up at Tony and smirked. "We're just too thickheaded."

"There is that."

"Jibril." Khaterah motioned to an overturned table. "The medical-kit display."

"Here," Jibril shouted as he rushed from the pile with a big silver case. Timbrel gaped as he flung a full medical kit toward her.

Khaterah flipped open the case, slipped on gloves, then handed some to Timbrel, along with a hypodermic needle.

Timbrel didn't hesitate. She pinched his skin at his shoulder and slid a needle between his rolled skin to administer a sedative. He'd never been the best patient in the first place. Beo huffed and lifted his head. "That's right," she said. "Tell me that bothers you." If he could complain, he had fight in him. His breathing was steady, though she could tell he was hurting.

Hands bloodied, Khaterah gently peeled back the cloth.

Dark red stains blurred against his gold and black stripes. Timbrel felt her own pulse shimmy down a bit—blood had coagulated. Stopped. "Will he be okay?" She'd never wanted the answer to be a positive as much as she did right now—wait. Not true. There was another disaster when she'd wanted more than anything to hear that the one tended would survive. Tony. Where was he?

"Yes, I think," Khat said. "I don't think the bullet hit anything major. We need to get him to a vet for surgery." Khaterah smiled at the two medics who carried a stretcher toward them. "Thank you."

Timbrel bent closer, but her dress defied her.

"May I?" Tony offered.

Timbrel smiled her appreciation.

He lifted Beo from the floor and set him on the long blue stretcher. They worked together with Khat to secure Beo.

"Anyway, looks like Beo saved the day. Again."

Timbrel turned to Tony, who squatted over Beo, petting him. Felt all the emotions of the evening tumble into one big glob. "Tony. . ."

He nodded. "We'll talk later. Let's get this sorted first."

"Dehqan, no!"

Timbrel jerked toward the eruption of noise. Only then had she realized how quiet things had grown in the last ten minutes or so. But what she saw stopped her heart.

A teenage boy aimed a weapon at Bashir, who stood handcuffed between what looked like two federal agents.

Shouts exploded as FBI, CIA, DIA, and special operators demanded the boy lower the weapon.

"No," he spit out. Face awash with agony and unshed tears, the boy shook his head. "You don't understand."

Bashir paled. "Dehqan." Shock morphed into rage. "How dare you! I gave you a home, a life!"

"You gave me torment," the boy gritted out.

"Dehqan, do not do this," Sajjan said as he inched closer. "It's over. Bashir will not be able to harm you anymore—"

"Don't you get it?" The raw pain writhed through his voice and expression. "He's already done the damage!" Tears sped down the boy's face as he slapped his own temple. "It's in here. Forever."

Timbrel felt nauseated, barely able to imagine what life beneath the thumb of Bashir must've been like for an impressionable teen. She darted a look to the mastermind and drew back at the sneer.

"Surah 11:101: 'We did not wrong them, but they wronged themselves.'"

"But you *did* wrong them." Dehqan aimed.

"Dehqan!" Sajjan scrambled from the side. "Do not give him what he wants."

The boy stilled. Shot Sajjan a wary glance.

"He wants to be martyred. You know what that means." Sajjan moved purposefully toward the teen. "Do not give him to that end. Do him no favors. Let him languish in an American prison, the ultimate shame."

"I do not want to see him again, and he is dangerous."

"I will make sure that does not happen," Sajjan said.

"He is dangerous. Cruel. He killed her."

Sajjan's face softened as he swiped a palm over the weapon and lifted it from the teen's hand. "I know."

Timbrel blew out a breath as her mother's fiancé led the boy to safety and the authorities carted Bashir off.

"We need to go," Khat muttered, pulling Timbrel back around to the stretcher, to her boy, panting heavily. She set her hand on Beo's shoulder as her gaze skittered around the room. SWAT team members had five men on the ground, hands cuffed.

A really tall guy—the same who'd thrown himself into the books—stood next to Burnett, holding the flashlight-like device. What was it and who was he? And perhaps the more important question—why was Burnett letting the guy take it?

"Australian Special Air Services, equivalent of Special Forces."

Timbrel eyed Tony, so grateful for his presence. His strength. His courage. He'd come back. He'd fought. Even with a missing leg.

A bit of confusion and confliction darted across Tony's face. "I think he's my replacement."

"Replacement?"

Tony's smile didn't reach his face. "I think it's time I turned in my keys, so to speak." He drew in a breath and shrugged. "Settle down. Find a wife."

" 'That's your plan? Wile E. Coyote would come up with a better plan than that!' "

Tony's eyes brightened. "*Farscape*. Baby, you're talking my language!"

Years spent watching the recoil of a weapon as the colonel fired it. Years of watching lives cut short by his hand. And now I almost did the same. Should I be ashamed when my actions would have wiped a very evil man from the planet?

But somehow, I knew Nafisa would not have wanted me to kill him. Ironic since it was for her, the love of her, that I wanted to hurt him.

I felt more alone now than ever as I waited in a chair at the back of the room, the police working the scene. The witnesses giving their testimonies. What would I do now? I had no home, no family. No Nafisa. With her—with her, I could figure something out. Plan a life. Together.

The pain washed over me anew with a fresh wave of grief.

"How are you doing?"

I looked up, startled. "How. . .how are you here? How have they not arrested you?" My mind struggled to assemble the crazy pieces of the puzzle. Him talking me down, stopping me from killing the colonel. Others. . . hadn't they called him Sajjan?

He smiled as he eased into a cushioned seat beside me, his back to the chaos around us. "It would be good if you did not speak of what you know."

I eyed him, afraid of trusting him. Afraid of *not* trusting him. "What do you want?"

"Be at peace, Aazim."

When I sucked in a breath, my mind choked. How did he know that name?

"I know what he did to the girl, to your friend. I know more about

Bashir Bijan Karzai than any person should have to know." He smirked at me. "There is nothing I do not know, even about his adoption of a street urchin named Aazim Busir. Son of Mehrak and Habiba Busir, two of the seventeen victims of a bus bombing."·

"How do you know so much, Maahir?"

"Because it is my job." He leaned a little closer, his presence both commanding and terrifying. His shoulders looked wider. Fists larger, stronger. "Can you answer a question for me?"

It sounded like a serious one. I was not sure my brain was up to that after all that had happened, but I still nodded. It seemed wrong to tell this man no to anything. "I will try."

"First, let me say that there are men in the world like Bashir, who are on a path so doggedly and with such determination and conviction they cannot fathom that it is a corrupt or wrong path. It is possible with anything, any belief, any concept, to take it and twist it into whatever one wishes."

"You fear he brainwashed me."

Maahir held my gaze without question and without speaking.

My mind flicked back to Nafisa, to our kiss, to my last embrace with her. After a blink, I met Maahir's gaze boldly. "I saw *truth* lived out. I saw love."

"You mean you fell in love."

"No. Yes." I frowned for a second. "Both."

A smile crinkled the edges of his eyes. But he said nothing.

"Is there a question?" I asked.

He set something on the table. When I looked down, I was surprised to find a picture. Of a man and woman. I shrugged. "I'm sorry. . .I don't—" Something pinged my mind. "Wait." I touched the edge of the picture, something terribly familiar. Achingly familiar.

"Do you remember them?"

"My. . .my parents."

The man smiled. "Yes. Do you have any pictures of them?"

Mutely, I shook my head, unable to tear my gaze from the image.

With two fingers, he nudged it toward me. "Take it."

"How. . .? Why. . .?"

"You will be taken care of, Aazim. I will see to it."

"Why?"

"In the future, I may have need of you. To help right wrongs. Bring justice where none is delivered. Where wrongs outweigh good." The intensity of his eyes made my heart thump hard. "Would you be interested in protecting the innocent, Aazim?"

Epilogue

Three Months Later
Oahu, Hawaii

It seems I owe you an apology."

Arms wrapped around her mother, Sajjan Takkar embraced his wife from behind and looked over the top of her updo at Timbrel. "How is that, daughter?" Something weird, warm, and wild corkscrewed her stomach at that endearment. The old Timbrel, the one who hadn't met Tony or gone through enough drama to last two lifetimes, would've told this handsome Sikh where he could shove that turban.

But this Timbrel, the one who stood on the beach as sunset caressed the crystal clear waters. . .the one who'd just watched her mother commit to love, honor, and obey—yes, Timbrel had snickered when those words met air—Sajjan Takkar until death parted them. . .that Timbrel found the words beautifully healing.

So much that she almost lost her train of thought. He'd just called her "daughter." Maybe it was an Indian thing. Nobody had ever called her that. "I doubted you, doubted who you were. Right up till the end."

"You were right to question who I was and what I was doing," Sajjan said. "The work I was doing was tricky and deceptive, something I take no pleasure in. But I believe God has gifted me with a talent for persuasion."

"Oh, definitely." Her mother crooned as she twisted and wrapped her arms around him. The two kissed as if they were the only ones left in the world.

"Ugh." Timbrel feigned disgust. "Get a room."

"Great idea," Sajjan said as he led his wife through the dusk and back in the direction of the cottage they'd rented for their extended honeymoon.

It was good. Really good to see her mom truly happy. Sajjan was a thousand times the man Don Stephens had been. And Timbrel knew the man who'd just swept her mom off her feet would never even conceive the thought of hurting Timbrel the way Don had. Sajjan genuinely loved her. They were both Christians, a surprise she'd discovered while the trip here was being planned. Sajjan wore the turban to honor his ancestors and heritage, but he had surrendered the religious beliefs years past and embraced Jesus, not just as a prophet but as the Son of God.

With a contented sigh, she turned and scanned the beach. Tony sat on the sand with Rika poised next to him. In shorts, Tony stretched out, his prosthesis showing. Timbrel loved the design with the flag and eagle. She smiled at how accurate it was for him.

He looked up as she plodded toward them. "You send the kids to their room?"

"They're worse than teenagers," she said with a laugh. "But I think she did this right—an intimate ceremony. No months-long planning. No drama. No paparazzi. It's the second-best thing."

"What's the first?"

"Eloping." Wait. "Where's Beo?"

Tony pointed down the beach.

"Ah." Timbrel joined him. "Thought any more about that medical discharge?"

He nodded. "Yeah." He sighed heavily. "I've been thinking about a lot of things, but that especially. When I woke up with my leg gone, I thought I was done with ODA452."

She eyed him, surprised. "Really?"

"God's given me a lot of good things, kept me alive to be here tonight."

"And I'm so glad He did."

"So, how you doing with that?"

"With what?"

"God."

Timbrel wrinkled her nose. "Things are still hard to understand—"

"Faith—"

"But"—she held up a hand silencing him—"ever since Pops gave me that card on the mission. . .I've been working through things, I guess. All my life, I had to take care of myself, protect myself."

Though Tony looked like she'd just bruised his ego a bit, he didn't say anything. And she was glad. It was hard enough fessing up like this.

"Anyway, I don't have to understand to believe or to surrender that illusion of control."

Tony's eyebrows rose. "Surrender." A heartbeat passed, then he smirked. "Good." His gaze rose to the star-sprinkled sky then back to her. "Do I need to hurt Pops?"

Grunting, Timbrel hid her laugh. "Will you always be *this* possessive?"

"Absolutely. And I call it protective. Not possessive." He curled an arm around her waist and kissed her temple. "I'm proud of you, Timbrel. You've come a long way, baby."

She would've thought the sun had come back up for all the warmth that flooded her. "Thanks. What about you, Hot Shot?"

"What about me?"

"You going back?"

Tony let out a long sigh and stared out over the water. "Speaking of surrender. . .I thought my days as a Green Beret were over, but now, I just feel challenged more. I'd like to keep working with the team, somehow."

Beo trotted toward them, sand kicking up as he ran.

Craning her neck forward, Timbrel tried to see in the ever-darkening day. "What's he got in his mouth?"

"Beats me."

Beo jogged up to them. Ignored Timbrel. Growled at Tony. And dropped his stash at Rika's paws. A dead fish.

Tony's German shepherd lifted her chin and shifted her seated stance. She stared out over the water. Glanced at Tony. But refused to acknowledge Beo's effort at wooing her.

"That's just cruel," Timbrel said with a laugh as Tony rubbed Rika's shoulder.

"Give the big guy a break, girl." Tony patted Rika's flank. "He's ugly—"

"Hey."

"But he's trying his best."

Beo nudged the fish closer.

Rika lifted her chin again.

This time, Beo nudged Rika's chin as if to say, "Do that again."

She did.

Beo dropped down. Wagged his butt. Barked.

Finally Rika slumped against the sand. Sniffed the fish.

Beo stood straight. Shoulders squared and chest out. Proud of his kill. Proud he won her over.

"C'mere," Tony said as he stood and dusted the sand from his shorts. He held out his hand.

Timbrel laced her fingers with his and walked with him.

"Remember that day in the hospital?"

"You mean, when you told me to get out of your life?"

Tony breathed his laugh. "Yeah, not my hour of shining."

Leaning into him, she held his arm with her free hand and rested her head on his shoulder. "Let's put it behind us."

"First," he said as they followed a stone wall around and back toward the main hotel. He stopped. "I kissed you in the hospital and you kept pulling away."

Timbrel blinked. "I did? I don't—oh." She released his hand, tilted her neck forward, and turned. "See the scar?"

He pressed a warm kiss to her neck, skittering goose bumps down her spine. "What's it from?"

"Brain decompression surgery." She faced him, brushing her long bangs aside.

Tony's brow knotted. "Brain. . .surgery?"

"I didn't know it, but in the blast, I got hurt. Thrown against a wall."

Tony gaped.

With a shrug, she caught his hand again. "When you kissed me, you were holding the back of my neck—it hurt."

Tony groaned. "And here, I thought. . ."

She turned to him. "You thought I was pulling away from you, in more ways than one? That I really was so bothered by Titanium Leg— Geez, you're shallow!"

"Hey, I was mortally wounded."

"Going all wounded-knee on me, now?"

Tony slowly met her gaze. "That day, thinking you were pitying me, was the darkest day of my life."

What she was supposed to say, she didn't know. She just didn't want this romantic getaway weekend to end here. Didn't want to sabotage what had grown back between them over the last three months. . .didn't want it to shatter. "Well, you filled that hole pretty quickly."

The confusion trickling through his face gave him away. Then he smiled. "Rika."

Shrugging, Timbrel started away. "You replaced me."

He tugged her back. "Not possible." Cupped her face. "Timbrel." Green eyes searched hers. That cockeyed smile as he traced her features. His expression went crazy serious.

"That's my name."

"Remember what you said back there?"

Retracing her verbal steps, Timbrel leapt and bounded from one topic to another. Her mom and Sajjan. Rika and Beo. What else. . .? *Eloping.* Adrenaline heated her body. She widened her eyes.

Tony smirked. "Earlier," he said, tilted his head behind them as if to point to the past, "you talked about surrendering control. . .so would it bother you if I reupped and requalified to work with the team?"

Oh. That. "Why would I mind?" She shrugged. "Isn't that who you are?"

"I thought if we had a status change"—he bobbed his eyebrow as he jerked his head to the left—"you might feel differently. What do you say?" Again he indicated for her to look at something.

Warily, Timbrel glanced to the side.

A man in a white Hawaiian shirt and pants stood at a table lit by a lone torch. A slight breeze drifted in off the ocean and rifled a piece of paper. The header was hidden, but somehow. . .somehow she knew what it was. *Marriage license.*

"Are you asking me to marry you?"

"Well, my dad said I can't come home without you and Beo, so I figure—"

"Your sister hates me."

"And my brother loves you. I gotta beat him to the punch."

Timbrel slapped his gut. "Jerk. Coward."

"Ouch." Chuckling, he nodded. "You're right. I am. When it comes to you, I most definitely am. And Stephanie will adjust. Baby, I don't want to fail you again."

Whoa. "Be prepared—you will."

Tony stared.

"You're human. And so am I—so be ready for me to screw it up." She smiled, trying to avoid the tears as her heart registered what was happening. What she was *letting* happen. "Because that's the thing I'm best at."

"No." Tony shook his head. "I know something you're far better at."

"What's th—?"

Tony pressed his lips against hers, and Timbrel eased into his arms as he deepened the kiss. Barking resonated in the back of her mind. Without warning, Tony punched into her. He jerked, breaking off the kiss. Spun around.

Beowulf dropped low, paws on the ground as he barked and growled, his tail going a hundred miles an hour.

Arms up and legs spread in a fighting stance, Tony wagged his fingers at Beo. "C'mon, you hound of hell. Bring it!"

Dear Readers,

Thank you for taking the adventure with Beowulf and his human counterparts, Timbrel and Candyman. I hope you've laughed, maybe cried, but more importantly—learned something about our military heroes (two-legged and four-legged) that might spur you to action! In fact, let me share an organization with you that I encourage you to consider supporting, either through donation or other support methods!

Before I stepped into writing military fiction, I had a profound encounter, meeting the family of a Navy SEAL who struggled with post-traumatic stress disorder (PTSD). Seeing the impact that hero's career had on him and his family altered my desire to write about our military heroes in one respect: I promised myself I would never write a military fiction novel without showing the repercussions the brutal role of combat has on these heroes. PTSD is real, it's daunting, and sometimes—the fight is lost.

A recent statistic stunned me: *"Through April, the U.S. military has recorded 161 potential suicides in 2013 among active-duty troops, reservists and National Guard members — a pace of one suicide about every 18 hours."* (May 23, 2013, article by Bill Briggs of NBC News)

Heartbroken by this alarming reality, I was happy to come upon (via Facebook) The Battle Buddy Foundation, an organization actively working to combat the stigma of PTSD and arm our military heroes battling PTSD with the help necessary to win the war on the mind. TBBF is also facilitating the training, certifications, and placement of service dogs with disabled veterans, as well as offering an equine therapy program. The service dogs—a real, hands-on "battle buddy"—caught my eye since readers meet a dog like that in *Beowulf*.

Once again, I am asking readers to put "boots on ground" and help our military heroes, this time by contributing to The Battle Buddy Foundation, which is not just money in a pot, but money invested in the life of a military hero! By donating, you may just save a life! If you cannot donate money, please help spread the word about The Battle Buddy Foundation, like them on Facebook (https://www.facebook/com/battlebuddy) and help spread their message of hope, therapy, and healing!

THE BATTLE BUDDY FOUNDATION

The Battle Buddy Foundation (TBBF), was founded by Marine infantry combat veterans. TBBF is dedicated to serving our brothers/sisters in arms struggling with PTSD and other combat related injuries.
http://www.battle-buddy.org
https://www.facebook.com/battlebuddy

The Battle Buddy Foundation is a nonprofit corporation registered with the Ohio Sec. of State. TBBF's 501(c)3 status is pending. TBBF will offer treatment for Post Traumatic Stress through individual, group, and marital counseling at our Battle Buddy Foundation Centers. TBBF will have separate programs with a special focus on both service dog placement, and Equine Therapy. TBBF will also work with local Veteran's Courts to assist with diversion/treatment programs. TBBF will work to remove the stigma associated with Post Traumatic Stress on a national level, educate the public, and help guide our nation's wounded Veterans to the needed resources.

TBBF is located at 8859 Cincinnati-Dayton Rd Suite 202 Olde West Chester, OH 45069

Specialized Search Dog - Gretchen J538
Afghanistan 2010–2011
Helmand Province, Sangin Valley, Afghanistan

"This is the crew chief. We should be arriving in Cherry Point in about twenty minutes. We have just enough time for everyone to wake up and pack up."

The voice over the speaker woke me from my sleep on the floor of a C130 cargo plane. Relieved to return to the U.S., I rubbed my eyes as I sat up and leaned against one of the 26 dog kennels lining the middle of the aircraft, the remaining space occupied by the Military Working Dog handlers. Farther down the aircraft, my dog was still asleep in her kennel. Gretchen, a six-year-old Labrador, was assigned to me by the Marine Corps for her third deployment (Iraq-2, Afghanistan-1). As I looked up at the red light that illuminated the aircraft, there was no stopping the memories.

Back in Afghanistan, I was tasked with assisting a Reconnaissance unit in the Sangin Valley. We moved to a secondary position and were settling in for the night. Gretchen and I were in a Marine Mine Resistant Ambush Protectant (MRAP) vehicle with two other Marines, chatting idly. Suddenly a massive explosive shook the vehicle.

Gretchen began to whimper. The blast originated from the direction of one of our positions, but we were unsure if it was a patrol. The Marines jumped on the radio and attempted to get hold of the others when a voice came through the radio. "We have a casualty. One of our night patrols stepped on an IED."

Our vehicle responded and arrived within five minutes. Three Marines had been on patrol when the IED went off. Because of the midnight hour, we were told we'd have to return at dawn since a Marine's rifle was still out there. So, the next morning, we drove out in three vehicles and stopped 100 yards from the detonation site.

I told the drivers, "Tell everyone to stay inside the MRAPS until I give the okay." Gretchen and I stepped out to search the area covered with small gray rocks and not 200 yards from a river. After she finished, I gave the EOD techs a thumbs-up. We continued in the direction of the blast area with Gretchen always 50 feet in front. I turned around and asked, "Yo, do you have a VALEN?"—the metal detectors used by the Marines. The tech replied, "What does it mean when your dog sits?"

I spun around, calling Gretchen to me. She had responded 20 feet from the original blast. It wasn't uncommon for the Taliban to put two or three explosives in one area. Binoculars up, the Marine said, "Well, looks like your dog found our rifle." I was glad we found it because that meant we could leave. Then I walked up to a piece of M4, now a broken, mangled piece of metal camouflaged amid the rocks. After checking for booby traps, the EOD technician retrieved the weapon.

Gretchen and I continued to search, then arrived at the blast site—a four-foot by three-foot deep hole in the middle of a dirt road that divided two fields of rock. As I continued to observe the area, I saw it: a red, purplish liquid. Blood.

I walked up to the puddle and found wrappings of emergency medical equipment, pieces of uniform, and trash. Angered, I began to pick everything up—the pieces of uniform, the trash, and. . .the flesh? I didn't realize that in my rage I was also holding a piece of flesh.

Horrified, I continued searching and found a shoe. Another Marine found a helmet. When I discovered an ID card blown in half, I put it in my pocket. The rage that ran through my body was unbearable. I wanted to fight. I wanted to kill. I wanted revenge. In my truck, the tears began, and I couldn't stop thinking about the mission. Couldn't stop the hate. Exhausted, I dozed off. . .only to be interrupted when Gretchen jumped on my lap and started licking my face. "Gretchen don't lick me," I said with a laugh. "I've seen what you do with that mouth."

When the airplane finally landed at Cherry Point, Gretchen and I made our way onto the runway. All 26 dog teams were lined up, awaiting the order to march to the building. A loud explosion made me cringe and look around in a panic.

The sky lit up with an array of magnificent colors. Fireworks. I hadn't even realized it was the Fourth of July. Relieved, I looked down at Gretchen and couldn't help but feel saddened—in only six months, I would return to California, and she would continue her mission without me.

About the Author

Ronie Kendig is an award-winning, bestselling author who grew up an Army brat. After twenty-plus years of marriage, she and her hunky hero husband have a full life with their four children, a Maltese Menace, and a retired military working dog in Northern Virginia. Author and speaker, Ronie loves engaging readers through her Rapid-Fire Fiction. Ronie can be found at www.roniekendig.com, on Facebook (www.facebook.com/rapidfirefiction), Twitter (@roniekendig), and Goodreads (www.goodreads.com/RonieK).

Also available from Shiloh Run Press...

Raptor 6

Hawk

Unabridged Audiobooks